THE MYTHS OF OPHELIA

THE CURSE OF OPHELIA SERIES

NICOLE PLATANIA

BOOKS BY NICOLE PLATANIA

The Curse of Ophelia Series

The Curse of Ophelia
The Shards of Ophelia
The Trials of Ophelia
The Breaker of Stars (a novella)
The Myths of Ophelia
The Curse of Ophelia #5 (Coming 2025)

The *Myths* of Ophelia

Nicole Platania

First paperback edition November 2024

© Cover design: Franziska Stern - www.coverdungeon.com - Instagram: @coverdungeonrabbit

Developmental Edit by Kelley Frodel

Copyedited by Grey Moth Editing

Proofread by K. Morton Editing Services

Map design by Abigail Hair

ISBN 978-1-965362-01-3 (Paperback)

ASIN B0D8LDDNVZ (ebook)

www.nicoleplatania.com

 Created with Vellum

For everyone tired of being a character in someone else's narrative. Your story is your own—write it however makes your spirit soar.

Author's Note

This book contains depictions of alcohol/drug dependency; loss of
a loved one; blood, gore, and violence; discussion of sexual assault;
depictions of mental/emotional neglect and abuse; organized
fighting; torture; PTSD; and some sexual content. If any of these
may be triggering for you, please read carefully or feel free to
contact the author for further explanation.

Pronunciation Guide
Characters who are crossed out were deceased prior to the beginning of The Myths of Ophelia.

Mystique Warriors

Ophelia Alabath (she/her), Mystique Revered: *Oh-feel-eeya Tuh-vahn-yuh Al-uh-bath*

Malakai Blastwood (he/him): *Mal-uh-kye Blast-wood*

Tolek Vincienzo (he/him): *Tole-ick Vin-chin-zoh*

Cypherion Kastroff (he/him), Mystique Second: *Sci-fear-ee-on Cast-Rahf*

Jezebel Alabath (she/her): *Jez-uh-bell Al-uh-bath*

Akalain Blastwood (she/her): *Ah-kuh-lane Blast-wood*

~~Alvaron (he/him), Master of Coin: *Al-vuh-ron*~~

Annellius Alabath, (he/him): *Uh-nell-ee-us Al-uh-bath*

~~Bacaran Alabath (he/him), Second to the Revered: *Bah-kuh-ron Al-uh-bath*~~

~~Collins (he/him): *Call-ins*~~

~~Danya (she/her), Master of Weapons & Warfare: *Dawn-yuh*~~

~~Larcen (he/him), Master of Trade: *Lare-sen*~~

~~Lucidius Blastwood (he/him), Revered: *Loo-sid-ee-yus Blast-wood*~~

Lyria Vincienzo (she/her), Master of Weapons and
Warfare: *Leer-ee-uh Vin-chin-zoh*
Mila Loveall (she/her), Mystique General: *Mee-lah
Love-all*
Missyneth (she/her), Master of Rites: *Mis-sin-ith*
Tavania Alabath (she/her): *Tuh-vahn-yuh Al-uh-
bath*

Engrossian Warriors

~~Kakias (she/her), Engrossian Queen: *Kuh-kye-yus*~~
Barrett (he/him), Engrossian Prince: *Bair-it*
Dax Goverick (he/him), Engrossian General: *Dax
Gahv-rick*
~~Victious: *Vik-shuss*~~
Nassik Langswoll (he/him), councilman: *Nuh-seek
Lang-swall*
Pelvira (she/her), councilwoman: *Pell-veer-uh*
Elvek (he/him), councilman: *El-vick*
Celissia Langswoll, (she/her): *Seh-lee-see-uh Lang-
swall*

Mindshapers

~~Aird (he/him), Mindshaper Chancellor: *Air-d*~~
Ricordan (he/him): *Rik-kor-din*
Trevaneth (he/him): *Treh-vuh-neh-th*

Bodymelders

Brigiet (she/her), Bodymelder Chancellor: *Bri-jeet*
Esmond (he/him), apprentice: *Ez-min-d*
Gatrielle (he/him): *Gah-tree-elle*

Starsearchers

Titus Verian (he/him), Starsearcher Chancellor: *Tie-tuhs Vair-ee-on*
Vale (she/her), apprentice: *Veil*
Cyren (they/them), Starsearcher General: *Sci-ren*
Harlen (he/him): *Har-lin*

Seawatchers

Ezalia Ridgebrook (she/her), Seawatcher Chancellor: *Eh-zale-ee-uh Ridg-brook*
Amara Ridgebrook (she/her), Seawatcher General: *Uh-mar-uh Ridg-brook*
~~Andrenas (they/them): *An-dreh-nuss*~~
~~Chorid (he/him): *Core-ihd*~~
Leo (he/him): *Lee-oh*
Seron Ridgebrook (he/him): *Sair-on Ridg-brook*
Seli Ridgebrook (she/her): *Sell-ee Ridg-brook*
Auggie Ridgebrook (he/him): *Aw-ghee Ridg-brook*

Soulguiders

Meridat (she/her), Soulguider Chancellor: *Mare-ih-daat*
Erista Locke (she/her), apprentice: *Eh-ris-tuh Lock*
Quilian Locke (he/him), Soulguider General: *Quil-ee-en Lock*

Non-warrior characters

Santorina Cordelian (she/her), human: *San-tor-ee-nuh Kor-dee-lee-in*
Aimee (she/her), Storyteller: *Ay-me*
Lancaster (he/him), fae: *Lan-kaster*
Mora (she/her), fae: *Mor-uh*
Brystin (he/him), fae: *Brih-stin*
Ritalia (she/her), Queen of the Fae: *Rih-tall-ee-uh*

Animals and Creatures

Astania, *Uh-ston-ya*
Calista: *Kuh-liss-tuh*
Elektra: *Ill-ectra*
Erini: *Ih-ree-nee*
Ombratta: *Ahm-brah-tuh*
Sapphire: *Sah-fire*
Rebel: *Reh-bull*
Zanox: *Zuh-nox*
Dynaxtar: *Die-nahx-tar*

Places

Ambrisk: *Am-brisk*
Banix: *Ban-ix*
Brontain: *Brawn-tane*
Caprecion: *Kuh-pree-shun*
Damenal: *Dom-in-all*
Fytar Trench: *Fie-tar Trehn-ch*
Gallantia: *Guh-lawn-shuh*
Gaveral: *Gav-er-all*
Lendelli: *Len-del-ee*
Lumin: *Loo-min*
Palerman: *Powl-er-min*
Pthole: *Tholl*
Thorentil: *Thor-in-till*
Turren: *Tur-in*
Valyn: *Val-in*
Vercuella: *Vair-kwella*
Xenovia: *Zin-oh-vee-yuh*

Angels of the Gallantian Warriors

Bant (he/him), Prime Engrossian Warrior: *Bant*
Damien (he/him), Prime Mystique Warrior: *Day-mee-in*
Gaveny (he/him), Prime Seawatcher: *Gav-in-ee*

Ptholenix (he/him), Prime Bodymelder: *Tholl-en-icks*

Thorn (he/him), Prime Mindshaper: *Thorn*

Valyrie (she/her), Prime Starsearcher: *Val-er-ee*

Xenique (she/her), Prime Soulguider: *Zen-eek*

Gods of Ambrisk's Pantheon

Aoiflyn (she/her), The Fae Goddess: *Eef-lyn*

Artale (she/her), The Goddess of Death: *Are-tall*

Gerenth (he/him), The God of Nature: *Gair-inth*

Lynxenon (he/him), The God of Mythical Beasts: *Leen-zih-non*

Moirenna (she/her), The Goddess of Fate & Celestial Movements: *Moy-ren-uh*

Thallia (she/her), The Witch Goddess of Sorcia: *Thall-ee-uh*

PART ONE
GAVENY

CHAPTER ONE
OPHELIA

WHY WAS IT SO ANGELSDAMNED HOT?

Condensation crawled down the side of my glass, pooling on the dark wood of the seaside tavern's bar one languid drop at a time. The heat of the Seawatchers' Western Outposts shoved itself down my throat, despite the fact that we were only nearing the end of the first month of the year.

I supposed it rarely got as cold on the islands as it did in other territories, but this was unseasonable. And aggravating. Snow lay atop various regions of the continent—thick white blankets of it likely doused Palerman in recent weeks—but here, nothing more than a breeze wound between the columns of the tavern. I inhaled as a spray of salty ocean air flecked across my skin, tempering the roaring heat.

And I *waited*—a word that had become the bane of my existence.

"Sure I can't get you anything besides water, Revered?" The friendly barkeep braced both hands on the aged wood, a towel slung across his shoulder.

"Thank you, Ivon." I offered him a warm smile, then raised the glass. "I'm fine with this, though."

He nodded, short dark hair bobbing over his forehead, and proceeded down the bar to his other customers. As he had every time we'd played this little game in the weeks my friends and I had been stationed in the outposts. In the weeks since the second Engrossian-Mystique war ended. Since Prince Barrett slayed his mother, Queen Kakias, and the Spirit of the Engrossian Angel Bant himself tore from her body, disappearing into the mountains.

I shook off the memories—the questions—a familiar restlessness twitching through my limbs at having to remain stagnant in these outposts.

Dormant, because the ruler of the fae, the bloodthirsty Queen Ritalia, was on her way to Gallantia, and according to her soldier, Lancaster, she wanted us pliant beneath her heel, but she did not deign to tell us precisely when she would arrive.

And I was forced to cooperate. She was a threat, and it was in the warriors' best interest to get her here and gone as quickly as possible. And because Lancaster held a bargain over Tolek's and my heads. If we failed to comply, we would be violating the deal and thus forfeiting our lives.

So, here we sat.

The tavern, The Sea Maiden, had become my favorite way to pass the days, and not only due to Ivon's attentive staff or the affable crowd they drew. The polished stone pillars lining the front opened directly onto one of the outpost's white sand beaches, soft mounds rising and dipping nearly fifty yards before melting into crystal blue ocean.

The waves were calm, peaceful, and an abundance of colorful wildlife occupied the coral reefs below no more than one hundred yards out. Ezalia Ridgebrook, the Seawatcher Chancellor, had taken us to explore them one day last week.

They were beautiful. I grew tired of it.

The waves curled lazily into the shore—my warrior hearing picking out the gentle roar over the voices in the tavern—and each sweep worked to dilute the dissatisfaction budding within me.

It was a bit like standing in the surf as it pulled away, the sand around your feet drifting, toes sinking further into the wet grains until you were certain you'd be taken with it.

I'd spent a lot of time on those shores these weeks. Spent a lot of time in the Sea Maiden, as well. Both to feed the spiraling creature inside of me that wanted out and to appear as we'd been bid.

My queen wishes your court to prepare for her arrival. And to cause no reason for delay.

Groaning internally, as I did each time Lancaster's warning fluttered through my mind, I pushed up from my seat at the bar and strode toward the veranda. Water in hand, I leaned my shoulder against a sun-warmed stone pillar.

I highly suggest you heed her instructions. You do not want to see what ruin she may unfold if disobeyed.

Fucking fae.

Who was a foreign queen to command warriors? But Lancaster had always been a solid force. A bit tricky, a lot deadly, but never wavering.

And he *had* wavered that day.

When he met my friends and me as we were about to depart the mountains after the final battle, heading for Soulguider Territory in search of the next Angel emblem—when Santorina shot him daggers with her glare, hand tightening on her knife—something in the fae had waffled.

My fingers curled into my glass with the memory. *Don't shatter another glass, Ophelia,* I instructed myself, but an inevitable agitation reared in my chest.

It didn't drown out the footsteps echoing behind me, though. Nor did it mask the unfamiliar, masculine scent that joined me on the veranda.

"That drink looks awfully low."

I turned toward the warrior leaning against the pillar opposite mine, his arms crossed and a bottle dangling between his fingers. Seawatcher, based on the coral and aqua gems adorning his ears. A symbol of rank among the ocean-farers.

Three of them lined one ear, poking out from beneath his hair, sun-bleached highlights gleaming against the dark strands falling past his shoulders. A thick beard coated his jaw, like he'd been on a ship for many days recently, and he wore a thin linen tunic instead of leathers. To accommodate the heat, if the sweat along his brow was any hint.

"I've been thirsty," I said, tipping the water to my lips again.

"Let me buy you your next."

I gave him half a smile. "Thank you for offering, but that won't be necessary."

"Come on." The man pushed off the pillar and stepped closer to me. Not close enough that I was threatened, but enough that I placed my glass on the table beside me and dropped my hands to my sides. Easy and relaxed, but within reach of my dagger. "Have one drink with me. My next patrol leaves tomorrow." His eyes crawled over my face. "And with the way you were watching the water just now, it's clear you have a lot of stories crowding that pretty mind."

In another situation, the invitation might have been light-hearted, warriors exchanging tales of travels over a drink. But he kept coming closer, until we were toe to toe, and his eyes fell to my breasts, to the way the binding of my leathers was tied so tightly, they pushed up with every inhale.

My *pretty mind* clearly wasn't what he wanted.

"I have many stories," I said, voice even.

"I have hours to listen. All night, in fact." No comment about the fact that I was clearly not a Seawatcher. No acknowledgment that he knew who I was—what title I held—which despite his invasive behavior, was a bit of a reprieve.

Shame for him I wasn't interested.

"I suggest finding someone who has hours to spare with you, then." *Waste your efforts elsewhere.*

He leaned closer, bracing a hand on the pillar above my head, and my back stiffened. Spirits, he smelled like a damp ship cabin baking in the cloying heat.

"I'm fine here." His other hand tucked an errant wave behind my ear, grazing my collarbone as it dropped.

And my patience snapped entirely, fingers curling around the hilt of my dagger.

"I suggest you remove your hands if you value them," a voice as familiar as my own sliced the air, low and lethal, and my heart fluttered like an Angel's wings. "Or that pretty little dagger at her thigh will be in your throat."

I hid my smirk, raising my brows at the man before me. He didn't back down, but his eyes flashed to my weapon—the only one on me, since I was meant to be acting docile—then dragged appreciatively up my body.

"Oh, now don't do that," Tolek tutted, his boots echoing from the wooden interior of the tavern to the stone porch, stopping feet away. "Now I'll have to join the reparations, and I *just* finished cleaning my weapons."

The Seawatcher's eyes flitted between us.

"Appears you have a choice," I whispered, inclining my head.

"He's not my type," he snapped.

"That wasn't the offer," I nearly growled, and Tolek chuckled. But despite the amusement, when I flicked my gaze to him, his stance was all defense. Claiming. Though we both knew I was more than capable of handling this, it sent those wings in my chest fluttering again.

With a disgruntled exhale, the Seawatcher pushed off the pillar, his musty scent falling away as he took slow steps backward toward the tavern entrance. The voices inside remained steady, no one noticing the threats we exchanged.

"The pissing contest isn't necessary," he said. "I was only offering a drink and some fun."

"*After* she declined." Tolek's voice was still calm, but his brows rose with the obvious misstep.

"And there's no contest," I added, flashing a devilish smirk at the warrior. He waved us away and turned to disappear among the patrons, off to find a more willing participant for his *fun*.

"Well, that was entertaining," Tolek said, stepping into the Seawatcher's place before me, one hand braced against the pillar as that man's had been, the other cupping my cheek.

He dipped his head, brushing his lips against my own, and the need for him snapped like a whip inside of me. I tangled a hand in his hair, the other wrapping around his back to pull him closer. Even through his leathers I could feel him harden, his length straining against the barrier as his tongue grazed mine and a moan slipped up my throat.

It took every ounce of Spiritsdamned self-control in my body to not wrap my legs around his hips and grind against him right here, pressed to this pillar, in full display of The Sea Maiden's patrons. My back arched at the thought.

As if sensing my desperation—and lack of logical decision making—Tolek pulled back, placing one more kiss to my forehead.

"Hi." He smirked, gaze traveling over my face. "I don't like when they do that," he added as our breathing evened out.

"Oh, but it's so fun when you threaten them."

How many times had something similar occurred since we'd been stationed here? I'd been *behaving* as demanded—awaiting Queen Ritalia's arrival as an oh-so-patient warrior and wasting away the afternoons where anyone she sent to tail me could see. How many times had I begun a friendly conversation with other patrons only for it to end with them presuming more than I let on?

It had become a game of sorts between Tolek and me, lobbying this jealousy we each harbored and using it to spur on our own fire. The challenge soothed the riling energy within me, the agitation at being commanded to wait for the queen abating if only for a few moments.

"It wasn't fun the day I nearly made good on one of those threats," he reminded me. His hair drooped over his forehead, and I absently brushed it back.

"That man was handsy. He would have deserved to lose a finger."

"More than that," Tolek mumbled. "And that woman who draped herself all over me in the gambling hall two weeks ago?"

"I only threatened to cut off her hair." I shrugged. "Jezebel taught me how. It wouldn't have been that hideous." *Unless I intended it to.*

He heard the words I didn't say, and a laugh burst from him. "You're ruthless when defending what's yours, Alabath."

Mine. As it did every time he said it, warmth spread through my chest.

Tolek Vincienzo was mine, and I was his. Infinitely. No matter what the Angels planned—what threats the fae queen brought down on us—that would always hold true.

So much had been uncertain these past months, but his steady presence settled a nerve. Still, the reminder of the queen had my teeth grinding.

"What's wrong?" Tolek asked, swinging an arm around my shoulder and tucking me into his side to face the sea.

I dropped my voice. "What do you think happened with Bant's Spirit?"

Tolek blew out a breath. "Can't be sure about that one, Alabath."

I toyed with the shard of my spear, Angelborn, hanging around my neck. The emblem of the Mystique Angel, Damien, containing a fossilized piece of his power. "It—he—disappeared into the mountains after leaving Kakias's body." I'd been rehashing the phenomenon ever since Barrett and I watched it happen—since the day he drove a dagger into the queen's heart and the Spirit of the Engrossian Angel that had been shed into her emerged —and we had yet to figure out what it meant.

Because we were *stagnant*.

I closed my hand around my necklace. "We still have two more to find." The Soulguider and Starsearcher tokens were out there somewhere. "And yet, here we sit."

"Here we sit," Tolek repeated, but he said it with an ease I didn't feel.

"If we have to wait, I want to feel like I'm doing something at least."

Tolek looked down at me and whispered, "We are, Alabath."

He wasn't entirely wrong. But restlessness buzzed beneath my skin.

"More than searching books and maps every night in the cottage. More than silently testing the Angellight I control. Even if I'm familiar with it, I haven't learned *why* I can manipulate it or *what* it's capable of."

Because Angellight was a substance of pure power known only to belong to the seven Prime Warriors when they ascended many millennia ago.

And now, it ran through my veins, too. Five distinguishable threads, one for each Angel emblem I found and bled on, all tangling together into a golden luminescence I was able to wield.

Tolek was contemplative as I went on, "Barrett is in Engrossian Territory, attempting to repair his tumultuous clan and earn his title again with *significant* pushback—Malakai with him. Cypherion and Vale are still off trying to solve the problems with her magic. And I'm"—I shook my head, facing the lazy tide and trying to be as calm as it was—"waiting."

"Sometimes, knowing when *not* to act is as wise as knowing when to," Tolek assured, placing a kiss to my temple. "We'll find answers to all of it. We just have a new challenge to work around. Wouldn't life be so boring otherwise?"

I laughed reluctantly. How did he see situations in such hopeful light, even when life had not always been kind to him?

Tol's voice was melancholic when he added, "Hopefully we'll resolve this business with the fae quickly and resume our lives."

"I have a feeling Queen Ritalia doesn't do anything quickly." When one lived as long as she had, days flashed by like minutes.

Tolek exhaled. "No, but it's smart to keep her as unaware of *your power* as long as possible."

"Lancaster and Mora saw it." The two fae—siblings, we found out during the final battle—saw me use Angellight against Kakias and fall into that realm where I manipulated the light to destroy the queen's power. "They would have told her everything. Been sworn to."

"Only what they saw," Tolek said. "Not how it felt to you or how you've gotten to know it recently, practicing in secret these weeks. For whatever reason, Ritalia thinks she has command over us—*your court*." I screwed up my face at the fae term for our councils and clans, and Tolek laughed. "Whether we like it or not, it's best for us to play along right now."

I sighed and met his eyes. We'd had this conversation many times, and always came to the same conclusions. "We get her here and out as quickly as possible. We do nothing to upset the balance of the bargain we struck with Lancaster, and we find whatever information they're willing to impart about the gods." Information we needed, given that it appeared the gods were tied to this mess with the emblems somehow. With our theory that Annellius, the first chosen, had hidden the shards of Angel power before his death, we needed every morsel of help we could find. Worry gnawed at me at the possibilities. "Then, we return to our Angel tasks and trials."

"That's my girl." Tol tilted my chin up to kiss me. Then, he added, "Looks like clouds are moving in."

Though it was early still, the sun was beginning to set—a blessing of the short winter days, given that we were primarily working by night—and thick gray plumes *were* rolling across the sky. Perhaps this heat wave would crack soon.

Tolek added, "I'd originally been coming here to tell you the girls returned." I looked up at him, the amber specks in his chocolate eyes flaming. "How do you feel about a flight?"

CHAPTER TWO
OPHELIA

UNFORTUNATELY, ANY HOPE OF A FLIGHT WITH Sapphire was drowned in the rain that cracked before Tolek and I even returned home. My heart twisted for my warrior horse-turned-pegasus, but I stepped across the threshold, wet hair plastered to my skin, and for a moment, my concern vanished.

A piece of me I hadn't realized was dulled ignited at Jezebel and Santorina standing in the small stone cottage we were staying in. Though *cottage* was a loose term given the six bedrooms flanking its gray cobbled walls, each with a slightly different style. Like they were added as needed rather than all at once.

The Seawatcher Chancellor, Ezalia Ridgebrook, and my sister's partner, Erista, stood with them.

"Jez, Rina!" I shouted as I hurried into the combined sitting-and-dining room strewn with books and notes on Angel magic. Warm wooden surfaces, worn couches, and the fire flickering in the stone hearth made the home cozy against the rain.

A high voice shrieked, "Tolek!" And Ezalia's young children bounced around the sofa, jumping on Tol.

"Seli, Auggie, you just saw him," Ezalia chastised with a laugh. But Tolek was already caught up in a game with the twins.

"Ezalia," I greeted, disentangling myself from my sister and Rina to hug the Seawatcher Chancellor. "I didn't realize the children were here."

Seron, Ezalia's partner, wheeled around the corner in the chair he'd had custom built after losing his legs in the hunt for the Seawatcher emblem. Guilt hardened in my throat as it always did when I remembered what he gave for this curse.

"They've been here for hours. They keep Tolek busy," he said.

"I don't think anyone's complaining about that," I joked as Seli grabbed Tolek's hands and starting spinning in circles, fast enough that soon her little feet were flying off the floor. Jezebel knelt beside her twin, asking what book he held. "You're always welcome here. Will you be staying for dinner?"

"Thank you, but I want to get them home," Ezalia said with a nod to her kids.

Herding them out the door proved a more difficult challenge than the chancellor expected, though, the kids continuously turning around to call one more thing to any member of our family.

"Thank you for everything," Rina added before Ezalia disappeared out the door with a wave.

As the latch clicked shut, I watched the spot where the chancellor had been. I admired how she held her family together amid loss and warfare, yet still managed to assist us with the Angelcurse. After that first trial, she and Seron had made an effort to spend more time as a family, and seeing her balance it all was inspiring.

It was how we'd ended up here, needing grounds to host the fae queen's court. The Ridgebrooks were already in the southernmost part of the islands for winter and happened to know of both a cottage we could stay in and a location for that impending meeting.

With a final grateful nod after the chancellor, I looped my arm through Rina's and led her upstairs. We both slipped into dry clothing, then ducked back down into the brightly lit kitchen. Pale blue lace curtains framed rain-streaked windows and a mosaic of coral tiles comprised the floor.

Jezebel and Erista were both in clean, dry clothes now, too, and they dropped onto the bench along the breakfast nook as Tolek placed a small tray laden with a carafe of crisp white wine, glasses, and snacks before them.

"Thank the Spirits." Jezebel snatched up a wedge of soft cheese and spread it on a chunk of bread. "I was *famished*," she hummed as she swallowed.

"We stopped to eat a few hours ago." Erista laughed softly, leaning back against the bench

"Hours!" Jez complained.

Chuckling, I fell into the seat beside Jezebel and pulled the book I'd been leafing through earlier toward me, toying with the cover. "Now you're fed and comfortable, so tell us everything."

Tolek tossed me a towel to finish drying my hair, then joined us at the table as Santorina pulled out a chair beside me.

"The human training camps are going...wonderfully," Rina said with a hint of what almost sounded like disbelief. "Ezalia took us to each of the key cities where Leo established contact. One is even nearing one hundred participants now." The chancellor had introduced us to her brother back in Brontain when we were hunting for Gaveny's emblem, and he'd been instrumental in Santorina's progress so far.

"And we stopped in the largest human town in Mystique Territory," Erista chimed in as Jezebel nodded with eager, wide eyes, cheeks stuffed. Half of the food was already gone.

"The soldiers Lyria sent are doing well, then?" Tolek asked as he poured glasses of wine.

"Phenomenally," Erista said, taking one from him.

Jezebel swallowed her mouthful. "Three of her lieutenants have spread throughout the territory, but this one, south of Caprecion, was up to ninety-two humans training to fight as warriors."

"Excellent." Tolek grinned, and I thought there was a bit of pride for his sister's soldiers' aid.

Our weeks here had been a facade of peace, but with the fae coming to Gallantia, it was more imperative than ever that we were prepared—and that meant everyone.

Despite the fact that the queen's court was to be contained to a plot of land off the coast, I didn't trust them. We'd told city leaders throughout the territories to be on alert.

Because the fae were coming to Gallantia, and their bloody history preceded them.

"What's happened here?" Santorina asked.

I summoned a bud of Angellight in response. It slipped around my hand, dancing up my arm. Then, I twirled it about the room, mingling with the lace curtains behind us and frolicking over the mystlight stove.

"You have better control!" Rina gushed between bites of fruit.

"Yes, and she terrorizes me with it," Tolek mockingly complained with a shake of his head. In answer, I sent the Angellight to weave through his hair, swaying and lifting the brown locks.

"I'm only trying to understand what it does," I said sweetly, calling the light back to my hand. Beside me, Jezebel watched it curiously, a crease between her brows.

"Didn't you learn what it does when you two went to that other realm?" Erista asked. Wrapping her arm around my sister, the Soulguider gently dragged her fingertips over her shoulder and Jez melted against her.

"The Spirit Realm," I corrected. We guessed that was where we'd been during the battle. "And we didn't learn much," I added glumly. Angellight slowed its dance around my wrist as if in thought. "But we were rather distracted."

"Yes, swallowing an unclassified vial of magic, traveling to a new realm because of it, and using your miraculous Angel power to blast a threat on this realm to smithereens *is* rather distracting," Tolek mocked.

"I'm glad you understand," I said seriously, but I sent that lingering thread of Angellight to twine around his head and flick him in the ear.

As we picked at snacks, everyone discussed tomorrow's plans. Santorina was venturing to nearby cliffs to assess the flora growing there. Apparently being in a different territory meant a whole host of new ingredients for her healing practice. She was already writing to our Bodymelder friends about it.

Jezebel and Erista had no agenda beyond lounging on one of the white sand beaches with a stack of books that could pertain to Jezzie's spirit-speaking power. We hadn't figured out why she was able to hear those on the verge of death or how she'd been able to control departing spirits in their final moments. But my sister had her cycle this week and swore she needed to rest to accommodate it, despite the tonic Rina gave us that made them less severe the few times a year we suffered them.

Beneath the table, Tolek ran a foot up my calf, silently calling my attention. He sat back in his chair, arms folded and a brow quirked as if to ask, *What would you like to do?*

With the way desire shot through his eyes—and my body—I had many ideas of what I'd like to do, but none fell under the order of remaining *visible* to any spying fae. Unless we truly gave them a show—

"Morbid reading choice," Jezebel interrupted the thought, nearly choking on her wine as she picked up the book beside me and flipped to the page I'd marked. At the title heading the excerpt in looping letters, any heat Tolek had ignited promptly dissipated.

"*An Angel's Fall to Magic?*" Erista read, tilting her head with more innocent curiosity than the rest of the table who all appeared various levels of concerned.

The mood sobered, and I leaned back against the bench, picking up my routine with the Angellight. "We still have to find the Soulguider and Starsearcher emblems, and while we now have a better grasp on *where* we should be looking"—the three we'd found were in sites sacred to the Angels, though that left many possibilities—"we don't know what they're for. I can't stop thinking about when Kakias died."

A chill swept across the room, but Tolek said, "Because when Bant's Spirit was released from Kakias's body, it meant something." He didn't add any qualifiers to the sentence. No *you thought* or *it might have*. I'd told him I'd felt in my bones that Bant's Spirit and the magic in the Angel emblems were connected, that the way the powers of Angels had warred in my blood had to indicate *something*, and he believed me.

"It...disappeared into the mountains." Why? And what would it do now? I continued, "I can't stop thinking about how much this connection to the Angellight seemed to change when Jezebel and I went to the Spirit Realm. Before then, I'd harnessed Angellight through bleeding on the emblems, but now..."

Light flared in the palm of my hand again.

A beat of silence passed in the room, the theories of ancient, unheard of magics pressing down on us.

"Those files your father found on Annellius said he died of blood loss, correct?" Rina asked of the first Chosen of the Angels. A pang went through my heart at the mention of my father. Jezzie's hand clasped mine under the table, and I nodded. "Maybe it was from using Angelblood on the emblems."

Tolek stiffened, ready to dissuade any more use of the Angel tokens if it risked my life, but I spoke up. "That could be, but it feels...wrong. I'm *supposed* to use the emblems—to unite them—so how could doing that have killed him and effectively stopped his efforts?" I held the shard of Damien's power hanging on my necklace. "No, I think Annellius did something he *wasn't* supposed to do in hiding them. And I think that led to his downfall."

"Greedy, greedy warrior," Erista said thoughtfully, watching my Angellight wind over the table.

Was he? Did that legacy ring true, or was there more buried beneath the histories?

As the thought itched deeper beneath my skin and the others returned to their leisurely plans, my fingers twitched against the side of my cup. The whirling light sped with my agitation.

"Excuse me," I said, popping out of my seat and wandering into the living room. I didn't stop until I stood in front of the window that took up most of the front wall, looking out over the small, rain-soaked garden and the ambling path beyond.

"Feeling crowded in there?" Tolek asked, wrapping his arms around my waist. I leaned my head back against his shoulder and inhaled the citrus and spice scent that calmed my nerves.

"A bit."

"We've been here a while," Tolek began.

I sighed. "I don't know how much longer I can do this." Spinning out of his grasp, I pressed a hand to the glass, watching raindrops I couldn't touch slip down. "I feel trapped. Stifled. These rules—I'm ready to tell Ritalia where she can put them."

Tolek huffed a laugh. Clasping his hands behind his back, he leaned against the wall beside the window. "Though I'd love to see you take on the fae queen—and while I'm certain you could win—we've made it this long. Let's keep planning, keep searching for hints of the emblems and your magic. Your sister is back, and when the rain stops, you can see Sapphire."

My warrior horse—pegasus—did always calm me. Flying with her secretly, under the cover of night these weeks, had been one of the few reliefs bringing me joy.

I took a deep breath, searching for the reasons I knew Tolek's suggestions were correct as I watched the empty road out front. "Remain docile here to appease the bargain, welcome the queen, receive our information, get her out quickly, and return to what's important."

"One correction," he said, voice rough. And he took a slow, tempting step toward me. My eyes flashed to his, those amber specks burning. Tol dropped his head, and his lips brushed my ear as he whispered, "Not too docile."

I sucked in a breath as he tugged my robe open, his hand dropping to skim the hem of my nightgown. As his calloused fingers brushed my thighs and heat pooled in my core, I didn't care that there were others in the cottage, that we were up against the glass, shutters thrown wide. My head rolled back as he kissed along my neck, every breath a rasp that absorbed my worries.

All I cared about now was the unsettled, restless creature inside of me and how Tolek could tame it, soothe it, give me an outlet to let all that wild energy peak—

A knock sounded on the front door, crashing through every indecent, lustful plan I was concocting. Based on Tolek's sigh as he stepped back and the way he adjusted himself, I thought he might have had his own plans brewing.

I followed him lazily toward the foyer, admiring the way his powerful back cut against his thin shirt. But when he opened the door and every one of those defined muscles stiffened, my own body tightened. Magic hummed in my veins, ready to be wielded.

Hurrying to Tol, I ducked beneath his arm and met two pairs of dark eyes. Canines flashed in the male's pointed smile, conveying every reason he was here without saying a word. And when he tugged his hood back, pointed ears peeked through his rain-soaked hair. At his side, his sister grinned fiercely.

"Ophelia?" Jezebel called from the kitchen. "Who is it?"

A scrape of chairs and a chorus of padding footsteps told me they were all coming to see.

"Plans are off for the week," I said without looking over my shoulder. And I matched Lancaster's and Mora's feral grins, curious magic riling beneath my skin. "Her Highness is finally ready to meet."

Chapter Three
Malakai

"The public will not accept—"

"We have been through this time and time again, Nassik," Barrett nearly groaned, but he maintained his *princely* demeanor and scratched his wolf, Rebel, behind the ears where he sat beside the prince at the head of the table.

"And yet you continue to be irrational," Nassik said, fingers clenching atop the onyx stone. It was cold and uninviting, much like most of the Engrossian Valley Palace, devoid of staff and comforts.

As one of the members of the former queen's dwindling council, Nassik Langswoll had been pressing Barrett on this matter and that matter every waking moment since the war ended. Even *my* head was aching from it.

At least the three remaining council members were all against Kakias and not entirely opposed to Barrett's rule.

"And you continue to be the biggest thorn the Angel has ever imposed in my side," Barrett drawled.

"The public needs a ruler." Nassik's voice was as icy as his blue-eyed stare, sharp cheekbones and jawline creating an angular, unapproachable expression. He folded his hands atop the table, a brutal scar peeking from beneath the cuff of his tunic—one of the Engrossian markings.

"They have one," Barrett sneered.

"Who chose to fight in the opposing army!"

Barrett's voice darkened. "And which is standing today?"

In the answering silence, I drummed my fingers on the table.

Two weeks. That's how long it had been since I arrived at the Valley Palace as one of Ophelia's representatives. She and Barrett wanted to present an alliance of the two major clans following the war. Mila and Lyria had been here even longer. And Barrett had been dealing with these challenges for nearly six weeks when the Engrossian-Mindshaper army forfeited on that battlefield.

No title, I'd told Ophelia when she asked if I would come in her stead. It was my only stipulation.

No need, she'd answered with a sly smirk.

I hadn't been sure what she meant, but I didn't question it. Lyria and Mila retained their titles. I was only here as a figure of the Mystiques and to assist Barrett. My brother.

And because Tolek had accused me of moping after Mila left the outposts. As the courtly bickering continued, my hand slipped beneath the table to squeeze her thigh.

She flicked her eyes my way, reproachful brow raised. When I returned it, one corner of her lips ticked up. Spirits, we'd been in this chamber for hours. It was nearly dinner time; I couldn't wait to get her out of here.

"Nassik," Barrett snapped, nothing but an erratic, cocky command. In contrast, his consort and general, Dax, was all calm intimidation where he stood behind the prince's chair. "Look around you." Barrett paused, allowing the older man to do so. The other two council members, Pelvira and Elvek, mirrored the action, taking in the six empty seats lining the long, rectangular table. The emerald velvet curtains were heavy with dust, the windows cracked open to allow thick, swampy air within the palace's stone walls.

Barrett lounged in his chair, one hand still stroking between Rebel's ears as the animal watched the council members with keen, sleuthing observation gifted by the God of Mythical Beasts.

"Now, tell me what you see," Barrett said after an intentional, lengthy pause.

"I do not understand," Nassik retorted, exasperation clear.

"Tell me what you see in this room." Barrett planted both feet on the floor and leaned forward. "Better yet, when you walk the halls of this palace—*my* home—what do you hear?"

"Hear?" Nassik scoffed.

"What do the staff say?"

"The staff is gone."

Barrett let that confession hang in the air. "Precisely, Nassik."

"I don't see what that has to do with anything," the man continued to argue.

But it was Mila who cut in. "Barrett, you were a guest of Revered Alabath for quite some time, correct?"

"An honored one," Barrett answered quickly. Tension between the council members thickened, but Barrett didn't flinch.

"I understand Mystiques have never been your ally," Mila said, "but I think we can all agree on one thing: Ophelia Alabath nurtured a warm culture in that palace upon her ascent to the Revered's seat, did she not?"

"She absolutely did," Barrett said.

Lyria continued her friend's argument. "The Revered opened the doors. She let the people know her."

"We cannot open the doors!" Nassik argued.

"I have to agree with him on that," Pelvira finally spoke, her long ash-blonde hair slipping around her pale shoulders, brown eyes alert in her narrow face. "We cannot expose the palace in that way."

"Confidential business is conducted here," Elvek added, nodding his plump head. All three of the council members' faces were stony.

Mila nodded. "Metaphorically speaking, though."

"General Lovall is correct," Barrett said. He folded his hands atop the table, seizing control of the meeting in that firm gesture. Dax remained stoic, his arms crossed. "We do not need to fully open the doors in order to make my reign more approachable. This table is empty—the palace is empty. If the people are going to understand that I defected to take my mother down for the good of all Engrossians"—soft flinches from the council—"they need to know me."

"They still will not trust you," Nassik said.

Barrett inhaled. That control was cracking, but he asked fairly, "And how do you suggest I negotiate their trust?"

All three council members considered. I had the distinct impression they had already discussed this very topic and were aware what was said next would not be well received, despite Barrett fighting to remain calm.

"There are rumblings of those who supported your mother's cause planning a coup against you," Elvek said, the final word dropping like steel against marble.

There had been warriors in Kakias's army who fought willingly. She had wielded the power of Thorn's broken crown—the piece of the Mindshaper Angel emblem allowing her to control a portion of the minor clan—over many, but some of the Engrossian legions had truly wanted to wage war on the Mystiques, and she'd given them the chance.

And they were the ones who would fight against the acceptance of Barrett's reinstatement as prince and any coronation to come.

"If we are going to beat the spread of those tainted beliefs, you will need an official partner to sit on the throne with you," Nassik proposed. "One to strengthen ties, the public perception of your allegiance, and belief in your capability of ruling this territory."

"Wonderful, Dax is already a general." Barrett waved a hand to where his consort stood, stony faced, as if braced for an impact that had yet to launch. "We'll happily conduct the ceremonies and rituals required by law."

Dax offered a small nod of agreement, but his expression held firm.

"Dax Goverick is indeed a general, yes," Nassik said. "But he defected as you did."

"We did that to support—"

"We understand, Prince Barrett," Pelvira interrupted, compassion softening her voice. "And I do agree that many of your people will see it that way. Many did not want this war, and we can ensure the truth spreads of who was responsible."

"The people will believe what they want to believe—"

Pelvira spoke over Nassik. "We can't open the doors, but we can bring back the staff. The late Queen Kakias dismissed them all, but we can return life to the palace. We get *them* to understand Prince Barrett's involvement and motivations. They will return to their homes each night, and the gossip will spread."

"It's true," I added. "After I was released from imprisonment, the news spread to every stretch of Mystique Territory in a matter of weeks. The vast majority turned against Lucidius quickly. The same will happen with Kakias."

Now, Mila placed a hand on *my* knee beneath the table, but no nerves bustled beneath my skin at the mention of my time in captivity.

Nassik stewed on what I said. "My point still stands."

"I seem to have missed your entire point in the first place," Barrett drawled, dragging a ringed hand through his dark curls.

"You need a proper partner to symbolize your commitment to the Engrossians." Dax's hand fisted at Nassik's words, and the blow echoed through the chamber with the cruel, curling smile of the councilman. "If you truly want to earn back your throne and lead this clan, you will bond with someone from a noble house, or you will lose your title."

∿

"*I WILL LOSE MY TITLE?* He will lose his head!" Barrett's storming echoed through the door of his suite hours later. It was the first time I'd seen the normally unflappable prince this angry.

When it came to Dax, there were no limits.

Taking a deep breath, I rapped my knuckles against the door. Dax opened it a moment later, giving me a terse nod. I followed him through the foyer, into the prince's office.

The King's Suite—the one Barrett and Dax had taken up residence in upon their return to the Engrossian capital—was bedecked in the deepest onyx and silvers, hints of emerald green splashed across the curtains and marble sculptures accenting the wealth.

Barrett prowled before the window muttering beneath his

breath. His head snapped up as we entered. "Brother," he greeted, his voice dark as a storm cloud. Rebel tracked his every step, the wolf up to his hip.

I nodded, tucking my hands into my pockets. I'd come alone, leaving Lyria and Mila to handle some correspondence.

"Barrett," Dax soothed, resuming their conversation with an unbelievably calm demeanor. "We knew this was a possibility when we left. We knew there was a chance of much worse than this."

"Execution, exile, et cetera." Barrett continued pacing, the sky outside dark. "I knew it was all possible, and still I took the risk."

"Then this should not be a surprise," Dax said. I hung back, allowing him to handle his prince.

Barrett wouldn't look at either of us; he just stared blankly out his south-facing window toward the city that wasn't visible thanks to the dense canopy of swamp trees and thick fog. He kept his gaze fixed on that direction each time he pivoted, though, as if he could see the warriors lining the streets. Beg them to accept him, to trust him.

"I'm not surprised there are challenges," Barrett huffed.

"Then explain, please," Dax asked, leaning against the desk with his arms crossed.

"I knew there was a possibility we would either die before returning here or I would not be accepted back." Barrett stopped, turning to face us with a hand dragging halfway through his hair. A torn expression flickered through the ire on his face. "I did not even consider the possibility that they would try to take you from me, to name you unfit or anything of the sort." His eyes dropped to Dax's gut, where Kakias had speared the general with a whip of dark magic that nearly killed him. "After all you've given for this, you deserve to be the one beside me."

"I am your consort," Dax said, his hand bracing his stomach. "That will never change, even if another takes a formal title."

Based on his stiff shoulders, he was saying this to push Barrett toward the future he'd always wanted, the one their people needed. I was certain the last thing Dax wanted was for Barrett to be with someone else even if only in name.

"Explain it to me," I cut in at the tick of Dax's jaw. The general cast me a slight nod of appreciation. "What is it they want exactly?"

"They want me to complete the official Engrossian partner rituals with a warrior of a noble household," Barrett explained, falling into a high-back leather chair and flinging his legs over one arm. "It involves two sets of vows. One is simply spoken before a priestess, followed by the scarring."

"Scarring? Like your..." I nodded at Barrett's chest. When their warriors came of age, Engrossians marked the accomplishment with scars and used a special ointment that did not allow the wounds to heal naturally. Barrett's were a brutal X stretching from collarbones to waist. Dax's, I had never seen.

"Similar," Barrett explained. "The same anointing tonic is used, but each partner takes a blade to the other, normally a small slice to the hand, and the blood is mixed. A vow said. The ointment applied. And by the blessing of the Angels"—his hands twirled through the air, voice thick with sarcasm—"your souls and spirits are bonded forever."

"And you two haven't completed either of the vows?" I asked.

"Trust me, if we had, this conversation wouldn't be happening." Barrett's expression darkened.

"We almost did once," Dax explained. "Kakias locked me up." And when Barrett freed him, they'd fled for Mystique Territory.

Perhaps it was obvious, but I asked, "Could you?"

Barrett looked ready to storm out of here and find a priestess, but Dax shifted off the desk, leaning against Barrett's chair with a wince, and said, "It takes days to recover. They'd know, and it could ruin any support Barrett has earned."

The prince huffed, sinking back into his chair. Absently, my hand went to my chest, where the Bind tattoo was now and forever inked.

"The last ritual is the consummation." Dax's throat worked over a swallow, his words hanging in the air.

"Is all of this about an heir?" I asked.

"No." Barrett sighed. "But they will claim that's part of it. I suppose the upside of that is they cannot select Nassik's heinous son for me."

Dax's fingers drifted gently through the prince's hair as he said, "We always assumed we had plenty of time to figure that part out, hoping Barrett would have centuries to rule."

"But now it's another fact they will use against us." Barrett let his feet fall to the floor with two loud thuds that had Rebel perking up.

"What was your original plan for an heir?"

Barrett lifted his sharp eyes to me, defined cheekbones casting shadows across his face in the dim mystlight. But there was a soft excitement in his words. "We always wanted to adopt, but if none of those children seemed fit for or wanted the role, we would watch the royal houses."

My brows shot up. "You would name another house successor to your throne?" It was unheard of in Engrossian history, as far as I'd studied.

But Barrett nodded. "Whoever had the best interest of our clan, the kindest but strongest heart, and the wisest mind. That was who I would train as my heir and nominate to transition power to when the time came, should the Spirits support them."

I crossed my arms, leaning back against the wall as I considered everything they'd said. The prince and his consort continued down their spiraled conversation.

"They want you to select a partner," I interrupted. "Do you have say in who?"

"I'm sure Nassik is already positioning his house as the wisest choice."

He seemed the type, the bastard. "Who will he offer?"

"He has three children that could be considered of appropriate age," Barrett said. Dax drifted to the side table, pouring each of us a measure of whiskey.

"You already presented an argument for why his son won't be chosen," I said, accepting a glass from the general. "Tell me of the other two."

"One daughter is nearly thirty years older than I am." Barrett grimaced. At our age, that was significant, but in a century, when

Angels-willing they were enjoying a prosperous rule, it would be nothing. "Vixin. She is vile, though."

"And the other?" I brought the glass to my lips. The liquor warmed my body on the way down, as if forging a plan.

"Celissia is wonderful, Barrett," Dax said before his prince could speak. "You've been close since you were children. You can't deny that."

Barrett rolled his eyes, but a small smile fought on his lips as he studied his whiskey. "She was one of my only friends as a child, actually." He looked at me. "She's two years older, stunningly beautiful, and has worked in the Banix citadel for the past decade. She's much smarter than I am and wickedly cunning with that mind, but kinder than most."

"Sounds like the obvious choice, then," I said.

Barrett frowned at me. "I don't want a choice."

Sighing, I set my glass on the shelf and sat in the chair across from his, a low, round table between us. "I know you don't want one, and I think it's awful you have to have one, but make the choice yours. Announce Celissia as your partner before another can be chosen for you, then prolong the vows as long as possible. Buy yourselves as much time as you can by going along with their plan."

Barrett glowered at me as if hating that my suggestion made sense. Dax nodded slowly, if reluctantly.

"Why are you being so rational?" Barrett asked. "It's unsettling."

Dax flicked the back of his head, but he added, "He finally cleared his mind now that he and Mila are f—"

"Not that it matters," I cut him off as Barrett burst out laughing, "but we haven't been." Really fucking wished we had, though.

Barrett cocked his head in an eerily similar way to Rebel. "Why not?"

I sighed. "Does it matter?"

"Very much so," Barrett declared, and Dax chuckled.

I pinched the bridge of my nose, squeezing my eyes shut. "If you must know, Mila went through...a lot in the first war." She'd been a prisoner. Had been tortured—just the thought had me seeing red. I pushed the fury down. "And the recent battles dragged up memories. So, while she works through that, we're getting to know each other." Away from a battlefield. Trying to do normal fucking things like normal fucking people.

When I opened my eyes, Barrett and Dax were exchanging a look.

"What?" I asked.

"She's too good for you," Barrett blurted.

Dax tugged the prince's hair. "*He means,* she's a good one."

"No, *I mean* he shouldn't fuck it up!" Barrett corrected. "We worked closely with her during the war. And Mila...well, she's special."

"Trust me," I said, unable to fight my smile, "I know that better than anyone." Standing, I clapped my brother on the shoulder and turned to refill all of our glasses. "You won't say those vows with anyone besides Dax, Barrett. We'll ensure it."

After I placed full drinks back in their hands, I dug through the drawers for a deck of cards, giving the prince and his true consort a moment to debrief on what I'd suggested.

I understood Barrett's reluctance to let his role control his life. Spirits, I admired him for it. I wished I had a bit more of that in me when I'd been younger. Perhaps things wouldn't have ended up as they had with Lucidius.

But sometimes you had to navigate within the world you were placed in rather than bending it to your rules. Make tough decisions—hate making them even—in order to benefit those relying on you and hope your plans worked in the long run. My knuckles whitened around the drawer handle.

Those decisions were worth it. At least, that's what I told myself while imprisoned.

The Engrossians needed a leader like Barrett. If it meant he had to play the game of politics for a while, he'd be victorious.

As I was slamming drawer after drawer, the prince's muttered words to his consort drifted over to me, the mournful but determined tones solidifying my own righteous intention.

"My love for you is deeper than the valleys, Dax," Barrett whispered, voice searing with promise. "No one will raise the valleys."

CHAPTER FOUR
MALAKAI

I ROLLED MILA ONTO HER BACK AND HOVERED ATOP her, the crisp, dark-gray sheets falling around us. "Good morning," I said, ducking to kiss her neck.

"It's nearly afternoon," she joked, blinking at the angle of the sun slanting through the fog outside the floor-to-ceiling windows. The dark, clouded glass sliced narrow gaps between the gray stone walls of the Engrossian palace. So much of this structure was turrets and angular towers like the one we were in now stretching to the heavens.

"Then we have time to make up for," I mumbled against her shoulder.

Her hands dragged down my back as she hummed, right over the scars warping my skin, but she didn't stop. Mila never flinched at my scars.

"I'm not sure how long we can get away with hiding in here," she said, voice breathy.

I kissed along the white lace-trimmed edge of her nightgown. Her back arched, peaked nipples pressing toward me in silent invitation.

One I wasn't accepting yet, no matter how much my cock throbbed at the thought of sinking into her.

"Where did we leave off last night?" I asked, skimming my hand up her side, the satin begging to be removed.

30

"What?" she gasped.

"You were telling me of your home when you fell asleep on the couch." I worked my way back up her neck. "Of the tradition your family had on Ascension Day."

Pausing over her with my hands on either side of her head, I kissed her once, briefly, then rolled off her and propped myself up against the pillows. Mila pushed up on her elbows and blinked at me with her mouth slightly open.

"What was it again?" I asked innocently. "The game with your brothers?"

Mila shook her head. "I'd rather not think about my *brothers* right now," she mumbled but rolled onto her side, tugging the sheet around her. "It was an obstacle course. Or a gift hunt. A mix of both, I suppose. My brothers would set it up overnight, and when I woke in the morning, it was a race to find my presents."

I smiled at the way her eyes drifted wistfully, like the memory was stealing her attention. "Four older brothers must have been a lot of fun. And mess."

I thought back to my own holidays, normally spent with my friends' families. Fancy long dinners that none of us cared for, especially as children.

Mila laughed. "My brothers are my protectors—sometimes annoyingly so—but they certainly guaranteed I had an eventful childhood."

"Do you ever think about going back home?"

She and Lyria may have met during the war, but Mila wasn't from Palerman. She was from a small town near Turren, bordered by the plains.

The door of her fortress pulled tight at the suggestion. Her gaze dropped, and I followed it—straight to the scars on her wrists. The horrible ones from her time imprisoned during the first war. The ones she normally covered with gold ivy-carved wrist braces, but that she'd been leaving bare more often when we were alone.

Silently, I sat up and took one of her hands between mine.

"I think," Mila finally said, eyes still on her scars, "when all of this business is said and done, I'd like to be able to return home semi-frequently. I'd like to help my parents as they grow old—

watch my brothers fall in love and have families and lives not burdened by war." She swallowed. Was she thinking of the one brother, the youngest of the four, who didn't make it out of the first war? "I don't think I could ever stay there. I've seen too much. Changed too much. But I also don't know if I could fight in another war."

Mila looked up at me from beneath her lashes, waiting for my opinion, especially on that last part. Like I might think it made her less of a warrior.

It was always a marvel when she cracked her walls like this. The general who did not need the opinions of others because she was strong enough to carry us all on her own, pausing to wonder if maybe she could let someone within those barriers.

The problem was, I didn't have much of an opinion on it. "I'd understand either way," I said, shrugging. "If you wanted to go back home to that sleepy small town surrounded by family, I wouldn't blame you. I don't know how you've kept fighting all these years." I took a deep breath. "But I also would understand wanting the opposite of a quiet life. To go out and seek adventure, even if not leading an army."

"Have you considered what you want?" Mila rolled onto her stomach, propping her chin on a hand as she looked up at me. That look was pure temptation, ice-blue eyes blinking up at me, cheeks slightly pink, and platinum hair wild.

What had she asked again? *Have I considered what I want?*

For starters, her.

But that wasn't what she meant. "No," I answered honestly. "I've been dealing with the past too much to map out a future beyond the assignment to assist Barrett. But I know I don't want anything chosen *for* me. Not anymore."

She smiled. "And how does being here make you feel about your father?"

I gritted my teeth at the question. Not because I was still uncomfortable talking about Lucidius, but because when speaking with me or even Barrett, Mila always referred to him as that: *your father*. Like she couldn't let us forget.

But I shoved aside the grating sensation it dragged through my chest—dug through all the work I'd done to reconcile the truth of Lucidius and the devastation he'd caused with Kakias.

"I think I let a lot of that go on the battlefield." Her fingers drew aimless circles across my stomach as I spoke, and the gentle touch soothed the agitation of a moment ago. "Or maybe it was after the Engrossians surrendered and the queen was gone." My muscles tightened as Mila's nails scratched along my skin at the mention of the queen. "I don't know when it happened, but fighting in the army actually helped me work through all the pain Lucidius left me with."

Charging into battle alongside the warriors he tried to ruin, proving to myself that though he wrecked us all, we could still stand.

"I don't feel as beholden to his mistakes as I once did, because now I'm fighting for myself." It was an unshackling of the heavy cage around my heart. One that I'd held in for far too long.

But I still didn't know where that left me moving forward.

Mila seemed to understand, not repeating that initial question but letting the truth of what I'd admitted hang between us. And I swore a bit of pride shone in her eyes.

Her gaze traveled up my bare chest. Though the worst were on my back, she cataloged each scar. She'd done this before. Studied them. Not in judgment or fear or any of the soiled feelings I felt toward them. Just observed.

But then her stare froze on something. My North Star Bind, dark against my tan skin. With her eyes on it, it was a beacon. Slowly, she traced each point.

Mila tilted her head, hair pooling over her shoulder. "How does it feel?"

Mila had the first two Mystique tattoos—the Bond on the back on her neck, and the Band, a recently-inked ring of flowers around her upper arm that declared her rank as general—so she wasn't asking how it felt to have the ink tether your soul the way only the ritualistic promises could.

"It's empty most days," I admitted. "Sometimes, we both feel a pang of emotion, but it's normally not clear why. I felt it during the battle."

I'd thought a knife was being driven through my chest, actually. I'd asked Ophelia if she felt anything similar, but if she had, her body had been under too much distress in the Spirit Realm to remember.

Mila's eyes swam with a mix of worry and something else. Something I thought might be...jealousy?

Tilting her chin up, I said, "It doesn't mean anything. I'll get us tea." Bending to kiss her forehead, I climbed out of bed, but she didn't follow.

"It might not *mean* anything to you two, Malakai," she said, "but those soul bonds don't go away that easily."

I nearly shuddered at the weight to her words, searching for that cage in my chest I used to lock all these feelings in. But the door had been blown wide open by the woman looking at me with raised brows. So instead, I let the discomfort her statement dragged up find a spot in the back of my mind. One where I wasn't locking it away, but it waited until I knew what to do with it.

LAUGHTER ECHOED from Mila's bedchamber before I even stepped foot in the door. It was a laugh I was beginning to recognize anywhere, and my own spirit lifted with the throaty, gleeful sound.

"Must you be so cheerful?" Lyria Vincienzo's voice echoed as I crossed the threshold, tray in hand.

Mila laughed again, propped against the foot of the bed with her arms crossed. I handed her a steaming cup of tea—the spicy, cinnamon one she loved, with ginger and clove—as she said to her friend, "I don't believe I'm any more cheerful than yesterday."

The Master of Weapons and Warfare was sprawled on one of the low settees before the fire, a damp towel spread across her eyes and head. Her long, chocolate brown hair pooled over the black cushion, curls nearly spilling to the floor.

"Lyria," I greeted, leaning against the bedpost near Mila. "How late did he keep you up then?"

"Until nearly dawn," she grumbled. "After he returned from

visiting Celissia with the proposal"—she pointed a finger in our direction without removing the cloth—"and you two snuck away, there was no chance for me to leave."

"Like you would have," Mila snickered.

"His Royal Highness wanted to *celebrate* his encroaching partnership, and I am nothing if not a loyal ally," Lyria drawled, waving a hand.

I stiffened. "How is he?"

At that, Lyria removed the towel and sat up. She closed her eyes for a moment, fighting off a wave of dizziness. "He's furious, asserting he will find a way out of this bonding, but I believe he's come to terms with the fact that they have to pretend for now."

"Was she with him?"

"No. He wants us all to meet her tonight, though. A formal introductory dinner, and we are all guests of His Royal Highness himself." Lyria flopped back onto the settee, the legs creaking.

I smirked at Mila, and she rolled her eyes but shot her friend a wary glance. Lyria had taken up the position of Barrett's comrade in drink, the two emptying many bottles of rich Engrossian wine in the time that we'd been here. Barrett, because his advisors were driving him to a rage as deep as the Blackfyre. Lyria, because...she hadn't said. But we supposed it went back to the war. To the pressure she'd had on her shoulders for months—Spirits, for her entire life. To the way it had cracked like a storm cloud when that final battle ended and the enemy surrendered. To the death count of Mystiques and alliance clans that had risen with the white flags.

She was processing, Mila said. Trying to come to terms with not only the war we'd survived but the conversations she'd had with Tolek regarding their father's manipulation.

Many long conversations, all driving her to a bottle now.

It hadn't become a problem yet. Merely a habit to watch, which Mila took responsibility for. It was her own way of coping. Lyria found distractions. Mila nurtured and organized. And I talked to Mila.

She was good at managing everyone's emotions. Checking in with each of us, helping us work through the demons at our backs.

So, I did that for her when flashes of blood-strewn, snowy mountains or a cage beneath the ground clawed at her.

"Let's get you back to your bed," Mila said, crossing the room to help her friend off the couch. The scars warping the skin across her legs shone in the morning sun. "You can sleep until dinner—"

Before Mila could finish that thought, the entire tower shuddered with two large booms.

"Oh, Damien's shining cock, can't I have one day of rest?" Lyria grumbled, and neither Mila nor I could help laughing this time.

～

JEZEBEL AND ERISTA strode into the entrance chamber of Mila's suite as Lyria made herself presentable, straightening her leathers and tugging her errant hair into a braid. Barrett and Dax followed on the girls' heels.

"We heard your entrance," the prince said, swiping a hand through his sleep-mussed curls.

"We weren't expecting you so soon," Dax forced through a yawn.

"Things have changed," Jezebel said, tugging off the thick leather gloves she wore when she flew.

"You really should be more conspicuous, Jez," I scolded, but hugged the younger Alabath tightly, her black flying leathers cold even through my tunic. "I thought we agreed you'd hide the khrysaor and make the end of your journey on horseback?"

Jezebel snorted a laugh. "Have you seen how dense the fog is across the swamplands today? We'd never be seen, especially landing on the highest towers."

I peeked around her shoulder toward the wide window of the sitting room doorway. A thick layer of gray rolled across the land below the tower.

"The canopies over the swamplands nearly block the skies from sight anyway," Erista added. The bun her curls were slicked back into today didn't so much as wobble as she nodded to assure us. "We didn't go anywhere near the cities in case the fog parted."

Barrett dipped his chin in appreciation, a slow grin spreading across his face. Jezebel launched herself at him, and he caught her with a sweeping hug.

Setting her down, he said, "I'll accept my well wishes and congratulations when you're ready. Has the Revered sent an offering?"

"What?" Jezebel's brows scrunched.

"Aren't you here because of Barrett's approaching partnership?" Mila asked.

Jezebel and Erista looked between the prince and his consort, and my stomach turned over. "What's happened, Jez?"

"Ophelia didn't want to put it in writing, but Queen Ritalia's arrival has been confirmed."

A cold chill passed through the room, every smile fading and every spine straightening. "When?" I asked.

"Two days from now."

"How do you know?" Dax crossed his arms, feet planted and ready for battle.

"Lancaster and Mora returned last night," Jezebel said. "Said she was three days out and we are expected to greet her. Ophelia wants us to fly back tonight."

"Who else?" I jerked my head toward the sitting room. We may as well be comfortable for this.

"The queen travels with her court and requests Ophelia do the same."

"Court?" I echoed.

"Bant's cock." Barrett dragged a hand down his face. "I'm getting flashbacks of my mother." The leader of the only warrior clan to retain titles and habits such as queen and holding court.

Barrett walked straight for the liquor cart beneath the window and poured himself a glass of deep red wine.

"Spirits, me, too, please?" Lyria said, falling onto the couch and stretching a hand out for a glass.

"Ophelia doesn't have a court," Mila said, returning our attention to Jezebel and Erista as they each took an armchair across from Lyria's couch. "Who is she gathering?"

"Ezalia is going to attend, given that the meeting is technically on Seawatcher land, but she's sending Seron and the children away. And Ophelia wants you three to return with us," Jez explained, nodding at Mila, Lyria, and me.

"I'll attend with the Mystiques," Erista added with a proud gleam in her eye. "And we're hoping Cypherion and Vale will return in time, and perhaps Vale will be able to read before, if her magic has been righted."

Having Ophelia's second present would be beneficial, but none of us had heard much from him recently. If he didn't make it back, we'd have to avoid the tricky mention that such a highly-ranking member of the council was missing.

I cast a look to Barrett, but he was already waving me off. "You three, go." The prince exchanged a glance with his consort. "We'll continue working on our matters here and begin introducing Celissia to the people as"—his jaw tightened—"my intended."

Jezebel opened her mouth to inquire, but Erista discreetly kicked her in the shin.

"Okay," I said to Barrett. Why was I worried about leaving him here? "But write to us should you need anything, brother."

Barrett's glee could have erupted at my use of the term. He teased me all throughout our preparation for the flight.

"This will always be your room now, you know," he announced as I gathered my things from my suite in the Valley Palace. I didn't tell him my chest clenched with the sentiment.

"Don't you want something to remember me by, brother?" he taunted when I intentionally left behind the book he'd loaned me when I couldn't sleep last week.

"Are you going to miss me?" he finally asked when I climbed onto Jezebel's khrysaor with her and Mila, no hint of teasing in his voice.

That time, I told him the truth. "I will, brother."

Barrett's victorious cries disappeared beneath the beating of the khrysaor's mighty leathery wings, tipped in razor-sharp scales.

I squeezed Mila's waist. "Ready for our next battle, General?"

And she shivered back against me as she replied, "Let's meet a queen, Warrior Prince."

Chapter Five

Damien

Bant sent a rope of gleaming light etched with inky threads rioting around the cavern, carving away walls and pillars, grand arches and a high-ceilinged foyer that allowed us to breathe for the first time in many millennia. Not that we relied on the air to exist, but the foreign, soothing inflation of my lungs nearly sent a rush of power to my head.

The seven of us gathered in the newly-defined space as Bant chipped away at worn stalagmites sand stalactites, revealing a design with a familiarity I could not place.

With his Spirit returned, he was the only one of us with strength enough to carry out this task.

My wings showered golden light upon the floor as I floated throughout the new space. Gaveny's ocean-tinged power drifted among mine, and Thorn's stormy clouds followed him as he zipped along the highest points, closely studying the detailing of the ceiling.

"It is grand," Xenique observed, a bit skeptical as she hovered near a rubble-strewn staircase to nowhere. It stopped just out of sight, only the illusion of an escape. Beside her, Valyrie studied the ceiling as if looking for the stars, our two sisters' unlit wings beating softly at their backs.

"It is as he demanded," Bant gritted out, wielding another

band of power to carve away an arch where an entrance would belong. I tilted my head at the precise placement, that inkling of familiarity budding further within me.

Ptholenix flew forward, placing the Angelglass he had reforged from shards in the spot.

"Firebird," Bant snapped, and Ptholenix raised a quizzical brow. "Not there."

"This is where he demanded," Ptholenix stated calmly.

"That is where a tunnel shall be carved for rooms," Bant argued, flexing his powerful arms as his light whipped out. So chauvinistic—the Engrossian always had been. And now, with his might unlocked...

Ptholenix sighed, his fiery wings crackling at his back with suppressed annoyance. "No, those belong beneath the staircase."

I tuned out their bickering, sweeping a gaze over each nook and cranny. My wings fluttered as the discomfort grew.

"What's wrong?" Gaveny asked, the ropes and scales of tattoos glinting across his shoulders and chest as he hovered before me, blocking out the senseless arguing.

"Ptholenix is correct," I answered. "The Angelglass belongs in the arch."

"I know he is," Gaveny said, crossing his arms. "Bant will hear for his stubbornness if he does not comply. But that is not what I meant."

The scar across my cheek twinged at the reference to the punishment our master would undoubtedly force upon his disobedient subject. The memory of Bant's wings being torn by shards of Angelglass lashed through me, the former, stifled cavern cramped with the heavy iron scent in my mind.

Heated, Bant moved the Angelglass from the arch to the center of the room, the scars across his wings catching the light. Two large gashes never to sprout feathers in their wake.

Gaveny lowered his chin, insistent. I always suspected that out of the seven of us, the Seawatcher Prime Warrior had retained the most of his mortality. The strongest human mannerisms and thoughts spilling from him.

I swallowed. "I do not know what is wrong here," I admitted. "But something about this is...amiss."

Gaveny studied the pillars, brown hair shifting around his strong shoulders as he turned.

Before he could say anything, a cruel voice sliced through the foyer. "*Bant!*" We all shot to attention as our master floated from an adjacent tunnel. "Why is the Angelglass not as I directed?" He spun a pale hand toward the archway at the head of the room.

And it was only as Ptholenix smirked cockily at Bant replacing the glass where it had originally been—as that large arch of reforged mirror took up the spot of a door—that the reason for my discomfort with Bant's design became evident.

Our master swept through the space, high and low, inspecting every inch.

"You have done a good job, Bant," he drawled. "I will ignore the defiance this time."

Bant's powerful frame inflated, and Gaveny shot me a surprised look, but I could not respond. I was too busy sweeping the details carved into the ceiling and walls. How was it so exact?

"Now that the glass is whole again," our master said, "look."

He wafted a cloud of glimmering white magic toward the Angelglass, and as it brushed across the surface, the Chosen Child's image shimmered to life. She sat on a bench, a book in hand and golden tendrils of power—*our* power—spun above her, as if it was nothing more than a light to study by.

A stoic silence settled across the seven of us, some enraged, some concerned.

"It's pitiful," Bant spat.

"It's manipulative," Valyrie added sharply.

Thorn released a high laugh. "*Kissed by Angels*," he cooed. His wails from the day the child retrieved his crown fluttered through the air as if carried on those strands of shimmering magic. *Kissed by Angels*, he had repeated.

My wings ruffled at the thought, the other Angels shifting as we awaited our master's direction. It was impossible. We mourned them for so long, they'd been forgotten to the rest of the world.

"The lock is poised to crack, despite any pity and manipulation your ranks may deem of the power," our master finally said. The gold of the girl's light reflected in his milky eyes as he hovered closer to the glass.

Bant raised his pointed chin, only a hint of wariness. "If I may," he said, waiting for a nod from our master to continue. "What is pitiful and manipulative is not only the magic. It is the fact that another opponent sails for her shores, and yet this child does nothing." Power ebbed around his ruffled wings, almost uncontrollable since the return of his Spirit. His emotions more volatile, as well. "She's wasting time."

Defensiveness whirled through me—only a taste of the protective emotion. Only ever a taste in this prison. But I had failed with the last chosen, and I would not fail again.

Before I could argue, our master asked, "Is she, though?"

A hint of satisfaction had my wings beating. On either side of me, Ptholenix and Gaveny noted the movement from the corners of their eyes.

Our master explained, "An enemy does indeed sail for her shores. One who could pose a threat to everything we've waited so long for." His milky eyes shone. "But perhaps this is what we need. The queen may not know it, but she may be the ally we have been waiting for."

"Sir?" Xenique asked, longing burning in her round eyes.

"The queen wants one thing. She will undoubtedly ask the girl for help, but should she mistrust this age-old enemy, it could be exactly what we need." His smile was chilling. "Perhaps she will tip the scales in our favor by being precisely the adversary history has painted her as."

And it was that word, *painted*, that had my gaze snapping to the ceiling. In my mind, the murals I had designed on ceilings identical to this rocky encompass flashed. Ones I had crafted with utmost care and passion and longing, placing them perfectly, like clues to future generations.

The discomfort I'd been feeling became a solid knot in my gut, this foyer so familiar and yet foreign.

For we hovered in a stony, buried rendition of my palatial home atop the mountains.

I lowered my gaze, catching my master's milky stare. His goals splashed across my vision, stained crimson.

And a seed of unease grew roots in my unbeating heart.

CHAPTER SIX
OPHELIA

A FEW MILES NORTH OF THE TOWN WE WERE STAYING IN
on the outposts, white sand sloped upward into a gentle hillside,
giving way to lush green grasses that ruffled in the breeze and
looked out over a calm, glassy sea.

It was a stark contrast to the Cliffs of Brontain where we'd
battled slapping gray waves to reach Gaveny's, the Seawatcher
Angel's, emblem out on those platforms.

Both were beautiful in their own ways, though. Rain-soaked
fog nearly kissed the hills tonight, providing the perfect coverage
for a flight.

A gentle nudge to one shoulder and a feathered sweep against
the other had me laughing. Turning, I met Sapphire's crystal blue
eyes. My warrior horse, who'd been harboring a secret all these
years. One that was revealed when something triggered the
unfurling of those beautiful, massive, snow-white wings now
flaring at her side in impatience.

"I miss you every day, girl," I whispered, dropping my head
against her side. "You know why it has to be this way."

She huffed, but I knew she understood.

Prior to the final battle against Kakias, pegasus were no more
than legends of bedtime stories. Until we knew more about how
she had become a creature of myth and what it meant, we had to
keep her a secret.

Her and—

A warm breath traveled down my neck, and I spun, meeting the slitted, golden iris of one of the khrysaor. The one who chased us down in the forest all those months ago. But where I'd been terrified then, now I only rolled my eyes at him.

"He's impatient," Jezebel explained, stroking a hand down his silver mane.

A mane, because the khrysaor was so very similar to my pegasus. Two or three times as large, but a body of a horse with wings and legs covered in knife-sharp scales, and feet ending in claws. I'd gotten a closer look at those wings recently. Realized that beneath the scales, which were a defensive reaction that could retract, the surface was leathery. Nothing like Sapphire's downy feathers.

The khrysaor appeared to be bred more ruthlessly, almost battle-ready, with a layer of armor and ferocious size.

"He's not as fearsome as I once thought," I said to Jezebel as we followed our mounts to a flat expanse of ground beyond the top of the ridge. We'd left Lancaster and Mora back at the cottage with our friends, sneaking out for some private flight time before our audience with Queen Ritalia tomorrow.

My sister avoided my eyes, quiet as she had been since they returned from visiting the human camps. I'd thought the excursion to Engrossian Territory yesterday to pick up Malakai, Mila, and Lyria would placate whatever bothered her, giving her extended flight time, but it hadn't.

"No, Zanox is truly a large baby," she said, distracting me. "He loves attention."

"Zanox?" I asked.

Jezebel stroked the side of her khrysaor's neck affectionally, his silver mane glowing in the moonlight. "He told me his name recently." I raised a brow. "Or he thought it. I can't speak to him, but one day last week I saw him and knew."

"And the other?"

"Dynaxtar," Jezebel said fondly, gazing at her khrysaor in a way that made me certain they were pieces of her soul the way Sapphire was mine.

"Have you ridden her much?" I observed the smaller female

khrysaor already fluttering through the clouds high above, nothing more than a shadow from here. Hidden enough that no one would even imagine what secret was sliding among the stars.

"Dynaxtar is different than Zanox," she explained, voice turning wondrous. "Zanox prefers me. There's a rightness to it. But Dynaxtar? She likes to feel the mist on her hide, free of the burden of a rider." Jez brushed her hair behind her ear. "Sometimes, I wonder if she'll find her rider one day. If there's someone besides me who's meant for her."

"Erista?"

"Dynaxtar allows Erista to ride her because of what Erista means to me." She said it like it was a basic understanding of the nature of mystical beings. "Dynaxtar and Erista don't share the bond, though."

I couldn't tell what was in her voice. Worry? Frustration?

"Do you wish her to find a rider?" I asked gently, Sapphire's wing brushing the ground around me.

"I do," Jez admitted, voice soft. "She deserves that."

I didn't know what that would look like—how to find someone *meant* for a khrysaor as Jezebel was.

"Let's keep Dynaxtar company for the time being, then." I swung up effortlessly onto Sapphire's back, legs tucking in above her wings. Zanox lowered a wing for Jezebel to scale, and something nudged at my brain as I watched her settle.

"Does Elektra get jealous?" I asked of the warrior horse she'd ridden for years.

Jez shook her head, looking down from Zanox's back. "She seems to understand. The bond I have with Elektra is a soul bond that we'll share forever. But what I carry with the khrysaor...it's different. I think the warrior horses grasp that better than we can."

It was a satisfying belief, hoping the world around us and the creatures teeming within it understood the nature of existence and fate at an intrinsic level. In a sense, it was comforting.

Winding my hands into Sapphire's mane, I indulged that pride and whispered, "Fly, girl."

Constellations twinkled above as Sapphire galloped for the cliff edge, and I sank into the peace with my pegasus.

We plunged down, and Sapphire's wings flared out, but we'd done this enough times now for me to be used to the dip of my stomach as her hooves skimmed the ocean surface. For me to relish the privacy as she disappeared into the low cloud cover and shot up above them. Where nothing and no one would see us save the stars in the heavens.

My fingers curled into her mane. And this feeling, this freedom of tasting the night air and the prickling of it against my skin, the thought of flying off into oblivion, trusting Sapphire to care for me, it was the most soothing sense of belonging to my restless spirit, here alone with her and the stars.

I'd always loved the stories constellations told as a girl. Loved the ancient tones of myths, the symbols and lessons they carried. I'd studied them with my father as part of my Second training. One of his many lessons: Any story could aid a leader.

But soaring through the clouds with Sapphire, the tales spun through me, weaving their own in my blood and bones.

Once we broke the fluffy surface and were surrounded by a dark sheet of sky peppered with stars, Sapphire hovered. I leaned forward, patting her neck. "Why are you stopping?"

Jezebel and Zanox broke through the clouds behind us. "I think they want us to talk."

I looked between my pegasus and the khrysaor. Over Jezebel's shoulder, Dynaxtar continued to loop freely through the sky, unbothered.

"Are you two scheming?" I muttered to Sapphire and Zanox, then met my sister's eyes. "What is it we need to talk about?"

Something had been off with Jezebel since she returned, and I thanked whatever Angels put these mythical creatures in our paths to ensure we addressed the problem.

"Your Angellight," Jez said, but Zanox huffed, his breath clouding the air. Jezebel cast him an admonishing look. "And my power."

I sat straighter. "What's wrong?"

"I don't know exactly."

Before I could respond, Jezebel lifted a hand, and a silver-blue light gathered in her palm. I froze. Certainly, that hadn't been what I expected her to reveal. Quicker than a whip, though, Jez recalled the light.

Where it disappeared, a white ring echoed in the navy sky.

"What was that?" I asked, finally finding my voice.

Her face was ashen. "That light—it's what we saw in the Spirit Realm. Ever since we've been back, it's been manifesting physically, too."

"Wh-what?" I stuttered, breathless. "You've been able to do that for weeks?"

Jez nodded. "I didn't realize what it was at first. Thought it was a trick of the light. But..." Her fingers curled into Zanox's mane as if for comfort, and though the soft beating of wings filled the night, her white knuckles were anything but relaxed.

"What happened?"

"It shot from me one day—I still don't know how. It sort of took on a life of its own and blurred into this arc across the sky like a falling star. And it"—Jezzie's voice trembled—"it killed something."

My blood ran cold, my own Angellight quiet. "What?"

"A passing bird, but...I don't even know how it happened."

As if satisfied that we were finally talking about this, Zanox and Sapphire started a slow trail through the clouds. Dynaxtar followed leisurely.

"And you're certain?" I asked over the breeze their wings created.

"Yes. Erista was there, too. We tried to figure out what could have caused it—if we may have been seeing things—but nothing else explains it."

"Have there been any other incidents since the Spirit Realm?"

Jez shook her head, but the weight of her secret unfolded from her. Up here, with Sapphire, Zanox, and Dynaxtar as our guards, a sense of assurance wrapped around us.

"My Angellight has been different since the realm, too," I confessed.

Jezebel chewed her lip. "What does yours feel like?"

"It feels like each Angel it stems from, rooted in me. There's

Ptholenix's fire and Gaveny's wild seas. Thorn's is a living storm, and Damien and Bant are both...sublime power."

As we coasted across a thick bank of clouds, Jez muttered, "Mine doesn't feel like any of that. It's...cold. Like a great loss."

I didn't say it aloud, but if Jezebel was able to communicate with departing spirits, that sensation of loss didn't surprise me. It all had to be connected.

"But there's a new instinct within mine, too," I admitted, wanting her to know she wasn't the only one feeling lost. "A vibrance even the five strings of the Angellight can't match. Like something seeking life and breath. I assume it's how they're merging within me, becoming mine. But I'm not really sure."

Jezebel was quiet for a moment as we flew. Then, she asked, "Can you summon it?"

And the uncertainty in her eyes was so uncharacteristic that I did. Starting with Damien's, I slowly unraveled the Angellight. The first thread pulsed, reaching from some archaic source right down into my very soul, golden and effervescent and wondrous.

One by one, I awoke each of the other four. Ptholenix's fiery orange and Gaveny's tempest of turquoise came first and easiest, the most controlled. The bright phenomenon of flame reflected and undulated against a glassy ocean.

Next, Thorn's erratic silver power rose like scattered storm clouds, the only one hard to wrestle into its strand, but still tethered to that source deep within me. Whatever power it was I didn't know I commanded. Something rooted to being the chosen child of the Angels, I presumed. To retaining the agent that activated my Angelblood, though we still were unsure what it was.

Finally, I engaged the last shred of power I held. The most unfamiliar and eerily sentient. Bant's.

With my eyes sealed tight and the other four patiently waiting, I prodded the Engrossian Angel's light. It was threaded with ink as dark the valley's pits and so reminiscent of those whips of tar the queen had wielded; it glowed and pulsed within me.

It had changed when Bant's Spirit disappeared into the mountains, like a beast raising its head and turning aware eyes on me. That connection was a little harder to fight for than the others.

But I caressed it, coaxed it to trust me. And I turned them from five buds of power into one solitary essence. A might unlike each of the Angels they stemmed from.

A magic wholly and intrinsically *mine.*

And as a singular force, the strands shot forward in a whirl of shining light, hovering high above the glassy sea. Warmth bathed my skin in a gust, and my eyes fell closed as I breathed in that strength.

Sapphire whinnied as the mass of power grew, a sound of pure encouragement and glee. Forming an effervescent braid, the light wound its way around my wrist, up my arm, teasing and tasting me. It sparkled against my skin, catching the reflections of the stars and winking to each.

Turning my face to the constellations, I swore they winked back.

I directed the Angellight to dance through the air over to Jezebel. Hesitantly, she pulled up her magic, as well. A delicate silver orb flickered in her hand, mist curling around it, twin to one of the stars plucked from the sky above.

For a moment, the magics mingled peacefully. I dug up more of that life-seeking source and fed it to the light.

Then, Zanox reared up, the scales on his wings snapping out. He roared, and I swore the back of his throat burned the same blue as the heart of Jezzie's magic. Sapphire bucked beneath me.

And my sister's power and mine careened into the sky like shooting stars falling from the heavens. The cold haunting sensation of loss combined with the vibrance of light.

"What's happening?" Jez shrieked.

"I don't know!" I gasped. "It's out of my control!"

Twin trails of gleaming gold and silver-blue collided with the force of meteors crashing to earth, and chills spread across my skin even as something within me burned. A shower of sparks rained to the thick clouds below, reminding me of both the dawn and the end of the world captured in one impossible moment—reminding me of the balance of power that held Ambrisk in its palm —shattering.

Both lights fizzled away into the dark sky, the night's silence heavy in the wake of crashing powers.

"Ophelia?" Jez said.

"Yes?"

"I don't think I want to use this magic anymore tonight." Starlight paled her features. Her eyes were wide and frightened in a way I rarely saw.

"We don't have to, Jez," I said, shoving all my fear aside to assure her. "We'll figure out what it means another time."

"Can we go back to the cottage?"

I wasn't sure if she was asking me or her khrysaor, but I nodded, and we coasted back toward the beach, clinging to the clouds.

Neither Jezebel nor I spoke—neither had anything worth saying—but the constellations and their legends wrapped around us. And I couldn't help but replay the golden light reflecting off Zanox's armored scales—the ones deployed when he sensed a threat.

CHAPTER SEVEN
TOLEK

"You never get over it," Erista said dreamily, watching the khrysaor and Sapphire take flight as she emerged from the willowing cypher branches at my back.

I raised my brows, turning away from the view as Sapphire's blue tail flicked into the clouds and disappeared. "Didn't want to stay in the cottage either?"

"The stone walls grew crowded."

That was an odd way to phrase it, but I huffed a laugh. "It's sort of nice having everyone back, though I could do without the fae."

"Such meddlesome tricksters." Erista perched at the base of a cypher, leaning back against the ash-white trunk with her feet tucked beneath her. "Did you fly much while we were traveling?"

"I told Ophelia to go on her own with Sapphire," I said, ignoring the abrupt change of conversation, "but she dragged me along with her almost every night the weather permitted."

A half-smirk twisted my lips at the memory of her pulling me onto her pegasus when I said they should enjoy the time together. Of Sapphire's impatient scuffing of the ground, agreeing with Ophelia.

Of how, hidden up in the clouds, I'd dipped my fingers beneath the hem of her skirt, teasing the slick heat between her legs until she was practically begging me to touch her. How I'd made her be *patient* until we landed and then given her an orgasm that could have shattered the stars and nearly had me following without her even touching me.

I cleared my throat, shifting to adjust the now-uncomfortable stiffness in my leathers. Spirits, would that girl ever affect me any differently?

I hoped not.

"It's magnificent." I cleared my throat again—damn the roughness. "The flying."

Every second of these weeks, being forced to pause the physical hunt for the emblems and be alone with Ophelia, had been magnificent truthfully. The unfamiliar domesticity I hadn't been sure we possessed. It certainly wasn't natural for us given it took a fae queen threatening an attack on the warrior continent to prompt it. But it had been a welcomed change.

"It's unlike anything else," Erista reflected, a bit mournfully.

"When she does fly alone, I don't even bring my journal," I said. "I just watch." This phenomenon that shouldn't be possible and yet somehow was with the Alabath sisters.

Erista hummed in agreement.

"Were you able to visit the desert on your way back?" I asked.

The Soulguider shook her head, curls bouncing. In only the moonlight, her eyes seemed as dark as night. Her unusual silence had me flicking a narrowed look her way.

"The Rites of Dusk have stopped?" I asked. She and her brother, Quilian, had explained that the swirling, sky-born dust storms were used to recharge Soulguider magic, but had been occurring more frequently as of late. Concernedly so.

Oddly in time with Ophelia's use of the emblems.

"Artale is quiet." Erista spoke softly, a waver of what I thought might be uncertainty passing through the words, but she recovered, slipping easily back into her usual lively demeanor. "I've studied them."

"The Rites?" I asked.

"The khrysaor." She gestured toward the sky, the gold crescent moons inked on her palms seeming duller than normal. "They are often mentioned with the pegasus."

"What did you find?" I asked.

The Soulguider's headband glinted between the dark coils of her hair as she tilted her head, her hands folded primly in her lap. "There are hardly specific accounts, but there are hints. Tales of beasts ridden into battle in ancient wars, with wings of scales and feathers. Always both. Where one was mentioned, the other followed shortly after."

A pair among legends.

"Sapphire's wings manifested when the khrysaor arrived at Ricordan's estate," I said. "But Sapphire had seen the khrysaor before."

She'd been there when the khrysaor first attacked us in the forest, on that journey to the Undertaking that set all of this in motion. The beast had reared up, thrashing its spiked tail and nearly impaling all of us.

That had been fun.

Jezebel explained she thought he was frightened then and was not truly a threat. Sometimes fear was the worst threat, though. The things it drove us to do...

"It has to be connected," I said, shutting down my own morbid thoughts. "If the khrysaor and pegasus are mentioned side by side in battle tales, there must be a reason."

My skin prickled at the consideration. Above, the clouds parted slightly, enough to allow the Mystique constellation to peek through, a shimmer of gold light reflecting off the clouds.

"And they happened to choose those two," I muttered.

"Both species are known for being incredibly loyal," Erista said. Warrior horses in general were devoted, but Sapphire had always displayed a heightened level of commitment to Ophelia. "They are recorded as holding allegiance to Lynxenon, Moirenna, and *others*."

I straightened. "Others?"

She shook her head. "It is hard to find a direct mention."

"Lynxenon makes sense," I said, scratching a hand across my stubble.

"The God of Mythical Beasts." Erista nodded.

"But why Moirenna?" I considered. "The only clan that has

any connection to the Goddess of Fate and Celestial Movements is the Starsearchers."

"Perhaps these beasts are not warrior. Maybe that's only who they've chosen," Erista suggested. Of us all, she'd studied the gods and goddesses the most. I trusted her instincts, though something about it still felt incomplete.

"And *others*?"

"I cannot be sure," Erista said, and that unfamiliar glint darkened her eyes again. "But the one recurring truth in every tale is that these highly loyal, mystical creatures were born for battle and chose their riders carefully. It's almost as tightly drawn as the hereditary bargains of the fae and the gods."

A chill rolled down my spine. "And if the pegasus and khrysaor are returning now..."

We both looked to the sky, the draping cypher branches swaying in the breeze. "What battles are they here to attend?"

And what did that mean for the riders they selected?

CHAPTER EIGHT
TOLEK

THE SAND SHIFTED BENEATH OUR BOOTS AS OUR PARTY climbed out of the small row boats that took us from Ezalia's ship, anchored out in the cerulean waves, to the little isle off the Gallantian coast designated for the fae arrival.

Ezalia and her people had been generous enough to offer the spot. We'd come to scout it with her a few times since residing in the outposts. It was the furthest from inhabited land that we could still access easily in the western Faelish waters.

The white beaches shone, grains of sand like diamonds in the sunlight and softer than an Angel's wings. Palm trees formed a staunch border at the edge of the thick jungle, beckoning as our group trudged up the beach. But Lancaster and Mora went left, heading toward the jutting white cliffs that arched out into the water.

Ophelia's court, that's how he had referred to us. How he had summoned our group.

"Where's the rest of them?" Malakai asked gruffly.

Ophelia walked ahead with Lancaster, making stiff conversation she hoped passed for pleasantries. To others it might. I nearly laughed.

"Wherever they made their camp, I suppose." I kept my voice low. While warrior hearing was sharp, fae senses were annoyingly strong. And who was to say what lingered in the trees?

"They didn't sail with the queen," Malakai muttered.

I glanced at him, keeping my expression neutral. "No, these two were already on the isle, but they got word her ship was docking a few days ago."

He frowned at the ocean. "Where is it?"

Besides the vessel Ezalia had used to carry us here, the ocean was a placid sheet of crisp, azure water. "Don't know."

My skin prickled. Malakai's hand drifted toward his sword. We were all baring weapons today. The Seawatcher bow and quiver of arrows at my back were a heavy reminder that this may be a diplomatic effort with a peaceful goal, but we still didn't know what the queen's reason was for being here.

I went on, "We don't know the intricacies of fae magic. When the treaty was signed between our people and theirs, we got the coveted magical land, but they got...."

Power and secrets.

Not in the ways the sorcerers of the Sorcia Isles did. No, that magic had been kept gated for thousands of years. But the fae were rumored to have unique abilities, varying even within bloodlines.

It excelled beyond warrior strength, speed, and commitment to the land we upheld with the treaty. Warriors did not need fae magic, though. It didn't align with our purpose, so we hadn't lost much with that agreement.

Or so I hoped, as we followed those pointed-eared immortals now.

"They've agreed to only remain on the isle, right?" Malakai double-checked. His stare was on Mila where she walked with my sister, those twin blades crossed at her back.

"The Revered's first stipulation," I assured, my own eyes locked on Ophelia's swinging golden hair. Jezebel, Erista, and the Seawatcher Chancellor walked beside her. Santorina stayed in the center of the group, hands stiff at her sides. "But the outpost leaders are remaining vigilant. Just in case."

Just in case the queen's court went rogue. *Just in case* they wanted to resume that bloody war of thousands of years ago, when humans were slaughtered at the hands of fae, before the warriors sent armies to assist them and opened Gallantia to the magicless.

How Santorina hadn't put a knife in Lancaster's throat was a testament to her maturity.

"And you wrote to Cypherion and Vale?" Malakai asked as the sea washed up, darkening the sand.

"I told him where to go to catch a boat and meet us here if we haven't returned by the time they're back." Angels, I hoped they'd make it here in time.

Not only because he was Ophelia's Second—the queen would likely find it a snub if he didn't greet her—but also because I missed my friend. Worry curled through my stomach at the thought.

"How far is this fucking camp?" I grumbled.

The closer we got to the cliffs, the more concern gathered behind my ribs. As Lancaster and Mora led us around the base of the towering rocky walls, across a natural bridge of flat stone that protruded into the waves, and watered crashed around us, I reminded myself this was necessary.

If we did not come to greet the queen, we would be breaking the bargain tying my and Ophelia's lives to Lancaster. We needed to ensure we kept this quick and peaceful.

Should be easy, I nearly laughed at myself.

As we rounded a bend, Ezalia let out a gasp. My stomach dropped, and I froze in my tracks.

There, built precariously into the edge of the cliff, was a palace that had certainly not been there before.

Ophelia glanced over her shoulder, eyes meeting mine. Though her mask was up, the message was clear. Her signal that what we feared was true: The fae came with tricks, and we must be ready to play their games.

Her hand flexed at her side, and I was jogging ahead in a moment, lacing my fingers through hers. We both released a breath.

"This is new," Ezalia forced through gritted teeth.

Though we were technically not on Gallantia, this isle belonged to the Seawatchers. And the queen had somehow constructed a *palace* on it seemingly overnight.

"It will be gone when we are," Lancaster growled, stomping ahead.

"Beautiful, isn't it?" Mora said, watching us expectantly. When no one answered, she pursed her lips and strolled after her surly brother. Ezalia and the others followed, the chancellor lobbing harsh questions at the female.

But Ophelia and I stood there for a moment, eyes on the structure more extravagant than even the Revered's palace in the mountains. All gleaming gold as if sunlight lit it from within. It's frame *actually shimmered*, a stark contrast to the bloodthirsty queen's reputation.

Balconies extended out over the cerulean water. Towers were carved into the rock side, and flags flickered in the breeze atop the highest points, the blood red rose and nemaxese's maned head set against a white backdrop. Lancaster directed our *court* to a spiral of stairs winding down to the sand.

"This feels...imposing," Ophelia muttered.

"It feels both out of place and ancient all at once." Because the rock *was* worn beneath the gold embellishments, if you squinted hard enough to catch it, and ivy twined up the southern facade.

"How could she think this is okay?" Ophelia's voice was hard. "To simply erect a *palace* for this meeting? On warrior land?" She fiddled with the shard of Angelborn strung around her neck, the other emblems tucked safely in her pack.

The entire structure before us glinted like it was crafted of the heart of the sun and something more. Something radiating power akin to Angellight.

"When you spend centuries ruling unchallenged, you forget certain things do not belong to you."

Ophelia looked at me, teeth digging into her bottom lip, but she nodded. As she stepped forward with my hand tight in hers, I followed, those flags flickering and the nemaxese's jaw stretched wide.

And I hoped we weren't walking right into its den.

∼

WITHIN THOSE WALLS, marble floors and pillars gleamed, stone seemingly crafted from this island's sand-warmed beaches themselves. A mural of blood red roses was splashed upon the foyer floor, catching the candlelight, and pennants with the royal crest hung between ornately-framed works of art—fae, not warrior.

The paintings glorified the brutalities of the war thousands of years ago. Elongated canines were bared in victorious smiles, weapons pointed toward the heavens. In one, the clouds parted, a heavenly figure looking down upon her subjects.

The Fae Goddess, Aoiflyn.

It was only that one silhouette that kept me from grimacing at the art and the fae lining the bustling balconies watching us. A reminder that we needed this partnership.

A representative stopped Lancaster before we walked much further. He cast a furtive glance over his shoulder at us, though only Ophelia and I were close enough to catch it, and a hint of something akin to protection glinted in his eye.

"I don't care what she wants," Lancaster snapped, but with an admonishing look from his sister, he reined in the ire quickly.

The rest of our warrior entourage were muttering quietly to themselves, pretending to observe the gold-framed artwork as they noted all types of threats. My sister and Santorina stood to the side, their backs to the wall and stares sweeping the second story walkways framing the foyer. I followed their gazes. A pair of fae stood in the shadows, observing in high-collared jackets and breeches.

The hair on the back of my neck rose further with every step into this palace. With every eye glued to us.

I locked my hand tighter around Ophelia's as Lancaster and Mora finished their quiet discussion, and the male stalked off without a word. With a shining smile, the female turned to us. "My brother has business to attend to, but I can show you where you may clean up before the queen's audience."

"Clean up?" Ophelia asked, not unkindly. She was curious about Mora after their first meeting in the Wayward Inn—when the fae had been posing as a warrior running from an abusive partnership. We'd never gotten the story on why or how she was there.

Now, she remained some odd combination of powerful threat and potentially friendly ally.

Peering down the hall Lancaster disappeared into, I almost wish he'd been our guide. At least with the male, we knew where we stood.

"We'll provide proper clothing to meet the queen." Without waiting for an answer, Mora turned and inclined her head for us to follow.

"Proper clothing?" I whispered to Ophelia.

Jezebel piped up from behind us, "This ought to be fun." For the first time in days, despite the questionable magic she'd shown Ophelia, she looked truly elated.

"What about you, Ria?" I asked my sister as we passed a set of wide doors, thrown open to reveal plaques and medals. "Ready to indulge in a new gown?"

"Of course," she drawled, and the flatness in her tone had my attention whipping around, but she strode ahead, not waiting for me to respond.

Ophelia grumbled beneath her breath as we followed Mora—cursing the formal fae fashion to the Spirit Realm if I heard her correctly—and digging her nails into her leather skirt. I stifled a laugh, kissing her temple softly, and she loosed a breath.

The palace's wide corridors were made entirely of gold-flecked granite. Spirits, was this whole palace made of gold? The floor, the window panes, even the shimmering velvet curtains?

"There's a dressing chamber that's been crafted for your convenience," Mora tossed over her shoulder.

Crafted?

She threw open a pair of heavy double doors with ease, leading us down another hallway lined with thick, deep green carpets. Those same red roses stood on pedestals beside each polished, dark-wood door.

At the end of the corridor, Mora turned expectantly to us as if waiting for some reaction.

When no one said anything, she pursed her lips, then continued with a wave of her hand to the left. "Through that door is a selection of formal attire, including boots and jewels. It will be much more appropriate to greet the queen in such." She waved her hand to the right. "Baths are through there should you need, and perfumes, oils, and other necessities can be found inside. Someone will return shortly to retrieve you, but guards will remain at the end of the hall should you need anything."

Should we try to wander, she meant.

Ophelia's fingers fidgeted against mine at the leash they subtly snapped around us. Ritalia may be centuries older, but she should be very careful how far she pushed Ophelia Alabath.

"Thank you," she answered, without even a beat of hesitation, despite the suspicious suggestion. "This will suit our needs well enough."

Ophelia's voice was cool. Even. As if this was precisely what she'd intended and the palace was grand but nothing unique. She flashed a virtuous smile that, on the surface, spoke only of pure gratitude.

But beneath the exterior, her teeth were as sharp as the fae.

⁓

"THIS DRESS IS HORRIBLE!" Ophelia called from rows away.

In the distance, Jezebel yelled at the rest of our party, assigning them each outfits from the fae's extensive collection. The dressing chamber was massive and honestly a bit obscene, with high ceilings and endless rows of options. Ruby red and gold hung from every candelabra, fire flickering off the dark wood and marble floors. Even the clothing racks and wardrobe doors were framed with carved gold roses, and the air smelled strongly of flowers.

Thematic opulence. Manipulative extravagance. A damn tricky show meant to make us feel relaxed and comfortable and entirely under their control.

I slid high-collared jackets along racks, looking for any in my size, not entirely caring which I wore. Baby Alabath would likely pick something else anyway.

"I'm sure it's not that bad," I called back.

There. I yanked a black piece with gold embroidery off the hanger and slung it on. I hated jackets—the sleeves never rolled up easily, so they were too restrictive—but I could wear it for this audience.

"Why does the queen insist we dress in the style of her court?" Ophelia grumbled. "And why am I listening?"

I laughed, striding around the end of the aisle. "Because—"

Every word, every damn thought, vanished from my mind.

Ophelia blew out a breath as she looked over her shoulder at me. "What?"

"That dress is far from horrible, Alabath." My voice was rough, but I could barely think enough to clear my throat. While the dress was different than anything I'd seen Ophelia wear before, and certainly not a warrior style, *her* in that dress was nothing short of spectacular.

The bodice was tight and strapless with a corset that was likely driving her crazy—driving me crazy, too. The gold fabric was so sheer that if it weren't for the lining beneath, I'd see right through it. A beaded design looped around the front—an intricate depiction of roses, I thought, but I couldn't focus enough to tell.

The skirts were full—she hated that, I was certain—but the material was thin enough that the outline of her legs was visible beneath. So fucking tempting.

And when she turned away from the mirror and stepped toward me... "I'm never going to survive this meeting," I groaned.

One leg ending in a high golden heel slipped out through a slit, all the way to her hip, and my cock twitched.

The queen's court may adhere to an outdated style of dress with the full skirts and tight corsets, but I could accept it if Ophelia looked like this.

"Jezzie added the slit for me," Ophelia said, voice sultry. Dammit, she knew exactly what she was doing. "There were long sleeves and a collar to my chin, but she cut those away, too." Golden hair tumbled around her shoulders, and her heart-shaped lips split into a tricky grin as she blinked those magenta eyes at me innocently.

"Not sure it still counts as fae fashion with your modifications," I rasped.

Ophelia flicked her brows up. "Are you complaining, Vincienzo?"

"Not at all."

She prowled toward me with a damn satisfied smirk I wanted to wipe off her mouth with my own, that dress cinching her waist and accenting every asset she had. All I could think of as she turned her back to me was bending her over here in the middle of the dressing chamber—our friends be damned—and burying myself in her heat. Her neck arched as she swept her hair over one shoulder, and I was ready to fall to my knees.

"Finish tying it for me?" she asked.

I didn't want to tie the damn corset. I wanted to rip it off her. The silk ribbons were suddenly my mortal enemy. She'd managed to get them mostly laced up. I didn't know why she hadn't waited for me, but I didn't really have enough blood in my head to ask.

Swallowing, I gripped the ends and tugged tightly. Ophelia inhaled, and in the mirror, her chest rose. Her eyes locked to mine, a challenge budding there.

"Rough, Vincienzo?" she asked as I finished lacing.

Ducking my head, I kissed the spot where her shoulder met her neck. Her eyes burned, and fucking Spirits, I was dangerously close to not being able to walk out of here.

"Surprised?" I skimmed my lips up her neck, and she inhaled, eyes fluttering closed.

"Intrigued," she corrected breathily. "Even though I hate this damn dress." She lifted the piles of skirts for emphasis. Her voice was calm. That wouldn't do.

"I'll make you a promise," I whispered, nipping her ear and tugging the ribbons tighter so her breath hitched. "You wear this dress now, and I'll help you take it off later."

CHAPTER NINE
OPHELIA

Tolek's words landed as a knock echoed on the door to our dressing chamber, and everyone's frolicking voices fell quiet. He stepped back, brows raised expectantly at me in the mirror.

"Going to answer that, Revered?" he purred.

My knees nearly wobbled, his promise still echoing, but I took a steadying breath and strode along the rows of jewel-crusted gowns, embroidered jackets, and Spirits knew what else. Jezebel, Erista, Malakai, Mila, Lyria, Santorina, and Ezalia popped out of the aisles one by one, joining us near the entrance with defensive expressions and warrior blades strapped across their fae clothing. Ezalia even had her bow in hand, the sharpened tips of her arrows peeking over her lace-clad shoulder. Lyria's sword hung ready at her hip. As the Master of Weapons and Warfare, she took a step ahead of the others, many eyes flashing nervously to Santorina. But our human friend only gave me an encouraging nod.

My sister had clearly found the accessory collection, adorning herself in a number of heavy bracelets that complemented her silver-threaded gown, but nothing gleamed as brightly as the fierce spark in her eye as I marched toward the door. The gilded handle was much cooler than my heated blood, the glint of the flickering candlelight across the shining surface a reminder of where we were and who waited beyond these walls—of the act we needed to play.

Wrenching the door open, I raised the mask of Revered. "Hello."

"Revered Alabath," the dark-skinned fae flashed a pointed grin. "My, do our styles suit you."

He leaned against the door jam, his high collar, breeches, and boots not suited to his casual demeanor.

"And you are?" I asked.

"Brystin," he replied with a cruel twist of his words. "Bry to those I favor."

"Brystin, then," I said. Behind me, Tolek laughed, and the fae male's attention snapped to him.

Something in those light-brown eyes heated as they assessed Tol, who stood patiently at my shoulder with his hands clasped behind his back. A challenge perhaps. A playful but lethal threat.

A growl nearly rumbled up my throat as the male's secret-shielding smile flashed again. "What are you considering?" I asked.

Brystin did not answer, but his gaze swept back to me, lingering on the tight bodice strangling my ribs. "Of the two of you, you might be the harder one to fight."

Not a direct answer to my question, but that was expected. The fae couldn't lie—not outright. Spinning tricks and devising avoidances were their ways around those rules.

"I'd love for you to find out," I murmured with false sweetness. "But I wouldn't want to keep your queen waiting."

Brystin stepped back, extending a hand toward the hall, and when he smiled again, I got the sense that blood could have dripped from the tips of his teeth.

"We are honored to receive you, Revered. And your lovely court." His stare raked over each of us as we filed into the hall, and my heels sank into the thick emerald rugs resembling jeweled moss creeping across the marble floors. Mora waited beside the candelabras, looking us all over with quiet satisfaction.

As Mora and Brystin led the way to the queen's audience chamber, Tolek muttered softly to Lyria about not taking any wine we were offered, to which the commander nodded impatiently. Warrior and human bedtime tales alike told of the risks of faerie drinks. I swallowed the reminder and hoped the rest of our party had been forewarned, too.

Malakai and Mila stepped up to Brystin. "Are you a member of the queen's guard?" Malakai asked.

The male smiled savagely, and my skin crawled. "For nearly two centuries now—though I'm the youngest and most promising."

Mila asked, "What secured you such a coveted spot?"

"My tracking abilities and methods for extraction of pertinent information are creative, and my queen adores creativity."

My skin chilled. As their conversation continued, Brystin answered each question with a slight twist of his words I was certain Malakai noticed.

I fell back a few steps, taking up Mora's side.

"Who is he?" I asked.

"One of the queen's most prominent guards." I thought a bit of disdain hid in her tone.

"Why would she send him to escort us, then?"

"Do you not send your most trusted advisors on the most precious of missions?"

As we wound through gilded hallways, bloodied fae art adorning the walls, my mind flashed to Cypherion, my Second, on an excursion I trusted only him to carry out.

But we were in the queen's palace—or at least, a temporary one somehow erected here. Could she not simply send any lowly soldier to escort us? Why one of her personal guards?

Mora's expression remained impassive. Much more guarded than when I'd first met her.

I dropped my voice so even Brystin wouldn't hear. "Why did you hide in the inn?"

Mora tilted her head, smiling endearingly. "I was not supposed to be trailing my brother. I certainly wasn't going to reveal myself to him. That was a surprise."

"You're welcome for keeping you on your toes," I said. "Was the story you told me true?" At Wayward, Mora had been pretending to be a battered wife, and I'd wanted so badly to help her.

"It was," she whispered, keeping that small smile up. "A very long time ago."

There was a story beneath her words, one laced with pain and the strength of a survivor. And something entwined within it tugged on my instinct to trust her, despite the fact that she was our treaty-born enemy.

"You've done well since then?"

"Very well," she said, chin lifting. "Better than his rotting self."

And I got the sense she meant *rotting* literally. "Good," I said.

Mora nodded in agreement and strolled ahead quietly, shrewd stare on Brystin.

I slowed my stride, falling back to the middle of our group between Rina and Tolek, away from prying fae ears. "Are you all right?" I asked Santorina.

"Fine." But her voice was much too high to be honest.

"Santorina..." I whispered.

"I'm focusing on my task with the humans and studying my healing practice," she said stiffly. "I'm proud to be able to represent the strength of a human force against the fae."

"Rina," I said even quieter, and she deflated a bit, "you can talk to us."

"It's—" Santorina's hands curled in the fabric of her deep purple gown—the shade was so dark it was nearly black. The shining onyx trim framing the bodice and weaving throughout the skirts shimmered as we passed under another wide candle-lit chandelier. "It's not the queen I'm worried about. She's tied to the treaty with the warriors through some sort of magic. Her court may not be, but it's a small comfort knowing the queen cannot harm me upon meeting her."

"What is it, then?" Tolek asked.

But when Rina's lips pressed into a line, I answered for her, "Lancaster."

Santorina nearly growled at the fae's name, the guards sparing us a glance at the inhuman sound. "You mean that cursed faerie who tried to kill me and then had the nerve to make bargains with both of you?"

I exchanged a guilt-laden look with Tolek. Though we'd talked to Rina extensively about our bargain with the fae, it was a sensitive topic.

Tolek's hand slid into mine. He blamed himself, but those bargains got us a place to hide in Mindshaper Territory during the war, and it brought Lancaster and Mora to our aid against Kakias.

Besides, Lancaster had healed Dax when he was within an inch of his life. Rina's anger was entirely justified—I was angry, too—but we'd needed the fae more than once.

"Neither of us have forgiven him for what he tried to do to you," Tolek growled.

"And if he ever touches you again, I will cut off both of his hands," I swore.

"Go a step further," Tol encouraged. "His tongue, his cock, whatever the male favors, it'll be gone in a heartbeat if he steps out of line."

That had Santorina laughing, but tension still framed her expression.

"If that fae dares to touch me again, I'll take care of that last one myself." And there was an inferno in her eyes as she said it, one burning as hot as the Spirit Fire itself.

As fierce as a warrior's heart.

I whispered, "Got your dagger?"

Rina flashed me a wicked grin. "Always."

We may not have brought every weapon in our arsenal as a show of the smallest sliver of peace, but a few blades were not mistrusting. They were simply smart. And would the queen wish to confer with unwise rulers?

Starfire and Angelborn warmed as if in agreement.

"Now, let's try to keep it out of Lancaster's neck," I mumbled, following the others down a set of grand stairs.

Heels and boots echoed on marble, nearly drowning Rina's next words. "Something tells me we're only running toward that fate."

I wasn't sure what she meant, and I didn't get a chance to ask, because we arrived at the grand wooden doors to the audience chamber, the arched frame stretching twenty feet high, and I strode to the front of the group.

As Mora and Brystin pushed them open, I slammed up my mask of Revered. Angellight whirled in my veins, providing silent strength. I lifted my chin, pressed my shoulders back, and assumed the aura of the ruler of the Mystique Warriors.

At the far end of the chamber, upon a regal, gilded throne carved with roses and their jagged thorns, a faerie brimming with power rose to her feet.

"Welcome, warriors." She spread her arms, a silver chalice in hand, her red gown coiled tightly around her. "This meeting has been waiting in the eons."

Queen Ritalia, the bloodthirsty monarch of the fae, grinned at me with nothing but immortal grace as I strode into the chamber with my council. An ancient gold diadem crusted in rubies sat above her high forehead as she beckoned us.

Tolek remained at my right, assuming the place of my Second until Cypherion arrived. Hopefully we'd finish these discussions quickly, before that mattered.

Santorina stood behind us, Mila and Malakai on either side of her, and Ezalia was on my left. Jezebel, Erista, and Lyria filled in our last line. We marched to the center of the audience chamber, stopping before the steps to the throne.

A string quartet played a dreary tune in the corner, and every attendee's movements seemed to flow to the music as we stopped walking. Fae gathered in clusters around the room, muttering so low, their words were nothing more than eerie whispers. Behind the throne, velvet drapes swayed against the wall ever so slightly.

"Seraph Child," Queen Ritalia said, and my attention whipped toward her, Angellight flaring in my veins. Brystin, Mora, and Lancaster took up positions behind her throne. "How I have been so curious of you for some time now." The queen's words slipped between a snow-white smile. Her eyes, green as the stems of the roses lining her halls, assessed me as I did her.

Curious of you. Not *happy to meet you*, or even *waiting to.* Simply curious.

"And I have wondered about you, Your Majesty."

Ritalia's head tilted, her hair piled atop it shifting like a nest of golden snakes. "What is it that you've wondered?"

"What you are doing here, most prudently."

She waved her chalice. "A matter we will get to after our welcome."

"In that case, I believe your welcome is better addressed by the ruler of this territory," I said, directing my attention to my left.

When we'd first arrived here and wandered around that cliff bend to find the palace perched above the sea, heat had flamed behind Ezalia's sea glass eyes. It returned again as the queen's attention fell to her.

"Might it?" Ritalia asked, sipping her wine. Not a drop of the maroon liquid stained her teeth. The unnatural, gleaming white smile worked a shiver down my spine.

"Ezalia Ridgebrook," the chancellor said, "leader of the fourth minor clan of the Gallantian Warriors, the loyal followers of his Prime Gaveny, Seawatcher. And the rightful ruler of the isle we now inhabit."

From atop her throne, Queen Ritalia looked down her nose at Ezalia. The condescension skittered beneath my skin, and I had to clench my hands in the folds of my gown to stifle the Angellight pushing at my fingertips. The ridiculous skirts were good for one thing.

Tolek cast me a subtle, wary look as Ritalia said, "Pleasure."

"You are very welcome for hosting you," Ezalia said.

"I do not recall thanking you."

"I know." I hid my smirk at Ezalia's words, the others shuffling behind us, and the chancellor went on, "Might I ask how this beautiful palace is here? Given it was not only a few weeks ago."

Ritalia seemed utterly satisfied by that question, a gleeful smile flicking up her lips. "You find our magic impressive, then."

I started because that wasn't what Ezalia had said, and the queen was not supposed to be able to lie. Tolek met my gaze from the corner of his eye, and I knew we were both considering it. But I shook my head, communicating in our silent way that apparently it did not matter whether what the queen said was true, only that she *believed* it to be true.

And as a conqueror who held her throne for centuries, she had learned how to twist others' words and digest them as truth. To her, us lowly warriors were enthralled with fae magic.

"We are quite curious," I cut in.

"Did you create it?" Erista asked, scanning the decor. The bright tattoos on her palms glinted in the candlelight as she gestured toward the elaborate details, candelabras dripping in rubies, and her full dusk-colored skirt shifted. "You must have, right?"

"Not I," Ritalia said, and her gaze landed on Mora and Lancaster. "A glam and a crete are poisonous weapons to have on hand."

"A crete?" Santorina gasped. With her and Lancaster's attention locked, every warrior present shifted into a defensive stance. Angelborn pulsed against my spine.

"What's a crete?" Jezebel asked.

Ritalia's eyes snagged on my sister, a flicker of something predatory and curious flashing through her stare. Both Jez and Erista stiffened at the attention, the latter shifting a step closer. My hand fisted at my side, and Tolek's slipped atop it, discreetly unknotting the tension.

"The young Mistress," Ritalia said, drawing out that word as she scanned Jezebel's silver gown and jewels, "requires an explanation."

"A crete is a branch of power for our kind," Lancaster said, voice stony as always. "It means I can conjure something out of nothing."

Silence fell across every warrior as that revelation sank in. My mind skipped back to when I'd collided with Lancaster in the Wayward Inn and how he'd mysteriously refilled his glass without needing to rise from the table.

"When we battled Kakias," Tolek said, "you dragged items out of the air as if it was nothing."

In the rush of Ricordan's manor and Sapphire and the Spirit Realm and *everything* that had followed, I'd forgotten about the powers the fae had displayed.

"And you," I addressed Mora, "a glam refers to glamour, correct?"

In an instant, Mora's facial features shifted to a near replica of my own. Around the audience chamber, everyone jumped. "Correct," the female answered in her voice, not mine.

"Not a perfect illusion, then?" Malakai said.

Ritalia glared at him as she answered, "As near perfect as any fae to ever grace my lands, Star Tied One."

I narrowed my eyes on the queen at her nickname.

That was the reason Mora was in this court, then. Why Ritalia kept the siblings around. Their deep wealth of power.

I swept the rest of Ritalia's court. What other threats lurked within?

"There are slight differences," Tolek said, looking between Mora and me. He didn't seem to notice Ritalia's stare narrowing on him, but I took a step closer. "The eyes are a giveaway."

I leaned forward, squinting with the little aid of the candlelight. Mora's likeness of my odd magenta eyes—a mark of the Angelcurse—were a deep purple, almost brown.

The female shrugged. "Nothing can be perfectly mimicked."

It was unsettling to see myself out of a mirror. Another fae trick to be aware of. Pushing my shoulders back and stepping forward, I tried not to grind my teeth.

"You two built this entire palace?" I asked as Mora shifted back into herself, a bit of reluctant awe slipping between my words. The ceilings towered impossibly high and ivy twined up the stone columns between the windows, cooling the sun piercing the glass.

"We did," Mora confirmed. The pride she'd displayed when she showed us to our dressing chamber resurfaced. Much of this place was only a glamour, then. Perhaps the decor? Lancaster had crafted the foundation beneath our boots out of nothing, and Mora adorned it with an impression of wealth.

The palace was elaborate. No wonder they'd been waiting here for the queen for so long. They likely needed days to recover after selecting the location and crafting it.

"That is very impressive," I told them despite the discomfort that level of magic planted in my gut. When I turned to Ritalia, her smile only fanned it. If these were merely her guards, what depths did the queen's powers stretch to?

"How diplomatic of you," she said and took another sip of wine.

"I give accolades where they are due." I nodded at Lancaster and Mora. "These two helped save our lives. We are here under pleasant circumstances, are we not?" I asked.

"Indeed, Seraph Child. Pleasant for those of us on this earthly plane." Ritalia assessed me, but before I could untangle those words, she declared, "You would have made a triumphant queen, Revered Alabath."

I inclined my head, and the quartet in the corner increased the speed of their tune. "You must be confused. Warriors do not honor queens."

"Don't they?"

The reminder of Kakias flashed in her stare. That she knew our business so intimately and was so comfortable wielding it against us.

She was picking us apart like carrion, even as we stood as honored guests in her halls. With every evaluating glance, every twisted turn of phrase, she was storing more and more slivers of us within her vaulted mind.

Every time she turned her eyes on another one of my party, my ire flamed. It only fanned it more that I had to *behave*. We were at such a disadvantage, thanks to the bargains and the unknowns of the fae's magic. I couldn't play the queen's games at her level for fear of how she'd react.

Did she have soldiers in boats heading toward Gallantia, ready to disturb the peace of those serene Western Outposts despite the truce? Did she have fae with abilities beyond Lancaster and Mora, with eyes trained on us? And did the tempo of the music increase as I spun questions in my head, or was I imagining it?

One wrong move from me could have her rewriting history. Have her saying *my* people crossed a line in the treaty if she truly believed it herself.

"May I ask, Your Majesty," I began, tempering my anger, "what intel have you gathered about your mission on our continent?" A subtle reminder that we'd known Lancaster had been on our land, but because he had been under instructions to play nicely with warrior leaders—and because we'd had battles among our own kind—we did not call her on the violation of the treaty.

But we could.

I shifted my hips so the slit Jezebel added to my dress flashed my thigh—and the dagger strapped to it.

A war could so easily be flipped in this very chamber if Ritalia wished.

"Studying the magic," she said frugally.

"And what were the findings?" I asked.

"You would think them interesting." Ritalia danced around the answer. "Things of gods twisting through the universes, dancing among realms. Of legends falling from the sky and painting the fields with deep crimson blessed by beings of winged might."

I picked it apart, each tidbit of information she hid within her words, buried so that us warriors would have to work to decipher what she meant. Gods and realms. Legends and blood. Winged might—

"But there is something more prudent to your arrival here, Revered Alabath," Ritalia said. The music's tempo increased, grating on my skin.

"Is there?" I asked. To me, there wasn't. I was here for three reasons: keep the fae away from Gallantia, ask questions of the gods, and appease the bargain.

The bargain.

If Ritalia's smile was any indication, she knew the moment I recalled the threat. My palms burned with Angellight.

"You made a deal with one of my own, and surely you knew something would have to come of that." Ritalia swirled her wine, the red liquid coming to the lip of the chalice with every pivot. "There is an abundance of Bounties seated among us, is there not?"

"Bounties?" Lancaster's deep voice rumbled through the room, a threat chilling it.

My head whipped in his direction, only for his eyes to lock on Rina. His nostrils flared.

Then, in a fit of rage, Lancaster exploded where he stood.

CHAPTER TEN
OPHELIA

FAE AROUND THE ROOM GASPED, BOOTS SCUFFING OVER pristine marble floors. We all reached for our weapons, pools of Angellight coiling around my hands.

All but Rina, who glowered quietly at the male clearly targeting her, confusion and animosity in the tremor of her bottom lip.

Lancaster's nails dug into the velvet drapery behind Ritalia's throne as if anchoring himself there, but his lips parted on a snarl, his eyes crazed. Even his jacket sleeves hung in tatters, corded muscles standing out on his forearms beneath the split seams.

"Your Majesty?" he ground out, every bit as animalistic as legend told of these immortal graces.

"What's happening to him?" I gasped, looking between Ritalia and Lancaster.

Mora gripped his arm, whispering something none of us could hear. Lancaster shook his head, but his gaze remained locked on Santorina. The veins in his neck strained, sweat beading on his forehead.

Rina stared back, as if frozen in wide-eyed shock. But her hand drifted toward the dagger at her thigh.

The room was otherwise suspended in silence.

"Your. Majesty," Lancaster repeated, each word stilted, and this time, there was a battle beneath his request. "What is the order?"

A lengthy beat of contemplation followed, during which every warrior balanced on the balls of their feet. Starfire and Angelborn were desperate weights against my body, begging to be unleashed, and the tension in the air pressed down on us.

Finally, Ritalia said, "Stand down, my hunter."

When I cut my glare to her, she was staring at my hands, where Angellight ebbed in golden tendrils. Disappointment crashed over me for exposing it, for giving this queen another fragment of control, but I reined it in and hid any reaction to my mistake.

Ritalia's haughty smile told me she'd already known and had only wanted to see it for herself.

A muscle feathered in Lancaster's jaw. Stress unspooled from his frame, and with one final knowing glance at Santorina, he stormed out a door behind the throne, Mora following in his wake.

Brystin snapped at a staff member with a smirk, holding his hand out for a glass of wine. "I forgot how much fun he promises when pushed."

"All of the warrior and fae courts, vacate the room." Ritalia's voice was calm but authoritative, ignoring her guard's remark. "I have something I must discuss with your Revered alone."

"Over my Angeldamned body," Tolek retorted beneath his breath.

"Tell me what that was," I demanded to Ritalia, nodding at where Lancaster had stood.

"I gladly will," Ritalia agreed to my shock, "once the others leave. We have various topics we must discuss."

"No." My voice rang through the room with the force of the Angels. "No one leaves until you explain that outburst. Then you and I can finish discussing why you're here at all."

It may have been foolish to command such a lethal queen, but she'd been toying with us all day. First making us change and wait to see her, then parading us here and picking through our appearances.

I may not have held the title of queen, but I was the Revered of the Mystique Warriors and the Chosen of the Angels. I demanded respect.

Ritalia twirled her chalice between her fingers. She almost seemed...impressed. "Very well." Setting the silver cup on the table beside her throne, she stood. "We do have the Queen of Bounties among us, do we not?"

The chamber was silent, Ritalia's stare locked on Santorina, whose voice was steel as she stepped up beside me. "Queen of what?"

"Enough of the riddles, Your Majesty," I clipped, holding on to the last sliver of reverence. "Tell us what this is about."

"What do you think the cause of the fae-human war was all those centuries ago?" Ritalia asked.

"You mean the human annihilation at the hands of your kind," Rina corrected.

Ritalia tilted her head. "That is the story as you know it."

"It's no story," Santorina said. "Fae slaughtered humans. My people had to flee Vercuella."

"The warriors took them in," I added.

"Fae slaughtered humans," Ritalia repeated, grimacing. "And humans slaughtered fae."

I blinked at her. "How is that possible? The fae—"

"Are stronger? Faster? More cunning?" Ritalia suggested. I sneered at the queen's words. Rina's hands tightened on the dagger she'd removed from its sheath. "All of those things are correct of the *average* human."

"And the non-average?" Tolek asked, noticing that specific word.

"The Bounties are not average humans," Ritalia said. And again, her stare sharpened on Santorina. "The Bounties are a race of humans born with a specific instinct and ability: to kill fae. It is because of the Bounties that the war began at all. We did not want to kill innocent humans; we wanted to exterminate those who sought to kill *us*."

Tolek and I exchanged a glance. In it, that one fact burned: *she cannot outright lie*. And, truthfully, this story was the least riddled Ritalia had ever sounded.

"Why wouldn't we have known this?" Jezebel growled.

"Because, Mistress Death"—Ritalia sighed—"we did not make

the truth of the Bounties known. Not with how susceptible it made us."

And I almost asked then why she would tell us now, but it was clear Ritalia wanted something, I just hadn't worked out *what* yet.

"What does this have to do with me?" Rina finally asked. Her heated stare was locked on the queen, knuckles white. "Why did you use that title for me? Why did *he* attack me?" She nodded once more toward where Lancaster had been standing.

"You humans are so slow," Ritalia mumbled, and Brystin's smile gleamed in answer. At his side, silver blades shone, etched with markings. "I scented it on you the moment you arrived, Miss Cordelian. You are the last of a great line of Bounties. A descendent from one who got away from our hunts. Their last true queen."

The declaration sank like a rock in my chest. Santorina...a queen? Of a race of humans born to kill fae? I looked to my friend, but her expression was unreadable.

She argued, "My family is from Gallantia."

"With how short mortal lifespans are, do you truly know the history back thousands of years?"

Rina's gaze shuttered. "You killed the Bounties."

"We killed all we found. Some fled, the cowards they were." Ritalia scoffed. "Some came here. Some to the Sorcia Isles. Some established their own homesteads in other parts of the world."

"And why did you tell Lancaster to attack her?" I asked, gaze flicking to the door he'd disappeared through.

"Lancaster was born long after the Bounty crisis, but he was bred for one thing in particular. Certainly his status as a crete is beneficial, but he was created to *hunt*."

Lancaster's snarl from minutes ago echoed through the room, my palms warming again with Angellight. I shoved it down, remaining focused on Ritalia.

"Did my hunter not seek you out as soon as he set foot on this continent?" she asked Rina. "He was bred to do such a thing. His senses set to destroy that which can kill our kind. You likely only still stand here because of those warriors around you."

It was the last thing Santorina wanted, to be at the mercy of warriors. But as she spoke next, voice loud and true, I realized the queen was wrong. Santorina Cordelian was her own force, her own will. She wasn't warrior; she wasn't human. She was a bounty of power.

"Does this mean I am your natural enemy? Will my head be on the floor of this throne room?" *Or will yours*, she didn't add. But every warrior shifted in anticipation of it.

Ritalia sneered. "I shall wake the hunter if you wish."

"You wake his instincts," I spat, my anger coiled and ready to strike, "and you say goodbye to whatever reason you wanted me here."

My threat crept across the room like a slow frost, and Ritalia grinned in return.

"I have no problem leaving your Bounty alive so long as she stays off Vercuella." Meaning she lost nothing in this arrangement, but she did expose a weakness. Why? "I know of the magic you seek, Revered Alabath."

There it was.

I didn't allow myself to blanch. "The magic?"

"That which was left behind, which was locked away but lives in your veins."

The emblems.

Tolek nearly growled beside me, his heated stare on the door hiding Lancaster from us. He appeared ready to break it down and fight the fae for sharing our secrets, but Ritalia only laughed. "Fear not, my hunter did not break your bargain. If he had, he would be dead upon this marble floor."

"How do you know, then?" Ophelia asked.

"I will tell you once we are alone," Ritalia said. "Your court and mine will both leave. I am going to briefly confer with my advisors and guards, but when I return, we will both have our answers."

"You don't visit with her alone, Alabath," Tolek muttered, and Malakai grunted his agreement, but I was ahead of them.

"We will keep an equal number of council," I stated. "After all, Your Majesty, the strongest rulers know when to listen to others. Isn't that right?"

Ritalia smiled sweetly at my challenge, but the lines around her lips were tense. "That is wise. We each may keep one."

I nodded, eyes flashing to Ezalia beside me. As the only other clan ruler, I was prepared to give her the honor of staying, but she shook her head. With a silent but poignant flick of her brows over my shoulder, I knew what she intended.

I turned, finding Tol's assured chocolate stare already on mine, and relief unwound within me.

"Tolek Vincienzo will act as my Second," I declared to the queen.

"Lovely," Ritalia sneered.

As the others left, I tried to catch Rina's eye. Tried to tell her we'd figure this out, that this Bounty declaration meant nothing if she did not want it to. She'd been powerful enough as a human, she did not need some ancient bloodline if she wished to scorn it.

But Santorina's stare was set on the antechamber, her emotions entirely closed off.

When the doors closed behind my friends with a bang, I felt further from her than ever.

Chapter Eleven
Malakai

Those doors closed, sealing us in an antechamber to wait for Ophelia and Tolek, and my chest tightened. I leaned my back against the wall, head thumping to the stone, and took deep breaths as I counted the flames flickering in the chandeliers.

There were so many candles in this fucking palace. Mystlight was so much easier.

How would they get extinguished tonight? Was someone expected to climb up there? There were no visible ladders or tools of any kind. Not a helpful thing to be seen. Sure as Spirits wouldn't be my problem, but it seemed impractical.

I dragged my hand down my face.

"What in an Angel's fuck are we doing here?" How had we *gotten* here? Emblems and bargains and gods. That was the purpose behind us making a temporary peace with the fae, but this —us being separated—grated nails through my chest.

Locked in. We were locked in. No better than—

I pushed off the wall and strode toward where the others consoled Santorina.

"I am fine," she was assuring everyone, no heat or ice in her voice. She'd likely boil over later, but Rina always thought a few steps ahead. She was likely waiting for the right time.

"We need drinks," Lyria chimed, drifting around the room and poking into cabinets.

"It'll all be faerie wine," Mila reminded her.

Lyria grumbled, sticking her head out from the cabinet with two of the bottles in hand. "Endless supply of the shit." She looked between them as if contemplating, then she sighed and returned them, slamming the door. "Why is there nothing else?"

"There's plenty of candles," I muttered, and Mila chuckled beside me.

"Lancaster will pay for that outburst," Jezebel swore, tucking into the corner on a settee with Erista.

"We aren't sure what he was after," the Soulguider tried to placate.

"I am," Santorina said, eyeing us all with an unaffected air. "He was after me."

Lyria sauntered back to the group. "Last mistake he'll make."

"As soon as Ophelia and Tolek are done, we'll get back to the ship," Ezalia said, latching on to her leadership roots. "We'll reassess everything back in the outposts."

Jezebel huffed a dramatic sigh, grumbling about how entitled the fae were, and Erista began kneading her shoulders. The Seawatcher Chancellor struck up a conversation with Rina, attempting to distract her from whatever had happened.

I nudged Mila, nodding my head to the side. She followed me across the room, near a second exit. I was about to tell her my idea, but Mila's attention snagged on Lyria, still shuffling through cabinets in a desperate search.

"She's okay?" I asked.

Mila nodded, almost reluctantly, and whispered, "Still refusing to talk." About the war, she meant.

"Is that unusual for her?" I asked.

"We talked about everything last time." Mila sighed, leaning against the wall and gently letting her head fall back. Platinum hair tumbled around her shoulders, unbound and silky. "Perhaps every recovery is different, though. Spirits know we've all changed over the last months." She gave me a shy smile. "Some of us have had the healing process easier this time, though."

"Healing is never easy," I said, shifting my weight. The ache to touch her was a pressure throughout my limbs, as if they might act of their own accord. Carefully, I brushed her hair over her shoulder, watching how it fell. "We all do it differently."

"Spoken like someone with experience," she joked, but a slight shiver went through her as I dragged my thumb across the bare skin over her collarbone.

"I was lucky this time. I didn't suffer how I did after the treaty, so I think it's easier."

The last battles had been victories for me, both personally and for the Mystiques. I'd survived on that battlefield and in my mind. But Lyria had faced so much more. If the screams of warriors echoed across the dark caverns of my memory on the hard nights, I couldn't imagine what she was going through.

"Some of us got luckier than others," Mila mumbled, eyes dropping to her shoes. Her deep teal gown stood out against her tan skin, making her eyes shine when she looked up at me. "I think I feel guilty at times. For being...happy. When so many aren't."

"*I* think that makes sense," I told her honestly. "Because we've both carried the weight of so many lives on our shoulders. So now that they're gone—to an extent—we don't know how to carry ourselves."

"*I* think," she mimicked, "that is very wise and spoken like someone who has truly evaluated his trauma and taken steps toward healing himself."

Something akin to pride warmed my chest. "I had someone smart helping me out." One corner of her lips tugged up. "You're allowed to feel guilty, Mila. But maybe being happy is how some of us move on. And it's okay to take a step forward and support the others as they catch up."

Those words sat between us for a moment, Mila's eyes on her friend.

"Enough of this," she finally said, straightening with a commanding breath. "What did you want to talk about?"

I cracked a smile because I'd forgotten I actually had a plan when I pulled her from the others, content to speak with her in this gilded antechamber flooded with candles, the two of us in ridiculous clothing.

But there was a point to this.

"I was thinking, we're here for a reason." Her brows shot up, urging me to continue. "Ophelia needs to handle what's going on in there." I waved a hand at the audience chamber. "But..."

Reaching around Mila, I pushed down the handle of the second exit, and the door clicked open.

"Looking for an adventure, Warrior Prince?" It was her general's voice with a bit of a taunt heightening it. Spirits, that thrill traveled through my entire body.

"I'm suggesting exactly that. Perhaps something *godly*." I swallowed, dropping my voice.

Mila smirked. "Wouldn't it be *unwise* of us to wander off after what happened in there?"

"Wouldn't it be *unwise* of us to risk being here without even attempting to get answers?"

Her eyes lit up, brighter than that damn dress. "What did you have in mind?"

"Do you think this palace has a library?"

～

"BRYSTIN SETS ME ON EDGE," Mila admitted, voice so low I could barely make it out as we strolled through the wide palace corridors.

Created this. Lancaster and Mora had created this entire structure, from the marble beneath our feet to the rich tapestries draped along the walls to every last candle.

"They all do," I agreed, and quirked my head to the left. "Let's try this way." We seemed to be traveling into the depths of the building.

"They do," Mila said, a step in front of me. Her long white braid swayed down her back, the soft, embroidered fabric of the fae gown draping across her hips and leaving little to the imagination. "But Lancaster and Mora seem easier to understand. They're here for their power. How they ended up here, where the rest of their family is, I don't know. But at least that makes sense."

I pulled my eyes away from her ass long enough to process what she'd said. "Did you hear what Brystin was saying on the way to dinner? About his tracking and *assignments?*" Bile built in the back of my throat.

"I did." Mila's eyes widened with concern. "Tracking power sounds dangerous. We need to be careful around him."

I nodded. It wasn't the implication that many of his assignments involved dismembering enemies, the memory of my own torture, or even Mila's torture, that haunted me. It was the twisted grin on the male's face as he'd said it—the way he'd seemed willing to do anything for the scent of blood in the air. For the *fun* of wreaking havoc.

That unsettling thought followed us as we continued winding through the palace. We passed a few pairs of fae, some carting linens or baskets of food and casting us wary looks, but not a single one stopped us.

"They don't seem to care that we're here," Mila observed, as a female with long black hair braided in a crown around her head kept walking, the pockets of her apron weighed down.

"Probably because we're being watched," I muttered. "They've likely been told not to engage unless we give them a reason, but to trail us." And without thinking, I slipped my hand around Mila's waist, turning her back to the wall, right up against a heavy tapestry.

She blinked up at me. "Yes?" But she bit her bottom lip, a sultry look clouding her eyes.

Dipping my head, I whispered in her ear, "Let's give them a reason."

Her hands curled against my chest, slipping under the lapels of the fae jacket to clutch my tunic as she exhaled. A decadent, breathy sound that had my cock aching. Maybe this was a bad idea.

She arched her back slightly, her breasts pressing into me, and my skin felt tight.

This was definitely a bad idea.

Placing one hand beside her head, I brushed a strand of hair behind her ear and brought my lips to hers. I kissed her, slowly and indulgently, my tongue stroking against hers.

Angels, I wanted her. More than teasing kisses, more than a show to weed out who was watching us—I wanted every piece.

My fingers dug into her hair, tilting her head back, and a soft moan hummed up her throat, begging me to hurry my pace.

How could I ignore a request?

I dropped my other hand to her ass, pulling her tighter against me, and the reins on my control were ready to snap when she writhed—

"Excuse me?" My head snapped up at the voice. The fae female with the braided coronet stood not two feet away, eyes wide. "May I help you with something?"

I flashed her a lethal look that said *why are you interrupting?* But Mila's cheeks flushed, and she falsely stuttered, "Oh, we-we're sorry. We were, um, looking for the library. But we seem to be lost."

The lustful daze in her eyes covered the lie nicely. Lost, distracted, hoping to lure out whoever was assigned to follow us when they thought us a pair of ambling warriors. Any excuse would work.

The fae assessed us, eyes shrewd. "Were you given permission?"

"Yes," we both answered.

Mila looked up at me, her grin sending my heart pounding, and I wrapped an arm around her waist, tugging her away from the wall with her back pressed to my front. The female tracked each movement, watched closely as my fingers tightened on Mila's hip, massaging the silk. Her expression softened at whatever she saw between us, believing us nothing more than lust-drunk young warriors.

Apparently she forgot warriors were entirely capable of lying.

"You aren't too turned around," she said. "Take the next two rights and go down the spiral staircase. You can't miss it."

"Thank you," Mila said, flashing a kind smile.

Weaving her fingers between mine, Mila pulled me down the hall before anyone could say another word, the image of an innocent couple scampering off for a rendezvous, with that female likely following our every step.

When we reached the library, the arched doorframe towered, a show of power and extravagance like every other damn thing in this palace. And there were more candles lining the aisles. Spirits, the sooner we got away from here, the better.

I checked over my shoulder, but there was no sign of anyone following us.

"Mora and Lancaster truly made this?" I whispered as we walked down the long aisle leading from the doors to the center of the domed room. The air was heavy with the scent of worn parchment, leather, and magic—the latter likely from the construction of such a massive endeavor. "Angels, there's an archive desk and all."

Mila spun around herself, eyes dragging over every shelf and shadow. Through the windows carving along the upper level, moonlight pushed against the clouds, silver spilling over every surface and leather-bound story. It reflected in her wide eyes as she strode up to the round desk in the center of the library.

"Hello?" she called, leaning over the counter, and I ducked around the side, looking down a few of the aisles. Books towered to the high ceilings, rolling ladders awaiting use, but no one lingered between the shelves.

"Maybe we can—"

"May I help you two?" A voice came out of the shadows, its owner rounding the far end of the circular desk with a candle in hand. Opening the waist-high door hidden in the wood, she entered the space and braced her elbows on the counter, tugging her shawl tighter around her shoulders.

"We're looking for books," I said. Of course we were.

"You are in the right place." Her voice floated on the air, comforting.

"Do you work here?" Mila asked.

She titled her head, black hair a night-drenched river over her shoulder. "I am a keeper of tales."

"We're with the warrior party visiting the queen," I admitted. She could probably tell based on our scent anyway. "We'd love to learn more about the gods, though."

A viper's smile split her lips, eyes glinting. "The gods?"

"Given we know little of them but they're imperative to fae culture," Mila said, returning a much softer grin, "and we are being so kindly hosted here, we thought it may be prudent to study Aoiflyn."

The woman observed us, then waved a hand toward the stacks to her left, gold bangles chiming a soothing rhythm. "That section focuses on the gods."

"Thank you," I said with a dip of my chin.

As we were walking away, her voice drifted after us. "I believe you'll find the third aisle the most helpful."

"Right," I nodded, and held out a hand to guide Mila ahead of me.

We started down the row she indicated, but after reading the first section of titles, my brows pulled together.

"The third aisle is all..." I scanned the words gilding spine after spine. *Death's Child, A Goddess' Dance with Death, Born in the Gates of the Desert...*

"They're all about Artale," Mila finished. She looked back toward the now empty archive desk. As I came up beside her, her shoulder brushing my chest, I followed her stare. She dropped her voice. "Why would she tell us the third aisle if this is Artale, not Aoiflyn?"

Stretching a hand above my shoulder, Mila tugged one book from the shelf, holding it down near the candle. I stepped closer to read with her, her warmth seeping into my body and that cinnamon scent making me want to finish what we'd started in the hall.

"Sphinx tales?" I asked, trying to focus as she leafed through the tomb.

She answered, "Apparently, they're a symbol of Artale."

"Sphinxes don't exist." Mila leveled me a stare as if to say *how many times have we been proven wrong about that?* I corrected, "They haven't been seen in a very long time if they do."

"Neither had the pegasus or khrysaor."

She stopped on a page that discussed how sphinxes were messengers, protectors, and advisors of Artale, and often communicated with the sprites of the Fae Goddess, Aioflyn, and delegates of the Witch Goddess of Sorcia, Thallia. The creatures were heralds of the Goddess of Death's blood across the land.

"Creepy," I muttered.

Mila shut the book. "Let's take a few of these with us."

"Why?" I asked, but held out my arms for her to pile them in.

"Why not?" Mila answered. Placing a second volume called *Godsblood Heir* atop the sphinx book, she grabbed my hand and whisked me toward another aisle.

"Aoiflyn. Finally," Mila exhaled as we reached the last row of the six marked for the gods.

"Many of these books are about bargains," I observed, studying the spines. *Deals with Gods, History of Locked Fates, Age of Bargains.*

I tugged the last one off the shelf, asking, "Do you think any of these have ways Ophelia and Tolek can get out of their bargain?"

Mila shrugged. "Only one way to find out."

She pulled one of the others and dropped to the floor. In the dim candlelight, I sat across from her. What I wouldn't have given for a hint of Ophelia's Angellight to read by, but I cracked the book open and squinted at the words.

"There's quite a bloody history around the *Age of Bargains,*" I noted after a long enough period of companionable silence that my ass was falling asleep on the marble floor. Truthfully, it had probably only been a few minutes, but this library was uncomfortable.

"Here, too," Mila agreed with a grim nod.

"Why is it all so entwined with blood?" I wondered aloud.

"I don't know," Mila said distantly, "but what's more interesting in this volume is those striking the bargains."

"What do you mean?" I asked, shifting closer.

"These are all accounts of the Fae Goddess' children." She chewed her lip, scanning the page. "Some she had with humans, most with the fae, and it's detailing infamous bargains they made."

"Does that impact the deal struck?"

"Not directly." Her eyes lifted to mine. "But it makes the fae strong beyond measure, and in fae culture, the more powerful they are, the trickier they tend to become."

And Lancaster was strong. We'd learned as much tonight when

Ritalia spoke of his creation magic. Which meant his bargain was undoubtedly iron-clad.

Mila went on, "Certain goddess' magic can also apparently repel other *ancient sources* of magic."

"Specific," I deadpanned.

"I'm not sure how it could come into play in deals. It all boils down to careful language." She paused, flipping through the pages. "Apparently the most powerful bargain magic can be hereditary, and many of the histories describe them as being used to lock secrets away."

I tucked that away to mull over later. "Are there any indications of ways *out* of bargains?"

Mila shook her head, opening her mouth to comment—

"What are you two doing here?" A sharp voice sliced through the library. Mila and I both jumped to our feet, slamming our books, which earned us a disapproving stare from the fae now striding down the aisle, a candle in hand.

"The librarian granted us permission," Mila answered as she tucked the book on Aoiflyn back onto the shelves, but I shifted to the side, hiding the two on Artale behind my back.

At least if we couldn't get anything on the Fae Goddess, we could take something with us.

"I am the only librarian who travels with the queen." Mila and I exchanged a glance. The female's tightly braided gray hair and wrinkled expression was certainly different from the first woman we'd seen. "The library is closed to visitors as of sundown unless accompanied by one of the queen's soldiers. Out with you. Now!"

"We're sorry," I rushed out, keeping my back to the shelves as we hurried away. "We misunderstood."

As we fled, I cast a last glance back toward that round desk, where the original librarian had disappeared. The memory of her melodic voice followed us down the halls.

❧

THE PALACE WAS quiet as we made our way back toward the antechamber. "Want to find somewhere private?" I asked. The slightest pink tinted Mila's cheeks, so I held up the books. "Research."

She smirked. "Research." But her eyes fleeted down the hall, in the direction our friends waited. "We should go check..."

She took a step toward me, then pressed onto her toes. With her hands firmly against my chest, every inch of my body was aware of her.

Mila, Mila, Mila, my fucking heart seemed to beat.

That cinnamon scent wrapped around me as she brought her lips to my cheek. "Perhaps we can do some research tomorrow night?" she whispered, a promise and a question.

"Tomorrow," I said.

I bent to kiss her, but we both froze when shouting echoed from the palace's foyer.

CHAPTER TWELVE
TOLEK

"YOU CERTAIN ABOUT THIS?" I ASKED OPHELIA WHEN Ritalia, Brystin, and the other fae had all left.

Her stare was locked on the door our friends had disappeared through, and I knew she was worrying about Santorina. What all this Bounty business meant and how we could combat it or embrace it.

Finally, though, she met my gaze, letting a hint of her worry show through the flinch of her brow. "I'm certain about very little right now," she admitted, and dammit did I want to kiss her and wipe away all those concerns, but she continued. "All I know is I need to feel like I'm doing *something*. Right now, I feel so out of control. If I can get some sort of command over this situation— secure us a kernel of truth to help figure out what's going on—I'll take it."

Determination and the strength of the Angels burned through those words. Spirits, she was magnificent.

"Spoken as a true queen," I said, kissing her hand.

She rolled her eyes. "Please, Tolek."

"Say what you may, but the title does sound nice when used toward you."

"The only queen we've known ruined our lives," Ophelia countered. "I'm not sure I'd want to be one."

Fair. "It's all about the intention. Barrett wears the title of king well."

Her lips twisted to the side. "Assuming he's able to get to his coronation," she reminded me. "I'm worried about him."

"I'm worried about all of us."

She laughed, tilting her head back. "This place is impressive."

"I hate to admit it," I agreed, following her gaze to the murals adorning the ceiling. More fae cruelty, if I had to guess.

Studying the artwork, Ophelia said, a bit sadly, "They remind me of the ones in the Revered's Palace."

I wrapped an arm around her, pulling her into me. "What was your favorite back home?"

Absently, Ophelia toyed with the button on my jacket. "I don't know. I never had enough time to really memorize them." She was searching through that mind of hers, trying to find a specific recollection from the home we hadn't seen in months, but with the way her magenta gaze dulled, she came up short.

"There was one in my office I loved," I said. "It was of a fox hidden in a berry grove."

Ophelia laughed, and my heart beat faster at the sound. "A berry grove?"

"Odd, right?" I shrugged. "That's why I liked it. When we get back there, I'll show you."

Not if. Because we were returning to the city atop the peaks if it meant my life. Ophelia belonged in the mountains, and I knew she missed them.

We talked about our favorite spots in the Revered's Palace, ignoring the presence of the fae and all sitting heavily on our shoulders, until finally, the door behind the throne opened. Ritalia and Brystin traipsed back into the audience chamber and stood before the throne.

Ophelia's persona of Revered instantly slid back up, and she wasted no time reiterating her earlier question. "If not from Lancaster, how do you know about the emblems?"

Ritalia looked to Brystin once before answering, but I couldn't read that fleeting glance. "I have sources—centuries-old sources—from whom I can decipher secrets."

What in the fucking Angels did that mean?

"And what do you want with them?" Ophelia pushed, not getting caught up in Ritalia's twisted words.

"I want them." Ritalia's fingers curved around her chalice. "Find those emblems, deliver them to me, and in turn, I will give you the precious information you seek of the gods."

"I cannot do that," Ophelia answered, without thought. "I've been tasked with finding them for the Angels. I have been tasked with fulfilling this prophecy, this curse. You are not part of it."

Not that we knew what Ophelia *was* supposed to do with the emblems, yet.

"You cannot do what they are meant for," Ritalia said, and we both perked up.

"Why not?" Ophelia asked.

"Because—" Her words cut off in a choke, the queen's eyes flaring wide.

Ophelia's eyes lit up, her fingers twitching against her gown. "You know, but you are bound from saying it?"

Ritalia sneered. "Find the items so cleverly hidden. And deliver them to me."

"They do not belong to the *fae*," Ophelia snarled, patience on the verge of snapping.

"They do not belong on Ambrisk at all."

And Ophelia's resolve shattered. "*WHY?*"

Ritalia was silent for a long moment, Brystin's keen attention bouncing between the queen and the Revered. Swallowing, Ritalia seemed to choose her words carefully as she said, "Make a bargain with me—"

"Absolutely not," Ophelia swore, her voice limned with power.

Ritalia went on, "Bargain that once you find what you seek, you will consider my offer."

Ophelia stewed on that. "What do we receive in return?"

"What do you request?"

"You cannot interfere in warrior matters," Ophelia answered quickly. "You cannot set foot on our continent, convene with our people, or use your magic to do so. This includes all matters pertaining to the Angels and this task."

Ritalia picked apart each word, casting another glance to

Brystin. Why did she keep deferring to him? After a moment, the queen nodded and looked down at us. "I will not set foot on your continent, convene with your people, or use magic to do so, nor will I interfere in warrior matters. And do not fret; my bargains are more powerful than my hunter's, laced with a deeper magic. To seal this, all you must do is drink from this chalice."

My skin tingled. "No. She's not drinking anything."

"I give my word there is nothing in here to harm her," Ritalia swore. "You made an indefinite bargain with my hunter. This is different. With my magic, you must only drink this wine."

Ophelia strode forward, taking the chalice. We both examined it, but Spirits, we didn't know what we were looking for.

I found Ophelia's eyes, and I lifted a brow. We had to trust the magic of the fae being unable to lie if we wanted to get out of here.

With one final glare at the queen and fingers clenching the stem, Ophelia tipped the chalice to her lips.

Damien's balls, I hated this. My heart rioted as she took one quick swallow, every fucking breath in my lungs tight. Her throat worked over the heady crimson liquid that clearly tasted horrible based on her answering sneer.

Outside the windows, the earth shuddered and lightning cracked. Magic tingled through the air. Ophelia took one last gulp and tossed the chalice aside, metal clattering against marble, but I watched her for three long breaths.

She showed no sign of harm.

Relief loosened the grip on my lungs.

We turned back to Ritalia. Once again, she stood proudly before her throne with Brystin. She lifted her chin, about to speak, but the main entrance to the audience chamber slammed open. The doors bounced against the stone wall with a boom, and the last person I expected to see ran in.

"*Cypherion?*" I shouted.

He was harried as I raced to him. The jaw he usually kept perfectly clean was dusted with auburn scruff, his eyes flying around the room like he didn't care what or who he walked in on, only that he'd found *someone.*

Malakai was on his heels, the two of us catching him right as CK's knees gave out.

"He has her," he repeated again and again, voice so low and broken. "He has her."

I met Malakai's eyes over Cyph's slumped form, sought out Mila standing in the doorway, and the matching subtle shakes of their heads were all the confirmation I needed. My lungs tightened, air escaping.

Vale had not returned with Cypherion. She was not waiting in the antechamber with the others or the main foyer, was not back in Seawatcher Territory at all.

"Cypherion?" Ophelia asked softly, the queen and her bargain forgotten. "What happened?"

"Titus—" His voice kept cracking, like he'd ridden so hard to get here, he hadn't slept in days, and now couldn't force the words that had played on a loop in his mind out of his mouth.

"CK?" I asked, gripping him tighter.

"Star Tied One!" Ritalia's voice sliced through the commotion, and my attention snapped up, following her venomous stare to...Malakai?

He raised his head, brows scrunching together.

The queen shoved herself forward, nearly stumbling, her diadem nowhere in sight. Mora, Lancaster, and a handful of other fae had raced back to their queen's side, from where, I didn't know.

Ritalia's jaw trembled, but her voice was ice as she looked between Malakai and Cypherion and commanded, "*Get your cousin out of here.*"

PART TWO
VALYRIE

CHAPTER THIRTEEN
OPHELIA

EVEN THE AIR WAS DISMAL AS WE TRUDGED UP THE stone-lined path to the cottage late that evening. Like the pressure of the ordeal we'd undergone was weighing down the clouds, turning every breath thick.

Cypherion was unconscious, though entirely okay according to Santorina's careful evaluation—his body had seemed to give out once he was back to us, as distressed as he'd been. Probably a defensive tactic, Rina guessed. Adrenaline and worry kept him fueled until he was safe and had told someone Vale was...

He hadn't gotten far enough to tell us the details. But Vale was with Titus, her chancellor and apparent captor.

And Cypherion was now upstairs, Tolek and Malakai watching over him in the spare room the latter claimed.

Jezebel and Erista left to check on the khrysaor and Sapphire, Lyria and Mila going with them as Ezalia returned home. That left Santorina and me in the cottage's cozy sitting room. Books and papers flooded the surfaces, a piano took up one corner, and it all felt crammed.

"Walk?" I asked Rina. Aside from evaluating Cypherion, she'd been silent since we returned, standing at the window overlooking the garden in contemplation.

She turned to me, nodding. "The beach."

Still in those ridiculous fae gowns, we left the cottage and descended the dusty path to the white sand shore, tall grasses waving us along in the breeze. Moonlight glistened across the gently crashing waves. It was hard to imagine that a short boat ride away, the fae queen loomed in her palace.

"It feels like a weird dream," I muttered.

"In a way," Rina agreed. "But it also feels like a fate meant to strike."

"What do you mean?" I asked, turning to her. My skirts slithered across the sand, the only sound besides the waves as I waited for Rina to continue.

After a long pause, she took a deep breath timed to the rolling sea and said, "I don't belong here, Ophelia."

"You belong wherever we are."

"No." She faced me, and the moon lit up the resignation in her dark eyes. "I don't belong with the warriors. I should have stayed at the human training camp in Mystique Territory, at least for a few months. Or traveled between the larger ones, maybe. Provided aid where I could."

The words landed like a blow to my chest, my ears hollowing out. "What?"

"Maybe that's where I should be. I can't help but feel like I could do more good there then I can with you all."

"You belong with *us*, Rina," I pleaded.

"I don't."

"Why would you—"

"Because I'm just a human!" She stepped back, opened her palms before her as if that would show me the truth. With her deep purple lace gown absorbing the night, she didn't look like *just a human*. She looked powerful. A creature that made the world bow to her whim. "I don't have warrior blood in my veins, Ophelia. I am not blessed by your Angels or descended from them. I'm a lowly human whose parents didn't even stand a chance when the first war landed at their door. I only happened to become friends with the Revered of the Mystique Warriors."

"You're not some meager being, and our friendship was not by chance, Santorina! You and I are meant to be in each other's lives —you can't tell me it doesn't feel that way."

How many times had she saved me? When Malakai left, when I kept drinking, when I fell on every bad habit imaginable, Rina never failed to smack much needed sense into me.

Or when her parents died, and she had been so alone, but I stayed at her apartment every night because she couldn't bear to leave it.

Our friendship was not some happenstance. It was an intention of fate and the Angels. I'd always believed that of each of my friends. My family.

"I love you, Ophelia," Rina said sadly, "but I'm not a warrior."

"I don't give a damn what blood is in your veins!" I pointed back toward the cottage. "None of them do either."

"By the fucking goddess, *I* do!" she growled—the sound barely human at all—and my eyes widened. For a moment we stood there, looking at each other, both panting.

The steadiness of her voice flayed my chest wide open. And with it, a bit of my grounding force slipped away. Spiraled right off into the heavens, tugging the tethers of control I clung to so tenuously.

My voice was small, vulnerable, when I asked, "Are you leaving?"

I wouldn't stop her if it was what she wanted—needed. But Spirits, would it wreck me to watch one of my best friends walk away.

Rina seemed to hear that pain. Her eyes softened. "No. I can't leave you all. I would be too worried being away right now." She framed it as if it was her choice, but a part of me was certain she'd made this decision for me. She took a few steps closer, facing the ocean again and hugging her arms to her chest. "Who would keep you all bandaged and safe?"

I nudged her with my elbow. "See, we need you."

Santorina breathed a laugh, the tension cracking between us. "It wouldn't be awful if I did leave. When that monster roared above me tonight, while I may have been stunned, I wasn't afraid. I *should* have been, but instead, I thought of where my dagger was. Calculated how quickly it would take him to leap across the room and where my blow would need to land to meet him."

I sighed, understanding. "And you want to help other humans feel that strength."

A bob of her chin had her ponytail swaying. "I wasn't afraid tonight, but I once would have been. And every human on this continent—on all of Ambrisk—deserves to understand that confidence. What good am I doing if I have a first-hand account of it and am hiding away?"

Leaning my head against her shoulder, I said, "You're not hiding."

But the words weren't only in defense of her, and we both knew it. They were a grapple at absolution for my own guilty conscience after so many weeks stashed away on Ritalia's orders.

Frustration riled in my chest at it all, but I tampered it for her.

"Once we're done with this Angelcurse mess, you're going to help train the most courageous group of humans to ever grace Gallantia."

"Thank you." The corners of her lips tipped up. "And thank you for the support, though I know you hate the idea of me leaving."

"I do hate it," I grumbled, even though a large part of my heart swelled with pride. "And I hate that you are such a damn morally admirable person that I can't even talk you out of it."

Santorina laughed fully at that.

"So," I said. "Bounties?"

"It's nonsense." She waved me off, staring back over the ocean.

"Sure." I shrugged and dropped the conversation. She clearly did not want to be pushed on it, but she had said it herself. Perhaps tonight—perhaps everything Ritalia had revealed—had been a viperous fate with its fangs bared, and the queen finally set it free from its cage, commanding it to strike.

And we were left to wait and see who it poisoned.

~

TOLEK, Malakai, and Mila were back in the sitting room when we returned, interrupting their conversation.

"Cypherion?" I asked.

"Sleeping," Tol said with a straight-lipped nod from where he stood beside the fire.

"I'll go check on him." Rina gathered her skirts and disappeared up the stairs. The ruffling of all that unnecessary material sliding against the wood agitated me.

The pressure of the day clung to the room, threatening to overwhelm me. I shook it off, looking to Malakai to address the next in a long line of questions. "Do you have any idea what Ritalia meant?"

Get your cousin out of here.

"That's what I was saying before you walked in." He leaned forward on the couch, keeping one hand on Mila's knee and grabbing a piece of parchment off the table. A letter, I realized. "I'm writing to my mother now."

Akalain. If anyone knew something about what Ritalia claimed, it would be Malakai's mom. Or Cypherion's, but we didn't have a way to contact her.

"Okay," I said, nodding at the letter. "We wait."

Again.

But Mila said, "There's something else."

Malakai grabbed two books off the table and tossed one to Tolek, handing the other to me.

"*Godsblood Heir?*" Tolek read the title of his aloud.

I flipped through the pages of mine, *Gate's Guardians*. It was all folklore about Artale and sphinxes.

"You took this from the fae library?"

Malakai shrugged. "I doubt they'll notice. We had permission...sort of." His gaze flicked to Mila, a secret exchanged in that split second.

"Thank you. Both of you," I said. Perhaps I should have been worried about *borrowing* from the queen, but a part of me was wholly satisfied. "These will be helpful since we didn't get to ask questions about the gods today."

And that reminder was the last I needed. Everything that had gone wrong today crashed over me, a roaring in my ears as my final semblance of control slipped through my fingers, my grip on the book tightening until I dented the leather.

We'd gone to the isle to meet the fae and left with little more than unexplained riddles and another bargain on my head.

Tolek saw it, setting his book down on the table and taking the other from my hands. "We'll deal with it all tomorrow," he said calmly, bidding goodnight to Malakai and Mila.

Then, he was leading me up the stairs and to our room, his spicy citrus scent filling all the voids dug out within me.

~

"TALK TO ME, ALABATH," Tolek said as he closed the door.

I strode across the small room, the walls tight and cramped, but in here it didn't bother me. In here, with only Tolek—the rest of the world shut out—it was safe instead of stifling.

Or it had been, the entire time we'd been on the outposts. This had been the one place I'd been able to stop worrying.

Tonight, not even that helped. My fingers scratched at my Curse mark.

"Did something else happen?" he guessed.

"How did it all go so wrong?" I muttered, looking out the window facing the calm sea. I thought I could see Ritalia from here. See the frazzled state in which she'd expelled us from her palace. Feel the questions I hadn't gotten to ask bubbling up in me.

"We're going to figure it out," Tolek assured me.

"Rina wants to leave."

That made him pause. "What?"

"After the emblem hunt is done, she's going to the human camps to help with training."

"And that upsets you because?"

I whirled toward him. With his hands patiently behind his back and a brow quirked at me, he was as tempered as the level sea beyond the glass. A counter to my unruly fire.

"Because Rina is my best friend," I said. He gaped, mockingly insulted enough to get me to crack a smile. "You know what I mean."

"Santorina is important to all of us," he said, leaning against the bedpost. "And that's why I know there's a part of you that's thrilled she wants to explore this."

Angellight stirred at my fingertips, a subtle band of gold twisting around my hand, much tamer than earlier. "There are so many unknowns right now. Sapphire, the Spirit Realm, whatever happened to Vale's visions. It scares me to consider anyone leaving," I admitted. "Makes me feel out of control."

"We'll get the answers we need, regardless of what we didn't ask today," Tolek said, not a waver of worry in his voice.

"What happened with Lancaster was a show of power," I said. "A command using whatever control Ritalia has over him, to make us feel like we're nothing. Like we're *hers*, though I am a ruler in my own right." My voice dropped, fear snaking through it. "I felt like prey, like we were positioned beneath them, and for what?"

"For assistance," he reminded me. "For answers to questions we don't even know how to begin asking. And because they are a very real threat, whether we like it or not."

My blood continued to boil beneath my skin, Angellight dancing around us. Thoughtfully, Tolek's hands drifted over my shoulders and turned me toward the window. "Think of every warrior out there. Of Rina's parents whose spirits were gone much too soon. Of every human who sheltered in Gallantia. That is why we allowed the queen to *think* she is above us and why you made that bargain, though I know you have no intention of delivering the emblems."

"Spirits," I said, my head dropping back to his shoulder. "I don't even want to consider what will come of that right now."

I didn't want to consider *why* Ritalia wanted the emblems so desperately—enough to expose what the Bounties were in order to win my favor.

Tolek dragged his fingers up and down my arm, leaving chills in his wake. "All problems for tomorrow. For now, we play the game." He dropped his head, placing a kiss to my shoulder, and his words shivered across my skin. "Remember, Alabath, I'm rather good at games."

"You don't play," I breathed, my heart rioting as he traced my collarbone. "You win."

Tolek had spent his life risking gambles, preparing for a standoff such as this with a queen whose hands were coated an unremorseful red.

"Every time," he swore, voice husky. "So, let's relax."

I needed to, he meant, though he wouldn't say it. Again, he was correct. But it didn't soothe the beast riling inside me, the one who wouldn't bow to this queen, this conqueror.

It needed another outlet.

I stepped out of Tol's hold. Strolling across the room, I turned to face him and leaned back against the small, wobbly desk. "We need to make a plan." I placed my hands on either side of me, fingers curling around the curved edge. I stilled for a moment, dismissing every concern, every threat into the furthest crevices of my mind and taking in the man before me. Hair in disarray, stubble darkening his chin, and sleeves pushed to his elbows. "But there are other games we could play first."

His stare turned hungry as he watched my fingers tap the wood.

The air between us became taut as a bow string, each breath only pulling it tighter. "I believe I was promised some assistance with my dress?"

Chocolate eyes flashed to mine, amber specks now molten, and I quirked a brow in challenge. "If my queen demands it," he drawled, "who am I to deny her?"

"I am no queen," I bit back, but my voice was breathy as he stalked toward me with slow, agonizing steps, each echoing on the wood floor with those fae boots. My wildly beating heart filled the silence between them.

No matter how many times we played these games, my body always did that. A rush of lust and adrenaline when he was near, setting every nerve on an anticipatory edge until I was nearly squirming.

I stifled it as he stopped before me, toe to toe, and feigned complete calm he likely saw through. Heat coursed through me, and it was an effort to stay still.

Tolek toyed with the bargain charm strung on my necklace,

studied the markings etched in the gold metal, a million observations passing through that beautiful mind.

As he gently set it down, he brushed my chest, goosebumps spreading across my skin, and a smirk lifted one corner of his mouth. He kept his gaze on his hand, unnervingly steady as he ghosted down my arm, right to the spot where I held onto the desk with a white-knuckled grip.

I knew what he was doing. He was lingering on every touch, every breath, to distract me.

And it was working.

His hand caged mine, slipping between the wood and my palm. Gently but demanding, Tol uncurled my fingers one at a time and guided me to turn. My back pressed to his front, and even through these ridiculous skirts, his cock jutted against my backside, hard and waiting.

Tolek gathered my hair over one shoulder, ducking his head and trailing his lips across bare skin. "You could be a queen," he whispered. "You can conquer any world you want, titles be damned. Queen, Empress, Revered...doesn't matter what they call you, so long as they say it from their knees."

My breath hitched at the conviction in his voice.

The binding of my corset loosened, a kiss landing at the top of my spine. "And you want help with your dress?" Another inch of relief, another kiss down my back. "Whatever my queen wishes."

And though I was not a queen—would never hold the title—the mix of reverence and antagonism in his tone had my thighs clenching together.

Tolek ripped through the remaining ribbons lacing up my back. "Fucking Spirits," he groaned as the dress pooled around my feet.

The skirts of that abhorrent thing were sheer; there wasn't room for layers beneath, so he'd known there had been very little standing in our way. But the top had required an extra, tighter corset beneath the thin fabric, and I'd hidden the details when asking him to tie up the back.

As I stepped out of the dress and turned to face him, his stare could have incinerated every inch of my body. Could have boiled through my Angelblood as he slowly tracked across my skin, up my legs—bare down to the heels I still wore, except for the dagger at my thigh.

That heated intensity traced over the high-cut arch of the lingerie around my hip and the gold lace fabric barely covering between my legs. The tight bodice connected to it hugged my body to the strapless neckline, that same material but accented with the smallest clear gemstones that shimmered in the candlelight.

"How are you real?" Tolek breathed, voice low and rough.

I rolled my eyes. "Cursed by Angels."

"My own personal gift from the winged bastards," he said, unable to stop staring.

It was better than being bare before him, hiding enough to drive him wild, accenting my curves and pushing up my breasts.

I was certain this wasn't what the fae had in mind when they'd placed the lacy item in that dressing chamber, but I might have to thank them. Tolek looked ready to fall to his knees before me.

Too bad that wasn't the game I had in mind.

Tugging the fae tunic over his head and tossing it aside, I ran my hands down the defined planes of his chest. He said I was a gift from the Angels, but Tolek's body was sculpted by them, every line and muscle perfectly crafted, the scars only adding to the beauty.

I undid the buttons of his pants—so different than the leathers I was used to him wearing—rubbing a palm down his thick length beneath the fabric. Tolek groaned at the touch, stumbling as he kicked off his boots.

I pulled down his pants and sank to the floor. Once he stepped out of them, I gripped him over his undershorts, and he twitched in my hand.

"What are you doing?" he asked a beat later, like his mind was still catching up.

"You said whatever your queen wishes." I smirked up at him, fingers curling around his waistband.

"But—"

"Please, Tolek." I dropped the game for a moment. My grip tightened, and his eyes flashed to it, not missing the slightest movement. "I need to feel in control."

It wasn't the first time I was on my knees before him, but it was the first time I *needed* to be like this.

Tolek nodded, and I tugged his shorts down. He was already hard, the tip gleaming, and even the sight had my core aching for him. I licked my lips, gripping him at the base, my other hand braced on his hip.

Slowly, I licked up his length, swirling my tongue around the crown before repeating that motion.

"Who's the tease now?" he asked, voice gravelly.

My gaze flashed up to his, holding eye contact as I took him between my lips, only an inch.

He groaned, bracing himself against the desk. His other hand tangled in my hair as I took more of him, rotating my hand to accommodate for his size, and he held tightly. Demandingly.

"By the fucking Angels, Alabath," he muttered.

I nearly smiled around him, using my free hand to grip his backside. My nails dug into his skin, and he hissed. In pleasure, I knew. Always pleasure teasing the edge of pain.

He was hard as steel now, and I finally took him all the way into my mouth, until his length hit the back of my throat and my eyes watered. He released another of those delicious groans, hand tightening in my hair, restraint causing the veins in his forearms to stand out.

I didn't want him restrained.

I wanted both of us wild and untamed. Free.

I moved faster along his length, sliding to the tip and sinking forward again and again, frantic and desperate. Tolek noticed the shift, gripping the back of my head tighter and meeting my pace.

"So fucking good, *apeagna*," he groaned, thrusting to meet me. It wasn't a punishing force, but it was luxuriating in the pleasure I was giving him. Granting me the power I so desperately needed after tonight. After these weeks stagnant in the outposts, indulging the queen's requests.

"Angels, Alabath" he purred, praise and lust deepening his voice. "Look how good you are."

I moved faster at the thought, taking him as deep as possible on each stroke. Heat pooled between my legs, and I squirmed for relief.

"Ophelia." The guttural growl of my name on his lips spurred me on. With my free hand, I cupped his balls and squeezed gently. "Fuck," he exhaled, the desk rattling as I drove him to ruin. "I'm close."

My gaze flashed up, his turning near savage to make eye contact with me while my lips were spread around him. With that stare I told him to let go. Commanded him to give everything to me now because I could take it.

He knotted his fingers in my hair, thrusting until he came down my throat with a groan that rippled along my bones and satisfied the ravaging need igniting within me.

Tol pulled me to my feet, lips slamming to mine and one hand curling into my hair, the other dipping between my legs to tease the soaked lace. He kissed me until I could barely breathe, until my knees were the ones threatening to give out. All I knew was him. Every sense was swarmed by Tolek Vincienzo.

When he picked me up, my legs wrapped around his waist, and he whispered, "Your turn." And I wasn't sure if it was a threat or a promise.

He spun, setting me down on the desk. I reached to remove my heels, but Tolek gripped my wrist. "Leave those on."

CHAPTER FOURTEEN
CYPHERION

IT SMELLED LIKE...MEAT?

Like something smokey, maybe. My head spun as the scent pushed in, and I pried my eyes open.

I was on my side, facing a glass of water. Condensation dripped slowly to the nightstand, everything else blurring around it. Spirits, why was it so hot?

Kicking off the soft blanket draped over me, I pushed myself upright with a groan. The room wavered. That was what I got for two weeks of riding non-stop from Valyn. But it had taken Vale and me three to get to Lumin before we'd headed to capital, and that was without the extra journey to the outposts.

Nothing on Ambrisk could have made me stop.

Not with her—

A harsh breath sliced through my chest. *You go, and then come back for me.*

I would. I fucking would.

Because she'd willingly returned to her captor after learning he held the answers to both repairing her sessions and finding Valyrie's emblem. After that fateful night in the Valyn archives, she'd volunteered to stay with Titus.

And I'd tear the Fates from the skies to get her back.

But first...where was I?

Light peeked around tightly pulled curtains, but it was early, judging by the pale glow. A second small bed sat on the opposite side of the nightstand, but the sheets were nearly untouched, like someone had either made it hurriedly or not fully slept. The light blue walls and soft linens seemed oddly comfortable, soothing my panic a little more.

My scythe, swords, and daggers were respectfully laid on the dresser across from the bed. I swiped up the dripping water glass and crossed to inspect them. My throat was thick as I drank; I must have slept for a while.

"All in order," I muttered. Every weapon was accounted for.

How in the damn Spirits had I gotten here? Everything before I passed out was a blur of riding through jungle and sand.

Stretching out my stiff limbs, I crept around the other side of the room and picked through the belongings. A nondescript pack and a cloak draped across a chair. Whoever it belonged to wouldn't need that in this oppressive heat. Those journals though—

Lucidius's.

Malakai.

Something nagged at my brain at his name. Something I was supposed to remember. I'd seen him, Tolek, and Ophelia before I'd passed out—

Get your cousin out of here.

Cousin.

"Holy fucking spirits." I sank against the wall, head falling back with a dull thud.

Cousin. The fae—I assumed that was Queen Ritalia—had spat that word at Malakai. About *me.*

My pulse beat against my skin, blood rushing in my ears.

"Malakai is my cousin?" I whispered to myself, evaluating his belongings stacked in the corner.

I listened to the words as if someone else had said them. Waited for them to hit me with the blunt force of a dulled blade. But nothing happened—nothing beyond foggy confusion.

"She had to be lying."

It was a question I'd asked my entire life—who was my father? One my mother had refused to answer. One I'd let tear me apart—

hold me back. And yet when a possible answer was dangled before me, I didn't feel any different besides the initial shock.

My heart was too shredded, my nerves frayed and anger hot in my gut.

How in the Angel's bloody realm could it be possible?

With a deep breath, I pushed off the wall and followed that smokey scent down the stairs to find the people who would likely be able to make sense of it all.

~

"WHAT DOES SHE MEAN SHE SUSPECTED?" The question was whispered, but even from the top landing, Ophelia's sharp voice was recognizable.

"I don't know," Malakai snapped. "I wrote back."

"To not tell him—"

A stair creaked beneath me, and Rina's softer question sliced off.

I shouldn't have expected anything else from my nosy group of friends. But where I'd anticipated feeling crowded from the attention, a warmth spread through my chest instead. One that gave me enough confidence to descend the staircase and round the corner into what appeared to be both a sitting room and dining room.

The windows were open, the ocean softly rolling in the distance. Ophelia, Santorina, Malakai, and Tolek sat on plush sofas in the center of the cozy space. Mila and Lyria were at the rectangular dining table facing the others.

But all eyes in this low-ceilinged room turned toward me.

I found Malakai, and he pushed to his feet as I said the only thing I could think of, "Akalain's brother—the one who died years ago—your uncle...he was my father."

Malakai swallowed. "Looks like he was."

I blew out a breath, and strode to the couch, dropping between the seat he'd vacated and Santorina, across from Ophelia and Tolek. Everyone in the room seemed to sag with relief, as if they feared I'd hole up in my room upstairs.

It wasn't a far cry from what I'd done in the past. Whenever they'd tried to push me on my father or my heritage, I'd brushed it off.

"How do you feel?" Ophelia asked, leaning forward. I had a feeling Tolek's arm around her waist was the only thing keeping her seated.

I shrugged. "The same."

"What do you mean?" Santorina asked, and I faced her.

"I mean, I've lived this long without knowing."

"CK, you've been wanting to find this answer for a while," Tolek said.

"Yeah." I sank back into the cushions and accepted if I didn't talk about this, they'd never let it go. "But I think I was only using it as an excuse. I'm the Mystique Second now, whether I like it or not." I raised my brows at Ophelia, who gave a smug smirk in return. "And I know I said I didn't think I was fit for it because I didn't know who my father was, but I accepted anyway. Now I know, and I feel...the same."

Actually, I was hollow inside, but that wasn't due to the revelation. It was about who wasn't here for it.

"Are you keeping the title?" Malakai asked.

I pretended not to notice the way Ophelia sat up straighter. "I am," I confirmed. "I still don't think I'm right for it, but...I'll keep it. I want it."

Surprisingly, none of that was difficult to admit. Like a band had snapped around my reservations the past few weeks after squaring off against the Starsearcher Chancellor and learning the truth of his own rule.

"Good," Mila said. Admiration shone in her eyes.

"You realize what this means, Cypherion?" Jezebel asked as she and Erista entered from what I assumed was the kitchen, carrying trays laden with breakfast.

That smokey scent hit me again, my stomach grumbling as they set them on the dining table, but I asked, "What?"

"You," Jez said, swiping up a berry and popping it in her mouth, "are a full Mystique Warrior."

The sentiment settled over the room, slipping between us all like the remnants of a lightning storm.

"I guess I am." And the electricity sparked through my blood, fueling a sense of belonging.

Malakai's mother, Akalain Deneski, had been chosen for Lucidius because her family had a strong Mystique heritage, and a Revered needed power. But her older brother—my *father*—had been the Deneski heir.

I'd heard of him for years. He was supposedly noble and brave, cunning and charming.

"Why didn't he ever show up?" I asked, deflating a bit. And as I said it, I only looked at Malakai and Tolek. Something in me felt like that question was only for us.

"He might not have known," Malakai offered. "I wrote to my mother as soon as we got back from the isle last night."

The isle. Right. Where the fae queen was. How had she even known the truth? There was still a chance she was lying.

Spirits, my head was spinning again. My crisis with my father didn't matter amid all of that.

But Malakai handed me a wrinkled piece of parchment.

Mali,

I wish I could say I am as surprised as you are, but a piece of me always suspected this might be true—

"She knew?" I gaped at my friends.

"And didn't want to share, apparently." Ophelia scowled as she picked at a loose thread on the couch. Tolek rubbed a hand down her arm as if this was a conversation they'd already hashed out.

"Keep reading," Malakai instructed. Even his voice was icy, though.

Cypherion's mother lived in Palerman many years ago, well before any of you were born. She and my brother were crazy about each other, though I thought they lost contact long before she would have had Cypherion.

I didn't know she returned until after you and Cypherion became friends, given her condition. She never came around to tell any of us she was back. It was only upon meeting Cypherion for the first time and hearing his last name that I guessed who he was related to.

Still, I thought it might be a relative. It isn't uncommon for warrior families to migrate to the same cities, as you know. But the more he came around, the less I could deny it.

And the older he gets, the more he is the spitting image of Riolan.

My eyes were misty, my throat crowded, but I continued.

He has the Deneski hair and eyes, certainly, but beyond that, he carries himself with the strength and gentleness of heart that made Riolan the warrior he was. He reminds me so of my brother, Mali.

Please tell Cypherion that I am sorry I never told him. I wished to, but it was his mother's business before my own. The one time I tried to speak with her about it did not end well. Tell him I have kept an eye on her ever since they returned to Palerman, and I will continue to do so as long as we are both here. She is not alone.

And neither is he. If Cypherion wants to take the Deneski name, we are honored to have him.

I exhaled, looking to the ceiling. Everyone was quiet. Waiting. Beside me, Santorina wiped her eyes.

And...fuck. She'd lost both of her parents. Ophelia and Malakai had lost their fathers, though to very different circumstances. And Tolek's relationship with his parents was...well, I didn't truly know what to call that. But it made me certain without having to say anything, they understood the weight of this letter in my hand. Of Akalain's acceptance.

"Can I keep this?" I asked Malakai.

He nodded. "Are you angry?"

"That Akalain didn't tell me?" I considered. "No. I'm angrier *my* mother didn't—couldn't," I corrected quickly. It wasn't my mother's fault something had addled her mind. "When did Riolan die again?"

"Maybe a decade ago now," Malakai said, dragging a hand across his jaw as he thought. "I think I was eleven, maybe."

"I wonder if that's what did it," I mumbled.

"Did what?" Ophelia asked, seeming to relax now that I said I wasn't mad at Akalain.

"Maybe that's what sent my mother into..." I trailed off. "It's been about that long."

Tolek said, "It could've been. Maybe she'd been in touch with him or was planning to contact him. I can imagine it would have hurt her to find out." He shifted closer to Ophelia at the thought.

"Maybe she loved him." Rina's voice was small. "If she learned of his death, her heart could have broken."

Guilt gripped my chest at the thought. Of a heartbreak so deep, it sent my mother into her current state, unable to even care for her son. I'd resented her sometimes for it, though I didn't want to. Now, I wished I'd known sooner. That I'd understood.

I imagined having Vale ripped away from me permanently, and my mind threatened to free fall the way my mother's had. Spirits, if she hadn't told me to come back for her—if she wanted to leave or if something horrible befell her—it would have been easier to give into the void than continue on.

I wished she were here. Everything was less painful with her around, her questions and reflections soothing as I processed.

A flash of what she might be experiencing right now barreled through my head. A cage she'd escaped, slammed shut once more. A master she'd broken free of, wielding her power as if it was his own. And if her readings were still malfunctioning, if she was hurting—

My fist tightened around the parchment.

At the crinkling I snapped back to the present.

Clearing my throat, I folded the letter and tucked it into the pocket of my leathers. The same dirty pair I'd been wearing for much too long, though everyone had the grace not to tell me they smelled like horse shit, sweat, and dirt.

"I think, more than anything," I said, "a part of me hoped he was still out there. That he might look for me one day. Now I have this void that I'll never fill."

"I'm sorry, Cypherion," Ophelia said. "But this doesn't make you anything less."

I shrugged. "I always suspected my father might have been a Soulguider. Because of the scythe." The one I found all those years ago in my mother's attic and had trained with ever since. The only piece I had of him.

I'd never told everyone to whom it belonged—but based on the benign reactions, they'd guessed.

"Riolan was the Master of Communication for Lucidius's council," Malakai said. "It's why I only met him twice. He was always traveling for different negotiations and meetings. Maybe he got the weapon during one of his trips."

As the only Soulguider in the room, Erista added, "He could have won it as an honor. Sometimes, if foreign warriors perform a service in our territory, they're rewarded with a scythe."

My heart inflated a bit. Had my father not only been descended from a powerful Mystique line but assisted another clan in such a meaningful way that he received an accolade? Pride swelled within me at the thought.

"And to make matters brighter," Tolek added, nodding at Malakai, "you now have a cousin."

I had a cousin who was already like my brother. And an aunt who had taken me in on more than one occasion when my house was too cold or my mother's silence too loud. The family that had always been there, by choice.

"Barrett will be thrilled," Lyria chirped as everyone moved toward the dining table and started piling plates with the steaming breakfast Jezebel and Erista had prepared.

"He and Barrett aren't related," Malakai said, almost defensively. "Not by blood at least."

Jezebel laughed. "You think that will stop Barrett from claiming so?"

Malakai groaned, held falling back to look at the ceiling. "He's going to be insufferable."

For the first time in weeks, a reluctant laugh slipped out of me. I grabbed a plate and piled food on, reminding myself I needed fuel to keep going. To get back to Valyn.

Ophelia came up to my elbow, her voice low. "After we've eaten, we need to talk about what happened."

What happened in Starsearcher Territory. Why Vale wasn't with me.

You go, and then come back for me.

I'll be back for you, Stargirl.

"We'll talk while we eat," I said. "I don't want to waste any more time."

"There's something I still don't understand," Erista said, eyes flitting between Malakai and me. "How did Ritalia *know* you two are related?"

"Because," a deep voice drawled from the foyer, and Lancaster strode around the corner, my grip tightening on my plate, "my queen can scent bloodlines."

Chapter Fifteen
Ophelia

"WHAT DO YOU MEAN SHE CAN *SCENT* BLOODLINES?" I asked, not the least bit surprised Lancaster and Mora were in our cottage. The immortals' presence swarmed the room.

Cypherion growled, knuckles white around his plate. "What the hell are you doing here?"

I didn't turn, didn't want to give Lancaster and Mora any advantage if we appeared disjointed, but from the corner of my eye, I saw Tolek place a hand on Cyph's arm and mutter something low enough that I couldn't hear.

The fae likely could, so I raised my voice and said with an air of perfectly cool control, "We prefer our guests to knock before they let themselves in."

"Your voices carried into the yard." Mora shrugged and floated over to the couch, perching on the arm of it. "It sounded as though you were busy,"

"Very helpful of you," Rina deadpanned. She glowered at the female sitting dangerously close to her, but she didn't so much as lean away, keeping her spine straight and attention poised.

Around the room, every warrior was braced for an attack. Plates slowly lowered to the table. Stances shifted.

If Lancaster noticed, he didn't comment. He only looked at me, as if no one else had spoken, and said, "Much like I can create something of nothing and my sister can mask an appearance, Queen Ritalia has a unique gift—far rarer than either of ours."

"She can sniff us out?" Tolek asked, skeptically.

"She can decipher where heritages merge along the course of the past. In our kind, she can scent powers before they've manifested to their full ability. It's a blood gift, like tracking, as opposed to our creation-based ones." Lancaster's eyes landed on Santorina, an unquenchable thirst burning there. "My queen can trace those alive today back to those she was once in the presence of."

Santorina didn't fidget under his stare, but tension crackled between them.

"You so much as flinch toward her," I threatened, "and I can count at least nine blades that will pierce your gut before you take a step."

Lancaster's jaw ticked, but he ignored me. "I am sorry for the outburst." The words almost sounded pained. "I did not intend to cause you any harm. It is a long story, for another time, but I mean no ill will to the Bounties, nor to you."

I held my breath, watching Rina as she swallowed. "You touch me, and my blade will be the first of the nine Ophelia counted. And I cannot promise it will only land in your gut."

"I am inclined to believe you." Lancaster grimaced, canines gleaming. In return, Rina offered a slight nod. Silence stretched between the two of them, lengthy and weighted with their temporary truce.

"How exactly does Ritalia's magic work?" Malakai asked, pulling us all back to the topic at hand.

"As I'm sure you can imagine, a power as subtle yet expository as the queen's can be imperative in the political world." Lancaster crossed his arms with smooth grace, leaning against the arched doorway into the sitting room. "It offers promise to your own bloodline and a threat to your enemies' secrets."

"Ritalia used her scenting to ascend the throne and ward off any competitors with threats of exposing their sordid pasts or magic they kept hidden," Tolek said.

Lancaster and Mora were silent, which was answer enough.

The queen had spoken in riddles yesterday; I wondered if any related to her power.

"Why was she so unnerved by Cypherion's arrival?" I asked, exchanging a glance with my stone-faced Second. "Did she scent something within him?"

Get your cousin out of here, she'd yelled.

Lancaster sighed as if exasperated by our questions. "You warriors do not understand how much of your world is prophecy to ours."

I straightened. "What does that mean?"

"It means they know a lot of shiny secrets about us," Tolek said.

Lancaster's gaze cut to Cypherion. "Did your mother or father ever tell you where your name originated?"

"My mother didn't." He shook his head. "I never knew my father."

Lancaster looked between Cypherion and Malakai, as if putting a new piece of the puzzle together. His throat bobbed. "I see."

"Regardless," Mora said, reclining against the cushions, "the name Cypherion is actually from an ancient fae tongue that's been lost to time."

Cypherion blinked at her. "My parents weren't fae."

"Over many centuries, the name has been adopted by warrior kind," Lancaster explained. "Now it is a reference to the conduits of magic in your land. In the closest literal translation, it means *of the cyphers*. The ones that have grown since the dawn of the world, but that were changed when the treaty was signed between fae and warriors."

"Changed how?" I asked.

"A sorcia enchanted the earth of Gallantia to reject fae spirits. The magic is rooted in the cypher trees."

"Reject fae spirits?" Jezebel echoed. "How are you here now?"

"We are allowed to walk on this land. Though the treaty specifies otherwise, magic of any kind does not prohibit that. But if a fae dies on warrior land, our spirits never find rest as yours do. Your Soulguiders cannot guide us home."

"That's true," Erista said. "We're always taught we can guide warriors, humans, and other creatures of Gallantia, but not the fae." Her brows scrunched. "I never knew it was because of the cyphers."

"It is a guardrail of the treaty—one of many." Lancaster shifted, leaning against the wall with a forced casualness. "To keep us in line."

"To keep you from launching an attack on Gallantia that would end in deaths on both sides," I elaborated. "Because the souls of the fae killed here would never find rest."

"What does this have to do with me though?" Cypherion crossed his arms, likely stifling his impatience with the fae. "It's only a name based on a tree."

Mora pushed upright and answered, her tone grave, "There is a fae prophecy given to our queen upon her ascension to the throne. She had a grand coronation, with all varieties of attendees. One carried the power of predictions in his veins, and when she asked for a reading of the future, he said: *He who is named for the trees will be the downfall of the royal bloodline.*"

"Ritalia heard you all say his name when he arrived and believed him the fulfiller of the prophecy, thus leading to her directive to remove him from her presence immediately." Lancaster looked between Cypherion and Malakai again. "She assumed you two already knew of your familial ties and would not have expected to be revealing such secrets."

Malakai and Cypherion both ignored that, the latter skeptically asking, "So I'm destined to kill the queen?"

Mora shrugged, her long brown curls swaying around her ample frame. "The problem with prophecies is they do not appreciate specificity."

I laughed. That was surely true.

"The young queen did not properly seal the request," Lancaster explained. "It was vague enough that the one who delivered the prophecy did not clarify *which* royal bloodline."

Cypherion asked, "The queen wants me dead, then?"

"She wants you watched. There were other parameters to the prophecy—for our kind, they operate similarly to a bargain. One cannot attempt to change the fate if they have been reckless enough to ask for it."

"That's cruel," Santorina said, voice low.

"It is our way," Lancaster gritted out.

"To be forced to live with knowledge of the future and let it taunt you?" she asked.

"If one does not wish to know what awaits, one can demonstrate enough control to not ask at all." Lancaster and Rina glared at each other.

"It's like Soulguider visions." Jezebel sliced through their debate, exchanging a look with her partner. "Except Soulguiders don't have a choice in receiving them."

I'd often wondered how it would feel to have access to Soulguider or Starsearcher magic, where the ends of lives or twists of fate were bluntly thrown into your path. And Soulguiders couldn't even disclose what they'd seen.

My heart ached for Erista and my grandmother, a bit of longing to know that side of myself better creeping in. I shook it away for now, though.

"How are you able to tell us this?" I asked Lancaster and Mora. "Won't Ritalia have your throats for exposing these secrets?"

"It is a show of good faith," the male replied. "In exchange for what she requested of you yesterday."

The emblems. Not a chance in the Angel-guarded realm would I simply hand them over to her because she asked, made a bargain, or revealed some secret that could be her own downfall. Truthfully, I found it a bit desperate and shortsighted of her to do so.

But Ritalia had been a queen for millennia. She understood the stakes. If she'd made this decision, there had to be more to the puzzle than I was seeing. It was best to keep the fae close while we figured it out and give them something in return to appease this partnership.

My head whirled with the possibilities. A warm hand braced my lower back, and I summoned some steadiness from Tolek, picking apart warrior secrets to decide what I could disclose to the fae.

"We *have* been hunting the Angel emblems. We don't have

them all, yet, and I am not comfortable making any binding agreements on their fate until more is known. We will however consider working with you in this open exchange, so long as Ritalia holds true to the bargains she made on the isle."

Lancaster nodded. "There are two left?"

"Yes," I said. No use attempting to lie when they'd seen me wield them against Kakias, but I didn't know if they understood the weight of the power I commanded from those emblems now.

"I have something that can assist with the sixth," Cypherion said. He took the stairs two at a time, returning with a stack of worn scrolls.

"These are from Titus. When he..." His words choked off.

And I saw it, then. The fissures he'd been fighting ever since he arrived at the isle, frantic and tortured. The ones he hadn't allowed himself time to express in his own panic.

Cypherion's fists clenched against the table, I imagined itching for a fight to give him some sense of power back.

I'd been waiting to ask. Waiting until he brought it up. But he was on the verge of shattering.

"Cypherion," I said softly. "What happened to Vale?"

His eyes glazed over as he stared at the sealed scrolls. "We went to Lumin first. I entered a fight, got us information that sent us to the city archives in Valyn. She shouldn't have gone there. Shouldn't have had to. Both of those cities are hard for her, but Valyn—Titus—"

His words broke off with a grimace. He looked like he couldn't keep speaking, too much rage tunneling through him. So, we helped.

"What happened when you got to Valyn?" Tolek asked carefully. "Did you go to the archives?"

"We did, and something came over her. The reading was"—his jaw ticked—"worse than ever."

I gave him a moment, then asked, "Did Titus know you were there?"

Cypherion nodded. "But we didn't know he knew."

My skin chilled. We hadn't been certain Titus was dangerous, only that he seemed to have ulterior motives for instructing Vale to lie to us. But now, with how disgusted Cypherion looked, it was clear we'd been wrong.

"Titus doesn't have any magic," Cypherion reported, mutters echoing around the room. "His fate tie barely exists, and he's never successfully conducted a reading. Even Vale didn't know."

Cyph looked at me, but I only blinked in response. Titus didn't *what?* "That's why he claimed what Vale read in Damenal as his own," I murmured. Vale had read of destruction and darkness across Gallantia—saw me entwined with it—and the chancellor had announced it as his own session. We only found out the truth during the Battle of Damenal, but...Spirits, how did Titus even hold his title?

Cypherion confirmed, "Titus has been using Vale's readings ever since he found out she was in the Lumin Temple when she was a girl and he *rescued* her."

He sneered that word, and the complications beneath the surface of Vale's past bubbled up, my own rage with them.

"He wasn't rescuing her at all," Cypherion said, leaning on his fists. His head dropped. "And now she's back there. In that manor she was so terrified of. The cage locked again."

"How did he get her?" Malakai asked. He and Tolek stood on either side of Cyph.

"He ambushed us, took us both back to his manor, and then presented a trade."

"What kind of trade?" I narrowed my eyes.

"Apparently the chancellor has an inkling of where Valyrie's emblem might be." He waved a hand at the scrolls. "These contain readings back to the Angel herself. He offered them in exchange for Vale staying with him. He claims he'll help her heal her readings despite the fact that he abandoned her for months," he growled those last words. "I'm sure that's a lie, as well."

"Why did Vale stay?" I asked, voice soft.

When I met Cypherion's eyes, self-loathing stared back. "Because she wants to help us. Because she cares."

Because Vale had been isolated for so long, and we'd begun to show her a bit of welcome. A bit of friendship. Maybe not after first learning of her deceit, but as time had passed and the waters began to clear, we understood that hadn't been her fault.

"She stayed for us," I muttered, my heart cracking wide for the Starsearcher.

"Then we'll get her back," Tolek swore, and around the room agreement echoed.

"Damn right we will." Cypherion's voice was laced with a brutal promise. One that said he'd walk through Bant's Blackfyre and burn with the stars to return to her.

"There's another reason she stayed," he added. "The bastard bound them together. That tattoo on her brand? The ink is imbued so she'll feel an inexplicable loyalty to him." Haunted memories dulled his eyes.

"Are you saying even if we get to her, she won't come?" Santorina asked.

"She'll want to if she thinks we no longer need Titus to work with us for the emblems. But she'll always feel this draw to him."

My skin prickled as I sensed where he was heading. "Unless..."

"Unless he dies and the magic in the tattoo breaks."

Silence hung over the room, thick and treasonous. Malakai asked bluntly, "Are you going to kill Titus?"

"I will if it comes to it." There wasn't a hint of mercy in his voice.

"And we'll be there." It was Mila who said it, twirling one of her gold cuffs around her wrist with vengeance shining in her eyes.

"Whatever it takes," I promised Cypherion. "Let's be smart about it, though. We don't risk anything—Vale's life or our own. We don't know what Titus will resort to."

"Can I ask," Tolek began, and all gazes swiveled to him, "why Vale? She was only a child in that temple."

Cypherion stiffened. "Starsearcher magic is dependent on their Fate ties—their connections to the eleven fates who convey readings to them. They're all born with one, they discover it sometime before they come of age." He swallowed. "Vale's Fate ties are *powerful*. More so than any Starsearcher I've ever met." He didn't elaborate, and I exchanged a glance with Tolek and Malakai that said we all understood it was Vale's secret to disclose.

Behind us, Lancaster and Mora whispered to each other. I spun around, raising my brows at them. The female said, "Powerful Fate alignments are not something even we would question."

"And?" I asked.

Lancaster seared me with a gaze. "If the girl has that much promise, we will help rescue her however we can."

I narrowed my eyes at him. "Why?"

"Because it would be unwise to upset the gods at a time like this." Lancaster gestured to the scrolls. "And it sounds as if it will lead to your next emblem."

"And what if you come with us and something triggers your hunter side to wake again?" Tolek asked with a concerned look at Santorina.

"I swear on Aoiflyn, only Ritalia can unleash it as she did at dinner. Otherwise, it is simply a sense that allows me to find the Bounties."

"I'm not a Bounty," Santorina grumbled, but she perked up. "If you are going to come with us, you have to agree to assist Ophelia with intel on the gods and goddesses. I know some, but it has been of little help to us."

I flashed Rina a grateful smile, and she returned it. Then, we both turned back to Lancaster and Mora.

The fae exchanged a glance, but if they were wondering why we were so curious about the deities, they didn't say.

"You have yourselves a deal, Queen of Bounties," Mora cooed.

"As unlikely an alliance as I ever expected," Lancaster muttered, still watching Santorina.

"Cyph, do you have any idea *how* we can get Vale out of Titus's grip?" *Short of killing him*, I didn't add. I wasn't against it, but the less chancellor blood on our hands, the better.

"I have a contact," he said, avoiding our eyes. I glanced at Tol, but he shook his head, equally perplexed. "Someone within Titus's manor who is helping form a plan that will either get us in or Vale out. Right now, though, we need to get back to Valyn." Desperation piqued his voice, heightening my nerves.

"What about Barrett?" Malakai suggested.

"What about him?" I asked.

"With the fake partnership he and Celissia are staging, it might be an opportune time for a tour of the continent." He shrugged. "Introducing her to leaders of various clans and cities, maybe?"

Mila continued, following his train of thought, "They can be in Valyn when we get Vale out, distracting Titus."

It was a good idea, but I deferred to Cypherion. He rubbed a hand across his jaw, looking at the pile of scrolls. "If Barrett is willing, that could be a huge advantage."

"Oh, I'm certain he'll be willing," Lyria chimed in, spinning one of her many small knives around her hand. "The king loves a worthy scheme, but he loves Vale more. The other night, when we were drinking, he went on about how they bonded in Damenal when she was a prisoner. How he'd go play cards with her when he couldn't sleep."

Cyph nodded, gratitude and sadness deepening his blue eyes.

Malakai clapped him on the shoulder. "I'll write to Barrett now," he said and disappeared up the stairs with Mila.

"I guess we better open those and find out what Valyrie left behind," Erista said, gesturing to the scrolls still sitting untouched in the center of the table, like everyone could feel the Angel's echoing presence radiating from them.

"They look very old," Santorina muttered, approaching as I carefully worked my finger under the first seal. Everyone cleared the plates and trays, breakfast forgotten, much to Jezebel's dismay.

The aged scrolls radiated power, tugging at the strands of my Angellight. Searching almost, for one I did not have yet.

"They feel it as well," I said.

"What do they feel like?" Tolek asked.

I weighed the first scroll again, biting my lip as I considered. "It's not quite like an emblem," I explained, selecting my words carefully. "Those call to me and beat, like a heart. These, though..." A wisp of a breeze danced along the back of my neck. "They whisper."

I unrolled the scroll fully, being reverent with its weathered state. "I can tell from being near this that it's tied to Angel magic, though not as potent as the emblems. It's more like sprinkles of who once was." I scanned the first paragraph, sighing.

"What is it?" Jezebel asked.

But I looked at Tolek. "You'll only brag."

He perked up, already scanning the parchment over my shoulder. "Excellent."

"What?" Cypherion asked.

Tolek grinned smugly as he snatched the scroll. "It appears the Starsearcher Angel kept her records in her language."

"It's all written in Endasi," I elaborated. "Which gives Tol the perfect opportunity to flaunt."

"Believe me, I don't need the excuse," Tolek muttered. I rolled my eyes, carefully opening the next two scrolls and laying each lengthwise on the table, mystlight illuminating them. "I can't translate it perfectly yet, so this will take me some time, but I've been working on it."

"That's amazing," Lyria said, flashing her brother an impressed smile.

Tolek returned her grin with utter confidence. "Thank you. I know."

I took the scroll he held and laid it beside the other two. "Can you translate the titles for us?"

Tolek laid a gentle, reverent finger on the first. His face sobered as he read. "This is an account of a reading Valyrie gave. One of her final ones, I'm guessing. The phrase doesn't translate directly but *mortos cus* roughly means death is near."

I shifted closer, scanning the unfamiliar words. "The Angels didn't die, though."

"Perhaps it's means *the end* instead of death," Mora chimed in, rising off the couch and joining the rest of us at the table.

"You can speak it?" I asked.

She shook her head, and I tried not to be surprised the fae was assisting us. "But I've learned ancient fae languages among others, and sometimes the interpretations of the oldest phrases are less accurate."

"What's the next say?" Lyria asked, watching her brother with an expression I couldn't quite place.

"That one says something about a game or a race. Perhaps referencing training of her warriors?" Tolek drummed his fingers on the table as if unsatisfied with that answer and shifted his attention to the final scroll. After a moment, his eyes widened. "This one is about the Ascension."

Tol leaned forward, and I followed. "Did Valyrie read the Ascension? Is that why they did it?"

"It's written very carefully," Tolek said. "As if in code."

Across the table, pulling out a chair and dropping into it with his arms crossed, Cypherion grumbled impatiently. "The Angels can never make this easy, can they?"

"Where would the fun be in that?" Lyria quipped.

"We've got a long couple weeks of travel ahead of us," I said, making eye contact with Cyph. "Plenty of time to work on translating these while we get Vale back."

He nodded, desperation and determination burning in his stare. "We get her back."

CHAPTER SIXTEEN
MALAKAI

THE DOOR ON EZALIA'S COMMANDER'S SHIP SWUNG
shut behind me, a soft thud muddled by the conversation echoing
from the deck and the wind out at sea.

The Seawatcher Chancellor was journeying back to the capital
with her family, but she'd arranged transport for us to get from the
outposts to the mainland a few days ago. Pink and orange streaked
the sky, crisp turquoise waves reflecting the sunset against the
rocking ship. I breathed in the briny air, and my chest unknotted, a
heavy sense having settled in it ever since Cypherion returned.

"Malakai!" Ophelia said, hurrying down the stairs from the
quarter deck. "We're docking in Starsearcher Territory in a couple
hours, and I need a favor, if you're able."

"What is it?" I asked. Low laughter echoed from the forecastle.
I almost turned on instinct, knowing Mila was waiting to get a
training session in. Truthfully, our daily workouts were one of the
few things keeping my head clear.

"Mila mentioned she'd written to Cyren," Ophelia began. The
Starsearcher General had been in touch. We'd shared what we
could about Vale's situation, seeing if they had any insight as to
what to expect with Titus. "And that they wanted to speak in
person. Would you two be able to meet them tonight?"

"Should be," I answered with a shrug. "They're only a little
way out of the town we're staying in, right?"

Ophelia nodded. "Thank you," she said, crossing her arms. One of Valyrie's scrolls dangled from her fingers, and a breeze danced across the back of my neck. My hand twitched toward my sword, whispers flitting through my mind. I shook my head, trying to focus on what Ophelia was saying. "I'd go myself but I need to see Sapphire and the khrysaor before Jezebel flies to pick up Barrett, Dax, and Celissia."

The prince had emphatically agreed to help and took the last few days of our travel to prepare the council for his departure.

"She and Erista are still leaving tonight?"

Ophelia nodded. "Jezebel can't wait, given how horribly seasick she's gotten on this journey." I laughed, only because Jez was sure to let us all know how miserable she found traveling by boat, bemoaning the entire trip. "They'll wait until the middle of the night, likely. Depends on the weather. But they'll be there and back in a few days."

"Those things still freak me out," I muttered, the breeze making me shiver again.

"Those things?" Ophelia gasped.

"The *khrysaor*," I corrected before I had an angry Alabath on my hands. "They're unnatural."

"Perhaps they're more natural than the rest of us," she challenged. "They were here first after all."

Not liking that argument, I changed the subject. "Mila and I will take care of everything with Cyren."

"Thank you," Ophelia said, and the smile she gave me was so genuine and carefree, it almost felt like we were younger versions of ourselves, and I'd done something as simple as hand her a book in school. She lifted the scroll, and whispering laughter trickled through my ears. "I have to get this to Tolek and Mora."

As she walked away, a small peel of twinkling secrets raised the hushed murmurs, as if trying to stir something awake. I batted them away, heading toward the forecastle where Mila waited.

∼

AFTER WE DOCKED, I helped Cypherion and Lyria with a bit of route planning for the next day's journey, then I headed for the stables. Mila was nearly done saddling Ombratta and her own sand-colored, white-maned mare, Luna. Creeping up behind her, I listened to her soothing coos as she muttered to her warrior horse.

Then, I pinched her waist.

"Spirits!" She jumped, spinning around, hand flying toward the swords at her back. But before she grabbed one, I gripped her wrist above her head. "Malakai!" she scolded as her heart pounded.

"Got to have quicker reflexes, General," I teased, nodding to where I had her caught.

Her eyes flicked up, her other hand shooting for my own, but I was faster. I snatched that wrist as well, and with both captured, I spun us away from Luna and pressed Mila against the flimsy wooden wall of the stable.

"Never thought I'd be stealthy enough to sneak up on you," I whispered.

"Apparently I'm becoming rusty in my time off." She tugged at her wrists.

"Better fix that."

Mila tilted her chin so her lips nearly brushed mine. Fuck, did we really *have* to go meet Cyren right now?

As I leaned closer, she twisted her leg around the back of my knee and sent me crashing to the ground. Mila landed gracefully on top of me, straddling my hips, my hands pinned on either side of my head.

"Don't get distracted, Warrior Prince," she said, voice sultry.

"I don't know," I challenged, nodding at how she was positioned. "I don't mind this."

With a roll of her hips that nearly had me groaning, Mila laughed.

But I wasn't joking.

Leaning up, I caught her lips with mine. She sank into me immediately, like our bodies were made to be fused together.

Mila released my wrist, one hand curling into my hair and tugging gently. Angels, the sensation went straight to my cock. I wrenched my other hand from her grasp and wrapped my arms around her, flipping us so I was above her. But it still wasn't enough—none of it ever was.

As I brushed my tongue against hers, a delicate, enticing moan slipped up her throat. I needed her closer—wanted to have all of these easygoing, unburdened moments with Mila. She seemed to agree, fisting my leathers. My hips rolled against hers, her legs bracketing my waist.

Fuck, we were supposed to be doing something here weren't we?

I bit down on her bottom lip, and she gasped in a way that threatened to undo me. I wanted to repeat that bite on other parts of her body and see what sounds she made. To worship each scar she bore and finally make her come so hard she forgot her own name—

Something hit the back of my head, and twin disgruntled huffs had us breaking apart, panting.

Ombratta and Luna looked down at us, casting us the most judgmental glares I'd ever seen.

"Damn warrior horses, had to be so smart?" I muttered, dropping my forehead to Mila's as I caught my breath. I brushed her hair behind her ear, pulling out a stray stalk of hay and studying those icy-blue eyes.

"Quite the inconvenience at times," she laughed, her words throaty. Spirits, even her voice was the best thing I'd ever heard. If I hadn't promised the others we'd go on this outing, I'd keep her here forever.

"Back at the isle," I said, and nerves rattled through me, "you promised me tomorrow."

I never got that tomorrow, though, distracted with everything that had unfolded with Cypherion.

She raised a brow, asking hesitantly, "Another tomorrow?"

"You can have every tomorrow, Mila. I'm not going anywhere."

As many tomorrows as she needed. They were all hers now.

～

"Good to see you again," I said to Cyren, shaking their hand as we met outside the town's market.

Given that it was such a small village, it hadn't been hard to find. It wasn't busy at this hour either, but Starsearchers milled about, closing up shop or visiting with friends. The white stone buildings and array of blue glass windows soaked up the starlight, the streets lined with silver sconces and cascading waterfalls of greenery.

"You, too," the Starsearcher said, adding "General," as they shook Mila's hand.

"How was the ride down?" Mila asked, inclining her head. Together, we strolled through the market, picking up supplies for the next few days of travel. We'd be camping as we passed major cities to avoid the busiest parts of the territory. Keeping out of Titus's network.

"It was quick," Cyren said. "I was only an hour east of here." Their long, dark hair was braided around their head so similar to when we were at the war front, but instead of battle leathers, they wore the sweeping silk robes some Starsearchers preferred. The fabric slithered over the cobblestones as we walked, melting into the low hum of business.

"No problems, then?" I ducked into a bakery stall and started loading their leftover loaves from the day into a bag.

"Not for me, no."

I paused, looking at the Starsearcher. "Not for you?"

"The friend I stayed with lives near a dense region of jungle. They harvest a lot of fruit, send it off to other territories, that sort of work. Supposedly, when so many were off fighting in the war, they were having problems with their produce."

"What kind of problems?" I thought back to the few times I'd been in Bodymelder Territory recently. Many of their crops were damaged, too.

But Cyren said, "Not like you're thinking. Not the quakes we felt in the mountains during the war or the unseasonable weather." They swallowed, and I paid the baker, following them to the next stall. "It's going to sound crazy, but they swore it was *birds*."

"Birds?" Mila tilted her head, weighing a bag of apples in her hands.

"Huge ones. A breed never seen before, at least in that region."

"And they, what?" I asked. "Ate the fruit?"

"Devoured it all," Cyren answered gravely. "Knocked down the trees. Ones that stood for centuries, providing for nearby markets."

Really large birds, then. A shiver spread over my skin, akin to the one I'd felt around the scrolls' whispering voices.

Mila and I exchanged a glance, but it was clear neither of us knew what to say, so we walked on.

Cyren filled us in on the rest of their leave. When they were done, they asked in a whisper, as if they didn't even want the stars to hear, "What of Vale?"

I sighed. "She's with Titus."

"Willingly?" Cyren asked.

I didn't answer. Mila fidgeted beside me.

Cyren swore beneath their breath, and I pulled them and Mila into a corner of the market. "Listen, Cyren, can you tell us what she might be facing?"

They worried the silk trim of their robe.

I continued, "Please, General. Cypherion isn't going to rest until we rescue her—none of us are—so anything you know might help."

"I don't know what the chancellor's immediate plans are, but I was surprised when his apprentice showed up with Ophelia at the war camp. Titus always kept her close because he didn't want others to know."

"To know what?" I implored.

Cyren said, "To know her. You can *feel* the power radiating off her."

"Feel it?"

"Starsearchers can. It's like my Fate tie—the alignment to one of the Fates that allows me to read the stars—calls to her. Like it wants to meld with hers."

"What would cause that?" Mila asked.

"A very strong sort of magic," Cyren whispered. "And if Titus has her in his grasp, I don't see a world in which he lets her go. Not now that others will know of her power."

"And Titus has none," I breathed.

Cyren's eyes widened. "What?"

Fuck. I wasn't sure if I was supposed to say that. Too late now. "Titus revealed to Cypherion that his Fate tie doesn't grant him any readings."

Cyren's jaw ground, eyes boring into us with urgency. "You need to get that girl away from him before Titus can use her anymore."

Mila stiffened at the warning in the general's voice, toying with her wrist cuffs. I braced a hand at her back.

"We will," I swore.

"Soon." Cyren looked between us. "A Starsearcher without a connection to the Fates is bound to become volatile."

Because power was a weapon that spawned one of the most dangerous things of all: greed.

"Can you read anything of them?" Mila asked, voice wavering.

"I've been looking for Vale and for the Angel emblem, but that's all been difficult to find." Cyren shook their head. "It's impossible to read an Angel or higher power, but her...I should be able to see her."

"Will you look for Titus, too?"

They nodded. "First thing tonight when I return. And I'll continue until you find her."

"Thank you," I said. "Write to us if you find anything."

"I will."

～

THE INN EZALIA had arranged for us to stay in wasn't far from the market on horseback, but the ride back was long enough that Mila and I were isolated in a way I was beginning to crave when she was involved.

"How do you feel about Cypherion?" Mila asked as Ombratta and Luna strolled beside each other.

Cypherion. My brother by choice turned cousin by blood. The topic I'd avoided talking about since we found out.

"You waited until I had no way to escape to ask, didn't you?" I accused. When Mila shrugged innocently, I couldn't help but laugh. "Doesn't really matter how I feel, does it?"

"Humor me," she said with a soft smile.

I sighed. "I wish I'd known, but at the same time, I'm glad I didn't. I wouldn't have felt right being the one to tell him, but I also wouldn't have been able to keep it from him." Not that the way he found out had been any better. I may not be the one prophesied to end any fae royal bloodline, but I was tempted to after the queen told him so carelessly. "I wish *he* had known, though. That he wasn't finding out now, amid this mess with Vale."

"It's poor timing," Mila agreed.

"I don't think he'll really process this news until he gets her back," I said. He only had one focus right now, and a part of me was sure he was using it as a distraction. It would be easier to process with Vale at his side.

"He seems to have accepted his role as Second, though."

"He has, and I'm happy that shift happened *before* he found out."

Mila nodded. "It's better he grew into it on his own."

"It is."

We were silent for a few moments. Then, since I seemed to already be talking about things I'd tried to avoid, I admitted, "I opened a new journal of Lucidius's last night on the ship."

Mila smiled over her shoulder at me. "I know," she said. My brows rose. "I wasn't asleep."

"Spirits," I grumbled. I'd been in the cabin she was sharing with Lyria late into the night, the commander and Mila gossiping until they fell asleep while I read—or so I'd thought.

She laughed, and the sound had me smiling, too. "What was that one about?"

"Starsearchers."

Mila considered, scanning the sky. "Have I told you I was obsessed with constellations as a child?"

I shook my head, but didn't comment on the abrupt shift of conversation.

"I always detested school, but I loved learning." She laughed as our horses ambled down the path. "I just didn't like others telling me *what* I had to learn. I would sit in lessons and read books beneath the table. Usually about stars and the myths surrounding them."

"Always so headstrong," I muttered, and Mila scoffed.

Then, her voice sobered. "When I was in that cage," she said, and my spine stiffened, "I watched the stars. Told myself to look up and remember what I was fighting to get back to." She swallowed, adding softly almost as an afterthought, "I hope Vale has someone to look to."

Angels, I fucking hoped so, too. I knew how torturous that sort of isolation was, regardless of anything else she was enduring. Hating the way that made me feel—and the way it dimmed Mila's voice—I nudged Ombratta closer to Luna. "Tell me about the constellations you love so much."

She brightened. "What do you want to know?"

"I want everything." Not only the stars above, but every damn piece of her. Because every hint of Mila I got only snared me further, and I'd spend every tomorrow learning the rest.

Mila laughed, the worries of moments before easing, but I wasn't sure if she caught onto my innuendo. "Malakai there are eons worth of information I could give you. Thousands of star maps and harrowing tales behind the legends. *Everything* might take some time."

With the way her cheeks tinged pink at the end of that sentence, maybe she did know what I meant.

"Then start at home. Start with the warriors."

And she did. As we found a trail that offered an unimpeded view of the sky, Mila began with the story of how the warrior constellations were placed one by one, by an all-powerful hand, the being rearranging the heavens for our Angels.

I knew of the constellations already—had them drilled into my head at a young age both in school and in the supplemental lessons I took in preparation for running our clan—but hearing Mila talk about them with such fascination was like learning them for the first time.

When told in her voice, the stories carried more magic than any rendition I'd ever heard.

Soon, the world was fading around us. Like the cavernous sky was a dome, carving out this patch between the cyphers for our total isolation, with a myriad of glimmering specks above.

The coos of birds and echoing gusts of wind faded. Sharp navy edges of the sky stretched down, giving the illusion of cutting off the rest of the world. It almost felt as if the stars were shifting and speeding, rearranging themselves in time with Mila's voice. Or perhaps the exhaustion was hitting me, combined with her lulling tone and Ombratta's pace.

"And Ptholenix's—the firebird," Mila said, reaching the sixth of the Prime Warrior constellations, "is said to burn a ferocious orange on select days every few decades, though few have truly seen it."

"That's fitting," I answered.

"It is," Mila said, her voice distant. My eyes snapped to her. Her gaze roved the stars, like she was intent on finding something.

"What is it?" I asked, alert. Screeches of impossibly large birds echoed in my imagination.

"Ptholenix's constellation is the firebird," Mila mused. "And Thorn's is the crown."

"Damien's is the sword." I shrugged.

"Spirits, Malakai," she gasped. "The answers are right here!"

"What answers?" I asked.

Tightening her knees against Luna's sides, she looked pointedly at me. "Are you up for a fast ride back?"

CHAPTER SEVENTEEN
OPHELIA

"HE'S EATEN SIX APPLES IN THREE MINUTES!"

I gaped at Jezebel as she held yet another ruby red fruit out to Zanox, which the khrysaor hastily chomped down—core and all.

"He takes after his mother," my sister cooed, scratching the beast beneath the chin. He nudged her palm, sniffing for more snacks.

Dynaxtar drank lazily from the stream running through the ring of sky-reaching trees and draping vines. Critters jumped about in the high, woven canopy, but fronds cover the path, keeping this tiny clearing isolated from those on foot.

"Shouldn't we find something more substantial to feed them?" I asked as I ran my hand through Sapphire's mane and she released a low whinny. "You know, they're rather large. Surely they can't survive on fruit alone."

The emergence of Sapphire as a pegasus altered more than her appearance. She was ravenous most days. As the thought trickled through my head, my hand stilled on my horse, and she huffed in complaint.

Well, revealing she's secretly a mythological creature didn't change her attitude.

"They can fend for themselves," Jezebel answered, tugging me from the thought. "They are rather large, you know."

I rolled my eyes. "You *are* observant. Come on, we should get back so you and Erista can finish packing and head out."

We'd docked a few hours ago, and while the others got settled for our one-night stay at the inn, Jezebel and I set out to find Sapphire and the khrysaor hidden in this jungle-shrouded clearing. They were incredibly smart, so when we told them the town Ezalia had arranged for us to stay in, the creatures knew to find shelter and await our boat.

Zanox and Dynaxtar would get to fly again tonight, and hopefully I could get Sapphire to stretch her wings if we found somewhere private enough.

We took our time doting on the three animals until their coats shone and their supply of apples ran low. Malakai said he'd grab more at the market tonight before we waded deeper into Starsearcher Territory.

As we left, I pressed one last kiss to my pegasus' nose. Then, we ensured the fronds covered the gaps between the towering trunks and set back down the short walk to the inn. Trees stretched to the sky, the branches high and sweeping, not a maze around the paths as many cypher forests were.

"It's so dark," Jez complained. "Why didn't we bring a lantern?"

"Here," I said, calling up a strand of Angellight. The gold flared to life, and the magic spiraled up above us. But instead of hovering, it cracked and sparked like a wild creature.

"Why is it doing that?" Jezebel asked. In the shimmering light, her tawny eyes were wide, recollections of our recent flight in the outposts and our colliding magic flashing between us.

"I don't know," I gritted out as the light tugged at me from within, pulling up toward something I couldn't see. "Keep walking."

I didn't tell her that it felt wrong. That I couldn't tell what Angel emblem I was siphoning light from or that it seemed to be searching for something. My breath quickened as we picked up our pace, and I fought to hold control on that malicious strand of magic—it pulled and pulled, stretching—

"Ophelia!" Jez shrieked at the same moment the golden tendril of light whipped into one of the towering trees.

It collided with the canopy with a riotous boom, a squawk ringing through the leaves, and a sensation like a thousand burnings wings fluttered through my body.

"Pull it back!" Jez screamed, gripping my hand.

"*I'm trying!*" I coiled that burst of gold light that felt so different than my Angel emblem threads back into the vacant heart of my Spirit, wrestled it until it was buried deep down. Until finally, Jez and I were left standing in the still, darkened jungle, nothing but our panting breaths filling the air.

I squeezed my sister's clammy hand as our hearts calmed. She startled at the touch, saying, "That was—"

But I never heard what she thought it was, because her words were drowned out by crying squawks.

And in the highest canopy of the jungle, a fire flared to life. It roared up in the branches, spreading out like a pair of wide wings. Then—

No.

It wasn't *like* a pair of wings. It *was* a pair of wings. A large bird of flaming feathers and tails swooped down, igniting the jungle with its fiery light and heading straight for Jezebel and me.

We dove to opposite sides of the path, the bird cleaving down the middle. I rolled along the dirt, jumping to my feet and pulling Starfire from my hip.

"What is that thing?" Jezebel asked, pulling her sword as well.

I didn't answer—not because I didn't know, but because I did not understand *how* my suspicion could be correct. And right at that moment, the bird of fire charged again, carving a figure eight through the sky and turning back toward me.

I swung Starfire, but the bird coasted on the wind, my blade only sliding through its feathers like they were no more than trails of embers. Its deadly talons swiped low, and as the creature turned around me, it dragged one of those three-inch nails across my shoulder.

"Holy Angels!" I swore at the sting, flooding the injury with Angellight to try to staunch the flow of blood.

"Are you okay?" Jezebel called. She backed toward a tree, the bird circling.

I pressed a hand to my wound. "Fine. But Starfire isn't doing anything against it."

"We might need something else!" Jezebel called as she plunged her own sword toward the beast, and it coasted back up on a wind.

"Like what?"

But the air shifted, the vines on the path ahead swaying. And then, Lancaster and Mora shot into view.

"Aoiflyn's tits!" the male swore at the same time his sister burst, "What fun!"

"Where did you two come from?" I gasped over the pain in my shoulder as the fae sprang into motion.

"We heard you scream from the inn," Mora explained.

I never thought I'd say it, but thank the Angels for that damn fae hearing.

Jezebel cried out, thrusting her sword again as the bird dove for her. Its sharpened beak snapped wide, clamping down on the blade. With a ragged shake of its head, the bird tossed my sister aside.

"Jez!" I screamed, running for her and keeping pressure on my shoulder. The wound tore further, and blood slipped between my fingers.

I ducked beneath those talons as the bird swooped low again. Lancaster reached out, and where I expected him to summon a weapon using that creation power, he instead grabbed—

A long chain connected to stone shackles.

Because stone could not burn.

I scrambled to where Jez was hunched over her knees on the ground. "What do you intend to do with those, fae?" I called. "The beast has no wrists!"

"No!" Lancaster growled as he swung the chain. "But it has a neck."

Mora snapped her fingers and a second bird sprang to life up in the branches. The original beast released another cry, this one filled with longing as it chased its twin up in the canopy. Fuck, we couldn't fight two. We could barely fight one.

I turned my attention on Jezebel, helping her sit up and lean against a tree. "What hurts?"

"Didn't catch myself right when I fell." My sister winced. "Something snapped."

I smoothed her sweaty hair down, kissing her head. "Get in the tree line."

Then, I was standing, pulling Starfire again and racing back toward the fight.

"Why the fuck are there two now?" I seethed, skidding to a halt next to Mora.

The female answered, "That's my doing."

I whipped my head from her to the second bird above. Mora squinted at it, resting docilely in the tree. "You're distracting it," I gasped, and Mora shrugged like it was effortless to glamour some small forest creature into a second massive, flaming bird.

Once again, I wouldn't admit I was impressed with fae magic.

"What's your plan?" I asked, deferring to the fae though it was against my better judgment.

"We need to get it low enough to touch," Lancaster said, and fire reflected in his dark eyes. "I'm trying to drag it down here but it's repelling my magic. And we don't have as much control on Gallantia as we do on Vercuella."

I shuddered to think *this* was the less controlled version of Lancaster's magic.

A high whinny pierced the air, and Sapphire came roaring through the trees, white wings flaring gold in the light of the flame. Zanox and Dynaxtar galloped along the path, corralling the rest of us as if in protection. The former quickly broke off into the jungle in the direction of my sister.

The khrysaor were too large to fly between the trees, but Sapphire, with her smaller wingspan, was a match for the bird of flame. She soared above it, driving it down toward Lancaster's waiting stone shackles.

It wasn't daring to fly low enough, though. My hand flexed around Starfire, but she was useless against the bird. If I got too close for too long, the heat might melt her blade, and my heart clenched at only the consideration of losing my sword.

But the shard of Angelborn at my neck burned. My weapons were not the only tool at my disposal.

It was reckless. I didn't know why the magic had reacted so wildly tonight—if it had alerted the bird of our presence or why—but I had to try.

"Sapphire!" I whistled, and my pegasus swooped toward me.

She barely even stopped as I leaped, landing on her back. The wound in my shoulder tore deeper, but I let it bleed. Sapphire wove in and out of the trees to get us nearer to our prey.

"All right, Angels, let's see what we've got." And carefully, one by one, I called up the five strands of Angellight within me, making certain of to whom each belonged. I looped them together, willing them to unspool into one unbreakable sheet, and circled the bird, forcing it closer to the ground.

I was careful with the magic, not using too much. Not touching the heart where that unnamed source seemed to come from earlier. I didn't want it sparking and rioting—didn't want to know what resided in there at all.

But this felt different than that uncontrollable force. The light I wielded now was the soothing magic, cascading through the air like a waterfall of gold, like the most natural thing on Ambrisk. I fed it steadily, warily, and let the power expel into the night.

"More, Mystique!" Lancaster roared after a few minutes.

"I can't give more," I hissed, sweat pouring down my skin. The slice to my shoulder stung, but I couldn't stop to heal it now. "I can only control so much."

The male gaped up at me. "What do you mean you can't control your fucking magic?"

"I haven't been alive and learning it for centuries like *some of us*," I spat, but I tried to feed more Angellight into the air. Since I was holding back to avoid that untamed heart, it wasn't as potent as usual, but a thin sheen formed around the path, like a bubble containing all the magical beasts within, warrior and fae alike.

It sealed across the jungle path, and together with my pegasus, we forced the phoenix down, down, down. A stray whip of magic tore off from the rest, wild and untethered. It lashed Mora's glamour as it fell, and the false beast stuttered out, a midnight dove once more.

"*What?*" Mora swore, but I had no answer for how it happened.

The original bird riled when it realized the trick, and I plunged the Angellight deeper around the jungle. Tunneled all of the magic I could into this bubble without losing control of it.

Sapphire's striking hooves and my light shoved the bird down, and when it danced above Lancaster, the male lunged. He shot into the air with a jump only fae strength could guarantee, and clasped one of the stone shackles around the bird's neck.

It squawked as it was dragged to the ground, scraping and clawing. Leaving long slashes across Lancaster's face and singing Mora's dress with those wings.

Sapphire landed, and I ran toward where Lancaster wrestled the bird. "Let's take it back," I said.

But it was too late.

With one final screech that wrenched through my heart, there was a crack, and the bird fell still. And with its silence, the aura of death—the loss of a destructive yet mystical and magnificent creature—settled over the jungle.

"Wh-why did you do that?" I stuttered, voice low as Lancaster stood. The entire right side of his face was covered in blood.

"*What?*" he seethed.

"Why did you kill it?" I couldn't explain it, but despite the fact that the beast had attacked us, the loss echoed along my bones.

"Because that thing should not be alive!"

"What?" I gasped, a hole widening in my heart.

"It needed to die," he emphasized with a wave at all of us, at the wounds still bleeding.

Zanox came galloping through the trees, Jezebel atop his back. "You killed it?"

"Enough!" Lancaster shouted, wiping blood from his eyes. The gashes across his cheek were deep. "We will discuss it back inside."

Then, he stormed through the trees, a silent assertion that if we wanted answers—and a healer—we had no choice but to follow. My ire ignited at the fae commanding us.

Jezebel and I solemnly returned Sapphire and the khrysaor to their hiding spot.

"Sometimes our people are locked to our tempestuous habits, though we'd rather not be," Mora muttered in an explanation I didn't understand as we traipsed back down the jungle path. "Come along. Tolek didn't hear you guys, and we didn't tell him where we were going when we left. He's probably worried we escaped to attack a nearby human settlement."

She rolled her eyes, but her attention drifted back to the clearing once again hidden by oversized fronds and sweeping vines. And a crease formed between her brows, dimming her immortal beauty in a moment of uncertainty.

CHAPTER EIGHTEEN
TOLEK

"WHAT IN XENIQUE'S NAME HAPPENED TO YOU?" ERISTA blurted as the door to the back room of the inn flew open, a sharp wind shuffling the scrolls and papers spread across the wide, polished square table.

Ophelia stormed in, and—

"Are you *bleeding*?" I blurted out.

"It's healing," she exhaled, falling into a chair at the head of the table. I crouched before her, forgetting the Endasi I'd been working to translate, focused instead on where crimson smeared across her skin.

Lancaster stomped in after her, striding past glass shelves crammed with books to the other side of the room and grabbing an apple from the basket on the sideboard. His feet scuffed over the wooden floors. Blood coated one side of his face, nasty gashes slicing his cheek. Mora and Jezebel followed, the former shooting a concerned look at her brother.

"And where in the Spirit Realm did *you* two go?" I threw at the fae.

"To save your Revered." With a growl—and no distinguishable response beyond that—Lancaster pulled out the chair at the opposite end of the table so he sat directly across from Ophelia and began slicing the fruit roughly.

"*Save us?*" Ophelia snapped at him, wincing as she leaned around me.

"Dammit," I muttered. "Erista, can you go find Rina?"

The Soulguider cast a worried look at Jezebel. Baby Alabath held her arm delicately, the skin nastily bruised and her face pale, but she nodded at her partner, and Erista swept from the room.

As Ophelia and Lancaster continued to bicker, I gently shifted aside the strap of her leathers and swung her hair over her clean shoulder. The gouge was deep. What in the fucking realm did that?

"Why did you kill it?" Ophelia yelled again at Lancaster.

I gaped at her. "What did he kill?"

"That thing isn't *supposed* to be alive!" Lancaster shot back, ignoring my question. "Don't you understand?"

"No, I don't understand any *fucking* thing that's going on here!" Ophelia's voice cracked, shattering the control I tried to hold onto.

"Quiet!" I roared. Ophelia gave me an impressed look, brows raised. "Now someone tell me what the *fuck* happened out there?"

Erista returned with Santorina, Cypherion and Lyria in tow. Rina handed me a stack of towels and a bowl of water, then scurried around the table with Erista to care for Jezebel. My sister dropped into a chair, sipping her drink and watching everyone curiously as if waiting for the fighting to resume, but CK stood behind Ophelia's chair with his arms crossed.

"It was a bird," Ophelia began, and as I delicately wiped away the blood staining her skin, she told us what happened.

When she was done, I reiterated, "A bird did this?" *A bird?* The claw mark ripped across her shoulder—Rina might need to stitch it. How had *a bird* done this?

"Yes," Ophelia answered, bitterness staining her voice. My attention snapped up to those magenta eyes burning with vulnerability. I brushed a piece of hair behind her ear, silently telling her to give me a thought.

"Not a *bird*," Lancaster interjected. "A phoenix."

A beat of silence passed as Rina continued wrapping Jez's wrist and Mora disinfected her brother's wounds so he could stitch them with his own healing magic. But Ophelia and Lancaster only glared at each other.

"Not possible," Cypherion claimed.

"No, Cyph," Ophelia said, her voice somewhere between tired and frustrated. "He's right. We've all seen renditions of them from storybooks and legends." She bit her lip, and I swore the fire of the bird's feathers flamed in her eyes. "It was a phoenix."

This time, the stunned silence was laden with fear.

"What in the everlasting Angel fuck?" I finally blurted.

Lyria echoed, "My question exactly."

"*That* is why I had to kill it," Lancaster ground out, slicing another chunk off his apple and eating it off the blade.

"*Why?*" Ophelia's voice was laced with venom, heaving with the pressure of yet another question.

Lancaster simply answered, "Because phoenixes are not meant to be alive."

"Are you going to kill Sapphire next, then? The khrysaor?" Ophelia growled, lurching forward and ripping open her wound again. Fucking Spirits, this woman.

"You lay a hand on them," Jezebel said, voice as cold as death, "and our Queen of Bounties won't be the only one hunting faeries." She hissed as Santorina set her arm in a sling, but the vicious look didn't leave her eyes. Rina wisely allowed the Bounty reference to slide this time.

"It does raise questions," Mora chimed in, her voice thoughtful as if oblivious to the tension thickening the air. Or pointedly ignoring it.

"Such as?" I asked.

"First the pegasus and khrysaor return," she said. "Now a phoenix. Why?"

Ophelia swallowed her anger. "You mentioned during the battle against Kakias that you've seen the khrysaor," she said to Mora, and she seemed to be teetering on some kind of nervous edge. "Do you know where they came from?"

Mora considered. The only sounds piercing the air were Rina's bustling about and the ice clinking in my sister's glass. When the female finally offered a response, the words rolled off her tongue with the heaviness of legends and magic. "Does the *fel strella mythos* mean anything to you?"

Angellight shimmered along Ophelia's palms, but she looked around the room, waiting for any of us to interject before saying, "It doesn't."

"That's an old folktale," Lancaster dismissed.

"Until recently," his sister retorted, gesturing toward the door. "It's a story—likely lost in the shorter warrior lifetimes—about brother constellations. Twins. An ancient being of the heavens was desperate for a babe, but her womb was barren, so she plucked the charted stars from the sky and breathed life into them. Pegasus was the first," she said, and Ophelia's spine straightened, glowing at the mention, "then his brother, Khrysaor."

Jezebel perked up.

"There were as many of them as there are common horses now. The pegasus with manes all colors of the rainbow and wings white as snow. The khrysaor gleaming the darkest night and silver.

"The accounts differ of what happened to the creatures after that. Some say they ruled the skies with a vengeful wrath; some say they were monsters of both peace and protection. And some swear they fought in the oldest wars, at the very head of their armies, with ferocious female warriors at their backs."

"The books I've found all speak of constellations," Jez said, "but I didn't know they meant so literally."

"It aligns with what we saw in the Spirit Realm," Ophelia said.

"During the battle, it was the arrival of the khrysaor that caused your pegasus to emerge." Mora shot her brother a victorious glare. "Only a folktale?"

Lancaster's scowl deepened.

"Can you think of why that may have happened?" I pushed, brushing my fingers over the back of Ophelia's neck absently as she bounced in her seat.

Mora considered. "A shed of power is the only trigger I can imagine."

"How would that occur?" Jezebel asked.

But Ophelia's tone was streaked with horror. "Blood."

She looked up at me, and those wide magenta eyes said, *Their blood has been used as mine has.* There was a kinship in that stare, a protectiveness that explained her outrage at Lancaster killing the phoenix.

She swallowed down the fear and explained, "When you crashed through the ceiling into the manor, Zanox was cut."

"We all saw the blood," I said, remembering the dark, sticking substance splattering the courtyard.

"There is something in his blood that caused the pegasus to emerge," Lancaster said, indulging the theory.

"And maybe"—Ophelia was searching now—"it finalized the reversal of Kakias's immortality ritual, too."

"What do you mean?" Lyria asked, leaning forward in her seat.

Ophelia explained, "When we tried to undo Kakias's immortality to make her mortal, we were missing an ingredient. She was weak, but still very much immortal, until Jez arrived." Ophelia shivered as if remembering the late queen's bloodcurdling shriek, but went on, "There's something in the khrysaor blood that set off that entire spiraling chain of reactions."

The room fell into a contemplative, myth-laden silence. Finally, Cypherion said, "There are too many occurrences for them to be coincidences."

Ophelia met my eyes, silently working through everything we'd been handed and uncovered. The constellations-turned-myths, Kakias's death, the fae queen's soldiers now at this table...

Her eyes widened, and I knew we put the pieces together at the same time. Ophelia's stare whipped to Lancaster, and she said, "It's connected to the reason you first came here, isn't it?"

"Yes," Lancaster clipped. "I think there is something on your continent—some kind of rot within the magic—that is causing all of these unnatural phenomenons to occur."

"Perhaps it's your presence," Santorina quipped, but even that flaming remark was tempered by weight of the threat.

Lancaster only offered a flat look in response. "I wish it were as easily exterminated as that." His gaze swiveling to Ophelia, he added, "You don't have a grasp on your magic."

"Not entirely," Ophelia ground out.

Lancaster sat back in his seat, twirling his knife around his hand. "What do you know of it?"

Ophelia and Jezebel exchanged a look, then Ophelia summoned a delicate strand of Angellight. Based on the pure gold sheen, it was connected to the shard of Damien's power around her neck. She sent it dancing around the fae, reflecting on the glass shelves lined with Starsearcher incense, candles, and books. Mora grinned, mystified, but Lancaster's hands inched toward his weapons.

"Not a wise choice," I threatened.

"Relax, Lancaster," Ophelia said, attention carefully honed on her power. "You wanted me to use it."

"You relax when an enemy's magic is close enough to strangle you."

"I thought we were allies." But Ophelia withdrew the power, having it settle across her shoulder—her wound—like a gold bandage. She relaxed, and in only a minute, she pulled the sheet away to reveal a fresh pink scar. "That's about all we know."

She didn't mention Jezebel's silver light or spirit speaking, but Lancaster narrowed his eyes on Baby Alabath, likely trying to draw a conclusion from her connection to the khrysaor.

All he said was "It's not much."

"I'm trying," Ophelia snapped.

"Try harder," the fae said. "You never know what things you'll unravel if you learn. What could be undone." There was a new edge to his voice. Less the commanding, ancient soldier and more distressed. Ophelia noted it, too; it sank into her frame as she chewed her lip, working through what she was going to say next.

"Damien, our Angel, has visited me a few times," Ophelia admitted, giving the fae a small peace offering as allies. An offering after they came to their rescue tonight, despite her disagreement with how Lancaster ended the situation. "Twice, he's delivered prophecies. During the later visits, though, he seemed...blocked."

"Blocked?" Mora asked.

"Like there was something he wanted to say, but he couldn't."

Mora exchanged a glance with her brother.

Ophelia cocked her head. "What?"

"That sounds like fae magic. A useful kind, but a rare one. To place restraints on another...it's complicated."

I asked, "A fae lock around the Mystique Angel?"

Interesting. Concerning.

"What in Damien's name happened to all of you?" Malakai gaped from the doorway. I hadn't even heard him and Mila enter.

As Cypherion helped Malakai with the bags from the market —including a large sack of apples for the khrysaor—we updated them on the night's events, right up to what the fae had claimed about Damien.

"We read about locks," Mila said. "In your queen's library."

Lancaster stood. "What were you doing—"

But Mora smacked his arm. "What about locks?"

"We were looking for ways to break them," Malakai explained with a nod at Ophelia and me. "Found things about goddess magic repelling ancient magic. About bargains being hereditary."

That sparked a memory—

It's almost as tightly drawn as the hereditary bargains of the fae and the gods.

I spun toward Erista. "You said something about that."

The Soulguider only offered a blank stare. "What?"

"In the outposts. While..." I glanced between Ophelia and Jezebel, unsure if they wanted Lancaster and Mora to know they'd been flying that night. "When we were talking about the pegasus and khrysaor."

"Tolek, I have no idea what you're talking about," Erista said, head tilting.

"I..." The thought trailed off, my attention swinging to Mora. On the beach, when Erista and I were speaking of legends and the khrysaor and pegasus, something had seemed off about her. A slightly different tone to her voice and darker eyes, her tattoos not a vibrant as usual.

Mora blinked expectantly.

"It was *you*?" I gasped.

"What was her?" Ophelia asked, slowly pushing up from her seat.

But Mora grinned. "I was wondering how long it would take you."

"When you and Jezebel went flying before the isle," I explained, "I *thought* I was talking to Erista, but apparently..."

Erista accused, "You impersonated me?"

Quick as a whip, Mora glamoured herself into Erista once again, flawless but for the off-shade eyes and dimmed gold tattoos. Every warrior in the room stiffened. "Your clothes are lovely," Mora said, holding up the edge of a Soulguider-style chiffon skirt. Then, she shifted back.

"That's disturbing," Jezebel commented, leaning defensively toward her partner.

But Ophelia studied the fae. "*Sometimes our people are locked to our tempestuous habits, though we'd rather not be,*" she muttered. "That's what you said outside." She braced her palms on the table, not even wincing over her injured shoulder. "You're under a bargain of some kind—forbidden from telling us something. And you glamoured yourself to point us in the right direction without explicitly saying it, didn't you?"

Mora's slight nod was the only confirmation we needed.

"You brilliant warrior, Alabath!" I burst.

Ophelia grinned, invigorated at a piece of the puzzle falling into place. "What else did you and *Erista* talk about that night?"

"The gods," I said. "Spirits, it was right in front of me. The khrysaor and pegasus are tied to the gods, that's likely a part of the *fel strella mythos.*"

"But the lock didn't keep Mora from speaking of the myth," Rina reminded us.

"Then it's the gods they're locked from sharing. Probably something specific," Ophelia suggested, still not looking away from the fae.

Neither said a word. Which was confirmation enough.

"We ask questions to pry holes in the wording of the bargain and discover what they can tell us—or what they can't that might hold an answer," I said.

Ophelia's eyes were alight as she nodded and recounted, "So the pegasus and khrysaor were brother constellations."

"It might be connected," Mila interrupted. When we all

looked at her, she added, "I think Malakai and I figured something out."

"Something about the pegasus?" I asked.

"Something about the emblems." Mila answered, and Ophelia straightened beside me, eyes wide as the general continued, "Where was Damien's emblem?"

"In Angelborn." Ophelia's eyes flashed to the ceiling, as if she could see the spear in our room above. "A shard in the hilt."

"A weapon," Mila said, nodding with a gleam in her eye.

Malakai snagged her train of thought as if they'd been discussing it already. "And Damien's constellation is—"

"The sword, yes!" Mila said, decisively. "Ptholenix's is the fire-bird, like Firebird's Field. It's related to the location of his emblem."

"And Thorn's is the crown," Ophelia continued, but her face quickly fell. "The sword and Angelborn aren't quite the same, though. And Bant's constellation is the ax, not anything like a ring."

"Engrossians often claim a second one, though," Malakai said. Snagging a blank sheet of parchment from the table, he sketched it out. "A few clans have claimed multiple over the millennia since the Angels. It's caused many fights throughout history."

"Did you know that before I told you?" Mila asked.

Malakai flashed her a sheepish glance. "Yeah."

She rolled her eyes but waved a hand for him to continue.

"The common symbol of the Engrossian clan is the ax because of its simplicity when they scar themselves." Many of the second major clan's warriors chose to immortalize their commitment to their cause with that symbol. "But do you know what their orig-inal constellation was?"

Malakai straightened, shoving his rough recreation of the star map toward us.

"The hydra," Ophelia breathed.

"Seven-headed monster," I said, realization clicking into place.

"How does that connect?" Lancaster asked, voice piqued with interest.

"Barrett's ancestors have had the Engrossian sigil ring in their possession for centuries," Ophelia explained. "So long that the story of *how* they won it has shifted over time, but it is said that one powerful Engrossian won the ring from a monster in their swamps. One with seven heads."

I added, "And are you aware that another clan fought for the hydra as their constellation back in the Age of Angels?" Moving around Ophelia, I scanned the glass shelves lining one wall until I found an encyclopedia and flipped through the index.

"Which?" Mora asked, enthralled with our lore.

"The Seawatchers," I said, finding the page I needed and flipping the mythos book around. "And a contrasting account of the hydra is a water serpent."

There on the page, an illustrated depiction of a many-headed serpent burst from a still navy sea, maw roaring wide and teeth glinting as long as my arm.

"The alpheous," Ophelia said. "They guarded the platforms. And Gaveny's known constellation is the conch. Which *can* produce pearls like his emblem, though they're rare."

"Do you see my theory?" Mila asked.

"The constellations are clever disguises," Ophelia said. "Some point to the emblem itself, such as Thorn's crown, some are an adjacent item like Damien's sword, and some are—"

"They're clues to what we might face or where we should look," I said. And when Ophelia smiled at me from across the table, there was so much hope shining in her eyes.

"This could change everything. Give us an advantage we need heading into those final two trials. And maybe...maybe even a reason for *why* this is all happening, if we look in the right place." Ophelia whipped her head toward Mila. "You're a genius. Thank you."

"Happy to help, Revered."

Cypherion said, "And the Starsearcher constellation?"

"Valyrie's Heart," Mila amended. "That's the nickname at least. It's a maiden and a huntsman." As she spoke, I flipped through the encyclopedia again. "The Fated Lovers legend says the two fell in love but were forbidden from ever being near one another, and Valyrie herself facilitated a way for their love to resound through the eons by casting them into the sky and creating her own constellation before the Ascension. Though no one can confirm or deny if it's actually true, it holds the name of her heart because she loved the two dearly and wanted their happiness enough to put some of her very self into the magic that bound them to the heavens. Each night, she would find them through her telescope to say a heartwarming hello from Ambrisk. It's a tragic story of sacrifice, really, but it's also beautiful."

We all stared at Mila for a moment as she finished, her eyes shining. Malakai shrugged. "She knows her stars."

"That she does," I agreed.

"We need to figure out what symbol could have to do with Valyrie's heart," Ophelia said, more alive than I'd seen her in days. As if this new promise swallowed up some of the stagnation she'd been wrestling with. "Then, maybe we'll be able to pair it with what Tolek and Mora are translating from the scrolls and decipher what's waiting in Valyn."

"Are we certain her trial will even be in Valyn?" Malakai asked, a bit warily.

"Titus seemed to know something," Ophelia said. "It's where we'll start."

And get Vale back, no one added aloud.

"What's the Soulguider constellation?" Lancaster asked.

Jezebel, who had been conferring with Erista, raised a brow at him. "Do you ancient immortals truly not know?"

But Lancaster merely sighed. "First off, Mystique, we are not immortals. We can be killed, but are simply highly skilled at avoiding it—"

Santorina scoffed.

Lancaster squinted at her. "Secondly, if we do not fall prey to foul play, it takes millennia for our natural causes of death to befall us, but they do. And third, the constellations are categorized differently in Vercuella. Not only do we see different ones based on location, but those that we all share have different meanings."

"We understand that," Ophelia said, rolling her eyes. "I think my sister assumed you'd gotten bored in those many non-immortal centuries and had researched them."

Lancaster groaned, apparently ready to continue this debate with Ophelia, but Mila interrupted, "Xenique's constellation has been right in front of us."

Erista and Mila exchanged a knowing look.

"What now?" Lancaster grumbled.

Ducking under the table, Mila pulled out the books she and Malakai had found in the fae queen's library.

The male narrowed his eyes. "Are those—"

"Yes," I interrupted, and Lancaster grumbled.

I still doubted Malakai and Mila had asked permission to borrow the tomes, but I didn't truly care. That queen was entitled. She deserved to have something taken from her after how she toyed with us.

Finding the page, Mila plopped the book down on the table before Lancaster and Mora and asked, "How much do you know about sphinxes?"

"Sphinxes?" CK echoed.

"Legends say Xenique had quite a preference of them," Erista said. "And they're largely a symbol of Artale, marking historic sites like our capital monuments, Gates of Angeldust, the Artiste of Artale's Corridor." She waved a hand as if to say *the list goes on* and pursed her lips. "None have ever been seen alive, so I'm not sure where it points, but the Soulguider constellation is the sphinx."

"Sounds like the exact thing that would be tangled up in a hidden piece of her power," Ophelia declared. "We head to Valyn first and chase the Fated Lovers, but then, we search for lost sphinxes."

And when Ophelia grinned, it was lit with as much fire as a phoenix's wings.

～

"READY FOR BED?" Ophelia asked, cutting through the swarm of theories my mind had become. It was only us left in the room now, the inn quiet. "Tomorrow's ride will be long."

My brain was too clouded with mashed up sentences some-where between Endasi and the common tongue to make a joke of the wording she'd chosen. Phoenixes, hearts, and races. Soul-guiders, gods, and Starsearchers. It all melded together.

I shook my head to clear it as Ophelia stood from her seat across the table and walked toward me.

"We're making progress," she encouraged.

"Is it enough, though?" When it was her safety—her damn life —at stake, would it ever be?

Ophelia gripped my chin, turning my attention toward her. "Give me a thought," she said, as I'd said to her before when she was afraid.

I blew out a heavy breath, leaning back in my chair. "I still see it, you know. All the time."

She stiffened, but I kept up the gentle tracing of her waist, grounding myself with the feel of her skin against mine and studying the scars on her midriff. "Not every night, but sometimes, when I jolt awake, I still see me having to cut Kakias's power from your arm. Sometimes the wound never stops bleeding. And..." My words faded into silence.

"Tolek," Ophelia said softly. She cupped my cheek, pulling my gaze upward. "I am alive because of you. So many times now, you've saved me."

"What if I can't one time? That's all it takes, and tonight, I wasn't even there." I waved a hand at the table behind her. "You need to survive this, Alabath. I need you to."

I wasn't above saying it, pouring my heart out to her and reminding her how desperately I needed her in this life or any other.

"I'm not going anywhere." Leaning forward, she brushed her lips against mine softly. I knew while she was equally angry and scared of the unknown, she was being strong for me right now. But Angels, kissing her was one of the best fucking feelings in the world, so I didn't care. "I know what you've been doing ever since we first went to the outposts."

"What's that?" I asked, tugging her a little closer.

"You've been holding everything together. Holding me together when I thought I'd implode, trapped on that little island waiting for Ritalia."

I laughed. "It's a bit bigger than a *little island*," I corrected her, but she only rolled her eyes.

"You kept me from going crazy, but you can let go, Tolek. It's not only your responsibility to protect me. It's our responsibility to protect each other."

"I think you're more inclined to risk your life than I am, Alabath."

"Yes, well, being chosen by the Angels will do that to you." She crossed her arms. "Regardless, we're a team, Tolek."

"Best damn team there is."

She smirked, and mine matched it. Even this small conversation, the tiny reassurances, made everything a bit lighter. With that weight lifted, I admitted, "I keep thinking about being in the outposts. About how nice it was to have a reprieve."

"Mm-hmm," Ophelia hummed, and I knew without looking that her eyes were on my hand, slowly creeping up her thigh.

"But they were also some of the cruelest weeks the Angels could have given us."

"What do you mean?" she breathed.

"Now I know what it's like," I said, and I leaned forward, placing a kiss to her stomach. "Now I know that semblance of a normal life with you. Being able to stay in bed for hours, to sit at a tavern or on the beach and indulge in every moment."

Ophelia knotted a hand in my hair, and I dragged my fingers up the back of her legs slowly, slipping beneath her skirt. Gripping her thighs, I pulled her closer.

"I know what it's like to have you whenever I want." I dragged my lips across her stomach, pressing those words into her skin. "And even after all this time"—I traced the seam of her lace undergarments, and she arched her back—"all I can think about is being between your legs. About what you taste like, how you feel around my cock."

I stood, hiked up Ophelia's skirt, and backed her toward the table. "Every day, it feels like there are collars around our necks." I teased over the lace between her legs, circling where she was so fucking needy, and her breath quickened. "They're pulling us further away, taken by some curses we don't understand. And if

I'm going to go, it'll be with the feel of you imprinted on my skin."

Ducking, I kissed beneath her jaw, and her head instantly rolled back.

"We really should go to bed," she gasped as I worked my lips down the column of her throat, still toying with the fabric that stood between us.

I brushed a knuckle over her clit, and her hips bucked.

"Right," I muttered. "Bed." The lure of her heat was driving me wild. "Are you sure?"

Ophelia's eyes were clouded with lust. A beautiful sight. "We can't here, Tolek," she scolded, voice breathy.

I dragged my lips back up her neck and whispered in her ear, "You can't say my name like that and expect me to not want to fuck you on this table."

Her thighs clenched around my hand, and I smirked against her skin.

"I love having that damn effect on you," I groaned.

"What?" She gripped my leathers.

"The way you show me you're unraveling as much as I am. The way it makes me feel like I might drive you as wild as you've been driving me for years."

"Tolek." She breathed my name again, and I was dangerously close to the edge. Ophelia's gaze was mischievous as she met my eyes. "What do you need?"

"I could think of a thousand different things I need right now, Alabath," I whispered, nipping her ear and keeping up a teasing pattern between her legs until she was nearly panting. "All of them involving you in various positions on this table—to hell with the Angels and their curses."

Slowly, I gripped both of her hands and removed them from my shoulders. I positioned them behind her, grasping the edge of the table on either side of her hips.

"Don't move," I instructed, my voice dark, and her magenta eyes flared with heat. "Not until I say you can."

Ophelia bit her bottom lip but nodded eagerly.

With taunting, savoring movements, I skimmed my fingertips

back up her thighs, relishing in each shiver she rewarded me with. When I reached the hem of her leather skirt, I was already straining behind my leathers, but I wouldn't fuck her yet. Not with my cock at least.

I hooked my fingers in the band of her undergarments, stripping the lace and silk down her thighs. Nothing else stood between us now, no other layers under her skirt tonight.

"Dammit, Alabath," I said. "This lace fucking wrecks me."

Her voice was breathy as she answered, "I think *you* wreck *it*."

I smirked. "A fair trade." I tossed them aside, standing, and Ophelia looked confused, likely expecting me on my knees. But I didn't want to do what she expected.

Instead, I kissed her deeply, and when her hands shot to my shoulders to find purchase, I grasped her wrists, squeezing tight. "I gave you instructions."

She placed them back on the edge of the table as I tugged her skirt up, spreading her legs and exposing her to the back room where anyone could walk in. A thrill widened her eyes.

"Do you trust me?" I whispered.

"Yes," she panted as I dragged one finger through her center. Fucking Angels, she already felt so good.

I swirled lightly around her clit, then dipped back toward her entrance, and she writhed against my hand, seeking relief.

"Careful you don't move too much," I whispered, dragging my teeth down her neck. "You wouldn't want to make a mess of the table."

"Fucking Angels, Tolek," she breathed.

I pulled back, repeating that pattern with my fingers as I peppered kisses and bites down her neck and breasts. I scraped my teeth across her nipple, and she arched into me, one hand fisting in my hair.

Freezing, I ordered, "Not yet."

She whined in protest—the sound making me painfully hard —but gripped the edge of the table again, using it as leverage against my hand.

I kissed and licked back up her neck until I was hovering right over her mouth.

No, I didn't want to be on my knees right now.

I wanted to be right here, where I could watch her writhe. Where I could watch every thought until all she could focus on was the pleasure *I* was giving her. On the promise woven between us.

And as I slowly sank a second finger inside her and gave her the satisfaction she begged for, those promises stitched even tighter.

She moaned, her head dropping back.

"One day," I swore as I pumped my fingers into her and memorized every breath and groan that slipped from her. "One day, we won't have to worry about any of this. One day," I added, picking up my pace, "we'll have weeks where the only curses we know are the ones you swear to the Angels in our bed."

Her hands clenched the table, desperate to let go as she began to flutter around my fingers. "One day," she panted, "we won't have to worry about the sacrifices."

And that word on her lips broke all the resolve I'd held to. I pulled my fingers out of her, quickly undoing my belt and dropping my pants, until I was slamming into her.

She cried out, neither of us giving a damn who heard. One of her hands gripped tightly to my hair, pulling my lips to hers as I pounded into her again and again and drove us toward that frenzied peak.

Tongues and teeth clashed, the room echoed, and as I hit that spot I knew would send her to ruin—as she squeezed my cock so tight I was coming harder than ever before—I memorized every damn reaction playing out across her beautiful face.

"I love you, Tolek," Ophelia breathed. "More than all the damn Angels."

"Infinitely, Alabath." I crushed her lips to mine. As we both caught our heaving breaths, I whispered again, "Infinitely."

Chapter Nineteen
Ophelia

"What's this part say?" I asked, leaning across Tolek's lap to point to a section of the scroll he was currently reading.

We'd been traveling on horseback today—I was riding Sapphire with everyone since we were in a secluded stretch of jungle and felt it safe to let her walk with us—and we stopped for lunch around midday. Tolek and I found a stream to wash up in, eating and resting on the piled rocks along the bank, slick from the spray of the current. Roots tangled down the sloping edge, disappearing under the babbling waterfalls.

"That part gets into the consequences and awards of the races," Tolek explained. "Below ground where the dead rest..."

"Where the dead rest," I considered, scanning the trees around us.

Tolek had been picking apart these scrolls since the day we left the outposts, using every available moment to translate Endasi with Mora, from which he and I were trying to build theories of what the next trial could contain.

The fae female seemed to have a natural talent for spotting patterns, so she'd been reading over the coded scroll in between our travels. Though she didn't speak Endasi, she and Tolek established a system. She would note down what she found, and once Tolek got through the other two scrolls, they'd shift focus to that one. No use wasting time fixating on the hardest one.

Tolek had picked through the first scroll about Valyrie's final reading while on the ship. Though it was interesting, we didn't think it held the answer to the Starsearcher emblem.

"Explain it from the beginning," I said. My hair brushed across his bare chest as I leaned back and his hand dropped to my leg. "The purpose of the races was..."

"For Valyrie to determine her fiercest warriors, the ones who received the honor of lining her cabal. They became her sworn protectors, daring advisors, and cherished friends."

I scoffed, eyes on the stream slipping across the stones. "Cherished friends, though many died to get there."

"Those ones weren't worthy," he said, brushing his thumb absently over my knee as he studied the ancient words. "According to the Angel. From what I can infer, she seemed to be ruthless. She barely knew the dozens of warriors who entered their names for the races before the games began. If they died, it meant little to her at that point."

Higher powers, always so careless of the lives they toyed with. Anger wound through me at the thought.

"What was the first stage of the races?"

"Duels," Tolek answered. "Physical battle first, then they moved on to one of wits."

I tilted my head. "Which was?"

"Poison. Deciphering what cups were deadly before the Angel drank them."

"Angels can't be poisoned."

"No longer. But before the Ascension—before they were truly flooded with almighty power—they were part mortal. I assume they were more fallible then."

A drop of poison would not likely have affected an Angel as it would have a mere warrior or human, but a stronger dose? Even the almighty could have feared it.

"Spirits, I hope this trial doesn't involve poison." I shivered. Tol's grip on my knee tightened, and I stifled my fear at the possibility. "How did it work?"

"The remaining thirty from the duel were each given a table of chalices and told to assess them. It was not only a test of their knowledge and precautionary thinking, but a way for the Prime Warrior to observe their cunning in the face of a timed challenge." Tolek blew out a breath. "It was the first time Valyrie saw them unmasked. Heard their voices."

"That's rather sad."

"Ruthless, as I said."

I leaned forward again, looking at the scroll as if I'd be able to interpret it. "How many progressed from that game?"

Tolek scanned the notes in his journal. "However many selected the correct cups."

And those who chose wrong...

I couldn't harp on it. Didn't have time to. "What was the final race?"

Tolek looked at me with a creased brow, as if seeing right through the defenses I was putting up, but he continued, "It doesn't say, but we do know where it was and what it led to. Which brings us back to..."

He tapped the paragraph I'd initially asked about.

"Below ground where the dead rest," I muttered, finger landing next to his on the worn parchment.

Tol nodded, dragging my hand along the line as he translated. "Only twelve would subsist the catacomb challenge, and with their survival, they forged an unending commitment to the Prime."

For a breath, Angellight shimmered across my skin, its iridescence subtle in the jungle but burning through my spirit, tugging insistently at my gut.

"That's where it has to be." My gaze snapped up to Tolek's. "Catacombs. We head to the catacombs once we get to Valyn. We bring strong fighters, we remain on guard, and we follow the tug of the Angelblood within me to look for a symbol of Valyrie's Heart, using whatever else we learn from here"—I waved at the scroll and his notes—"to prepare."

I withered at the consideration of the underground tombs and the things that may lurk down there, but I buried my fear lower than the corpses and let the heat of the Angellight seal it away, at least for now.

If we wanted answers, if we wanted to wrest control of our lives back from those who had refused to give us answers, we needed to do this.

"What have we learned from the coded scroll?" I asked, pushing to my feet and dusting off my hands. We had to return to the others and get moving.

Tolek rolled up the parchment, stowing it carefully away. "There's a name repeated multiple times, though we don't know who it is."

"What name?"

"Echnid," Tol said. He handed me a canteen to add to my pack.

"Do you think it's one of the Fates?" I asked. "Since their names are only given to Starsearchers."

"Could be." Tol dragged a hand across his scruff, considering as we clamored up the bank and onto the jungle path. "There's a lot of mentions of sacrificial stars and other ominous things in all three scrolls. The word Fatecatchers was used a few times in the final reading."

"Fatecatchers?" I repeated.

Tol shook his head. "There's no explanation for them. Or at least not one I've deciphered yet."

He slipped into a tense silence, eyes narrowed on the branches above. Soon, our friends' voices echoed from the road up ahead. Before Tol and I came into view, I grabbed his wrist. He turned his chocolate eyes on me, a brow raised as if to say *yes?*

"Is something else bothering you?" I asked. "Besides the threats and mentions of sacrifices."

His jaw ticked at the word, but he peeked around the trees, making sure the others were far enough not to overhear. "Lyria," he admitted.

"What about her?"

"I've tried to talk to her a few times since she came back from Banix, but other than group gatherings, she's been avoiding me. Mila said she won't talk about the war, but I know it left scars."

How could it not? "Do you want me to try to talk to her?"

"As a Revered?"

"As whatever she needs," I corrected, and took a step closer. "Whatever you need, too, Tolek. I'm here for you."

He brushed a strand of hair behind my ear, fingers lingering along my jaw. "I know, *apeagna*. Thank you."

At that moment, Cypherion's voice rose through the trees, reminding everyone we had to hurry if we were going to make it to our stop tonight—a fact he was disgruntled by. Malakai and Tolek had been dragging him off his horse at every rest point, forcing him to sleep and eat, though he wanted to keep riding.

"He's worrying me a bit, too," I whispered to Tolek.

He narrowed his eyes on the swinging vines ahead. "He's been a bit cagey about this contact of his in Valyn and what the plan is."

I sighed. "I trust him implicitly, but..." I didn't want to admit it. To even suggest Cyph was allowing nerves to rule his decisions. We'd all be acting the same way if it was us in his position.

Tolek seemed to understand, squeezing my hand. "He'll relax once we get her. Let's keep going."

As we walked on, I squeezed Tol's hand back. "Thank you," I told him. "I couldn't do any of this without you."

And I knew how much pressure he was putting on himself. To decode the scrolls, to translate the Endasi, to keep me and everyone else here safe.

Tolek lifted my hand to his lips and placed a chaste kiss there, though the promise burning in his eyes was anything but. "It's my pleasure, Alabath."

∿

THE NEXT MORNING, I woke to Cypherion prodding me in the shoulder.

I rocked upright, blinking away the sleep as the jungle canopy and closely packed trees swam into focus. "Is everything okay?"

"I heard from my contact in Valyn." Cyph's voice was frantic enough to rouse Tolek beside me, his hair standing on edge and stubble thick. "We have a meeting place and time."

Chapter Twenty
Ophelia

Valyn had changed since our summer exchange when we were sixteen. We'd stayed in one of the old temple academies then, one they'd converted to house visiting trainees. The halls had been packed with teenage warriors. Flirtations, trysts, and fights waited around every corner, but it had been grounded. A routine and tours of the historic sites of the city, ending each day in common squares on the temple grounds mingling among the warriors. Festivals, sneaking out, getting caught...

Now, nearly six years later, as Cypherion and I wound through the streets of the furthest edge of the capital, the air was heavy with an untoward combination of magic and gritty, hostile spirits. Every breath was ominous, like a Fate could tear through the heavens, reach out celestial hands, and pluck us from the cobblestones.

"What district are we in again?" I asked.

"Technically none. This is a twelfth zone that doesn't fall in a district," Cypherion answered from beneath his hood. "Be careful where the incense is thickest." He jerked his chin toward a dense cloud of lilac haze up ahead, glittering in the orbs of mystlight hanging from brass lanterns over each doorway.

"That's not the kind meant for Starsearcher sessions, is it?" I asked.

"Not in this part of the city," Cyph muttered. "Those ones don't only affect Starsearchers."

Needing my head free of drug-induced haze, I kept a wide breadth from the clouds and followed Cyph quickly down more winding walkways, all surrounded by various shops and draped in greenery that began to feel like a maze.

He'd been relentless getting here. Once he received word of tonight's meeting place from his contact, we'd ridden hard for three days. He likely wouldn't have stopped once if the exhaustion wasn't about to drag him off his horse. I offered to fly ahead with Sapphire, but she could only carry two of us at a time, and travel by night. His informant had been very specific that we'd need everyone for this plan.

Only Cypherion and I were meeting him now, but that didn't stop Tolek and Malakai from trailing us to be safe. Looking over my shoulder, the two warriors were feigning interest in a tavern window where the barkeep could pass beverages out to the now-empty courtyard.

"You're sure you trust this person?" I triple-checked with Cypherion, studying him for any sign of faltering.

I was certain he'd never willingly lead us into danger, and I was watching to ensure his sharp mind hadn't been affected. As far as I could tell, he was as calculating as ever—acting quickly but not rashly.

Pushing a hand through the greenery draping tightly across the stone walls and shoving lightly, Cyph said, "I would trust the man we're meeting with very few things in life. But this..." He walked a few feet and repeated the action. "This, he cares about." A subtle click, and a door creaked open in the flora-wrapped wall, a sliver of dim light pouring over the stone walkway. "And he has reparations to make."

~

IT WAS...WELL, it was a hidden tavern.

One with booths cut into the walls, and low, curved ceilings forming shadowed meeting places. It was buried two floors beneath the ground, as the fighting dens I knew Cypherion frequented often were, or the less savory gambling halls I'd visited with Tolek.

Cypherion led us to the bar and ordered two of the cheapest ales. "For appearances," he said, looking over my head as he leaned against the chipped granite counter.

Based on the shuffling of two pairs of boots from the stairway behind me, our guard had arrived. Or maybe it was the citrus and spice scent that somehow found its way to me through the stale air, masking the festering liquor spilled on the bar.

Without acknowledging them, I accepted the mug Cypherion extended to me, then followed him down the aisle between small wooden tables and the alcoves. When we reached the last booth, he ducked inside. I slid along the wooden bench beside him, both of us keeping our hoods up.

"Cypherion," a low voice said.

"Harlen," Cyph offered.

Harlen. My head whipped toward Cyph. "The one who works for Titus?"

This was his contact? No wonder he hadn't wanted to tell us his name. My hand drifted toward the dagger at my thigh, the only weapon Cyph had let me bring, given that the others were too noticeable.

"He's trustworthy."

I kept one eye on the Starsearcher hidden in the shadows. "Didn't he sell you and Vale out by passing your movements to the chancellor?"

"I did do that," Harlen said. "But I was manipulated—as Vale was. Titus used me to get to her, and then punished me to get her to cooperate. But yes, I am guilty of what you claim, Revered Alabath." Then, Harlen leaned forward, and—

Cypherion swore. "Spirits, Harlen. You look...are you okay?"

One of his eyes was swollen shut, a nasty gash stitched sloppily across his cheekbone, and yellow and green splotches faded along his jaw.

"I'm fine." Despite the bruising, he flashed a grin, but it tugged gruesomely at his stitches. "And before you ask, he hasn't touched her."

Cypherion swallowed. "What's happening to her?"

"She's...different. She's spent most of the time locked in a room we used to think Titus used for readings." He exhaled. "Though we now know that's a fucking sham."

Cyph's jaw ticked. "Is he making her read?"

"Yes," Harlen answered. "He beat me to make her cooperate because he won't dare lay a hand on her. He can't risk it given that she's the only reason he's maintaining a facade of power." Cypherion's knuckles turned white from how tightly he clenched his fists, and I laid a hand on his arm to remind him where we were. "She's stubborn enough that she refuses to read when I'm there, for fear of what he'll do if she's not paying attention. But Vale has not been harmed physically."

"Physically?" I asked. Cyph was nearly shaking with tension now.

"Like I said, she's different." Harlen seemed to choose his words carefully. "I don't get much time alone with her, but even when it's only us for a few moments, she's hardened. Like there's an impenetrable force around her."

When we'd imprisoned Vale following the Battle of Damenal, she'd solidified that steel-will around herself. She became distant, *hardened*. This sounded even more severe than that.

"Titus held true to his word about helping her fix her sessions, though."

"Of course, he did," Cyph muttered, flexing his fingers. "It's in his best interest."

Harlen nodded. "He hasn't asked me to read once since she's been back."

So, Vale was the chancellor's puppet again. I straightened, one hand laying on the hilt of my dagger for support, the other remaining on Cyph's arm. "How are we getting her out?"

"We?" Harlen asked.

"Harlen," Cyph growled, "you *do* have a plan, correct?"

"I do." The Starsearcher nodded. "But you two will not be going into that manor."

Cyph's voice was laced with a threat. "I'm getting her back, even if I have to tear this entire city apart."

"Yes, but it won't be *you*." Cypherion opened his mouth to continue, but Harlen waved him off. "Everyone in your little cabal has a role to play, but yours is not there." His expression turned serious. "I promise, I've thought it all through, Cypherion. This is the only way."

"What am I doing, then?" Cyph's words were gloomy but layered with authority.

"Tomorrow night, you will be in the fighting rings downstairs while Malakai and whoever he deems the best assistant break into the manor."

"Why Malakai?" I asked.

"Because Titus remembers his careless disposition from the Rapture and deems him the least threatening. The least important to watch."

"Watch?" I asked. My gaze flashed over the quiet tavern.

"Titus likely already knows we're here," Cyph whispered.

"And he likely knows I'm meeting with the two of you," Harlen added.

I turned back to the Starsearcher. "Why the theatrics, then?"

"Because it's what he would expect. I don't want him to think I know he knows. I'm certain I will receive a grand punishment for this, but it's all part of my plan. And because his people are probably watching us closely at this moment, I'm going to take this bag"—he dropped a heavy burlap sack on the table, and the contents jingled—"and give it to you to have your friends bet on Cypherion tomorrow. Because I've earned quite a reputation these last few weeks for being involved in the fighting rings, so it's only fitting I called a sure-fire contestant back here. And Titus fears we are working together to try to earn enough to purchase Vale from him."

"She's not something to be bought," Cypherion said, but he grabbed the bag and tucked it under his cloak.

"Trust me, I know." Harlen grimaced, but went on, "You said the future Engrossian king is your ally? He's set to introduce his queen-to-be to Titus tomorrow evening."

"That's when this all happens, then," I said.

Harlen had orchestrated all of this. Directing us to the bar upon arrival. Having the money for the bet ready. Even carefully placing Malakai as the one to break into the manor instead of me or Cypherion. It had all been strategically plotted.

"How can we be sure Titus doesn't have someone reading this plan?" I asked.

Harlen answered as if having anticipated that question. "He won't expose to anyone other than Vale and me that he isn't able to read it himself."

The chancellor's own pride would be our biggest ally. At the corrupt thought, a slow, savage smile split my lips.

Harlen matched it.

"While Malakai gets into the manor to find Vale," I said, "Barrett will keep Titus out of the way."

"Yes. And you—"

"I'll be taking care of something for the Angels."

"Vale didn't give me any details, but she said there's something specific she's trying to read when Titus isn't using her. That the readings are powerful. Whatever you have to do here, Revered, I assume it's tied to that."

I nodded. "We'll take care of it while they get her out, Barrett distracts the chancellor, and Cypherion keeps himself very visible in the rings since Titus's people will be watching him closest."

Cyph grunted in agreement, crossing his arms.

"Precisely." Harlen leaned forward, and the bruises shadowing his face gave him a haunting impression. "Let's discuss the details, shall we? This plan can't have any holes in it if we're going to succeed."

～

AFTER HARLEN LEFT, we lingered in the tavern for appearances. It was late when we finally stood, and I asked Cypherion, "You trust him?"

For the first time in days, he grinned. "I'd already worked out his entire plan. I'm surprised you hadn't, Ophelia."

"I would have!" I crossed my arms, fighting the urge to hit him for not divulging what he suspected. "When you went quiet as he started telling us his idea, I had a feeling you were two steps ahead, but I'd been so focused on *you*, I hadn't had any time to scheme."

"Come on, Revered. If we're going to lead the Mystique Warriors, we need to add scheming into our schedule." We both laughed, but then his expression softened. "I'm sorry I didn't tell you. I wanted to see what Harlen had to say organically, without anyone else guessing."

I waved off the apology. "Damien knows I haven't always shared my plans. We all just want to make sure you're okay. And Vale."

I still didn't know what exactly had changed between them when they traveled alone to Starsearcher Territory, but it seemed too intimate to ask.

"This plan is strong," he said, reassuring himself as much as me. "We'll get her back."

"I swear on Damien's unholy dominion, tomorrow night, we're getting Vale back and leaving here with Valyrie's emblem."

And I prayed to the Angel himself it was true.

CHAPTER TWENTY-ONE
OPHELIA

"Hello, Ophelia," Lyria said when I found her behind the inn the next morning, dragging a sharpening stone down her sword. As the Master of Weapons and Warfare, she commanded the blades like they were her own limbs.

I dropped onto the step beside her and pulled a piece of rope from my satchel, practicing my knots to the steady sound of her work. "How are you?"

"Good," she drawled. "Visiting Sapphire?"

A breeze wound through the air, warm with heavy gray clouds darkening the sky. A storm was coming—I only hoped it waited out the one we had planned for tonight.

"Yes, though I wish I had more time to properly fly with her." My chest twisted at the separation, and I tugged the rope tight, immediately loosening it to start the pattern over. "I hate that she's hidden, especially since Zanox and Dynaxtar were gone until early this morning."

Lyria hummed in thought. "Tolek said he's flown with you."

"He has," I said. "As you can guess, he loved it."

The commander avoided my eyes as she had been her brother's.

"Lyria," I whispered, gently touching her elbow. And finally, leaning the sword against the railing, she looked at me. "Is everything okay?"

Those chocolate irises—twin to Tol's—searched mine and seemed to see straight through me. She sighed. "Should it be?"

And that was all she had to say for me to understand. Lyria wasn't hiding from us as Tolek feared. She was searching.

"No," I told her honestly. "No, it does not ever *have* to be okay. Especially not after everything we've done and seen."

Not with what we were preparing to face tonight.

"How are you doing it?" she asked softly. "Continuing?"

I deflated a bit. "I don't have a choice."

"Don't you?" When I cocked my head, she continued, "Why must you listen to the Angels?"

It was a sacrilegious question almost, but it stuck thick between my ribs. A root winding around the bone—one I was afraid to let grow, but also afraid to pull out.

"I've cursed them on many occasions, but there is something within me that cannot stop." My hands tightened on the rope, and Lyria tracked the motion. "Maybe it's the Angelcurse, maybe it's the way my spirit is woven." I shrugged. "Whatever it is, it's incessant. It needs answers."

Lyria gazed down the path winding away into a vineyard in the distance. "Purpose," she mused, looking a bit sad.

"You could call it that," I agreed. "I accepted the title as Mystique Revered. I have to keep pushing to make the world better for them."

For a moment we were quiet, sitting in each other's company. Echoes of life drifted from inside the inn—our friends and family waking, cooking, scheming.

"You're good at it, you know," Lyria finally said. "Leading. You're an easy person to want to believe in." Her words stretched out and wrapped tight around my heart. "And I'm happy Tolek has you. Happy he's had you all these years, in one way or another." She laughed. "Even happier that the woman he's with will challenge him when he needs it."

I hid my smile as I watched my hands. "Trust me, Lyria, he challenges me more."

"I believe it," she said. "I remember how you two were as children. I may have been older, but I watched the training sessions sometimes. Watched you go head-to-head. Saw him fall in love with you, too."

My heart skipped a beat over those summer days and what I hadn't even realized they meant.

Lyria continued, "All those years he spent yearning make these moments—like flying on the back of a pegasus—so much sweeter."

Inside, doors opened and closed, and Barrett's energetic voice called, "Who's making breakfast for the royal couple?"

I laughed, partly at the prince, but softly said, "They do for me, too." I may not have been yearning, but I think a part of me was always waiting to fall in love with Tolek. It was that part that breathed a new life now.

And when Lyria stood and extended her hand to me, I swore there was a bit of that life in her voice. "Come on, Revered. Let's go eat before those scoundrels devour it all."

Thanks to Harlen's careful plotting, the inn in the twelfth, unclaimed zone in Valyn was empty except for our traveling party. It was poorly furnished and had one bathing chamber for the entire building, but it was private and convenient for our plans. With the scattered square tables having been pushed together, mismatched chairs, and creaking floorboards all bathed in the morning sun from the windows lining the front wall, it was actually cozy. The wear and ease a bit like the Cub's Tavern.

Due to the quality and the ruse, however, the Engrossians were staying at a much nicer inn in the heart of the city. That didn't stop them from seeking us out for breakfast. Having arrived in the early morning hours with my sister and Erista, no one was aware they were here yet.

Barrett stood proudly in the center of the dining room, hands on his hips as he looked over the group of us. Everyone was here, my sister and Erista noisily singing folksongs in the kitchen as they prepared breakfast. I smiled at the hint of normalcy she insisted on whenever there was a kitchen present. Cooking calmed her nerves.

When the prince's eyes landed on Lyria and me, his grin widened. "I hear we have plans to discuss?"

"That we do, Your Majesty," I answered. My heart inflated,

traitorously daring to hope with each step of the plan that slid into place.

Barrett nodded, a subtle gratitude in his eye. "And I have someone to introduce." He held out a hand, and a woman with dainty features and raven-dark hair falling to her curvy waist stepped around him, standing squarely in the center of the room. Round eyes swept over the scene, not seeming the least bit phased at the number of warriors staring back at her—or the fae. "May I introduce to you my promised partner and my oldest friend, Celissia Langswoll."

Celissia sank into a curtsey, her hair swinging around one shoulder to reveal a brutal purple scar in the shape of an ax on her collarbone. "It's a pleasure to meet you all."

"You don't need to be so formal with them," Barrett said.

Celissia's gaze snapped up, a brow quirking at her prince and a soft smile puncturing her round cheeks. She folded her hands in the skirts of her dark purple gown and whispered, "I'm only attempting to play the role of a good and kind queen." There was a joking reprimand in her voice that had Barrett rolling his eyes.

"Angels, you're just like him, aren't you?" Malakai said.

Celissia's eyes sliced to him. "You must be his dear brother," she cheered and Barrett barked a laugh.

"Dear brother?" Malakai echoed. "I'm going to need a drink."

"It's not even midday," Mila snickered.

"Doesn't matter." Malakai stomped across the dining room to the bar, digging around the stocked shelves.

Tolek, lounging in a chair at the long table with Lancaster and Mora, notes spread before them, jested, "I love family reunions."

"Me, too," Barrett said. With a wistful sigh, he sank into an empty seat.

I stepped forward, holding my hand out to Celissia. Before I could even say hello, her keen stare landed on my North Star tattoo, then swept up to my magenta eyes. "Ophelia Alabath," she said. "Revered of the Mystique Warriors." Beside the bar, the door to the kitchen flew open and Jezebel marched through carrying a tray laden with bread and pastries Harlen had delivered. "And Jezebel's sister," Celissia finished.

"Observant," I said with a nod of approval.

"Where I'm from, it pays to be." As the daughter of an ambitious noble household, I understood what she meant. Most councils were filled with schemers, and based on what I'd heard, Kakias's court was no different.

As more food was brought out from the kitchens, others around the room introduced themselves—Celissia watching the fae curiously.

Mila said, "Your father is Nassik, right?"

Celissia lifted her chin, her hair falling behind her shoulders. "Yes."

No one voiced an opinion on the councilman, taking chairs at the table in a rigid silence, but Celissia's hardened stare matched both Barrett's and Dax's. Even Malakai, Mila, and Lyria appeared tense.

Finally, once almost everyone was seated, Lancaster drawled, "Who is Nassik?"

"He's on my council" was all Barrett offered at my side. I exchanged a look with Tolek to my left that confirmed none of us were entirely trusting of the fae yet.

"And you don't like him," Mora stated, intrigued eyes flicking between us all.

Barrett scoffed. "That's an understatement." He looked at Celissia, wincing. "Sorry." But she waved a hand to tell him to continue. "He's the biggest opponent to my crown and one of the main reasons I have yet to formally claim the title, along with other unrest."

He didn't elaborate, speaking to the fried eggs on his plate.

"We can talk about that later," Dax cut in, placing an arm on the back of Barrett's chair. "Tell us what's happening tonight."

The air in the room thickened. Beside Tolek, Cyph picked nervously at his food.

"It's a four-pronged plan," I explained. "Cypherion will be in the fighting den with Tolek and Lyria supporting him. You three will be entertaining Titus while Malakai and Mila sneak into the manor to find Vale using Harlen's careful plans of the building, and my team will be in the catacombs, hunting for Valyrie's emblem. If all goes to plan, we'll retrieve both Vale and the token tonight and be gone before the morning. You can continue on your tour of the city with the chancellor and play completely innocent."

"Innocence—such a ruse." Barrett sighed heavily. "It's a wonderful thing I'm a good actor."

"Are you, Bare?" Celissia quipped with her arms crossed. "I don't seem to recall that."

"You wouldn't, dear," Barrett said, smirking. "My best performances are in the privacy of—"

With the arm wrapped around his chair, Dax covered the prince's mouth before he could finish that sentence, but laugher burst along the table. "Some things are okay not to share," the Engrossian General muttered.

"Are you stifling your king?" Barrett argued, words still caught behind Dax's hand.

"Someone has to," Malakai said.

"Treason!" Barrett blurted.

"Can it be treason if I'm not pledged to the Engrossians?" Malakai asked. A smirk played around the corner of his lips. Seeing him tease Barrett warmed the cold tattoo beneath my elbow. He seemed a bit like his old self—lighter in a sense.

Unfortunately, it was a weightlessness the prince didn't seem to hold. As everyone slipped into discussion of the night's details, I tapped Barrett on the shoulder and nodded toward the other room.

He followed me along the bar and into a small alcove lined with a thick brocade rug worn with holes. Dim lanterns hung from the ceiling, lit with candles and bearing sticks to burn incense.

"How are you?" I whispered, letting the clamor of voices from the other room mask my worry.

Barrett waved off my question. "Fine, as always."

"Are you okay with this plan?"

"Of course I am," he swore. "We need to get Vale back."

"You agreed so quickly, though, when you already have so much to worry about in your territory. Are you certain?"

"I promise. We don't want to be anywhere else." His throat

bobbed on a swallow. He peeked back around the corner, and when he faced me again, his eyes were darker than their usual glinting green. "But there is a part of me that's wondering if this plan is a bit reckless, even for my liking."

"How so?" I asked, not entirely disagreeing.

"We're the rulers of the major clans, Ophelia. We shouldn't be wandering into catacombs and breaking into manors."

"You're fairly invited to that dinner," I reminded him.

"You know what I mean."

I nodded. I did understand his fear, but it wasn't one I could give in to, so I tried Barrett's joking tactic. "Are you saying you can't protect yourself, Prince?"

"Please," he scoffed. "I know you can as well. And I learned in my time in Damenal that you aren't likely to remain back in the palace while others risk their lives, but perhaps we both have to start considering that alternative."

"I may be the Revered, but I will never rule from an ivory tower." I dropped my voice as a playful disagreement rose from the dining room. "And I know that's not in your nature either, Barrett. Not the prince who fled his home and allied with his enemy to save his people. So, what is this truly about?"

Barrett pursed his lips. "I'm concerned about my clan. A tour is one thing, but I can't be seen adventuring all over the continent making reckless decisions if I'm hoping to sway them to let me retain my title."

A longing ache went through my chest at his distress.

"How bad is it?" I'd heard from Malakai about the debates Barrett had been facing, but not from the prince himself.

"It's bad, Ophelia." His confession was barely a whisper. He leaned against the wall, hands in his pockets. "I hold the palace, sure, and the few loyal council members, but none of that means anything. I need something to prove myself from this tour."

"Celissia?" Wasn't that the point of the facade? To win over his people through a strong partnership?

"Celissia is merely a temporary solution to buy us time, and a good friend to do so for Dax and me. But I won't let her life become a figurehead for longer than is necessary." Brotherly love wound through every word.

"I'm sorry, Barrett." I squeezed his arm. "I faced challenges in claiming my own title, and I will stand by you in any way I can. Your love and respect for Celissia is admirable." He brushed me off, but I continued, "Many rulers wouldn't care for the well-being of an individual warrior. But I think you may be one of the few who cares for each person as much as the whole. And I can tell you love her as a sister." My attention flicked back toward the rowdy dining room. "We have to keep our family close in times like these. We have to protect each other and do whatever it takes to escort them through the darkness."

"If anyone can, it's you with that Angellight," Barrett said, his regal smirk returning.

I thought back to what Lyria had said about me being an easy person to want to follow. I wasn't sure if I agreed—I'd made many mistakes along my path so far—but if there was someone worthy of being a ruler, someone who truly wanted to bring his people nothing but brighter days and plentiful years, it was the prince before me with his messy dark curls and playful smile.

"You've got an abundance of light yourself, Barrett," I swore. "Your people will be lucky to feel it."

~

"I'M so tired of these damn scrolls," Jezzie groaned, flopping back against the thin blankets on the bed in Tolek's and my room. Erista laughed at my sister's dramatics.

"Me, too, Jez," I commiserated. "I'll be happy when we never have to see them again."

Tolek was stretched out on the floor behind me, propped on one elbow and scribbling in his journal. "If we play our cards right tonight, we may not have to."

He'd been working night and day to translate the Endasi, stretching the limits of what he knew and doing his best to make sense of what he didn't. He'd even visited the libraries and book-shops in every small town we could afford to stop in, searching for anything that would help me find and capture Valyrie's emblem tonight.

"Anything new?" I asked, brushing Tol's hair back from his face.

His lips twisted to the side. "It's going on about Valyrie's friendship with Xenique and Ptholenix. About how imperative it was during the years the Angels were exiled from one another. And"—Tol sighed, frustrated—"I'm not sure. Some of it isn't making sense."

He'd been saying that for days now.

I peered over his shoulder, though I'd only learned enough to know a few basic words. "Is this the one about the final reading?"

Tol shook his head. "In the one about the races."

That wasn't what I expected. I didn't see how the other Angels tied into Valyrie's brutal games, but I shrugged. "Maybe we know everything we're going to find."

But Tolek's eyes continued to rove the document, his free hand toying with my hair, completely consumed.

"Where the dead rest," he mumbled. He'd been stuck on that phrasing since he first translated it, claiming something about the repetition didn't feel right. What didn't feel right to me, though, was having to visit *where the dead rest* at all.

I suppressed a shiver, not needing to show anyone that the thought of visiting ancient catacombs didn't exactly excite me.

"Let's try the Angellight again," Jezebel said, swinging her legs over the side of the bed.

She scooped up the emblems from the side table—all but Damien's, which remained around my neck—and dropped onto the floor beside me. Then, with a delicate dagger, she pricked her finger, a droplet of bright crimson beading.

I couldn't help but think of what Mora had said of the khrysaor's blood. Of how it likely caused Sapphire's pegasus to emerge and that it may have been the final step to reversing Kakias's ritual, as well.

What had it been? As the only two present on Daminius, Barrett and I had been wracking our brains to no avail.

"As much as I hate this ritual, and it makes my magic feel

riled," Erista said, entranced as she watched Jezebel pinch her finger to draw more blood, "this part *is* fascinating."

"I agree with the first sentiment at least." Tolek's eyes lifted from the scroll. "Bit cliche for a Soulguider to be interested in blood rituals, no?"

"Blood, death, spirits." Erista shrugged. "All are simply tools at our disposal."

Tolek blinked at her, then a crooked smirk bloomed. "Fascinating."

Erista turned back to Jezebel and me. "Remind me again what this is supposed to do, though?"

"Jez and I both ended up on the Spirit Realm. If it was only my active Angelblood that caused it, she shouldn't be able to travel there. Plus, it changed how both of our power feels and manifests. There has to be more to it."

Erista stared at the drop of blood on my sister's finger knowingly, as if waiting for it to do something.

"Right, but we already proved she can't produce Angellight as you can," Tolek said.

We'd tested the emblems with Jezebel's blood thinking maybe her Angelblood had somehow been activated, but she didn't create any Angellight. Not a drop beyond that silver-blue glow.

My sister and I were trying other experiments.

"Maybe there's a way to awaken something within Jezebel using my blood. Lancaster said we need to be testing this magic in different ways." I held up a hand and my dagger as Tol opened his mouth. "Before you complain, Tolek"—I made a tiny cut on the back of my arm and winked at him—"I can heal it quickly."

Angellight was already wrapping up my wrist in a golden tendril. It licked at my blood, crimson coating the iridescent strand, and before our eyes, the tiny sliced sealed over.

My light could heal even quicker than the mountains could stitch up an injury. I'd realized I could do that when Kakias attacked us at the trench months ago and again when my body seemed to recover unnaturally fast during the final battle. I hadn't known at the time what it was, but apparently Angellight—especially the kind I could now wield outside of my body—was helpful for at least one thing.

If only I knew its other secrets.

They were there, beneath my skin. I could feel them, but every time I tried to tug them free by yanking on those threads of magic, my body protested. I didn't know what it meant. Didn't know how I'd figure it out, either, given Damien still refused to appear.

Regardless, I shoved away my discomfort and looked at Jezzie. "Ready?"

She nodded. "Do you worst."

I stared into her tawny eyes, alive with possibility, and all I heard was Lancaster's demand that we learn more. That we push the boundaries of this newfound magic.

"What are you—"

Before Tolek could finish his sentence, Angellight shot from my hand, right toward Jez.

"What's the point of the blood?" Erista asked, watching warily as my golden power wrapped around her partner, toward the wound on Jez's finger.

"A direct link," Jezebel said, "hopefully."

"It feels different," I said through gritted teeth. "It feels like... something waking." Like something growing wings and taking flight.

I willed the power to wind around my sister as it did through my bones. Envisioning it, I directed it to learn her as it had me, to wake whatever might be resting within her along with that untamed spirit power.

"How do you feel?" I asked.

"It's warm. Good." Jezzie studied her hand, where my power skimmed right over her blood, but left it untouched. Slowly, she unwound her own silver-blue light and threaded it against my own. "Where the ability to talk to the dying feels like a cold release, this feels like...life. It feels like something greater than any warrior—"

Her words were slashed into silence when the strand of Angellight reared up.

Like a beast lunging for its prey, the golden tendril whipped back and shot for Jez, releasing a vicious hiss.

"Ophelia!" Erista shouted.

I tugged it back. Tugged and tugged that wild, savage magic, recalling it to me.

But it pulled for Jezebel.

Jezebel, who was now scrambling away as the power stretched for her, as it wrapped around her neck.

Threat, something in my head echoed. *Sister, adversary, fellow.* Terror seized my lungs.

The room was full of shouting, and I begged the magic to listen.

Jezzie tore at the strand as it spread. As it slithered around her shoulders and down her spine. And the voice of the power, the thing that had woken, chuckled in my head.

"I don't know what's happening!" I panted.

Hastily, I gathered all the emblems in my hand and dug deep within the cavern of my spirit.

Angellight was spreading over Jezebel's limbs now, consuming her.

"*Get off my sister!*" I growled, and I ripped at the Angel strands.

A burst of silver-blue light erupted from Jezebel. It spiraled against mine with the icy pressure of vengeful destruction. A roaring wind spun between them.

My Angellight snapped against it like a twin force—or an evenly matched opposition. A balance. One building me up and the other set to destroy.

With an echoing crack and a flash, my power whipped back into me, and Jezzie's into her, sending us staggering. The lamp beside the bed toppled over as Jez hit it, and I crashed into the wardrobe, breath *whooshing* from my lungs.

Tolek was beside me, checking me over and helping me sit up.

The gold light settled back beneath my skin where it belonged, purring contentedly and spitting energy back into my muscles, fueling me.

But Jezebel and I panted, wide-eyed, her face hauntingly pale. Her frame was so small as Erista held her, kissed her temple.

"No more tests," Erista demanded when neither of us spoke.

I blinked at them in silence, my stomach turning at what the light had done. That power slithered along my bones, and in its wake, a tainted feeling lingered. I was a creator of ruin with that untamed magic.

"No more," I agreed. Not if it would risk anything happening to Jezebel, Lancaster's taunts be damned.

As the two of them left, taking the emblems other than Damien's for safe-keeping, I lashed at the wild magic inside me. I beat it down, forcing it to submit to my will, because it would not attack my sister or anyone I loved again. Not as long as I breathed.

I remained on the floor, staring blankly at the door, until Tol moved in front of me.

"You didn't know," he said, reading my guilty thoughts plainly on my face.

"I shouldn't have tried."

"Your sister is strong. She'll be okay." But there was a defensive edge to his voice that said he agreed. That the Angellight might be more volatile than we thought.

"It always listened to me before," I said morosely. "Maybe not fully in my control, but it bent to my will."

"I know," he said, kissing my forehead. "I know. But we'll figure out what happened later. For tonight, put it behind you. Because we're walking into an entirely different battle."

Tonight...the catacombs. My stomach dropped.

"I can't use this magic."

Tol cupped my cheek. "You're strong enough without the damn Angels, Alabath."

I closed my eyes and allowed him to ground me. Not without checking on the power in my blood, though. Not without taking one more moment to make sure it was locked away tightly. A beast shoved in its cage.

When I was certain it couldn't get out, I stuffed all my questions inside with it and forged a lock over the uncertainty.

I wouldn't let them out. Not again.

If that was what the power of Angels did, I would be stronger.

Chapter Twenty-Two
Cypherion

"WELL, I'VE PLACED A VERY LARGE BET ON A WARRIOR who's new to the territory." The door to the basement preparation chamber clicked shut behind Tolek. He strode to the wooden stall where Malakai and I stood, dropping into one of the rickety chairs before the mirror. "And I did so rather loudly, so everyone was aware of who to challenge."

I ripped the tape wrapped around my knuckles, flexing my hand. "Thank you."

No one but us was in here, most already upstairs watching the earlier fights. Though the stale air and cracked mirrors weren't a luxury fitting room, it was calming to have a silent space to prepare.

My mind was descending into that focused place, shutting out all other concerns. It was the reason I fought—to find a fixated calm when everything else was overwhelming—but tonight, I needed it more than ever.

I couldn't let my attention slip.

"You're sure about this?" Malakai asked again.

They'd been asking all day as we reviewed Harlen's plans. As if every decision I was making needed to be checked because I wasn't in my right mind. Spirits, who was I kidding? I hadn't been fully in my right mind since Vale agreed to stay with Titus.

I'd been willing to do *anything* to get her out of there. To get us both out of there. Together.

She'd had other plans.

You go, and then come back for me.

I'll be back for you, Stargirl.

I rolled my neck. I needed this fight, even if it hadn't been a distraction for Titus, I would have wanted it, but at least now it was contributing when I couldn't be the one to rescue her from the manor myself.

"This is the best chance we have of getting her tonight," I said. "I can't leave her there longer when there's a possibility of rescuing her."

Malakai said, "We all need to be smart. If Titus really is—"

"She stayed for us," I snapped. A knot formed in my throat. "Vale stayed with Titus because she knew how desperately I needed to get back to you guys. How much we needed those scrolls. We have to make that sacrifice worth it and return the favor." I paused. "She deserves to be free."

"CK?" Tolek leaned his elbows on his knees. "What happened with you two?"

Malakai cut him a look, but they'd been tip-toeing around it all week. And the truth of what developed—or re-developed—between Vale and me when we went on that mission had become a wedge between us all. All I'd been able to think about today was the last time I fought, when she'd been at risk. How I'd still been pushing her away, but terror clawed at my chest.

I didn't want to share that with my friends. The secrets weren't driving them away, but they were leaving a very large chasm in the floor they were about to walk across for my sake.

"I'm sure you can imagine," I confessed. "But I was wrong about her. And we amended those differences." Billowing steam from the hot springs rushed to my mind. The scent of starlight and her voice crying my name.

What I wouldn't give to be back there with her now, free of every other threat in this damn world.

Tolek grinned. "I knew it!"

"If you already guessed, then why did you want me to admit it?" I asked.

"Because if you can't admit it to us, you damn well won't admit it to anyone else," Malakai said, practically giddy.

But a roar of the crowd upstairs reigned in their amusement.

Tolek crossed his arms, challenging, "And we're all putting our asses on the line for you tonight. Rescuing Vale could result in drastic inter-clan contention and cause many problems for the Mystiques. We needed to be certain you were serious."

His speech was harsh but not false. And in it, I recognized that defensive guard. He was here for me tonight, willing to do whatever it took to rescue Vale, but his priority was Ophelia. And if this went poorly, we could cause severe political conflict.

"I'm more serious about Vale than anything," I snapped.

Tolek's usual gleam returned to his eye. "Let's not get caught then."

"Bright idea, genius," Malakai mocked. They started bickering as I finished preparing.

At the door, I stopped Malakai with a hand on his shoulder. "Listen," I said. "I'm trusting you. I trust you more than almost anyone on Ambrisk." Tolek gave an affronted scoff that I ignored. "I need you to get her out." I hated myself for even saying it—for implying that I doubted him as he doubted himself sometimes—but Vale was too fucking important to let it go unsaid. "Whatever you do, don't freeze."

I waited to see if he'd take offense to the reference of all those times he'd tensed up after his imprisonment. I never blamed him for it—I understood why it happened—but it wasn't an option tonight.

Malakai only nodded grimly. "I'm past that now, Cyph. I promise. I wouldn't risk going in there otherwise."

"Thank you. Both of you." I looked between him and Tolek, swallowing the last bit of fear that pushed at me. "I love you, guys."

"Love you, too, Cypherion," Malakai said, clapping a hand to my shoulder.

Tolek pulled me in for a near-strangling hug and whispered, "Let's go get your girl back."

As the three of us Mystique Warriors marched into the den,

with revenge marking every step, the roar of the crowd faded. Shouts and jeers melted together, and all I could hear were those parting words.

You go, and then come back for me.

I'll be back for you, Stargirl.

All I saw was the last ring I'd been in, when Vale had fallen ill, and I'd sworn I'd shred through that opponent to make sure she was okay.

A pressure settled on my shoulders as my vision tunneled into the dirt between the ropes. It was the weight of not only Vale's life, but of the Mystique Warriors I was now helping lead. Of all those who deserved a fair and just rule, not a manipulating liar, as the Starsearchers had. But it was also the strain of my mother's life and the Deneski legacy, the confusion from all of those fucking secrets.

I shoved them down as I had since I'd found out the truth, and I shook out my hands.

I was vaguely aware of Malakai and Tolek flanking me as I approached the ring. Of the former falling back into the shadows with Mila and the latter pressing up to the rope beside his sister with rambunctious cheers.

Of everyone sliding into place for this act.

But really, all I saw was her.

I locked it all up in my mind, ducked beneath the rope, and braced myself. Titus wanted to put on a show with Vale's power? I'd give him an even bigger one.

CHAPTER TWENTY-THREE
TOLEK

"You're hiding it well," Lyria said, leaning against the post beside me as CK climbed into the ring. I didn't take my eyes off my friend as he stretched, facing the back wall away from his first opponent. A wiry, lean-muscled warrior who bounced quickly on his feet.

"What?"

"It's killing you that you're here instead of with Ophelia," Lyria mumbled. She watched the crowd with disinterest. Playing the part of rich, bored commander who was merely here to collect.

I braced my elbows on the rope. "Not going to deny it. But this is my role."

I let out a rowdy cheer for Cypherion, and the crowd answered in turn.

"Your role..." Lyria turned the words over as Cypherion and the first fighter began. Over her shoulder, Malakai and Mila slipped away into the shadows.

"We all have a role." Cypherion took a hit to his ribs, and I grimaced and called out a random insult to the warrior, though I knew CK had allowed that one to sneak by him. "That's his. And tonight, this is mine."

Lyria pondered. "What's mine?"

"What?" I asked, pulling my attention from the ring.

"What's my role in all of this?" She sipped her drink, a strong liquor that burned even from here.

With a drastic blow, Cypherion had the first warrior down. The crowd erupted, and I used the excuse to shift toward my sister. "Lyria, you're our commander. You're the reason we won that war."

"Everyone—"

"Every general, lieutenant, every damn soldier in that alliance survived because of you. Yes, they all played a pivotal role, but it was your steady direction that kept them there. That helped them all survive. Because you're a damn good commander."

CK's second opponent was already climbing into the ring, the first guy dragged away to recover. The crowd was wilder, now, and Cypherion was a solid wall against them, focus solely on the fight.

"I don't think I deserved that role," Lyria admitted.

"You earned it."

"Did I truly? I had a good team behind me and used Danya's plans." Grief twisted her features as she mentioned the former commander.

"Not only did you execute them, but you adjusted where needed. You listened to that team and collected the best ideas for the most favorable outcome. And it *worked*."

"It could have been better."

"That's our father's voice in your head, and you know it."

Lyria shrugged, lifting her chin, and, facing the ring, she maintained that illusion of perfection she'd been bred to embody. "I don't know what my role is now, though."

"To be truthful, Ria, I think most of us are figuring it out." Cypherion nailed his opponent with a fast combination, and the crowd roared. "Beyond Ophelia and CK, who have official titles, the rest of us are adjusting. And I think even they're treading uncertain ground most days."

That damn Angellight and how it had stolen from Ophelia and attacked Jezzie today flooded my memory. How fearful it had made her. Ophelia was nearly always determined enough to temper her fear, but when someone she loved was threatened, she cracked.

So, I didn't tell her the Angellight had not only assaulted

Jezebel, but it had consumed Ophelia, transformed her. It had *felt different*, pouring from her at an uncontrollable rate when the two sisters tried to enact their unknown power together.

Lyria said, stealing my attention, "It feels empty now. *I* do."

"What do you mean?"

"Everything. I put so much energy into the war. And when it was over, I looked over that battlefield. Nothing but death looked back, Tolek," she said, pensive. "Not survival, not the lives we saved. Only death. And I felt responsible for all of it. That knowledge took something from me that day."

"What do you want to do next?" I asked. She could dwell in the past, but maybe moving forward would help.

"No idea," Lyria said. She threw back her drink with alarming ease and flashed me a grin. "But I'm happy I can be here with you while I figure it out."

I smiled back as Cypherion knocked out his second opponent. "I am, too, Ria."

"I don't remember him being quite this brutal," she said as CK wiped a drop of blood from his lip. The only one he'd earned thus far.

"He's been forced into it," I agreed. "He's still as soft as ever on the inside, though. When he wants to be."

"Vale is a lucky woman," she muttered.

I barked a laugh. "That she is."

Lyria took a fresh drink from a passing servant. "I haven't seen any of these tasks Ophelia has completed, but they sound extreme."

"They are," I gritted out. Again, that nagging feeling returned. My hands tightened on the rope.

"She went into this one with an idea of what to expect, though," Lyria comforted. "More so than any of the others, at least."

"That's what's bothering me," I said. "Why was this one so easy to figure out?"

Reluctantly, as if afraid to worry me, Lyria suggested, "Perhaps the Spirits aren't exactly rising to the occasion as expected."

"Rising..."

And there it was. The translation adjustment that had been nagging at me for days. A rearranging of words—an imperfect match in the common tongue.

"It doesn't..." My mind whirled, fear turning as icy as Xenique's damn soul magic. "Ria, I need you to take over for me."

"What?" she hissed.

"You can do it. Just be as obnoxious as I would," I encouraged. "This is your role now."

Lyria assessed me, and whatever she found forged her stare into steel. "Go," she instructed.

I swept through the crowd, raced up the zig-zagging staircases, and burst out the hidden door into the flower-lined alley. Jumping on my horse, I shot for the catacombs across the city.

Because I had to warn Ophelia. Before it was too late.

Chapter Twenty-Four
Ophelia

THE REEK OF DEATH CLUNG TO THE AIR, SNAKING UP the stairway descending into the catacombs. Not the grotesque scents of loosened bowels or the iron tang of bloody wounds that smothered the battlefields. No, this was different. This was the musty odor of sordid things long locked beneath the earth. The cloying, assaulting influx of a wooden crate cracked open only to be stuffed with spoiled, rotten truths.

It was unnatural and wrong. A denied decaying.

"Tread carefully, Mystique," Lancaster whispered in a voice that spoke of centuries of understandings of the world around us. "Things not meant to be disturbed are below these grounds."

"How do you know?" Santorina muttered. I searched the darkness creeping up the stairs.

Where the dead rest, Tolek had read from the scrolls.

It was Mora who answered, the ornate hilts of her twin short swords peeking over her shoulders. "I can feel them. They are...displeased."

"Exactly how I like haunted spirits to be." I sighed.

It was only a resting place, though. If spirits lingered, they could not harm us.

Perhaps I should have brought Jezebel as opposed to the fae or Santorina, who stood between Mora and me. But Jezebel and Erista were staying with the khrysaor and Sapphire, prepared with our belongings in case something went wrong and we needed an escape. And she was guarding the emblems—all but Damien's which hung around my neck.

"How has your magic been faring?" Lancaster muttered.

Terror from the inn earlier snaked between my ribs. "I won't be using it."

He growled, "Mystique—"

"It attacked my sister," I snapped, glaring up at him. "It attacked Jezebel." With the voice of the Revered, I added, "I'm not touching it."

Lancaster evaluated me. "You may not have a choice."

"Did the scrolls mention anything about what specifically waits down there?" Rina asked, thankfully changing the subject.

"Only that the dead of Valyrie's chosen warriors are entombed below. It was an honor to be buried in the Prime Starsearcher's crypt." One bestowed upon few throughout history, not even chancellors.

"Lovely," Rina deadpanned. But she threw her shoulders back, long ponytail swinging down her spine and night-black leathers hugging her frame.

I'd had reserves about her accompanying us, but Santorina had trained hard. She was a skilled fighter, and as she'd so confidently put it, "*What if you injure yourself like you often do?*"

I told her the Angellight I could summon was enough to heal me, but she didn't trust the magic. And I trusted her more than any Angel, even if the light was threaded into my being.

So, she was here, the fae flanking us on either side, our guards on this trial.

I wished they were Tolek and Cypherion, but Harlen had been right in his strategy. Out of all of us, Cyph was going to be the most watched in this city. Titus knew we were here; it wasn't about hiding our presence so much as evading his notice. Hoping Barrett kept his attention elsewhere.

And the two of them were much better use in that fighting den tonight.

Swallowing the fear twisting through my chest at the many ways this plan could go wrong, I evaluated the archway framing the catacomb entrance. The cream-colored stones were aged and porous, a layer of dark moss creeping up the sides. Across the top, carvings had been dulled by the centuries, but they were visible in the mystlight lamps hanging on either side of the stairway.

"Can you tell what it says?" I asked, pressing onto my toes.

"It's Endasi," Mora answered beside me, her voice clear and out of place with the haunting presence twirling up the stairs. "Something about the fates of the Angel's tributes."

Exactly as the scrolls implied. I shivered at the many travesties that could have befallen them.

"Did they die down there?" Rina asked.

"Perished or were punished," Lancaster mused. "Doesn't matter. That's where they are now. We're only wasting precious minutes, and the Engrossians will already be with Titus."

Which meant Malakai and Mila would be attempting to breach the manor soon. Our time was now.

"At least Harlen was right," I said, taking a step forward so my boots toed the edge of the descent. "There aren't guards stationed here."

Lancaster grunted, his many long knives glinting. "That implies that what's inside is too ghastly for a patrol to be necessary."

As if in response to his words, a chill wind whipped from below, wrapping the musty odor around us, but I clung to every bit of confidence it tried to drag from my body, warmed myself with the light of the Angels, and smirked over my shoulder at the fae. "Good thing we're more deadly than what rests beneath."

Without waiting for a reply, I stepped to the top of the stairs and descended into the catacombs.

CHAPTER TWENTY-FIVE
MALAKAI

"I'M SURE IT'S USUALLY BEAUTIFUL HERE," MILA whispered as we crept around the back of Titus's manor. "But tonight, this place is unsettling."

"Maybe it's the fact that we know he's keeping our friend hostage inside," I said dryly.

Mila shuddered, shuffling closer in the shadows of a crooked cypher tree leaning against the side of the manor. "Probably."

"Mila," I said, turning so I blocked her from the grounds beyond. "Are you sure you're okay doing this?"

When Cypherion and Ophelia told me what role I'd be playing tonight, I didn't even consider disagreeing. Also didn't consider who I wanted to accompany me when they said it was best if I only took one person.

"Of course, I am," Mila answered too quickly, blinking those crystal eyes up at me as she fidgeted with her wrist cuffs.

I nodded, taking a step closer. "What's happening to Vale isn't happening to you, Mila. We're going to get her back, and neither of you are ever going to be imprisoned again."

Mila sighed, dropping her hands. "I don't want to go back there, but the thoughts keep pressing in."

Grabbing her hand, I brushed my thumb across the top of her ivy-carved cuff. A weight seemed to rise off her with the gentle touch. "I made you a promise during the war that we were going to survive. Together."

Her swallow was audible. "Being here is...hard." A slight laugh. "Maybe that's not the right word. I keep seeing flashes of my own imprisonment, but this is a very different type of cage." Mila looked at the high walls of Titus's manor. "No one deserves to live in a cage, regardless of the metal the bars are forged from."

The light pouring from windows three stories up peeked between the cypher branches, highlighting the walls of her fortress, and solidifying as her gaze snapped back to mine. Not keeping me out. Never keeping me out anymore. But a barrier for the rest of the world.

"Even though I'm scared, I'll do this." A waver of uncertainty went through her words, though.

"When you were in that place, you said all you could do was look up, right? At the world waiting for you. And make yourself a promise that you'd get back there." She nodded, and I jerked my chin to the wide sky sweeping over the sleeping jungle. "Then keep looking up, Mila, and remember the promises you made to yourself to live freely. Always remember to look up."

"Look up," she repeated. And the steel fire of her heart glinted in those words.

It was an inferno that ravaged my soul—one that Mila captured with her very being. Repeating that gentle drag of my thumb across her wrist cuff, I took in her expression. The way the moonlight sloped across her nose and rounded her jaw. The way it somehow both softened her features and highlighted the sharp points.

I made sure her eyes were clear, then I leaned forward, attention on her lips. She inhaled right as I met her and pressed against me, hands sliding up to lock around my neck.

For a moment, I let what we were about to do fade. Let the branches of the cypher trees mask us from the world, and I kissed the woman who consumed me.

I'd once kept so many words bottled up. I'd let all the things I wanted to say to the last woman I loved bury themselves in the depths of my shredded soul. Never again.

"You're so strong, Mila," I said as I pulled back, lifting her wrist. "Every damn day, it's admirable." I pressed one more kiss to the thin barrier of metal hiding her scars from the world.

"You can show me how much when we're done here," she said, assuming a low confidence that had my cock stirring. If she gave me the chance, I'd leave no doubt in her mind about how much I admired every inch of her.

"Motivation," I said, casting a look over my shoulder. "I like it. For now, let's get in and out of here unnoticed."

"That'll be my job, Warrior Prince." She smirked up at me, the mischievous glint I'd missed back in her eye. "I'm much stealthier than you."

"Lead the way, General." I flattened my back against the wall, letting her creep past and step carefully over the bright flowers and garden decor.

Titus was certainly a creature who adored opulence. I didn't understand it, but it was one word I could use to describe this entire estate. From the distant iron gate where Harlen told us to leave our horses to the abundant groves of a variety of fruit trees, he spared no expense.

"Watch your footing," I whispered, nodding ahead.

Mila followed my gaze to where a small snake slithered through the stalks and wrapped up a cypher. "I hate snakes."

"We'll be inside soon," I assured her.

Mila nodded but kept an eye on that creature winding its way up the trunk and into the branches. And I kept an eye on the clenching of her hands, the flinches toward the swords across her back.

A few feet ahead, a window large enough for Mila to slip through had been propped open. Harlen had laid out the plan perfectly, though my skin prickled with each step.

"Be careful," I whispered as she sank into the dark cellar. A stupid warning. Of course she would be careful.

But her answering smile was grateful, moonlight filtering through the dense branches to halo her expression. "Always." And she faded into the shadows.

I waited impatiently, fingers tapping a silent beat against my palms until she unlocked the door into the ground level for me to join her. We shut it behind us in case someone came down here, and tension wormed through me at the click of the lock.

It was long, quiet minutes of creeping up staircases, wending around corners, and ducking behind the ostentatious drapery. Endless listening for footsteps or voices, though we found none.

Thick gray rugs lined the halls, so at least that was a blessing of the Angels. Neither our steps nor small noises carried as they would on the bare ivory marble beneath.

If only the curtains had been pulled across the windows. But as we ducked under the tall frames so as not to be seen by any outer patrols, the grounds stretched beyond. Harlen swore there wouldn't be too many guards, but Titus had doubled his routine system of sentinels since Vale returned. Including a team of escorts at her chamber.

Those would be our biggest threat. One we were approaching quickly. My hand drifted to my sword across my back.

I nudged Mila as we turned down another hallway. We didn't need to communicate out loud given how we'd drilled the layout of the manor into our heads today. I knew every turn she was about to take and that Vale's corridor was the next over.

I tapped my nose. *Smell anything?*

Mila sniffed. Shook her head, brows furrowing.

Harlen had said he would set up the incense hours before we arrived. Some slow burning oil combination barely detectable until it was too late, imbued with a powder that would knock out the Starsearcher guards.

Why anyone would sell such a thing, I didn't know. But it would work in our favor tonight.

That is, assuming Harlen was able to light it properly. But given that the subtle lavender scent supposed to lull the guards outside Vale's door into a heady session was undetectable in the hall, my chest tightened.

I raised my brows at Mila, a silent, *Your call, General.*

She peered around the corner. Held up three fingers.

Three guards.

Mila turned back to me, and I caught her stare.

I tried to communicate to her that there was no way in Damien's sorry existence I was leaving this manor without Vale— not with Cypherion's voice in the back of my mind telling me how much he trusted me—but if Mila didn't like the odds, I understood. She'd suffered enough for unjust causes.

But she nodded at me with wrath in her eyes. And silently, she pulled a knife from each thigh.

With the light prowl of a jungle cat, she danced around the corner, long braid whipping in her wake, and let both blades fly.

I had barely stepped into the hall when I heard the unmistakable squelches of knives sinking into throats. The thuds of the bodies falling.

And the shout of the one guard left standing.

Mila charged, ducking his sword and swiveling behind his back, meeting his blow with a solid strike. With his attention on her, I charged.

Another guard shot from the perpendicular hallway, intercepting me before I could reach Mila. He launched a series of triple-bladed Starsearcher daggers at me, like stars hurtling through the sky.

I ducked the first two, the third slicing along the skin of my neck. It sheared off a small section of hair with it, and I growled at the guard.

Pressing my hand to the wound, I dodged another dagger. Over my opponent's shoulder, Mila unsheathed her second sword and crossed them to meet a vicious strike aimed for her head.

She stumbled back a step, but the guard pressed forward. He slammed his sword on her wrist as she twirled around him, and he knocked one of her short swords to the ground.

Shock widened Mila's eyes. Shock—and *fear*. Something she never allowed to slip into her fights.

I saw red at it.

With a grunt, I blocked my guard's final dagger and slammed my shoulder into his gut, sending him toppling into a marble statue. His head cracked back with a nasty crunch.

Unremorseful, I charged toward the Starsearcher now towering over Mila.

And I didn't think as I sheathed my sword in his back. As the blade poked up through his chest, dripping with thick crimson.

I shoved the guard off it and wiped the blade on his tunic, trying to stop my own damn hands from shaking. I couldn't lose myself again. But Mila—

Only once I mastered my breathing and knew my panic was tamped down did I look at her. And I saw past the hardened stare, the nod she gave me in thanks. Pulling her to me, I pressed my lips to hers and indulged the desperation that had become a live and pulsing thing within me.

"You're okay?" I muttered against her mouth, one hand cupping her face.

She nodded, the fear evaporating from her eyes, but a question resting there. "You?"

"Yeah," I assured her. *Since you are.* Stroking a thumb across her cheek, I added hurriedly, "Let's get going before more guards show up."

We didn't waste time hiding the bodies. They'd know we were here when Vale was gone.

I jammed my heavy boot against the handle, the lock splintering and doors flying wide.

Mila and I barreled into a suite bedecked in as grand decor as the rest of the manor. With a lavish bed staring at a row of windows exposed to the night sky, rich rugs and large mirrors adorning the space.

But—

"Where is she?" Mila panted, racing around the room and into the depths of the bathing chamber while I checked the balcony, but the doors didn't open.

"She's not here," I said. "Harlen said she'd be here. She's here every night as soon as dinner ends, which was two hours ago now."

Vale's routine was clockwork. A repetitive pattern meant to lull her into mundane compliance and appease her magic.

"Do you think Titus demanded an emergency reading?"

My mind whirled. Did we go through the rest of the manor or

retreat? I couldn't face Cypherion if I chose the latter. Couldn't return without answers and his girl safely in tow.

"I don't know." I gripped the hilt of my sword and stepped toward the door. "But we have to find—"

A sharp, icy tip pressed into the skin of my neck, and a gravelly voice threatened, "Not another step."

Chapter Twenty-Six
Ophelia

Despite the lightness of our footing, our boots echoed against stone so aged, I feared it might crumble beneath our feet. Moss clung to the walls, trapping in that eerie chill and compressing the air. It trailed all the way down the stairs, stretching along the narrow tunnel at the bottom. Even with my heightened vision, I couldn't see the end of it.

My boots thudded as they met the dirt floor, unnaturally loud. As if some celestial presence wanted to ensure whoever entered the Starsearcher Prime Warrior's private space was announced.

I kept my hands within easy reach of my weapons as we crept down the tunnel, the walls arching overhead. Mystlight orbs gathered intermittently along the ceiling, glowing as yellow as the fire of the Spirit Volcano.

"Mora?" I whispered. She hummed low in response. "Do you recognize anything from the scrolls?"

Her voice drifted through the tunnel like a wind. "They told of an ancient resting place, as old as Valyrie herself." Tolek had told me as much. "Where the third of Valyrie's races was held, and the only one of the locations that still exists."

The first had taken place in a long-destroyed coliseum, the second in the Angel's private estate, the location of which was now unknown.

"It did not specify what was faced in this race, though," Mora added.

Santorina stopped short. "If they didn't say what the third race was, what *did* the scrolls say?"

Mora's answer became a lulling melody in the too-still air as we took careful steps forward, each loud and summoning. "That this is a place where the dead rest, the eternal home of her precious victors."

Absently, I brushed a hand over the wall, and something behind the stone hammered distantly in response. My second pulse beat faster.

"Valyrie is one of the Angels whose magic had a connection to the gods," I thought aloud, eyeing Mora and Lancaster. "Through Moirenna and the Fates. Is there anything you can infer based on what you know about them?"

"Every god has sacred grounds spread across Ambrisk," Lancaster said. "Not unlike these sites you search for your emblems in."

"Do you know of any of Moirenna that resemble this?" I gestured to the draping curtains of moss and crumbling stone—to the cloying presence of death.

"No," Lancaster said curtly.

Mora added, "Many of Aoiflyn's are kept close to her bloodline, locked securely. They are seen by few but are thick with power and abundant blessings." She spoke wistfully, as if she'd seen them personally.

Rina and I exchanged a look at the vague comment, but we kept walking down the narrow tunnel. The weight of Starfire and Angelborn were steady comforts against my body, especially with the uncertainty of my Angellight.

"This is all a brutal, bloody game worthy of a higher power," Lancaster muttered.

In the distance, a faint rumbling sound echoed. We froze, and my eyes flashed to the fae.

Breath fogging before me, I whispered, "Let's not speak ill of them while at their mercy."

He nodded, eyes icy as he watched the depths of the tunnel.

As we resumed walking, I wrapped my hand around the shard

of Angelborn at my neck and summoned what strength I could from the singular emblem.

The metal warmed against my palm, my blood pounding faster through my veins as if to remind me why I was here. That steady pulse matched my steps, beating in my ears. I resisted the urge to summon Angellight to the tips of my fingers, even enough to let it hover there.

The stillness crawled across my skin, each second making me fidget more.

"Mystique," Lancaster growled, flicking a glance at my necklace. "Why have you not studied your magic better?"

I stiffened, jaw clenching. "I haven't had the time."

"That is a poor excuse. You should be experimenting with this light despite the havoc it caused."

Santorina scoffed, but my heart pattered behind my ribs. An icy chill crept down to my bones. It was that uncanny wind from before. The mystlight flickered with discordant warmth, and a part of me wanted to pull up that Angellight. To feel its safety and comfort, but I couldn't know how it would react.

The end of the tunnel loomed closer. A darkness so vast and swirling with endless secrets. It pressed in on us. Called to me.

"It's grown beyond what I've wielded before," I admitted, hating showing the fae that weakness.

"What do you mean?" Lancaster asked. And then, because he likely sensed my growing discomfort, he tacked on, "What does it feel like?"

"It's energetic and animated," I answered. The light whirled within me, floating those comforting sensations through my blood. "Like something that could truly instill hope and life, that could heal."

Lancaster and Mora exchanged a look.

A bead of unease slipped around my chest, spreading wings that rustled beneath my skin.

"What?" I asked.

The male's jaw ticked, and Mora scanned the tunnel curiously. "Why did the power attack your sister?" Lancaster asked pointedly. There was something in the glare he gave me that I didn't understand, like he knew about Jezebel's contrasting spirit power, though we hadn't given the fae any details beyond her connection to the khrysaor.

"No idea."

Lancaster sucked in a breath. "Learn the magic," he demanded, and annoyance riled within me. "There may be possibilities beyond the mortal bounds—things bolted by the hands of higher powers that could be cracked."

As his words trickled off, we neared the end of the tunnel and the looming, black chamber. Another shudder went through the walls. It rocked into my bones and spurred my frustration with it all. With the fae acting superior, with the Angels leaving me without answers, with the magic indeterminable as friend or foe.

"I want to master it," I swore. "I *will* master it. But I won't risk the lives of others to do so."

Before Lancaster could respond, I faced the chamber. I allowed myself one moment to study the darkness, then, I took the final step across the threshold.

The stone beneath my boot shivered and dropped an inch as if a lock had flicked. To our left, the wall burst in a spray of rubble and dust. Decaying, bone-white fingers punched through the air, intent and searching, horror sluicing through my veins.

And those hands latched around my throat.

CHAPTER TWENTY-SEVEN
MALAKAI

"HANDLE US A LITTLE ROUGHER, WHY DON'T YOU?" I sneered at the guard whose knife was dangerously close to piercing the skin of my neck. The manacles he'd slapped around my wrists rattled.

"Don't tempt me," he mumbled as he dragged me along the halls and wrung his massive hand around my arm. Even through my leathers, my skin burned, but I bit back any show of discomfort, glaring at him.

"Or?"

He dug the knife in, enough that a line of blood trickled down my throat. But I reached deeper within myself, into the place I went during the years I'd been tortured. Into the ghost I'd forced myself to become for each lashing, each hot iron against my flesh, each blade recently sharpened and held tauntingly before me.

To when none of it mattered, because the reason I was there outweighed it all. I dragged up the unfeeling beast I'd let myself become and stared blankly at this Starsearcher guard.

"I've had worse," I said.

"Keep talking and I'll do my best to top it." I refused to give him a reaction. "Or maybe she will." He jerked his chin ahead of us to where a tall female guard led Mila.

Damn fools if they thought she couldn't take out that woman

because she was smaller. Mila could have a grown man on his back faster than many male warriors I knew.

Still, the threat was enough to make me bite my tongue momentarily. To make him think they had an edge here. Clearly, they didn't realize Mila was a general or that we had both survived torture and walked free.

They'd taken our weapons. Slung them in their own belts and across their backs. Fools. That only kept them within our reach as they led us through a veritable maze of hallways. Sure, our hands may be chained, but the iron links were another weapon.

In this situation, everything was.

This manor was palatial, the chancellor within conceited enough to build himself such a grand home. But it lacked the antiquity of the Revered's Palace, which stretched back to Damien himself. As the guard shoved me around corners, I took stock of every piece of artwork that marked various halls, counting as I committed the path to memory.

Finally, after twists and turns that were unnecessary given I'd seen the layout of the building, a pair of ivory doors towered ahead, what looked like pure silver outlining the frame and handles.

"Welcoming us for dinner?" I grumbled.

Mila shot me a half-smirk over her shoulder, and I knew we were thinking the same thing. They could do their worst, and we'd survive it together. We'd see all the tomorrows. "They really should learn to treat their guests more kindly," she intoned.

Her guard gripped her neck, jerking her around aggressively. "No talking."

"Touch her like that again and I'll rip off your hand," I swore, voice lethal.

"You're digging your own grave with those pointless threats." Mila's guard said, flicking her braid over her shoulder. "And this isn't a dining room."

Before I could answer, she shoved the door open, and a gleaming chamber laid beyond. Everything from the floors to the towering pillars to the only other exit across the way was carved of ivory and white crystal, shining and inlaid with silver. All except the domed ceiling made of stained glass, twelve panels within, each depicting what I guessed were stories of the Fates. One remained dark, that twelfth Fate that no longer existed.

And beneath it, standing proudly in the center of the room, was Titus, a fine silver silk robe billowing around him.

My heart leapt into my throat.

Where was Barrett?

I didn't ask on the off chance that Titus hadn't figured out the Engrossians were part of our plan, but I glared at the chancellor as guards dragged us forward. Until we stood mere feet from their boss.

"Welcome, welcome, Mr. Blastwood." His eyes traveled over Mila. It took all of my control not to lurch in his direction. "I'm afraid I don't know you, miss?"

"Mila Lovall." Her voice rang clear through the room, playing his game of formalities. "General of the Mystique armies. With the status of my title, I command you release me and my soldier from these chains."

Titus contemplated, not even bristling at her demand. "I believe chancellor outranks general, does it not?"

"And Revered outranks chancellor. Shall we summon her?"

What was Mila saying? She knew full well that Ophelia wouldn't be able to come here tonight. I flashed her a warning look quickly enough that Titus wouldn't see.

But the chancellor waved a hand and said, "I don't think that will be necessary." His robe swished with the motion, and a pile of soft blue fabric was briefly visible behind him. "Besides, we wouldn't want to disturb your Revered, would we?"

My stomach bottomed out.

"What are you talking about, Chancellor?" *Use his formal title,* I reminded myself. Play the game.

"Your Revered is currently...occupied, if I am correct." He observed mine and Mila's blank faces. How the fuck did he know where Ophelia was? "Or was that not the plan? I was sure my apprentice had set it up as so."

A growl rumbled in my chest. That untrustworthy prick, Harlen, sold us out? I swore to Damien—

The door opened behind Titus, and a man was dragged in. Dragged because he could barely stand, his knees buckling and head drooping.

I hadn't met Cyph's Starsearcher contact, but judging by the distress blaring beneath his bruised features, this was the man Cypherion and Ophelia had met with. The one who had concocted this entire scheme to rescue Vale.

And if those injuries said anything, he hadn't sold us to Titus. No, Titus had figured this out on his own.

Harlen was hauled into the room by two bulky guards, and behind him—

"What the fuck is this?" I shouldn't have let the outburst win, but three more figures followed Harlen. Unchained, but very obviously prisoners based on the warriors escorting them.

Panic gripped my chest, ignited by anger.

Barrett, Dax, and Celissia, the latter blinking wide eyes at a spot behind Titus. The general had nothing but a coolly lethal stare for the chancellor, and Barrett maintained the unbothered princely demeanor he often wore in front of others, hands tucked into his pockets.

"Malakai, brother, what are you doing here?"

"I could ask you the same," I answered Barrett, then turned my attention back on Titus. "Prince Barrett is the future Engrossian king, and Celissia is his queen-to-be. Let them and their guard go this instant!"

"Even nobility does not get off when conspiring against other clans."

In his most regal, bored voice, Barrett drawled, "In what realm have we conspired against you? I thought we were having a rather nice dinner."

Titus gave Barrett a scolding look. "Denial will not end any of this quicker, Your Royal Highness."

"To detain them is an act of war," I countered.

Mila chimed in, "And I believe even here, cowering in the far stretches of the continent, you heard how brutal the Engrossian forces can be."

"Well, I suppose it's good the majority of the clan does not support this king apparent." Titus tilted his head, a creature of cunning and wit. Those years of manipulation when he'd gained his seat being put to use within his mind.

"What are you *talking* about?" I growled. Barrett's jaw ground.

"Oh, nothing. Nothing." Titus picked at a loose thread on his sleeve. "Truthfully, your half-brother and I were having a peaceful visit before you spoiled the fun." He looked over his shoulder at the Engrossians. "His partner is lovely, by the way."

I didn't know if he meant Dax or Celissia, and I thought that was the chancellor's intention. To show us he was on to their plan. After so many years of secrets and tricks, Titus had learned to spot them in his opponents. We'd been out-manipulated.

Was he any better than Queen Ritalia, wielding other's lies against them?

Behind Titus, Celissia caught my eye. She inclined her head slightly to the side, toward Titus, but I didn't understand what she meant.

"Yes," Mila said, "Celissia is beautiful and kind. Together, they will demonstrate a harmonious rule for the Engrossian clan. But I suggest you release them so that may happen."

Titus pinched the bridge of his nose as if exhausted by these games. "We have more important things to take care of right now."

And when the chancellor stepped aside, I saw what Celissia had been gesturing toward.

The world tilted, and my heart rate sped. I clenched my hands, forcing myself to focus through the panic. Vale was sprawled on the floor, her light brown waves fanned out like a starburst around her head. Pale blue dress so out of place against the harsh marble floors, and her eyes closed.

"What did you do to her?" I demanded.

"She's fine," Titus said, but Harlen lunged at his master, the move sloppy and weak, one of his ankles seeming gravely injured. The chancellor looked toward his apprentice with disdain. "She is only reading, Harlen."

"She shouldn't be unconscious from a reading!" he said through gritted teeth, his cut lip splitting open.

Titus looked adoringly down at Vale. "Sometimes the most powerful sessions take their toll."

"That's not how it—"

"*Silence, Harlen!*" The chancellor's command bounced off the crystal and stone chamber. "Vale will wake soon. Pay her no heed. We only had to bring you all to this seeing chamber because your timing was so poor."

My jaw ground as I watched Vale strewn on the floor, willing her to move. The steady rise and fall of her chest promised life, but all I could hear was how Cypherion would scream if something happened to her.

For them, I gave up the game. "Congratulations. You know why we're here, Titus. What do you want?"

"I want my apprentice to stay here. I want her to remain at my side, conduct readings for me, and to do so happily. I want the girl who looked at me as if I hung the moon for rescuing her to return and do my bidding. But ever since that imbecile left, she has been... difficult." He sneered over the word. My blood heated at his insinuation of Cypherion.

"Let her go. Let her be her own person."

"I cannot do that," Titus said. "I lose her—I lose everything. It was hard enough the months she was gone."

"Why didn't you help her, then?" When Ophelia sequestered Vale as a prisoner, Titus did nothing.

"I always intended to get her back. At first, I truly thought the way to fix her readings might be in your mountains, and she was of the most use to me with her magic full. Until I realized the potential of this chamber." He waved a hand at the pristine pearlescent walls. I didn't understand what he meant, but he went on, "I've relied on a less than satisfactory replacement in her absence. I *need her.*"

Needed her to be the mask to his sham. Needed her as a wealth of magic and fate. But...Titus didn't needed Vale. No, he only needed *power.* Thrived off it.

Cypherion needed *her.*

And Vale needed...I didn't know what she needed. Especially

not with that tattoo warping her decisions. But she deserved the choice.

I looked Titus dead in the eye. "What will it take?"

"You two," Titus said, looking between Mila and me, "broke into my home tonight. That alone is worthy of a punishment, regardless of your intentions with my apprentice."

The way his lips curled over the word punishment sent my stomach churning and palms sweating.

"And they"—the chancellor smoothly inclined his head toward the Engrossians—"entered my manor without honor, intending to fool me. That calls for reprimands, as well. I could allow you all to leave, make you swear you will not repeat your attempts to steal my apprentice, but I doubt that will be enough to placate some of your friends."

As if to accent his words, a sharp crack echoed through the chamber.

A sound I'd thought I'd left in a cold damp cell within the mountains. Leather snapping against stone in warning. And I knew what came next. Where it would land next.

Swallowing my fear, I dared a look over my shoulder. My guard had drifted away, back toward the door. And from his belt he'd taken a leather whip, warming it against the stone pillars. Only gentle strikes, more to unnerve the prey than to actually serve any purpose.

The scars on my back ached.

Shut it out.

Shut it all out.

"What will it take to let us go?" I repeated.

He lifted his brows in Vale's direction. "She stays, and I lower the punishment."

"Not a chance."

"Then the whip it is."

My brows pulled together. It was too easy. "So beat us a little bloodier, and then you'll let Vale go?"

"No." He shook his head, smiling. "Then, I'll allow you to walk out of here without breaking your legs."

Barrett and Dax roared their arguments.

I looked at Mila, at the Engrossians. All so innocent. All so undeserving of the pain waiting at the end of that device.

Mila...I found those crystal blue eyes that had become a source of strength. Mila had been tortured once in her life. For nearly one hundred days she'd suffered. I'd be damned if I allowed it to happen again.

I *couldn't* watch it happen. Her gaze pleaded with me as if guessing what I was about to say next.

"Malakai, don't..." she said softly, as if it was only us.

I couldn't let any of them endure it.

But I was quiet for too long, apparently. Because the guard behind Mila ripped a blade from her side and held it to Mila's neck. She swallowed thickly, her throat bobbing against the steel. And still, Mila shook her head to tell me no.

Don't do this.

You don't have to.

But it was too much, seeing that glint of silver against her skin. Barrett and Dax were yelling, words I couldn't make out over the roaring in my ears. Celissia was inching closer to Vale. Harlen was staggering as he tried to stand, tried to help.

Titus ignored them all.

The guard behind Mila waited for a signal, but Mila held her wrist, ready for a chance to fight back.

And it was the tremble of her lips that sealed my fate.

"Fine!" I shouted, and everyone else went silent. "The lashings, broken bones, whatever you demand in order to leave here, but only me. I will take the punishments."

Mila's shout was guttural. "*No!*"

I gripped the chain between my wrists. "If you so much as fucking touch *any* of them, Titus...You can kill me right here, and my spirit will haunt every day of your pathetic life."

"Not wise to threaten the man calling the shots on your ministrations, Malakai."

"A lesson I've never learned, it appears."

Titus smirked. "You have my word."

Too bad your word means nothing, I almost said, thinking of the tattoo inked over Vale's brand. The one tying her to Titus with a sick and twisted sense of loyalty when the man was supposed to offer her protection.

But because his word was all I had, I swallowed the biting remark.

And I nodded.

Then, I shut out the rattle of Mila's chains as she struggled against her captor, and the guard behind me shoved me to the floor —blocked out Barrett's curses at the chancellor as a dagger sliced up the back of my leathers, exposing my scars to the air.

How had I gotten here again? On my knees before a whip. A subject meant for nothing greater than torture. For nothing grander than torment for other's protection.

I'd take it. I'd accept it as I had every other beating because it kept the people I loved safe. Mila, Barrett... None of them would feel this pain.

And that was the thought I repeated as the first blow landed. As my flesh tore beneath the leather, ripping open the scars I'd healed.

A familiar warmth spread across my back. Blood.

I found Mila's eyes through the pain, crystal irises glistening with furious tears as she yelled profanities at Titus and the guards. This punishment wouldn't rip open every scar I'd worked so hard to mend. Not the ones she'd stitched up within me. It would be okay.

The guard behind me shoved my shoulder, the pain across my back searing through my bones.

If I'd completed the Undertaking, I'd heal even faster than my non-ascended warrior blood did. Now, it would likely take all night for the wounds to stitch. Longer probably, given we were further from the mountains than when I'd been whipped before.

But I hadn't attempted the ritual. I'd refused time and again because I was a coward, afraid of what I'd face in there. It had been easier to return to the void inside me that didn't feel this pain. To bury myself there.

As that person swam to the surface, and the second blow tore through flesh with a familiar sting, I kept my stare locked on Mila.

All I could picture was them doing this to her instead. Had

that been one of her punishments? She'd never mentioned. The scars I'd seen weren't consistent with it but—

A third lash landed, nearly making me scream.

I buried that pain deep, deep down. Curling forward, the skin of my back stretched, the wounds burning.

Mila shouted again, tears streaking down her beautiful face.

I couldn't look at her anymore. Wrenched my stare away and counted the seconds before the next blow landed.

Three was a kind day, in the life I once endured.

I could survive three again.

Even five. It was when it got toward ten that I would start to feel dizzy.

Perhaps I'd pass out around then. I used to force myself to stay conscious through it all, but maybe I could allow myself that reprieve now. Trust that I was absolving the pain from my friends and they would get us out of here. Hopefully Vale, too, if there was a way.

I'd take however many lashes Titus demanded if it meant they were safe.

In the guard's shadow, I watched his arm rise again. I clenched my teeth and searched Titus's beady stare—a stare heavy with greed and torment. I opened my mouth to spew hatred at him, to lessen the sting searing through my flesh, but—

Over his shoulder, Celissia was crouched beside Vale. She touched the Starsearcher's shoulder, listened to her breathing.

Vale's head snapped up. And her expression was not the dazed, searching gaze of a reading.

It was a brutal, vengeful glare aimed at her captor's back.

No one but Celissia and me saw her. One hand was clenched around something small, shining with a glittering blue.

But with the other, she unbuttoned a panel in the waist of her dress and removed a delicate triple-bladed dagger.

And with the guards' eyes all on me, with everyone's attention trained on my blood seeping across the floor and their cries masking her movements, Vale sprang to her feet.

And she didn't hesitate as she sank that dagger into Titus's neck.

Chapter Twenty-Eight
Ophelia

"RUN!" I SHOUTED HOARSELY, THE SKELETAL FINGERS crushing my windpipe, nails digging into my skin. Its touch imprinted itself on my throat, something haunting passing through me.

I reached for Starfire, but I was shoved back. Rock came crashing down, and a body—a *decayed* body—exploded through the wall, rising from its eternal resting place.

It was a warrior by the looks of its tattered clothes—or it had been. Shrunken and withered, any skin remaining on its bones barely clung there. Long hair flowed from its scalp, and hollows stared out of where its eyes once belonged, yet it watched me with a sentient, knowing intensity.

The corpse clenched its fist tighter around my throat, and as spots popped before my vision, a deep hatred burned in that vacant stare.

My feet scrambled for purchase as it forced me back, back, back. I slammed into a wall, my head snapping against stone. Angelborn dug into my shoulder blades.

"What in the fucking Angels are you?" I gasped.

Its yellowed, rotting teeth split into what I thought was a feral grin, snapping before me.

The corpse pressed harder on my throat, shoving me up. My back scraped against the rough wall, and my feet dangled over the floor. I kicked and kicked, aiming for all the weakest spots on a body, but it didn't flinch or crumble.

Nothing harmed what no longer lived.

My vision swam. Shouts echoed, and blades sang through the tunnel.

Tugging, I clung to the warrior's wrist, but its grip was as stony as the walls of these catacombs. My dagger at my thigh would do nothing, and there wasn't room to pull Starfire.

I swept my hands against the rubble piling up around us, searching for something loose. A stone I could use to deter the corpse. Its grip was tighter than a cobra's.

"Mystique!" Lancaster yelled from somewhere down the tunnel. "Use your magic!"

I can't, I couldn't say through my crushed throat. I didn't know how the power would backfire—who else it would hurt.

The corpse squeezed my neck tighter until I thought it would snap.

"I call in my owed debt!" Lancaster shouted, his voice laced with an authority only magic could grant.

"*No,*" I barely gasped.

But already, my body was bending to the will of the bargain.

If I didn't do as Lancaster demanded—if I did not pay this debt—Tolek would suffer for it. Die for it.

What little air resided in my lungs tightened as the dead bore down. The bargain tugged at me, taking what it was owed and stealing my autonomy.

"Blades are no longer your only weapons, Mystique," the fae panted through whatever fight he was also facing. "Use your fucking magic!"

With both hands latched around the corpse's wrist, I stashed my fears and gave into the insistent fae magic pressing on me. I used the breath fading from my body to reach toward my own power.

And as I channeled every bead of withering desperation, every morsel of air snaking down my throat into the magic in my soul, power mounted beneath my skin.

It rose, a beast awakening. With claws and teeth and wings flared, but—

But it was too much.

It wasn't the warmth I had come to recognize. "*No*," I muttered again, kicking wildly.

This wasn't the glorious Angellight I commanded. This was the hissing thing that had launched itself at Jezebel earlier.

And with a burst rivaling a shattering star, light exploded between my clenched fingers. Gold, effervescent, and *burning*. It was reckless and uncontrollable, coiling fear through my gut.

The dead screeched, an echo that would haunt me for all eternity, but its hold slackened.

I fell back to my feet, hunching over my knees, and gulped down air. My ears rang with a dull buzz. Damien's emblem scorched my skin, but I pulled the heat into my bones and let its healing properties repair whatever was damaged in my throat.

As my vision adjusted once again to the dim tunnel, I froze at the sight before me. The rotting corpse of the warrior was nothing but a pile of ash.

The presence it had carried was gone, as dead as any resting spirit should be.

After a few moments, the world stopped spinning and the ringing faded from my ears, only to be replaced by the clash of metal against stone. Through the dust of the crumbling wall, in the dark chamber at the end of the tunnel, Lancaster, Mora, and Santorina rotated around a second corpse warrior.

Unsheathing Starfire, I ran toward them, hurtling over chunks of rock. In the damp, death-filled air, my sword sang.

This one was different than the one I'd fought. Where that had been precise, using strength gathered within ancient bones to pin me to the wall, this one was wily. It swung a claw-nailed hand at Santorina's face—scraped across her cheek—before pivoting quickly to pounce on Mora.

The fae female struck, swiping one of her shining blades toward its neck. But the creature slyly dodged, much nimbler than the dead should be. Instead of decapitating it, Mora severed a chuck of dead flesh and bone from the warrior's neck.

Lancaster shouted to his sister to turn, to dodge, but it was too late. In a slow, calculated movement, the creature swiveled its head toward Mora. It lunged forward, and—

"No!" I gasped.

The corpse sank it's cracked and rotting teeth into the female's shoulder, through leathers and skin. Mora shrieked as the pair tumbled into the wall.

Lancaster launched himself at the dead with the force of an Angel. Mora, wrestling with the warrior atop her, gritted her teeth in a snarl. The corpse was wild, a being who—when living—had likely been untamed. One who lusted after blood and warfare. And now, in death, it appeared those traits had festered. Or maybe it had been locked up for so long, instinct had taken over.

Lancaster gripped the hungry one with a brutal force I'd never seen of fae or warrior. "I'm sorry!" he roared to his sister.

Then, he ripped the corpse off her.

And a chunk of flesh went with him, Mora's tunic quickly soaking crimson as she cried out. Lancaster went after the corpse without remorse, dismembering him. One finger at a time.

Santorina scurried around us, crouching beside the female. With Lancaster, I circled the predator. Those jaws still snapped, now coated with Mora's blood. And each gleaming drop of crimson that flew was another strike against the dead warrior's existence.

"Magic, Mystique!" Lancaster demanded.

"I don't know how!" I argued.

"You just did!"

I gripped Starfire tighter. "I don't know what I did. It can hurt you all!"

"I command—"

But I was not taking another demand from him tonight.

Before Lancaster could finish speaking, I clung to my last flimsy hope, and I struck with steel.

Starfire sliced clean through what was left of the corpse's neck. Head and body toppled to the ground in opposite directions, and finally, the dead stilled.

"Decapitation," Lancaster contemplated as we approached the body. "That's what happened to the other one?"

"No," I breathed. "But it's something even the mountains can't fix." I turned away from the corpse and shoved Lancaster in the chest—hard.

"What in Aoiflyn's—"

"You do *not* command me during a battle again! *Never* pull the bargain when it could get others hurt!"

"It didn't," he argued, canines flashing.

"But it could have! And you're damn lucky it didn't backfire because my one stipulation was that anything you demand of me cannot harm anyone I care for." I backed down a step, glaring. "If it had—you'd be dead right now, fae."

"Perhaps if you actually learned what power lies within you, I wouldn't have to be your excuse for using it." And with that, Lancaster spun away, hastening for his sister.

I took one breath to steady myself, looking down at the beheaded corpse, and remembered the feeling of my agency being ripped from me with that bargain. Distasteful and wrong.

I didn't want to feel that way again.

The body twitched once more, then laid still. An unexpected silence weighed the air as his screeches faded, the pressure of the ancient secrets of the catacombs a viable force beating upon our skin.

The lack of a presence that had long resided here.

Raising my sword, I sliced through the body a few more times for good measure. Then, suppressing a shiver, I returned to the group.

Mora's face was ashen, eyes flat. Lancaster stood shirtless, his broad chest on display as he ripped off the layer of soft, thin tunic he'd worn beneath his leathers and gave it to Santorina to clean up Mora's wound.

"We need to get you out of here," I said.

"We need to get your damn emblem," Mora growled, trying to push to her feet with Santorina's hands supporting her. Her knees nearly buckled.

I swung her good arm around my shoulder as Rina said, "You

can't keep going." She looked between Lancaster and me. "Nothing I do is helping it. I'll have to work on her back at the inn."

Lancaster's jaw ticked.

"You two head back," I said.

But Mora gritted out, "I don't have a choice." Her words were grave. In her pallid face, anger burned. She panted, "Ritalia has sworn us to help you."

She couldn't get out more words, but I understood. If she or Lancaster abandoned me, despite me pushing them to turn back, Ritalia had some sort of bargain threatening them. The fae would die trying to do this.

It sparked the question again of why? Why did their queen want these tokens so badly when only I could wield them? Why did she think I'd ever hand precious shards of magic over so easily, and why was she willing to risk two of her strongest guards for the mission?

I swallowed back all those fears, because there was nothing we could do about them now. I wasn't leaving these catacombs without that emblem.

Lancaster assessed his sister's shoulder. "Even my magic can't heal this entirely."

Leaning closer, my stomach turned at the deep, bloody hole where a chunk of flesh had been torn out. Crimson gleamed across her skin, but what was worse was the way her veins shone pale and blue beneath the sticky mess. And either my vision was still adjusting after nearly being choked, or the lines were ebbing. Like something swam within.

Still, Lancaster did his best to staunch the bleeding. He and Santorina used the remaining strips of his tunic to fashion a makeshift sling while I supported the female.

"This is going to take a long time to heal. Once we're safely out of here, Mora, I promise, I'll do it." Lancaster's eyes shone with a deep intensity as he swore to his sister.

"I can't die," she said with mock humor. "She won't let me."

I wasn't sure what she meant, but Lancaster growled, "There are worse fates than death."

As he said it, a clatter of metal, like weapons swinging on belts, rang down the tunnel. Slowly, fear thick in the air, we all pivoted.

"Mystique," Lancaster said, voice chilled.

"Yeah?" Starfire was in one hand. Angelborn in the other.

"I think now is when we run."

CHAPTER TWENTY-NINE
VALE

BLOOD POURED ACROSS MY HAND, STAINED MY DRESS. The blood of a man I once thought my father, my savior.

The blood of the man who had become my captor.

Everyone in the room stopped moving as I sank my dagger deeper into Titus's throat. As I rotated the weapon, the second blade pierced his skin and sliced diagonally across his neck.

Titus gargled on his blood, the choking bouncing off the walls. I shoved him forward, and he collapsed into the crimson puddle, looking up at me from his back.

Malakai stared at me with his eyelids drooping, trying to lift himself off the ground but his hands slipped in his blood, an awed look on his half-conscious face. The woman I didn't know who had helped pry me from my session stood resolute at my side.

I stared down at Titus. It was odd, how he seemed so small now. So...powerless after holding my leash for so many years.

And I stood above him, holding the power of endless Fates in the palm of my hands.

And as I panted over the body of my impounder, a deep, roaring satisfaction spread along my bones. The Fates sang within me, all of their ruthless hearts cheering for the death of the man who had ruined me.

My chest seized, an ache budding in my shoulder, but all I could focus on was the revenge simmering within me as Titus bled out. Crimson stained the hem of my gown; his stare burned with betrayal.

I did it, I nearly sighed in disbelief, clutching the item in my hand to my chest. I had written the downfall of Titus. After years of isolation and manipulation, months of abandonment and torment, I had become his breaker.

It was only when his eyes stopped searching and limbs ceased twitching that I gasped.

The small inhale was loud in the seeing chamber—or perhaps that was merely the echo in my ears.

The echo that turned into a roar of starfire.

And then, I was screaming, a long keen echoing with the power of my Fate ties.

Something inside of me was shredding.

It wasn't the pain of a knife wound or the discordant readings. It wasn't the ache of all those times Cypherion pushed me away and I let him go.

This was something much more intrinsic, like roots were wrapped around my heart, and they were being grossly ripped from my spirit. A wrenching, world-shattering type of pain that began in my shoulder and spread through my entire body.

My careening cries fractured everyone else's stillness, and they sprang into action. Weapons clashed and fresh blood poured. I collapsed, bones crashing to the cold marble.

The same gentle hands that had roused me moments ago were on either side of my face, swiping away the tears and calmly asking me what was wrong.

But I couldn't find the words for the vacancy in my soul.

Chapter Thirty
Ophelia

Lancaster picked up his sister and charged deeper into the chamber.

"Go!" I said to Rina, pushing her in front of me. She had a dagger in each hand, more strapped to her person.

I took off after her, diving into the abyss beyond the corridor. My breath sawed through my chest as I skidded through the darkness. I cast one glance over my shoulder—afforded only one second —and a wave of deadly soldiers met it.

Ten at the most, but they charged as fast as any living warrior. All in that same state of decay, all with dust swirling around them. Crumbs of stone fell from their tattered clothing as if they'd burst from the walls in some other part of the catacombs.

They screeched as their brethren had. Hollow, aching, wanting sounds that wrenched through me.

I sped into the dark.

Mystlight flared to life as we ran through the heart of the catacombs. Rows upon rows of wooden shelves stretched through the long cavern, ceilings low and rimmed with weakly fluttering sconces.

Artifacts laid scattered about their surfaces, bones trimming the base of the walls.

"Gods be damned," Santorina called. "Any of these could be the emblem."

I scoured the shelves as we ducked between aisles. Ahead, Lancaster fought to get his injured sister away, winding through the rows and finally setting her down to lean against the wall.

"It's not any of these," I called back to Rina over the howls and growls of the dead. Something beat beneath my skin. Greater than only my second pulse.

The dead were getting closer, their rattling breaths slinking around the chamber.

Lancaster hurtled past Rina and me, into the center aisle. He didn't look at me as he asked, "Can you find it?"

There was a tug in my gut, that beat solidifying into a steady, demanding pulse. "Yes!" I yelled.

In answer, he summoned a long sword—one of the largest and most ostentatious I'd ever seen—out of thin air and faced the corpses flooding the main aisle.

"Go with her." Lancaster nodded at Rina. He took a few steps forward, positioning himself firmly between where his sister was crouched and the enemy.

"You can't face all of them on your own!" As Rina said it, the first dead warrior reached Lancaster with a bumbling, childlike run, and the fae sliced clean through its neck.

"Want to say that again?" Lancaster asked, fury limning his body as he kicked aside the crumbling corpse. "You're more help to her. The quicker we find that emblem, the quicker we can get my sister help."

"Come on." I tugged Rina up the aisle toward the head of the cavern.

Lancaster stood as a wall against the catacombs' defense. But—

The dead didn't storm toward him as the hive-minded horde we'd expected.

"Shit," Lancaster muttered, bracing himself.

Splitting down the rows, the corpses wound with the uniform actions of a group who had practiced this routine many times, shrieking as they pursued all four of us.

They were a team trained to defend this place and what it contained.

Mora fired off daggers with her good arm—grunting in pain

with each—but all they did was slow down the creatures, cause them to stumble. It wasn't enough to kill them.

I skidded to a stop. Rina gripped my arm, trying to push me ahead, to force me after the emblem.

"We have to take care of them first!" I snapped, magic bubbling to the surface of my skin, rebelling against its cage.

A corpse leapt from the nearest aisle, raising a rusted old sword preserved about as well as its body toward Rina's back.

"Move!" I shouted.

Rina dodged to the right, and without thinking, I blasted a burst of hungry magic at the corpse, withering it to ash along with the ancient blade.

"Holy gods," Rina swore.

"Nope," I panted. "Just me." And I dove at the next corpse. Our blades met repeatedly between us as it cornered me down the aisle.

Rina slashed at another, letting it close enough to grab her before she sank a blade through where its eye would have been. Its screech was silent as she dragged a larger knife through its throat, severing right down to the bone so the creature collapsed before her.

"Smart tactic, Bounty," Lancaster called.

"I'm not—" Rina's words cut off in a gasp, and I whirled, dodging my opponent.

Lancaster was hunched over, a wooden staff protruding from his side. Blood oozed around it, the fae barely able to stand.

With some immortal and almighty will—or perhaps merely sheer determination—he lifted his sword with one hand, the other pressed to his side. And the male sliced through the neck of the warrior grinning a yellowed smile down at him.

Then, Lancaster toppled into a shelf, sending silvered artifacts clanging to the stone floor. With a sharp inhale, he wrenched the staff from his side. It wasn't jammed deep, not even an inch coated in blood. Not enough that he should be so weak and pale.

"It's made from a cypher," he wheezed. "There are splinters..."

I shook my head, walking backward as the creatures closed in from the side rows. They pressed forward, segmenting me off from my friends. "What does that mean?"

"It means I can't heal it. And I can't access my magic."

The cyphers. The trees we'd thought were nothing more than magic conduits across Gallantia but were actually gifted to repel fae spirits. In more ways than one.

"Rina, help him! Get to Mora, both of you!" I called. And I braced myself with Starfire and Angelborn. At least if I didn't have friends fighting beside me, I could ground myself with the weapons that were extensions of my body.

The corpses rushed in from all sides. And my pulses pounded, pounded, pounded. Warred with me to run elsewhere.

One jumped at my left, and as I spun to meet it, another tugged my foot out from under me. I went crashing to the ground, my cheek scraping against rock and teeth slicing into my lip.

I flipped over, the tang of blood sharp in my mouth, and tried to scramble back, but the warrior loomed closer. I tightened my grip on Starfire and Angelborn. No way in the Spirit Realm I'd let them go.

This corpse hovered above me, seeming even older and more aware than the others. It assessed me with a vacant stare, seeing Angels knew what within my spirit. I adjusted my grip on Angelborn, waiting for my opening.

But the dead surged, lifting his foot in an unnaturally quick motion, and stomped on my ankle.

And even through the thick leather of my boots, something cracked. A cry ripped from my throat, but I bit it back, refusing to show him pain to widen that horrifying smile.

The shadows of the other corpses shifted, surrounding me.

Predatory magic called within my blood. It wanted out, wanted to feast on the bones of these corpses.

Use me, it begged.

"*No*," I gritted out, forcing it back.

It was too risky to use—too explosive.

I clenched Angelborn tighter. If this one got a step closer—

"Alabath!" The last voice I expected to hear called through the void of the distant tunnel, and my heart leapt.

"Vincienzo!" I yelled over the pain in my ankle. "Get out of here!"

The corpse closed in on me overhead, long, gangly limbs flopping almost puppet-like.

Tolek emerged from the darkness, the dead forming a wall between us. His eyes widened as he beheld what was happening. I could hear his wrathful growl as he captured the surprised dead's arms and wrenched them behind his back until his decaying shoulders popped, and he kicked it in the spine.

Tolek threw the warrior to the floor. "Not a fucking chance."

"Decapitate it!" I shrieked, and he followed the order.

Panting over the pain of my ankle, I swung my own sword, forcing the others back. Tolek helped me to my feet, my step buckling.

"Injury?" he asked, standing in front of me with his sword up.

I tried to take a step and hissed. "Likely broken."

I didn't have time to pause to use Angellight to heal it fully. Couldn't wait for the mountains to set it.

I willed a quick flash of Damien's light through my veins, straight from the emblem around my neck. Only enough to soothe the ache. It was sloppy, didn't quite work right, but between that and the adrenaline coursing through my body, I grabbed Tolek's hand and pulled him into a limping run.

"Let me carry you," he demanded.

"We both need our hands to fight, Tol." It sounded more like a plea than anything—something within me calling out for help as the four remaining warriors pursued us.

Only four, though.

We'd taken out more than half.

As I stumbled over my wrecked ankle, I thought we stood a chance.

And despite the shrieks of the dead and the tang of fae blood coating the air, despite the fact that he was a reckless fool for charging in here, gratitude for the man beside me unspooled like soothing Angellight in my chest.

Tolek Vincienzo always came to my rescue.

At the end of the aisle, the cavern opened into a circular chamber, ceiling draping low over a dais in the center and mirrors surrounding us. Though we were far below ground, a window was carved into the overhang.

"That has to be it," I gasped. A silver box sat atop a metal stand, mystlight blaring down on it.

"Wait!" Tol said, whirling around with his sword raised, but I was already moving. He had to fight four against one—

No, two.

Because Santorina was speeding up the aisle after them, daggers in her hands and vengeance in her eyes. Right as she leapt on a corpse from behind, I jumped onto the platform, landing on my good foot and sheathing my weapons.

"Ophelia, don't—"

"What?" I called to Tolek.

My pulses pounded. That tug in my gut persisted.

There was no latch on the box. It was made of mirrored glass with unblemished silver trim. As I leaned over it, my necklace swung into view in the reflection, and a flare of heat raced through me.

Maybe it wasn't a lock to be picked. Maybe it answered to magic.

Blades clashed behind me, mingling with Tolek's and Santorina's curses as they fought the dead.

My hands shook, but I gripped the pedestal. For them, I'd do this.

Carefully, so carefully, I pulled a thread of tethered Angel power from my veins. The one I trusted and knew. I tried to control it, to summon only the strand connected to Damien and press it against the box.

Nothing.

But I didn't dare draw up more. Not with its erratic state.

"It's not opening!" I shouted.

"Can you grab"—Rina sliced at a warrior—"the whole thing?"

Swiping Starfire up, I limped off the dais, landing beside her. "It's welded to the stand."

"That's part of why I came here," Tolek panted, dodging a close blow. "I realized a mistake in the translation. This emblem—

for whatever reason—the chosen can't take. It'll harm you, Ophelia."

"*What?*" I gasped. In my shock, my attacker got a step closer.

"It's why Ptholenix and Xenique were mentioned so frequently in the races. We got the translation wrong. It didn't say the dead *rest* here, but rise. And the chosen is meant to fight them while another retrieves the emblem."

We'd mistranslated. It was an easy mistake to make with an ancient language.

I caught my corpse's strike with Starfire. "Someone else—"

"You get them in, they grab it. A friend, Ophelia," he gritted out. "It's all about friendship and how necessary it is to survival. The damn Angels are trying to preach to us now, too." His arms strained as he held back a dead warrior. "How are you so fucking strong? Are you training in the damn afterlife?"

My mind whirled.

"Rina?" I clenched my teeth, trying to balance my weight on my good leg and still fight.

But she was already up those steps. Already had a hand on each side of the mirrored box. And before I could take another breath she cracked the seamless lid, and—

Santorina swore. "It's empty!"

"By the fucking Spirits," Tolek cursed as he took out another corpse.

"What do you mean?" I yelled.

"There's nothing here, Ophelia."

"But I could feel it. My blood—"

But that pulsing sensation in my veins wasn't tugging toward the box at all. It wasn't the beat of a nearby emblem as I'd thought.

No, that second pulse was lurching toward the remaining dead warriors.

"I can't..." I mumbled.

"What?" Tolek asked.

"My power. It wants...it wants to be used."

They were pressing in. Closer, closer, closer. Tolek and I were both so worn, so injured. Somewhere, Lancaster and Mora might be bleeding out. Blood trickled down Santorina's cheek, her human healing not nearly as quick as ours.

For them, I would do what scared me.

"Stay behind me," I said.

And without another thought, I answered the call in my gut. I tugged not at the five threads tangled through my soul, but at the thing unnamed. With the strength of the Mystique Angel himself, I lashed it out across the chamber like a violent snake striking.

The dead screeched as their brethren had.

As the magic tore from me, it searched. *What do you seek?*

It was full of possibility, full of life. But it couldn't find whatever it hungered for.

Instead, it wrapped around the remaining corpses. And beneath my light, they burned and howled. Bones charred to nothing but ash.

My magic writhed through the air, longing for more, more, more. Begging to consume.

You cannot have anyone else.

It tried to tug me forward, to take and gnaw, breathe and expand.

In my mind, I pictured myself back on that plane Jezebel and I had traversed, where we stood among the power of myths. I cupped a steady hand around the magic and absorbed it back into my vacant spirit.

It rioted against me, but drop by drop, the waves of gold cascaded into me. As they did, my mind flickered between here and elsewhere. Somewhere with a misty plane and gray-coated skies, another land of grand, sweeping mountains that kissed the clouds.

My knees buckled, wounded ankle barking, and Tolek caught me around the waist. Silence screamed in the wake of the dead, my panting breaths and rioting heart fighting it. Greedily, I leaned into Tol's grounding warmth and fought to remember what was going on. To remain here.

"I don't...it's not here," I muttered. Even to my own ears, the defeat in my voice was crushing. "The emblem. It was all for nothing."

"Let's get out of here," Tolek said, scooping me up. "We'll figure it out later."

We found Lancaster and Mora nursing their injuries and the five of us made our way back to the entrance of the catacombs in wounded silence. Heavy with the scent of jasmine, the night breeze winding through the air was a welcome relief to the crushing stench of decay below.

"Just a second," I said as we reached the archway atop the stairs.

I gazed up at that stone curve and the fading Endasi atop it.

Something squirmed within me, the power that had been fed wanting more. And perhaps it was unwise, perhaps it was reckless, but I wrenched up those strings of soul from the emblems.

And with the power of Angels, I lashed light down the stairwell, whipping it sharply against the stone walls.

Ancient rock caved in with the cataclysmic force, echoing down the descent and sealing the way into the catacombs.

Then, we left the dead to rest.

Chapter Thirty-One
Malakai

The chamber erupted as Titus stilled, drowning out Vale's shrieks.

Starsearchers charged to their fallen chancellor's defense; the room became a mess of clanging weapons and my blood beneath my hands and knees.

My blood...fuck. It was so warm down my exposed back, my gloves were sticky with it.

And the scars that had been ripped open burned.

Mila flipped her guard over her shoulder and slammed the woman into the floor effortlessly. With the Starsearcher's own dagger, Mila impaled her through the throat. Fucking incredible.

Then, she was ripping her twin swords from the guard, and she got to work on the other opponents.

Heal, I wanted to scream at my wounds. I needed to get up. I needed to help.

I breathed heavily, each inhale painful as my ribs expanded. It hadn't hurt this badly last time. Maybe because I'd given up, then.

Now I was desperate to help. I focused on the way crimson was smeared across the ivory floors, marring the reflection of the Fates in the dome's glass, something oddly poetic about the seeing chamber resulting in so much death.

As the pain in my back became a steady ache, I assessed the fighting through swirling vision. Dax and Barrett had weapons now, too. Harlen, stumbling and face contorted in pain, had his chain wrapped around the throat of a warrior. There were maybe eight of them in Starsearcher garb.

Too many...

There were too many.

Vale was still collapsed on the floor, biting back cries of pain. Celissia crouched beside her, whispering to the Starsearcher and pressing her hands over Vale's shoulder, as if that would absolve the ache.

With tears streaming from her hollow eyes, Vale nodded at Celissia. One hand still clutched something to her chest, but with the other, she ripped a dagger from Celissia's waist. The Starsearcher grunted, launching it at an approaching guard. It landed squarely in his eye.

Celissia pulled a hatchet from her belt and joined, skillfully beating back a Starsearcher guard while keeping one eye on Vale.

Vale, who poured every ounce of desperation—of rightful vengeance and tormented tears—into crawling toward that guard's body. Into relieving him of his other triple blades and fighting as fiercely as anyone.

Because she had a reason to fight, too.

The open wounds across my back stung as I stumbled upright, feet slipping in my blood. There was so much of it, my stomach turned. I wasn't used to seeing it in such bright light. My cavern prison had been a blessing in one way, I supposed.

The warrior who had been seeing to me was fighting Mila now. In a flash of steel, they danced about the room. There was no way I could lift a sword or throw a dagger, but...the chains hanging from my wrists clanked together. My vision swam, and an idea took shape.

Tightening my grip around the chain, I waited to catch Mila's eye—

There it was.

A flash of a glance, not enough to lose her opponent, but enough to check on me. And see that while blood dripped down my back, I stood.

Her eyes swept over my hands, and she understood my plan. I crouched down.

Back, back, back she drove that Starsearcher.

I couldn't lift my arms, not enough to wrap my chain around his throat. But I could—

With a stumbling step, the warrior's ankle met the iron. I bit my cheek to keep from screaming at the pain driving through my body, and he crashed backward to the floor with a cry that cut off in an echoing thud.

Mila crouched before me, hands on my face, knees in my blood. The others continued to fight, but she was here. I nearly collapsed at the relief.

"It'll heal quickly," she said, voice wavering as she reassured both of us. "It'll heal, Malakai." She pressed her forehead to mine, hands shaking against my cheeks. "I'm going to get you out of here. You saved me before... I'm going to save you now."

I saved her?

I tried to ask what she meant, but I moved too quickly and a bolt of pain went through my back.

It didn't hurt as badly as it should. Not when I could see she was safe. But even opening my eyes was hard. So much blood was on the floor. My head swam.

I had no concept of time as the fighting silenced. I didn't try to count the seconds. Just tried not to move too much with each rasping breath.

"Malakai," Mila said softly.

Everything hurt, that last effort to stand draining all the adrenaline keeping me upright. My back was flayed open, raw skin sticky and throbbing.

"Mila," I muttered, keeping my eyes closed.

"Yeah?" she asked shakily, and I forced my eyes open. Looked into her watery, ice-blue ones. So fucking beautiful, even with the tears. If she was the last thing I saw before dying, I would go happily. One day, perhaps...but I wasn't done living with her yet.

I croaked, "We have to look up, right?"

Mila bit back a sob, tears tracking down her cheeks. "Look up, Warrior Prince."

"Is he okay?" Barrett's voice was close and piqued with panic. Everyone had to be alright if he was checking on me.

"We need to get out of here." That was Celissia.

"Malakai, we can't carry you," Barrett said. Spirits, they couldn't even put their arms around me for support without my back screaming.

"I can walk," I wheezed. "Help."

Barrett and Mila helped me out of the rest of my torn leathers so the fabric wouldn't brush the wounds. Then, they stood on either side of me as I ever-so-slowly rose, holding each of my arms, bracing steadying hands against my ribs, but not daring to move any closer.

I draped my arms across their shoulders, hissing at the pain of lifting them even that much. Every shift sent daggers through my back.

Dax was carrying Vale, who looked on the brink of unconsciousness. One hand gripped her shoulder, the other clenched to her chest. Whatever that tattoo severing had done to her was drastic.

"Aren't you coming?" Celissia asked, her curious stare on Harlen.

He shook his head. Three of the Starsearcher guards stood behind him, three who had fought with us. That small reminder that there was good in this manor unwound a knot in my chest and made me grateful I stood for my friends so they could remain unharmed alongside that good.

"I'll take care of this," Harlen said, waving a hand at Titus's prone body. "You all get somewhere safe."

"Thank you," I slurred as we slowly fled.

And Vale mumbled a faint, "You're a good friend, Harlen."

CHAPTER THIRTY-TWO
OPHELIA

"LOOKS LIKE IT ISN'T BROKEN AND IT SET WELL," RINA said, gentle fingers assessing my wounded ankle. She fluttered hastily about the dining room of the inn, barely taking time to stop before any of us.

She'd gotten Lancaster seated atop a table in the back corner, Mora laying on two pushed together beside him. The male, his shirt off and wound ghastly in his side, tracked his sister's every breath as she tried to hide the pain lancing through her shoulder.

Knee bouncing impatiently, Cypherion sat before the dining room's lone window, my sister, Erista, and Lyria attempting to distract him as he nervously awaited Malakai's party's return—with Vale, hopefully.

Thanks to Tolek tossing me on his horse with him, I was able to use my Angellight to heal my injured ankle almost all the way as we rode back to the inn, despite the rapid pace we kept to get the others back quickly.

I wasn't quite sure how the magic worked, but I tucked away the knowledge that it could both heal an injury—which I'd learned before—and singe the dead. That one sent a chill down to my bones not even Angellight could warm.

I grabbed Rina's hand as she flitted by, and her gaze snapped to me. "Thank you," I said. "How can I help?"

She pursed her lips, evaluating her two patients. "I need to get the splinters out of Lancaster's wound." She dropped her voice, frustration burning in her narrowed stare. "Mora's is worse, though. It's...it's nothing I've ever seen."

"Show me," I said.

With Tolek bracing me, I limped over my sore ankle, stopping before the fae.

Rina spoke with calm authority. "The blood isn't clotting. But it's running more...congealed than it should." She dropped her voice. "It's almost like poison was in that bite."

The fae female tried to suppress a shiver. "It's fine." A sheen of sweat gleamed on her forehead, her skin gray.

"Mora," Rina said softly, nervously, "I'm going to try to put together a tonic for you, but I may need to get more supplies."

Through slitted eyes, Mora tossed a glance her brother's way. "Fix him first."

"No," he argued. "You're much worse."

"Fix him"—she inhaled sharply—"then he can use his magic to keep me stable while you figure out a remedy."

Rina sighed, looking to Lancaster. "She has a point."

"Fine," Lancaster grumbled. "Be quick."

"I'll be as quick as I can," Santorina assured with as little bite as possible as she gathered supplies.

I evaluated the ebbing veins through Mora's shoulder, how they pressed against her skin with a sentience rarely seen.

"Those corpses seemed as if they were enchanted by something," I muttered to Tolek, not bothering to drop my voice since Mora would hear regardless. Damn fae senses.

"Valyrie must have charmed them to guard the power she left behind," Tol said. "Until the chosen arrived and fought through that twisted version of the races. The physical duels. The metaphorical poison if you grabbed the emblem yourself. The defense of the Angel."

I blew out a breath. It *had* all been right there, every stage, but not in a way we could have expected. "How did Annellius do all of this?"

"Perhaps he wasn't alone," he offered.

But Vale had seen him in one of her readings, on his knees and begging. Very much isolated. Which meant those who had helped him hadn't survived.

The wound on Mora's shoulder beat.

I didn't want to do it. I didn't *trust it*. But the fate of what might happen if I remained complacent flashed before my eyes. This horrid bite of the dead could infect Mora, her queen's bargain tethering her to life until it tore her apart, her spirit remaining restless in our land.

Though I still did not want to hand the emblems over to the fae, I couldn't allow Mora to suffer.

"Can I try something?" I asked.

Her eyes were closed, but without even asking what, she nodded. Whether it was implicit trust or the verge of unconsciousness, I wasn't sure.

Carefully, slowly, I called up Damien's strand of Angellight— the one I was the most connected to. It pooled in the air before me as I watched the shimmering layer of gold with a steady focus. Tolek and Lancaster did, too, the latter guarded.

This magic had healed me—but the untamed side of it had also destroyed. As I directed golden light toward Mora, I prayed to the Angel it stemmed from that it would behave.

It hesitated at first—as if something *more* than a lingering Angel charm infected the fae's skin—and sniffed around the wound like an unsure pup. Then, it soared into her.

Mora gasped.

"I'm sorry!" I rushed out.

"Knock it off, Mystique!" Lancaster roared as Rina scolded him for moving.

But Mora gritted out one word: "*No.*"

The gold trickled around her wound, wrapping it like a sheer bandage. But through that sheen, tendrils were visible. Little offshoots winding through her veins, targeting whatever taint festered there.

I didn't understand how it was working—it was only my will controlling it—but I asked, "It's helping?"

Mora's brow relaxed. "A bit."

I didn't know how long we stood there. Cypherion paced the

room, checking on us every so often and demanding we recount our tale. Jezebel, Erista, and Lyria pressed for details. Rina worked on Lancaster, claiming there were hundreds of impossibly small shards of cypher in his wound, and I worked on Mora.

Until the door to the dining room flew open, and we all braced ourselves. In my mind, the shrieks of the dead echoed.

But it was Dax's broad shouldered-form that filled the frame. And in his arms—

"Cypherion?" the Engrossian General shouted, Vale curled against his chest and Celissia walked at his side.

Cyph, striding swiftly around the tables hosting the fae, was in front of Dax in a moment. "Vale?" His eyes snapped up to Dax and Celissia. "What happened to her?"

Behind them, Mila and Barrett pushed through the door before the Engrossians could answer.

"By the fucking Spirits," Tolek cursed, and we both raced forward—Mora assuring us she was okay to rest now—to where Malakai's arms draped around their shoulders. The reek of blood stung the air, and Malakai could barely stand.

Tol reached to help support him but Barrett snapped, "Don't touch his back."

"His back?" I asked, scampering around Mila. And I gasped. Tolek swore viciously.

"It's not that bad, Tol," Malakai slurred, attempting to lift his head, but it only bobbed back down. His entire body winced. "Not like before."

Before.

Rage roared through me as I took in the torn, ragged flesh. That's what Malakai's back had become. The scars from his imprisonment were shredded, and three large lashes ripped the surface, turning his back into a cross work of bloody, gleaming skin.

I never saw Malakai's wounds this fresh—when I'd found him in the cave nearly a year ago, everything had been healed. I'd witnessed plenty of ghastly injuries in my life, but nothing like this.

Nothing that gave a new life to the wrath beneath my skin.

But with it, nausea swept through me. How had tonight gone

so wrong? How had so much blood been spilled? And all for these emblems we didn't even understand—one we didn't even find. For the Angels who seemed to think us their puppets.

"What the fuck happened?" I growled.

"Titus happened," Mila ground out.

Santorina was already preparing a table for Malakai, laying down towels. "Put him here."

But Mila swept the scene. "I can take him," she offered. At Rina's nervous look she added, "I dealt with worse during the first war."

Santorina wrung her hands. "Okay. Take whatever you need." She nodded to the bar, strewn with her supplies.

"Thank you," Mila said, a sigh of relief floating through her words. "Barrett? Tolek?"

Together, they helped a barely conscious Malakai through the dining room and up the stairs. I wasn't sure how they managed to get him all this way, but I was grateful they had.

"Cypherion?" Vale stirred, voice timid. We whirled to face her —now in Cyph's arms—as her eyes blinked open slowly. "It hurts."

"What hurts, Stargirl?"

"My soul," she whimpered. My heart squeezed in my chest. "Like a piece was cleaved off."

Cypherion's brows pulled together. His gaze drifted across Vale, down the powder blue chiffon gown draped gracefully around her, and that was when I saw them, too. The crimson stains.

Rage darkened Cyph's voice. "What happened?"

"It's not her blood," Celissia answered. "It's Titus's."

My breath left me in a *whoosh*. "Titus?" I asked. Cyph looked between Vale and the Engrossians as if reluctant to take his eyes off her.

Dax's lips pressed into a line, and he mouthed, "She killed him."

The whole room fell silent.

Vale had murdered a chancellor—*her* chancellor. Another gone. I looked up at Tolek as he reentered the room, eyes hard.

Worried. Jezebel, Erista, and Santorina—even the fae—were all still, as if the heaviness of this new threat weighed on everyone.

With Titus dead, who would come for us? What punishment waited?

But Vale shuddered into Cyph's arms, whispering again in a voice so broken, "It hurts."

Her soul, she'd said. Her soul hurt. And Titus had died.

It wasn't a physical injury, nor was it sadness. It was something deep within Vale that ached, that felt like a piece had been sliced off, because the chancellor had bound them on a soul level through the tattoo on her shoulder.

And to kill him was the only way to sever that oath. The result...something irreparable torn within her.

Reluctantly, my eyes dropped to my own tattoo, the ink beating an ominous tune on my arm. And then my gaze lifted to the ceiling, as if I could see Malakai's matching North Star resting in that bed above.

A warm hand rubbed my shoulder, and I swallowed thickly at Tolek's comfort, shoving down the fear writhing within me. The fear this entire night planted.

"Vale," I said softly, limping toward her and Cypherion, "do you need a healer for anything?"

Her head rolled to the side. The tear tracks on her cheeks glistened in the mystlight. "Ophelia," she muttered. "I have something for you."

"For me?"

With tremendous effort, she lifted the hand clutched to her chest. I stepped closer, palm outstretched.

And she tipped her hand toward mine, an abstract gemstone tumbling between us. It glinted an array of deep sapphires with iridescent rainbows in the light.

Instantly, my skinned burned in welcome. A slice of something both familiar and foreign slid into place in the gaps within my spirit.

Based on the jagged bit of gold on the bottom, it might have been ripped from a setting in a necklace, or maybe a statue. And though I had no clue how Vale had found it, I knew exactly what it was.

"Valyrie's heart," I muttered, awe coating my words. Blistering heat spread through my palm, up my arm, soaking away a bit of the fearful chill that had claimed me.

"The Fated Lovers," Vale exhaled.

As she said it, I looked closer. The crystal wasn't an abstract form. It did appear to be taken from something, and it was worn with age, but it almost looked like two individuals wrapped around one another.

Turning back toward Cypherion and letting her eyes fall closed again, Vale breathed, "I hope you didn't go to the catacombs. I tried to write to tell you I had it, but Titus found out. Spied on me and Harlen. Think that's how he put together what he was planning. I'm sorry."

Her words were thick with sleep, so I didn't bother to tell her we *had* gone to the catacombs. That it had been an utter disaster and a pointless mission. Based on the warning in her slurred words, it seemed she knew what waited down there.

I didn't ask her now, though.

Instead, I said, "Don't be sorry about anything, Vale. Thank you." I curled my fingers around the emblem. "Thank you for getting this for us. Perhaps later, you can tell me how you managed it."

She nodded, those silent tears still slipping down her cheeks.

"We're so happy you're back. Why don't you take her upstairs, Cyph?" I offered.

Vale didn't need a healer. No one but time and perhaps the man who held her could mend the wound to her soul.

Cypherion nodded. "Let's go, Stargirl."

As they left, Barrett came back downstairs with a list of things Mila requested. Malakai's blood was smeared across his clothes, dampening the dark fabric. Lyria helped him, disappearing upstairs, arms laden with shredded stretches of linen, a bowl of water, and whatever ointments Rina recommended for later.

Celissia turned to Santorina, her eggplant-colored gown torn around the hem. "Can I help with anything?"

"What do you know of healing?" Rina asked, not unkindly.

The Engrossian queen-to-be fidgeted with the hatchet at her waist. "My family has a rich healing practice. I've inherited much and studied at our citadel."

It wasn't the magic of the Bodymelders or the fae, but it was expertise. Santorina visibly sagged at the offer. "I'd love help monitoring Mora." Celissia nodded, following Rina's muttered directions in the corner of the room.

My head swam, but I clenched my eyes for a moment and fought to hold it all together. Mora, Lancaster, Malakai. Vale —Titus.

Another dead chancellor. Another possibly fractured alliance. Wounded warriors and fae in my own team, new scars on our souls to recover from. And a mounting burst of power within my own veins that I didn't know how to trust.

After a deep breath, I turned to Dax. "What happened?"

He recounted how the Engrossian dinner with Titus had been interrupted when the chancellor learned Malakai and Mila had infiltrated his manor. That they were *escorted* by Starsearcher guards to a seeing chamber. That they didn't know exactly what had happened to Vale before, but she'd been seemingly unconscious upon the floor, and Celissia had woken her while everyone else was distracted.

"He did what?" I asked, voice barely more than a whisper, when Dax got to the part where Malakai had volunteered to take the punishment for the others. The air in my lungs compressed, so much pressure squeezing and trying to pop them.

He'd been tortured for two years. He'd been whipped and burned and taunted. And yet, when the people he loved were shoved to the end of that leather strap, he kneeled before it. Bile stung the back of my throat at the thought.

There had been so much blood on him. So much lost.

"We need to set up a guard tonight," I forced through a thick throat. "In case someone comes looking for us after Titus."

At the hoarseness in my voice, Dax asked, "Ophelia?"

The shrieks of the dead warriors pressed down on me, the ghostly drafts of their spirits burning to ash warring in the air.

"And we have to get out of this territory as quickly as possible. Once everyone is healed, we can't waste any time."

I was tired of us losing. Of innocent people being tormented for this sick game among the Angels.

"Alabath," Tolek said softly.

"I need a minute," I said, striding from the inn with as sure a step as I could muster before anyone could follow—though I knew one person would.

I wound down the path leading toward the vineyard, leaving behind the room I'd been grateful to see earlier but that now reeked of blood. Leaving behind the memories of tattered and torn flesh, of mangled screams from withered corpses frozen in the last, desperate moments of life.

Or at least, I tried.

With each blink, they followed. With each inhale, the stains clouded the air. With each step, a dozen charged after me, chains chiming around their bones. The ones that had locked them in that prison beneath the earth and the ones figuratively capturing their souls.

I walked all the way down the path surrounding this edge of Valyn until I reached the line of willowing branches that opened onto bare grapevines.

"Alabath," Tolek finally said when I showed no sign of stopping.

"Need air," I clipped.

His hand—so warm and steady and full of life—gripped my arm, gently tugging me to a stop in the shadows of a cypher. "We can get air right here."

He spun me toward him, and I tried my hardest to drop my gaze to the speckled gray stone, but in the night those spots looked like dark blood frozen on the surface. My eyes instantly snapped up, locking with Tolek's.

A wild wind whipped through the trees, and over Tolek's shoulder, a waving branch became a hunched, decayed figure.

I flinched, clenching my eyes shut.

"Don't run away." Tolek stepped close enough that his heat warmed my chilled body. "Was it Malakai? Or the emblem?"

"No," I muttered. My breath was tight in my chest. The air prickled with misty rain, curling the ends of my hair and sticking to my skin.

"Talk to me."

"*This is all my fault*," I snarled. In the distance, thunder rumbled.

"It isn't—"

"Don't tell me it isn't because it is, Tolek! Everyone—my father, the council, countless soldiers and allies—have died because of this curse, and tonight, I watched more people nearly die for it, too! I watched—and—"

Malakai's back flashed before my eyes. Mora's ruined shoulder. The bloodied staff from Lancaster's side.

And Jezebel, with those tendrils of Angellight choking her. Squeezing tighter, tighter.

"This is bigger than you, Alabath. This is *bigger* than all of us."

"And we're *all* losing." The words were rough. "How long until one of us loses everything?"

"We aren't going to lose everything."

"We are puppets for the Angels, Tolek. We are their toys and their weapons." I sucked in a breath, pressing my hand to my mouth to hold in an angry sob. "They're loading their bows with warriors as sharpened arrows and aiming us at their targets. And each time, it is a solid, inarguable strike of the bullseye. All because of this agent in my blood that activated the Angelcurse and whatever prophecies were spun in the stars *eons* ago! And why? Why is that fair?"

"It's not fair!" He threw his arms out, stepping back as if to capture the whole mess—to contain it so I wouldn't feel its wrath. "None of this is fair. None of the hands we've been dealt, none of the shit we've survived, is fair."

He rushed to me, taking my face between his hands, and only then did I realize tears streamed down my cheeks, hot and angry and unquenchable. "Every damn emblem you go after, every battle you walk into, I am terrified of the most unfair outcome of all. I fear life will deal the worst hand yet, and the long string of unjust patterns will continue."

My lips trembled as something inside of me cracked, and my throat grew too thick to speak. More and more with each word he said. But Tolek's thumbs stroked my cheekbones with the steady confidence he always radiated.

"But do you know what I do when I'm dealt a bad hand, Alabath?"

My voice was so small as I said, "What?"

A smirk quirked one side of his lips. "I play smarter, not harder."

"We can't outsmart the Angels, Tolek." I shook my head slightly in his hands.

Another stroke of his thumb across my cheek. "Where's that confidence I love?"

"They took it. Siphoned it away with each of the dead they chased us with tonight. With each of their spirits I had to burn, they took it."

"Alabath," he tutted, "are you saying you doubt I can outplay the Angels? That together, we can't tackle the eternal bastards?"

A lump formed in my throat, the battle of my heart warring to say yes—yes, I knew that together, he and I were invincible, that this love between us could forge the stars—and my head beating it down to say no.

No, we were nothing against the Angels.

No, there was more at play here.

No.

He read each of those fears in my silence. Then, one hand dropped to the small of my back, the other remaining sure against my cheek, and he pulled me a step closer. Forced me to come to him, to feel his beating heart and the certainty spilling from him.

"Don't you dare disagree with me, Alabath," he growled, voice spiraling into the night, crackling with fury. "The Angels—all of this—none of it matters when we're here. None of it can touch us as long as we're together. You and I, we're the constant." His thumb brushed across my lips. "There is nothing any Angel, god, or Fate can do to change that, no matter how many curses plague us or trials unfold at our feet. Because as long as they do, we are infinite."

As he said it, the sky above cracked, the clouds finally giving way to the milling storm.

Under the downpour, I cracked, too.

"I'm tired, Tolek," I admitted, sinking into him as the weight of the words left my shoulders. "I'm tired of fighting enemies we can't even see. The ones I can raise a blade to are one thing, but I don't even know who we're after anymore. Or who's after us. I'm confused, and I feel so used, and...I'm tired."

Warm rain drops pelted the stone, each one loosening a piece of the rock cemented in my chest.

"I know. I'm tired, too, Alabath." He pressed his lips to my forehead. "I'm so damn tired of seeing you weighed down with this pressure. Do you know another reason I liked being in the outposts so much?"

I sniffed. "Because the archery stations are always open?"

Tolek laughed. The rain picked up speed, nearly drowning his next words so they were only held between us. "Because despite the restlessness the queen's orders instilled in us, we were allowed to breathe. To indulge in something we have too little of."

"Peace?"

"Time."

A roll of thunder echoed his words, my skin icy and hair plastered to my cheeks.

"I'm scared we're running out of time."

Tolek's eyes darkened. "Never." He walked me backward until my spine hit a cypher, the two of us cocooned in the tree's willowing branches. One hand tilted my chin up so I could look nowhere but at the pure, molten fire of his eyes. "With you and me, there is always going to be time. As much time as there are stars in the skies. The cosmos doesn't run out of time, *apeagna*, and neither will we."

"What if—"

"No." Nothing but pure demand radiated in that voice. The rain lashed down harder. "I don't give a damn about the Angels. I don't care what threats they wield or what power they employ. I'm starting to think they are nothing without you—and I know I am. You are the thing holding this all together, and there is so much power in that, Ophelia. You can command it as you wish. Have us all on our knees at your mercy because *that* is your right."

His words snapped through me, emboldening me. "And if I want this entire task to end?"

Tol rested his forehead against mine. "Then we put a fucking end to it."

The rain-soaked air stung my skin, but the iciness didn't reach me. All I knew was the utter power in Tolek's voice. It burned, igniting the Angellight woven through my very soul, into the hollows my spirit failed to fill.

"So be tired if you must," he said, gripping my jaw tighter. "You deserve it. Tell the damn Angels they bend to your will, Alabath, not the other way around. And if you need a break, I'll carry you." He paused, searching my gaze. "We've all questioned our purpose here. Questioned how we're tethered to the prophetic fates of Bounties and cyphers. Of stars and spirits and Angels. Perhaps I'm not tied to any of those things but you. When you're tired, I'm here to help you surmount the Angels."

Tolek's waterlogged hair drooped into his eyes, but even that couldn't mask what burned there—something as potent as my Angellight and as venomous as the beings it was birthed from.

It soared through me, searing the dark voids of doubt. And in answer, without even a conscious thought, Angellight shone through my skin, tendrils wrapping around my waist and Tolek's, banding us together.

"It would be my honor to conquer the everlasting with you," I said as thunder rumbled overhead.

His words were sharp against my lips. "Let's make the Angels fucking scorch."

Chapter Thirty-Three
Cypherion

SHE'S BACK, I REPEATED TO MYSELF AS I CARRIED VALE up the stairs to our room.

But though she was curled into my chest, she was different. Smaller somehow, like the loss bleeding into the air was ripping her apart at the seams. She shuddered, her hand braced on my chest, and the movement was so wrecked. Shattered.

"What do you need, Stargirl?" I whispered once I was sitting on the bed with her tucked in my lap.

"He's dead," she muttered, voice hollow.

I swallowed past the thickness in my throat. "I know, Vale." I sighed. "I know."

"Everything hurts."

I clenched my eyes, breathing in deeply to cool the molten ire lodged behind my ribs. Spirits, I wished I could kill Titus ten times over. Wished I'd killed him that night Vale had offered to stay in his manor instead of leaving with me.

I'd been so close to it, staring at the knife on the dinner table like a lifeline. But I'd given into what she wanted instead. Guilt speared through my chest, making my next words thick. "Where does it hurt worst?"

But there wouldn't be an answer because that aching emptiness was beneath the skin. It was the price of an imbued warrior tattoo being severed—a sacrifice that would change her forever.

With one hand still on my chest, Vale pressed the other to her own, right over her sternum. "Here." Her voice was flat. "It's a void. Something's been taken."

My heart was being ripped out of my chest with every faint word. Titus could die a thousand deaths and they'd never be enough.

"Listen to me," I said, tilting her chin up. Even in the low mystlight, her expression was distant, skin pallid. "He cannot take your spirit, and he cannot take your heart. Those things belong to you, and you are damn rich in both. You *never belonged to him.*" I paused, letting those words settle into the torn pieces of her soul, and I prayed to the Angels they could fill the vacancies. "You are in charge of your own fate—curses, you are the commander of them! And you belong to no one."

A possessive part of me knew she belonged to me, but not in the way Titus had tried to command her. Regardless, as her lips trembled more with each sentence, that protective voice in my head screamed *mine*. Screamed for retaliation and the ashes of the chancellor lit in her honor.

Vale repeated, "I belong to no one...because I killed him."

My spirit crumbled at the loss in her voice. "I know, but that is not why you belong to no one." I soothed a hand down her back. "You belong to no one because you're free, Stargirl. I told you once that you're not some unimportant piece of the universe, no matter how small he tried to force you to be. If you had truly existed as nothing more than an extension of Titus, his death would have done a lot more than take a piece of your spirit. I know what's missing is irreparable, but you're still here because you're so much more than that."

My fate, my universe, my damn heart. Whatever you wanted to call it, that was what Vale was.

She was silent for a long moment, muffled echoes of the others downstairs and in Malakai's room drifting through the inn.

And for all of those quiet, processing minutes that she needed, I held on to her. I stroked her hair and soaked in the sound of her heart beating so strongly despite what she went through.

And eventually, she whispered, "I'm happy I did it." Vale

curled her fingers around my linen tunic in an iron grip, and that
—that sign of life, of strength—unwound the knot in my chest.

I swiped away the tears slipping down her cheeks. "Happy
doesn't even begin to cover how I feel, Stargirl." Relieved, elated,
desperate—those were a start. "I'm sorry it hurt you, but I'm
proud of you, Vale."

"Proud?" she asked, blinking up at me.

"Yes." I nodded. "Yes, I'm really proud of you. You survived
him, Stargirl. You fought your way out, and you delivered revenge
for everything he'd done to you."

Vale considered that and muttered, "Titus was never proud
of me."

His name on her lips was a wrench through my lungs, and a
fire ignited in my blood. But he was dead already, and while a part
of me wished I'd been the one to do it, a larger part was satisfied it
had been her.

The girl he'd kept as a prized trophy. The girl he'd used and
manipulated. The girl he'd tried so hard to break, but who was an
Angelsdamned expert at forging shattered pieces into works of art.

"Titus was a fool," I said.

Was. The force of that word hit Vale like a knife to the gut, her
breath stuttering. Her eyes drooped closed. When they opened
again, her vacant stare landed on her dress—on the crimson stains
darkening the powder blue fabric, and her breath hitched.

I stood and placed her on her feet, not saying a word as I
tugged her dress off her. A part of me wanted to burn it—to turn
every reminder of tonight to ash for her—but Vale watched me
closely, and something in that focus told me she wasn't ready.
Instead, I folded it, stains hidden, and saved that challenge for
another day.

Striding back to where she stood beside the bed, I asked,
"What can I do?"

Spirits, I felt so helpless. It was disorienting, not knowing how
to solve this for her. But I feared there wasn't a strategy to healing.
None but time.

Vale tangled a hand in the front of my tunic again, eyes on the
thin white fabric. "Can I wear this?"

I inclined my head toward the dresser. "Do you want a clean—"

Her trembling lip cut off my question. Swiftly, I pulled off my tunic and helped her into it, lifting her hair out the back so her wild waves fell around her shoulders. The wrinkled material swam over her frame, but she tugged the sleeves around her hands and held the collar close to her face, inhaling.

"Smells like you. Like home," she mumbled, and the fucking relief in those words could have sent me to my knees.

"You're home now, Stargirl. Wherever we are together—that's home. Us against the Fates."

Scooping her up, I took her back to the bed and leaned against the pillow. "When you want to talk about it," I said, "I'm here."

She traced absent patterns around the hem of my shirt, the white linen resting softly against her thighs. It was a steady movement, even if not eager. A better state than she'd been in when Dax passed her off to me, but still hollowed out.

"Not tonight. Tomorrow—I'll talk to everyone tomorrow," she answered, and her words lacked inflection. It reminded me of the tone that spoke through her weeks ago in the archives. When something had overcome her, her eyes swirling silver, and a different voice claimed to be there when Endasi was created.

She rested her head on my chest, and as the moment passed, her breathing leveled out, her fingers tapping a musical beat against her skin, like she was using it to soothe herself.

"Okay," I said, but if she wasn't ready tomorrow, that would be fine. She'd somehow retrieved Valyrie's emblem, and that was more than enough. We'd give her all the time she needed to recover.

Needed.

I'd asked her what she needed when we first got up here, but fuck need. Vale had been provided her basic *needs* for years—just enough that it warped her understanding of living—but she had been deprived of choice all that time. Perhaps taking small steps toward decisions would help restore her grasp on her freedom.

"In this moment, Stargirl," I asked softly, dragging my fingers up her spine, "what is it you *want*?"

"Want?" She considered, twisting her sleeve around her hand. Her eyes lifted to mine, searching.

I elaborated, "What will make you feel better?"

Vale studied me, and slowly, silent tears streaked down her cheeks. Her breaths grew shallow and aching. "I want..." Another breath, and words cascaded out in that disjointed, haunted voice. "I want it all erased. I want you to take me back to when we were in the hot springs. Before Valyn, before the archives. I want you to make me remember the freedom." Her cheeks were tinged pink, like only the mention of that dream was breathing a bit more life into her. Like the piece of her soul cleaved off with the tattoo bond was dampened compared to this—to us. "When we were there, I thought for one night, I could take my own fate into my hands—I could seize it, own it. I want that back."

"You can have it, Vale. Tonight, you had something taken from you, but it's not you. That part of you that was tied to him—the past he compromised and ripped away—it may be gone, and it may hurt like all Spirits, but it isn't all of you." I brushed away a tear. "Now you can seize every dream the Fates spin up."

She hiccupped. "I feel broken."

"No, Stargirl." I kissed her cheek and whispered, "You're not broken. But sometimes we have to rip out the toxic roots of ourselves to make room for the healthy ones to grow."

The ones that were tended with love and kindness, the ones I'd show her, because if there was one thing I was certain of, it was I could love Vale the right way. I'd messed up before—pushed her away and punished her. I'd never be such a fool again.

"Kiss me?" she asked, and though she still sounded like she was teetering on the edge, my heart thundered at the request.

"Cursed Spirits, you don't have to ask."

I swept her down onto the bed so she was on her back, hair fanned out around her, and when my lips met hers, relief unwound in me. Based on the way her body went pliant, she felt the same.

This wasn't a kiss like in the hot springs—it wasn't frantic and clawing. This was grounding.

I slipped one hand into Vale's hair, holding steadily to her and glided my tongue along her lips. When she opened for me and the kiss deepened, that sensation of starlight ignited in my chest. Of everything right and free and promising. Of the possibilities the future held for us to repair what Titus had shattered.

"Cypherion," she whispered against my lips, tugging me closer.

"Yeah, Stargirl?" Fuck, it felt good to kiss her again. To have her heart beat against mine and feel her skin warm beneath my hands.

Vale's fingers crept along my stomach, to my waistband. "Remind me," she begged, her voice cracking. "Remind me of that night."

She gripped my cock over my pants, and though I wasn't sure if it was a good idea given all she'd been through, I was powerless against her touch. It was only seconds until I was sinking into her slowly, watching every gasp fall from her lips. Kissing the tears slipping from the corners of her eyes.

I dropped my forehead against hers, nearly breathless. "Tell me to stop."

"Please, don't," she said, desperate in a way I'd never heard from her. Like if I stopped, she'd crack. Vale's hand tangled in my hair, pulling my mouth to hers. "I need you to replace every memory of tonight."

I did. Slowly and tenderly, I reminded Vale of the moments we'd spent together before I'd left her in Valyn and the promises of our future.

"I love you, Vale," I said into her skin, kissing down her chest. "And you belong to no one but yourself." I paused, pulling my hips back and adding with a small smile, "And me."

"I'm honored to belong to you, Cypherion," she gasped as I sank forward again.

"You looked so beautiful in those hot springs, Stargirl. With the steam beading on your skin and curling your hair. The starlight in your eyes. You looked like you were made to be there." I moved faster, still being gentle with her, but giving her what she'd asked for. "I'd wanted you so desperately, then. Breaking that control was the best decision I ever made."

She let out a small moan, biting her lip to keep quiet.

"I'm going to take you back there," I swore, feeling us both ready to combust. "We're going to relive those memories and make so many others."

Vale pulled me down to kiss her, and we both rode out our climax like that, entwined in each other without giving a damn to even the Fates.

After, Vale curled into my side, still in the shirt I'd worn all day.

"Thank you for coming back for me," she whispered.

"Always, Stargirl."

And as she waded through the darkness, finding her way without that piece of soul, I'd continue to rescue her as long as she needed me to.

Chapter Thirty-Four
Damien

Valyrie and I knelt before our master in the large suite Bant had carved out for private dealings. Our wings draped along the stone floor, palms open atop our knees in submission.

The towering round ceiling was perfectly smooth, as if carved and polished by an ancient, mystical hand. But the echo of my home overlaid itself on my surroundings, replacing the stale air with mountain-crisp breezes in my mind.

And beyond the walls, a presence beat.

So close. We were so very close now.

Our master's frame shimmered with untapped power. It was becoming a lively beast inside him, more each day.

He lifted a hand, studying the misty white wafting around his fingertips. "She is being pushed, as I had hoped."

"You were correct," I said, head bowed. "The enemy queen we did not predict may be a greater asset than originally considered."

"But that Starsearcher..." His eyes flashed to Valyrie, and in those milky orbs, galaxies swirled, adopting her power. "She could share very dangerous secrets."

"I have still not been able to read," Valyrie said with her head bowed, silver rings glinting as she folded her hands. "Based on the Angelglass, her block is still in place, though I believe she is pushing her way through it. She is bound to Moi—"

"Do not speak the traitor's name!" he snapped, a cloud of misty power flooding the chamber.

"Apologies," Valyrie said, leaning further forward, voice high and clear, though her eyes were rimmed with red after what we witnessed in the Angelglass tonight. "The Starsearcher is a catcher of Fates, a clawer of those that slip through godly hands, and a definer of destinies, but I do not believe she knows of where we are or why. I will continue to watch."

He hummed in response, a noise that nearly rattled the walls, my bones with them. So much might festered within him, seeping out. "Despite the Starsearcher, the Chosen Child is poised to ask questions that doomed us before. We saw with the return of Bant's uselessly discarded spirit that she is more than we intended."

Guilt wound through me at the mention of the misstep I'd once made. Though Bant's was more drastic. Entirely intentional and whole, where mine had been a sliver before being withdrawn.

Bant though...

That day echoed through my mind. His endless shuddering as what he'd so carelessly handed over to the Engrossian queen slipped back into place. As millennia of feeling danced along his bones.

For the rest of us, it was different. Our spirits not given over to a mortal in such an unholy way. We had not suffered an utter severing from our eternal bodies, but a warping and tearing. A suppressing into...elsewhere. We retained enough to recall those emotions that came along with a lively, intact spirit. Though it was only an echo.

My wings ruffled at the consideration of how that desperate decision, a scheme against me and my descendants, could have led to the ruin of what we'd fought for over millennia.

I growled, "Bant was reckless."

"He was a *fool*," my master raged. And in his words, that power —the one I often thought I should fear—swam. "To think any one warrior could be the Chosen. That any one warrior could complete our tasks when they are laced with the endless magic of those who betrayed me."

He drifted around the chamber, hovering over a throne of carved stone. "It is much more complicated than shedding a spirit into a mortal. Bant should have known the intricacies of these games, ever since the day you all ascended to me here. It requires sacrifices of blood spelled by our own hands to shatter those ancient locks."

My wings shifted in agreement, tips of my feathers dragging along the dusty floor, but determination to not fail again solidified my words, and I turned us back to the more important matter. "The girl is clever, yes. But we have known her heart for a long while now. She is resilient. We know we can deliver her to the end we need."

Restlessly, he shifted back to his feet and paced the chamber, form more corporeal than I had ever seen. He *walked* across the stone floors, though with his power, he did not need to. It was a choice. To feel solid ground beneath his feet.

He murmured, "We may still be surprised yet."

I exchanged a look with Valyrie. "What do you mean?"

"She has power we did not anticipate. Power that has stirred things, and it gives her an advantage."

I considered how she'd wielded the Angellight. First with only the emblems—now, more freely. It was never before seen, even with those long-banished foot soldiers and guardians. Even those kissed by Angels couldn't wield the power of seven.

"We have seen the beasts awakening," I began.

"Not only that," our master said. "Two tales have merged to become one." At his words, a surge of golden light burned across my skin. *A memory*, I assured myself. It was only a memory. "I knew the curse of Ophelia might spell our reign or our downfall, but I did not think like this."

Stars had fallen from the sky, but was he saying two prophetic fates merged within the child? He had gone on about a fate millennia in the making, and I thought it had been gleeful rambling, thought it had been a reference to the chambers sealed around us finally cracking.

But perhaps it had been about that other unseen and unpredictable force. The beat of wings long clipped and the burn of magic long silenced.

Were the two utterly fused by the hands of the great mist and the power within a child's blood? How...*how* would that end?

Kissed by Angels.

I turned a hardened stare to my master, awaiting direction.

"She needs to learn of this power carefully, at our discretion to avoid the bridges it may open prematurely." His milky eyes darted smoothly from Valyrie to me. "You will need to guide her."

Valyrie, long silver hair stirring in a wind around her shoulders, asked, "And Xenique?"

"When the girl is ready, Xenique's legacy will be our final piece. She already has it, but point her to the discovery now, you two."

We stood, beating our wings in the golden glow from my own light, pushing the boundaries. Valyrie's lilac ether spilled around our feet.

And our master flashed a gleaming smile. "Now...*Fly.*"

CHAPTER THIRTY-FIVE
TOLEK

"WATCH DUTY?" LYRIA SAID, HOPPING UP ON THE PORCH railing beside me as I nodded.

"Told Ophelia to get some sleep." She probably wouldn't until I switched shifts, but it was worth a try.

The door to the inn swung shut, Lancaster and Rina's low bickering wafting out. "They're getting along well," I deadpanned.

"As best as we can hope," Lyria said with a shrug. "I don't know what to make of the fae."

I blew out a breath. "Me neither. They appear to be trying to help." Especially tonight, in the catacombs. They'd risked their lives. How much of that was only because their queen commanded it, though?

I yawned loudly as I considered it, and my sister guffawed at my theatrics.

"Go get some sleep, Tolek," Lyria said when I failed to stifle yet another yawn.

"I'm fine," I argued.

She leveled me a stare that reminded me of our mother.

"Angels, you look exactly like her when you do that. Ready to reprimand me for coming home with the knees of my pants torn once again or dirt smeared across a fresh tunic."

Lyria stifled a laugh. "She did hate having to patch up our clothes."

"You mean having to cart them to the seamstress," I corrected.

"That walk was long," Lyria countered. "She made me do it for her sometimes, once the triplets started adding clothing to the pile on top of ours, and we were all growing so rapidly."

Even when it had only been Lyria and me, though, Mother never did her own sewing. Certainly not when three more children added to the family.

When I was little, a part of me hated that. Wished I had a mother like Ophelia or Malakai, who stayed up late to ensure those little things were done for us. But every time I thought that, I'd remember I was lucky to have a mother at all after my birth, and guilt replaced the longing.

Now, with distance, I didn't care what kind of chores she'd done, only wished she'd been a bit more attentive overall. The rest didn't truly matter.

"I'm only saying, you could have avoided the walk if she did it herself or taught us," I joked with a yawn, running my hand through my already-messy hair.

Lyria eyed the strands standing on end and shook her head. "Go to bed, baby brother. I'll take over the watch."

"You're not tired?"

"I didn't have quite as thrilling a night as the rest of you," she reminded me.

I quirked a brow. "You didn't enjoy the fighting den?"

"Oh, I had a wonderful time," she corrected. "Won quite a lot of money and watched men get jealous for it. But it wasn't the same as battling risen corpses or getting to slay that cocksucker of a chancellor."

I laughed at the description of Titus. "That is true." But remembering our conversation in the rings, my tone sobered. "I know you probably would have preferred to be in the thick of the fight"—she had earned the title Master of Weapons and Warfare, after all—"but thank you. Not many of us could have commanded attention as a spectator in the den, and if you hadn't been there, I wouldn't have made it to the catacombs in time."

I didn't even want to consider what that could have meant.

Seeing Ophelia on her back, that corpse baring down on her, had been haunting me all night.

Lyria seemed to swell with pride at the comment—only slightly. But it was there. And it brightened my spirit to see.

"You're welcome," she said thoughtfully. I didn't know what considerations were running through her head after my gratitude, but from the way she stared out over the vineyards, it was something heavy.

With a quiet goodnight and a kiss to her cheek, I left my sister to contemplate under the watch of the stars.

"I'm heading to bed," I said to Santorina and Lancaster. The two stewed in tense silence as Rina continued to carefully pluck cypher splinters from his wound.

"Goodnight, Tolek," she said.

Lancaster only grunted, "Warrior."

I shook my head, fighting a laugh as I climbed the stairs to the bedrooms. Exhaustion pulled at me as I neared the door thinking of everything that had happened tonight. The catacombs and the manor, the words I'd vowed in the rainstorm.

I'd meant every one, would lay my life down for them.

Ophelia and I swore we would scorch the Angels, and as if in answer, the very air burned as I crossed the hall to our room. An inferno hot against my skin, like an iron fresh out of the forge.

Like I was being held directly to those fiery coals, and—

"Alabath?" I called, throwing open the door and racing into the room.

There she was—asleep, twitching with pained whimpers atop sheets sticky with sweat.

"*Ophelia?*" I pulled her to me, her skin burning worse than the Spirit Volcano. Hot enough to blister my hands, but I turned her face toward me. "Wake up, *apeagna*."

In the moonlight slipping through the inn's curtains, blue-tinged lips parted on small, gasping breaths. Her eyes flickered beneath pale lids, brows pulling together.

My chest caved in, my own breathing desperate as it sawed through my throat.

The heat seared, and Angellight shimmered across her skin, like it was seeking a way out. But whatever had its claws in her had the iron will of eternity.

Chapter Thirty-Six
Ophelia

The muscles along my back burned. My ribs were molten lava, and distantly, so very far away, I thought someone screamed my name.

There was a second voice trying to smother it, though. One that boomed like thunder and washed over my senses like rain.

Now...fly, it commanded.

Another wave of fire rippled down my muscles, and then, it was my agonized screams drowning out the voices. My pain spearing through my body, sizzling away the calming cool rain.

No one came to help at my cries—no cool hands along my brow or whispered assurances. Nothing to remind me that I was okay or tether me to consciousness.

But there was...*something* pushing past the pain. A breeze dancing along my burning flesh, carrying a hint of fresh—

Wildflowers.

Like those decorating Damenal and splashed across the Mystique Mountains, tangling on a crisp breeze, but these were stronger. Headier and dreamy. I clung to that scent, and with impossible force, I wrenched my eyes open, shooting upright to a pain rocking through my body.

"Where in the Angels?" I muttered, even that slight movement aching.

A land of abundant, verdant mountains surrounded me, but

these were not *my* mountains. No, these were far grander than anything Gallantia bore—grander than any range I'd ever heard of on Ambrisk.

These peaks stretched to the clouds, disappearing among fluffy white masses well before they tapered to their points. It felt as if I wasn't even halfway up this range, but puffs of those clouds danced along the tips of the wild grasses, as if cleaved off by an almighty sword and left to drift down to earth.

As if even this valley was high enough in the mountains to tangle with the heavens.

Gritting my teeth against the pain, I stretched a feverish hand out to one. The misty residue cooled my skin, licking away the burn in my muscles, and a relieved gasp slipped from me. The cloud sliver coiled around my arm, alleviating the soreness until it evaporated into nothing but shimmering, magic-filled air.

Groaning at the aches ricocheting down my spine and abs as if I'd been through a rigorous training, I forced myself to my feet and stepped fully into the nearest wafting clouds. With the world fading in their fog, I forgot where I was and let the magic lick away my pain.

"Wherever I am," I muttered, "this is glorious."

As the clouds drifted apart, scattering through the valley, I took in my surroundings. Between sweeping peaks, tall lush grasses curled up around my knees. Vibrant greens were awash with tiny pink, white, and yellow buds bursting in clumps between the stalks—

A golden light flashed across the valley, and when it cleared, I gasped. "*Damien?*"

"Hello, Ophelia," the Angel said with a familiar smirk. His voice was warm with affection. "Welcome."

"Welcome *where*?" I asked.

The Prime Mystique blinked at me. "It is your dream, child."

"But I—" I looked around at the abundant trees—not a cypher in sight—and the clear blue sky. "These aren't the Mystique Mountains."

Damien surveyed the land. "No, it appears we aren't at home."

Wistfulness dripped through his words, but before I could inquire, his purple eyes pulled mine again. "You have accessed the light."

His lips were tight, wings beating softly as they held him gently aloft—or perhaps it was the magic he thrived off of here. He glowed brighter than when he visited me, those wings casting an effervescent shimmer around the earth. Where it touched my skin, my own Angellight purred in recognition. Damien's feathers ruffled at the sight.

"Yes," I answered honestly, ignoring his shrewd stare.

"And?"

"*And*?" I blurted, lurching forward. Pain bolted down my shoulder, and I hissed, massaging my arm. Where was that remedy cloud now? The fire was quickly returning to my muscles. I went on, though, because I needed answers. "It terrifies me. Have you seen what it's done? How it's destroyed and consumed?"

Did he know how it had slayed the dead and choked my sister?

"I— " His word cut off, only silence coming from his open mouth. The Angel collected himself quickly. "I have observed the powers lurking within you, and they are not what you think." His brows pulled together, and he looked...pained?

"What does it do? Why do I have it? Is this Angellight something I need to use to absolve the Angelcurse?"

Why? I wanted to shout to the heavens.

"Learn the light, Ophelia. Reach into the depths of your heart and spirit and let it beam, but do not be fooled by its might or presume what it means."

"Fooled how?"

"Magic—like any form of power—is as tempting as a voracious lover. It will eat at you, steal you away." Damien's eyes were serious. "Become its master, but stay true to yourself. Stay true to your task."

Stay true. The words of the Mystique Warriors rang through my blood, straight from our founder himself. The leader meant to guard us as we did the magic of the mountains.

But it had been months of this journey without a lick of help.

And I was so tired of being a toy to the Angels.

"Where have you been, Damien?" I asked. "I—I haven't known what to do. I've had so many questions."

"I have heard them all," he swore. "But alas, I do not hold the answers."

From the bob of his throat, it was clear that was a lie. He held the answers, he simply could not divulge them. Like the fae queen's magic commanding Lancaster and Mora, it obstructed his speech.

"What—"

"Look to the stars," a voice cracked like a whip behind me. And from the grove of pink-blossomed trees, a second Angel emerged.

A sparkling, lilac light that resembled the sky right after dawn ebbed at the edges of her wings, and silver hair as silky as a flowing river cascaded around her tan shoulders.

"Valyrie?" I gasped.

Her delicate lips tipped up into a smile, but it was somber.

My voice was small. "Did you see?"

A shallow nod.

"I'm so sorry," I swore, guilt heavy in my chest. "I—I didn't know the power at my hands." I looked between her and Damien. "I didn't know it would destroy the dead."

That it would ruin those corpses, the ones I suspected were the victors of her races. Confidants who had rested in that chamber since she ascended. I hadn't known it would obliterate the warriors that were her friends.

I wanted to cast the Angellight from my body at the memory. I'd killed before but not like that—not uncontrollably and on the whim of another. I wished I could expel the ability, as Bant had shed his Spirit into Kakias. This power was not meant to be contained by a mortal body, and I couldn't stand another being trying to use me.

But Valyrie said, "It did not kill them, child. It only returned them to where they belonged."

Her face tipped to the sky, eyes falling closed for a moment. The mourning in her words was offset with an apparent under-standing, a satisfaction perhaps.

It ripped at my heart, my confusion, my uncertainty. Did I dive into this power or shun it? Which would benefit my family and my people more?

Which would solve this Angelcurse? That was what I was here for wasn't it? To be the answer for these immortal beings. For whatever it was this mission was after. Whatever Annellius had been greedy and failed at.

Annellius...

Had he been greedy? Or had he...had he felt the power thrumming through his veins as I did and resented it? Perhaps it had hurt someone he loved, as Tolek suggested?

Was that his fatal flaw, loving too much that he ripped the power from his body to atone for it?

As if reading the thoughts flooding my mind, Damien and Valyrie stiffened. The Prime Mystique warned, "Do not follow his path."

"What *was* his path, though? What was the mistake that ended his life? At least tell me how to avoid it."

"You must rely on faith, child," Damien commanded. "It is the doctrine of all we do. Of all we are."

I'd carried faith in the Angels my entire life. Faith in their causes, their guidance, their rituals. But...my eyes dropped to the tattoo beneath my elbow. The faith that I was always doing the right thing had led me down painful paths. The Undertaking and the Bind were fallible. Were the Angels, as well?

I was nothing but a puppet to them. How did faith play into that? Was faith the agent of the strings they pulled, or was it another misguided attempt?

"Trust fate to guide you," Damien emphasized. "Do not stray from this path, but do not dig too deeply into the whims of the stars."

The stars?

Were they talking about Vale? Her sessions?

"Why?" I asked, voice shredded and so out of place among this haven. "Why shouldn't we arm ourselves with whatever knowledge the stars can provide?"

Valyrie's eyes softened. "Because it might show more than warriors are meant to know."

"What does that mean?" Irritation bubbled beneath my skin, the feverish heat mounting.

As if in response, the soothing clouds drifted closer, wrapping tighter around us. They slipped between the everlasting Angels and me. And as they formed that wall, fire mounted in my body.

"Spread your wings, Child Kissed by Angels," Valyrie said, voice as light as the mist. "Spread your wings and learn. Go to the ones who recount the histories in the land of your ancestors and find out the truth."

"What does that *mean*?" I cried.

But it was fruitless.

The clouds swallowed the Angels, and at their disappearance, my body faded in a burst of golden light, heat scorching to my bones.

Part Three
Xenique

CHAPTER THIRTY-SEVEN
SANTORINA

"THESE GODSDAMNED SPLINTERS ARE IN DEEP," I grunted, tilting my head so the mystlight could illuminate Lancaster's wound further. All the torn flesh and exposed muscle, gleaming red.

When had I become so desensitized to it? To the way blood shone against my skin—even that of my enemies. Perhaps it was when my friends and I first left Palerman. That cataclysmic shift that had occurred within all of us on the journey, preparing us for the people we were meant to become.

Or perhaps it was even earlier, when the war had swept through our home. When it had been my parents' blood on my hands.

It should have unsettled me. Even now, it didn't.

No, now, after carefully—painstakingly—finding the many, many minuscule splinters in Lancaster's wound for an hour, the work was rhythmic. Like a beat beneath my skin to operate to.

I tweaked a particularly brutal shaving of the cypher spear, and the fae stiffened.

My eyes snapped up. "Did that hurt?"

"No," he said brusquely. "If you can get them out so they stop blocking my magic, I'll heal the rest myself."

I scowled at his tone, but one look at the gash in his side and the remaining slivers of wood impacting his magic had me biting back my retort.

Still...I jerked the next splinter from his side, and he hissed. I flashed a small, saccharine smile in response. "That one was in deep."

Lancaster only glowered. Mora was resting upstairs, under Celissia's care. If I helped Lancaster, perhaps together we could all restore Mora.

With them gone, though, and having sent everyone else to bed for the evening, the emptiness of the dining room was a weight on my chest. Every plink of my supplies or shift of Lancaster pretending his stifled magic wasn't a pain was thunderous.

"How does your healing magic work?" I asked, more to fill the silence than anything, the routine of fishing out the splinters now steady.

"It's an innate force in the fae," he answered in that bored, flat tone. "To use it on a wound such as this or from a knife is simple. You only imagine the injury being stitched together, and it is done."

"Is that how you healed Dax, then? When Kakias attacked him at Ricordan's manor?"

"Yes, though that wound was inflicted with something much more lethal than a dagger. That time, I had to pull out the toxins. Deadly enough ones that a fae of typical power wouldn't have been able to heal it."

Arrogant prick. Of course, he had some deep wealth of magic. I was loathe to admit Dax only lived because of this immortal creature and that seemingly endless power.

"Why is yours so much stronger?" I asked, shifting so the light hit a new area of the wound, a dozen fresh ash-white splinters illuminated.

"My what?"

"Your magic."

Lancaster stiffened, and my gaze shot up. His eyes were narrowed on me. I straightened, wiping my hands. "Why is *your* magic—and your sister's—so much more powerful than a typical fae?"

He dragged his tongue over his teeth. Ground his jaw. And—

"Why aren't you answering, Lancaster?"

Nothing beyond his nostrils flaring as I said his name and hatred pooling in his dark eyes.

"It's related to the Gods and Goddesses you're blocked from speaking of." Somehow, the fae siblings' magic was connected to them. That was an interesting fact I'd have to tell Ophelia later. It was also one to be wary of, given we still didn't know how the gods were involved here.

I continued my questions, seeing what he *was* able to say. "Does fae healing magic work on things like disease? Or common illnesses?"

Lancaster relaxed a touch. "My kind does not suffer from them, and we haven't been around humans in the correct capacity to test it."

Because when they were, the humans were chattel to them. I tempered that response. He could talk about the magic, but not its origins. "Is healing considered a unique gift?"

"You have many questions," he dismissed.

"I worked hard to hone my skills. To become reliable and trustworthy with the lives of others." *As my mother was*, I didn't add. I wouldn't give him that piece of information. "I only wonder if what I worked so hard to do comes naturally to your kind."

"For most, yes. To small extents usually, but Mora and I are fortunate that healing runs in our family line." His words were tight, but it appeared he was trying to force them out. To share something. "We have stronger abilities than most in addition to our own unique gifts."

Blessed by the Goddess. We'd have to figure out what that meant exactly.

I plucked another small splinter from his side, the ridiculous number of muscles across his abdomen flinching. "I've gotten most of the large ones out," I said.

Lancaster grunted as if to say *I have nothing but time* and reclined on his hands. The wood groaned beneath him, but I tried to ignore the taut pull of those stupid muscles. He was a beast bred to hunt. The strength, the canines, the speed and grace were all weapons that could end my life in a moment.

Perhaps I was a fool to help him. I should leave the splinters, allow him to suffer for all the blood his kind spilled. For all the humans they slaughtered.

"I know you're considering it," he said, deep voice slicing through my trance with the wound.

"What?" I feigned nonchalance and dove back into the carnage.

"You're wondering why you're helping me. You're contemplating the repercussions of leaving this wound to fester, of letting me bleed out." He paused, eyes burning into the side of my face. "Or perhaps you're contemplating stitching it up with that thread your Bodymelders make and healing me with the splinters still inside so I will never access my magic again. That would be particularly cruel, but you are a human after all—"

"What does that mean?" I snapped.

"It means humans are callous."

I scoffed. "Some humans may be, but certainly no more than you heartless, unforgiving immortals."

Lancaster mimicked my scoff. "Your kind lives such short lives, you don't truly understand the rushes of emotions you get. Everything is felt so intensely, but for barely a wink of time. You cannot deeply understand the words *heartless* or *unforgiving* in a matter of decades." He spoke so casually that I could barely believe the claims he was making about *my* kind. "Your decisions are emotionally-driven and passionate, but you lack understanding of those things and therefore do not truly consider the consequences."

"And you immortals—who care so little of life and beauty that you would slash countless human throats—understand consequences?"

"Who said we only slash throats?" Lancaster's eyes gleamed, a predator baiting his prey. My pulse thrummed, but not in fear.

I tightened my grip on the tweezers. "That's right, you don't. You brutalized innocent humans during those wars. You tormented them and dismembered them. Do you think I don't know? I grew up hearing the horror stories." I leaned closer and pressed the metal against his open wound. His jaw ticked, but he didn't react. "The ones who got their throats slashed were the *lucky* ones."

"They were." His tone was solemn, but I wouldn't name the other thing within it. The one that almost sounded regretful.

"How can you say any of this?" I retorted. "You were *created* to hunt the remaining humans who stood against your people." I still didn't know what that meant, but I ignored the curiosity. "Humans who had nothing to do with the wars, whose ancestors died so long ago, we don't even know their names."

"Another sorry fact of the short-lived." *Much like your existence*, he didn't need to add.

"Apparently humans are cleverer than you think," I hissed. When he raised a skeptical brow, I roughly tugged a splinter from his side, taking extra care to prick the torn flesh and draw more blood. "It is unwise to insult the person with their hands in your open wound, faerie. Especially when they are someone as careless as a measly human."

He growled as I jerked another splinter. "Perhaps not one so rash, at least."

"*Rash?*"

"You do realize you're only proving my point with this vindictive game."

I simmered. He was right, of course. I was allowing my emotions to control how I healed him right now. Exactly as some hysterical, overly-sensitive, unable-to-make-wise-decisions human would.

Not at all how my mother taught me.

Swallowing the mix of indignation and longing that wrought within me, I cleared my throat and got back to work. "You imply that feeling human emotions is so bad, but I would rather feel than live centuries in a cold and cruel mind, serving a monstrous queen."

"We don't all have choices," he muttered.

I breathed through the irritation still bubbling in my chest. Humans could be kind, humans could be *good* and worthy of peaceful, passionate lives. I would not stoop to his games again.

"If that is the case, you'll understand how so many humans feel, having had many of their choices taken away from them, too." I removed another splinter—only a few left that I could see. "It is because of prejudiced beliefs such as yours that I'm leaving as soon as we find the last emblem."

"Leaving?" he asked, uninterested.

"I'll be traveling back to our human training camps and working with those who wish to no longer be defenseless."

Lancaster cocked his head, hair slipping across his shoulders. He watched me, an indeterminable look in his narrowed eyes. "You are training them?"

"I am. Encouraging them," I explained, a rush of pride warming my cheeks. "You say humans don't understand our emotions and the consequences, but I'd argue we feel everything so much deeper because we understand on the same level, yet it's compacted into a much quicker, more heartfelt timespan."

Heartbreaks were more monumental, deaths more life-altering, injuries more damaging because the years were so few.

Lancaster said, "When you live for thousands of years, you understand more than you care to."

Ignoring the heavy presence of his stare on my face, I gently removed the last few splinters and straightened up, wiping my bloody hands on a damp cloth.

"There you go. Try your magic."

Lancaster gritted his teeth, both of us watching the wound. After a long, tense moment, I gasped.

Before my eyes, the gash began to heal. In small stages, given that his magic was still recovering from the impact of the cypher spear, but I waited in stunned silence as ancient faerie power clotted the blood and slowly began restructuring the torn skin.

I'd never seen something like it. I'd always appreciated the beauty of healing, of the strenuous, precise work mending took. And while this magic alleviated a lot of what I found so satisfying about my practice, it added a new wonder to the art. Chills spread across my skin.

Eventually, Lancaster closed the wound.

"It'll scar?" I asked, looking at the spot where a fresh white mark marred his torso.

His abdominal muscles tensed under my stare. "With the cypher's curse, this one will."

I studied the scar. It wasn't a neat, stitched up disfigurement, but one with points stretching away from it, almost like a sun. It stood out among the numerous others covering his strong body.

"Why not make it even?"

"Because it is a mark of something I survived in the catacombs, and a simple slice could belong to anyone." He grabbed his tunic and tugged it back over his head, hiding the wound. "This will always be a reminder of where it came from."

I considered that, reluctant to admit it was somewhat poetic. Godsdamned fae probably thought I couldn't understand that either with my small human mind. Well, this human had managed to get him to hint toward what he couldn't share of the Gods, and that was important.

"And by the way, you were wrong about one thing you said, Bounty."

I glowered at the name. "What?"

"You said my kind care so little about life and beauty." He paused. "I can assure you, I appreciate beauty more than most."

He stomped up the stairs, leaving me in the echoing silence of the dining room.

～

I WAS DUNKING my tools in disinfecting tonic when footsteps sounded down the stairs.

"Can I help clean up?" Celissia asked.

"Sure, if you want to start gathering the towels and sorting them into those we can salvage and those we'll discard, that would be great. Thank you."

She nodded, and I turned back to the bucket. Thank the Gods Harlen had arranged for this inn to be private. I didn't know how we would have handled tonight otherwise. With so many deep injuries, access to the kitchen and dining room were imperative.

Plus, there was something comfortable about working here. Organizing my supplies along the worn bar top was familiar.

"Santorina?" Celissia asked after a moment, and I glanced over my shoulder. "Why are you helping the fae?"

I sighed, letting the metal tools rest in the bucket. "He may be a twisted, deadly, entitled predator"—Celissia snorted a barely audible laugh—"and he may be bred to *hunt* me, but my mother was a healer."

Celissia sobered. "Was?"

"She died during the first war." I turned to start re-corking my various jars of supplies and noting which would need to be refreshed. "A fatality of an attack on Palerman." The memory of that day tightened my chest, but I breathed through it.

She approached the bar, setting down a pile of folded towels. "I'm sorry for all the pain these wars have brought between the clans. So much of it seems unnecessary for the masses."

"It does," I agreed. "But Ophelia was the one who picked me up when my parents died, so I'll face anything for her."

Celissia smiled softly. "As I would for Barrett. He supported me similarly when we were young. I didn't suffer a loss like your own, but in my worst moments, Barrett was always there." She spoke of the prince with such tenderness, one that he'd earned based on what I'd seen of him.

"He's going to make a great king," I said. "A leader the world needs."

Celissia cast a wistful glance toward the stairs. "I only hope he sees that, too. He's the only person I can envision ruling our clan the way they deserve."

"Is that why you agreed to the ruse with him?"

"He didn't even need to ask," she said. "That, and, selfishly, I've always dreamed of seeing the world. Of getting away from Banix for a while."

"I've heard your father..."

"My father should not hold power," Celissia snapped. It was clearly not directed at me, so I let her continue. "He's fine as a councilman, likely balances out some more impertinent decisions, but as a ruler?" She scoffed. "I fear him."

"Why?" From what we'd been told, he was greedy, but dangerous?

"Some people base their hopes on injustices that have already been redeemed. They get stuck on them. I think he believes he's fighting for a worthy cause, when truly, it's one that does not involve him."

"What sort of cause?" I asked.

"The kind that, frankly, I think wants to be forgotten." Celissia shrugged, picking up a pile of bloodied rags and moving toward the door.

She disappeared outside, ducking back in as I was finishing tidying the bar. "Your mother was human, correct?"

I nodded.

"Where did she learn to heal with warrior practices?"

"She didn't have magic, but she studied with a very inclusive group of Bodymelders when she was young. She adopted their techniques. It took more work, more time, since Bodymelders can use their power as influence and she couldn't, but it only made her want it more. Work harder for it."

"That's why you're helping Lancaster, isn't it?"

"My mother taught me most of what I know, but the best thing she taught me was that no one deserves to suffer. I can't say I necessarily agree, given the crimes the fae have committed." I scowled. "But I can't dishonor her by forgetting."

Only the thought of her careful ministrations as a healer and her thoughtful guidance had me outlasting the disdain the fae wrought.

"Lancaster implied something earlier," I began as we extinguished the mystlights and traipsed toward the staircase. The rest of the inn was quiet, thank the Gods. Everyone needed to rest after tonight. "I asked why his and Mora's magics are so strong, and he wasn't able to answer. I think it's connected to the gods."

Celissia's gaze drifted to the dimly lit hall above. "Did your mother ever teach you about healing practices besides those of the Bodymelders?"

I shook my head, not following that train of thought. "Did your tutor in the citadel?"

Celissia clasped her necklace, a large oval stone with a rainbow hue when it caught the light. "No, but my family has ties to very powerful healers, so I've always dug deeper into the practice."

"Bodymelders?" I asked.

"Some old, ancient bloodlines that tended toward it. Mostly dormant now. But I've found that there are some sources of magic we really should be learning more about. Things from the isles and beyond."

"The Sorcia Isles?" I asked, and Celissia nodded.

Sorcia magic had been locked behind their gates for thousands of years. No one on Gallantia knew details of it, save the rogue nomadic sorcerer. They used spells and talismans to work, things that Bodymelders didn't rely on given their abilities came from the land.

"How did you pull Vale from her session tonight? Not even Cyph can normally draw her back."

Celissia avoided my eyes as we stopped at the top of the stairs. "I tapped into some unique branches of healing practices while in the citadel."

"Isn't that sort of study restricted?"

"Isn't it difficult for humans to learn warrior ways?" she countered. I was about to argue that *restricted* and *difficult* were not the same thing, but perhaps that was her point. "Your mother sounds like a spirit the world could have used more of."

"She was," I said. "Especially with the hatred and greed stemming through Ambrisk today."

Celissia smiled. "Much like your mother, I want the world to suffer less."

"Thank you for your help tonight," I said, the sentiment wrapping around my heart. "I couldn't have done it all on my own."

"Of course." She nodded. "Good night, Santorina."

"Good night, queen-to-be."

She waved off the title, but I couldn't help but think that if it hadn't been a ruse, if she and Barrett actually were to rule together, perhaps they'd create a throne worth bowing to.

CHAPTER THIRTY-EIGHT
OPHELIA

"THEY SAID...WHAT?" TOLEK ASKED. WITH MY HEAD resting on his chest—right above his heart—I couldn't see his face, but the unease was clear in his voice.

"That I shouldn't dig too deeply into the whims of the stars."

"And that was Valyrie?"

"Yes," I sighed, sitting up to face him. "Which only makes me more uncertain about all of this."

Tolek's head fell back against the pillows, and he rubbed his eyes. "Valyrie knows something she doesn't want us to see."

"And what could be a part of this Angelcurse that I'm not meant to know?" I bit my lip. My skin was still sticky from the sweat that had beaded during my dream, but the rain-soaked breeze from the open window was helping.

That storm would slow us down in the morning, though. The knot of worry in my gut tightened.

"Once she's feeling better, we'll talk to Vale." Tol reached up, tugging my bottom lip from between my teeth and resting his thumb on it. "She got that emblem somehow. Perhaps she knows something about what Valyrie may want to hide."

Taking his hand in mine, I traced circles across the back as I thought. "I'm supposed to be their chosen. The one to solve this curse, and yet..."

"Yet?"

"Yet lately, I'm wondering if Annellius was right." Even saying the words felt dangerous. Damien had insinuated he was watching my every move.

I continued, "Damien warned me not to follow Annellius's path. History remembers him as greedy, but when Kakias died, she implied maybe that wasn't the case. She'd said he was a fool and gave up power. That he *hid* the emblems."

All of Kakias's last moments came back to me. *History is written by the survivors, girl.*

Annellius surely hadn't survived his battle with the Angels.

"You think he devised the trials, then?"

I shook my head, enchanted corpses screeching through my mind. "No. Those reek of higher power. I don't think Annellius was capable of it. But perhaps he found the emblems—found out what they did—and returned them rather than used them? Damien and Valyrie want me to complete these tasks, unlike whatever Annellius did."

"It sounds like they would prefer you didn't even know about Annellius."

"Why, though?" I asked.

"Maybe what the Angels want isn't what's best for you," Tolek offered. "It did *kill* Annellius." His hand tightened on mine, pure terror in that vicelike grip.

"It did," I mused, staring out the window to where those stars I was not supposed to question gleamed tauntingly, peeking through scattered storm clouds high above the earth. In them, I saw my ancestor staring back at us, and I wished he could speak to me again. "Why do you think Annellius's eyes were brown when Vale saw him in a reading?"

"Instead of magenta?"

I whipped my gaze back toward Tol's, remembering the time in Seawatcher Territory when I bled on the emblems as Vale read. She'd seen Annellius, then. "If my eye color is a sign of being chosen as we thought, why did he not share it?"

"I don't know, Alabath," Tol said, defeated.

Sighing, I crawled back into the warmth of his arms, allowing the nearness to steady both of us. "There are so many questions, Tol. So many things that haven't been what they've seemed."

He stroked my arm with gentle fingertips. "What do you want to do about it?"

"We're finding that last damn emblem," I swore, and he laughed at the conviction in my voice. "We've come this far, sacrificed so much, we're finishing this. But then...then we'll need to find answers before we act." I sighed. "Perhaps giving the emblems to Ritalia *would* be best."

"You think so?"

"I don't know." I nuzzled closer to him, my mind whirling though sleep beckoned after the ordeals we'd gone through.

"We'll talk to everyone tomorrow," he assured me. "Go back to sleep, Alabath."

I kissed his chest, right over his heart, and watched the stars until my eyes grew heavy.

⁓

THE STORM RETURNED FEROCIOUSLY in the morning. I was drenched head to toe after one minute outside, trying to visit Sapphire. She couldn't fly in this; with how it was pelting down, her wings would be waterlogged in seconds.

We were stuck here. If someone from Titus's manor found us...

The possibility made my skin prickle, fingers jittering over my tea as I sat before the fire in the dining room. Rain and wind lashed the windows, cyphers swaying. My boots tapped on the stone hearth.

"I give her one day," Jezebel muttered where she sat with Erista at the table nearest the grate. The wooden surfaces had been cleared of the bloody linens, ointments, and satchels. Santorina was upstairs checking on her patients now.

"Two," the Soulguider challenged.

Jezzie scoffed. "You have such faith?"

"Four hours," Lyria snickered as she leaned against the bar, a half-empty glass of whiskey in hand. *If we're stuck here all day, we may as well drink,* she'd claimed upon finding us down here minutes ago.

I whipped my stare to the commander. "I can hear all of you!"

Tolek laughed and sat beside me, gently brushing my hair across my shoulder and massaging the back of my neck where the Bond was inked. The tattoo beat impatiently. "What's your bet, Alabath?"

I crossed my arms, the tea in my cup sloshing with the abrupt movement. "I am not betting on how long before my patience snaps."

"That's because I'm right," Jezebel chimed, kicking her boots up on the table and draping a thick wool blanket over her lap and Erista's.

"Right about what?" Cypherion's voice carried from the doorway as he led a pale-faced Vale by the hand.

I straightened, looking over the Starsearcher. She'd donned that powder-blue dress again, crimson stains splattering it, but her hair was washed and skin cleaned of gore. "How are you?"

Vale took a seat at my sister and Erista's table, Cypherion claiming one beside her and slinging his arm across the back of her chair.

"I'm okay," she answered. And I heard the words for what they truly said, recognizing something deep within them: *I am breaking.*

"We're happy you're back," I said. *I see you, and I understand.*

"Thank you, Revered." She looked around the group. "Thank you all, truly, for coming for me. I didn't..." Her eyes flashed to Cypherion, the vacancy of losing her soul bond still clear. "You didn't have to."

"You're a part of our family," Tolek said without room for argument. His thumb stroked my knee. "We stay true to our own."

"Our cabal of damaged warriors," Jezzie suggested.

"Our troop of everlasting spirits," Erista chimed.

Vale tried to smile, adding, "The fiercest core of relentless hearts."

"And an incredibly attractive group to boot," Tolek supplied.

I rolled my eyes, but despite his ridiculous contribution, the sentiment of our family settled over the room like an early morning mist. Something so natural and certain, you *knew* it would always be there to cool your skin when the sun rose, but a small, effortless wonder of the world, regardless.

That moment of bliss shattered when a knock sounded at the inn's main door. Immediately, Lyria popped up, the rest of us tensing.

"Who is it?" Tolek asked, but his sister swung the door open, unconcerned, and a hooded figure stepped across the threshold. Rain dripped from their cloak as Lyria closed the door to the pounding storm.

The guest pulled their hood back, and Cyren—the general of the Starsearcher armies—smiled at us. "Heard we were strategizing today."

"What are you doing here?" My concern threatened to unwind, but I remained on edge. Cyren was a member of Titus's council.

"Lyria wrote to me when you got here, and again last night—" Their words cut out, scanning the room and landing on Vale. Taking in the stains on her dress. "I heard what happened."

Vale inhaled, pulling up a trembling bravado. "It's true. I did it. Are you here to take me?"

Cypherion stilled.

But Cyren shook their head. "I'm here to see how I can help ensure stability moving forward. And I brought you some things." The general opened their pack to reveal soft, moss green fabrics.

Clothes. They'd brought Vale fresh clothes from one of the nearby markets so she wouldn't risk being seen. They were on our side—would buy us time so everyone could heal before we had to travel. I relaxed into Tolek's side.

Shocked, Vale blinked at Cyren. "Thank you." She pulled out the chair on her other side and nodded to it.

Cypherion redirected the conversation, but kept one eye on Vale as he asked, "So what was Jezebel right about?"

"That Ophelia won't hide in this inn for long," Jez explained. Even Cypherion smirked, agreeing.

I lifted my chin. "I'll wait out the storm. I won't leave until

Sapphire can travel comfortably." Angels be damned, those eternal bastards could practice patience for once. I was so *tired* of following their schemes.

"And where are we going when we leave?" Jezebel asked.

For a moment, my heart inflated. At the steadfast assurance in the way she said *we*, in the assumption that no matter what or where, we'd all go together.

It extended beyond this room, too. Upstairs, where Malakai was still sleeping soundly under Mila's care. To Rina and Celissia, who were tending to the fae. To the Engrossian Prince and his consort, our unlikely friends, who had disappeared after breakfast to write to their council.

"That's what we need to figure out." I blew out a deep breath, spinning so my feet were firmly on the floor and setting my cup on a nearby table. "Last night, Damien visited me in a dream."

"You dream of your Angel?" Erista asked, head tilting, gold band glinting in the firelight.

"I don't think it was a dream. I think it was actually Damien. With a message."

"He hasn't visited in months," Cypherion said.

"I know, and I tried to ask him where he's been but something cut him off. As something always does." I sighed. That damn block on whatever the Prime Mystique wanted to tell me.

That warning bell rang in the back of my mind, shrill with temptation to walk in Annellius's footsteps because I deserved to be more than a toy to the Angels.

Lyria, propped atop the bar now, asked, "What did he have to say?"

I recounted how Damien's words felt like a warning. How he told me to become the master of my magic before it ate away at me, but to not allow it to fool me. Even here, away from wherever we were in that dream realm, my skin chilled at the memory.

"He's right," Erista said. "Power can become enthralling if unchecked. I've seen it happen with Soulguiders."

"I've seen it happen on a battlefield," Lyria added, shadows behind her eyes, "with a very different sort of power. When one is unprepared for the high, they often hit the lowest lows afterward."

Jezebel countered, "Ophelia is prepared, though. We both are. We may not know what our abilities do, but we're being careful."

In my mind, Angellight whipped around her throat again. She struggled and struggled.

My stomach turned over. I pulled and pulled and *pulled*, but—

Tolek's arm wrapped around my waist, tucking me closer to his side as he said, "We're being careful, but we need to stop waiting for answers to find us. At the very least, Damien's warning made it clear that Ophelia has to figure out what this power does." With a pointed stare at my sister, he added, "And I'd wager that extends to you, too, baby Alabath."

"There was more," I said when the room fell silent. My eyes met Vale's, color slowly returning to her cheeks. "Valyrie was there, too."

"*What?*" she and Cyren both gasped.

I nodded. "She was present and ethereal as you'd imagine, but not quite as vibrant as Damien."

Vale leaned her elbows on the table. "What did she say?"

"She went on about listening to the stars, but to not dig too deeply into their whims because we may find things warriors are not meant to know."

These balances the Angels presented seemed so delicate, so precarious. And truthfully, so terribly frustrating.

Find the emblems, but do not ask questions. Listen to the stars, but do not try to see too much. Risk your life, but do not fail. A series of contradictions that dug beneath my skin and pried at the slippery foundations of my own beliefs.

"Did Valyrie mention me?" Vale asked.

I shook my head, and—was that a flash of disappointment in her eyes?

"How did you come by her emblem?" I asked softly.

Rain beat against the window, filling the silence as Vale toyed with the ends of her hair. "When Titus said he could help fix my readings, he wasn't lying."

Cypherion, watching her intently, was silent, as if she'd already told him this.

"How did he do it?" I asked.

"He forced me into very powerful reading chambers like the one I was in when Malakai and the others showed up." Vale's eyes closed for a moment, and she shook her head as if fighting off a memory.

"The first time was the day after Cypherion left. It was...awful. I couldn't fight it anymore. That chamber was too powerful, and it pulled the suppressed readings to the surface until everything cracked." She watched the rain, her voice vacant. "A deluge. It slowed eventually. But that chamber snapped whatever lock was baring my way. I think Titus had it built out of stone infused with precious resins and powders."

"To try to draw out his own power," Cyren muttered like a realization had just dawned.

Vale nodded.

Cyren said, "I'm sorry he forced you into that." Vale smiled appreciatively. Cyren tilted their head, braided coronet shining like a halo. "I wonder if..."

"If?" Vale asked.

"Perhaps that seeing chamber can be used to enhance Starsearchers of a normal power level."

Vale considered, her first genuine smile spreading across her face. "Find a way to turn his deceit into something advantageous for our clan."

"Why stop there?" Lyria asked. "Maybe that level of magic can be converted to weapons of some sort. A mobile strength for Starsearchers."

"It's something to consider," Cyren agreed.

When there was a lull in their theorizing, I asked, "You can read again?" Vale nodded. "How has it been?"

"Intense," she said. "At first, the sessions were painful and all-consuming. I wasn't—I'm still not—used to it. This magic was always something I understood and embraced. Until recently, something I felt proud of."

"And you don't anymore?" Tolek asked.

"It's not that I don't, but I'm relearning it. The first few sessions were excruciating. So many images flooding by after being suppressed for far too long, I still don't know what to make of them all." Vale swallowed. Cypherion gripped her thigh, squeezing gently, and she met his eyes. "Once I adjusted to it, I found out I can do something no other Starsearcher in known history can."

"What?" My skin prickled, Angellight stirring.

"I can read the fates of higher powers."

Stunned silence fell across the room like a sheet of ice. "An actual reading?" Cyren asked.

"Yes."

Erista said, "Aren't you only supposed to be able to read the fates of warriors and beings of similar power levels?"

Vale's lips pressed into a line. "Exactly."

Cypherion interjected, "It seems like what Vale saw in Seawatcher Territory—with the Angels and gods and Annellius— was part of this sect of power she has and possibly why her magic was malfunctioning."

"Which started when I first came to Damenal," Vale added.

"When you were first around the emblems," I muttered, gripping my necklace. It couldn't be a coincidence that Vale's magic initially stopped working when she was near a potent source of Angel power.

"And when I first read about your future, Ophelia," Vale said. "That reading that spoke of darkness without a cause."

"Why, though?" I considered.

Vale stole herself. "I don't only have one Fate tie," she said of the connection Starsearchers have with the beings who transfer them readings. "I have nine."

My eyes widened. Jezebel's jaw unhinged, and Lyria nearly choked on her drink.

"*Nine?*" Tolek repeated. Cyren and Erista both blinked rapidly at Vale.

"Nine," she confirmed.

And it all made sense. Why Vale had been taken to that temple as a child, why Titus was so set on keeping her, why her magic seemed to work differently than any other searcher we knew of.

Lyria, chin propped in a hand, utterly rapt, asked, "And there's never been another Starsearcher with that many?"

Vale shook her head. "Not to my knowledge."

Cyren elaborated with an awed look at Vale, "Even two is uncommon."

"I think the way it manipulates my magic is why I was able to see Annellius in the past."

Tolek asked, "And that's how you found the emblem? You read Valyrie and saw where her emblem was?"

"Yes," Vale said. "She was in the catacombs with a brass telescope—"

"A telescope?" I asked, looking concernedly up at Tolek. "There was no telescope there."

"There wouldn't have been," Vale confirmed. "It was where the heart was stored, within that glass box, but I had to wrench it from its fixture."

Tolek's brows flicked up. "Had to?"

"The dead wanted the telescope," Vale deadpanned. "But it didn't seem to care about Valyrie's heart."

Shivers danced down my spine. "You escaped them? All of those corpse warriors?"

"All of...There was only one?" Her words turned up at the end like a question. "When I gave it the telescope, it fled, and I was able to leave with the heart. I hid it from Ti—" Her words cut off in a choke, but she sniffed and lifted her chin. Beside her, Cyren's lips twisted in disgust at their chancellor. "I hid it. My plan last night was to get it to Barrett. To ask him to pass it along to you so you could do what you must while I remained here to keep the chancellor distracted."

Cypherion leaned forward, tugging Vale from her seat and into his lap. His hand stroked her hip, right over the bloodstained fabric. "Doesn't matter now. And we have another emblem, regardless of how."

Though he was only trying to keep Vale from having to relive everything, he was right.

"We have one more left to find." I stood from the fireplace, pacing in a slow circle. "When I spoke to Valyrie, she said to *go to the ones who recount the histories in the land of your ancestors, and find out the truth*."

"The mountains?" Jezebel asked, brows scrunching together.

"That's what I thought she meant at first," I answered, "but I don't feel like there's much in the mountains that can help us. Who are our other ancestors, Jez?"

Jezebel grinned, and that—the camaraderie, the flutter through my gut as we prepared a plan—it all chased away the chill wrought by the unknown. "Grandmother's side of the family..."

With a smile, I turned to Erista. "Are you ready to return home?"

Erista's feline grin was dazzling. "Oh, Revered. I thought you'd never ask."

"I assume we should start at the capital?" I asked, mentally mapping how long it would take to get to the Soulguider capital, Xenovia, near the Mystique Mountains. "It will be a bit of a journey."

"Who recounts the histories, though?" Lyria inserted, hopping off the bar to stand beside me in the middle of the room. Her eyes brightening at the choice to strategize—to hold a position on this council—warmed my spirit. "Are there some grand historians to the chancellor in the capital?"

"Or," Tolek blurted, shooting up, "perhaps it's not Xenovia." Without further explanation, he hurried up the rickety, creaking staircase.

Erista continued, one eye on where he'd fled, "We don't have historians beyond the usual of any clan. But we do have a wealth of Storytellers."

Storytellers.

Warriors who abstained from associating with any clan formally when feeling the call of a particular rare brand of magic. They instead joined the cult roaming freely across Gallantia, giving life to the tales of antiquity. They kept them sacred and preserved by word of mouth alone.

I'd seen one once, in the Wayward Inn when I was on my way to rescue Tolek. She'd spoken of the foundations of the Angels. Of their feuds and struggles and eventual succession, all things I'd now seen firsthand.

Storytellers were increasingly rare, though.

"You have many?" I asked.

"Compared to most territories." Erista shrugged. "Some claim they listen to the stories they share from the souls of warriors past, so they flock to our deserts. They are to be trusted more than any historians."

"And I bet the ones we need aren't in the capital," Tolek said, racing back down the stairs with a journal in hand. He flipped open to a dog-eared page, displaying a shoddily sketched map of Ambrisk.

"What is this?" I asked, noting the random markers he'd drawn across Gallantia.

"This is a poorly copied rendition of the map Dax and I found in the forest during that final battle. When we were separated from you, Santorina, and Barrett, and you all went to Ricordan's manor, Dax took me to one of Kakias's old camps. She kept this map there —something to do with the proximity to the mountains—Dax was never highly ranked enough to know the exact reasoning—but this is how we were going to find you before I called Lancaster for help."

Lyria shook her head. "I'm not following how it's supposed to help now."

"Because, dear sister, something about this map has been bothering me. It was clearly imbued with magic somehow." He grimaced, but went on, "For a while, I thought the nagging feeling was only because of that, and I told myself to forget it. But maybe it can help..."

Tolek dumped the map on the table in front of Cypherion, and everyone gathered closer.

"When we're done with this hunt, don't go into cartography," Cyph muttered, leaning around Vale's shoulder to study Tol's handiwork.

"I'd be wonderful after I learned properly, and you know it," Tolek argued. "But that's beside the point. Kakias had these markings on her map. I copied them down, see?"

He gestured to small *X*'s strewn about the continent randomly. "Do any of these locations seem familiar?"

"That could be Palerman. Maybe Brontain." I searched the

scattered markings for any other familiar areas, and my second pulse sped. "Firebird's Field?"

Cypherion pointed to one in Mindshaper Territory, an inch south of the mountains. "That could have been where the pit was. We were below ground, so we can't be sure. And there's one in Valyn."

"Kakias's map charted the emblems?" Jezebel gasped. "But why? Or *how*?"

"Kakias was once supposed to search for them," I recalled. "It's why Bant shed his spirit into her. It didn't work properly, but Kakias wanted power and knew if the chosen found these, they could stop her. She may have been rotten and twisted, but the queen was smart. She must have narrowed down ideas, so she could stop me from getting them when the time came." I shook my head, tired of playing the game of our dead enemy. "What's more important now is, where are the Soulguider ones?" I leaned closer, searching the desert on the small rendition.

"What's in that region?" I asked Erista, pointing to an *X* that was far west in the desert. I knew some about Soulguider terrain, but not enough to specify something so important.

Erista's brow furrowed for a beat, then her mouth popped open. "Valyrie said to visit the land of your ancestors?"

I nodded enthusiastically, something finally, *finally*, coming within reach.

"She may have meant it literally." Erista looked between Jezebel and me. "Your grandmother hails from the Lendelli Hills, does she not?"

"She does," I said.

"This mark looks to be in approximately that area."

"The Lendelli Hills," I muttered. Where our maternal grandmother was born, a land she'd told us stories of our entire childhood. Of sand dunes and whispering secrets on the wind.

I stared at the map, wings fluttering in my chest as the group moved around me, and wondered what tales the spirits held for us there.

CHAPTER THIRTY-NINE
MALAKAI

I WOKE TO THE SOUND OF A WHIP CRACKING IN MY EARS.

Jolted upright to a sting shooting down my back.

My vision blurred, blood coated my skin, and my breathing was heavy—

"Malakai." Cool hands cupped my face. "Malakai, it's okay."

That voice sent a soothing wave through my body, tempering my racing heart. I blinked furiously and did my best to get my bearings, to count what was tangible in the room. No whips, no blood. There was a desk and a wardrobe and a fire in the hearth— that's what I had heard cracking, not a whip.

My hands...they were on soft wool. Not a sticky marble surface, nor a chilled cavern. I rubbed the blanket between my fingers, the material grounding me.

And my back didn't sting. No, it was sore, but surprisingly whole as I caught my shaking breath.

"You're okay, Malakai," that voice before me said again. The one that had come to mean comfort and warmth and support.

Mila. I met her eyes, so wide with concern. Or perhaps it was fear. Torment, maybe.

Mila. The inn. We were back in the inn. In Valyn.

Titus...he had me whipped. And Mila had to watch, but she...

"You're okay?" I asked frantically. Gripping her wrists over her gold cuffs, I turned my head to kiss her palm.

She smiled slightly, brushing my hair back from my face with glassy eyes. "I am. And so are you."

It was coming back in flashes. Getting here from the chancellor's manor. After Vale had...Spirits. Vale had *killed* him. That was going to be an issue.

The ride back had been one of the most disorienting experiences of my life. Ombratta was gentle as she carried us—me leaning heavily on Mila to compensate for my back—but every step had sent a bolt of pain through my open flesh. Every breeze had stung like my skin was lit on fire.

"How long have I been out?" I asked. A storm raged outside the windows, so I couldn't tell what time it was.

"About a day and a half," Mila said, and my heart sank at those words. She spoke so clinically, as if she were a healer reporting casualties to their superior. "Your wounds are fully healed, though I'd be careful for another day so you don't reopen them."

She'd bandaged my back and wrapped a dressing around my torso. That tender care made my chest feel crowded. Now that I noticed it, the white linen was tight with every breath, but that firm brace against my ribs was another comfort. Another reminder that someone had been there to heal me this time. That I'd taken a punishment, but things were different.

My voice was thick as I asked, "And is everyone else okay?"

Before she answered, the door slammed open, and Cypherion filled the frame. "I'm sorry," he said. "I heard your voice. Figured you were awake."

Cyph approached the bed, looking over my bandages. Emotion burned beneath his stare, piercing down to my fresh wounds.

"I heard what happened. Saw—" He swallowed, choking up. "Thank you."

It was only a few words, but it said enough. Thank you for taking that punishment. For withstanding it. For getting Vale out.

"I promised I would get her back," I said.

Cyph looked between me and Mila, his cheeks slightly pink. "I'll leave you to it."

The exchange was over so quickly, his words brief, yet his gratitude was thick in the air. He left, and that feeling of accomplishment lifted my bones and spirit.

"Everyone made it back," Mila answered my previous question, still in her orderly tone. "There were some injuries, but they're all here."

They were all alive. Mila and I were alive. I dragged my hand up her arm, solidifying her presence. No cells or chains or bars were keeping us apart.

We survived.

I repeated that to myself as my fingers danced along her leathers, from shoulder to wrist, counting our breaths. Her skin was likely so warm beneath the material, so soft and scarred. Fucking beautiful and real. I wanted to cement the feel of her in my mind.

"Did they get the emblem?" I asked, voice hoarse. My forehead fell against hers.

Mila swallowed, the air heavy as she breathed, "We can talk about all of that later. You should rest now."

My eyes flashed to the door Cypherion had left through, his gratitude ringing in my ears still. Gratitude because he loved Vale and wouldn't waste another day pretending otherwise.

I looked to Mila. Took in those bright blue eyes and full lips.

"I don't want to rest," I told her. "I could have died a few nights ago. Everything could have been taken, and all I can think is life is too damn short to not live it." I may have had new scars slicing across my old ones now, but we'd damn well made it out of the manor. "So, I don't want to rest, Mila." I sighed, locking my eyes with those crystal blue ones. "I just want you."

She inhaled. "What?"

Leaning forward, I caught her lips in a gentle kiss, one that was almost a caress. But even that taste drove me wild. I cupped the back of her neck, tugging gently to angle her head so I could kiss her deeper.

"*Please,*" I said against her lips.

"Your back...you need..."

"I'll be fine, Mila. I swear." Angels be damned if I let these stupid wounds stand in the way of being with her. "You...you are what I need."

And at the raw desperation in my voice, her eyes flared. Like that was exactly what she needed, too, but she hadn't wanted to say it.

"I thought—" She whimpered, and the walls of her fortress came crashing down. "I thought you were going to die. When they kept—and there was so much blood—it wasn't stopping." She shook her head, tears slipping between her lashes.

The sight of them took me right back to the chamber, when she'd been assuring me I was going to be okay, and the words she'd claimed.

"In the manor," I began, "you said I saved you. Did you mean in the Labyrinth?"

"No." Mila took a deep breath. It rattled through my own chest, made me feel on the verge of a free fall I didn't understand. Then, she added, "The reason I was freed during the war was because the war *ended*."

Only our heavy breathing filled the air as I waited for her to continue. Did she mean...

"When you signed the treaty, Malakai, I was freed from my imprisonment. *You* saved me."

I saved her. She'd never told me how her imprisonment ended, and I hadn't pushed for details. She'd said she was released. But *I* had saved her.

Through a treaty I'd come to think meant nothing more than deceit.

But it had meant something to Mila. To others out there, I was sure, but to this woman before me who I fell for more and more every day.

I'd saved Mila when I signed that agreement, entered myself into torture...but she'd walked free. Somehow, knowing that cleared every sordid feeling I'd associated with that decision. Made every scar worth it because they kept more from her skin.

"I saved you."

"You saved me," she repeated, blinking away tears. When she

looked at me again, an inferno burned behind her irises. "I think we've always been connected because of that. A part of me was always meant for you. And I'm tired of waiting for the future with you, too."

Mila kissed me desperately, and I swept an arm around her waist to turn us, her back falling to the sheets. Ducking my head, I dragged my tongue along her bottom lip, nipping until she opened for me.

"Why didn't you mention that before?" I asked against her mouth.

Her hands dug into my hair, pulling me closer as if she'd never let me go again. "I didn't want you to think that's why I'm here. As some twisted debt."

"Even if it was," I said, kissing along her jaw, "I'm not dumb enough to let you go because of it."

Tiny tremors wracked her body. I grabbed one of her hands, locking our fingers, and her palm shook against mine.

"Relax, Mila," I whispered with a kiss to her cheek, then one to her wrist. "I'm here, and I'm not going anywhere."

"I know," she breathed. And slowly her hands stopped shaking. "I know."

Then, she leaned up to catch my lips, pulling me back down to her. We both grew more frantic, my cock aching. Her legs were braced on either side of my hips, and when I rocked against her, the most satisfying moan vibrated up her throat.

"Fuck, Mila," I breathed, ripping my mouth from hers to explore her neck. I pressed her hand into the pillows beside her head and rolled my hips against her center once more, getting rewarded with another one of those needy moans. "If you already sound like that now, you're going to ruin me when I'm inside you."

Her laugh turned into a breathy gasp when I bit down on the skin of her neck, sucking gently. Even through her leathers, her heat taunted me. So much, I could barely feel the pain in my back.

"What are you waiting for?" she asked, and it was the only permission I needed.

Pulling her to her feet, I first unhooked the empty weapons belt slung across her hips. Carefully, I set it aside. Then, I moved to the many clasps adorning her leathers, stripping them off her in slow layers. I kissed across her chest as more skin was exposed, down her stomach and hips and thighs, not pausing where she wanted me, but keeping my eyes on hers the entire time.

The air in the room sizzled with each inch I lowered, and this waiting game almost felt symbolic, torturously so. Like all these weeks we'd been hiking the path of recovery together had finally led us to the summit.

And dammit if the view wasn't spectacular as she stood before me in nothing but white lace undergarments and those gold cuffs.

I pressed a kiss to her hip, the bottom of her ribs, between her breasts, until I stood and skimmed my hand up her side. "You're perfect," I whispered, brushing my thumb across her peaked nipple, and I nearly groaned when she inhaled, arching into me.

I stepped closer, keeping that hand toying with her breast and cupping her cheek with the other, and kissed her with a searing intensity that said, *we survived*. The sound of the fire crackling through the room filled the space between our rushing breaths and her soft moans.

She writhed against me, and I was ready to sink into her, but there was one more thing we needed to discuss.

Pulling back, I lifted Mila's hand and looked at her wrist. I wouldn't push this. Not if she wasn't ready. A nervous waver flickered across her face.

"You can keep them on. It doesn't change anything," I promised. "But when you're ready, I want all of you."

She swallowed, her pulse racing. "I know you've seen the scars, but I've never taken them off while sleeping with anyone."

"You don't have to." I kissed her and muttered against her lips, "One day, if you want, you can."

Something in my words settled over her, and Mila studied the intricately carved ivy design. The gold shimmered in the firelight, such beautiful pieces to mark an ugly span of history.

Then, she looked squarely at me, cheeks flushed. "I'm ready."

And somehow, those two words were more significant than any secret between us—than anything else we might do.

The heaviness of it settled on my chest. The audible click of

Mila unlatching those cuffs and setting them delicately on the shelf beside the bed—her turning to me with her past on display—was a different level of vulnerability.

The scars along my back—both fresh and older—tingled as if in understanding.

As she stepped back to me, close enough that her lace-clad breasts brushed against my chest, she placed one hand on my shoulder. She looked right at the scars that would forever mar her skin and studied where they met mine.

After a moment she lifted her eyes to mine and said, "Thank you."

My brows rose. "For what?"

"For making me feel safe." My heart nearly cracked at the sincerity weighing those words. Like she'd needed that comfort but hadn't realized it.

And a part of me thought I'd needed to be able to give that to someone again.

Gently, I brought her wrist to my lips and kissed her scars, holding her eyes as I did. Noting how her breath hitched.

"You're so fucking strong, Mila." I walked her back toward the bed, guiding her to the pillows, and her eyes sparkled. "So fucking strong for all you've survived." I settled between her hips again, rocking against her core. Through the thin layers of her undergarments and my shorts, I could already feel how drenched she was, and fuck did I want her. But she deserved to be worshiped first. "Now—tonight—I want you to remember that." I crawled back down her body. "And I want you to *let go*."

I started with the scars on her legs and worked up. The large one around the back of her ankle, the ones peppering her calves and thighs, and a jagged one slicing down from her hip. I pressed kisses into them to remind her she was a damn survivor.

"Every one of these scars is a sign of what you endured," I said. "I love them."

As I finally settled between her legs, I pressed a languid kiss over the silk covering her center. Dragged the sensitive bud between my teeth and her back arched off the bed.

"Please, Malakai," she said as I repeated that.

"What?" I asked, holding her hips still. "Eyes on me when you ask."

She lifted her head, looking me directly in the eye, but she didn't ask. "Touch me."

I nearly exploded. Hooking my fingers into her waistband, I dragged the silk down her toned legs. I took in every inch of her, stroking myself through my shorts to alleviate the ache.

"Fucking Spirits," I breathed.

I ducked my head, tongue exploring exactly where I'd dug my teeth in. I stroked up her center, learning what patterns made her squirm the most. What had her back arching and hands kneading her breasts—a damn beautiful sight. Pushing two fingers into her, I pumped in and out.

"So good, Mila," I hummed against her. "Exactly as I knew you'd be." She was every good and sinful thing I'd envisioned. Every damn dream I thought I'd never want or deserve again, and somehow more. "Better than anything I could have imagined."

I crooked my fingers inside of her, and she cried out. But then she tangled a hand in my hair and tugged. When I looked up, she said, "I want to come with you," and I almost lost it again.

Mila pushed onto her elbows, catching her breath as I discarded my shorts. The way she flushed as my cock bobbed free, taking in my length with an impressed look, was nothing short of satisfying. A sight I'd be committing to memory.

I stroked myself as I settled between her hips. "One day, I'm going to watch you ride me," I said as I dragged the head of my cock up her center and she stifled a moan. "I've been imagining it for a while now."

I pushed into her slowly, barely an inch. She was hot and tight, and I wanted nothing more than to see her unleashed like that, but even I wasn't masochistic enough to try that with the fresh scars on my back, though I barely felt them as she consumed me.

"For now," I panted, "I want to watch you unravel."

To memorize every expression on her face as those walls came tumbling down.

"One day," Mila answered on a gasp as I pushed in further,

clutching my arm, "I want you to take me every way you can imagine."

"Is that an order from my general?" Another slow inch. So slow, I wasn't sure how I'd make it, but I wanted every second of pleasure to last for her. Wanted to erase every ghost haunting her.

Mila smirked, panting, "Spirits, yes, it is."

And I slammed forward, making her cry out.

I kissed her as I pulled my hips back and sank forward again. "Relax," I muttered against her lips, sweat already beading on our skin. "I've got you."

Like my words unlocked something within her, she eased around me, and I sank to the hilt again. Mila gasped, but I swallowed the sound, moving slowly. Pulling back and plunging forward again to hit that spot deep within her that was making her moan.

"Just like that," she said, knowing exactly what she wanted, and dammit if that wasn't one of the most attractive things I'd ever heard. Her telling me she knew what she liked, she knew what she wanted *me* to do to her. It had me thrusting into her quicker, meeting every request she had, every angle she moved her hips to.

Her hands dragged so gently over my back, like she wanted to feel my scars but didn't want to hurt me.

"Your scars are beautiful, too." She exhaled as I brought one of her knees to her chest and sank into her.

Breathing heavily, I told her, "We wouldn't be here together without them."

Maybe it was true, maybe it wasn't, but as I watched Mila's eyes cloud with a dazed lust and felt the beginnings of her orgasm fluttering around my cock, it felt like the most promised thing in any realm. This. Us. Like we were those constellations she loved and had always been connected, even if the map of our scars traced them.

"Promise me," I grunted as I picked up into a punishing pace. As I knew I was hitting that edge and felt her careening toward it, too.

"Anything," she gasped.

"You always said tomorrow." I captured her lips, a kiss too

sloppy and desperate and needy. "Promise me all your tomorrows, Mila. Because you have every one of mine."

"I promise," she said. "Every tomorrow is yours."

And then she clenched tighter around my cock, and with only a few more strokes we came together.

And those constellations I thought had written us? I was damn wrong.

We wrote *them.*

Forged them out of the fires we'd walked through, remapped their paths through the scars etched into our flesh as our own courses had changed.

We weren't just two warriors who'd stumbled upon this earth. In this moment, with every damn tomorrow sworn between us, we were as fated as the stars.

~

"VALE HAD THIS?" I repeated, holding Valyrie's heart before the flickering flames and watching how the light shone through the shades of blue.

Ophelia and Tolek sat in chairs beside the fire in my room in the inn. Mila was at the foot of my bed beside me. We'd barely left the room since I woke up yesterday.

"She did," Ophelia confirmed.

That's what she'd been clinging to in the seeing chamber.

"Do you feel anything from it?" Tolek asked.

"Yeah." I nodded. "Yeah, it feels like all the others. Warm and... a bit alive."

Unhooking her necklace, Ophelia strode across the room and held it out to me. "This, too?"

I grabbed Damien's emblem, and that familiar, faint beat pulsed through it. "Yes, but I never felt it in the spear before. When it was mine."

"How is that possible?" Mila asked me, then turned to Tolek. "You don't feel anything?"

"Nothing."

"Interesting," Mila mused.

"Very interesting." Ophelia reclasped her necklace. "You said they feel alive?" I nodded. "I have a theory."

Tolek's eyes were trained on her as she strode toward the fire. "Enlighten us, Alabath."

Ophelia watched the flames flicker. "What if the Angels' spirits are in the emblems, and that's what we feel pulsing in there?"

"Bant's was in the queen, though?" Mila asked.

"We know he shed it. Perhaps he somehow found a way to get it from the ring—which was already in her possession—into her body." Ophelia rubbed at the dark webbing on her wrist, her original Curse mark.

I shifted on the bed, the wrap around my wounds itching. "You think this whole thing—the hunt for the emblems—could be to set their spirits free?"

"It's not a bad theory," Tolek said, crossing an ankle over his knee. "But it still doesn't answer how or why."

"No, it doesn't," Ophelia answered, shoulders slumping, and Tolek rose to mutter something to her.

"You really feel something in there?" Mila whispered to me.

I nodded, evaluating Valyrie's heart in my palm. A stone carved to vaguely resemble two entwined figures. "Not sure why."

When Mila said nothing, I lifted my gaze to find her eyes narrowed. "What's wrong?" I asked.

She shook her head. "It makes me uneasy. All of this."

"Me, too," I admitted on a groan. "A part of me wishes we could forget it. That I didn't drag you into this."

"If you're part of it, I want to be, too, Warrior Prince."

At the name, I kissed her wrist then turned back to Ophelia and Tolek. "When are we getting the final emblem?"

Tolek laughed as I tossed the heart back. "Someone's eager."

The words he wasn't saying were abundantly clear: He'd missed this ambitious side of me. I did, too. And a big reason it returned was the woman sitting beside me.

At the thought, I wrapped an arm around Mila's waist.

Ophelia rolled her eyes at Tolek's comment. "The storm looks like it's clearing. We'll leave tomorrow, Angels willing. Cyren went to Titus's manor and is going to work with Harlen to cover for everything that happened here."

For explaining the dead chancellor and the instatement of a new one.

"All right," I said, tightening my arm around Mila. She squirmed. "Is there anything you two need from us before we go?"

Tolek fought a smile at my question and ushered Ophelia toward the door. "Not a thing. We're taking care of all the plans and correspondence."

"Terrific," I said.

And as the door clicked shut behind them, I flipped Mila onto her back and spent the rest of our time in Valyn in that room.

Chapter Forty
Malakai

"The horses aren't fans of sand," Dax said, falling onto his ass beside Barrett—on a slope of the very stuff the mares didn't like.

Soulguider horses were used to the give of the sand beneath their hooves, but Mystique horses and many other clans' hated it, just as they didn't favor the icy terrain of Mindshaper Territory. Sure, they survived it during the war, but we all tolerated conditions then.

When we were traveling south from Valyn, through the Starsearcher jungles and toward the Soulguider border for the past week, Ombratta had been her usual, well-tempered self. The moment we stepped into the desert, all the horses had been riled.

I shook the small, intrusive grains from my boots and sat beside Barrett and Dax in the shade of a cypher tree for a quick break before continuing on to Lendelli.

"I hate sand, too," I grumbled.

I peeked through the willowing branches toward where the mares gathered, unsettled under their own canopy as Cypherion and Vale took their turn to feed them.

Ophelia, Jezebel, and Erista were traveling with Sapphire and the khrysaor, but Tolek, Mila, and Lyria took a moment to spar, the fae observing shrewdly. As I watched, Lancaster muttered something that made Tolek scoff and Mila tip her head back with laughter. The sound wasn't audible from here, but it rolled along my bones nonetheless.

As if feeling my stare, Mila looked over her shoulder, quirking a brow. I grinned at her, and damn did my chest inflate when she smiled back.

Celissia ducked beneath the branches, stepping in my line of sight. When I jumped, she laughed, flicking a glance toward Mila. "Enjoying the view?" she teased. I'd gotten to know Celissia better on the journey down from Valyn. Found her to be quick-witted, compassionate, and with a keen interest in taking all of Tolek's money in every round of cards.

"Absolutely," I swore.

The queen-to-be tossed Dax a canteen. The general lunged to the side to catch it, grunting. When he sat up again, he massaged his abdomen.

"That scar still bothering you?" I asked Dax.

"More than usual lately."

Barrett's jaw ticked as he watched the spot where Dax had been stabbed with Kakias's dark magic with heated intensity, like he could see beneath his consort's tunic.

I narrowed my eyes at the general, but Dax assured us, "Scars often hurt."

"Not like that," Celissia said, eying him carefully. "It makes me nervous that nothing I do is helping." She clasped the pendant hanging around her neck and muttered under her breath. Dax watched her with a blank expression, shaking his head.

Barrett was unusually quiet through the entire exchange. He sat with his elbows propped on his knees, folding and unfolding a letter between his long fingers.

"From my uncle?" Celissia asked, following my stare to my half-brother. Elvek, one of the members of Barrett's council, was apparently the queen-to-be's uncle on her mother's side and as distrustful of Celissia's father, Nassik, as the rest of us.

Barrett's head snapped up, shaking off the thoughtful daze he'd been in. "Yes, and Rebel."

"Rebel?" I asked of the wolf.

"Since we left, Elvek's been sending Rebel on regular patrols for a few days at a time." His tone was calm, but Barrett's knee bounced.

"And?" I said, eyeing the tick.

Dax answered, "Barrett's concerned Rebel is going to be recognized as belonging to him."

"Our people are unsettled," the prince explained. "Those who support me are doing so quietly, but those who don't are..." He groaned, leaning back against the cypher. "They're stirring. Rebel has found up to four separate clusters of warriors gathering against my rule."

He passed me the note, and I scanned it quickly. They were small groups, nothing concrete, but it was the spark that could ignite an internal war. Elvek sent Rebel out again a few nights ago, so they'd have another update within the next couple of days, and were hoping the issue was waning. Beyond that, Nassik had been reclusive, not stirring up trouble for the council.

"Elvek doesn't sound concerned," Celissia said. "Typical postwar propositioning."

"And what if it's not?" Barrett snapped. He winced, casting her an apologetic glance. "Sorry." She waved off the apology, and Barrett went on, "What if this is all for nothing, though?"

"What if it is?" I asked. Dax sliced me a warning glare. "What if these people present an opponent to your throne? You're the last of your line, so it would be difficult, but imagine for a moment they found someone willing and able to challenge you? What would that mean?"

Barrett scoffed. "I'm not narcissistic enough to think I'm the best person to be king. Simply the best option right now. If there was someone out there who I genuinely thought wanted to lead the Engrossians from a place a goodness, with the training and mind for it, I'd gladly abdicate." He shook his head. "But there's not. Not that we know of, at least."

"Even if that person came about," I said, "even if you lost your damn throne through an uprising, you changed the tide of the war when you joined us. Some of your people may not like that choice, but every other clan will remember it for history." I passed the letter back to his capable hands. "I believe you're going to reclaim that throne rightfully, but even if you didn't, what you've done wouldn't be for nothing."

With one hand resting on his stomach, Dax placed the other on Barrett's shoulder. "Malakai's right."

Frustration rippled off the prince's frame. He leaned forward bracing his elbows on his knees. "There's something going on, though. I can feel it."

"What do you mean? Did Elvek's recent letters say more?" I asked.

Dax swiveled to face me, again wincing, and watched intently as his prince said, "Nothing of notable concern." Barrett dragged a ringed hand through his dark hair. "I was certain that, with me gone, Celissia's father would make strides toward his own agenda."

My brow furrowed. "Then why leave him in reach of the crown?"

"Because I wanted to see what those efforts would be." I was silent, not quite following that strategy, so Barrett continued, "I thought that while Nassik did not support my initial plans for reclaiming my position and moving our clan forward, he would fold once his daughter and I were promised. And he has, on the surface. But I expected he would still be working to fortify the territory against our *enemies* as he fears you all might be. That he would be rebuilding the armies and ensuring our defenses, nurturing that innate refusal of me being king. And I wanted to catch him in the act."

"But he hasn't done any of that?" I asked as a warm breeze coasted between the branches.

"Not a thing to push back against any of the initiatives Elvek and Pelvira have instituted."

"Which are?"

"They've opened the doors," Dax said.

Barrett elaborated, "The palace is flooded with staff again. There's life being breathed back into our home." He clasped his hands between his knees and—dammit, pride glinted in his green eyes.

"It's truly marvelous to see," Celissia said, practically radiating. "Or so a friend wrote to me. She said there hasn't been this much warmth and levity in Banix in years. It sounded hopeful. Restorative."

"The people are happy, then," I commented. "Aside from those Rebel uncovered."

Barrett glowed at the words. "Those employed by the palace are elated, and the nearby districts in Banix are already benefitting from the available work."

"What risk could Nassik possibly see with this plan, then? The majority of the people are happy, his daughter will be queen as far as he knows, and even though the palace staff is back, you're not there, so there can't be a threat to the crown. Maybe Nassik realized that, and that's why he's been silent?"

The prince flopped back in the sand, reaching up to pick at a loose piece of bark on the nearest cypher.

"Nassik was on my mother's council for decades before I was even born." Barrett sighed. "Sometimes, I think he's the one who kept her in line."

"What do you mean?"

"He has a certain"—Barrett's head tilted, contemplating his next words—"audacity to him. He's not afraid to speak his mind."

"Regardless of the opponent," Dax added gruffly. Celissia's agreeing laughter bounced across the dunes.

"So I've seen," I said. "You think that makes him irredeemable, then?"

"It makes him a confusing adversary, because I can't figure out his motives. He was against my mother at times, but now he's against me, too?" Barrett shook his head. "It doesn't make sense. I fear he's planning something...bigger. And biding his time, allowing us to get comfortable."

Celissia dragged her hands through the sand. "He has a lot of secrets."

"So don't get comfortable," I said simply. "You orchestrated this tour, remember? *You* still have control here, Barrett. You and Celissia have met with leaders of multiple cities since leaving Valyn —won them over. They'll back your claim for the throne if it means the Engrossians won't be a threat."

It was clear from Barrett's silent fidgeting that he agreed, though reluctantly. He didn't *want* this tour—this facade. Barrett wanted the man he loved to wear the crown beside him in full truth. To take the Engrossian vows with Dax, his general and king consort.

And every day he spent indulging this bluff was driving him closer to snapping. Celissia gave me a grim nod that said she understood and only wanted her friend to be happy. Barrett had been raised with the games of royals, and while his heart was staked on his clan, his spirit was not in the manipulation.

"You'll sit on that throne," I swore, "and you'll do it with Dax by your side."

The prince looked up at me, and gratitude shone in his eyes. The kind you felt when you couldn't voice what you wanted, but were thankful someone saw it anyway.

Dax shifted closer to his prince's side and brushed back his curls. "We have other plans in place. Other dreams that you and Celissia have been discussing since you were small. This is how we're going to achieve them."

"He's right, Bare," Celissia agreed. "There are bigger goals to remember."

I wasn't sure what they meant by that, but Barrett blew out a rough breath, continuing to chip away at the cypher. "It's all so worrisome."

I snorted a laugh. "Sounds like the simplest way to describe politics."

They all cracked smiles.

"I think Nassik cares about one thing over all else," Dax said, exchanging a nod with Celissia. "His house. His daughter is promised to the crown so he isn't openly rebelling, but we'd be foolish to assume he won't take an opportunity to do so."

A power-hungry ruler whose boundary had not been tested yet. How far would he go?

"I think Dax is right," I said, thinking back to all those years I spent studying history as the heir to the Revered. Picking apart the movements of past rulers and the reasoning behind their decisions. "Nassik, like so many in politics, doesn't truly care about his people. Many might when they first start out." I shrugged. "But somewhere along the line, the power overtakes them. It becomes less about the greater public and more about...*more*. More land, more wealth, more accolades for their family. We've seen it time and again in the past."

"I studied that pattern, too," Barrett muttered. "It's one no one has ever come up with a way to combat."

"Pure hearts?" Celissia drawled.

"Are few and far between." Barrett pried up the wood chip and flicked it out across the dunes. He sighed. "At least we'll have more news from Rebel soon. Come on, let's eat before we head back out."

"I'll be right there," I said as they stood.

Barrett wanted to combat the greedy tendencies of men, but was there truly a way to fight warrior nature? We thrived on the magic of the land; it made sense that so many sought power in other forms once they'd had a taste. Whatever made them feel stronger, more prominent. Invincible.

I contemplated the sun-kissed dunes and budding cyphers for a few silent minutes, tossing the pitfall of warrior instincts around in my mind.

But my eyes kept landing on that stubborn chip of wood Barrett had flicked away, lonely and sinking in the sandy sea, and I couldn't help but wonder if that was how being a ruler often felt?

Being pulled in so many directions that you found yourself alone, drifting, and drowning in your surroundings.

CHAPTER FORTY-ONE
OPHELIA

ZANOX ROARED SOMETHING FIERCE AS SAPPHIRE LOOPED around him.

"Competitive?" I tossed over my shoulder at Jezebel.

She leaned forward and stroked her khrysaor's neck, her voice carrying on the wind. "He's a big baby."

In response, Zanox bucked. Not enough to actually dismount Jezebel—that creature would dive in front of flaming arrows before he let harm come to my sister—but she did pop off his back, airborne and laughing for a moment.

Sapphire sped ahead. As I peered back at them, the khrysaor's wings beat among the wisps of clouds stretching into the sky high above Soulguider Territory. Dynaxtar soared peacefully to his left, carrying Erista.

My heart inflated, a bubble of bliss expanding between my ribs. I curled my fingers tighter into Sapphire's mane and released a wild laugh to the stars.

After everything in the catacombs and the rescue—everything with Damien's odd dream visit—*this* was what I needed. To feel unbridled, unbroken, lost among the clouds with my myth-born warrior horse.

"Cypherion and Malakai said we need saddles," I called to Jez as Sapphire swooped around Zanox again.

"No thank you!" From the lift in her voice, it was clear she shared that utterly freeing and intrinsically right feeling spreading throughout my body. Erista whooped in agreement, the sound trailing along the clouds. Sapphire shook her head as if to agree she wouldn't be saddled again.

"That's what I said." I laughed. "Tolek told him there wasn't a chance we'd agree." Not when the heart of these creatures *was* freedom after being contained for so many years.

"Knowing Cypherion, he'll find a way to create them regardless," Jezebel said.

She was likely right. "Tol gets it because he's flown with me. Cypherion and Malakai only see the dangers."

"It's something you don't understand until you're a part of it," Erista said wistfully, in a way that made me wonder if she wanted to be a part of it—a khrysaor rider as the girl she loved was.

"Your friends are rather overprotective, sister."

My next laugh echoed through the heavens. "I don't think I'm allowed to say that."

Jez did have a point. The boys were a mix of curious and cautious when it came to us flying. Tolek less so, understanding that Sapphire and the khrysaor would never let us get hurt. Still, they bickered over it.

And it warmed my heart each time.

"Landing soon?" Jezzie called to me.

"A little longer?"

She nudged Zanox so he circled high above the earth, carving a path back through the clouded skies with his razor-tipped wings.

～

DYNAXTAR FOUND a burst of speed at the end of the flight, her clawed feet digging into the sand as she landed first, sending it spraying up around those midnight-black scales I would have thought would be retracted with only us around.

Sapphire had been unsettled since we left Valyn, too. As her wings tucked in, I searched the dunes and cyphers, but the low, sloping mountains of Soulguider Territory appeared empty for miles.

We were at the edge of the expansive Lendelli Hills that stretched across a central section of the clan's domain, nothing but desert until you hit the town a mile east, but no stragglers from the market or nomadic parties dotted the sands.

Still, I remained on guard as I dismounted Sapphire, keeping my weapons close.

"That's my girl. Both of them," Jezebel cheered as she slid from Zanox's back and raced to her other khrysaor, helping Erista down and kissing her with all the exhilaration of the flight.

I turned my back, giving them a moment of privacy. Angels, I was so happy Jez had her. When we began the hunt for the emblems, there'd been strife between them. A debate of loyalty versus love.

Jezebel had always been a force, like a well of power was packed in her bones, but those weeks Erista was gone had taken something from her. Dimmed a light only love could restore.

Now, she'd become an even stronger version of herself, bolstered and encouraged by her partner's wild spirit and curious nature. She was scared of the magic within her—unsure what it did still—but her confidence shone with Erista's support at her back, and it was a sight I'd never tire of seeing.

"Come on, girl," I whispered to Sapphire, running a hand across her downy-soft wings.

We led the way into the series of caves Sapphire and the khrysaor would hide in while we were here, ensuring the curtain of brush was secured across the entrance. Our steps were muffled by soft sand that turned to stone as we crept deeper into the tunnel, finally rounding a bend into a wide-open pocket set beneath a high, domed ceiling.

Sapphire and the khrysaor immediately strode to the shallow pool in the center, dipping their heads to drink. Thin streams trailed off, leading deeper into the caves.

Between the height of the tunnels and the fresh water source, it was the perfect spot for the creatures to hide out. Almost as if this Soulguider land was meant to stash secrets.

An ache went through my heart as Sapphire crossed back to me, wishing for the day she wouldn't *have* to be hidden. When we had explanations to the myths. It ebbed from her, as well—the need to be free, though she understood why she wasn't yet. Why none of us were, truly.

Sapphire and I had always been connected at a soul-deep level, our spirits entwined by the ether, but ever since she sprouted those beautiful wings, something between us had shifted. It was like a latch hovering over its lock, needing a final nudge to seal it.

An extension of myself, that's what I'd always thought my horse had been. I'd assumed that's what everyone's relationship with their warrior horse was. But perhaps we were more, written in the *fel strella mythos*—though we were still figuring out exactly what that meant.

We sat along the bank of the pool, Sapphire's wing draped beside me and my fingers gently stroking her feathers.

"Do you think there are more out there?" Jezebel turned to me at my question. "More like us? With these...connections? More of the pegasus and khrysaor?"

Jezebel was silent for a moment, watching as Zanox and Dynaxtar took up guard positions near the entrance to the cavern, folding their wings in and settling down for the night. "I don't know."

As she admitted it, for the briefest flash of time, we could have been back in our manor in Palerman, exchanging secrets beneath the covers. Like we were sketching our warrior leathers by the light of a Mystique lantern well after our parents told us to go to bed. Like we were innocent young girls again, wondering about the secrets held in the future's palm.

I gazed up at Sapphire. Were there more pegasus out there, waiting to spread their wings? More phoenixes? How did we find them?

The shift in my warrior horse's countenance since her wings emerged was impossible to ignore. Like she claimed some stifled destiny. Stretching my arm up to weave my fingers through her mane, I swore I'd find them, too.

"So," Jez began, and from the way Erista rolled her eyes at the too-casual tone of her voice, I knew I wouldn't like what she asked next, "do you want to work with our magic?"

I stared out over the pool. "Now?"

Ever persistent, Jezebel crawled into my line of sight. "We know what happened in the catacombs. How it became...destructive and burnt those corpses to their bones."

"*Fucking Vincienzo*," I simmered. I'd given Jezebel the overview—told everyone what they needed to know. Apparently, based on the concern widening her tawny eyes, Tol told her how scared it made me. "He should keep his mouth shut."

"He won't ever do that where your safety is involved," she retorted.

I gave her an admonishing glare. "My safety is not the issue here." It was everyone else's.

"We don't know that, Ophelia," Erista said softly. Dammit she was always hard to argue with, her words coming across as understanding and empathetic no matter how little she said. A part of me wondered what her Soulguider magic derived of the future that she couldn't share and how it shaped her opinions.

Jezebel placed a hand on my arm, asking, "Are you scared because of what happened at the inn? With me?"

Had Sapphire stepped closer to me, too? Her wing cocooned us from the world, forcing me to talk to my sister. I glared up at my pegasus.

And though it twisted my insides, as I met those crystal blue eyes, I admitted, "Yes."

"Ophelia," she began.

I cut her off. "It singed those corpses to ash. What if that had been *you*?" I shook my head. "I don't ever want to use it again if I don't have to."

"None of that was your fault."

"That's even worse!" I pushed to my feet. "That means I can't control it."

"It means you need to train it," Jez said, following me. Erista remained on the bank, allowing us to argue. "We both do. And I know it's scary, but I don't think running is our answer."

It wasn't. I'd never been one to run from power. But this wasn't a title or a sword, this was beyond any conceivable realm. Any territory we'd encountered.

It was another seed planted within me that I was afraid was only there to *use* me.

"You've been spirit-speaking for years, though, Jez. You have a familiarity I'm still learning."

Her eyes widened as she nodded, as if that was the point. "Then let's learn."

"Why don't you?" I threw at her.

"My magic requires death, Ophelia!"

"And mine seems to cause it!"

"Not always," she challenged. "There are two sides to all of it. A balance." As she said it, she called up the silver-blue light. It pulsed around her for a moment, seemingly useless, and faded back into her frame.

"How am I even supposed to train Angellight?" I sighed, throwing my arms out. "There are no Angels here. They abandoned us. They abandoned *me*." The back of my eyes stung, and I didn't fight it. The caving in of my chest, the jilted hurt, seared my words. "They cast the curse and then they *left me to fight it*. To figure out what the fuck I'm supposed to do."

"Figure it out!" she yelled. "Damien said to use the Angellight."

"No," I growled.

"Do it." She took a step forward, and something buzzed beneath my skin.

"*No*," I asserted with the command of the Revered, but it was pushing, *pushing*.

"Jez..." Erista said softly.

But Jezebel wouldn't be deterred. "Unless you're truly so sacred of it, do it! Unless you're scared of what the Angels may do and want to hide instead!"

My armor was cracking, power ebbing closer to the surface.

I wasn't. I wasn't one to hide. I wasn't one to run. And as those truths settled into me, I screamed.

And light burst from my skin. Searing and all-consuming. Uplifting but not devouring.

This. This was the Angellight from the battle against Kakias, the pulling of different hollows of my spirit, each tethered to a thread of magic in the emblems. The euphoria, the fulfillment, it all flooded me.

Gold light filled the cave and pulsed against my skin, begging me to use it.

A fearful thought broke through: *I don't know how.*

It is in your blood, a voice echoed—a voice I knew, but I couldn't place. Not in this haze of burning.

Searing.

It didn't singe the brush. Didn't melt the sand. If anything, it seemed to feed life deeper into the earth. To restore weeds withered in the cave corners and crystalize the soft grains beneath my boots.

Even the khrysaor and Sapphire looked curiously at it, neither attracted or repelled. And Jezebel—

Jez had erected a precautionary silver-blue shield before herself and Erista. But unlike in the inn, this light didn't hunger for hers.

As our eyes locked, she dropped that wall, a ring of charred earth left where it had been.

And still, my Angellight did not harm her. It didn't lunge, didn't lock around her throat. Did nothing but slowly, curiously, slip across her skin with affectionate licks of greeting.

"How does it feel?" Erista asked, eyeing the gold shimmering up Jezebel's arm.

I tugged at Damien's thread, warmth gathering in my chest. "It feels how it used to. The safe version."

"Can you do anything with it?"

With another pull on Damien's string, I sent it shooting toward my pack. It dug within, spilling the five emblems across sand that glowed like diamonds.

The gold light wafted the emblems to me as if on a breeze. I crouched down, running my fingers over each, luxuriating in the distinct presence of each connection.

It was the newest one, though—Valyrie's heart—whose pulse beat the loudest. I scooped up the carving and felt into the shrinking hollows of my spirit.

"There," I muttered. A bead of power swirled like the depths of the cosmos, unspooling within me. It stretched out, longing to meld with its five counterparts.

I latched on to it and pulled, feeding that source into the power within the emblem. It fueled me in turn.

Until a might like the stars flooded the cave, darkness and silver stars shimmering through my Angellight in a canopy across the rocky ceiling.

"That's Valyrie," Erista gasped, constellations reflected across her awed face.

"It is," I agreed.

An instinct screamed in my bones, wanting to be united with this emblem as it had the others.

My gaze flashed between the fated lovers in my palm and the magic painting the ceiling. Then, I took my dagger from my thigh. With a prick to my finger, I smeared a streak of crimson across Valyrie's heart.

And her magic reared up, shooting stars and trails of white fire among those cosmos. Jezebel released a laugh, and I tugged on the other threads of light. Gaveny's turquoise-tinted tides and Ptholenix's burning fire frolicked with the constellations, the colors of Angellight tangling in the air. Thorn's silver storms rioted through them, and Damien's and Bant's brute forces cracked like lightning strikes.

Together, they forged a new world around us. The crystallized grains of sand rose into the air, swarming among the light, shadows painting them deep maroons.

And through me, that empowering sensation I'd come to associate with Angellight flooded. It burned and ignited all my deepest hollows, restoring my magic.

Light looped around the cave, dancing among the khrysaor's and pegasus' wings. Carefully, I separated the six distinct magics so each Angel's hovered above us, six ancient sources. Then, I allowed them to melt back together.

"Look at how you're controlling it," Jez encouraged.

And as precisely as I had been toying with the magic, I recoiled that mass of power back into me, like a snapping of a band against my spirit. I stopped burning, and the world fell into stillness again.

Jezebel opened her mouth, but Erista gasped. "Come on!" she demanded, racing to the mouth of the cave.

We followed, a swell of noise mounting.

"What is it?" Jezebel asked.

But as soon as we parted the brush curtain, I knew. Far in the distance, away from the city, in a haze of burning ruby reds and deep violets, a sand storm swirled high above the desert.

"The Rites of Dusk," I gasped. Swarms of Soulguiders danced among the dunes in the ritual.

"How does it work?" I asked Erista.

"The sands are blessed by Artale," she explained. "It's how we connect to her, though we revere the Angel more. The Goddess of Death's magic laces the land, and when it's stirred up, it pools in the air, like it's being set free. As it falls on you and you say the ritual words, perform the acts, your own Soulguider magic is replenished."

"How often do you have to take part?" Jezebel asked, likely counting the last time Erista had.

"Not frequently, once a year is typically enough. The Rites have been occurring more lately, though. In various places across the desert, mainly near major cities." Perhaps the increasing warrior populations caused that. "They used to only be a few times per year, and timed fairly evenly. Now they're sporadic."

Sapphire brushed a wing over my shoulder, and I glanced down at the still-burning emblems in my hand, then back at the swirling Rite.

As Jezebel and Erista continued discussing the ritual, I recalled the magic unspooling across Ambrisk. Unusual temperatures and riled creatures.

And my skin chilled at the idea that it may all be connected.

CHAPTER FORTY-TWO
OPHELIA

THE DAY FOLLOWING THE RITES OF DUSK, THE Lendelli Market was alive with the abundance of magic flowing through its warriors.

"Have you and Jezebel been here before?" Rina asked as we strode through the stalls. All around us, the scents of richly-seasoned meat wafted through the air; shouts about fresh fruit, newly-forged jewelry, and hand-spun scarves carried down the aisles beneath the woven fabric roof, sunlight dappling the streets.

"Once, when we were young, but I barely remember it." Our entire traveling party followed Erista's bouncing curls and trilling explanations of the vendors lining the sand-strewn stone streets. "My grandmother always shared dazzling stories, though."

"She was born in Lendelli, right?"

I nodded, side stepping a man with a crate full of pomegranates. "And lived here into her first century. Once she turned twenty and came of age, she spent nearly a hundred years training to be a priestess of Xenique."

Santorina halted. "The training is a hundred years?"

"It can be." I looped my arm through hers and tugged her back into motion. "Her magic isn't particularly strong. In Soulguider temples, priestesses make rank, so she already had the basic title and was slowly climbing up."

"A hundred years," Rina considered. To a human, that was a long lifetime. "What made her give up all that work?"

"Love." I smiled fondly. "My grandfather was on an assignment from Palerman when they met. It only took him two weeks to convince her to run away with him."

"Knowing Grandmother," Jezebel interrupted, appearing at my shoulder, "she decided that first day that she loved him and was making him work for it."

Santorina laughed. "That does sound like her."

Jezebel skipped ahead to catch up with Erista, looping her arm around her partner's waist.

"Sometimes I wish I'd learned more about that side of my heritage," I admitted to Rina.

"Didn't she teach you and Jez when you were young?"

"The basics, yes. But I don't *know* it the way I do the Mystiques. I've never been able to tap into the magic or recite the histories." Digging a few coins out of my pack, I exchanged them for two silk scarves, draping one around Santorina's shoulders and the other around my own.

Something about the thin maroon fabric, gold trim catching the light, helped me feel closer to my grandmother.

"We always thought I'd inherit my father's position as Second," I continued, "so Grandmother understood why I focused on that dominant side of my bloodline, but I completely shunned the other piece after the first war."

When the option of the Undertaking had been ripped from my future, I became sullen and disinterested in anything that didn't have to do with restoration for the people I was meant to lead.

"Your grandmother knew a great love worth running away for. I'm certain she understood why you reacted as you did." Rina shrugged a shoulder. "We all knew."

"Still," I said, rubbing the silk between my fingers, "I wish I'd tried harder. I wish I hadn't been so awful those years."

"You were heartbroken, Ophelia," Rina intoned. "Over more than one loss. No one is their best then."

I'd made amends with my friends and family for how I'd acted, but that didn't mean it didn't haunt me. I didn't think my grandmother begrudged me the time I took to grieve—if anything, she seemed to understand better than most—I only wished I did so differently.

I gripped the silk tighter. "It was her stories of my grandfather, actually, that made me believe in the idea of all-consuming love."

"You never met your grandfather, right?"

"No." I shook my head, following the rest of the group around the next corner where the clangs of steel rang from the blacksmith's tent. "She spoke of him with such adoration, though. It was always what I thought Malakai and I had—that sort of enthralling love. But she'd always seemed a bit resigned about him and me."

"Really?" Rina's brows shot up. "She never showed that."

"Not outright. She did—*does*—love Malakai, but she was never emphatic about the pairing." I shrugged. "I always thought it was because it sealed my fate as a Mystique and led me to focus even less on our Soulguider heritage, but maybe..." I looked over my shoulder to where Malakai walked with Cypherion and Tol, laughing with a few of the Soulguiders Erista had introduced us to. To where the quartz pendant my grandmother had gifted me for my twentieth birthday shone proudly on Tolek's leathers. "I think a part of her might have always known that it wouldn't be Malakai and me at the end."

Perhaps she'd seen it in one of her Soulguider visions—that it would be Tolek and me hand in hand until our dying days.

"I love your grandmother as if she's my own," Rina began, examining a hooked knife.

"She feels the same toward you."

"She's told me." I smiled at that. "And as someone who also loves you, I'm certain she only wants you to be happy. We all do, and that's why we were so frustrated following the first war. Not because of the heritage you shunned." Rina squeezed my arm. "Be happy, Ophelia. We're here now—you *can* learn."

Ahead, Erista called Rina's name to point out a stall full of tonics and herbs.

"Thank you, Rina," I said. "Go shop to your healer heart's desire."

She laughed, never having been one for shopping, and ducked into the tent.

Learn, Rina had said.

I picked up the knife she'd been looking at. With its delicately crafted, rounded blade, it was a pristine Soulguider weapon. I didn't know the exact name, but Rina was right. I *could* learn.

As I stood on this land my grandmother may have walked on, I couldn't help but wonder, had these markets been here when she shopped? Had she roamed these sand-strewn stone streets? Were the vendors old friends, or descendants of them?

Where was her home? Her place of worship and schooling? Her *life*? Before she gave it all up for the man she loved.

Someone tugged at my hand, breaking through the thought.

"You okay?" Tolek asked, those brown eyes searching my expression, amber flecks burning right though me, all the way down to the soles of my boots, rooted on Soulguider ground.

"Yeah," I said, a bit sadly. But the market around us was bustling with both shoppers and magic, and for once, the day didn't feel burdened by the Angels.

It was clear in the intensity of Tolek's gaze that he knew I wasn't being entirely honest. Obvious in the very intentional step he took toward me. In the way he tilted my chin up with his free hand and kissed me so passionately, I could almost forget the remorse swirling through me.

Whatever it is, I'm here, his lips spelled. My heart raced at the sentiment, at the feel of his tongue stroking mine, at the warmth of his body, evident even in the dry desert heat and making me squirm.

"Don't get lost, you two!" Jezebel's voice drifted from down the street.

Tolek smiled against my lips. "I'm tempted to do exactly that." Keeping his hand beneath my chin, he surveyed the area. "It looks private behind that tent. We could..."

Wings fluttered in my chest, my core aching for him at only the thought. "Later," I said, kissing him chastely, but I didn't miss the way his stare heated at the promise. I rolled my eyes. "Come on, Vincienzo."

"Yes, Revered," he said, smugly satisfied.

I pulled him after me, invigorated at the promise of being in the land that held a piece of my ancestry. As we wound down the aisles, I committed every sight and sound, every smiling warrior and bartering seller to memory.

I got my wild, dreamer soul and proclivity for magic from my grandmother. I hoped, while we were here, I would be able to connect with her.

~

A PLEASURE HOUSE was not what I had in mind.

"You're certain this is the best way?" I asked Erista again as she, Cypherion, and I stood at the bar of yet another inn our party was commandeering for a few evenings.

This one, unlike the one Harlen had procured in Starsearcher Territory, wasn't cleared out for our stay. It was quite the opposite, with residents littering the dining room and filling the rooms above. The front door was propped open directly onto a hectic market street.

Given that we were in ally territory now, the Engrossians were staying in the same inn, seated around our table in the dining room with everyone else. Even the fae were there, with hoods up. Mora had been increasingly quiet since the catacombs, but things had been more amicable with Lancaster. As if us tending to his sister formed a temporary truce.

"The pleasure houses are the best option," Erista said confidently, elbows resting on the turquoise tile bar as we waited for drinks.

Water was placed before me, and I spun the glass between my hands.

Cypherion asked, a bit stiffly, "Why, though?"

"The Storytellers of Lendelli have formed nests," Erista explained. "Something about the freedom of the pleasure houses attracts them."

It made sense when she put it that way. Brothels didn't usually operate under strict rules. It likely made for a comfortable, reclusive space for those of the famous cult to withdraw from the world, even if they were not working members of the establishments.

"Then, I can't wait to see." I tipped my glass to hers, and the Soulguider flitted off to claim a seat between Jezebel and Vale with our friends.

"Have you heard back from the Bodymelders?" Cypherion asked, his attention drifting to the table.

"Not since Esmond's last letter. He said the chancellor has declined any aid being sent now that they got the flames under control and didn't lose too many crops." A devastating fire had swept through villages near Firebird's Field a few days ago.

"That's good," Cyph said. "But it's still unprecedented. Do they think it was sabotage?"

"It is," I agreed, "and they have no idea. Esmond is leaning toward no." He'd been the Bodymelder Chancellor's apprentice in Damenal, had been stationed with Lyria's troops at the border, and spent some time with us in the outposts post-war. Esmond was one of the best of the healing clan; I trusted his insight.

"That's worrisome in a different way, then," Cyph said, but his attention was still snagged on Vale, so I let the conversation drop.

"How's she doing?" I asked, nodding to the Starsearcher.

Cypherion observed her, sitting quietly in her seat but smiling at the conversation. Cyph's lips twitched upward, too.

"She's okay," Cypherion said. Then, he dropped his voice. "I think she's grateful Harlen had also been named apprentice and few people knew she was back. It was fucked up that Titus treated her that way, but maybe it's for the best. Harlen is acting-chancellor until the council decides what comes next and she..." His gaze drifted back to Vale, nothing but pure adoration glinting in those blue eyes.

"She's free," I said, understanding.

No more oaths, no more toxic savior relationships, no more tattoos and brands and temples. *Freedom.*

"Yeah," Cyph said, wonder in his voice. "She'll get there. The loss of the tattoo has been the hardest part."

The breaking of a soul-bond. Automatically, my hand drifted to my own North Star.

I brushed it away, clearing my throat and looking over Cyph. Scruff still adorned his chin and longer auburn curls stretched to his shoulders. "And how are *you* doing?"

Cypherion looked at me, nodding. "Better now."

"Good," I said.

"And thank you."

I raised a brow. "For?"

"For—" He blew out a breath, laughing. "Dammit, I didn't want to admit it. But thank you for making me take the position of Second. For waiting for me to accept it."

"I pushed pretty hard."

"You wouldn't be *you* if you didn't push us all, though," he said, and I rolled my eyes. "But I mean it. Thank you, Ophelia. I realized when Vale and I were dealing with Titus that I may actually like it. That I could be good at it."

Cypherion had always been an asset in meetings and strategy sessions, but there was a marked change since he returned. Like he now understood those strengths within himself. How he'd organized Vale's entire rescue with Harlen, how assertive he'd been. Sure, it was because her safety was at risk, but those dire circumstances only brought the qualities he always had to the surface.

I didn't add aloud that he'd come to these understandings without the knowledge of who his father was.

"You're perfect for it," I swore, gripping his arm. "We're only getting started, Cyph, but you and me...we've got quite a partnership ahead of us."

"Taking the Mystiques to new heights." He chuckled. "I suppose that's literal with Sapphire."

My warrior-horse-turned-pegasus born from the stars herself would certainly help us soar.

A thought struck me then. "We have a while until we head out, correct?"

At the mention of tonight, Cypherion nodded minutely, fidgeting with his ale.

My brows drew together, but when he didn't comment, I downed my water and said, "Vale and I will be back before then."

~

THE CAVERN WAS cold compared to the dunes we walked to get there, a welcome chill cooling the sweat beading down my back.

"As much as I love the cryptic nature of this all, Ophelia," Vale whispered, voice still a touch hollow, "I hope there's a reason you're bringing me to this dark cave."

I laughed. "I promise, nothing nefarious. I owe you too much to wish any ill will against you."

We rounded the final bend, and Vale let out a small, awed gasp.

"You were gone for so long, and then the way we've had to stagger our travel times for secrecy, you've yet to see Sapphire."

My pegasus stood across the pool, flaring those magnificent white wings. The gold woven among her feathers glinted in the mystlight lanterns set up throughout the cavern.

I nudged Vale. "You can go closer. She's as docile as ever."

As she took an eager step around the pool of water, the shadows in the depths of the cavern shifted, and Zanox emerged.

No—it was Dynaxtar. The quieter of the two beasts, a bit smaller and timid. Zanox stood behind her, almost a shadow against the dark rock as he observed Vale with an approving snort.

Dynaxtar, though, came to stand across the water, wings relaxed at her sides.

"Curious," I said.

"What?" Vale asked, without looking away.

I shrugged. "Dynaxtar usually only cares about Jez, and Erista by extension."

Vale considered, watching Dynaxtar's silver mane tumble over her neck as she shook her head. "She's beautiful."

"She is," I agreed. I'd once thought the beasts fearsome, but these weeks with them had taught me to look beneath the armored scales, beyond the unfamiliar. "They're incredibly smart and patient with us, too. All three are."

"Mystical beasts tend to understand us better than we expect," Vale said.

I jerked my head toward Sapphire. "Come on."

We rounded the edge of the pool, and Sapphire beat her wings gently in excitement. A twin sensation fluttered through my body, down to the shreds of my soul.

Vale circled Sapphire, admiring her.

"You can touch them," I said, and Vale started. I gently trailed my fingertips along the downy feathers. "She doesn't mind. I think she likes it, actually." As if in confirmation, she released a low nicker.

"That's my girl," I purred.

Vale was silent as she explored Sapphire, casting curious glances toward the khrysaor.

"I'm sorry for what you had to do." I whispered it so quietly, I thought she might not have heard at first.

But after a moment, she said in a tone that chimed like a bell, "I am, too," and continued tending to my pegasus.

"I know I wasn't in your situation, but I've had to do a lot of things I never thought I would. Spilled blood I'd never imagined would stain my hands."

Lucidius, all those months ago within the confines of the Spirit Volcano, was a loss that had become a festering wound between Malakai and me. Then, shortly after, the Mindshaper Chancellor, Aird. I carried less guilt for that. When he'd attacked me during the Battle of Damenal, I'd been left with little choice. Still, an entire clan had relied on him. Had I doomed them to a worse fate by slaying him or cleared the way for a more just ruler? Only time would tell, given that no political movements had been made clear from the Mindshapers.

But Vale...what she'd done was different than either of those circumstances.

I continued, "I won't pretend to know how you feel or presume to understand how your relationship with Titus truly unfolded, but from what I do know, and from what I've experienced myself, it's okay to grieve while still being happy you made that choice."

"There was no choice," she answered. "And yet, sometimes, I find myself torn. I fluctuate between being angry I didn't have an option, wishing there could have been another way, and grateful I was allowed to be weak enough to let the Fates decide." Her words twisted with ire at the end—ire for herself or for the circumstances, I wasn't sure.

"Death is not simple, nor is it clean. And in my experience, it is rarely easy to come to terms with." My father's presence settled around me, as if his spirit was with us.

Vale watched her hands. "Sometimes I feel nothing at all toward it, and I worry that being able to kill someone who had given me so much at one point means I'm heartless." She bit her lip. "The night they found Cypherion and me in the archives, the Fates showed me a reading that said I would be Titus's downfall." I perked up, wondering what else she saw and how it had built to that moment. "I didn't think it was possible, but I suppose I was meant to do what I did. And now, sometimes I'm numb to it."

I strode around Sapphire and took Vale's hands between my own. "Everything you feel—be it loud crashes of tidal waves threatening to drown you or the still calm sea—is all a part of healing."

"Thank you," Vale whispered. And it was only two small words, but they were layered with such sincerity, like it was exactly what she'd needed to hear. Vale hugged me to her, gratitude seeping from her body in waves.

As she pulled back, the silver on her shoulder glinted.

"May I ask?" I said, and she followed my stare to the ring of stars, her fingers tracing over it as her own eyes dropped to my Bind, and she nodded. "How did it feel?"

"It was something I'd never wish on my worst enemy, Ophelia. It was the root of myself shredded—a piece lost to eternity. And now, I have to learn the consequences of it."

I gripped my arm around the Bind, rolling my lips together. There was nothing to respond, nothing but fear cascading through my body, so I nodded.

Vale stepped back, saying, "I'm going to go meet the khrysaor, if that's all right."

"Of course," I said around the dread crowding my throat. "They prefer apples if you want to feed them. We had to tie the baskets shut in an attempt to keep them out."

Sapphire's wing curved around me, and the soft sound of Vale muttering to Dynaxtar and Zanox filled the cavern. She spent an hour tending to Dynaxtar in particular, and the entire time, all I could see was the outline of the North Star inked on my arm. All I could wonder was if I would one day learn to live without a piece of my soul.

Chapter Forty-Three
Malakai

I sprawled on one of the couches in the Lendelli inn's many lounges. Mila and Lyria were in chairs across from me and one of Lucidius's journals was in my hands—Soulguider Territory this time. One of the fae books on the sphinxes lay open on the table between us, but as much as I tried to focus, I couldn't help but eavesdrop on the girls' whispered conversation.

"I don't know what I want from it," Lyria said, watching the bright mystlight dancing in its lantern in the chandelier strung over the table. "I like being back with everyone, though."

"Oh, my company wasn't enough?" Mila teased.

"Shut up," Lyria groaned, laughing. From the corner of my eye, I noticed Mila exhale, relieved she and her friend were settling back into their old routines. "You know it was, but that was before. We were traveling the territories, there was always something new to explore."

"I know what you mean," Mila said. And I swore I tried to read the journal instead of listening.

The damn gates would not let me in but legend spoke of them and the ones who tell tales of legends whispered of it too so this must be it.

What gates was Lucidius on about?

Mila continued, "Being with a close-knit group reminds me of the early days in the army, but I miss getting to see new places. A mix of both would be nice."

"I did miss my brother." Neither acknowledged that the different lifestyles they discussed would force them to be separated. I didn't think either wanted to accept that until the time came.

"Have you told him that?" Mila asked.

Lyria was silent for a moment.

"Lyr…" Mila prodded.

"No," Lyria groaned, and a dull *thunk* led me to believe she'd thrown a pillow at Mila. "No, I haven't. I've avoided more important conversations with him as I avoided the decision to retain my title since the war ended."

"You do realize—" I cut myself off, not looking up from the journal.

"We know you've been listening, Warrior Prince," Mila said.

I whipped my head toward them. "How?"

"You haven't turned a page in minutes," Lyria answered.

I groaned, but went on, "You realize that in not making a decision, you're keeping the title?"

Lyria nodded. "I'm not ready to let it go, yet." There was a hopefulness in her voice that I hadn't heard since before the Battle of Damenal.

"What are you reading over there?" Mila asked, leaning across the table to swipe Lucidius's journal.

"I'm looking for mentions of the sphinxes," I said. "Lucidius had been in Firebird's Field where we found the Bodymelder emblem. Had likely visited Brontain, too. I'm trying to map where he went in the desert and compare it to this book we stole from Ritalia."

Mila and Lyria looked about to comment when a voice interrupted from the doorway, "There you are."

I craned my neck to find Cypherion and Tolek waiting, the latter leaning casually against the wood and surveying the room.

Sitting up, I asked, "What are you guys doing?"

"*We* are getting ready for tonight's agenda," Tolek said.

"Which is?"

His answering smile was almost too devious for my liking. "Pleasure house."

My brows shot up. "That's truly what everyone's doing tonight?"

"Certainly is," Tolek said, falling onto the couch beside me.

I looked to Cypherion who hadn't moved from the doorway. "You're going?"

He shook his head, jaw tense, and Tolek looked cautiously at him. I didn't know what that was about, but all Cypherion said was, "Erista told Vale where she can get some unique tincture in the market. She's going to take us. The Engrossians are going to stay back here with the fae. Jezebel and Santorina are going with them, though." He inclined his head toward Tolek.

"And do I even dare ask *what's* at the pleasure house?" I asked.

Tolek smirked, "Well, Mali..."

"Fucking Angels," I muttered.

Tolek spoke over me, "Many people who enjoy some more depraved proclivities seek out pleasure houses for—"

"For the love of the Angels, Tolek," Lyria said, holding up a hand. "Please do not speak from personal experience."

Tolek laughed at his sister, then directed at me, "Erista said it's the most likely place to find Storytellers. Their magic thrives with the lack of restrictions."

"Storytellers," I muttered, looking down at the books I'd placed upon the table, then up at Mila, exchanging a knowing grin. "I guess we're going to the pleasure house."

～

"*This is a pleasure house?*" I muttered, my eyes widening at the large sandstone facade, intricate carvings creeping up the sides and around the window frames, most with thick curtains tightly drawn.

Mila laughed, brows raised. "You act as if you've never seen one?"

Ophelia and Tolek started up the grand staircase leading to the bronze-carved door, clouded glass marring the figures within. Lyria, Santorina, and Jezebel followed.

"I've seen them," I quickly corrected.

Mila laughed again at my flustered response. "Oh, do you frequent them? Good to know."

I blew out a breath as we climbed the steps to that looming doorway. "I meant that the brothels in Damenal and Palerman... from the outside, they were never so..." I waved a hand at the ornate decor. "Grand."

It was a kind way to put the difference. The Damenal brothels were tucked on private streets on the edges of the Merchant Quarter alongside gambling dens, apothecaries-turned-vice-dealers, and other less than reputable establishments. The brothels were legitimate, at least. Just not quite so stately.

"You're spending time in *disagreeable* brothels, then?"

"Spirits, Mila," I swore. "I'm not visiting any! It's not to my taste."

"Too good for it?" Mila asked.

"I don't have a problem with it," I grumbled. "But I preferred to meet women in taverns or shops." The doors were heavy as I held them open for Mila after the others. They had to cost a fortune.

"So many women," Mila whispered, shaking her head as she ducked beneath my arm to follow into the entryway, and I caught the teasing gleam in her eye.

"Pain in my ass," I mumbled, and she released another low laugh.

It wasn't that I thought myself too good for a brothel. But every damn day since I was imprisoned, I'd received pitying looks. If I was going to fuck someone, I didn't want it to be in exchange for money. I wanted to be wanted. That twisting need I experienced when Mila looked at me the other night. How she'd looked at me every time since.

I didn't say any of that as I stepped across the threshold into a dark hallway, thick violet curtains draping across windows, scarves tossed over mystlight lanterns to cast the entire space with a hazy hue. Stone archways lined the entryway, branching off into a maze of rooms and corridors, everything gleaming with rich textiles and fixtures.

I glanced back at those heavy doors. Definitely cost a fortune, then.

Stepping right up behind Mila, I whispered low in her ear, "Maybe there were other women before." She shivered against me. "But not anymore."

Mila looked over her shoulder from beneath her lashes, but her eyes weren't on mine. They were locked on my lips as her own parted. So close, her exhale drifted across my skin.

"How committed of you," she taunted.

I gripped her chin. "You expect anything else at this point?"

"You two are my *favorite* sort of customers," a sultry voice purred from my left.

Reluctantly, my attention whipped to a woman dressed in nothing more than a silk shawl. She leaned against the archway, her bronze skin glowing in the low mystlight, curves on display and dark hair tumbling over her breasts. But what really caught my attention was the hungry spark in her eye.

"What do you mean?" I asked, ignoring the curious stares of our friends and keeping one hand on Mila.

"Young and naive, but true feelings lie between the two. Always makes for a decadent evening." The woman sauntered forward, dragging a finger over my shoulder. "So much jealousy to play with."

Reflexively, my grip tightened on Mila. It didn't escape the woman's notice. "Oh, that is divine." She held a hand toward the nearest archway. "Shall we?"

"Nolletta," a voice snapped from the gloomy hall ahead. "You have a client coming tonight. Go bathe."

The woman didn't cower or flinch at the harsh command. Dragging one last gaze over both Mila and me—hunger still burning in her eyes—she turned without a word, hips swaying as she disappeared back beneath the archway.

"Pity," Mila said when she was gone. "That could have been fun."

"Always the teasing," I muttered against her lips, pulling back before she could seal that kiss. I suppressed a laugh at Mila's disgruntled scoff, taking a few quick steps to catch up to the group where they stood before the woman who had instructed Nolletta.

"You two done?" Lyria asked with a brow quirked.

"No," I said bluntly.

Tolek chuckled. "Careful, or you'll end up bedded before we get the information we need."

Right. Information. We were here—at this pleasure house that should be called a pleasure palace—for very specific, necessary information.

"They will certainly try to win you over," that critical voice said again. "But they understand what no means."

The owner stepped into the light, her tall, reed-thin frame adorned in similar scarves and shawls—of the richest silks and shimmering threads—as the men and women visible through the archways, though hers covered her entire body from shoulder to toe.

"The Madame?" Ophelia asked.

"At your service," the woman answered with a flourish, tucking a pipe between her puckered lips. Onyx-black hair was coiled tightly above her head, giving her entire face a shocked expression, and gold dripped off her hands, neck, and ears.

The house was not the only thing lavished in wealth, then.

Angular, dark eyes surveyed our group. "I do hope some of you are here to enjoy the amenities. Such a wealth of opportunity. Such overwhelming distress clouding your minds."

Erista had warned us that no matter what, we'd feel swayed to participate. To spend days here fucking and feasting and forgetting whatever plagued us outside these walls. As an alluring silence settled over us, I wondered if there was more to it than simple temptation. Even the air in here, the way the light swayed in sultry puddles and distant moans carried through the corridors, had my cock hardening and my resolve fading.

"We will be indulging in what you have to offer," Ophelia answered for us. Carefully chosen words.

"Excellent," the Madame nearly moaned, taking a hit of her pipe. "I was told you'd like to roam free. To see what we host within." She waved a hand. "One rule: you touch it, you pay for it."

"Understood," Ophelia said.

"Then by all means," the Madame purred, "welcome to the pleasure house."

∽

"This place is a labyrinth," I muttered to Mila.

She hummed in agreement, and the sound went right through me. "It would be very easy to get lost in here."

Spirits, I wanted to, but I shoved off that desire again.

We passed yet another room where the arched wooden door was closed, but moans and slaps of flesh against flesh carried through the walls. This entire corridor was full of them—some doors opened to reveal luxurious beds, silk cushions, and tapestries adorning the walls—as were the last three corridors our group had walked down since ducking under one of the archways off the foyer.

At the end of the hall, Ophelia turned to face us. Mystlight cast a wavering haze over her features, purple from the shawl draped across the orb. "These are all private rooms."

Sure enough, from behind the door over her shoulder, a chorus of lewd cries echoed off the stone wall.

"And they seem to be hosting quite a bit of fun," Lyria noted, eyes gleaming.

"Please, Ria," Tolek said. "I don't need to know what you find *fun*."

"As if you—"

"I think we should split up," Ophelia interrupted, and I was grateful for it. "Whoever finds a Storyteller first, you know what to ask. And use the shells from Rina to alert everyone if we need something."

I palmed the method of Seawatcher communication in my pocket, a trinket the ocean-faring warriors had given Santorina and the humans to pass along messages. Rina had spread them among us weeks ago, teaching us how to send basic alerts.

"Good plan," I agreed. "Mila and I can head that way." I

nodded down one of the twisting corridors. There were plenty of empty rooms—

"You sure you two will be all right on your own?" Lyria teased.

"By the Angel, Lyria." I sighed, tipping my head back and pretending I hadn't been thinking precisely that. "We told that woman no, didn't we?"

In a sing-song voice, she said, "She didn't try very hard to persuade you."

"We'll be fine," Mila said with a laugh. "We'll meet you all out front?"

Ophelia nodded.

As Mila and I left the rest of them to figure out their groups, I wrapped an arm around her waist, whispering in her ear, "This worked out well for us."

And she flashed me a feline grin. Because Mila and I had come here with the intention of finding the Storytellers—and asking our own questions about history.

CHAPTER FORTY-FOUR
OPHELIA

"YOU KNOW THEY HAVE THEIR OWN AGENDA TONIGHT, right?" Tolek whispered, nodding after Malakai and Mila.

"Definitely," I said. "But they're also here to help, so if they want to keep a secret, that's okay."

Tolek nodded. "How are we splitting up?"

"You two go ahead," Santorina said to Tolek and me. "It'll be easiest for you to pass as a couple looking for a bit of fun if none of us are trailing after you."

"I'm going to go on my own," Lyria said. "See you all outside." And she flounced down the darkest corridor, her steps nearly inaudible.

Jezebel pointed to one of the remaining halls. "We'll take this one, you go that way."

"Be smart," I told her, but she merely rolled her eyes and walked away, Rina laughing as she followed.

And with that dismissal, Tolek and I strode down the final corridor, the moans and gasps through the walls certainly living up to the establishment's name. My skin heated with every door we passed, knowing what was happening beyond these doors, feelings Tolek's body brush up against mine at every turn. The allure in the air was thick and hard to ignore, but I tried to listen for the poetic tones of Storytellers.

"What do you say we make this task a bit more fun?" Tolek asked, voice gravelly.

I blinked up at him. "How so?"

"Up for a game, Alabath?" And the smirk he gave me was pure evil.

Tolek pulled me through the nearest archway, into a room of writhing bodies. A whirl of ornate, woven tapestries and low-sitting divans were scattered about as he pushed me up against a waist-high partition. The edge of the wood dug into my spine, but since it was in the center of the room, it gave us the perfect sightline to see who was speaking with whom. If any crowds gathered.

"What's the game?" I asked, hands crawling up Tol's chest as he surveyed the employees of the Madame with keen observation. A blur passed through the corner of my eye, piquing my attention. Whoever it was seemed familiar, but they were gone too quickly to know for certain.

"See if you hear what you need," Tol murmured, ducking to kiss my neck, "while I take care of our disguise."

I dug my fingers into his hair, behaving like a lust-drunk young girl here for solely one thing. Tol lifted his head, brushing my hair back from my face. A shimmer of mystlight fell across his defined features, darkening the shadow of scruff along his jaw and highlighting his lips.

Who was I pretending to fool? I was entirely enamored with Tolek Vincienzo regardless of where we were. We didn't need to put on an act to play his little game.

"CK would have hated this," Tolek commented.

I scoffed, pushing at his chest. "Are you truly thinking about Cyph right now?"

"Should I not be?"

"How would you feel if I was?"

Tol's eyes darkened, and he stepped closer, wedging one leg between mine so he pressed against my center, and I gasped. He nipped at my ear. "I would be forced to bury my best friend if he was on your mind right now, Alabath." As a very clear sign, he dragged his teeth up my neck, biting.

A moan vibrated up my throat.

"Hear anything?" he muttered in my ear.

I thought past the throbbing in my core and quickening of my breath. Swept my gaze across the room of couples lost in one another. "No," I whispered.

Tol kept up his game.

"I only mentioned CK," Tolek muttered, voice rough, "because his mother used to work in a brothel. Decades before he was born."

"I didn't know that," I said.

"He didn't either for a while, but I think that's why he was so touchy about not wanting to come here tonight."

"Interesting." I tucked away that observance and dropped my head back to give him access to my neck. "I don't hear or see anyone that looks like a Storyteller."

"On we go," Tolek said, grabbing my hips and turning me. He walked me backward beneath the arch and across the corridor into another room. All the while, a ravenous heat ignited those amber specks in his eyes.

"We probably don't have to pretend to be patrons while looking, you know," I muttered, but the words were breathy.

"Not pretending, Revered," he said, and my title on his lips sent a wave of heat through me. I shoved him against the nearest wall, the tapestry behind him fluttering with the motion. A grin split his lips, and he kissed me roughly as if to say *two can be aggressive, Alabath*. Leave it to Tolek to turn this into a game, too.

He spun me so I leaned against his chest, brushing my hair over one shoulder, and goosebumps peppered my skin. "Besides," he whispered as he pressed slow kisses to my neck, his scruff a bristly drag that I felt in my core, "it's so much more fun to get to tease you in public. In view of so many. Let them know you're mine." His hands roved over my body. "Find your Storytellers. I'll be here."

I observed the room, trying my hardest not to get lost to the desire building within me. There were even more couples in here than in the last room. A few were groups of multiple people. Three or even four, all moving harmoniously in the combination of dancing, scarf-tampered mystlight and firelight.

One man lay on his back, a woman sinking down on his length

again and again, and a second man pushing into her from behind at the same time. From here, with so much flesh on display and equal moans of pleasure leaving all three of them, it was impossible to tell which one—or two—belonged to the Madame and who was the patron.

I wanted to feel Tol's body against my own, wanted our leathers gone. I pressed back against him.

Tolek's breath was hot against my neck as he asked, "See something that interests you, Alabath?"

Their bodies continued to writhe in a synchronous rhythm, lips clamping around breasts, hands exploring as Tol's crept around me and dipped beneath the hem of my skirt. His hard length jutted into my back, and his fingers...Spirits, he teased the edge of my undergarments. A shiver wracked my body, and I imagined what he'd do if he flipped up my leather skirt, bent me over the couch, and claimed me right here.

I gasped, some combination of watching what was happening in this very room and feeling Tol against me sending an ache straight to my core.

Angels, what was this place doing to me? Need clawed at me. Right here, even in a room full of people.

I tilted my head back against his shoulder, catching his lips in a sensual kiss, and ground my ass against him. One hand cupped my jaw as Tolek groaned, tongue commanding mine with all the power and strength that he was.

"I'm curious, yes," I whispered, breathing heavily as we broke apart. "But I don't like to share."

"Me neither." He smirked, kissing me again. "I think we should keep going."

"Keep going?" I asked and rocked back against him.

Tolek laughed. "Not like that."

I pouted, but he nipped my ear, murmuring, "We're gaining an audience, *apeagna*."

Blinking away the lust that had formed a senseless haze around me, I noticed a man standing across the room, leaning casually against the wall beside one of many flickering fires, his eyes hungry as he watched Tolek's hands on me.

We're not here for this, I reminded myself, though truthfully all I wanted was for Tolek to spin me around right now and take me up against that wall with punishing force. I bit my lip at the thought, heat gathering between my legs.

As if reading my lascivious thoughts, Tol groaned. "Alabath." Gripping my hips, he turned me to face him, kissing me so hard I thought I'd see stars from that alone. When he broke away, panting, he said, "Don't fucking tempt me."

"But it's so fun," I said breathlessly, the roles reversed from his earlier taunting.

"I'll show you fun when we get out of here."

I was about to respond, but a melodic voice drifted from the other room.

"Gather, children," it said, and notes of a legend poured through the wide doorway.

Tolek froze, too, head cocked.

"That voice," he muttered. And then, he was pulling me through the door, my boots scuffing over the piles of chiffon trailing across the floor in the spacious room, cushions and tapestries overflowing onto every surface, comfort fit for a veritable den of proclivities.

Tolek stopped before the biggest divan, a circular, turquoise velvet cushion large enough to hold four bodies.

It only hosted three currently, though. Two of which were very intimately involved, but the third sat with her legs crossed at the round edge nearest us. A small gaggle of warriors lounged on the floor before her as she spoke, utterly entranced with her words.

Tolek sliced right through her sentence. "What are you doing here?"

"You know her?" I asked, gaping up at him as something hot roared in my gut. "Spirits, Vincienzo, I don't think I want to know—"

"Not the way you're thinking, Alabath." His hand tightened on mine, but his eyes remained locked on the woman on the divan.

And it was then that I followed his stare. That I traced up her bare feet and legs, the gold jewelry adorning them. Right up the lilac and brown chiffon scarves that wrapped around her hips and breasts.

Those long, willowy limbs were...familiar. The dark hair spilling around her shoulders, the tenor of her voice...

"I saw her once," Tolek explained, "at an inn we stayed at in Bodymelder Territory, on our way to Firebird's Field. She was telling a story about a prince who sacrificed himself for his kingdom." He blinked as if the thought was scattering.

The Storyteller's dark eyes met mine, and a memory came crashing back to me. Not in Bodymelder Territory...no, I had not seen the Storyteller there.

But I had seen this woman once before. In a different inn, many miles away across the mountains, on my way to rescue the man now standing with his hand locked in mine.

"Aimee?"

She gave me a bold grin. "It's lovely to see you again, Revered."

CHAPTER FORTY-FIVE
CYPHERION

"GOT WHAT YOU NEED, STARGIRL?" I ASKED, FINDING
Vale at the front of the tent Erista had led us to. Or *pretending to*
find her.

I never wanted to let Vale out of my sight again. She called me
overbearing, but she smiled every time she said it. And every one of
those smiles seemed a little more like she was coming back to life,
finding her new self after the ordeal of the tattoo severance. Like
she'd been forged into something new, more ruthless and determined than ever.

Now, as my hand landed on her waist, stroking that bare inch
of skin above the band of her long skirt, and she flashed me that
same knowing smirk, I waited for her retort.

"Acting as if you didn't see me pluck it from the crate over
there?" she teased and gently placed the tinctures she'd been after
into the draw-string pouch hanging across her body.

"I'll be more discreet next time," I said, bending to kiss her
forehead and turning her back to face the street.

I could have feigned innocence, but the way her voice had lilted
up at the end...I'd missed that. I'd missed her. I was soaking up
every minute, especially the ones as simple as strolling through a
market together without Titus on our heels.

Even if it took every ounce of carefully-honed control not to
take her back to the inn and make up for those weeks we'd been

apart. To remind her I came back for her, she was free, and no one could take anything else from her.

My hand tightened on her waist, and she froze, turning to face me.

Damn all the people in the stalls—all the vendors and patrons and even Erista, kindly pretending not to overhear our conversation as she wandered ahead with Celissia. Because Vale's face was serious once again, her eyes dim.

But *she* asked *me*, "What's wrong?"

I blinked at her, my other hand resting on her waist. "What?"

"You're tense." She rubbed her hands down my chest. "What happened?"

I sighed. "I prefer being the one doing the observing. My mind was wandering," I admitted, and she understood where it had gone.

"Mine does that often."

"I can tell," I said as we ambled down the street. "A light fades from your eyes when you're thinking about it. Like all the stars in the sky have gone out."

"Sometimes"—Vale swallowed—"it feels like they have. But when that happens, you're there. You're brighter than the stars, Cypherion. When I can't fight through the darkness, you're brighter."

"You're more than all the damn stars, Stargirl," I whispered.

From the soft tones of our voices, I wouldn't have thought we were in a public place. The lack of privacy somehow made the conversation more intimate. Deciding to forget the bartering vendors and children running around, to be able to have this conversation right here and share this reassurance.

I kissed her, thinking of how she tasted under the moonlight in the hot springs. When a Soulguider in the tent across the alley whistled, I pulled back, bristling.

"Let's go," Vale said, catching my hand and tugging me toward Erista and Celissia. The Engrossian was asking Erista about how her magic replenished during the Rites as they browsed elaborately embroidered blankets woven with shimmering gold thread.

"Where to next?" Vale asked the Soulguider when they were done.

"I told Celissia I would lead her and Barrett to the city council hall first thing in the morning," Erista said, nodding at the Engrossian. "We're going to head back to the inn to wait for Jezebel and the others." She turned her amber eyes on me, brows raised.

Vale tilted her head questioningly. I hadn't mentioned this idea to her yet, mainly because I was afraid I wouldn't follow through. But I had asked Erista for directions in case I wasn't a damn coward.

I cleared my throat. "We'll be visiting that vendor."

～

"ARE you going to tell me what this is about?" Vale asked, voice soft.

I squeezed her hand as we wound through the market, moonlight and an increasingly-searing heat paving the way. "Pretending you haven't figured it out, Stargirl?"

"I was going to allow you to explain first," she said with a mocking sigh.

I laughed. "I'm tired of us living without answers."

Us.

Something in this entire mess—her staying with Titus, me finding out about my father, the mission to get her back, everything it had devolved into—had cemented the concept of *us* in my brain. I'd been ready to lay my life down for hers before, to sacrifice anything for her, but it was somehow more real after all the risks.

Perhaps it was being back with my friends. Seeing how they considered Vale a part of our family certainly made the weeks we spent in Starsearcher Territory less of a dream and more of a foundation for a future.

But I wouldn't lead her into that future without a sure understanding.

I pulled her to a stop in front of the tent Erista had told me about. Orange light glowed from the sliver between the flaps, heat sliding underneath the unsecured edges.

I took a deep breath, but before I could enter, a hand cupped my cheek, turning my attention toward her. "Whatever is said in there, it doesn't change a thing." Vale's thumb stroked across my cheekbone, her olive eyes boring into mine.

I nodded, kissing her palm softly.

She could have gone on, but Vale always knew precisely when to speak and when silence said more than anything. Tonight, the support flooding through the quiet was louder than words.

Perhaps that was something everyone felt with the person they loved. Perhaps it was some deep understanding she read in my spirit, some rightness that proved we were it. Regardless, as I pulled back the tent flap and held out my hand for her to cross the threshold first, I swore I'd do anything to nurture that stability.

"We're closing up soon," a gruff voice hollered from beside the forge. Spirits, it was hotter than the volcano in here.

"We're looking for the owner of the shop," I said.

The man brought his hammer down, the clang against steel ringing in the small space. "Yes."

"We were wondering if we may ask a question?" Vale peeked up at me, a warning of *we better tread carefully* in those olive eyes.

"And?" he asked.

Could he have been less communicative?

I cleared my throat. "We were told that if we wanted to inquire after any sensitive information, you were the man to seek out."

Another ring of hammer against hot steel, and sparks flew. "Yes."

With the sinking feeling that this might be entirely fruitless, I released Vale's hand and slung my scythe from my shoulder. "It's about this." I held the weapon before me, angling it as Erista had demonstrated. "Have you seen something of this make before?"

I didn't know if it was my tone of voice or pure curiosity, but the man set his hammer down. Wiping a dirty rag across his deeply-tanned face, he turned toward me.

And when his eyes landed on my scythe—my father's scythe— the white's shone.

"Where did you get that?" He stood from his stool, taking a few steps closer.

"That's the question," I huffed. His eyes shot to mine. "It was my father's. But I never knew the man."

The Soulguider held out a hand, almost reverently. His guard was still up behind his inquisitive stare, though. "May I?"

My teeth ground, but Vale answered with a pointed look at me. "Of course."

Handing over the weapon that was as precious to me as one of my own bones, I asked, "What's your name?"

"Elyrio," he muttered, "*friendly* clients call me Rio." That hit my gut so hard, I ignored his warning emphasis on friendly. Rio. That's how Akalain had referred to her brother in the letter she sent Malakai. It was a coincidence, but one that sliced through a wall I'd built.

"Rio," Vale said, purposefully, "what can you tell us of the weapon?"

Elyrio ran a hand along the shaft. "These three gold bands at the end are significant."

"How?" I asked, narrowed eyes on his expert grip as he assessed my scythe.

"One would mean the owner of this weapon was an esteemed solider in our army, or a distinguished guider of the dead." He dragged a finger around that first band of gold in the wood. "A second belongs to the personal employ of a chancellor or a sacred site across our territory. Those who are the most prominent in that guard."

The fire of the forge flickered across the weapon, gold bands glinting. "And the third?"

"A third band is rarely given." He hummed, as if digging through his mind. "Only two dozen times in history have they been awarded."

"And what have they been for?"

"It is an honor reserved for those who have direct involvement in a matter of our Angel. In forging, the blade is dipped in a sacred source and imbued with a rare but powerful magic." My stomach dropped with his words. "Three bands are given to warriors when a chancellor—or someone with as much sway—called for assistance, and the barer was clearly successful."

"Would this chancellor have been Meridat?"

Elyrio frowned, likely at my casual use of the chancellor's first name, but I'd met her numerous times and she'd insisted.

"In the last century, yes," Elyrio said. "This weapon was likely forged by a chancellery smith." Reluctantly, he extended the scythe back to me.

"Thank you," I said. "And those can only be found in the capital?"

I didn't truly know what I was asking. These were questions I never thought I'd face. The weapon was mine; why did I care where it had come from?

I knew *who* my father was, that he did something truly incredible to earn the scythe. But still, having pieces of the story without the whole picture nagged at me more than I wished.

"Unfortunately, yes." Elyrio led us back toward the door. "If you ever find out the story, I'd love to hear it."

I nodded, lips pressed tight.

"Thank you," Vale said demurely as we left. She slipped her hand back into mine.

Once we were out of the market and heading toward the inn, she asked, "How do you feel about that?"

Tension rolled from my shoulders the further away we got. The desert night wrapped around us, temperatures quickly dropping, and Vale shivered. I tucked an arm around her as I thought.

"When I'd assumed my father was alive somewhere, chasing after him held no appeal to me. He could find me if he wanted to know me. But now...now that I know he isn't coming back, and that maybe it wasn't his choice..." I shrugged. "It sounds like he did some incredible things. Maybe his legacy deserves to be remembered. To mean something."

"His legacy does mean something," Vale said, rubbing a hand down my back. "*You* are his legacy, Cypherion. Last name or not."

Deneski or Kastroff, did it matter?

I once wouldn't have cared to carry on the life of a man I didn't know, no matter how much the lack of information had tampered with my own beliefs of myself. But perhaps we all deserved to be remembered.

Chapter Forty-Six
Malakai

Following Mila through the web of the pleasure house without ripping her clothes off was one of the hardest things I'd ever done. Spirits, I was half tempted to pull her through the next open door, even if I had to spend all the money to my name to rent it for the night.

Her leathers hugged her body perfectly as she wandered ahead, and my cock hardened at the memory of what it felt like to sink into her. She disappeared around the next turn, and I paused, pressing a hand to the stone wall and shaking my head to clear it.

We had answers to find tonight.

"Get off of me." Mila's low threat sliced through my thoughts and I raced around the corner.

A barely-dressed man, muscled skin gleaming with oil, pressed her up against the wall, grinning sleazily.

"I paid lavishly for an evening with anyone I want," he said, looking Mila over, oblivious to how she kicked at him.

"Let go." She tugged at where he gripped her wrists against the wall—right over her gold cuffs—and rage blurred my vision.

"I'm not used to the leathers, but we can play." He leaned further down. "Pretend you're an active warrior."

"Who do you want to pretend I am?" I growled.

He barely looked up before my fist slammed into his jaw.

The man went sprawling to the tile floor with a loud smack,

the thin scarf wrapped around his waist falling. With him completely naked, I dragged him up by his hair and threw him against the wall, my arm pinning his throat.

Blood trailed down his chin. Fucking satisfying.

"What the fuck do you think you're doing?" he asked.

"What do *you*?"

He pushed at me. "Getting what I paid for."

"Think again." I threw another punch to his jaw. "She's not a worker here, and frankly, I don't think any of them would deign to touch you—no matter how much coin you spent."

A small crowd had formed behind me, spilling out of the nearby rooms—many half-dressed—but I didn't pay them any attention. If this got us thrown out, so be it.

Among them, I found Mila. Hair in disarray, but pure fire in her eyes.

"Are you okay?" I asked.

She nodded, jaw tight.

"You're lucky, then," I said to the piece of filth. "Oh, and you missed one crucial piece. She's not just any active warrior. She's a general of the Mystique armies." Fuck, it was gratifying when his face paled. "And if I hadn't been here, I'm sure she would've been happy to show you how she earned that title." I shoved him down the hall, his bare ass nearly crashing back to the tile. "Now get out. Of the entire house."

Once he was gone, I spun toward Mila, taking her face between my hands. "You're sure you're okay?"

She nodded again. The silence rattled my chest. Last time she'd stopped speaking was in the Labyrinth when the cave-in had triggered memories of her captivity.

"Words, Mila." I dropped my forehead to hers. "I need to hear you say it."

"I'm okay," she swore, voice containing more steel than I'd expected. Her fortress solidified. "Shaken, but okay. I could've handled him on my own."

"You don't have to," I told her, brushing a loose strand of hair behind her ear.

"I'm happy I don't," she admitted. And she didn't seem to feel weak for confessing that she wanted someone to help her. Mila never found weakness in that sort of vulnerability. It made her even stronger.

Made me love her more.

Slipping my hand around the back of her neck, I tilted her head and kissed her hard enough to forget that prick. Sealed the fact that I was the only one kissing or touching her tonight. Ever again.

"Excuse me?" a soft voice asked beside us.

Without turning, I grumbled, "I swear on Damien's grave if another one of you tries to approach us."

But Mila kissed me once more and looked around my arm. "Yes?"

A Soulguider with golden skin bedecked in dusty purple scarves and bronze jewelry stood a few feet away. "I only wanted to apologize for the patron and make sure you know we've escorted him out. You're welcome and safe here, and if there's anything we can do, let us know."

I exchanged a glance with Mila, trying to shove away the rage still burning through me. "Actually, there is," I said. The woman's head tilted. "Do you know where we can find a Storyteller?"

She smiled. "Come with me." Her scarves whipped around her frame as she turned.

I took a step to follow, but Mila grabbed my wrist and whispered, "I have to say—jealousy looks great on you, Warrior Prince."

～

"YOU ASK AFTER THE STARS?" The Storyteller before us was incredulous, twisting a long braid around her hand. "Surely you know my gift of legends is not about the Fates."

"Technically," Mila argued kindly, "Storyteller magic is about relaying history, correct?"

The Storyteller—Parrille, her name was—straightened. "That is correct."

The worker who had led us here found her walking with two of her comrades, sharing some tale the wind had whispered to her

—or whatever the fuck the explanation for their magic was—and pulled her aside in this stretch of hall, abstract tapestries and orbs of shaded mystlight dulling the chill from the stone walls.

We started by asking her about the Angelcurse, but the Story-teller claimed there was no such information in their cult's history. I was skeptical—Ophelia would certainly be discouraged by that—but once we'd asked a number of different questions that we thought could unravel some tale in her mind, Mila and I had moved on.

"We don't need to know of *the* Fates exactly," I said. "But I was wondering if you are able to speak of fates of those who had passed?"

"Since that is deemed historical fact," Mila explained.

The Storyteller pursed her lips, locking her arms across her ample chest. The teal scarves wrapped intricately around her body bunched with the movement. "Who is it you ask after?"

Ophelia came into tonight with questions about the Angels and the emblems. But Mila and I had been talking, and we kept coming back to one person—one story he'd written.

The damn gates would not let me in but legend spoke of them and the ones who tell tales of legends whispered of it too so this must be it.

Anything could help. "What about gates?"

"Gates?" Parrille perked up.

"Are there gates that are...I don't know, special? Where someone would go to worship the Angel maybe?"

"You search for where the legends rest?" I was silent, because I didn't fucking know what she meant. "I cannot tell you of that." She spun, her waist-length twin braids nearly hitting us with the movement, and took a step down the hallway.

I groaned. This was useless. But I'd saved one last card to pull, and Spirits, I didn't want to, but I had to try. "There's someone else. Another name."

The Storyteller flicked a judgmental look over her shoulder. "Stop wasting my time, warrior."

"I promise," I said with a swallow, "you will know of this one."

Parrille turned back fully, gesturing to me to continue. The

Angelcurse had somehow been absent in her histories. An alarming development, sure, but one to worry about later.

Mila nodded, encouraging me to voice the question I'd only shared with her.

"Lucidius Blastwood." My father's name hung in the air between us. "I want to know about Lucidius Blastwood."

Parrille lifted her chin, eyes drooping over me. "I see it now. He is your father, no?"

I reared back. "How do you know that?"

"When you are born with the gift of speaking to the winds—when you sacrifice your connections to your clan and family to practice—you learn a great many things." Apparently not about Angelcurses, though. She tilted her head as if listening. "I know of the man you ask after. Have seen him with my sisters and brothers. Have heard tales of him. He was a tainted, tainted man."

"Trust me, I know." My fingers curled at my sides, the scar along my jaw tingling. "But I think he died with secrets. Ones that are becoming more and more imperative to our lives. Can you tell me anything about him?"

"I take it you know much already?" When I nodded, she continued, "Ask a particular question. Telling stories of one's entire life can take years."

I ground my jaw, choosing my words carefully. I didn't have time to start her on a random tangent. "He was looking for something across the continent. What was it?"

Parrille closed her eyes, seeming to search the archive of her mind. After a moment, her lips popped open, and her voice became that rhythmic tone of a Storyteller again. "The former Mystique Revered was curious about the seven Primes. He spent long decades of his life roving the continent, in search of power that may have been left in their wake."

My eyes cut to Mila. *The emblems.* Lucidius *had* known about them. We'd suspected, based on the locations his journals referenced and the fascination with the Angels, but a part of me had always thought—or maybe hoped—it was a coincidence.

So much for denial. The scars across my back ached with the realization.

"He was successful in finding what he sought, though he was unaware. He did not possess whatever vital source it required. And in the process, he lost pieces of himself to the attempts."

Lucidius found the emblems but didn't have Angelblood. I didn't have Angelblood. Why, then, was I able to feel the emblems beat?

"Lucidius drove himself toward the edge of insanity on this desperate mission."

I dragged my tongue over my teeth, letting what I already knew sink in. As if sensing that mounting wave of turmoil, Mila slid her hand into mine, lacing our fingers together, and I calmed.

It gave me the strength to organize my thoughts. "How did he know of this lingering power if he wasn't meant to find it?"

"He learned of them from a female of a different clan." *Kakias.* She cared enough about Lucidius to share what Bant's original plan was when he shed his angelic Spirit into her. "But neither of the two were ever fully honest with each other. A bond of true love, warped by desperation for power."

"I guess that means Kakias and Lucidius *had* loved each other at one point," I whispered to Mila. "Even with her soul tarnished and sacrificed to immortality, she'd loved him."

"Or he'd loved her," Mila said. "Unrequitedly."

"A waste of emotion if so," I sighed. Regardless, it still didn't answer the most important question. "Why?" I asked, voice breaking. "Why did he want them?"

It couldn't only have been for Kakias. The queen knew of the emblems because of Bant, but had not cared about them before she learned Ophelia could use them against her.

The Storyteller shook her head. "I cannot know that."

"What do you *mean*?" I argued.

"The winds only whispered the story of what unfolded. Lucidius was clear that he sought these remnants of magic, but he never shared with anyone why. That remained buried within his soul, a secret he took into the Spirit Volcano with him."

"Can you tell me *anything* else? A—I don't know—a reason? What was wrong with him that made him do such horrific things?"

Ophelia was searching for the emblems, too, and she was not Lucidius. She did not have the cruel, twisted heart he bore at death.

And Lucidius wasn't a chosen. Why look in the first place?

Parrille's stare softened. "Sometimes, it is best to let the dead rest and forge your own path through the hottest fires of the continent, Warrior Prince."

I fidgeted, fingers aching to touch the scars on my back.

"We're going," Mila snapped. She laced her fingers through mine, a solid reassurance, her voice thick with sarcasm when she added, "Thank you for being oh-so-helpful."

Parrille dipped her head, and glided away down the corridor, twirling that long braid around her hand.

As we rounded the corner, we slammed straight into Lyria. The commander's eyes were wide and harried, gaze darting around the corridor.

"Oh," she exhaled. "It's you."

"Are you okay?" Mila asked with a step toward her.

"Fine," Lyria snapped, flinching.

Mila eyed her. "Lyr, what happened?"

My hand drifted toward my sword as I looked over Lyria's shoulder, but the hall was empty, the sounds of the Storytellers' low conversations drifting from adjacent rooms.

"Nothing. I'm fine." Lyria nodded too enthusiastically, running a hand through her long hair, taming the disorder. "I don't like it here."

"Come on," I said, shaking off the remaining chill from the Storyteller. I fished the Seawatcher communication shell out of my pocket as it started to heat with a warning from the others. "Let's get out of here."

Mila's narrowed eyes stayed on her friend the entire walk out.

CHAPTER FORTY-SEVEN
OPHELIA

"YOU KNOW HER?" TOLEK GAPED AT ME.

Aimee cocked her head, curiosity pursing her lips. Yes, it was certainly her. She may have adopted the Soulguider style of garments and accessories with the flowing silk and body jewelry, but that voice was undeniable.

"She was in the Wayward Inn when I rescued you from Mindshaper Territory." I squeezed Tol's hand. "She was telling a story of..." Aimee smiled, nodding. "Of the Angels."

"That I was," she purred.

"It was about the foundations of the Prime Warriors and the clans," I said, thinking back to that night. "How they came by their magic from the land, how they created their descendant warriors." Aimee's eyes seemed to glow at the mention, something enchanting about her presence. "They fought among themselves, the magic eating away at them, until they eventually ascended. And left magic behind."

Reflexively, my fingers curled around Damien's emblem at my neck. It had been Aimee's words that stuck with me, all through Mindshaper Territory and on the trek back to the mountains. Through the Battle of Damenal, when I'd first seen Angellight burst from the necklace.

It had been that story that finally helped me piece together what the Angelcurse was about. And so, the hunt began.

"I believe you felt the repercussions of those feuds between brother Angels this winter, did you not?"

"What do you know?" Tolek's eyes narrowed on Aimee. He seemed distrustful—a bit unlike himself, but I wasn't sure why. Perhaps what he'd heard from her in Bodymelder Territory had been worse than he implied.

Aimee unfolded her lithe body, rising from her seat as gracefully as the winds that whispered to her. With a wave of her hand, the crowd scattered, the pair of warriors on the divan behind her unfazed in their activities.

"I know the stories that are whispered to me," she said, leading us to a glass side table, delicate gold carvings twining up the legs. She poured herself a glass of deep red wine. "I know what happened with the dead queen." A lengthy sip of maroon liquid, the notes wafting through the air around us stronger than they should be. "I know where you and your sister visited."

"The Spirit Realm," I breathed, that plane of murky light and falling stars flashing through my mind like bolts of Angellight. Quickly recovering myself, I asked, "Is that where Jez and I were?"

"I have only heard legends of the place," Aimee said.

"Isn't that what everything you speak is? Legends?"

Her full lips tipped into a smile. "The ones that are true, yes." With a swirl of her wine and a pivot on her heel, Aimee glided through the nearest arch and down the wide corridor. "Coming?"

Tolek and I exchanged a glance that said *it's why we're here*, and we followed her. All the way into a chamber packed with even more plush divans, wide cushions, and trailing silks. They filled the low-lit space between the fireplaces at either end, not a stone of the floor visible.

This was the true Storytellers' nest. Half a dozen of them were scattered throughout, voices low, but there were no escapades taking place beneath the bronze chandeliers.

As Aimee wound through the room, nearly floating on her jewel-covered feet to a divan before one of the gaping fireplaces, the others each nodded in reverence to her. She was not only a Storyteller, then, but a leader of some sort. Or at least someone respected.

Tolek and I took one of the plush seats opposite Aimee's. Over her shoulder, someone pulled sheer maroon curtains across the doorway. An illusion of privacy, though we were far from alone.

I pretended we were, though. "What legends have you heard of the place my sister and I visited?"

"I do not know much of that place," she said, still swirling that glass of wine, "but I know of the place to which it connects."

"Connects?" I asked.

"The plane you were on is not quite what you think. It is a bridge. A bend between two very real realms."

"Where does it lead?" I asked. "And how did we end up there?"

Aimee smiled at that, and when she spoke, her voice was the mystical but authoritative tone of a Storyteller. "So many questions from the minds who know so little."

"Answer them, then," Tolek snapped, not taking kindly to the insult.

I placed my hand on his knee, dragging my thumb in soothing circles. Though, truthfully, I'd been about to say the same thing.

"Relax, connoisseur of cards, I mean no offense."

Tolek only said, voice icy, "Explain."

Aimee reclined against the rolled back of the divan, turning her eyes to the fire. "Those who roam this continent—this planet—are aware our magic benefits other worlds. There is the Spirit Realm, the one we are most comfortable discussing. But beyond that there are many, many more. They are all locked away by the precision of that very magic."

"Our magic doesn't work that way. We can't walk between worlds," I hedged.

Aimee turned those dark eyes on me. "Warriors know but a drop of what the earth commands. Your pact with the magic binds you to the land, feeds it to your souls, but you do not retain the ability of manipulation that is required to open those doors. Warriors are no Realmspinners."

"Who is?" I asked. Then, my blood chilled, and I dropped my voice. "Can the fae?"

But Aimee shook her head, and the reassurance steadied my pulse. "The pointy-eared near-immortals cannot either."

"Then who?"

"It does not matter who," Aimee said, "but what and why." When we were silent, she sat up, long bare legs curling beneath her. "What do the realms hold, and why were two young warrior sisters able to travel to a bridge between them?"

What did the realms hold? The concept of them existing was nothing unusual. Aimee was right; we'd always known other realms subsisted. That the magic of the mountains was so potent in our land because it seeped into all worlds in existence, providing for them, as well.

But if each realm varied...

"Are the bridges unique to the realms they lead to?"

Aimee said, "It is believed so, but that is where legends diverge."

"Assuming that's true, though, a bridge would likely reflect either end of its scope?" I'd practically seen our world imprinted on that murky gray sky when Jezebel and I had been there. The mountains and Kakias's power spearing toward them and...

"Does the *fel strella mythos* mean anything to you?" I asked, heart thundering. That's what had been at the other end of that plane. The constellations falling and winged creatures. Aimee's answering smile was indulgent. "It's true then? How the pegasus and khrysaor came to be?"

"I'd heard claims that the beasts roamed our lands once again," she muttered, almost reluctantly, a stark contrast from that smile a moment ago.

"They do. I—" I bit my lip, loathe to give up this information, but I forced the words out. "My horse is one of them."

That was enough to win over her curiosity. "You saw that on the plane?"

"I saw beasts flying through the sky and constellations crashing to earth."

Aimee evaluated me. Tolek remained silent at my side, allowing me to lead the conversation and reveal what I found necessary, though he doubtlessly tracked every movement Aimee made.

Finally, she crossed one leg over the other and said, "You

learned of the creation of the two? Did you learn who ruled them?"

"They were plucked from their positions in the sky by a holy being who desired children," I answered.

"Correct." Aimee nodded. "But that is who breathed life into them. What about who *controlled* them?"

"Is it not one in the same?" I asked.

But Tolek answered, "Apparently, there was someone else."

"You are clever," Aimee told him with an approving once-over that had my hand tightening on his knee again. Before I could let out my snappish response, her voice became mystical again. "There were others. A pair of formidable sisters—long before the warriors you stem from walked Ambrisk. The very same being who formed her sons from the stars imbued these two with the powers of life and death. One to raise the constellations, another to hold their leashes. A summoner of myths, and a destroyer of them."

Chills spread along my skin, and my heart nearly stalled. Beside me, Tolek was so very still.

"The mark of the gods was within them," Aimee went on. "It was always told they would come again. Though no one knew how, when, or why."

A pair of formidable sisters. The rulers of the pegasus and khrysaor, set to walk Ambrisk again.

It shouldn't have been possible. And it didn't explain *how* we'd ended up on the bridge or what waited at the other end, but regardless...

Angellight pooled in my palms. No, it was the other magic. The untamed one.

Imbued these two with the powers of life and death.

We were...my sister and I were—

As if summoned here by the Angels themselves, Jezebel's voice flooded the room. "Ophelia!" She burst from behind the sheer curtain, Santorina right behind her.

"Jez!" I shot up from the divan, but at the frantic look in her eyes, every thought of the *fel strella mythos* faded, the light in me winking out. "What's going on?"

"We need to go," Jezebel insisted.

"Ah, Mistress Death," Aimee purred. The name shot through me—Ritalia had called Jezebel the same.

I glared at the Storyteller, looking between her and my sister. "What—"

"Ophelia, please, let's get out of here." Jezzie's face was so pale, her hands shaking in mine. Rina was whispering something to Tol. As I looked her over, I realized her hands were stained crimson.

"Let's go," Tolek said in response, shepherding us toward an exit. By the look in his eye, I could tell he'd noticed the distress in Jez's voice.

My sister whispered, "There's a spirit. I could hear it."

I blanched. "You mean..."

"Someone died." Her lips pressed together with a flinch.

Even Aimee's face paled. "Go, warriors."

Jezebel had my hand tightly in hers, Rina on our heels, pulling her Seawatcher shell out to notify the others. Tolek was a step behind her, his family dagger discreetly at his side as he reached over us to pull back the curtain.

As we spun around the corner, I looked back at Aimee. Spirits, I hadn't even asked her about the entire reason we'd sought her out. "The Angelcurse. The emblems," I began, not wanting to say too much. "You know of them?"

Aimee nodded, face tight.

"We have one left." I looked around. "Xenique. Can you tell us anything of it?"

"The sphinxes." She bowed her head, saying in a voice I thought was hesitant and forced, "The legends run true. Find them."

"Where?" I gasped, holding tightly to Jez as she tugged me down the hall.

"Where all dead and riddled secrets lie."

～

"JEZ! JEZZIE!" I held her, trying to stop her shaking as we stood outside the pleasure house.

She was frantic, eyes whipping between the shadowed corners

of the quiet street and the stairs leading back inside, like she expected someone to follow her.

"Jezebel!" I said firmly. "Look at me!"

Her eyes found mine—wide and something tortured in them —and I held her cheeks before she could look away again.

I softened my voice. "What happened?"

Tolek and Santorina stood around us, watching carefully while also monitoring our surroundings. Tears tracked down Jezebel's cheeks. Up the stairs, Malakai, Mila, and Lyria were emerging from the pleasure house.

"I heard—I heard something die," she said. "A Storyteller, I think. But I don't know—I couldn't see, didn't get to hear their thoughts fully—"

My heart cracked at the tremor in her voice.

"I'm sorry, Jezzie," I whispered, kissing her forehead and tucking her close to me.

I met Rina's eyes over Jezebel's shaking frame as the others joined us, and Tolek whispered an explanation to them.

"It felt like someone was following us. There was some odd sense in the air." Santorina shivered, eyes on her crimson-stained hands. The back of my neck prickled at her tone. "Then, a scream came from another room. And it cut off abruptly. I tried to go help, but I was too late. It was a weapon I didn't recognize."

Something within Jezebel crumbled.

There was something that didn't line up here, though. As torturous as it was, Jezebel had been hearing the dying her entire life. More horrifically during the Battle of Damenal. Why had one transitioning spirit caused her to melt down like this?

My own heart raced as I held my sister tighter and whispered, "What else, Jez?"

And she took one huge, shuddering breath, stealing herself. "I think I killed her."

I couldn't feel my limbs at those words. At the utter terror lacing them.

I think I killed her.

"What do you mean?" Tolek asked, bracing a hand on my back.

Imbued these two with the powers of life and death.

Jezebel gathered herself. "When I heard—my power reached out. I didn't realize it was doing it, it just *did*."

I met Tolek's eyes, and it was clear we were thinking of the same thing. Not only what Aimee had said, but of that day in Valyn when my magic had acted of its own accord as Jezebel's had tonight. Rage tunneled through me, singeing my panic and fear to ash—anger at the control I lacked that day, at what Jezebel was suffering right now.

"Normally, it only listens to them. It doesn't speed up or delay the dying." Jez's tears stopped, but she leaned on me. "This time, though...I don't know how it did it. But it felt like it ripped her spirit from her body. Like I did. Like *I* wiped that life from Ambrisk."

"How..." Rina trailed off.

"I don't know." Jezebel shook her head and looked up at me. "Can we go home, please?"

"Of course." I smoothed her hair and tucked her into my side, starting down the dark street. As we made our way back to the inn in the creeping quiet of Lendelli, I couldn't fight the feeling that more had unraveled in the pleasure house than we saw.

CHAPTER FORTY-EIGHT
VALE

CYPHERION WAS SOUND ASLEEP WHEN I SLIPPED OUT OF our bed. I kissed his forehead, and his hand flexed over where he'd held me only a moment ago. But he'd been under so much pressure recently, I didn't want to wake him for my own restlessness.

Instead, I slipped one of his tunics over my head, grabbed the bag of tinctures I'd purchased in the Lendelli Market last night, and crept out of the room.

Slivers of twilight slipped between the curtains in the hall, bathing the wooden planks and my bare feet as I padded to one of the spare rooms on this floor. Cypherion's tunic slid against my thighs with each step, providing the comfort only he gave me. The one I recalled to get me through those days in Valyn. In the quiet, it wrapped around me, bolstering the hollow Titus's death had carved in my spirit. Those edges, as sharp as a jungle cat's deadly claws, were slowly dulling, forming something new.

Soon, dawn would strike, and the inn's patrons would wake, the cooks arriving to prepare breakfast, but for now it was silent.

Except for the Fates pushing at my mind. They'd been excessively loud ever since the seeing chambers broke through the blockage, and I was still struggling to decipher what they wanted.

As the calamity crashed through my mind, I rounded the corner and came to an abrupt halt.

"Good morning, Vale," Barrett greeted from his seat before the crackling fire. He folded and refolded a piece of parchment in his hands.

"Sorry, I didn't know anyone would be in here."

"Not a problem." He gave me an attempt at one of his characteristic smirks.

"Is everything all right?" I asked, stepping further into the room.

Barrett sighed. "Fine. Received more correspondence from home. The same as before, Nassik has not been present." He fiddled with the paper again, but it was obvious he didn't wish to speak of it further. The pressure of the Engrossian people had been weighing on the crown prince, despite the fact that their tour had been successful so far.

"I can leave you to your writing," I offered.

Barrett sat up straighter. "Nonsense, I love your company." He nodded at the bag dangling from my hand. "What were you coming here for?"

Placing the pouch on the low oval table taking up the center of the room, I unloaded my supplies. "I couldn't sleep, so I thought I'd read. Erista helped me track down a few new tinctures and candles I'm very curious about."

I set a line of six small jars along the edge of the table, their dark glass reflecting the firelight.

"What's so intriguing about them?" Barrett asked, leaning forward. The chair creaked beneath him, it's amethyst velvet overstuffed and worn.

"They're from a shopkeeper known to work closely with Artale's magic," I explained, and Barrett's eyes widened. I was afraid to say what I hoped these specific tinctures would do—what higher power I wanted to access with them.

I looked away, pulling out one of my usual blends and igniting an incense stick, propping it over a small silver dish. "I need to conduct a session to warm up first, though."

Had to clear the pressure my Fate ties were pounding on my mind.

"By all means," Barrett encouraged. He reclined in his chair, tilting his head curiously as I went about my reading.

Once I had all of my supplies set up as I preferred, I sat back on the thick russet rug and crossed my legs, taking a few focused breaths. My eyes slipped closed, and I fell into the space where the Fates ruled my mind. White fire blinked to light, stars calmly zipping across the sky.

I started with a familiar topic. Cypherion.

Ever since I returned to him and found out the truth about the fae queen's prophecy, I'd been attempting to read his fate and see what may come of it. Unfortunately, foretold futures of the kind were hard to access. Still, I conducted a daily check to ensure nothing tragic had changed.

As I tried to pull up his future and open my connection to any one of the Fates that may know of him, a blinding trail of starfire flared behind my eyelids. Fate voices collided, and I couldn't tell one from the other.

I sighed in frustration.

"Everything okay?" Barrett asked.

I cracked an eye open. The prince still folded the letter in his hands. "Technically, yes. But my readings are still muddled."

"I thought the seeing chamber fixed that?"

"It did, but it wasn't instantaneous. I can access all the Fates again, but they're like a riled hive of bees. The messages are blending together rather than being communicated one at a time."

It had happened in the Valyn archives, the first time I'd been able to access my Fates in months—when I'd been told I would be Titus's downfall—and every day since. It was difficult to decipher clear readings currently, but it was slowly healing.

"Try again," Barrett said, his dark green eyes soft with understanding. "Keep going."

And I did.

For long, quiet minutes, I tested the future of every person we knew, pulled at every Fate tie laced through my magic and tried to peel apart the voices. But they were stubborn, shouting to be heard over the others, gathering in my chest until it was hard to breathe.

Clearly, these lower readings weren't working.

I could try...

My mind went to the emblems, to the Angels and gods no

Starsearcher in history was able to read. Except for the flashes I'd been granted of them in the seeing chambers.

I shouldn't push the magic, not when it was so new. But the pressure in my chest squeezed tighter, my head pounding.

I pulled at one, one tied to who I thought was the Fate of Fertility, though it was hard to tell among their swarm. It was no more than a corner of a godly reading, though.

And the beat of my session crescendoed in my mind. One of my Fates spewed shooting stars, the trails of starfire igniting brighter than I'd ever seen, and images spilling through them.

I gasped, elated at the return of proper magic. Finally, after weeks of empty attempts, a figure burned in that white fire.

"Who is that?" I asked the Fates in my mind.

She was a tall figure, her features masked behind a mist. But her palms were open at her sides, and from them, a thick crimson liquid dripped to the earth.

Blood.

And from that blood, humanoid creatures rose. A number of them, of all sizes, and each had one tether leading back to her. She turned her face to the sky, hair slipping around her shoulders and—

Pointed ears caught the light.

"Fae?" I gasped.

Who was this woman? Based on the accounts Ophelia shared of Ritalia, this wasn't her. Was it a former queen? Were those on the leashes her subjects?

I scanned the crowds of fae, but the trails of starfire were dimming, this strand nearly reaching its time. The Fate who had given it to me—whichever it had truly been—did not speak, did not elaborate. I tried to gather any remaining clues as the white dimmed. There, at the very edge of the vision, were two faces I knew. Two who slept in this very inn.

What did Lancaster and Mora have to do with this? What did any of it mean?

Please, I wanted to beg the Fates. My shoulder ached. *Please, I've lost so much already. Have mercy on me. Show me something.*

But the star was past its time. For now, the reading was forfeit.

"Vale?" Cypherion's voice pierced the dull starfire, and my eyes snapped open. He was dressed in his leathers, his weapons strapped to his body and hair half pulled back. "I'm going to work out with Tolek and Malakai. Do you need anything?"

"No, thank you," I said, and despite my still clouded readings, his attention softened my frustration. I allowed the sage and bergamot from his tunic to calm me, combatting those sharp edges of my voided spirit.

Cypherion nodded, leaving, and Barrett went, too, off to meet with the city council. I turned back to my supplies, preparing to fall back into the Fates, those six tinctures lining the table taunting me.

CHAPTER FORTY-NINE
TOLEK

"CHEAP SHOT!" I CALLED AS CYPHERION KNOCKED MY sword to the sand.

"*How?*" he barked back.

"You distracted me with frilly moves."

Malakai laughed from where he watched. "I think that's strategy. It's one of your primary means of fighting, Tolek."

"Yes," I called, sheathing my sword and unbuckling my vambrace to stretch my wrist, "and it's more fun when I'm the one using it against you two."

I met Malakai on the sidelines and uncapped my canteen as we rested for a moment. It was early, so we'd come out back to spar in the clearing behind the Lendelli inn. We should have gone further away to stifle the noise, but none of us wanted to be too far while everyone slept.

Not that we should need a guard in Soulguider Territory—they were our allies—but with everything stacked against us lately and how the pleasure house ended, it unwound a knot in my gut to stay close.

"So, who's going to explain what happened last night?" CK asked, taking a long sip from his canteen.

Malakai and I exchanged a look, both waiting for the other to continue.

I sighed, cracking first, and explained the cryptic hint the

Storyteller shared about the Soulguider emblem and that she was someone both Ophelia and I had seen before. "That's not even half of it," I added. "Aimee told Ophelia some interesting things about where she and Jezebel ended up during the battle. About different realms and bridges between them and the *fel strella mythos*."

I recounted the details quickly, and when I was done, Cypherion crossed his arms. "You think Ophelia and Jezebel are these sisters from the myth, somehow returned again?"

"I don't know if I believe in all that." I shook my head. "Perhaps it's a continuation of the story."

"It would make sense why the pegasus and khrysaor flocked to them," CK reasoned.

"I don't like any of it," Malakai said.

"I'm not sure I do either." I loved that Sapphire had this newfound power and that Jezebel had her khrysaor, but fear wrapped around my chest at what it meant.

"It's a lot more intense than what I learned," Mali added. Cyph and I gave him a look with raised brows. "After I was done beating up a man who deigned to touch Mila—"

"*What?*" Cyph sneered.

Malakai grumbled, "That fucker is lucky all I did was hit him."

I looked to his wrapped knuckles. "Good job."

Malakai nodded. "After that, we found a Storyteller, but she knew nothing of the Angelcurse."

"How is that possible? Aimee knew," I said. "She didn't reveal much about it, but she'd heard of it. Enough to tell us to go *where all dead and riddled secrets lie*."

A confused silence settled over us, the call of desert birds cracking the morning air.

"I also asked about Lucidius," Malakai offered.

Cyph and I exchanged a glance. "And?" he asked.

"And she confirmed Lucidius knew about the magic the Angels left behind—likely from Kakias herself—but she couldn't tell me why or what he wanted them for."

"Why not?" I asked.

"Because Lucidius never told anyone, and she can only deal in concrete historical fact." Bitterness twisted his words.

There was clearly more he wasn't saying—little details that rattled him. Last night had done a number on all of us. When we returned, Jezebel was still trembling from...whatever had happened.

It was all cryptic. Truthfully, it felt like a pile of lies.

"Did Lyria say anything when you guys met in the pleasure house?" I asked Malakai.

"Like what?" he asked, wiping a cloth over his face.

"She was quiet on the walk home." It wasn't entirely unusual lately, but there had been a haunted look in her eye.

Malakai rubbed the back of his neck. "She was jumpy. Mila was worried about her, too."

I nodded, re-buckling my vambrace. Something had shaken my sister, Jezebel had possibly killed someone, Rina had felt followed, and we received a pile of confusing information from the Storytellers. Excellent.

At least we had a hint for the emblems. For right now, that needed to be our priority.

Or...in a few hours, once we all worked off a bit more frustration.

"Let's go again," I said, pulling my sword.

Malakai shook his head, laughing. "Accept the defeat, Tolek."

"He's always been a horrible loser," Cypherion mocked.

"That's because he rarely loses to anyone but me." Ophelia's taunt rained out from the porch. Based on the still-disheveled state of her hair, she'd only just woken and tugged on her leathers.

When we all retreated to our rooms last night, a nagging feeling had kept me up. It was obvious from her ranting of hypothetical scenarios about Jezebel's magic and the *fel strella mythos* that she felt it, too. Now, when she flashed me a challenging grin and braced her hands on the railing, I raised my brows and returned it. "Care to put that claim to the test?"

Come on, Alabath. Play with me.

Ophelia examined the short sword strapped to her waist, her leathers looking as flawless as ever on her toned body. "You're in the mood to be embarrassed?"

"I'm in the mood to win," I corrected.

"Then you should keep fighting these two," she said, waving a hand at Malakai and Cypherion, who both retorted in offense.

"I don't know, Alabath. You haven't been training with swords as frequently lately." With the constant travel, we'd all had less time to work out. Ophelia and Jezebel spent most of their time experimenting with magic, only joining us for short circuits and sparring sessions.

Ophelia scoffed. "Let's do this, then." She descended the stairs, her sword drawn in a breath.

Meeting her in the center of the sandy clearing, I set my stance. We'd been here before, she and I. Had stood blade to blade to practice or teach or burn off excessive energy—especially that last one. Something about the way my muscles fell into that perfect position, ready to catch her first attack, was even more natural than our usual drills. With Ophelia, everything was a little more natural.

She struck first, surprising me. She didn't usually lunge like that.

I met her blow, our blades clanging a few times before she dodged to the right, spinning behind me. I whirled to meet her, catching her next strike with my vambrace.

"Close one," she taunted.

"You're quick."

"Always have been."

I shook my head as I met another blow, swords vibrating between us. "Quicker than you used to be."

I'd fought Ophelia my entire life. Her style was practically ingrained in my own muscle memory. Something had changed, though. Almost so minutely, it could have gone unnoticed, but every move had been smoothed out. Every attack a breath quicker. Angels, if she wasn't entrancing.

Sweat beaded along my skin as she nearly beat me time and time again.

"You're holding up well, Vincienzo," she said through gritted teeth.

"Been training harder," I said. In the spare hours when she was with Sapphire, I trained. In the down time when I couldn't find it in me to rest or read, I prepared this way. We'd had too many damn close calls. I'd do everything in my power to avoid another.

Memories of the Fytar Trench—of Ophelia screaming in pain as Kakias's power ate at her—flashed through my mind, followed quickly by Ricordan's manor, and how Ophelia had gone to whatever fucking bridge in her mind.

And I'd been so...helpless.

My attacks sped up with each image. I sliced my sword through the air, meeting Ophelia's. Channeled all the fear and rage those moments ignited within me into *this* fight.

Ophelia's eyes widened as I nearly snuck by her defense, the magenta glowing with something akin to fire—

No. Not fire. *Angellight.*

The very essence of the immortal bastards scorched through her stare, laced every sweep of her sword. It burned away the shadows claiming my memories, seared right down to my very soul.

There she fucking is. My heart beat in a way that I swore mirrored hers, some kind of melody.

And every time our swords met, it was another spark between us. Another word written in the silent poetry we wove, only her and me able to read it.

Finally, she got that deadly tip of Starfire beneath my chin. I breathed heavily, grinning down at her.

"I yield," I purred. She dropped her weapon, but before she could step back, my hand snaked around her waist. Our sweat-drenched skin pressed together as I pulled her to me and kissed her desperately.

I didn't really care who won, only that we shared the impassioned fire burning between us and the steel of our blades was forging new vows to the cursed stars.

"Want to go again?" Ophelia panted.

"Absolutely," I said with a smirk, stepping back. And that time, as we sparred, laughter barreled between us.

We fought—unfairly on some part, like when I gripped her by the waist and tossed her over my shoulder—and Malakai and

Cypherion trained beside us. Santorina joined, and the five of us took turns, forming a tournament of sorts.

Soon, Mila and Lyria came outside, and I watched my sister closely for any hints of shadows from last night. She seemed unusually chipper, and I couldn't tell if it was forced.

Jezebel and Erista added to the rotation, the former having recovered a bit from last night, but she and Ophelia both seemed to want to use steel instead of magic today. Neither seemed ready to talk about whatever Aimee had implied.

The Engrossians and even the fae lined up to join. We started our roster over, pairing up to battle throughout the rest of the morning. The only one missing was Vale, who CK said was testing her new supplies inside.

Maybe we should have been on the move again. After last night, we should have been refocusing everything on finding the final emblem. On figuring out whatever *where all dead and riddled secrets lie* meant, along with all the other information Aimee revealed and what happened with Jezebel's magic, but we needed this reprieve. This chance to breathe because we were only a group of young warriors and the Angels had dealt us a damn unfair hand lately.

So even if it was only a few hours, we allowed swords to clash, taunts to be thrown, bets to be made, and for a little while, in those hours behind an inn in the Lendelli Hills, everything didn't feel so damn threatening.

~

"LYRIA WINS!" Mila called.

"You're a biased judge," I cursed.

"You're a sore loser, baby brother," Lyria mocked.

My jaw dropped open. "Such unsportsmanlike words."

"I assure you, I could have said much worse. Do you not recall the things you heard shouted across the war camp a few months back?"

I certainly did remember, and I certainly laughed about them, too. "But you are the Master of Weapons and Warfare," I teased.

"Then it's only fitting that I have the best insults, no?" She lifted her sword, pointing it at me in a mock threat. "Would you like to hear some of my favorites?"

I knocked aside her blade with my own. "I'll allow you to throw the more colorful language at your other opponents. It wouldn't be brotherly of me to respond, and you know I can't resist a challenge."

"A wise choice." Lyria grinned and flounced to the side of the makeshift sparring ring beside Mila. It was the happiest I'd heard her sound in a while, so I didn't argue the ruling, instead traipsing to where Ophelia sat beneath a cypher.

"Resting?" I asked, dropping down next to her. The sweeping branches stretched all the way to the sand, some of the only trees able to persist the desert.

She flashed me a welcoming smile, eyes drifting over our still-sparring friends and the trees dotting the perimeter. "It's pretty hot," she said. Her eyes narrowed on Lancaster and Mora, sitting on the outskirts of the circle opposite us.

"True. What are you doing there?" I nodded to where she was using her dagger to whittle a branch fallen from a cypher into a lethal point.

She searched the trees again. "I wanted to keep my hands busy while I watched."

That meant she was agitated. Not at us or she would burst with it, but at *something*. Likely the influx of information from the Storyteller.

Ophelia tilted her head, studying the carving, then scanning the sparring ring. "Rina?" she called.

Santorina jogged over, wiping sweat from her brow. "Yes?"

"That was a good disarming of Celissia."

"Thank you."

"You're dropping your left elbow a bit. Watch out for that," Ophelia said, and Rina nodded. As she turned to go, Ophelia added, "If you'd gotten that last jab through her defenses, and it went through her shoulder, would that be a killing blow?"

Rina's brows tugged together. "I would have pulled it."

"I know," Ophelia said confidently. "But I'm not as skilled at healing as you are. Would it have been?"

"Not here, with the trained healers. But during a battle? With dirt and grime getting in the wound? Sure."

"Interesting," Ophelia considered.

Rina and I exchanged a curious glance, but I shrugged and she walked away.

"What was that about?" I asked once it was only Ophelia and me again. She looked at me, biting her lip, and my eyes dropped to the cypher stake in her hands again. "Alabath?"

Instead of answering, she pressed the hand holding her dagger to my chest and kissed me. And Angels, if that didn't make me forget everything I was going to ask her. She moved closer, fingers curling into my leathers, and I swore something akin to Angellight sparked between us.

When she pulled away, cheeks beautifully flushed, I took a deep breath and tried to focus.

Leaning back on my hands, I lifted my eyes to the trees and waited for Ophelia to answer the questions I could barely remember. When she didn't, I tried another distraction. "I'd never thought about why the cyphers are able to grow throughout the continent when others can't."

She tilted her head, studying the willowing branches. "What do you mean?"

"Why do the oaks and pines only grow in certain regions, yet the cyphers are in every territory?"

"Because of the magic within them, I suppose. How they pump the ether of the mountains into the rest of the world as conduits." She brushed a hand along one draping limb, leaves returning from the winter and a few buds sprouting. "Perhaps since they contain an extra defense against the fae, they're able to weather all terrains?"

I nodded. "All good explanations. I never thought it was odd until recently."

"Sometimes we forget to question what we're told is normal."

Her voice was so fucking heavy when she said it, dipping with a weight I wanted to wipe from her shoulders, from the planet. Ophelia had been forging ahead for so long now, taking everything the Angels threw at us with only minor tremors to her facade.

And I was the only one she truly let see them.

As she watched our friends laugh and spar today, *I* watched *her*. And while the infectious energy in the air made her smile, the pressure it was adding was evident. It swam beneath the surface, wormed its way into the small cracks in that mask.

To protect them. To find the solutions. To end this but have us all standing on the other side.

And the part that twisted me up the most about that? I didn't have the answers. I didn't know what to do to make her feel better. Whatever the fuck it was, I'd do it. Cut up my own arm and bleed across those emblems in her stead if it would provide some sort of clarity for whatever the fuck we were doing.

Sighing, I scooted closer to her, throwing an arm around her shoulder and kissing her temple. "I love you, *apeagna*," I whispered. "Infinitely. You know that, right?"

She blinked up at me. "More than anything."

"And we're going to figure this out. We're going to find the answers about..." I blew out a breath. The pegasus, Jezebel's and her magic, the Storyteller's revelations, the emblems...there were so many obstacles competing for our attention. "About all of it. I promise."

With a sigh that seemed to curve her entire frame, Ophelia hugged her knees to her chest. "I love you, too, Vincienzo." Based on the way her voice seemed a bit freer, it wasn't fear that sank through her bones. It might have been relief. Like that reminder had been enough to make her feel invincible once again. "Let's take today to enjoy, though."

"If you insist."

And with that, I wrapped my hand around the back of her neck, tilting her chin up with my thumb, and kissed her more roughly than before. Damn everyone in his clearing; I didn't care what they saw.

I slipped my tongue against hers and coaxed one of my favorite little moans from her throat, devouring her as I wanted to every damn time she was near me.

Only when she was absolutely breathless did I pull back and rest my forehead against hers. "We're going to scorch the Angels, Alabath. Remember that."

A vicious, beaming smile and dazed magenta eyes that only tempted me to do wicked things in her honor looked back at me. "Infinitely, Vincienzo."

A throat cleared daintily beside us. Ophelia looked up, but I kept my eyes locked on her.

"Vale?" she asked.

"Please don't stop on my account," the Starsearcher joked, sounding a bit more like her old self.

Cypherion echoed, "They can stop. They do it enough to get by with a break."

I flipped him off for that one, still looking at Ophelia, but based on the gentle grunt, Vale elbowed him.

Ophelia laughed. "What is it, Vale?"

"When you're done, I have an idea."

"Oh?" That mischievous smile was back on Ophelia's lips.

I finally looked up to see Vale matched it, and Cypherion instantly appeared exasperated. "I'm ready to read the gods."

CHAPTER FIFTY
OPHELIA

EVERYONE IN OUR PARTY JOINED FOR THE GODS' reading. Once the moon slipped into the sky, we traversed the dunes to the cave system Sapphire and the khrysaor were hidden in.

As Vale set up a series of six candles in the dim mystlight lanterns of the cavern, each with a different incense and tinctures burning ahead of it, Lancaster stepped to my shoulder.

"One per deity," he muttered.

I nodded. "Do you think each is specific, or is it the amount that matters?"

Rina answered from my other side. "I'd guess they're each attuned to the god's or goddess' principle domain and the properties they're abound with."

"Perceptive, Bounty," Lancaster grunted in appreciation.

Santorina bristled. "Don't call me that."

"Just because you do not like what is within you, does not make it untrue."

My narrowed stare swiveled from Vale, lighting the final incense, to the fae male. But I didn't need to reprimand him, because Santorina snapped, "I am perfectly happy with myself, thank your ego for the inflated opinion."

Lancaster sneered, stalking away to stand beside Celissia. She'd bonded with the fae while assisting in their healing process, the

397

two gravitating toward the Engrossians often now. Barrett and Dax joked with Mila and Lyria at their side.

Stress lined the prince's expression, and when our eyes met, he nodded grimly in acknowledgment, but he dragged a hand through his curls and plastered on a smile, gaze flicking to Vale.

And I was reminded again that everything we did—every decision we made to try to appease the fae while they were here—was not only in pursuit of the Angelcurse. As Barrett said in Valyn, we were rulers, and the stakes to keeping our people safe were mounting.

I turned back to Rina and asked, "Are you all right?" I spoke low enough that hopefully even the fae's immortal eavesdropping wouldn't pick it up. I was extra wary of that lately.

"With him?" she asked with a pointed glare at Lancaster. "Entirely unconcerned." I wasn't certain if it was a lie or not, but Rina went on, waving a hand at Vale's set up, "With this? I'm immensely curious."

"Do you think it's a good idea?" I whispered. Vale was settling into her reading, the cloud of melded incense swarming around her, frizzing her hair.

A few feet away, Cypherion perched on a rock, stare intent on his girl. Tolek and Malakai stood on either side of him, attempting to calm his agitation.

Rina said, "I don't know if anything we've done lately is a good idea, Ophelia." She had a point. "But this is even more precarious. If it's not the gods' will to be reached..."

We would suffer the consequences of their wrath.

But I didn't want to raise that concern with anyone. Not after the levity we'd all expressed today. We would deal with that fate if it befell us. Instead, I forced a smirk to my lips and said, "We already have the Angels breathing down our necks, why not throw in the gods, as well?"

Santorina gave me a scolding look, but based on how she shifted a bit closer, nudging me affectionately with her elbow, she knew we may not have a choice. We were at the will of the higher powers.

I was grateful to have these people by my side through the storm.

We drifted over to Tolek, Cypherion, and Malakai, the four of us doing our best to distract Cyph, but his attention was only focused on one person.

Sapphire draped her wing over my shoulder, and I ran a hand down those downy-soft feathers, wishing for some kind of explanation as to everything the Storyteller said. How she was here, if Jez and I truly fit into the myth, and what it all meant.

My sister sat across the small pool in the cavern with the khrysaor and Erista. We hadn't had time yet to unravel what we'd learned last night, and she still seemed sunken within herself from the supposed death, but tonight, I was determined to get some answers—some pieces. Angellight whirled within me as if in response to that call.

Finally, Vale's head snapped up.

"How do you feel?" Cypherion blurted.

The Starsearcher swiveled toward us, her eyes mostly clear and her body seemingly under her control. "I *feel* fine." She pouted.

"Were you able to see the gods?" I asked. Sapphire's wings ruffled with my anticipation.

"Somewhat," Vale explained, eyeing the new tinctures. "I could see them more definitively than before, but it wasn't a clear scene or anything. It was"—she shivered—"a twist of power, I think. Tempests and lightning and iron doors slamming shut."

My gaze shifted to Lancaster and Mora, both with attention honed on the Starsearcher. "Any idea what that could mean?"

Lancaster looked to his sister, then said, "It sounds like she was seeing a display of their power in its cruelest form."

"What's the cruelest form?" I asked.

"It depends who you ask," Mora answered, her face a bit pale.

Santorina took a step forward. "What would you two say?"

And Lancaster forced out, "Bargains."

Tolek and I exchanged a glance, my hand coming to the charm at my necklace.

"Bargains are the cruelest..." Rina murmured, assessing Lancaster and Mora. "And you cannot speak of the gods and goddesses because your magic is connected to them, as is this entire Angelcurse, if we're correct."

We were all silent for a moment, trying to put together those pieces.

Finally, Vale said, "Part of the scene almost felt locked away."

"Locked?" Malakai echoed, brows raised. And I knew what he was thinking. Locked, like the bargains of the strongest fae he'd read about in the books he stole from Ritalia.

Vale nodded. "There was some kind of veil segmenting off part of it, like its locked away." She huffed, glaring at her new supplies. "I truly thought that, combined with my unlocked magic, these would do the trick. Open those final floodgates."

I chewed my lip, suppressing the demanding power within me. But we needed this information, even if the Angels had warned against digging too deeply into the stars.

Especially because of that.

My eyes found Jezebel's across the pool, sitting safely on the bank between Zanox and Dynaxtar, Erista and Mora beside her. My sister, understanding exactly what memory was harassing my mind, nodded in encouragement.

And though fear coiled between my ribs, I had to stop letting it freeze me.

"By the fucking Angels," I grumbled, unclasping my necklace and dropping to my knees before Vale. "Try again."

"What are you doing?" Tolek asked, warning in his voice. Cypherion stood from his perch, hovering.

But I ignored them both, watching only Vale as she inferred my plan and silently agreed, a honed confidence in her strength, one that had been dampened before she returned to Valyn. Dumping out the contents of the pouch at my side, I scattered the emblems across the earth and unsheathed my dagger.

"Alabath!" Tolek swore as Cypherion said, "Ophelia, don't!"

But my blade was already slicing across my hand, deep enough to sting, sending blood raining down across all six Angel tokens. The shard of Angelborn, the ring, the pearl, the gilded petal, the broken crown, and now, Valyrie's heart—the crystal carving of the lovers—were all sprinkled red.

And the boys' shouts were muffled by a barrier of Angellight shooting up around Vale and me, a tunnel stretching to the top of the cave.

Vale's session had been empowered by my light that day in Seawatcher Territory when she first seized, but now she'd fixed that ailment. Now, we had to find out what else she could read.

I squinted against the light as it brushed against my skin like a harsh wind. It was effervescent and euphoric, the way the power used to always be while under my control. It fulfilled all those searching, hollow pieces inside of me.

And it burned like an Angel's cruel heart.

But it didn't sear painfully. No, this was restorative as I called up the strongest essence of it I could. It lit the candles and licked across Vale's skin.

Beyond the barrier, Jezebel sat safely beside the pool between her khrysaor. Relief swooped through my stomach. It wasn't harming her this time.

Gold ether wrapped around Vale and me, and I nodded to the Starsearcher, her eyes falling closed as she reached out to the Fates. And after a moment, she gasped.

And in the tunnel of Angellight, her reading unfolded. As it had in Seawatcher Territory when the frames of Angels seem to appear above us, pieces of what Vale saw came to life.

There were flashes of tempests and lightning streaking the skies, fires raging through the lands and beasts bounding, untamed. The stars whirled, those iron doors slammed shut, and even the mountains cracked.

As I watched it play out, Vale spoke, tone breathless in disbelief. "The gods...they're walking with the Angels."

"I see them," I said, but I wasn't sure where they were, only seeing a blank canvas surrounding their forms. They laughed, though. The six with features obscured and seven with wings beating at their backs, all seeming...amicable.

"Do you know where they are?" I asked.

"Wildflowers," Vale said. Behind her closed eyes, in the depths of her readings, the trails of starfire and her nine Fate ties were showing her more. "They're overflowing like an explosion of fire. All oranges and yellows across the rolling hills."

There was only one place I knew of that fit that description. "Keep reading," I urged, smearing more blood across the emblems. The tunnel flared around us.

On the other side, Tolek paced, his hands locked behind his back to stop himself from interfering. I kept my focus on Vale.

"They're exchanging power. It's like the magic I saw earlier, but tamed. The winds and creatures, the heavens and mountains... everything is docile." Her eyes shifted back and forth beneath her lids. "Peaceful. But something is being...traded, I think? And —*no!*" Her lips pressed together, eyes clenching tighter.

"What is it?" I leaned forward, dug deep inside myself and the emblems to pull up as much Angellight as possible to help her strengthen the reading of the Prime Warriors.

"The gods and goddesses, they're—they're hurting the Angels." And I saw it as Vale narrated. The Angels were on their hands and knees, grabbing for their throats. The power was everywhere, exploding all around them.

"I can't hold on to it," Vale said, her hands tightening into fists, words rushing. "The magic they're trading, it's harming the Angels, some sort of sacrifice. And they're—"

Lightning cracked across the image, Angellight sparking, and Vale's eyes flew open. "They're gone," she panted. "A burst of light and they were gone."

I released a breath and dropped the Angellight tunnel to the cavern floor. Vale and I both slumped, our gazes locked as we tried to interpret what she'd read. Her eyes still swirled with silver stars.

Cypherion and Tolek dropped beside each of us.

"Dammit, Alabath," Tol said. Taking my bleeding palm in his hand, he began cleaning the wound. "You truly are trying to send me to the Spirit Realm."

I gave him a small, flirtatious, and hopefully forgivable smile. "If I do, perhaps I can travel between the worlds again and find you."

"You'd fucking better," he said and kissed my forehead.

I quickly healed my hand with Angellight and tucked the

emblems away, but as I was finishing up, Vale voiced the question gnawing at my mind, loud enough that the entire cavern froze. "Do you think that was the Ascension?"

I bit my lip. It was exactly what I'd thought of when she described the scene. "It might have been."

"But then, how were the gods involved?" Jezebel asked.

I worried less about that than about what Vale asked next, "And why was a process that was supposed to be thrilling and harmonious displayed as a brutal trading of magic?"

"I don't—"

"Quiet!" Erista's voice cracked across the cavern. Slowly, her gaze drifted toward the entrance. "Something is wrong."

I had one beat for the ice in her voice to turn to panic, then, she was running.

Jezebel was on her heels, calling for her partner, and the rest of us sped after them, sand kicking up as we hurried through the tunnel.

"Erista, what's happening?" Jez shouted again.

But Erista didn't answer—she didn't have to. Because when we all stumbled to a halt at the mouth of the cave system, we froze. Hands immediately flashed toward weapons.

"What is this?" I asked.

Erista swallowed, voice shaky. "It's the Rites of Dusk."

"But..."

The Soulguider nodded. "Something is very wrong."

Dread chilled my blood. This wasn't the Rites we'd seen recently. That was frivolity and empowerment. It was warriors beneath the swirling sandstorm, waves of maroon and amethyst bathing their dancing and offerings.

This, though...this was a horror dropped directly upon the market town of Lendelli.

Dark purple sand clouds shredded along the streets a mile away, obscuring the buildings and wrenching up tarps.

Without another thought, we ran. The soft sand slowed our progress, my legs burning much sooner than usual. Lancaster and Mora tore ahead of the rest of us with their fae speed.

"This shouldn't be happening like this!" Erista called. "The sands don't fall."

Neither do constellations, I thought, digging my feet into the earth to speed up.

The screams got louder as we breeched the town limit. Cries from families who had still been out enjoying the last of the evening's warmth—from children searching for their parents.

"What's the plan here, Alabath?" Tolek called over the roaring wind. The sand was swirling closer, and I squinted against it.

"Get as many people inside as possible!" I yelled. Only Tol, Jezebel, and Erista were close enough to hear me, the others breaking off into smaller groups and winding through the town.

Heads down, we sprinted around corners and up alleys. Soulguiders ducked beneath stalls, behind crates, anything to get out of the harsh, gravelly winds. They tore at my skin, the force leaving small cuts along my arms, and grains of sand stung my eyes.

"Get inside!" Erista yelled to her people, keeping a hand above her face. "It will stop soon!" And she sounded so confident, but when she met my narrowed gaze, the uncertainty was stark.

We cleared one street and started on the next, holding up woven tarps and scarves to cover the worst of the blasts. Soulguiders carried their young, braced windows with splintering wooden table tops.

Up and down we ran, helping families secure their doors and sealing shutters closed. Ducking through another alley, Tol, Jez, Erista, and I stumbled to a halt.

"Children," Jez panted. They hunched on the ground, heads tucked to their knees against the powerful gusts. When they lifted their stares at our approach, their eyes were red and glassy.

"They must be from a nearby boarding school," Erista yelled over the roar of the winds. "It's before curfew."

"We need to get them inside," I said.

A boy who looked about twelve popped to his feet beside me, the wind rifling his long braids. "The doors are all locked!"

By the Angels.

"We'll get them open!" I called down the alley so all the children could hear. Spinning, I coughed over the sand shoved down my throat, and asked, "Tol?"

He nodded, eyes red and determined, and unsheathed his sword. Wood cracking and splintering pierced the howling wind as Tolek jammed the hilt of his weapon against one of the nearest locks until it broke, and he shoved the door wide.

Jezebel and Erista raced inside to secure the windows on the other side of the empty shop as Tol and I ushered the children in.

The last of the bunch, a small girl about five and who appeared to be her younger brother, were the slowest.

"Alabath!" Tolek called, nodding down the way.

A mass of sand was gathering at the end of the alley, roaring toward us. We raced forward, and Tol scooped up the girl while the boy locked his arms around my neck, his face tucking into my shoulder. I cradled the back of his head and raced for the shop.

The dense cloud tickled my legs as I ran, whipped my hair around me, and I clutched the child tighter, willing the Angels on our side for one damn time.

I sped inside as the force of the cloud hit. We slammed the door on the winds, the walls rattling as it passed, but the sand that had managed to be swept inside with us fell quiet.

I leaned back against the door, panting. The boy shook, but I looked down and steadied my own breath. "What's your name?"

"Dennon," he answered in such a trembling voice.

I set him on his feet and crouched to his level. "Do you go to the nearby school, Dennon?"

He shook his head, long bangs drooping into his eyes. "We were going to Father's stall to bring him home for dinner."

By *we*, I assumed he meant his sister and himself. Tolek stood over his shoulder, the girl clutching his leg.

"Once the storm passes, we'll help you find him." I looked around the small shop, vacant shelves lining the perimeter. In the center, Jezebel and Erista were gathering the children. "Do you see that girl?" I asked, pointing to Jez, and both Dennon and his sister nodded. "She tells the best stories. Go ask her for one, and I bet by the time she's done, this little storm will be over."

They brightened, locking hands as they flew toward Jezebel. I pushed to my feet, blowing out a breath.

"*Little* storm?" Tolek asked as sand battered the windows.

"This is because of the emblems," I whispered, guilt thickening my throat.

Tol shook his head, gaze drifting toward the door. "No, *apeagna*. The timing lines up, but I have a feeling this is because of something much bigger than your blood on some shards of metal."

"But during the war, the Rites always coincided with the emblems being used."

"Yes, but nothing as tainted as this," he reminded me.

I chewed over that for a moment, watching the children now gathered in the center of the room. Their scared, innocent red eyes and the scratches against soft skin.

And my resolve hardened. "I'm going back out there."

"You can barely see!"

"Right now, yes." And I dismissed every misgiving about this decision—every uncertainty about the lengths the magic within me could go, mustering up the courage to flash Tol a smirk. "But if I caused this, I have to have something that can counteract it, too."

I held up Damien's emblem, shining around my neck.

Tol's eyes flicked between the shard and my own, reading the idea from my wicked grin. And though he clung to the verge of asking me not to do this, though he hated every time I was lost to the power of my light, the amber specks in his eyes ignited.

A slow smile spread across his face. "Make it fucking scorch, Revered."

With his confidence turning my body molten, I tore back into the alley, Tolek guarding my back.

And as we ran, I gathered up all that power ebbing within me from the reading, all the magic I'd been suppressing for weeks, forming six unique strands, and I wove them together.

We sped down the cobblestones, toward the center of that swirling mass of clouds above Lendelli, and charged right into the dense, dark-purple heart.

Then, without a slice to my skin or any form of blood splashing across the emblems, I wrenched up every drop of power and blasted Angellight into the sky.

Golden beams parted the swirling clouds like beacons in the night, melting together into one unstoppable force. The sands warred against the warmth of my magic, sizzling as it burned at their depths.

I dug into my spirit and thought of all those bracing against the repercussions of the unspooling magic across Gallantia. Of those sheltering in this very town, of those ravaged by the fires of Bodymelder Territory or whose food sources were depleted by untethered creatures.

I thought of those forced into smaller, weak positions and those who didn't deserve the wrath of whatever curse this was.

And I poured all of the rage and hurt and aching in my soul into my Angellight, flooding the storms.

"Alabath!" Tolek yelled as my magic consumed me. As my skin glowed gold and heated, *burned*, but his hand held steadfast to mine. "How much more will you give?"

Wind whipped my hair around my face. Through gritted teeth, I swore, "As much as it takes."

CHAPTER FIFTY-ONE
SANTORINA

GODDESSES BE DAMNED, I RARELY WISHED TO BE ONE OF the fae, but as I tore through the Lendelli Market and my lungs caught on fire, I wouldn't have minded having their stamina or physique.

A gust of wind slammed down the alley, shoving me into the wall.

"Gods," I cursed as my shoulder caught my weight.

I braced a hand on the stone, struggling upright, but a much larger, warmer hand dwarfed mine. I opened my mouth to argue, but the body pressed me to the wall as another blast of wind shot down the street, and the frame of the person behind me eclipsed me from the force.

When it passed, a voice growled, "Keep your head down, Bounty."

I spun, pain radiating through my shoulder, and came face to face with Lancaster. Pressed firmly between his disgustingly honed immortal body and the building, the sand barely lashed me.

"Get off of me!" I forced.

His brows flicked up, and he stepped back in time for a smaller gust of wind to throw sand in my face. Over his shoulder, Mora scolded him and Celissia eyed us. Barrett and Dax had gotten separated from us when a burst of wind sliced between our party a few blocks down, but they were with Malakai, Mila, and Lyria.

"She's human," he shot at his sister. "She shouldn't be here."

"Why do you care where I am?" I asked, wiping the dirt from my eyes.

Lancaster paused, narrowed stare flicking over my face. "You helped my sister."

"Then I am perfectly capable of helping here, too!" I shoved his chest to step around him, but he barely flinched. Lancaster eyed the shoulder I was still massaging. Damn immortals and their quick healing. The storm barely seemed to rock his sturdy frame.

"Stay with us," he demanded, and he took off down the alley, Mora and Celissia waiting for me to go ahead.

We helped the Lendelli citizens cover up windows, the worst of the storm being in the center of town. Cypherion and Vale were in this stretch with us, the Starsearcher beneath a shelter reading. Cyph flicked nervous glances her way as he helped me latch a set of broken shutters with a strong length of rope, Soulguiders, Celissia, and the fae working hurriedly opposite us.

"We should get inside," Cyph called as the howling wind picked up.

But it was Vale, in a distant voice that didn't sound like herself, who called, "Wait!" She emerged from beneath her shelter, unbothered by the sand and wind. Her eyes swirled with silver. "Something is happening."

Vale turned toward the center of town, head tipped to the sky.

And then, light pushed through the clouds. It was incremental, a scattering that peeled back the storm and bathed the city under siege. It crept around corners and alleys, piercing the dark night with a warm golden glow, and reached to something within me.

"What is *that*?" Lancaster asked, squinting as his stony features were illuminated.

"That," Vale gasped, voice still eerie, "is Ophelia."

Cypherion and I exchanged a look. *Angellight.*

～

OPHELIA'S ANGELLIGHT stopped the storm. I didn't understand how—the citizens of Lendelli were even more confused—but it calmed the riotous sand clouds tearing through the market enough for us to begin restoring the alleys.

Using a small amount of magic, Mora glamoured her and her brother's ears. She, Celissia, and I took charge of one lane where barrels and crates had been overturned, stalls shredded like claws of wind had ripped right through them.

As the fae righted a cracked barrel, grain spilling over the stone street, she rolled her shoulder. I paused my sweeping, bracing an elbow on my broom.

"Is it still plaguing you?" I inquired. Mora turned her keen, immortal stare on me, and I nodded to her shoulder.

She checked down the alley, ensuring she wouldn't be overheard. "Yes, but I do not want to alarm my brother."

Celissia's head lifted from where she was folding empty burlap sacks.

I balked. "Why?"

Mora went on rearranging the stock of the stall we were restoring, the tent shredded but some of the goods still intact. "Because it is beyond his capability of fixing."

"Why?" I pushed, hands tightening on the broom.

Mora's lips rolled between her teeth.

"Right." I sighed. "Locked."

So whatever reason Lancaster's magic wasn't working was tied to the secrets the fae had been sworn to. And as we'd guessed so far in our gentle prodding over our travels, all locks tied back to the gods.

Though it felt like days ago at this point, questions from Vale's reading nagged at my mind.

"What did you think of what was seen before the storm hit?" I chose my words carefully. While Lancaster, Cypherion, and Vale had all drifted away to aid other parts of the market, there were still plenty of warriors around. I dropped my voice even lower. "Of the Gods...harming the Angels."

Mora shuffled about the shredded tent, her step not faltering, and I pretended to focus on the pile of rubble I was amassing as she said, "The Angels mean very little to me beyond a subject of study such as the scrolls."

"But does that justify what the Gods may have done?" Celissia asked, stacking her neatly-folded pile along the back wall.

"There is no proof the Gods and Goddesses did anything," Mora said, not unkindly.

"Suppose they did, though," I challenged.

A cluster of Soulguiders passed the stall, arms laden with goods from shattered crates. Mora took a step closer, voice sharp as the blades at her thighs. "I have studied my...Aoiflyn in depth in my many centuries, and there is no account of her walking this land with the Angels."

"Perhaps it's been forgotten. Like those bargains that hold your tongue, perhaps the histories have been similarly tied up." I shrugged, but Mora averted her eyes. "You clearly do not believe the Gods are guilty of the acts Vale thinks she witnessed. It unsettles you."

Celissia's eyes flicked between us as I pushed the fae.

"No," Mora said. "What unsettles me is that the warriors do not know what the Gods and Goddesses are truly capable of."

"What do you mean?"

Again, her lips rolled together.

"Gods and Angels, Spirits and Fates. Even those beings not worshipped on this continent. They are all masses of power. They have wrung *wars* through the heavens, leveled worlds at the blink of an eye." Mora shivered, the motion so quick it could have been my human eyes playing tricks. "Your friends find my queen brutal? They find the cruelty of their own leaders hard to grasp?" Her face paled. "They are small compared to the might of the six."

Her words raised goosebumps across my skin.

"Then you do find the Gods capable of harming the Angels?" I asked, searching her expression for any hint of what she wished to say beyond this vague warning, but it was veiled. Damn tricky immortals.

"Capable, certainly." Mora sighed. "But there is no account of

Gods gracing your continent in the long fae histories, so I do not believe it happened as the Starsearcher saw."

She turned back to the barrels, hefting another up with a grunt. Celissia went on with her work, largely staying out of the conversation, but I didn't believe for a moment she wasn't tucking away every syllable. I grabbed my broom again, but didn't resume sweeping. A clawing instinct gripped my gut, my fingers tightening on the wood.

"I have worshipped the Gods my entire life," I whispered. "My parents instilled the practices in me. They taught me my morning and nighttime prayers as a girl and told me when I was in distress or lonely, the Gods would care for me."

A warmth filled Mora's eyes when she turned to me now. A kinship. "And it pains you to consider that the Gods and Goddesses may not be as wholesome as you were led to believe?"

"It is a hard fact to reconcile." A dichotomy my brain couldn't understand.

She nodded. "From what I have seen, your friends are dealing with similar questions of their own Angels. Who to trust, who to follow."

Celissia scoffed, striding across the alley to another tent. "That's simplifying it."

"And now that it appears the Gods may have harmed them, does that not throw our beliefs into question?" I hated that I used the term *our*, but even though I would never admit it out loud, humans and the fae did share this one common ground—the Gods. It was ironic that the most basic foundation was the only similarity we could acknowledge.

That was all I'd consider of that, though.

"There is a complexity in all religions. One most humans have not lived long enough to grasp." I glowered at Mora, but she held up a hand and continued, "I do not mean offense by this, but it took me many centuries of study to fully understand. I still am not certain I do. In a way, we all believe the same thing, though."

"What do you mean?"

"Many species and races tend to claim their deities for similar reasons. For guidance, protection, and solace in the face of the unknown. A story of creation, a fear of destruction. Life and death and rebirth. We tell similar carvings of the world's beginnings and endings, but with different symbols and figureheads."

I considered what she meant, digging into my expansive—or limited, according to her—knowledge of the Gods and Angels. The magic may be designated differently between them, the powers they instilled or protected varying, but there were trends that could not be denied.

A Goddess of Fate. An Angel of Starsearching.

A God of Nature. Angels whose territories tended toward the seas and land.

A Goddess of Death. An Angel who guided souls.

They were segmented differently, but when names and titles were removed, it was impossible to deny that the symbols they represented, the comforts they provided, were similar.

"But how does that change when the Gods and Angels are no longer only symbols or figureheads?" I dared to ask.

Celissia, back in our stall, added with a sympathetic nod, "How does all of this change if they walked among us?"

Mora didn't argue that the Gods had never walked the earth this time. Instead, she said, "I suppose that is a question only fate's misty hands can answer."

My brow furrowed at that frustratingly vague response, but before I could answer, a shadow shrouded the stall.

"We're returning to the inn. The warriors will continue tomorrow," Lancaster stated, not even looking at me.

I scoffed, finishing the quick tidying as the siblings discussed the work they'd done to help the market.

As we walked back, Cypherion and Vale in conversation with Lancaster, Mora stepped beside me and Celissia. "Did you truly not know you were a Bounty?" she asked.

I narrowed my stare on her brother's broad back, not making eye contact with the female. I wasn't in the mood to be taunted when my beliefs were already so unsteady. "I knew nothing of the Bounties, nor did I know their blood ran through my line. Before my parents died, we lost contact with all remaining family."

Something sharp twisted inside me, a key almost nudging into a lock. A piece that claimed it would like to know where this power came from, and who survived the slaughter to lead them to Gallantia. Did I truly have the senses to track the fae? Who were my ancestors, and were there more of us out there? How had they evaded such powerful soldiers?

My eyes locked on Lancaster; how had they outrun *the hunter*?

Mora tracked the subtle stare, of course. Damn observant fae. "He hates it, you know."

"What?" I blinked at her.

"My brother hates what he was born to do. Hates that she can snap her fingers and order him to kill."

A harsh breath sliced through my chest. "How did it happen?"

"That is not my story to tell," Mora said. "And it is not one he will share freely."

"How is it you do not have the instinct?" Celissia asked as we rounded a corner, carefully avoiding a pile of shattered glass. The air still held that eerie purple and maroon glow of the Rite, and the shards winked with it.

"Fae magic is all tied to blood, but it varies. It is not guaranteed that because we are of the same line, our power will manifest the same. And beyond that, we do not share fathers. Our mother had many, many children."

"Is she in the queen's employ?" Celissia asked. "Is that how both of you ended up there?"

"Not her employ, no." Mora's voice tightened, and she didn't elaborate.

Another unclear response. I sighed. "Do your other siblings share your tendency for glamour or the stronger healing magic?"

"Our line spans expansive territories of power, but Lancaster is the only family I remain in contact with."

"Truly? With so much family, how could you turn your back on them?"

"When he turned of age, he was summoned by the queen, to the capital where I lived and worked." Her voice sobered. "He did not take kindly to it."

Her words faded; she was unwilling to share anymore of her

brother's business. And in those last words, ire burned. A familiar kind, but I was uncertain to whom hers were directed.

"I imagine anyone would hate having their autonomy taken in such a way," I said, defensively. It didn't make this fae male different than anyone else. In fact, it aligned him with humans more than he probably cared to acknowledge.

We don't all have choices, Lancaster had said of his status serving Queen Ritalia when I was healing him. When I had called him cold and cruel.

"I only say it because I do not think you are as different as you believe."

"Yes," I deadpanned. "I was bred with an instinct to kill him as well. He should be careful when he sleeps tonight."

"In a sense, weren't you?" She inclined her head, and—

"*Aoiflyn's tits*," I swore beneath my breath, kicking a rock. Personal retribution aside, she was correct. Perhaps it explained that carnal need for revenge for the civilizations I never even knew.

"You share his attitude, that is certain." Mora laughed, and even Celissia snickered.

"Thank you for the opinion," I said, voice thick with sarcasm.

The female clicked her tongue. "Santorina, it was not meant to be rude."

"Forgive me if I do not care to be compared to someone whose sole purpose in life is to kill me. Queen or no, that is a difficult bridge to cross."

"You're correct," she said, and I blinked at that agreement, coming to a stop in front of the inn. "We are all players in a game of legends long spun. The moves we make, the sacrifices at our hands, it was all decided long, long ago."

My anger sank. "That's a rather sad way to look at life."

"Or it is freeing. To know there are powers out there guiding us," Celissia suggested.

"It is both," Mora agreed, and for someone typically so full of jubilant hope, she sounded starkly remorse. "I envy the shorter warrior and human lifespans at times because of the naivety it allows you all to live under. But the realms appear to be shifting."

She eyed the piles of sand littering the streets. "Though I do not believe what was read in that cave tonight, it is important to remember the game. To prepare for unexpected strings to be pulled, and the most enchanted of royal hands to be played."

I followed her stare to the sand stirring in the breeze, contemplating precisely what moves the Gods had in store.

CHAPTER FIFTY-TWO
OPHELIA

THE INN WAS SILENT BY THE TIME TOLEK AND I returned from the market. Angellight still buzzed beneath my skin, warm and indulgent. After the Rites, no patrons lingered downstairs, not a single one loitering in the hallways as we traipsed to the third floor our party had commandeered.

"Come on, Alabath," Tol whispered, taking my hand to lead me into our room.

I stepped inside as he held the door, his palm warm against mine settling something in my spirit that hadn't quieted since Vale's reading.

The rooms in this inn were bedecked in the rich, lavish colors of the Soulguiders. Deep amethysts and sage greens, pops of turquoise and bronze dangling from mystlight chandeliers and framing decor, adorning the headboard and four posts on the bed. Desert marigolds bloomed on the desk, the stark yellows as bright as those I imagined in Firebird's Field, which only brought my mind back to Vale's reading—

The lock clicked shut, and Tol tugged on my hand. Turning, I surveyed him. He leaned against the wood, his head thudding back. With a sigh, he stroked his thumb across my knuckles, tingles erupting up my arm.

He watched that spot where his skin brushed against mine

repeatedly for a long, heavy moment, tension crackling in the air around him like he was about to splinter.

"Tol?" I asked, stepping toward him.

"I love watching you wield magic—wield pure power, *apeagna*." When his eyes snapped up to mine, they were *burning*. "But I hate those fucking emblems."

There wasn't another word before he hauled me to him, spinning so my back pressed to the door, the smooth wood cool against my spine, and his lips crashed into mine. It wasn't a fleeting, gentle kiss like the ones we exchanged at any given point in the day, and it wasn't quite languorous and sensual like when he showered me with adoration each night.

No, this was tongues warring, teeth clashing. It was desperate and awed, furious and terrified. It was the baser instincts dug deep down within us that we suppressed in the face of all the obstacles outside these walls, finally breaking free.

He told me with every sweep of his lips how scared he was when I used Angellight, but also what else it did to him. How it made him want to worship me, how it drove this desperate need because he didn't know when it might take me from him.

Guilt wound through me as he kissed me harder, but there was no choice when it came to the Angelcurse.

There was no choice.

At that, the anger that fueled me when I shot Angellight into the skies incinerated any remnant of regret that had been blooming. Anger at the Prime Warriors, at the gods, too, if they were truly involved. For toying with our lives, for ravaging this beautiful man before me and planting a war within his own heart.

Biting Tol's lip, I dug my hands into his hair and hitched a leg around his hip to tug him closer. His thick length rocking against my core rewarded me in the most delicious way.

With a growl, Tolek nimbly slung Angelborn from my back and both of our sword belts from our hips. Then, he grabbed my other thigh, hoisting it around his waist as he kissed me so I was slammed back between him and the door, the wood shuddering.

He wrenched his lips from mine, dragging a path along my jaw, down my neck, and rolled his hips against me. "Every fucking time you use the emblems," he growled into my skin, "every time you feel like you disappear from this world, I'm ready to throw myself off the edge of the realm to get you back."

The rough edge to his voice ripped at pieces of my heart. But his hands gripped tighter to my body, like he needed to confirm I was here.

"You tether me. I would wade through the Angellight to find you, Tol," I panted as his teeth scraped my collarbone. He gripped my ass beneath my skirt, but his fingers weren't where I wanted him. Where I so desperately needed him.

He quickly untied my leathers, tossing my top aside so my breasts were free. Tol dragged his teeth over my nipple, and I moaned, head falling back. He bit down, running his tongue over the peak to soothe that pain before moving to the other.

"You get further each time you use those things, Alabath," he said, breath hot against my skin. "That magic gets stronger. Spirits, it's impressive, and I promise to show you exactly how impressive." At that gravelly tone, I met his eyes. "But make no mistake—I will slaughter the Angels if they try to take you one of these times."

"If that ever happened, we would slaughter them together," I swore, and I kissed him to seal that vow, rolling my hips against his. "Now prove your words, Vincienzo."

He laughed, a low and tantalizing sound. Drifting his lips along my jaw, he pinned my hips to the wall. But he didn't move. No, he kept me in the most wanting state.

Tol nipped my ear, voice husky as he whispered, "Do you want me to fuck you against this door, Alabath? To show you how impressed and *desperate* I am for you?" His hands gripped my backside so tightly, I thought he'd leave permanent marks. His fingers curved around my thighs to tease my center.

"Yes," I begged. My hips strained to writhe, needing him inside me, but his hold was firm.

"Or do you want it up against the window over there?" My dazed vision flicked to the glass spanning one wall. The curtains were still pulled back, ravaged market stalls and streets stretching into the distance. "Hands on the glass? So anyone passing by can see you're *mine*, despite what any Angels may think?"

Spirits, I wanted him everywhere. Every damn spot in this room—in every room. "Everywhere, Tolek." I pulled my gaze back to his, tugging greedily on his hair until he hissed. "Across every realm, atop every mountain, show the world I'm yours."

A crooked smirk. "Then hang on."

Keeping me pressed tightly against the door, he dropped to his knees, my legs slung over his leather-clad shoulders, so broad and firm and supportive. In a breath, he had my skirt hiked up and undergarments torn on the floor. He left my boots on and my dagger strapped to my thigh, fingers tracing the hilt.

Tol's gaze roved over me as I was bare and breathless before him, and his stare spoke of worship and possession. He dragged a finger through my slick center to circle at the apex of my thighs.

"So fucking ready for me, *apeagna*," he muttered.

I was so sensitive from the wait, I shivered at his touch, unable to hold back a moan. "Do that again," he commanded, and I couldn't help but obey as Tolek repeated that teasing motion, adding more pressure. He watched for every gasp and jerk of my hips. With his eyes on me and him on his knees, I felt like the most prominent of Angels.

Without looking away, Tolek pressed a kiss just above where I wanted him, and he laughed when I whined in impatience.

"Is this what you want?" His wicked tongue flicked out in a pattern that had me breathless, my hips jerking. He was so good with that tongue, even better when his fingers joined it, plunging into me with one clear intention: to remind me this was beyond the gods.

His tongue dipped inside of me then licked up my center, circling with pressure that had me swearing to every Angel above. His fingers replaced it and crooked, brushing against my sensitive inner walls.

"Do you like that, *Revered*?" he demanded, annunciating the word.

"Yes," I panted. "I love you on your knees. I love you saying my title."

"Ride my fingers and show me." That deep tone, so full of

authority and devotion, had my hips swiveling against his hand, angling up so he went even deeper. "Good girl," he purred.

"Keep going," I gasped, my head falling back and hands grappling against the wood.

And he did. Tolek listened to my commands, my cries, until constellations were starting to fall before my vision and my entire world ended with the man on his knees before me.

And for every stroke, lick, and bite, Tol muttered a combination of salacious and sweet promises. Things about fighting through the realms for me, vows to always stand at my side. He embedded the memories in my skin, right down to my very bones and cursed spirit.

"Ophelia," Tolek said as I fluttered around his fingers. I dropped my gaze to his. "Come for me."

Between his commanding words, his fingers crooked inside of me, the return of his tongue, and that blazing stare looking up expectantly from between my legs, I crashed into oblivion.

The door shook against its frame, but I didn't give a damn if it splintered and broke. Didn't give a damn if anyone on the street saw or heard. How could I when this utter state of bliss Tolek instilled in me took over?

Once my climax passed, Tolek set me on my feet, on legs that barely worked. But when he rose, he didn't kiss me as I thought he would.

No, he strode to the window, tugging the curtains shut and turning back to me. *No more witnesses*, his searing gaze said. *The rest is mine.*

Tol undid the buckles of his leathers, discarding the layers in smooth movements as he crossed back to the center of the room, until his perfectly defined muscles and the assortment of scars littering the right side of his body were on full display. The pale, jagged lines caught the light, and the sight twisted through me with an odd combination of desire and vengeance.

With a nod to me, Tol said, "Take off the rest of your clothes, and get on the bed."

His stare didn't leave me as he did the same, boots, pants, and undergarments all littered across the room. The only thing left on me was the dagger at my thigh, which Tolek watched with a curious gaze as he prowled toward me.

I perched on the edge of the bed, and he stood between my legs. His hard length jutted up in front of me. I licked my lips as I gripped him at the base, wanting him, but Tol grabbed my chin.

"Not tonight," he said. "Tonight, I need to be inside of you."

That raw desperation was back in his voice, and it ignited something within me. Heat pooled in my core.

Wrapping an arm around my waist, he hitched me to the center of the bed and settled between my legs. For a lingering moment, his gaze swept across my face. My heart clenched with the intensity of his stare, like he was committing me to memory in case his worst fears really did come true. It tugged at that anger at the Angels, had me clawing for him.

He kissed me with the same careful commitment, and though the desperation remained between us, something else shifted. Every movement also became reverent and impassioned.

The head of his cock nudged my entrance, and I was already squirming. He ran his length up my center, intentionally teasing my sensitive clit.

"Tolek," I breathed. "*Please.*"

"Always so beautiful when you say my name," he said, and he sank into me.

Gentle thrusts and rolling of hips. Gasps of pleasure and groans caught between kisses. That's what we became, my hands curling into those silk sheets, his firm on my skin.

Tol gripped my thigh where my dagger was still sheathed, and with his other hand, he laced our fingers together, a lifeline of our souls.

He was a part of my soul. Always had been.

As he repeatedly sank into me, our bodies and lips and that unspoken communication we shared reminded us both again and again how desperate we were to hang on to one another. How when we were broken down to our most fundamental pieces, when we were nothing more than the essence of a warrior that existed in the universe, it would always be us together.

"I love you, Tolek," I gasped.

He devoured the breath on my lips. "When this is over"—his forehead fell to mine, and he spoke as if he was convincing himself, too—"no matter what remains, we will."

And I swore, "In every infinite realm."

Because that thread that had always been between us, that had tethered our souls together at such a young age, was made of something stronger than the Angels. Stronger than gods and fate and time.

An unending, unyielding, infinite sort of love.

At my promise, Tolek pounded into me. Our breathing increased, the rhythm of our rolling hips picking up speed. Our hands stayed laced beside my head, and when we reached that climax together, we held tight to that grip, unwilling to let go.

As our hearts calmed, Tol pressed his lips to my forehead, and whispered, "I love you infinitely, *apeagna*. When the Angels scorch to ash and the gods fade to fate, I will be yours across every realm."

Across every realm, beyond any fate, Tolek Vincienzo was mine. And I'd be damned if I let the Angels ruin us.

We laid there as those promises solidified, cocooned from the world as if nothing beyond these walls mattered. I drew lazy patterns across Tolek's chest, tracing the scars left on his body, and he teased his fingertips up my spine.

Too soon, Tol rose from the bed, striding naked through the room to pour us glasses of water from the pitcher on the side table. The scar on his powerful thigh from the Engrossian ax when he'd tried to give his life for mine was stark in the night, thicker and less neatly healed than the others decorating his skin.

I pushed off the bed, gathering the five Angel emblems from my pack and setting them on the nightstand. Mystlight flicked along the different arrangements of gems and metal. Only the shard of Angelborn remained around my neck.

The worries Tolek had distracted me from started to push in.

"Will you hand me my nightgown, please?" I asked without turning.

Tolek's strong hands slipped around my hips, his lips against my ear. "No."

I laughed, turning in his arms. The heat of his skin against

mine and the smile on his face—so easy and with an edge of teasing
—chased away the worries. "No?"

"I prefer this."

He always did. Most nights I didn't mind; it only gave us fewer
barriers for the morning.

I looked back at those emblems, resting so perfectly on the
nightstand. I considered telling him what was worrying me, then,
but...my gaze flicked to the window. The thin door. Too risky.

"Temperatures are dropping in the desert."

Tol's lips skimmed mine. "Body heat, Alabath."

I rolled my eyes, pushing against his chest to grab my nightgown myself, but Tolek beat me to it, carefully swiping it from the
dresser and handing it over. Then, he put on a pair of undershorts.

"Open the curtains?" I asked as I crawled into bed. "I want to
sleep with the stars."

He flashed me another of those dazzling, worry-defeating
smiles. "Whatever you wish, Revered."

~

SLEEP PULLED US UNDER QUICKLY—THE satiated, insistent
kind that only came when Tolek's arms were around me. But it
didn't keep my mind from perking up at the smallest sound.

At the drift of a breeze through a curtain when the windows
should be closed.

At the brush of a seemingly silent hand who'd spent centuries
sneaking.

I kept my eyes closed, my breathing even, and stifled the Angellight whirling protectively beneath my skin. Those ears would pick
up even the slightest shift in the rhythm of my heart.

But he couldn't hide his presence, looming over the
nightstand.

I waited until his attention was snared with my delicately laid
trap. Then, faster than the cats prowling the Starsearcher jungles, I
struck.

Tolek jumped from bed, his family dagger immediately soaring
toward the intruder. He ducked, but I bore down, driving the

stake I'd whittled from the branch of the cypher into the male's shoulder.

Until his knees cracked to the wood, his grunts of pain loud enough to wake the entire floor. I followed him, pinning his hips. One arm hung uselessly at his side, his magic incapacitated, but he swung up with the other, dragging a nail down my cheek. Blood tickled my skin, but I didn't flinch.

The door to our room crashed open, our friends pouring in, but I only twisted the stake deeper, where Rina had told me it wouldn't kill.

I snapped off the tip at a rough angle, ensuring it splintered.

Rounding the bed to glare down at the intruder, Lancaster snarled, "What in the Goddess's afterlife are you doing here?"

The man beneath me grunted.

"Hello, Brystin," I purred down at him, flicking away a drop of blood from my cheek. "I was wondering when you'd finally show your face."

Chapter Fifty-Three
Tolek

"Okay, Alabath," I exhaled as Cypherion, Malakai, and I heaved Brystin into a chair. Dax bound his wrists and ankles, the fae's shoulder still bleeding freely with the tip of the cypher stake in it. Santorina and Celissia cleaned some of the major mess from the floor—to assist the innkeepers, Rina suggested.

I stalked toward Ophelia, carefully wiping away a lingering drop of her blood the fucking fae had drawn. My hand tightened on my dagger, but I swallowed the rage. "Tell us how this happened."

"He broke in to steal the emblems," Ophelia said, crossing her arms and glaring at the fae male. His blood still smeared her hands and nightgown. I lifted my dagger at the sight. But—

The nightgown.

"You knew he was here, didn't you?" I asked Ophelia, my eyes narrowing. Every head whipped toward us, but she merely grinned up at me as if this was one of our games.

She asked sweetly, "What makes you say that, Vincienzo?"

"Insisting on clothes before we went to sleep," I began.

Malakai grunted, arms crossed, "I think we're all grateful for that."

"Definitely," Lyria confirmed, leaning against the wall behind Brystin, her eyes trained on the fae and flooded with threats.

"I don't know—" Barrett started to joke, but Dax cut him a

426

harsh glare. The general flinched, hand on his stomach as he muttered something to the prince. But Mila shushed them all, stare intent on Ophelia.

"First of all," I continued, still wearing nothing but my undershorts, "you would all be so lucky to see me naked."

"Some of us have seen more than we care to," Cypherion complained. "Now, continue."

I turned back toward Ophelia, her wide magenta eyes blinking expectantly up at me. "You insisted on clothes tonight because you suspected he was going to attempt to break in. It's why you've been preparing that stake, too." I gestured to the shattered pieces of crimson-stained, ash-white cypher now atop the dresser, and Brystin grunted. "You were whittling that thing all morning, and it's why you wanted to sleep with the curtains pulled back."

"I'm surprised it took you so long to notice." Ophelia smiled wider, and I'd be damned if I didn't meet it. We made quite a pair of deviously charmed warriors, grinning across crimson-stained floors.

Until a pillow slapped into the side of my face. Ophelia laughed, but I spun, finding Jezebel perched on the bed with her ankles crossed. She shrugged a shoulder. "Slipped."

"Baby Alabath," I grumbled.

"Stop looking lustfully at my sister while there's blood on the floor, and I won't have to throw things."

I tossed the pillow back to her, not adding that I always looked at Ophelia like that.

Jez continued, "Why did you insist on leaving the curtains open?"

I answered, still in awe of Ophelia's mind. "Because when we returned to the room tonight, Ophelia and I had a fun time in full view of that window, and I assume she wanted Brystin to think we were vulnerable and exhausted."

Which, truthfully, I had been. Sleeping soundly as I often did nowadays, I may not have woken if I hadn't felt Ophelia beside me.

She nodded approvingly at me.

"Disturbing," Jezebel said, hopping up from the bed and

giving it a wary look. I didn't bother to tell her the bed wasn't the only place we'd been.

Ophelia turned toward Lancaster and Mora, expression hardening. "Did you two know he was here?"

"Not entirely," Lancaster bit out, eyes trained on the splintered piece of cypher inside his comrade's shoulder. "I scented him recently. Figured Ritalia sent him on some jaunt for her own purposes. Reconnaissance like she had me doing previously, now that I'm occupied. I knew nothing of his thievery attempt," he sneered.

"Don't act like you're above it," Brystin taunted, breaths heavy between his words. Ophelia really hadn't been merciful. Spirits bless her, she was fucking magnificent. If I had my way, I'd clear the room of everyone else right now to show her how impressive this plan was.

No, Vincienzo, I scolded, eyeing where Jez sat, armed with another pillow. There was a fae bleeding in the middle of our floor. I'd fuck Ophelia into oblivion later.

Lancaster stalked forward and gripped the arms of the chair Brystin was tied to. "Thieves are dishonest."

"But killers are morally fine?" Santorina interjected from the corner of the room, a bloodied rag in hand.

Lancaster flicked a gaze over his shoulder, his hair drooping in his face. "Defending him even though he would have killed your friend?"

Santorina snorted, unfazed by the bait. "Gods, no. Only wondering where the line is drawn."

"I think the line of fae morals is not what we're here to discuss," Ophelia said, looking between the two of them with a creased brow.

Thieves were dishonest.

Apparently that was where Lancaster's boundary stood. If fae really could not lie, only twist their words, was dishonesty truly the problem? Or maybe it was loyalty and trustworthiness. Trickiness against the vulnerable.

Lancaster still had that bargain with Ophelia and me. One he could use against us any day—and we him. One that if any of us broke, our lives were taken with it. And he had not tried to trick us, even when it was supposedly in his nature to do so.

In fact, Lancaster had been on Gallantia for months, and we'd heard nothing of it. He'd found and befriended Mindshaper rebels, helping us locate them during the war in the winter, but beyond that, he'd kept to himself. Hadn't tried to hurt any innocents, besides the time he held a knife to Rina's throat. And though I wouldn't forget that, perhaps the damn fae was trustworthy after all?

Or it was all a trick. I supposed only the Fates could know. My gaze flicked to Vale, her eyes still swirling silver. Maybe tomorrow she could seek out the fae goddess in those readings. We could see if the Fates would finally share about her.

For now, though, we had an interrogation to get underway.

Santorina and Lancaster continued to spew barbs, but the fae male pushed up from Brystin's chair and took a step back, crossing his arms. "Did she send you?"

"Of course," Brystin scoffed.

"Why?"

But Brystin's gaze swiveled to Ophelia. "Do you care to fill him in?"

She assessed him, looking right down her nose with those bloody fingers drumming on her arm. "Your queen doesn't trust me."

A grin. "Not in the slightest."

"She's smart, then," Ophelia retorted.

And it wasn't a joke. Both Ritalia and Ophelia were too wise to easily trust the other. Not without proof. Even when you could not lie, word only went so far. Ritalia, ruler for centuries and manipulator of secrets, likely guessed as much.

"She realizes this won't make us any more likely to give her what she wants doesn't she?" I asked.

"Her Majesty has grown unconcerned with a peaceful partnership, so long as she gets the outcome she desires."

My skin prickled at that vague explanation, gaze cutting to Lancaster and Mora. The former's attention was still locked on the fae bound before us, but Mora watched Ophelia curiously. Almost...admiringly?

"What's changed?" Ophelia asked harshly.

"Who said anything has?" Brystin smirked, still as casual and unaffected as always. "Perhaps this has always been her plan."

Lancaster and Mora exchanged a brief, confused look, and Cypherion tracked it. "It wasn't." He looked to Ophelia. "Ritalia is pivoting. Otherwise, she would have had Lancaster and Mora steal the emblems."

The former snapped, "I wouldn't sink—"

"Shut up," Ophelia barked, looking among all three of the fae. "I'm not sure I trust any of you right now. We might be better off impaling you all with cypher stakes and leaving you locked in this room."

"Sweet Mystique," Mora cooed, "you'd have to prepare those lovely weapons first."

Ophelia flashed her a saccharine smile. "Who says I haven't already?"

She very well could have them hidden in this room somewhere. I hadn't realized she tucked the one beneath our pillows tonight.

But Ophelia only waved a hand at Mora and Lancaster. "You two may stay for now since you've been genuinely helpful, but we're watching you closely." As she said it, the energy in the room shifted. None of us moved closer to the fae, but it was like everybody angled slightly, every hand drifted closer to a weapon. On the word of the Revered, any of us—Mystique, Soulguider, Starsearcher, or Engrossian—would strike.

"What I'm curious about, Brystin," Ophelia continued, turning back to the male, "is why you're here *now*. You've been trailing us since we left Valyn." One blink was all that belied his shock, but Ophelia didn't miss it. "Oh, don't look so surprised. My pegasus was unsettled, and I thought I saw you in the pleasure house last night. So briefly, I wasn't sure who it was, just someone familiar."

"Was it you?" Jezebel blurted, striding forward. "Did you kill that warrior?" Her question landed with a heavy silence.

"It wasn't a warrior," Brystin grunted.

"That's a yes," I confirmed.

Brystin smiled. "I started it. I did not strike the final blow—I don't know how she died."

No one said anything—none of us dared look at Jezebel—but she shrank back beside Erista who whispered soothing words to her.

"But why did you act now?" Ophelia asked, returning us to the topic at hand. "Before we have the final emblem. You want to steal them, do you not? Surely, having all seven would be more useful."

"Having six would be enough." He did not technically *disagree* with what Ophelia claimed.

"Curious," Ophelia mused. "I suppose they're useless to Ritalia no matter how many she has."

"Useless?" Malakai asked.

"No Angelcurse. No Angelblood. The fae queen is nothing but a futile statue in this prophesied fate. Perhaps she doesn't need to wait for all of the emblems." Ophelia scratched at the blackened veins from her Curse scar. "She just doesn't want me to have them."

Cypherion, still standing defensively near Brystin, echoed the earlier point, "Something in the queen's hand has changed. Something that means she does not *want* to wait."

Ophelia maintained her controlled mask, but a bead of nerves bubbled in her searching stare. "Or she *can't* wait."

Mora chimed in, gently massaging her injured shoulder, "She would only adapt her plans in extreme circumstances. In her centuries, the queen has learned to be very patient." Why was she giving us that information?

"What could she have discovered?" Ophelia asked, and Brystin scoffed. Ophelia stiffened at the noise, an instinct snapping as sharp as a bolt of lightning. She sighed, striding across the room to where her weapons lay. "Very well, then." She picked up her dagger. "Would someone else like the honor of convincing him to speak?"

"Say the word, Alabath," I said eagerly. That fucker broke into our room while we slept, drew Ophelia's blood.

"Wait!" Lancaster blurted, turning to Brystin. "Did she give you any rules?" Brystin remained silent. "If they harm you, are you to do something?"

That had both Ophelia and me freezing. That fucking queen... She'd given all her soldiers cleverly worded orders, things they could not deny, likely woven into bargains. Instructions on how to react, pulling their strings even from far, far away.

Brystin jerked toward Lancaster, hissing as pain shot through his shoulder. "Why are you helping them?"

"I am not."

"You have orders."

"Orders that nearly got my sister killed," Lancaster sneered. "Oh, but thank the Goddess that wasn't allowed. Not like that put her through excruciating pain."

Brystin looked over Mora, who, despite her pale face and shadowed eyes, glared back at him. "She is fine."

"No thanks to our queen," Lancaster spat. "Now, is there a stipulation bargain if you are caught and tortured?"

Brystin's silence rang through the room.

"Answer enough," I said, shrugging and grabbing my sword. "We'll simply kill him then."

Mora disarmed me impossibly fast. "Never play a game in which you don't know all the rules."

Anger roiled through me at having my weapon taken. I stepped up to her. "Good thing I don't lose."

But it was Ophelia's voice—small, soft, and meant only for me—that drifted through the room. "Tolek..." A hand on my arm.

Her mask was dropped as she looked up at me. Here, in front of everyone, a bit of her uncertainty shone through. She ignored the audience, silently pleading with me to be with her. To play the game and survive to scorch the Angels.

I sighed, backing down a step from Mora and placing a kiss to Ophelia's forehead. Then, with an apologetic but taunting smirk, I added to the fae female, "I'd appreciate my weapon back."

She extended it. "Don't be stupid. It is unbecoming." The tension in the room cracked at her words.

"He doesn't die, then," Santorina said. "Unfortunately."

"The beautiful Bounty Queen has a bite," Brystin joked.

"Wouldn't you like to know," Rina snapped without looking at him.

Lancaster grumbled, "Despite his aggravating presence, it is my advice that he is not harmed further than he already has been."

Ophelia evaluated him. "Fine. But we're moving tonight. Now."

"Where?" Jezebel blurted, shooting up.

I was already gathering weapons and belongings as Ophelia strode for the bathing chamber, hopefully to wash that blood from her hands.

Ophelia's voice drifted over the splashing water. "Ritalia has plans. We don't know what they are, but I'll be damned if she catches us unaware again." Emerging back into the room with a drenched towel scrubbing at her skin and water sprinkling her nightgown, Ophelia added, "We're going to find the Soulguider emblem."

"And you know where that is?" Malakai asked.

"And we have to leave *now*?" Barrett added, gesturing to the pitch-black sky.

"I've been working it out since the pleasure house, and yes, we do. The Storyteller said *where all dead and riddled secrets lie.*"

"Not catacombs again," I nearly whined, but continued preparing, because Ophelia was on a mission, and I'd follow her anywhere.

"Those precise words had to be important," Ophelia said.

"What about sphinxes?" Mila asked. "They have to be connected somehow, but the Storyteller didn't say anything of them."

"No," Malakai gasped. "But she did say something about a place where legends rest. She said she couldn't tell us anything of it."

"What did you ask her?" Erista asked.

"About gates," Malakai said. "Lucidius's journals mentioned some gate he visited, and the Storyteller referred to it as where legends rest."

"Sounds a lot like *where all dead and riddled secrets lie*," I added.

Malakai looked to Erista. "Is it to the city?"

"No." Erista grinned. "It's not a city border. I think we need to visit the Gates of Angeldust."

And that title...I'd heard it before. "Is that—"

"Galleries dedicated to the souls my people lead along the way, reliquaries for blessed items, and the hearts of replenishment of the streams across our land? It is indeed. There are a handful across the territory, one not far from Lendelli." Erista's eyes glowed as she put together pieces. "And framing the gates of the archaic building are carvings. Very rough recreations, barely accurate, but some call them the *riddled* sphinxes."

Ophelia grinned, a mix of exhilaration and worry in her expression. "We leave immediately. I don't care that it's late."

Shame we wouldn't have time to finish cleaning the blood-stained rug.

Chapter Fifty-Four
Ophelia

The Gates of Angeldust glimmered as if coated with the magic of the divine beings they were named for. It was reminiscent of the gold brushed through Sapphire's white-feathered wings, tucking in as Tolek and I dismounted.

In the time it took us, Jezebel, and Erista to get back to the cavern for Sapphire and the khrysaor, the others had gotten a head start to the gates on horseback. It barely wasted any precious time, and I wanted the creatures nearby in case something went wrong with this trial tonight.

It almost didn't seem possible that anything bad could happen within those gleaming gates, though.

Regardless, the heavy presence of wandering spirits clung to this place.

The toes of my boots met the line marking the entrance to the labyrinthine complex. Towering alabaster walls carved a perimeter around the gallery's land, that shimmering gate designating the entrance ten feet on either side of where I stood.

Wrapping a hand around the bar, the presence of storied histories washed over my skin. A ghostly hand brushing across my own, a lingering hint of life.

"Do you feel it?" I whispered to Jezebel beside me.

She nodded minutely, setting her hand on the bar beside mine. "Must be our Soulguider blood."

Though we never trained that heritage—couldn't, given we chose the Mystique line—it would always flow through us. Weaker, but *alive*.

In the distance, deep within the heart of the complex, streams babbled. Those weren't drinking waters, though. No, these streams were laden with magic. Much like the cyphers, the thin network of waters trickling through the land was a conduit. It bore spirits to their final resting places, weaving patterns through the deserts as they carved the sands.

And these—the Gates of Angeldust—were a well of that power.

It was intricate magic, details remaining private among the Soulguiders, but with simply the blood in our veins, that presence spoke to my sister and me.

I gazed up to the top of the gates, the metal sculpted like a pair of flourishing wings. And on either side, perched atop the stone walls, a carved woman's head watched over the rising and falling dunes.

"Follow the sphinxes," I muttered. They could have easily been female warriors if I didn't know better.

Jezebel whispered, "There they are."

Waiting for us. A clue from the constellations.

For a mile in any direction, all they saw was sand, streams, and scattered cyphers. An old defense from the age of Angels, leaving the land closest to the sacred site bare of dense hiding spots for any nefarious thieves or attackers.

But Lendelli, with its prosperous markets and packed rows of apartments, stretched beyond to the east. A steadfast of warriors providing another boundary.

Turning my back on the glimmering bars and sphinxes, I faced the group. They looked at me with determination in their eyes, weapons strapped to muscled bodies.

"I don't know what will be waiting in there." I summoned every bit of strength I could, used all the twisted rage Damien's vague warnings sprouted within me. Deathly catacombs and platforms bursting in the sea flashed before my vision. "I won't deny any of you who wish to come inside, but I want you to know what the possibilities are before you agree. We've lost good warriors to these trials." My eyes landed on Mora. On the festering wound wrapped beneath her tunic. "Some have been gravely injured. Assuming we're right, and this is where Xenique's emblem is hidden, we're likely to face very dangerous threats."

"Actually," Erista interrupted, clearing her throat, "the fae can't come."

"And why not?" Lancaster growled.

Erista straightened, curls bouncing as she flipped a sharp look on Lancaster. "I advise you watch your tone. You believe in the Goddess of Death, do you not?"

Lancaster and Mora both nodded. We all conveniently ignored a restrained Brystin as he mumbled beneath his breath.

Erista seemed to choose her next words carefully. "Then trust me when I say her magic is woven deeply into this earth. Partnered with Xenique's, it ensures any enemy of the warriors who enters the gates will fall on their swords immediately."

"The fae will die if they step foot inside?" Barrett asked, wide-eyed.

"Magic can be cruel when it comes to *riddled* things" was all Erista said, her expression twisting.

I didn't try to evaluate the haunting twist to her words or the way my sister looked questioningly at her.

"Mora," Tolek said, digging in his pack, "can you wait out here and search the coded scroll for more patterns? We need to figure out if it's giving away anything about the Ascension after what Vale read tonight."

The female nodded dutifully and took the rolled parchment from Tol.

"The fae remain out here," I said. "And a few of us will need to stay as their guards."

"I'll do it," Cypherion offered. All of our heads whipped toward him.

"Are you sure?" He'd been hurt when I told him to escort Vale back to her territory rather than staying with us in the mountains for the final battle, pain flooding his blue eyes when he thought we felt he was unnecessary.

Now, though, his stare remained sure. Calm. And he said, "As your Second, I will guard the fae out here while you retrieve the emblem."

Spirits, I truly had made a wise decision in appointing him, hadn't I? Despite his initial doubts, Cypherion was truly stepping into this role and all it meant. Even if he would rather cross through the gates with us.

"Thank you," I said with a nod, and for an unexplained reason —perhaps because we'd all come so fucking far since last spring and that growth was digging into my chest—my eyes stung.

Hearing the heavy weight behind my words, Cypherion said, "Of course, Revered."

"I think I should go inside," Vale said, loudly enough for us all to hear, but it was clearly intended for Cyph. Not asking for permission, but ensuring he was okay with that choice.

He was silent for a brief moment, swallowing as he searched her silver-tinted stare. "You should, Stargirl." Then, he kissed her forehead, adding in a whisper I barely heard, "Remember—you belong to no one. Us against the Fates."

"The least you could do is make the pretty Starsearcher stay, too," Brystin interrupted.

Shooting him a glare sharper than his scythe, Cypherion tugged the rope around the fae's wrists so he stumbled forward, grunting.

"I'm pretty enough to entertain you," Cyph growled, watching where blood leaked from Brystin's shoulder—cypher stake still intact—to the sand. "Look at her again and more than the ground will be stained red."

Brystin had the sense not to respond, but an amused glint that I didn't like entered his eye. One that had Malakai saying, "I can play guard, too."

But I spoke up. "No, Malakai. I think you should come with us." His brows pulled together. "You're the only other one who can detect the emblems. I need you in case—"

In my memory, cold, skeletal fingers curled around my throat. Air snapped from my lungs.

But Tolek's arm wrapped around my waist, a silent reassurance.

I found my voice again. "I need you in there."

That sense of purpose seemed to fall over Malakai like a well-suited pair of leathers. Like a sword's grip worn perfectly to his hand, one he wrapped his fingers around and gave me a confirming nod.

"We'll remain out here," Barrett said, exchanging a glance with Dax and Celissia, and that sent a flutter of comfort through me. Though Cypherion was more than capable, at least he wouldn't be outnumbered by the fae.

"Everyone else?" I asked. Tolek, Jezebel, Erista, Santorina, Lyria, and Mila.

They all nodded in turn, ready to enter the sanctity of history and legends of the Soulguiders.

Fear gathered behind my ribs, but I shoved it down. "Better not waste any more time, then."

I made to turn back to the gates, but a hand locked around my wrist.

My eyes flicked up to find Tolek's burning into me, and just like that, the rest of the world fell away. The hushed conversations of our friends melted into the desert winds.

"Yes?" I asked, my heart fluttering.

"Take a breath," he reminded me. I did as he said, the crisp air filtering through my lungs as a soothing reminder. "How are you feeling?"

"Fine." We didn't have time for me to feel any other way.

But Tolek only lowered his chin, waiting. I groaned, dropping my voice to ensure no one else heard. "I'm worried about what's inside these walls. I'm afraid of..." I summoned a small bead of Angellight to my palm, dimming it before it flourished out of my control. "After tonight, I'm even more uncertain about what it can do or why."

We hadn't fully talked about what I did during the Rites. How much power I'd summoned or why it pushed back the storm.

"It can work miracles, Alabath. *You* are pure power and strength."

A lump formed in my throat at his words, but I swallowed past it.

"I'm tired of being strong without answers, though. The questions...they're piling upon my shoulders, and I fear I may crumble." Ire heated my voice as I added, "And I am *so* tired of having to be resilient. It's exhausting getting back up every time I'm knocked down. Pretending it doesn't hurt me or scare me."

"Don't pretend with me, *apeagna*," Tol said, twining his fingers between mine. "I get why you put up a facade for everyone else—for yourself, sometimes. But not with me."

I breathed in that thought and allowed his presence to be my infinite tether to the world.

"What else?" Tolek asked, brushing his thumb across the back of my hand.

I watched the place our fingers locked. "I'm really fucking angry that everyone is either giving me cryptic commands or trying to harm us."

Tolek smirked and gripped the back of my neck, kissing my forehead. "There she is."

"What?" I tilted my head to peer up at him.

Tol retreated an inch but kept his grip firm. "Be fucking furious, Alabath." His gaze cut sideways to Brystin. "Spirits know I am. Let that rage take wings and soar all the way to damn the Angels."

I grinned up at him. "You're not telling me to be smart?"

He shook his head, thumb stroking my neck. "You're making as wise of choices as any leader could when they don't have all the answers. We've been smart. We've been careful. Now, let's fight."

"Spirits," I breathed with a laugh.

"What?"

"I just...really fucking love you, Vincienzo."

"Infinitely." And he sealed his lips to mine.

Then, in a move that felt as intimate as anything we'd done, Tolek pulled Starfire from her sheath at my waist. He took a step back and held her before me across his palms. Chills danced along my skin.

"Now, let's retrieve our final token of the Angels, Revered."

I shivered at that title on his lips and wrapped my fingers

around the handle of my short sword. Her presence and familiar strength settled into my arm. Briefly, my memory flashed back to the day I'd gotten her. A gift from my father on my tenth birthday. When her weight was too mighty for me, but I was as determined as ever to wield her.

Though I'd lost him to this war, I still had this constant.

And combined with Angelborn on my back, I truly felt I could send the world to ruin.

Erista used the crescent moon tattoos on her palms to open the gates, something only Soulguiders of a certain status were privileged enough to have, she explained. After a wrenching goodbye to my pegasus and a final glance exchanged with Cypherion, we filed inside after the Soulguider.

A long stretch of sandy path awaited us beyond the walls, but cyphers bloomed on either side, elthem flowers closed to the night. The air was rich with their floral scent, almost out of place after weeks traveling through the dry desert, and those streams babbled faintly, out of sight between the ash-white trunks.

It was as serene as a temple, but a place of worship didn't lay within these walls.

Silently, our party walked up the path toward the stone gallery in the distance. Tolek was on one side of me, Jezebel on the other.

Voice so low it was barely distinguishable, my sister asked, "How do you know this is where the emblem is hidden?"

My heart thudded, and I considered snapping up that brave mask, but one look at Jez from the corner of my eye had my defenses dropping. We were tied to so much unknown together, she deserved to hear when I was faltering.

"I don't." I shook my head. "I'm going on the faintest of whims here, Jezzie. Whatever it is in my gut that tugs toward the emblems, combined with Erista's knowledge."

Damien and Valyrie had told me to come to the Lendelli Hills to find out the truth, to learn my magic. It all had to mean something.

If it wasn't within these gates, we'd journey to the next city, and the one after that. All the way to the capital if needed. We were finding this emblem, though.

Jezebel tucked her hand within mine. "Let's prove you right."

The alabaster steps loomed ahead, leading to this house of spirits and souls, the heart of replenishment for the magic of death's hands.

I searched my gut for any hint of that Angel instinct, finding it concernedly quiet.

CHAPTER FIFTY-FIVE
MALAKAI

"I don't like it," I muttered as we stepped into the atrium and the doors closed behind us with a thud.

No one had opened them to allow us in. At least, no one visible. I cast a perturbed glance over my shoulder, and my chest tightened. The streams were louder now, the babbling crowding my head.

"It's not that bad," Tolek tried to assure me, but even he was surveying the chamber with a narrowed glance. Four archways led off the atrium, positioned like points of a compass.

I gave him a blank look. "It's practically a house of death."

Tolek chuckled as we all shuffled deeper into the room, hands in reach of our weapons. "You can return to the pleasure house instead if you'd prefer."

I shoved his shoulder. "I *would* prefer that to spirits and their secrets. It's unsettling in here." My heart thundered.

"It's like any other historic site." He seemed unbothered by the ghostly presence wrapping through the air, but his eyes flashed to the hand I hadn't realized was rubbing my sternum and back to the closed doors, and he understood why it was stifling to me. Tolek clapped a hand to my shoulder. "Let's do this as quickly as possible."

"Yeah," I agreed.

As Tolek continued ahead, a hand squeezed mine. I turned to

Mila, and she brushed her thumb across the scar on my jaw, silently saying she knew what memories the sealed doors woke. That she was here to remind me I got out.

Lifting her hand, I kissed the gold cuff around her wrist, returning the favor. Mila inclined her head, and we stepped deeper into the atrium.

Mystlight hung in a giant orb high up in the point of the vaulted ceiling. Veins of bronze and speckles of amethyst dotted the alabaster marble, shining in that glow. It draped all the way through the spacious chamber, highlighting the towering winged statue of Xenique in the center that Erista strode straight toward.

She knelt at her Angel's feet and muttered a prayer. Vale, Mila, Lyria, and Jezebel mimicked her routine, offering their own respect to the Soulguider Prime Warrior.

Ophelia and Tolek exchanged a look, the latter inclining his head, and they followed.

"Aren't you going to offer prayers?" Santorina whispered to me.

I shrugged. Perhaps it was sacrilegious—it definitely was—but I wasn't sure how I felt toward any of the Angels, let alone one of another clan. "We'll see how tonight goes, then I'll decide."

Santorina hummed in agreement, ambling ahead to catch up with the others as they migrated away from the statue. I stood at Xenique's feet for another moment. She didn't look down at the warriors before her. No, the statue's gaze was directed out, toward one of the only blank stretches of wall between the arches. At her feet lay two creatures, carved from the same bronzed metal.

"Sphinxes," Mila said, lingering with me.

Unlike the carvings atop the gate outside, these were not only the bust left to be determined. These were bodies of lions—almost like a nemaxese—each with the head of a woman and great wings tucked into their backs. And this pair laid protectively at the feet of their Angel.

I swept my gaze over the rest of the atrium. This was the only statue but between the arches off the circular room, tapestries depicted the Angel in various states. Sphinxes littered the decor, but in tiny details. The borders and backgrounds, never the center.

"Not only at the gates, then," I observed.

"I suppose we were right about them," Mila said. "Now let's hope whatever riddles their house holds are nothing too arduous."

A chill trickled down my spine, and we turned our backs on Xenique and her mystical creatures. A part of me hoped it was for good.

The others were headed toward the archway directly ahead, at the top of the large, bronze crescent moon carved into the marble floor, amethyst speckles twinkling like stars around it.

As Mila and I caught up, a groaning echoed to our left. We all spun toward it, swords whining as they were pulled.

"What in the fucking Angels?" I muttered.

There, in the bare stretch of wall Xenique's statue faced, a fifth archway now loomed.

This one was different than the others. Where darkness pressed behind each of the original four, waiting for mystlight to flare within, this one glowed with a very dim silver-blue light and swarmed with fog.

"It's a Hall of Wandering Souls," Erista breathed, as if we should know what that cryptic explanation meant.

"Looks inviting," I deadpanned, rubbing at my sternum.

Tolek choked on a laugh at my side, but Erista remained serious. "It's where those who don't flow within the streams remain. There's supposedly one in every Gates of Angeldust, but they've never been seen except on rare occasions."

"You mean"—Rina gasped, looking between Erista and the new arch warily—"the spirits in there never find eternal rest?"

Erista shook her head, curls framing her mournful expression. "Not all souls find peace. Some are rejected by the streams' waters, some die with such unresolved disputes, they can't move on. Some simply are not ready and linger in this realm. They can't be given free reign over Gallantia, so they reside in a Hall of Wandering Souls."

I peered into the Hall's misty gray. The same speckled marble floor continued from the atrium, veiled a few dozen feet in by...was that stuff that seemed like fog actually spirits? Floating there between the marble and stone carvings lining the walls? Angels, I hoped not.

"Sounds like a sorry existence," I muttered to Tolek.

"What would possess a soul not to rest?" he whispered back.

"Unfinished business?" Lyria suggested, and I didn't want to know what that could mean.

A chill spread down my spine, and I shook it off, shifting closer to Mila. "Should we keep going?" I angled my head toward the original archways.

The group started to turn, a bit reluctantly.

But Erista stood her ground. "The Hall does not usually open."

And all of our attention swiveled to her. Her eyes were slightly glazed, like the magic was taking a toll on her.

"What do you mean?" Ophelia asked.

"It is not meant to welcome newcomers." Her voice drifted with breathy worry. "And if it does open, it is said that anyone nearby with Soulguider blood must respond."

"Respond how?" I asked, eyes narrowing.

Erista looked at Jezebel and Ophelia. "We must enter."

In the silence following her words, only those damn streams in the distance could be heard, soft enough that they grated on me.

"Okay," Tolek said, "then let's get it over with." He waved a hand toward the arched doorway, and...did the mist within recoil?

Erista blinked at him. "*Only* those with Soulguider blood, Tolek."

He sighed, head tipping back toward the ceiling. Instinctually, Ophelia reached for his hand. "Why?" she asked.

Erista appeared conflicted. "It's been the Angel's rule since she was first gifted with her magic. The doors rarely open, but if they do, we are not to question it."

Spirits, this ambiguity drove nails into my brain. And those fucking babbling streams weren't helping.

I asked, "So only you three can go?"

Erista nodded.

Ophelia chewed her lip. "Will it help us find the emblem?"

Looking into the depths of the dark hall, Erista said, "I hope so."

Great. More vague answers.

Jezebel was at Erista's side, a silent commitment that she'd go wherever her partner directed, but Ophelia and Tolek watched each other silently. His jaw ticked, and her eyes searched his. Neither said a word aloud, but they definitely were saying plenty to one another.

I wrapped an arm around Mila's shoulders. Not a chance on an Angel's burning wings would I separate from her while in this creepy fucking gallery.

But she and I weren't the chosen of the Angels, thank the Spirits. We'd survived enough shit and could stay together to see all the tomorrows.

Finally, Tolek groaned, "Fuck these damn Angels." He kissed Ophelia, whispering something to her, and then stepped back.

Ophelia's eyes found me, Starfire tight in her grip. "Keep looking for it," she said, somewhere between a plea and an order. "I don't know that it will be"—she flicked a glance over her shoulder into the hall—"that it will be in there. In case it's not, search this place."

Because I could also detect these emblems. I guessed I wasn't as uninvolved as I'd hoped.

I nodded. "Of course."

"Thank you." And there was a quiet *until the stars stop shining* beneath that gratitude. With a slight dip of my chin, I sent the sentiment right back, attempting it through our broken Bind.

Ophelia smiled as if she felt a hint of it.

She instructed us all to be careful, and then the three warriors with Soulguider blood stepped beneath the archway, into the field of swirling spirits and mists, or whatever it was exactly.

A part of me hoped they didn't find out.

Chapter Fifty-Six
Ophelia

The Hall of Wandering Souls called to me the moment the archway revealed itself in the marble. Dull, ghostly voices, like whispers through the trees, echoed down that hallway, the towering walls stretching impossibly high and deep.

As I stepped through with Jezebel and Erista, some untended part of me woke. Something wanting and lively.

Something powerful.

A groaning of marble had my head whipping back toward the atrium, catching the final slivers of mystlight as the door slid shut of its own accord.

I'll be waiting at the end of wherever that damn hall takes you, Tolek had whispered to me before he'd stepped back.

It was only a corridor, I told myself. No cause to be afraid. But my blood pounded faster in my veins.

At the last glimpse of the atrium, I met Tolek's eyes. *I love you,* I mouthed. But I didn't get to see him say it back as the final crack in the doorway sealed over with a dull thud.

And with it, my heart rioted.

I straightened my spine, locking away the fear. The was no room for it tonight. We had a chance to find the seventh and final Angel emblem by venturing through this hall, and I would return to the Spirit Realm before I let it slip away.

Especially with Ritalia scheming somewhere off the shores of our continent.

Gripping Starfire's hilt and siphoning off the strength only my weapons could provide, I stepped forward.

"What's the haze from?" I asked Erista as we proceeded cautiously. Even the Soulguider was watching her steps, as if unsure what lay beyond.

"A side effect of so many lingering souls," she explained.

Eyes on the thick mass of fog ahead, Jezebel asked. "It's not their actual spirits, is it?"

Something within me writhed at the possibility of having to go *through* restless spirits. I thought back to the ones who had tested me during my Undertaking. There was a similar misty essence in the hall.

But Erista shook her head. "I don't think so. Spirits would likely be in their bodily form still, not scattered." She paused, walking a small circle as her gaze scoured the ceiling. The hooked sword at her hip glinted in the mystlights piercing the haze. "These are remnants of those lost."

Grief twisted through me at that explanation.

"Can you hear them?" I asked Jez.

My sister shook her head, and in a voice cracking with sorrow, she said, "No." Jezebel paused, listening more intently. "I think they're too far gone, even for me."

Lingering somewhere between.

Though that was devastating, a piece of me thanked the Angels or Artale or whoever planted these powers in Jezebel that she did not have to walk this stretch of hall with a myriad of wandering spirits shouting through her mind.

We continued on, entering the thickest of the fog. I could barely see Jezebel and Erista beside me. My sister slid her hand into mine, securing us together.

The hall felt endless. *This will drive me mad*, I thought. These voices that weren't quite voices whipping around us, echoes of thoughts that were no more than drifting winds. The mist tickled my skin, unsettling and invasive.

I could go mad in here.

The fear pounded at my mind until, finally, the fog parted

ahead. And at the end of the hall, towering twice my height, was a stone sphinx.

"I guess the constellation didn't only refer to the entrance," I said.

The beast was carved of the same alabaster that made up the perimeter and the steps into the museum, like she'd been here as long as the Gates of Angeldust had existed.

The paws of her lion's body were the size of my head, her face incredibly beautiful, even frozen in granite. With a strong, square jaw, broad planes, and a shrewdness to the stony eyes, she was powerful. Should they beat, the wings at her back likely would have been stronger than Damien's, larger than Sapphire's.

I looked into that statue's face, and I swore she looked back.

Tearing my eyes away, I searched behind her. Nothing but a bare wall waited.

"It ends here?"

Jezebel and Erista had the same thought, peering around the statue. "Was anything else said about the Hall of Wandering Souls?" my sister asked her partner.

Erista didn't meet our eyes, studying the sphinx. "Only rumors and myths."

Myths...

Again, my eyes found those of stone. So many myths surrounded us. Our entire lives, they had, and Jezebel and I had never even known our existence was written in the stars.

A pair of formidable sisters, long before the warriors you stem from walked Ambrisk.

Imbued with the powers of life and death.

Those harsh stone eyes belonging to a legendary, mythical being bore into me.

One to raise the constellations, another to hold their leashes. A summoner of myths, and a destroyer of them.

"Jezzie," I said, not looking away from that hard stare. "I think I have to use the magic."

"The Angellight?"

"No," I said, fear creeping in. "The part of my magic I haven't been able to control, whatever the *fel strella mythos* gave us. It's more than a connection to the pegasus and khrysaor, it's part of why they're here, and..."

"One to raise the constellations," Jez echoed my thought.

"But isn't that what attacked Jezebel in the inn?" Erista asked, watching us warily.

Disgust twisted my stomach. Repulsion at the magic I didn't understand within me, at the possibility that it could hurt Jez if I used it.

Her choking breaths echoed in my memory, the sounds of corpses shrieking as they burned to ash.

I explained, "I've been thinking about the catacombs. Comparing how the magic reacted there to the Angellight. The latter always feels so...definitive. I can read it as tethered to a specific emblem or Angel. It's mine, instilled in me, but it has a clear property."

They both nodded, and Jez asked, "And the other magic?"

"The rest..." I thought back to the desperation flaring through me as we fled the corpses down in the catacombs, like alarm bells ringing in my head. I hadn't known what I was casting out at them, I simply *did*. "It's burning and effervescent like the Angellight, but it's alive in a way that magic isn't. It was searching that night."

One to raise the constellations.

The two magics were often so similar, I wondered how many times I'd had both powers at my fingertips and didn't realize it.

"I think it was trying to instill life into the corpses, but for some reason it backfired, and singed them to the ground instead."

"Two sisters," Jez murmured, searching my stare, "imbued with the powers of life and death."

"One to raise the constellations," I continued what the Storyteller had said.

"Another to hold their leashes." At Jezebel's words, her control over the alpheous flashed through my memory. Her gazed tracked over the marble at our feet, stopping at the enormous paws of that sphinx. Up, up, up, until it landed on that female face, so beautiful even etched in stone, and she voiced the words I'd been afraid of. "You need to wake her."

"I do." A familiar enthusiasm swirled in my chest, and instead of shoving it deep down, I allowed it to gather.

"Do you know how to do that?" Jezebel asked.

Not for the first time tonight, I was brutally honest about how lost I was. "No idea." I forced a laugh, sheathing Starfire. "But I have to try."

"What are you going to do?" Erista's voice was guarded, her hand drifting toward her hooked blade as she moved between both Jezebel and the sphinx, and me, as if protecting the girl she loved and this precious work of art from an unknown magic.

"I promise, Erista," I said, taking a step forward, "nothing the Angels haven't sent me for."

I'd been led here, and without any kind of direction, I had to trust what wove my bones and being to guide me.

Hesitantly, Erista stepped aside.

"Jez, put up your own shield," I instructed, because while I wanted to test this magic on the sphinx, I would let it take my own life before I set it on my sister again.

Immediately, one of those silver-blue veils shimmered in front of Jezebel and Erista. If we were right, and Jez's power was death while mine was life, maybe they'd repel one another as they'd fought before. I thought that was what they'd been doing when we flew with Sapphire and the khrysaor and that day in the inn, fighting after stifled for so long.

"Start slowly," Erista cautioned, not harshly.

I took a deep breath, cementing that memory of Jezebel struggling to breathe in the back of my mind as my own warning.

Watching the beautiful stone face, I dug deep within myself. To the same place I pulled the strings of the Angel emblems, the hollows that filled in my spirit. But this time I ignored each one of those connections. Shifting them aside, I searched for something else. Something that had always been there, but that had woken on the bridge to another realm and longed to be unleashed.

There.

Hidden beneath the cover of Angellight, another source of magic welled within me. And when I finally acknowledged it, saw it for what it truly was, it rose like a great beast spreading its wings for the first time in long, long centuries.

Now that I knowingly called it forth, named it for what it was, the power to raise myths answered my call.

Magic budded through my veins, emerging at my fingertips. It looked so strikingly similar to the Angellight, as if both were meant to weave together within me. As if, perhaps, it was my being that decided what form they took.

Carefully, but not timidly—I didn't want the power to believe it owned me—I cast a gentle stream of shimmering light toward the sphinx. It bathed the air like a shooting star.

My muscles tightened, shaking as I struggled to retain control over a power born of myths, and set to work raising a constellation.

Gold light poured around the sphinx, down over her head, across her shoulders and that powerful lion's body. It explored those magnificent wings—

The feathers ruffled.

"It's working," I breathed. It was the most minute flutter in the drafty hall, the stone facade slipping away to reveal the softness beneath.

But like a veil falling one draping inch at a time, white stone melted down her features.

It started at the highest points of her wings and the top of her head. Her flowing black hair and sharp green eyes. The nose and dusty-pink lips. All the way down to the massive paws and back to her whipping tail.

And when all the stone was melted upon the floor like an oily spill, the sphinx rose before us. My power recoiled into me, purring and satisfied after being intentionally fed for the first time in Spirits knew how long.

"By the fucking Angels," I muttered.

I'd woken a sleeping myth. A creature long gone from this world, that many believed no longer existed. That many believed had *never* existed, much like the pegasus.

Before I could truly allow that to sink in, the sphinx opened her mouth, and she said in a voice like warm honey that showed no indication of having been frozen in stone for millennia, "Welcome, Alabath sisters. I have long hoped you would rescue me."

CHAPTER FIFTY-SEVEN
CYPHERION

"You remember that prophecy your queen is so afraid of?" I kept one hand on my horse, Erini, and my voice emotionless. "Stop talking or my count of fae lives taken won't end with the royal line."

"But what's the point of so many blades?" Brystin nagged again. By the fucking Spirits, he was relentless. The howling desert night air was a better sound than his voice.

"You carry your own weapons," I responded without looking at him. I hadn't given in to his incessant questioning since the others left, and I wouldn't now. "If you have to ask, then perhaps you're using them wrong."

His answering smile was evil. "I am a weapon myself. I carry a few, but not so many."

I turned a blank stare on him, saying in a flat voice, "That's foolish of you."

"Is it foolish?" He tilted his head, pretending to wonder. "Or is it a well-honed tactic to disarm my opponents with my lack of protection? Surely, we could find out right now." He held out his tied wrists. "If you want."

I sighed with a shake of my head, not exasperated in the slightest. "You can try to deter me all you want, but my best friend is Tolek Vincienzo."

Brystin sneered. "I don't want to become your friend."

"I wasn't offering."

"Then why mention it?"

"Because I've become an expert at chatter as a means of distraction, and I certainly won't fall for any of your tricks."

Barrett and Dax snickered. Even Lancaster, sitting in the sand with his elbows propped on his knees, added, "Cypherion has a point. That Vincienzo warrior is insufferable when he wants to be."

"See," I said to Brystin. "Half of my life has been spent with Tolek. I can tolerate your games."

Brystin smiled an infuriating, smooth grin, but I tugged the rope attached to his wrists until he stumbled again and redirected my attention back toward the gates Vale had disappeared through.

Behind me, Barrett picked up bantering with the fae prisoner. A worthy opponent, as Dax's occasional interjections reminded him. Where Brystin appeared to be trying to win with cool control, Barrett was wilder. Willing to say whatever would sway the argument.

Currently, he debated the male over whether warriors or fae made better candies.

Fine by me. Freed up my time babysitting to watch the Gates.

Malakai and Tolek wouldn't let anything happen to Vale. Ophelia wouldn't either. They'd all proved in rescuing her that she was embedded into our family as much as anyone else.

But fucking Spirits, last time we attempted something in a historic site like this, Vale and I had been in the Valyn archives. She'd fallen into her most consuming reading ever, and Titus captured us. The scars lingering on my mind from that night had yet to fade. And she'd been consumed by the Fates all night.

"I have a feeling Vale will not only be safe in there, but she'll serve a purpose with that magic of hers," Celissia said, approaching my side with her eyes trained on the structure behind the wall.

"What do you mean?"

Celissia gave a small smirk that was so much like Barrett's, they could have been siblings, but hers was softer. "Call it intuition."

I blew out a breath. Vale and Celissia seemed to have bonded since meeting. Perhaps it was because they were both newcomers to our tight-knit group—though they were eagerly welcomed, it had to be an adjustment. And Celissia had a way about her that made you *want* to like her.

"What's wrong over there?" I asked, inclining my head to where Mora sat with her back against the alabaster wall, one hand stroking Dynaxtar, the other holding one of Valyrie's scrolls.

Celissia's lips twisted to the side, and she dropped her voice. "That injury is still plaguing her. The arm is losing function by the day."

I blinked at the fae. At the way she kept her injured arm cradled to her chest, but casually so. "Why didn't she say anything?"

"She doesn't want to frighten her brother. His magic isn't helping, for whatever reason. Santorina and I have been doing what we can, but I worry it may not be enough."

"She'll die?" I barely muttered, but the others were loud enough that none of the fae could hear.

"Not if I can help it."

The possibility twisted through me with surprising sadness. I may not have known Mora well, but she'd done nothing but help my friends. She'd fought by their side in the final battle against Kakias and in the catacombs.

Sure, she had orders from her queen to obey, but Mora presented such a genuine front, I wouldn't have been surprised if she helped us all on her own.

Celissia's eyes were on Mora as she said with a curious air, "There's more to them than we know. I can tell."

"Why do you think that?" I asked.

"Because there's more to me, as well."

I wasn't sure what she meant, but she had an interesting background, from studying in the citadel to her father's house. There had to be secrets to her. "It's been good for Santorina to have someone besides our incompetent asses around."

Celissia laughed. "You're all very skilled in other areas. It's been interesting watching your unit function as a group these weeks."

"How so?" I asked, as the chatter behind us picked up.

"You're all strong fighters and intelligent minds, but you excel in very different areas. Or perhaps you prefer slightly different subjects." She shook her head, waving off the distinction. "You balance each other. Much in the way ether winds through the world to ensure the balance of power, your group instills harmony."

I swallowed past a thick throat. "We do."

And if one person was removed from that carefully-crafted machine, the balance was lost. I watched the gates again.

"What in the name of Bant's golden cock are you on about now?" Barrett blurted with a laugh.

Brystin groaned. Somehow, the prince had turned the fae into the exasperated one. "You cannot truly believe your magic is *that* defensive?"

Celissia and I faced the pair. Dax, Lancaster, and Mora all observed at a safe distance, equally amused. Except Lancaster. His face remained as impassive as ever.

"You've exposed the cyphers as being a path to harming the fae." Barrett waved a hand at the injury in the male's shoulder, still bleeding slowly. "The land of Gallantia is *against* you."

"But you do not know how to use it. In our culture, words are the sharpest weapons."

I stiffened. "What are you saying?"

Brystin flashed me another of those infuriating smirks. One that had the hair on the back of my neck standing and said, *I'm glad you finally caught on. This was getting so boring.* "You truly think a simple bargain is keeping my queen off your land? Imagine the facade…"

Mora's head snapped up, worry widening her eyes.

Facade?

"What kind of facade?" I snapped, grabbing Brystin by the collar. He smiled cruelly at Mora, and her face drained of color.

Facade…Glamour.

Shoving Brystin back against a tree, I snarled. "What the fuck did your queen do?"

Dax and Barrett jumped on the fae, interrogating him to pick through his half-truths and evasions.

"Ophelia," I growled, whirling back toward the gates as a storm rumbled through my chest, "hurry the fuck up with that emblem."

Because it seemed we had much more immediate problems brewing.

Chapter Fifty-Eight
Tolek

The Angels clearly don't want me to participate in their trivial hunt for emblems.

I sighed.

The hunt wasn't trivial, I was aware of that. But watching that damn archway seal with Ophelia behind it—being separated from her *again* when these trials had nearly taken all of our lives—was like a nemaxese's claws sinking into my gut and shredding, tearing, bleeding.

"Come on," Malakai said with a hand on my shoulder. "Let's get this over with so you can get back to her."

"Where do we start?" Santorina asked. The crescent moon carved into the marble floor, inlaid with flawless bronze, could have been indicating any direction, depending which way you looked at it.

But it was Vale who said, "That way." With a sure hand, she pointed down the looming tunnel all the way across the atrium.

She took off without waiting for us, her boots ringing out on the speckled floors and skirt swishing around her ankles. Malakai and I exchanged a glance, then I hurried to the Starsearcher's side. He hung back, bringing up the rear of our group.

"How do you know?" I asked Vale as we crossed the expansive atrium.

Her eyes were trained on the tunnel as she answered, "Ever

since my reading of the gods, the connection with the Fates hasn't broken."

"You don't always have a connection with them?"

"I do, but typically between sessions it reduces. Like a hum instead of a full song." Her hand pressed to her breastbone as if alleviating an ache. "Now, they haven't quieted."

"Without the incense?"

She nodded. "They're rather persistent, it seems." Her voice was melodic, the same tone as when she'd read earlier, and when she looked up, her eyes swirled like shooting stars.

If her nine Fate ties were speaking, it had to be important. "Let's listen to them, then." I shrugged, looking at the archway ahead. "Wait!" I gripped Vale's wrist right as she made to step into the tunnel.

My sister was behind me, her defenses raised. "What is it?"

I nodded to the stone carving the entrance. "Endasi." Faintly, framing the arch and barely visible in the mystlight, the Angelic script was etched into alabaster stone.

"It was above the entrance to the catacombs, too," Santorina reminded us.

"I suppose we're going the right way, then," Mila said. "Can you read it, Tolek?"

I scanned the overly-intricate carving. Xenique loved ostentatious designs, it appeared. "Roughly," I began. "*Half of the seer's treasure lies within.*"

"The seer?" Malakai asked.

"Likely a way to hide Xenique's name," Mila guessed. "A way to refer to the power of Soulguider visions."

Half of Xenique's treasure. It was practically a map to the emblem itself.

"Let's go then," Malakai said, determined and nodding at Vale to lead the way. She tilted her head for a moment as if listening, then started down the tunnel.

Malakai, Mila, and Santorina followed first, but I hung back a step, checking the translation one more time.

"Come on, baby brother," Lyria cooed, looping her arm

through mine, and I walked along with her, hoping this time my translation was correct. Why only half of the treasure?

The tunnel was made of the same marble as the atrium, with veins of bronze that caught the mystlight flickering from sconces along the wide walls. Though not as towering as the entrance, the ceilings were high. How had a place this massive been built?

And how strong was the power that lay within to require such a cage?

Ahead of us, the others chatted quietly over the distant streams. Malakai bent low, whispering something in Mila's ear that had a laugh bursting from her, adding some much-needed ease to this spirit-shrouded corridor. Lyria smiled at the sound ringing against the marble.

"You approve?" I nodded to Malakai and Mila up ahead.

"More than." My sister flashed a dazzling smile, but it didn't meet her eyes.

I put a hand on her shoulder, so slim beneath the leather. Had she always been that thin? I held her back a step. "Ria?"

Lyria's eyes searched the expansive corridor. "It's an odd place, isn't it?"

"Not the most common," I answered, shrugging and continuing to follow the others, "but it's fitting for what we're here for, I suppose. It would be interesting to explore it without the pressure of the Angels bearing down on us."

"The damn Angels," she swore, shaking her head. I let out a small, relieved laugh at her disgruntled tone. "Do you think spirits really linger here?"

"Truly, I'd never thought about it until Erista said what the purpose of the hall was." I had always figured we were delivered to the afterlife by the Soulguiders upon our death. Mystique bodies were returned to the earth through the volcano and our spirits rested in the Spirit Realm.

Some felt differently about it. Believed in ways of divine intervention or reincarnation. I supposed they were possible. The idea of my spirit finding Ophelia's in every life after this one was a thought so right it almost made me convert my beliefs on the spot. But it wasn't something I truly spent much time considering.

Why worry about an afterlife when we had this one?

But from the way Lyria's next words rushed out, it was clear *she* had contemplated it. "I think the idea of a spirit persisting can be quite romantic or torturous, depending on the person."

"What do you mean?" I asked.

"If their life was so full of abundant beauty that they couldn't bear to leave those they loved behind, even to wait in the Spirit Realm for the day others met them, well that's quite a romantic view of life, is it not?"

"It is," I whispered, ambling slowly behind the others.

"But if they're trapped, if someone is ready to go and is somehow held here for eternal unrest..." She shivered. "I believe that would be one of the worst tragedies that could befall a warrior who has already given their life."

Her brown eyes flashed up to mine, like looking in a mirror, and every life she saw taken on the mountainous battlefield died again behind them. The deep hues rippled with a pain that sliced through my chest.

"I like to think every spirit will end up where they belong," I said.

Lyria's voice was wistful when she answered, "That would be beautiful."

Damien's unholy cock, I wanted to rip the haunting memories from my sister. To take those wounds in her stead.

Lyria was too good for it. Or perhaps, none of us were truly good. To simply say someone was nothing but *good* trivialized the complexities of their spirit.

At her heart, Lyria was so much more than that. She was courageous and clever, but also compassionate and understanding. She, unlike so many commanders, had found a way to balance the two sides.

And because of that, she was carrying this weight of responsibility that was poised to shatter her bones.

"Where do you wish to end up?" I asked.

Lyria shrugged. "Wherever I'm meant to be, I guess." A heavy *I don't know where that is* echoed in the shadows of that sentence. "We can't really be certain of the purpose of any of this, can we?"

Lyria asked as we followed Vale around turn after turn, her reading leading the way.

"Which parts?"

She laughed, invigorated. "Of life. Of every damn day. It all builds to something, I would believe, but—I don't know. Perhaps it's because I'm surrounded by the energy of the Soulguiders and their heart of magic, but it feels like being in *this* place serves a purpose."

"Every decision we make, Ria, contributes to our lives. The small and the large ones, whether they support what the Fates have planned for us or riot against it, it all weaves together. That's what comprises our stories."

"Being here, though"—she searched the tunnel, the endless halls branching off it— "makes me consider the point."

Following the war, Lyria had been concerned with her role, with finding her place after witnessing such tragedy. She thought she was responsible for it, but I wouldn't agree to that. Lyria was a part of the war, but she wasn't the war. Just as the lives lost on that battlefield weren't her. Thank the Angels.

In the shuffle of our boots against marble, I asked, "And what have you decided?"

"I think it's you, Tolek." Her eyes darted to mine. "I think we were robbed of so much time in our childhoods that the Spirits and Angels are trying to make up for it."

My chest hurt at the thought.

Lyria continued, "To be honest, I don't give an Angel's ass about these emblems. I'd be thrilled to hand over my title now that the war is over. But we lost enough time thanks to our father. So, I'm here."

I was the purpose for my sister. The sentiment tightened my throat and didn't quite fit into the disjointed lines of my life.

Not after I'd had my worthlessness beaten into me at such a young age.

Not since I'd learned to accept that, while my life was filled with unconditional love from my friends, I would always lack those foundational pieces.

I was unlearning those lessons every day, chipping away at the dam they'd built within me. Now, my sister's words flooded that barrier.

And between us, the dam cracked. "I don't know much about life purposes or secrets of the world, but I know for a fact that I'm damn lucky to have you as a sister. To have survived what we did as children, the manipulation we clawed our way out of individually, and be able to stand together now? That feels pretty rare to me."

She smirked. "The name Vincienzo means something pretty good, doesn't it?"

"Because *we* made it so," I said. "Not him."

Our father was not the name Vincienzo. We would carve our own legacy.

I continued, "Maybe you're right, and I'm your cause. If you need to think so, that's okay. But I think it's more likely that a small piece of both of our purposes here is to help the other. To assist in mending the scars he caused." A shake of my head. "I don't think that's either of our full stories, though. I love you, Ria, but neither of us is each other's entire purpose. You've got a shining future ahead of you, title or not."

I tilted my head, whispering, "And by the way, if you don't want the title, tell Ophelia. She won't bat an eye at your reluctance."

Lyria pursed her lips. "It's not so bad." A soft smile curved the corners of her lips, much softer than anything I usually saw from her. It was a bit more peaceful. A bit unburdened. "There's something else I've been thinking about."

"What?" I asked. If it was within my power, I'd help her achieve it. My sister had given so much of herself to the Mystiques, to our father's grand delusions, she deserved whatever her heart clawed for.

"I want to get our siblings out of his hands."

I stopped walking. I never claimed to be a good brother, but Spirits, perhaps I was worse than I feared. Because I'd been so focused on repairing this relationship, I hadn't considered how our father might now be playing his games with those we left behind. The ones I barely had any relationship with because I'd spent as much of my adolescence as possible away from our manor.

When they were born—when my mother had miraculously delivered him three perfect babies after my birth nearly killed her— that had been the last day he'd shown any ounce of care for me. It was the day it officially became *my* fault that I nearly killed my mother. And because of it, a ruined and jealous part of me silently wrote off my siblings altogether.

As if a fire flared in my gut, my guilt over those actions forged into determination. "We'll get them out before his claws are in them."

"If they aren't already," Lyria muttered, striding ahead to catch up with the group. Though mystlight wavered in the tunnel, my skin chilled.

"If they are, we'll help them. If it wasn't too late for us, it isn't for them," I said. "Once this mess is over, we'll return to Palerman and tell father we think it would be good for them to train in Damenal. That it would reflect well on the family or whatever horse shit will appease his ego. We'll fight for them, Lyria."

As no one had fought for us.

"That we will, baby brother." She looped her arm through mine, and I was grateful I'd let the dam between us crack.

I'd stopped trying to track where Vale was leading us many turns ago, but the babbling of the streams grew louder, Lyria and Mila filling the silence with jokes. But we wound around another turn, and even their voices broke off.

The corridor opened into a chamber larger than the atrium, and we stood on a platform jutting out from the wall with a steep drop off into a river. It rushed endlessly in either direction, twelve feet below us.

Glass windows were cut into the marble walls all the way to high ceilings, exposing swirling tides within. Some moved as quickly as the Solistine River, some trickled like those cutting through the dunes.

And directly across the river from our platform, a thick wall stretched halfway to the ceiling—a dam holding the water at bay.

"The streams," I said.

"This must be the source," Vale breathed in awe. "The heart of the magic Soulguider power comes from."

We peered over the ledge.

"Down there?" Lyria asked skeptically eying the spirit-laced water.

"Not fun enough, Lyr?" Mila quipped.

My sister smirked at her. "Sounds like exactly our kind of fun, actually."

"Then as always," Mila said, "let's find a way." She raised her brows at Vale. "Can you confirm?"

Vale closed her eyes. "Yes," she affirmed. "Yes, down there, deep beneath the earth, is where the heart lies. Stemming from the mountains, as all sources of magic do."

Then down there was where we had to go.

I searched the walls, but they were smooth. No signs of hand- or-footholds, no ladders or hints of climbing gear. Like one needed damn wings to fly down to the floor and retrieve whatever waited below.

But Ophelia needed that emblem, and if going down there could help her, I'd do it.

As I was looking over the edge of the platform, a groan echoed through the chamber and the floor lurched beneath me.

"What's that?" I asked.

An earth-shattering creak split the air, the water below shivering.

Then, much like the one that had cracked within my heart at my sister's melancholy, the dam trapping the flood of magic-spun water burst.

Chapter Fifty-Nine
Malakai

Water cracked from every angle. Like somewhere, something had triggered a release of not only that dam, but from the walls above, too. Behind us, waves swept through the corridor, shooting over the ledge and swiping my feet right out from under me.

Mila's shriek rang out as my stomach tumbled. I took a breath, and we plummeted into the rising spirit river. When my head plunged beneath the surface, all roars of rushing waves and shouts of the others faded.

The weight of my leathers and weapons dragged me down, and pressure pounded on my ears. The water was as cold as the frozen lakes of Mindshaper Territory, spearing right down to my bones.

It was all murky, gray-green down here. Not like a sandy wave crashing on the coasts, but like...

My lungs iced over. I didn't want to think about the haze in the Hall of Wandering Souls. Couldn't consider what lived in the source of magic responsible for guiding spirits to their afterlife.

Definitely not while I was submerged within it.

The water churned faster, *faster*. It flipped me head over heels. I whirled around, trying to find which way was up.

And poking through the noise-dulling pressure on my ears, for a brief moment, music trickled along the current. A much less vicious melody than the burst dam, and *much* more alluring. Suspended beneath the water, my head and lungs at the point of pain, that drifting song tried to turn me into a cypher in the breeze. It called me to follow the swirling tide wherever it might lead.

In my chest, right above my heart, a bead of an ache shot through, and out of the corner of my eye, a flash of pale hair drifted along the current. I whipped toward it.

And my stomach sank to the depths of the pit.

A plume of crimson clouded the water, and Mila limply floated through the gloom.

The air swept from my lungs—a damn foolish mistake with such precious supply down here—and I blocked out the tempting song, the luring waves.

She was my only focus.

Swimming toward her, I gently looped an arm around Mila's waist and kicked toward the surface, high above and growing higher. Spouts of water poured from the sides, raising the tide all the way to the platform we'd been standing on.

Mystlights pierced the murky water, those mottled orbs growing larger until I was bursting through the surface. My lungs were tight, body aching. I gulped down air like a greedy fucker as I hauled Mila out of the water first. Lyria was there already, carefully gripping her beneath the shoulders and rolling her onto her back so I could pull myself out after her.

"What happened?" Lyria coughed, dripping head to toe. The dam had slowed, no longer an endless flood. "Mila?" she asked, gently turning Mila's head toward her.

And behind Mila's ear, a gleaming red gash looked back at me, shining gruesomely in the mystlight. Her silky platinum hair soaked up that blood like a parched plant desperate for life.

"Fuck." With tired limbs, I dragged myself toward her and ripped off the layers of my leathers to get to my soft undershirt beneath; I hastily tore that off, too, and pressing it to the wound with tender care. It wasn't as sopping wet as the rest of me, but it was better than nothing. "She must have hit her head when we went under."

"On the marble?" Lyria gasped. When I nodded, her eyes flooded with worry.

"Hold this," I told the commander.

Then, carefully—so fucking carefully because I didn't want to jostle her head wound—I leaned down. Kept my hands from shaking out of sheer will and shoved away the terror ripping through my body. Mila didn't have time for that.

Pressing my ear to her chest, I nearly cried when that steady beat greeted me. My panic unwound further when I held my hand below her nose and felt the small puffs of breath. I listened, counting each dull thud until my own heart rate slowed.

"She's breathing." I shifted to take Lyria's position applying pressure to the wound. "Where's Santorina?" I called out.

"Here." Rina's tired voice echoed from further down the ledge.

She cradled her wrist to her chest, and Vale stumbled after her. But no pack was strapped to Rina's body. *Spirits*. All of her healing supplies were gone.

"I'm sorry." She shook her head when she saw the panic splitting my features. "The tide ripped it from me."

"Damien's balls." Tolek exhaled from over my shoulder. I hadn't heard him approach, but he was there, removing his undershirt, too, so we would have it to replace mine, which was quickly staining crimson. Both were too wet to help much, but he dropped it beside me.

Lyria scooted out of Santorina's way so she could evaluate Mila, adjusting my hand with her good one to better apply pressure to her wound.

"Are you okay?" Tolek asked her, dragging a hand through his hair to slick it out of his face.

"Feels sprained," Rina said through a tight jaw.

Over their voices, that melody drifted along the waves again. The bead of pain panged through my chest, more insistent and in time with the rise and swell and dip of both that music and the stirring river.

Shifting closer to Mila, I brushed her hair back from her face. It went against every instinct in my body not to pull her into my lap, but I had enough composure not to risk messing with a head injury. Her eyes were closed, lids paler than usual. Her lips were— dammit they were blue from the icy water.

The melody rose again, my chest aching like an arrow went through it.

"Fuck, what is that?" I snapped, glancing over my shoulder.

Tolek dropped beside me, warily asking, "What's what?"

"That music," I growled.

Everyone was silent. I kept counting the rising and falling of Mila's chest, my own squeezing tight.

"What music?" Rina hedged.

My head snapped up. "You don't hear it?"

Lyria, Santorina, and Tolek exchanged nervous glances that told me everything. I nearly laughed, the sound mingling with a sob in my chest as I looked back down to Mila. "You've got to be fucking kidding me."

Right as I'd thought the Angels couldn't fuck me over again…

"What?" Tolek asked.

I held the fabric to Mila's head, ignoring where blood seeped through to stain my hands. "The Angels can go fuck themselves. I'm not doing it."

Not with Mila unconscious. We needed to clean and stitch this wound. To get some sort of tonic in her that would speed up the replenishing of her blood and strength.

To get her to open her eyes.

"Not doing what?" Lyria whispered.

I ground my jaw, refusing to acknowledge the truth.

But Vale, who had been silent since emerging from the water, said with the dazed eyes of a Starsearcher waking from a reading, "The Soulguider emblem is beneath the spirit river."

~

"I won't leave her." How many times did I have to say it? A dozen didn't seem to be enough for them.

"She'll be okay with us," Tolek promised.

"Her head is *bleeding*!"

"It's staunching," Rina assured, nodding to my hand. "Her

body is healing itself. There's magic in that water—even if it's for different purposes, it comes from the land. It's speeding up the process." Sure enough, Tolek's undershirt had barely absorbed anything after I'd switched to it minutes ago.

Still, I wouldn't leave Mila while she was unconscious.

"The magic isn't healing your wrist," I argued.

Rina's lips pulled into a line. "I'm human," she reminded me, voice soft. "I heal slower."

"Technically," Lyria corrected, "you're a Bounty."

"Oh, for the sake of the Goddesses," Rina grumbled.

I only looked back down at Mila, counting the rise and fall of her chest again. *One...two...three...*"I can't."

"You must," Vale said, but it wasn't her voice. This tone rang with an untoward authority.

"I don't give a damn about those emblems."

"We need you to," Tolek said. "Ophelia needs it."

That alluring song wafted through my head again, and I snapped. "You do it, then! You go get it for her! You're the one she loves." I didn't mean it the way it sounded. Not in a jealous rage.

I only—I didn't understand.

Why was I the one required to do these things? To be the second piece of chasing these emblems? The one who wasn't truly meant to lead our people, called in as the reserve for the chosen one.

There was an irony to it that I couldn't quite find with the woman I loved bleeding before me. Spirits, I hadn't even told her I loved her. And now...

I counted her breaths. She was breathing. Alive. She'd wake up.

Tolek knelt next to me, and in a low voice the others wouldn't hear, he admitted, "Trust me, Malakai. If there was a way I could take this responsibility from you, I would. I would sacrifice *anything* to keep you from carrying more burdens for us." He squeezed my shoulder and continued, "You've damn well done more than enough for seven lifetimes, brother. But there are certain things"—he swallowed, and when I looked up his eyes were on my Bind tattoo—"there are certain things I can't be for Ophelia. At least not right now." His gaze lifted, hardening. "So it has to be you. And not only for her, but for all of us. For every single warrior who will suffer at the hands of whatever this Angelcurse hides if we don't succeed. Because I have a feeling we only know a fraction of the secrets hidden in the legends."

I ran my tongue over my teeth, gaze falling back to Mila. Brushed a strand of hair behind her ear. "You'll take care of her?"

"With my life," Tolek swore.

Swallowing, I closed my eyes. Allowed that echoing melody to rise above the waves and wrap around me.

It was calling me, twisting and writhing beneath my skin. And I couldn't shut it out.

Reluctantly, I brushed a kiss to Mila's forehead. "Your tomorrows, Mila," I whispered. "Every one of them. I'll be back to collect, General."

I carefully transferred the care of her wound to Tolek's hands, ensuring he had the placement Rina had shown me.

Then, I rose and walked back to the edge of the water. It wasn't churning as roughly as before, but the hum still flowed along the current. I removed my boots and weapons, hating the way it left me so bare but the extra weight would drag me down.

The music grew louder, and I counted the beats, taking deep breaths.

Then, I dove in.

Chapter Sixty
Ophelia

"You were...waiting for us?"

The sphinx nodded, onyx sheet of hair cascading around her lioness form. "For many years now. Long before your births, the lingering spirits in this hall told rumors of the universe stirring. Of the two sisters who could raise and slay myths returning to us."

"It *is* us?" I asked, my mouth dry. "We're the sisters from the myth?"

"No. Think of yourselves as the next generation of them."

As if summoned, voices rose among the fog. It was almost a gleeful sort of laughter tinkling off the marble. Something off-kilter and distant that made Jezebel shiver.

The sphinx turned her dark, slitted eyes on my sister. "I am sorry about that facet of the power."

"What do you mean?" Jez asked, chin high.

"Is it not haunting to hear their dying, remorseful thoughts?"

"Sometimes, yes," she admitted. "But often, the honor outweighs the misfortune."

The sphinx tilted her head with feline grace. "Honor?"

"To be the one to remember them, the last connection their spirits experience to the living world. I can think of few greater honors than escorting them through that final hurdle of life."

Angels. My ferocious, myth-born sister. Only she would find the glory in such a power rather than seeing it as a curse on her spirit. And to have kept it a secret for so many years, carrying both the heavy burden of life and the sanctity of it.

Jezebel was a true warrior at heart, worthy of the legends spun around her, of being the rider of khrysaor and destroyer of myths. Only one who handled the title Mistress Death with such grace earned it.

Stepping closer, I squeezed her shoulder, hoping she felt that admiration in the gentle touch.

The sphinx bowed her head toward my sister. "You have a noble heart, Jezebel Alabath."

"Thank you," Jez said with something I rarely saw: a modest blush.

"You said you've been waiting for us," I began, and the sphinx's attention swiveled back to me. "For what exactly?"

She smiled, and even that grin was mischievous and feline. "I have a tale. One I can only share with the chosen, but it required the sisters of the myth to free me."

"What about me?" Erista asked, and based on her step back, she was prepared to leave, but the sphinx shook her head.

"You may stay, Miss Locke." And there was something knowing—something rich with understanding—in that ancient voice. Something that reminded me of how Damien and Valyrie spoke to me in that dream.

"What is the story?" Anticipation fluttered through my chest.

"We must start at the beginning," the sphinx said.

"Beginning of what?"

"At *my* beginning, Ophelia. Of how I came to be in this hall with a story to bear." Walking soundlessly to the back wall, the sphinx turned a circle and settled on the floor, her paws crossed primly before her.

When she began, her voice was bathed in truth and legends, almost like that of the Storytellers. "I once roamed the Soulguider lands freely. Until the fateful day the Angels were tricked into ascending by the wiliest of higher beings, and their divine power was imprisoned. On that damned day, I was turned to stone, and have not woken since, much like many other lives slipped from this world."

Jezebel and I exchanged a look, brows furrowed. *Tricked?*

"But before that, the dunes were mine to traverse, and the warriors were subjects to overlook, so that they might not cause harm to my Angel and mistress." A venomous glint shone through the sphinx's jade eyes.

"I was a gift to her from a god himself when she asked for a defender." She chuckled. "Though, she meant a *lover* or a *friend*. But as I said, gods are tricksters, and Xenique did not properly frame her request. He gave her a half dozen of my merciless kind to stand by her side instead. To defend her."

"Why?" I asked. "Why would a god give an Angel a gift when warriors were so uninvolved with them?"

A devious smirk flitted across the sphinx's lips. But she turned to Erista. And she bowed her female head, wings rustling with...excitement? "A true guard of secrets. Your service is appreciated."

Erista's face remained impassive.

"E?" Jez asked softly, voice wavering. "What does she mean?"

"She cannot tell you," the sphinx said, cruelty painting her voice. "No Soulguider may share this deepest secret. But I can."

My sister's eyes flicked nervously between her partner and the half-feline, once-stone beast.

"What is it?" I asked.

The sphinx tutted. "My kind does not reveal secrets so easily, Ophelia. That would be careless."

Everything she had said thus far was not the point of this tale, not if she'd been able to offer it up. Nothing about the Ascension or how she came to be was the true mystery.

I groaned internally. Of course, I had to prove myself. Being chosen by the Angels was not enough for anything—except offering them my cursed blood. I was growing so tired of this, the frustration heating my veins, but I mustered up all the strength held within my title and asked, "What must I do?"

Was this the trial for the Soulguider emblem? My hand drifted to Starfire's hilt, but the sphinx shook her head at the movement.

Where all dead and riddled secrets lie...

And sphinxes were not known for their physical feats.

I dropped my hand from my sword and quirked a brow. "What is the riddle?"

The sphinx lifted her head proudly. When she spoke, her words drifted through the mists, obscuring those wandering spirit voices and coating the marble walls, voice like a song:

"Older than the stars,
and more powerful than the mists.
A rarity of crimson crowns,
guide by starlight and tides,
rule of death and fate,
veins of renown ebb rarely through the world.
Gifted to the Angel guiding souls
by a womb of pure intention.
What am I?"

The final note rang along the marble walls, and the sphinx settled into her position.

My mind was blank. Truthfully, I didn't know what I expected. A riddle of the sphinx was surely meant to be difficult.

"Choose wisely, Alabath sisters," the sphinx said with a smile that could only be called sinister. "For if you provide the wrong answer, you become my prey."

My stomach bottomed out. All the rumors about the sphinxes were true, then.

"And if we don't answer?" Jezebel asked.

My head whipped toward her. "What?"

She gave me an incredulous look. "If we aren't certain, we shouldn't try. We'll find another way to get whatever information she has."

But there wouldn't be another way.

I may not have been certain what the sphinx knew—whether she was simply guarding the emblem or something else—but whatever it was, Damien and Valyrie had told me to come here. To find the secrets in the Lendelli Hills.

Whatever those secrets were, we needed them.

"If you choose not to answer, I will open the door through the mists." The sphinx waved a paw behind us, where that original archway had been. "But I must forewarn you, you will not be given a second chance."

"Ophelia," Jezebel whispered, a note of pleading in her voice.

I brushed a strand of her cropped hair behind her ear. "Let's think for a moment, Jez."

Think.

This riddle was not vastly different than the prophecies Damien had delivered. A varied motive, certainly, but the rhythmic cadence and ambiguity rang with the same haughtiness.

If Damien had delivered this, where would I have started?

"What words seem important to you?" I asked Jezebel. Erista stood silently at her side, avoiding our eyes.

Jezebel sighed, clearly still against this idea. "Something older than the stars," she mused.

"That jumped out to me, too. And more powerful than mists," I echoed.

"Angel of Souls...so it's related to Xenique."

"Makes sense." I looked around us. "Given all of this."

"Crimson..." Jez trailed off, and I nodded. "Crimson is not typically a clan color of the Soulguiders."

"And veins and land," I said, voice low.

Jezzie's nose scrunched. "I didn't want to think about that one."

"It could be referring to the streams," I suggested. "They cut through the dunes like veins."

"Could be." She nodded, more comfortable with that suggestion, but unless the answer was a reference to Xenique's magic, I wasn't sure what the veins would signify, and what could it possibly be about the Angel's magic?

"More powerful than mists..." I repeated, looking at that haze crowding the ceiling. Mists couldn't be the Spirits, though. That wouldn't make sense.

"The Angels are more powerful than the Spirits," Jezebel said, following my sightline.

"Crimson and veins," I repeated. My gaze dropped down to my scarred hands, where my blood had been used too many times to count.

Angelblood? I didn't want to voice it aloud lest the sphinx think it was a guess, but could the answer truly be so obvious?

Crimson...ran through veins...more powerful than mists...but—

"Older than the stars," I muttered.

The Angels were not older than the stars. To be older than the stars would be to be older than Ambrisk itself. Neither the Angels nor their blood stretched back those eons.

But...others did.

Stars and tides. Death and fate.

Crimson, veins.

My eyes sliced to Erista.

She'd mentioned it once. Only once, and so many months ago, it felt like another life entirely. There was no way she'd known this moment would come—that she had seen it in one of her visions. Because Soulguider visions only predicted death, and none of us would be dying here tonight.

The Soulguider met my stare, and hers dipped ever so slightly. An indication that when she mentioned this substance all those months ago, on a mission to the Southern Pass in the Mystique Mountains to head off an Engrossian host, she thought it was a piece of information we may one day need.

I turned back to the sphinx, knowing if I voiced the incorrect answer, my life would be sacrificed.

And I said the word Erista had spoken on that mountain night beneath the stars. "*Godsblood.*"

Chapter Sixty-One
Malakai

The water washed the stickiness of Mila's blood from my hands with each stroke, and a part of me hated it. A part of me wanted, needed, to feel that on me and remember nothing down here mattered with her waiting for me. For all of those tomorrows we hadn't yet gotten.

The tide was pressing down on me, the song swirling louder as if in protest to my thoughts.

So, I did what was like carving out my own heart.

I shut it out.

Shut out the image of Mila's blood and her shallow breathing.

Shut out the dead weight of her body as I heaved her from the water and how her limbs had flopped to the marble. The crimson-soaked, platinum hair sticking to her face.

I locked it all deep within me and kept swimming toward the heart of that song. Down, down, down I went, trying not to worry about how long the air in my lungs would last.

My chest was getting fucking tight already. Maybe if I'd completed the Undertaking, I'd have an advantage in strength and stamina.

But I was a stubborn fucker who couldn't do it.

And I was too far down now to turn back. I had to trust in the fucking Angels, as everyone else insisted.

I counted my strokes as the music mounted around me and the

marble gave way to rocky walls. I was beneath ground now, in the bowels of Gallantia, where magic ran thickest.

Finally, as the tightness in my chest was nearly unbearable, a chamber opened where the wall met the floor. The song called me to it, and when I swam in and up, my head burst above the water.

The music cut off immediately, a haunting silence hanging in its place. I made for the ledge and hauled myself from the water, rolling onto my back. With my arms splayed against the warm rock, I steadied my panting, counting the cracks in the cave's ceiling.

Ten—that was all I allowed.

Then, I forced myself to my feet, crouching in the low-ceilinged alcove. This definitely would have been easier for Ophelia. Ascended warrior, Angellight power, and all that, but also nearly a foot shorter than me.

Pressing my hand to the ceiling to keep track of where it sloped downward, I crept toward the bend in the cave. The water sloshed against the bank, lapping at my ankles and making the rock pretty damn slippery.

I approached the turn slowly, my heart racing as I peeked around it, but—

"A dead end?" My low words echoed.

I took a few more steps around the corner. There was only a small half-circle of rocky space, but sitting on the bank, cradled in an aged bronze stand that appeared to have been waiting there for thousands of years, sat a sparkling, moon white orb.

There was nothing else. No defenses, no humming power. Looking cautiously around the space, I nudged the shimmering ball with my foot.

Nothing happened.

"This can't be it," I muttered. In Firebird's Field, the earth had erupted. The statue of Ptholenix had roared and flamed.

Here, the water sloshed lazily against the rock and the air remained still. Stale, if I was honest.

Crouching down, I pressed a hand to the glassy orb. It was as hot as the rock around me—a warmth that could only come from *power*—but still, nothing happened. Not beyond the racing of my heart and the sharp pang piercing my chest.

I stood, turning in a circle and rubbing my sternum. "It can't be this easy."

But I wasn't going to look too closely at a gift from the Angels. Perhaps the test was the swim down here. Or perhaps hearing that music marked you as worthy.

Am I?

The thought only blinked through my mind, but something about it tightened my throat. Worthiness wasn't a sentiment I'd associated with myself after I'd been imprisoned. After that sacrifice I'd made to end the war hadn't actually made anything better, instead allowing Lucidius and Kakias to devastate the Mystiques, I'd lost a lot of personal faith.

It had driven all sense of value from me for a while. And still, when I considered my worth, it wasn't anything like...this.

Wasn't anything a warrior deserved. No Undertaking, no titles. Nothing more than a quiet existence away from this mess.

But...

When you signed the treaty, Malakai, I was freed from my imprisonment. You saved me.

That decision hadn't been all bad. Perhaps there was some worth yet to recover.

I turned back to the orb, crouching again to examine it. My reflection was distorted in the glassy surface, but after a few seconds, it cleared and I saw the high points of my life. The ones in recent months where I'd come back from the dead and fought for myself. The moments I'd felt and seen the purpose of life again.

Mila. I saw a whole lot of her in there. Every tomorrow, every redemption.

Maybe that was what made me *worthy* of getting here. Of hearing that song in the depths of the chasm. Because I'd been as good as gone and had fought to stand on my own two feet.

If that's true, though, I thought, watching my muddled reflection return to only me and the cave, *what does that mean for me next?*

Damned if I knew.

Whatever had gotten me here, I didn't care. I swiped up the moon-white orb from its stand and waited for any sort of reaction.

Minutes passed, the scars across my back itching, and I rubbed my fingers along the rough indentations cut into the orb.

Still, nothing happened.

I didn't stop to question it, though I worried a trick was breathing down my neck, an Angel laughing at my naïveté.

But instead of paying heed to that unavoidable possibility, I waded back into the water and got the fuck out of there.

CHAPTER SIXTY-TWO
OPHELIA

"GODSBLOOD."

The answer rang through the air, so confident and yet so uncertain. Because it shouldn't be possible, not within the warriors or the Angels.

The sphinx's teeth gleamed something ferocious as she grinned, and for a moment I thought that might be the last thing I ever saw. That I had been wrong in that guess and was now to suffer the tragic fate of a failed riddle: death at the maw of the sphinx.

Those teeth, the length of my hand, glimmered with predatory intent.

But then, she purred, "Very good."

A relieved breath swept from me. "How is that possible?"

"To understand that, you must gaze upon the heart of the stream's magic."

Before we could ask what she meant, the sphinx rose. And behind her, stone grated against marble, another archway forming in the wall. The babbling of water returned, much louder this time.

The sphinx lumbered on her great paws through that door, a silent instruction to follow.

Uncertainly, Jezebel and I looked to Erista. She nodded, and despite the fact that she knew of something going on here that she hadn't told us, I trusted her. Our Soulguider grandmother had instilled the importance of secretive predictions in us from a young age.

We crossed into the new chamber, waterfalls of all sizes and speeds cascading from spouts and gaping mouths up the sparkling alabaster walls, cut to look like craggy cliff sides. Through pockets in the stone, rivers rushed.

Cyphers dotted the room, a veritable abundance of magic pouring into a central pool taking up the majority of the chamber's floor.

The sphinx sat in the bank's long grasses, her tail swishing behind her, and tucked in her wings. "Step forward, sisters of myths." She nodded to Jezebel and me, and with eyes carefully searching our surroundings, we did.

"Now bow over this core of magic and allow it to enthrall you and sweep you away, so you may find the answers you seek."

I whipped my gaze to her. "How can we be sure you won't hurt us while we're distracted?"

"You can't truly," the sphinx purred. "But you must take my honorable, god-given word as enough."

To trust a god-blessed creature? Never in my extended lifetime did I think I'd do that. But I didn't have an option if I wanted answers. And I supposed, as a woken myth, she may not be so different from Sapphire, whom I trusted intrinsically.

"You okay with this?" I checked with Jezebel.

She cast Erista a look I couldn't read, but there was hurt layered within. Later. We'd figure all of that out later. "We've come this far," Jez said.

Together, we knelt at the pool's edge.

"You do not need to submerge yourself," the sphinx instructed. "Simply, *look*."

Skeptically, I gazed into the waters. It reminded me of the pool in the cavern we'd kept Sapphire and the khrysaor hidden in, but much larger and flooded with a more potent form of magic. One that reached out to even me, with my meager Soulguider inheritance, and tugged on the possibilities of my power.

The dazzling water rippled gently, like a breeze wafted over it, and the crystal surface clouded.

The sphinx began speaking again, that same melodic tone as when she'd given us the riddle. "My mistress was always more than an Angel."

A mural swirled—a story unfolding. Beside me, Jezzie inhaled and grasped my wrist as Xenique's beautiful face filled the image. Her wings flared behind her and cast a sheen on her dark skin and kind smile.

"The blood of the gods beat through her veins, a daughter of Artale herself."

What?

I meant to ask it aloud, but it seemed the sphinx's magic had stifled our words as she spoke.

"Xenique, the Prime Warrior of the Soulguider clan, was a demigod. Child of the Goddess and a human consort, a powerful, powerful being born of *true* love." Two shadows wavered on either side of the Angel, a golden tether between them. They stood in a chamber much like this one, cascading waterfalls and cyphers haloing their forms.

"The influence to see death ran through her veins, a magic straight from her Goddess mother. To Xenique, death was a portrait layered over the true world, a veil of sorts, through which she saw every fate that would befall those around her."

The image shifted, Xenique's surroundings blurring and dulling. Lives extinguishing. Everything but the Angel's exquisite face took on that gray-tinged veil she saw through.

And the smile that had seemed so kind, so loving—it didn't truly reach her eyes.

No, in those amber depths, fear and sadness lurked. Loneliness.

The sphinx went on, "Because she saw destruction everywhere she went, Xenique asked the gods for a defender." The Angel fell to her knees in this very chamber, muttering unheard prayers to the waters. "But she made a mistake. She asked her questions too broadly. And instead of her mother or a more understanding God, Lynxenon answered."

The God of Mythical Beasts. Lynxenon had heard Xenique's plea, and in return—

"That is how I came to stand at her side. He chose the sphinxes for our tie to Artale. A defender. A protector who kept all others away, something which may have actually made her lonelier and less understanding of her own magic."

Sure enough, as Xenique sat in her revered seat above the desert, the rest of her warriors were nothing but blurs on the landscape. And that murky veil remained around her.

"Of all the Angels, she most longed for the connection of the seven to return after their inner feuds caused them to split. Because while she may be distanced from her warriors and guardians, at least those higher beings understood her." A dignified scoff. "Or, she hoped. She was always different than the others, thanks to her status as a demigod. It is why she demanded the secret never be spread among all seven clans. That only *her* people may know."

Flashes of images sped through the rippling waters. Of Xenique, isolated and alone, wings drooping behind her. Of her attempting to reform relationships with the other Angels and being handed denial after denial. Only Ptholenix and Valyrie deigned to meet with her after many years of pleading.

"I, and my sisters, were her companions," the sphinx went on. "Until that wretched Ascension Day."

Wretched?

The water splashed like an explosion beneath the surface, shooting high above us, and the entire scene dissolved into seven Angels gathered in a field of burning flowers. Six others stood at their sides.

Are those—

The image went up in flames.

No—not flames. It was a flaring, golden light streaked with different facets of power. Turquoise and orange and lilac wove without, more colors there and gone too quickly to name.

"That day, the Angels were forced to sacrifice all the might they bore on this continent, in order to uphold another." The light burned and burned. The sphinx's voice rose, crashing through the chamber. "They left behind stagnant pieces of magic, meant to be uncovered so that the chosen may break the curse the Ascension locked them away in. So you may free my mistress and the others from that horrid prison."

It is *their spirits locked away? That is what I need to free?*

The sphinx ignored my silent questions. "It is that curse which runs through your blood, the Angelblood the marking of it. Activated by the blood of the gods."

That final sentence rang through the air, and the water stilled, the light fading.

The vision released its hold on me, the chamber swarming around us in a rush of cypher-and-magic scented air. I fell backward onto the bank, panting. Dozens of questions bombarded my mind.

"The agent that activates the Angelblood." I met the sphinx's gaze, my breath shuddering from my body. "The answer I've been searching for as to how I was struck with this curse—it's Godsblood?"

The sphinx sat, her tail swishing behind her proudly. "That it is."

"How did I—" I swallowed. "How did *I* get Godsblood?"

"Your grandmother hails from Lendelli, the home of Xenique when she once lived. After the Ascension, the capital was moved east, nearer the mountains. But this land, these dunes, they were of my mistress' own soul. They are where she lived, where she bore her children, and where they bore theirs for many generations to come. Until one strayed, falling in love with a Mystique, and abandoning her home here."

Chills spread across my skin, and I swore I could feel that ancient thread of Godsblood beating through my veins.

"Are you saying our grandmother is a descendent of Xenique?" Jezebel asked. "Of a demigod? That the blood of the gods runs through our mother's line?"

The sphinx nodded.

"But...we were always told her family was of the lower Soulguiders," Jezebel argued. "An unimportant line."

I let out a breath, my eyes falling closed. "Of course, we were."

I turned to my sister. "Xenique went to lengths to hide her Gods-blood. Probably tampered with the histories and ruling classes to elevate other lines above her own."

"Why?" Jez shook her head, but I didn't quite understand her denial when I could see in her eyes she already knew the answer.

"It made her feel isolated. Why would she want her descendants to experience that, too? Something as powerful as the blood of a god could cause problems between clans." I looked to the sphinx for a confirming nod. "It sounds like Xenique wanted peace between them all. She wanted her people to feel included, so she wove the secret of the Godsblood into their magic, their history, so no one could know."

Did our own mother even know what ran through her blood?

Jezebel whirled on Erista. "Did you know?"

"Not everything." The Soulguider's eyes were wide and pleading. "I'll explain later, I promise."

Something stiff passed between them, and the fear clearly played out on my sister's face. Had Erista known secrets about her throughout their entire relationship? Had that been the impetus for their bond in the first place?

Spirits, I hoped not. The heartbreak was already cracking across Jezebel's features.

She shut it down, though. A coolness I wasn't used to took its place.

Godsblood, I repeated to myself. We needed to figure out the rest of what the sphinx had to share, then we could leave, find the Soulguider emblem, and free the Angels—or their spirits—from their prison.

I plucked another question from the waiting line of them in my mind. "If we both have Godsblood, why is only my Angelblood active with the Angelcurse?"

"Twentieth birthdays are so important for Soulguiders, are they not?"

I blinked at the creature. My mother had always instilled that in us. When a Soulguider turned twenty, their true purpose was revealed to them. *Twenty is an important year in your heritage,*

Ophelia, she'd said again and again as my birthday approached last year.

We'd shirked the idea, my sister and I, choosing Mystique traditions, but for half of our mother's side, it had been an important year. And it was precisely that night, following my birthday celebration, that Damien appeared to me for the first time.

When I'd been drunk off sparkling wine, drowning the thoughts of what the night should have been. Only days after finding Malakai's spear. Heartbroken and longing and so damn naive to the workings of the world around me. To what was waking within me at that very moment. When I'd stumbled upstairs to my room in my family manor and crawled into my bed only to be awoken by blinding Angellight for the very first time.

The magic within the Godsblood must have been potent enough to overrule my claim on the Mystiques and initiate the Angelcurse. Little could, but the will of a god? Not much could trump *that*.

But...twenty—

A new fear lodged a breath in my throat. "Will Jezebel receive the Angelcurse when she comes of age?" I gripped my sister's hand tightly, her cold front remaining up. I'd been ravaged by this damn curse. I wouldn't let that happen to her.

But the sphinx shook her head. "Not if you complete it. Finish the task, and the curse will never touch another again."

I released a breath.

"We thought the Angelcurse was the cause of my magenta eyes. If Jezebel has the potential for it as I did, and the fate wasn't activated until my twentieth birthday, why were *my* eyes always a sign of it?"

Spirits, it was such a frivolous thought, but my mind reeled.

"Only one life can harbor the curse at any time." She shrugged those powerful shoulders, her wings ruffling. "It is my suspicion that if you fail, the curse will transfer to your sister upon her twentieth birthday, and the signs will show, as well. Now that the bloodlines of Angel and Goddess have merged naturally, anyone born unto you will know the same fate. Always the oldest first." She added again, voice dark, "Should you fail."

Should I die, she meant.

If I failed, Jezebel would be left with the Angelcurse. My chest hollowed at the consideration of it. I'd been uncertain if I even wanted to complete the thing or if perhaps Annellius was correct in hiding it. That the Angels had toyed with our lives enough and it was time to fight back.

This wiped all possibility of that from the table.

"If we have Godsblood from our mother's line, how did Annellius get it?"

The sphinx answered, "Annellius discovered the curse within Alabath Angelblood and activated it himself. He tracked down a descendant of the goddess and *drank* from the source."

My stomach turned. So desperate. He was *so desperate* and greedy for power, he took a warrior's blood in the worst possible way to activate this curse. One he turned his back on in the end, anyway. It was a cruel kind of irony.

What could have been that bad? What did he learn that made him decide he didn't want to complete the curse cast when the Angels ascended and instead doom future generations of Alabaths to carry on a cause he was too cowardly to face? Especially when he had already gone to such egregious lengths.

Could freeing the spirits of the Angels truly be that bad?

There was only one way to know for certain. I looked up at the sphinx, steeling myself to ask the question.

Briefly, a part of me faltered—didn't want to know.

A scared, shriveled piece of my wayward spirit wished to remain in denial for a moment longer. To hug naivety because certainly, *certainly*, it would be easier to face than whatever I learned next. To hear the reason I'd been exploited.

But I knew, deep in my soul, that was never truly an option. I was saddled with this Angelcurse and the heavy decision that would follow once I heard the truth.

I took a breath, and it weighed down my lungs like it was a life-changing inhale. One that would alter the trajectory of everything that followed. The last innocent one of my existence before I was forced to make choices no mortal should be responsible for.

With my sister's hand locked in mine, the Godsblood and

Angelblood and Spirits knew what else pumping through my veins, I asked, "It isn't only the Angels' spirits that need to be freed, is it?" A shake of the sphinx's head. A squeeze of Jezebel's hand. A breath through my traitorous, dry throat. "Then, what is the purpose of the Angelcurse?"

The sphinx smiled all those sharp teeth. "The purpose of the Angelcurse is to free the Warrior God."

CHAPTER SIXTY-THREE
OPHELIA

I BLINKED AT HER, THE ROOM UTTERLY STILL.

Finally, I forced out, "Wh-what?"

"Fulfilling the Angelcurse, replacing those seven emblems into their statues where Annellius should have, and bleeding across the lot, will free the Warrior God."

"Warriors do not keep the gods." A stupid statement, clearly.

"Not anymore," the sphinx purred. "But once, there was a seventh god. The most ferocious of them all. Strong enough to break the precious balance of power that cradles every world in the palm of its hand."

I met Jezebel's wide-eyed stare. Behind her, even Erista was frozen in shock at this revelation.

"H-how is that possible?" I stuttered. "What *happened*?"

The sphinx's voice turned melodic again, a story etched in truth. "Longer ago than any living memories can recall, *seven* gods oversaw the realms. And when they were created out of the mists of the universes, their power was equal, each with domain over a designated denomination, not unlike your Angels.

"But over time, the power warped in some." She tilted her head —pityingly or ruefully, I couldn't tell—and her onyx hair slid over her shoulder. "The beings they commanded on Ambrisk grew much more powerful than the rest. The Warrior, Sorcia, and Fae deities became the strongest of the gods, as their children were on land. And still, among those three, one's power stretched bounds beyond the others. Spanned capabilities the other two could only dream of."

The sphinx settled her chin on her paws, dreamily saying, "But oh, did he wish to use it. Oh, did he look down at his children and see how *they* could supremely rule this world. What other realms they could access bridges to." She sighed, reluctantly tacking on, "This kind of thinking, this greed...it is very dangerous to peaceful existence. Especially when greed melds with such power. And so, the known gods devised a plan to entrap the rapacious Warrior God within his own power. To imprison him and lock him away."

"They simply...trapped him?" I asked. Was he still alive? Could a god die?

Spirits, this was unbelievable.

The sphinx nodded. "Each of the six known gods and goddesses sacrificed a kernel of their magic to build the prison."

Pushing back to her feet, the sphinx rounded the pool. Waving a paw above the water, the known gods formed above the calm surface. Their faces were blurred, but their frames highlighted one by one as she went on, "Thallia, the Witch Goddess of Sorcia, gave the most as the strongest of the six. She forged the lock that keeps the Warrior God bound.

"The Fae Goddess entwined her magic into the histories, staying the tongues of those who remember this account. Making it so that the Warrior God was wiped from texts and unable to be spoken of. Another tale left to be forgotten to the winds." Aoiflyn's glowing image dulled, a book snapping closed in her hand.

I gasped. "That's why Damien could never share this. Why he looked so pained when he tried to."

The sphinx nodded. "The Fates, even, cannot tell of the Warrior God, thanks to Moirenna's promises to honor Aoiflyn's tongue-tied bargains."

"And why Vale's magic malfunctioned," Jezebel whispered. "She was trying to read things that are locked, until Titus broke through the block with the imbued seeing chambers."

"And while that helped clarify most readings, the gods have still been muddled," I said.

Spirits, it all made so much sense once we had this final piece.

A latch switched.

The sphinx continued, "Nature contains the god and does not whisper his name. Mystical beasts disappeared as their lines died out. Creatures walking in death, whom he wished to rule and who bowed to him, were trapped in their fiery realms."

One by one, each of the gods' images dimmed, fading into the water as the sphinx named their sacrifice.

"Every one of the six gods weakened themselves?" I clarified. "They handed over their magic in order to keep this one god away?"

The sphinx nodded.

I watched the known gods vanish into the water's surface, mournful auras around their pristine bodies.

Was he truly that horrendous, then? His nefarious greed a possible ruin of the world?

Or was it their own jealousy that caused them to imprison their brother?

"How does this pertain to the Angelcurse? How did it begin?"

"All magic requires a loophole, as you well know," the sphinx purred. I thought back to Kakias's immortality ritual, to which my very life had been the loophole. "In order to seal the lock, the balance of power demanded there was a way to reopen it."

"Why?" Jezebel asked, a bit skeptically. "If he truly is that horrible, why allow for that?"

"The balance commands all that we are."

"The gods cannot overrule it?" Jez braced her hands on her hips.

But it was Erista who said, voice shaking, "Even Artale cannot negotiate with the balance of power. It is a pillar of our world, something we are taught the moment we start guiding spirits."

The sphinx nodded.

"So," I began, fingers curling around the shard of Angelborn at my neck, "my combination of Angelblood and Godsblood and these emblems are the key to unleashing this Warrior God upon Ambrisk?" Another silent nod. "And if I don't, this Angelcurse will transfer to the next Alabath? To Jezebel and all who come after us?"

"Yes," the sphinx said, and there was no echo of the melodic tone in her voice. Nothing persuasive or malicious. If anything, she sounded a bit remorseful. "You must do it, Ophelia Alabath. Complete the Angelcurse, unleash the god so that my mistress and all the Angels may roam freely again."

That struck me. "The Angels..." Damien's stilted presence, his inability to return recently. "They're locked away with the god, aren't they?"

Melancholy dimmed her stare. "Ascension Day was more than the Angels assuming their full scope of power and leaving this plane. It was an immediate removal of it all and fragments left behind, though that part is left out of the stories thanks to the known gods. The day you all celebrate and honor your Angels—the one to renew your promises as warriors—was the darkest day in our history."

My gut churned.

"The Warrior God had already been imprisoned, but he was becoming restless, so the known gods reinforced their locks. They tricked the Angels into that prison with him, as well as many creatures under their domain or with tethers to the god, using their residual magic to seal the doors. The sphinxes, the pegasus, the khrysaor, and all the others—we were all gone shortly after."

"The khrysaor?" Jezebel gasped, anger flaming in her eyes.

The sphinx turned to her. "There were once so many more of them than the two you now know. They carry the blood of the Warrior God himself, as does the pegasus."

"Is that how she emerged?"

"What do you mean?" Jez asked.

"Zanox *bled* when he crashed through Ricordan's manner. It sprayed everywhere, triggered Sapphire's transformation." The searing pain that had radiated through my body echoed now.

And gradually, every piece was sliding into place, like a veil was lifted across my mind now that I had them.

"That was the last step in Kakias's ritual. My active Angelblood was why she needed *me* specifically to become immortal, but that ingredient we forgot..." I racked my memory, and finally, as if the Spirits were waiting until I'd understand to allow me to remember. "The power of the fallen," I gasped.

The Fallen God.

"He has been referred to as such, yes. The queen obtained and used his power in ways I do not understand," the sphinx confirmed. "And when your khrysaor bled, it sealed the reversal."

"How did Kakias find out about the Godsblood and the Warrior God?" I asked. "How did Annellius if all of the stories were rewritten?"

"As I have said, all magics have loopholes to balance them. You were able to wake me for the full story, but Annellius sought it out. He dug into myths and found tales that did not align. Rearranged the inconsistencies as if they were a puzzle to be solved." The sphinx's chest inflated. "Confirmed it with your Angel himself, though he could not speak of it."

I swallowed over a dry throat.

"And Kakias?"

"Bant shed his spirit into her. It transferred unspeakable knowledge, though the queen was so singularly focused, she did not wish to use it."

It should have soothed a piece of the uncertainty gnawing at my mind to finally have this one answer. But there were too many others to focus on for relief.

"The rest of the khrysaor and pegasus," Jez said, returning back to that question, "they live?"

"They wait, sleeping in the stone. Lesser, now forgotten gods and beasts born of them all lurk. Slowly, so very slowly, things are unraveling. The ether seeping through the world is budging at the growing hands of the Warrior God." She leveled us with a stare. "He is growing stronger for the reckoning."

"The dying land," I said, voice hollow, "the unusual Rites of Dusk, the fires, and tainted creatures. It's all because of this isn't it?"

"It is." She bowed her head, seeming to appreciate our understanding of the severity.

Ambrisk itself was rebelling against this god being locked up.

The known gods had each given a kernel of magic to trap the Warrior God, but magic was a force impossible to control. It was unraveling.

We'd noticed it so many months back; how long had this truly been going on? Had it been mounting since I was born? Since those first drops of Angelblood mingled with Godsblood in the Alabath line?

I tightened my grip around Damien's emblem, seeking some sort of stability.

"What does all of this have to do with the *fel strella mythos*?"

"Ah," the sphinx said, smiling, "the very legend that allowed you to wake me. To restore the creatures of myth that were lost with the imprisonment of the god."

"It cannot be a coincidence," Jezebel said.

I was tempted to agree with her. How was it we were *blessed* with these two prophetic destinies?

"It is not," the sphinx agreed. "The stories once existed separately, but the Godsblood was the key. Only sisters with that source could revive the tale. Only they could have the power to brings the myths to life and destroy them again."

A sister of life, a sister of death.

Not only communing with departing spirits. Jezebel had the power to execute them, too. To restore constellations to the sky by slaughtering myths, as I could pull them down to earth and wake them.

"Are Storytellers born of myth?" I asked.

"Their unique brand of magic is something of legend, yes."

I turned to Jezebel. "That's what happened at the pleasure house. When Brystin attacked that Storyteller, your magic reacted, Jez. Because the power of a Storyteller is something of myths, and she was dying. You have the power to *destroy myths*. To control them. It's why your magic didn't harm warrior spirits during the war, but it did that night."

I went on, the magic buzzing in my blood, "And mine...mine is the counter. To pluck constellations from the sky and give them life. That's what this power was trying to do in the catacombs. It was searching for a life to restore in those enchanted corpses. When it found none, it imploded. And it woke a phoenix that night in the jungle—something preserved in the trees." I took my sister's hand. "When we traveled to that plane— the bridge—it woke these powers fully. We are each other's balance, Jezzie."

She considered, eye's gleaming with a dark promise. A true Mistress of Death. "Sisters born of myth," she whispered.

Sisters who could conquer the gods.

The sphinx assessed us proudly. "Something stirred on the day of your birth, Ophelia Alabath. The myth magic you bear, thanks to the Godsblood, ignited something that enables you to wield the power of Angels." Her jade eyes gleamed. "A breath and blood not seen in...long enough that even the Angels had lost hope."

They had written us off, it seemed. I gritted my teeth, fighting the urge to let them rot in that prison for eternity in retaliation. To show them the might of a warrior who held their fate in her veins.

The sphinx tilted her head, the move entirely feline. "What legacy will you leave behind Revered of the Mystique Warriors, Chosen of the Deities, Seraph Kissed by Angels?"

"I do not plan to find out soon," I growled.

Because, while I wasn't certain I trusted the gods or the Angels —didn't know if I should unlock the prison or not—I was going to see the end of this bloodstained battlefield.

"We all must learn one day," the sphinx chuckled. Then, reading the fury burning through my stare, she added, "Do not turn your back on this fate. I can see the temptation. The daring in your spirit. To do so would be catastrophic. For you, for future generations, and for all the realms."

But which path *was* more daring?

To free a reckless, greedy god, or to turn my back on him?

"If I am to do this," I began slowly, "*how* do I free the god?"

Jezebel and Erista shifted beside me. In encouragement or to deter the idea, I couldn't tell, but I needed to know. Needed all the information I'd been lacking this entire time in order to make a decision of such consequence.

For months now, my life had bent to the whim of this Angel- curse. I was supposed to be the weak thing catering to divine interventions, running without an answer as to *why*, just blindly taking the steps.

I was done.

Finally, I was taking that power back, with striking claws and sharpened teeth and the wings of Angels' might beating at my back.

"There is a theater in the midst of mountains. Buried beneath stone and magic. Within it, a statue has been worn to time. Return the emblems of the Angels to their rightful bearers. Pour your blessing upon them."

I swallowed past the ache in my chest, the tangle of relief and uncertainty, like sliding a final piece of a puzzle home.

"This theater," I began, swallowing. "Have I been there before?"

The sphinx lowered her head, and something in the heaviness of the moment had the pressure in my chest threatening to crack. The backs of my eyes stung and my breath came in small gasps.

We had it.

We had an answer.

I wasn't sure how I was going to navigate it, but at least we knew.

Rising, the sphinx circled back toward the archway into the Hall of Wandering Souls. "Go now, child. Complete what others before you have failed."

CHAPTER SIXTY-FOUR
DAMIEN

THE DEMIGOD'S POWER PULSED AROUND HER LIKE A beast trying to wake. We were inching ever closer to a dream millennia in the making.

The Angelglass still remained in that foyer, the seven of us gathering in Xenique's new chamber when the tremor went through us, tugging at all of our magic, but that could only mean one thing. The final pieces were in their hands.

When Xenique's power beamed as the rest of ours—when the deep amethyst toyed with Ptholenix's flames and Gaveny's roaring tides, Thorn's storm clouds and the galaxies at Valyrie's fingertips —that would be it.

The last shard of the lock to this caged prison acquired. All we had to do now was wait.

The seven of us gathered closer, forming a circle in the great empty space within this new palace encased in stone.

"Soon," I said.

"Are you certain this time?" Bant threw at me.

"She is not like the last." I grimaced at him, a wave of untethered emotion flaring through me and sending my eyes widening.

The others watched me cautiously. Eagerly.

It was exactly as it had been that day in Firebird's Field, when we were sentenced to this prison to contain his might. Seven Angels, side by side as we should have always been had our internal feuds not torn us apart. As we should always be in the future, power soon thrumming through our veins again.

Only this time, we were on the cusp of freedom.

With barely a thought, I summoned a beam of my light, sending a gold column toward the ceiling. Glittering ether dripped from my feathers in answer.

Gaveny grinned, elation clear in the beating of his wings, ocean blues spilling from them. With a dramatic twirl of his hand, he cast a matching beam soaring toward the top of the chamber, the cresting waves awash with his turquoise signature.

On my other side, the Firebird's stare flamed. Then, an inferno licked down his tawny arms and stretched toward the ceiling as if pouring from the maw of a long-sleeping creature.

Beside him, Valyrie turned her face toward the heavens, eyes closed and a brutally beautiful smile taking over, as if she could see the stars and Fates she missed so dearly. The friends she mourned. And she opened her palms, stars twining up. Higher and higher until that fourth column of magic met the light and tides and burning embers.

Even Thorn, hovering between Gaveny and Bant, cast a roaring tunnel of storm-kissed magic. The gusting winds blew my hair behind my shoulders and whispered secrets in my ears. It swirled Valyrie's and Xenique's long skirts around their ankles and fanned Ptholenix's flames.

Directly across the circle from me, I met Bant's stare. Even he appeared wistful, his scarred wings rifling as he gathered his stronger power. A sixth beam of light burst to life, emitting a pure gold glow similar to mine, but laced with inky ropes of magic.

Xenique watched us all, a small, hopeful smile piercing her full lips and dreams spinning to life in her eyes. After so long exiled from her peers while on earth, this was what she wanted. The future she envisioned—seven Angels united.

And a twisted, deceitful piece of me that had awoken with the return of stronger magic wished it would remain only the seven of us.

Part Four
Thorn

CHAPTER SIXTY-FIVE
TOLEK

"TOLEK!"

Fucking Angels, Ophelia's voice had never sounded so good. Except—

"What's wrong?" I asked, catching her as she stumbled up to me outside the Gates of Angeldust, a frantic edge to her expression.

Cupping her cheek, I tilted her face up, exploring those magenta eyes. There was something new there, a heated and haunted light igniting her entire expression.

"We found it," she gasped over her rapid breaths. "We—we got all the answers."

Ophelia's eyes dragged over me, where my leathers were unbuckled and my undershirt gone. "Where's your shirt? And why are you soaking wet?" She ran a hand through my hair.

Then, Ophelia glanced over my shoulder to Santorina— cradling her now-wrapped wrist—and the Engrossians guarding the fae prisoner. To my sister and the others, on alert with weapons in hand. To Mila draped across Malakai's lap, still not awake.

And she jolted into action.

"What happened?" she asked, ducking from my arms and rushing to their side. Jezebel and Erista followed, our entire group gathering around Mila as Lancaster worked, with Santorina and Celissia watching over his tending. We'd had no choice but to move her. We needed the fae healing magic to stitch up her head wound.

We recounted what happened in the flooded chamber after Ophelia disappeared into the Hall of Wandering Souls with Jezebel and Erista. The dam breaking, the water sweeping us all in, how Mila hit her head on the way down.

"Shouldn't it be easy to heal with your magic?" Ophelia asked Lancaster.

"It will be." He gritted his teeth. "But given what lurks in the water, I have to separate anything that could infect her bloodstream."

Malakai spoke for the first time since the fae began working, his voice as dark as the khrysaor's scales. "What do you mean?"

"Those waters are tainted by spirits," Lancaster ground out.

"They're not tainted," Erista snapped. "They're blessed by the Angels and Artale."

"Same thing," Lancaster muttered, his lethal hands braced tenderly on Mila's head.

"You'll be able to get it out?" Malakai asked, focused solely on the woman in his arms. "She'll be okay?"

Lancaster nodded. "She'll live."

I didn't point out that wasn't what Malakai had asked, but I met CK's eyes over the group. Based on his stony stare, he'd noticed, too.

"There's something else," Cyph said. He dragged Brystin forward a step, demanding, "Tell them."

Brystin pursed his lips, but Ophelia stormed toward the fae, that light in her eyes slipping across her skin and gathering in her palms. "Tell us what?"

She was a threat brought to life. I stepped up behind her, hand on the hilt of my sword, and glowered at Brystin.

But the male remained quiet. Cypherion looped the rope tighter around his hand and tugged, Brystin's blood pouring from that wound.

"He's been toying with us," Cypherion grumbled. "He hinted at a *facade* in the bargain with Ritalia."

The sand swarmed around our ankles as Ophelia's light flared, my own stomach knotting. She clenched her fists against the power, and I braced my hand at her back, her shoulders dropping an inch at the touch.

"How can we know that's true?" I said. "Could be a twist to his words."

Based on the glimmer in Brystin's eye, he was having a damn good time with this.

"Because Ritalia would have been a fool to not have a loophole," Ophelia muttered. Angellight dimming, she looked up at me, and that stare could burn a thousand corpses to ash. "We knew there was a catch. This...*facade* is it."

"We think it has to do with a glamour," Dax growled, arms crossed as he glared at the fae.

"He's been quite secretive," Barrett said. Under his breath, he added as if in a personal challenge, "Persistent, too."

"Glamour," Ophelia repeated, her mask of Revered fully slammed up and voice harsh. "Keep an eye on him. Do whatever you must to get answers, but don't trigger whatever Ritalia swore him to."

A fine line to walk, but Barrett and Dax looked positively gleeful at the permission, shoving the fae down to the sand and questioning him under Cypherion's watch.

Ophelia took in the new information, a thread of tension winding tighter between us all. Her eyes drifted across Mila and Lancaster, and it was clear she wanted to question the male but wasn't willing to disturb his healing.

Looking over her shoulder, she found Mora sitting against the high wall. She took a determined step toward the female, but froze. "Are you okay?"

I followed Ophelia's stare. Mora's skin was even paler than it had been earlier. Her energy drained. Despite the glamour threat and the fact that the female was the only glam among the fae present—and a powerful one at that—it was clear in the look Ophelia, Celissia, and Rina exchanged that they were concerned.

"Just tired," the female said with an unconvincing nod. Dynaxtar's wing curled tighter around her. "Tolek?" she called, voice weak.

I jogged over, Ophelia and Celissia on my heels, and asked, "What's wrong?"

Mora extended the scroll with the coded language about Ascension Day. "I noticed something in the patterns. I think it's mentions of warriors."

"Of the ones from the age of Angels?" I asked, looking over the passage Mora indicated as Celissia whispered to Ophelia behind me.

"At first that's what I took it to mean," Mora said with a heavy breath. "But if the tense of the language works like our modern one, it's speaking of *future* warriors."

Future warriors? Was it about Ophelia bearing the Angelcurse?

I took the wrinkled parchment from Mora. "Thank you. I'll continue on this."

"Mora?" Ophelia asked crouching before the female with a much more tender stare than she'd given Brystin. "Can I look at your shoulder?"

The fae nodded, and I stepped back beside Celissia as Ophelia and the fae discussed in low voices. Ophelia pulled back Mora's bandage to reveal—

Fucking Angels. My stomach turned. The wound was… festering wasn't quite the right word. Because it didn't seem to be infected in any way, but it wasn't healing nor did it bleed. A gaping loss of flesh stared up at us, an eerie blue swimming through Mora's blood.

"It's some kind of tainted magic," Celissia whispered. "Her brother can't heal it, so she's trying to hide it. But…"

Ophelia could try to soothe the wound with Angellight, as she had after the catacombs.

She hated using the power. Feared what it would do, especially after how big it proved itself to be during the Rite.

But there, crouched in the sands of her grandmother's land, Ophelia seemed to glow. That difference I'd noticed in her when she emerged from the gates, her eyes wild with a thrill, it was radiating around her now, almost a visible sheen to her skin.

No. It *was* a visible sheen—all around her. Similar to the

Angellight wall she'd erected while fighting Kakias in the final battle, but now it wrapped her frame like the thinnest, softest silk.

With her hands gently braced against Mora's arm on the borders of the wound, Ophelia pushed that light into the fae, and gold slithered around Mora's shoulder.

I stepped closer to pick up what Ophelia was saying to the female. "This is the Angellight—the gift I can control because of the Angelcurse and the emblems. It's different than the mythos magic. That's the one I don't know as well. The one we saw with the phoenix and in the catacombs."

The *fel strella mythos*...the one the fae and Storyteller had told us of? What else did she know of it?

I didn't ask yet. Only watched as Ophelia glowed—both literally and figuratively. Because not only was her frame alight, but each word she spoke carried utter strength and dominance. Every blink and breath filled with wonder and ecstasy that crept along the sand and straight into me.

Angels, she was a manifestation of myth and power itself, and it consumed her.

"How's that feel?" Ophelia asked after the thin sheets of magic formed a bandage. It was similar to what she'd done immediately after the catacombs, but it was somehow *more*. Like she'd untangled the threads of power living inside of her and stopped being afraid to use them.

Mora nodded, but her face remained gaunt. "That venomous instinct is still there." She closed her eyes, leaning back against the wall. "But it's easing. I think I'll stay here and rest while the magic takes hold."

Celissia seemed satisfied. She squeezed Ophelia's shoulder before heading back to the others.

"Damn phenomenal, Alabath," I said, dragging her to her feet and walking a bit away from Mora.

She gave me a dazed smile I wanted to see every day of my life. "The magic practically has a life of its own. It wants things to be whole and pure; I simply willed it to achieve that."

"Alabath," I laughed, shaking my head.

She pulled her attention away from Mora, blinking up at me. "What?"

"You say it like it's such an easy thing to do." She opened her mouth to argue, but I pressed my lips to hers to stop her. "You command the power of Angels, Ophelia," I whispered, against her lips. "There's nothing simple about it, or you."

She looped her arms around my neck, kissing me with fervor now. Spirits, was this all over? Could we go back to the inn and lock ourselves in our room for days?

Too soon, she was pulling away. "Come on," she said and slipped her hand into mine. Right...we still had Brystin and the emblems to deal with.

When we traipsed back to the group, Lancaster was saying, "It's done. She should wake soon."

Sure enough, the wound on Mila's head was sealed, the blood crusting her platinum hair dried. Malakai's chest—still entirely bare and streaked with blood—sagged. Though his eyes were locked on Mila, he was clearly not speaking to her when he said, "You haven't even asked about the emblem."

"Because I already know you have it." I looked down at Ophelia, but she continued, "Can I see it?"

"Here." Vale's voice drifted over the group as she pulled out the orb—the glass shining like a moon plucked from among the stars—and passed it to Ophelia.

In her hands, it lit up. Images swirled within, obscure and storm-drenched.

But Ophelia frowned at it. "Something's wrong."

"What do you mean?"

"It's the right one," Malakai said confidently. "I could feel it."

Ophelia nodded. "It is, but..." She rolled the orb between her hands.

"It's not burning you?" I asked. Ophelia looked at me, confusion in her magenta eyes. Squeezing her hip, I added, "That might be a good thing."

"All the other ones burned," she mused, attention dropping back to the emblem, a token of Xenique's power held in the palm of her hand. Sapphire nudged her, and Ophelia looked up at her pegasus. "Any ideas, girl?"

She handed it to me, and CK and I observed the thing, dumbfounded given that neither of us could feel the magic like Ophelia and Malakai could. It seemed laced with ether of some kind, but truly, I would never have been able to identify it.

I rolled the orb between my hands, a ridge in the otherwise-flawless glass scraping against my palm. "What's this?"

Ophelia leaned closer, casting a small bud of Angellight between us. An indentation cut into the surface, etched and worn by the centuries, but still clearly there.

"It looks like a crescent moon," she said, brow furrowed.

"The symbol of Xenique," CK said simply.

"Yes, but..." Ophelia fingered the carving. Then, her gaze snapped to her sister. "Jezzie...give me your necklace."

"What?" Jezebel's hand flew to the chain around her neck—where a crescent moon pendant hung inlaid with an amethyst. A gift Erista had given her when their relationship was still a secret.

Erista gasped. "By the Angel!" Her sandaled feet flew over the dunes as she circled the group, stopping at Ophelia's side to trace the symbol in the glass

"Can someone please explain?" Lyria huffed, kicking the sand.

"I think baby Alabath's necklace fits into this carving on the orb like a puzzle piece," I guessed.

"Why, though?" Jezebel asked, unclasping her necklace.

"Because this emblem—out of all of them—is most precious," Ophelia said, eyes locked with her sister. "It's a tie to the Angels *and to the gods.*"

"The gods?" Santorina asked.

Erista said, "My father has always claimed we had items that belonged to Xenique in our family trove. That's where I took the necklace from. And perhaps..." She looked at Jezebel, hope shining in her eyes. "Perhaps it was always meant to belong to you, J. That's why I gravitated toward it."

Jezebel scoffed, crossing her arms and looking to the Gates, still shining gold beneath the night sky. Something about the Soulguider's words clearly bothered her, but Ophelia frowned and mouthed *later* to me.

"That doesn't explain the gods," I interjected, failing to keep up.

"Sorry," Ophelia said, shaking her head. "We have to start at the beginning to explain."

And Damien's unholy cock, did she weave a story. That this magic of the *fel strella mythos* literally allowed her to raise myths, and she'd used it on a sphinx inside the hall. A sphinx who had once been a guard of Xenique—the Prime Soulguider Warrior—who was not only an Angel but a fucking demigod.

"But this emblem wasn't the hardest to find," Malakai proposed, still cradling Mila in the sand. "Shouldn't it have been if Xenique held that esteem?"

"Not for you," Ophelia corrected, "because you could hear the siren song. One I bet I triggered when I used the mythos magic to wake the sphinx. I bet only you and I would have been able to hear it, making us the only ones who could find the orb. And without Jezzie's necklace," she added, fitting the crescent into the mold, "it's useless."

She pressed down on the pendant.

And golden light erupted like a burning wind. It was feral and uncaged, a being freed after millennia of pounding on its glass enclosure. It speared toward the sky like a pair of wings fluttering and tasting the desert air for the first time.

It wrapped around us, and *everything* felt more possible and powerful as it explored, but it was followed by a weightlessness—like a Spirit floating through the world, untethered.

Finally, after whirling and dipping across the night-bathed dunes, the light seemed to realize it wasn't finding what it sought. And it retreated back into the orb.

"What the fuck was that?" Malakai asked.

"I have no idea." Ophelia's voice was awestruck, but sobered quickly. "There was more the sphinx said, though. She told us the purpose of the Angelcurse."

Everyone froze, the air heavy. As if the eyes of every Angel and god were turned on us now.

"Which is?" I asked.

"To free the Warrior God from the prison the six known gods locked him in."

No one said a damn word, until—

"What in Bant's everlasting fuck?" Barrett blurted.

"My reaction exactly," Jezebel deadpanned.

"There used to be a seventh god," Ophelia explained. "A Warrior God. But the known gods locked him away."

"And you want to *free* this thing?" Lancaster growled, stepping closer.

"I have to." Ophelia's fingers curled around the orb in a desperate grasp, and dammit, I wanted to peel away the pressure on her shoulders. "Jezebel and I have Godsblood as descendants of Xenique. That's what activated the Angelcurse in the first place. And since it merged with Alabath blood—Angelblood—the curse will be active in every Alabath to come. If I don't do this, someone else will have to."

Full of immortal arrogance, Lancaster argued, "Or we destroy the emblems, as my queen wishes, and no one has to."

"The cage is already being pried open!" Ophelia challenged.

"You can't let him free," Lancaster roared, storming toward us. "Are you insane?"

"I'd back off right now, fae," I threatened. "You take one more step toward her, and it won't only be the Revered of the Mystique Warriors you deal with."

Cypherion grunted in agreement.

Lancaster ignored me, sharp stare trained on Ophelia. "Give the emblems to my queen. Allow her to end this."

"She won't be able to!" Ophelia shouted, voice cracking. "Don't you understand? All magic has a loophole. The very balance demands it. The magic trapping the Warrior God is unspooling."

Lancaster blanched. "What do you mean?"

"The Rites, the phoenix, the unsettled magic that sent you here! It's all connected. The gods each had to sacrifice a bit of their power to lock him up, but because Godsblood and Angelblood have permanently united within the Alabath line, it's all unraveling. It's only going to get worse."

Shock fluttered over Lancaster's sharp features. Shock and a tugging, causing him to stumble back. "I have to get to the Queen."

Ophelia's eyes widened. "It's in her bargain with you, isn't it? When she sent you here, she said once you have answers about your magic, you're to return to her?"

Lancaster nodded, teeth gritted. "Once I find the source of our magic's stirring and who is responsible, I am to return with haste."

Good. Now his bargain following Ophelia and I would be relieved for the time being. Hopefully long enough for us to figure out how to get out of placing the emblems in the queen's clutches.

My hand clenched at the thought, and I realized I was still holding the scroll from Mora. Unrolling it, I scanned the Endasi passage again, trying to interpret it as if it was about the future. Though it never outright used the word warrior—even in the ancient language—there were a few repeated phrases that did directly translate. And if those were about warriors...

"Damien's cock..."

Ophelia whirled toward me. "What is it?"

"Power challenges and stifled warriors," I read, the translation not exact, but close. "Magic as mighty as the enemies across seas, gone beginning with the Ascension." My gaze snapped up. "Did the sphinx say anything about warrior power growth?"

"What?" Ophelia asked.

"If this is right, the gods trapped *warrior power* in that prison, as well. It's why our natural speed and strength and senses are stronger than humans but not quite as strong as..."

Every warrior eye turned toward Lancaster. "*Fae,*" Ophelia breathed, and her voice turned venomous. "Is that why Ritalia doesn't want us to do this?"

Lancaster shook his head, but his eyes narrowed skeptically, as if he too was putting together pieces of his queen's motives.

"Don't worry about Her Majesty," Brystin taunted. "She's already on her way."

We all whirled toward where Dax held his leash, the male hunched in the sand.

"*What?*" Ophelia snarled.

Shoulder still bleeding, Brystin grinned. He'd been waiting for this moment. *This* revelation was why he'd shown himself tonight, why he'd toyed with us. "Queen Ritalia knows where the emblems belong."

Ophelia bowed over the male, grabbing him by the collar. "How in the Angels' realm is she on our land?"

"She had some help. Don't trust bargains based on what you see."

Those words hit Ophelia like a boulder—sank my stomach, too—and she demanded, "What is she planning?"

"To make sure you *never* fulfill this curse. That no one can."

Shoving Brystin away, Ophelia spun to face us. "We need to get to the mountains. Now."

CHAPTER SIXTY-SIX
MALAKAI

WE WERE FUCKING *FLYING*.

We had been for a while now, and still, I didn't understand it. The desert soared hundreds of feet below, wisps of clouds around the sphinx's wings on either side of me, and the sunrise teased the tips of the mountains we sped toward.

The sphinx had emerged out of the Gates of Angeldust shortly after Ophelia, Jezebel, and Erista. I'd stared at her dumbfounded for a few minutes—Ophelia had *woken* this mythological creature —before being pushed toward her with Lancaster and Mila while the others broke off toward Sapphire, Zanox, and Dynaxtar, more piling onto the larger khrysaor with Ophelia and Tolek leading on her pegasus.

But I couldn't enjoy any part of this miracle because the woman I loved was still unconscious in my arms.

"Come on, Mila," I whispered, gently turning her face to me. Her lips and eyelids were tinged blue, her usually-tan skin icy.

"She'll wake," Lancaster grumbled from behind me.

We coasted over a pocket of air, my stomach dipping. I tightened my thighs around the sphinx's sides, bracing my free hand against her lion's body, and tossed a quick glance over my shoulder. "She'd better."

"I could feel the poison leaving her," the fae said over the roaring wind. "It was wound very deep thanks to that injury. It will take time for it to fully seep back into the land."

Mila's lips parted on small breaths, each one fueling my crazed hope.

"How could you *feel* it?"

"My healing is not a trained skill as your human friend's. I was gifted with a very strong type of magic." Lancaster's words were tight. "Therefore, I can feel the effects of it. Unlike even your Bodymelders, who must manipulate their ingredients and the body rather than fall in tune with it. It is a slight nuance to one who does not practice, but an imperative one."

I'd have to take his word for it, despite the fact that I didn't trust this fucker.

But relief loosened a knot in my chest when the majestic voice of the sphinx carried on the air, "He is right, warrior." Her words rumbled through her body beneath us—as large as Dynaxtar's.

"How can you know?" I asked. Mila's chest rose and fell, pale morning sun bathing her profile and highlighting the dried crimson staining her hair.

The sphinx only laughed in response.

Another time, I would have pushed her to answer. Now, though, I narrowed my eyes on the mountains looming ever closer, and held Mila tighter.

Come on, Mila. You promised me your tomorrows.

We followed Sapphire at the helm of our flying party, toward the wide mouth of a cave carved high into the mountains, her white wings reflecting the breaking dawn. She swooped in, Zanox and Dynaxtar on her tail.

"Do you have any idea what your queen is up to?" I asked Lancaster.

The only reason I hadn't insisted we impale him with a cypher stake before this leg of our journey was because Mila might need his healing. He, Mora, and Brystin had been split among our party, though, the other fae each on one of the khrysaor.

"No," Lancaster clipped, and if I wasn't mistaken, there was a tinge of distrust to his voice.

"She wants the emblems," I led as the dark tunnel engulfed us and we kissed the fresh breezes goodbye. We both stiffened against the sudden shift, the air thick with the scent of damp stone and something I couldn't name.

"She does," he agreed after a tense moment.

"And beyond not wanting this supposed Warrior God to be freed, do you know why she would want them? What she could do with them?"

Lancaster scoffed. "Is not wanting to free a tyrant not reason enough?"

Was the god a tyrant? Or was Ritalia?

"Answering a question with a question to avoid the truth," I pointed out. A chill whipped through the tunnel as we dipped and rose with each powerful flap of the sphinx's wings. It was colder within these mountains than I remembered.

"You're familiar with the tactic?" Lancaster asked.

"You admit you're evading something?" I almost smirked at his resounding silence. "Answer this—do you know what her plan is here? What we need to look out for?"

I wasn't stupid enough to think he would admit it to me, direct orders from his queen or not. We were warriors—the fae's enemies for centuries.

And yet—

"I do not."

A chill that had nothing to do with the mountains speared through me. Because Lancaster's tone was graver than ever at the confession that his queen withheld her plans from him.

"And you trust her decisions?"

He was silent for a long moment, the beating of wings filling the cavernous tunnels we swept through. "She placed rules on my sister's life that have caused her a great deal of pain, and she took more than I can name from me. I have felt the ill will of bargains that reign through the generations and will do what is in my power to guide hands to unravel them."

I dug through his masked words.

Lancaster and Mora had suffered from bargains *that reign through the generations*. Certain fae magic—goddess gifts—were said to cause hereditary bargains. And Lancaster was unable to speak of certain depths and origins of his magic...

Exactly how powerful *was* Lancaster?

The male had used Ophelia's and Tolek's bargains twice. Recently, to save their lives in the catacombs. And before that, to force us to answer to Ritalia, which was likely the queen's doing with her power over him as her hunter.

The question stood, was it the bloody fae queen moving pieces around her board here?

I thought of the one queen we'd faced before, and how deep her desperation ran. How twisted her motives and methods became. As Sapphire's graceful body arced over a stone bridge and swept back down—white coat gleaming even in this shadowed network of tunnel—one thing was blatantly obvious. We would need to be prepared for all manners of brutality from the queen of bloodshed.

I swore it internally, tightening my thighs around the sphinx as she ducked beneath the bridge. I was about to warn Lancaster that we'd do whatever it took, would show no mercy for fae on warrior land, when a strangled whinny pierced the air.

"Aoiflyn's tits!" Lancaster swore.

And Sapphire was careening toward the floor, an arrow through her wing.

CHAPTER SIXTY-SEVEN
OPHELIA

SAPPHIRE WAS FALLING, CRIMSON STREAKING THE AIR from her wing, and my heart sank to the bottom of my stomach.

"They fucking shot her!" I yelled, voice tearing through the wind. My hand locked around Tolek's wrist at my waist as we careened toward the rocky floor.

Sapphire's pain shot through my body like it was my own, her agonized cry ripping out a piece of my spirit. The gap flooded with rage.

Tolek shouted back, "*Who?*"

I didn't need to answer. We both knew who.

Tolek's arms tightened around me as the ground loomed closer.

"Catch yourself, girl!" I yelled to my horse. And, not wanting her to worry about saving us in the landing, Tolek and I dove as Sapphire's hooves clattered against stone. We rolled across rock, my skin scraping and stinging, but that didn't matter. In the mountains, a surface level wound would heal in minutes.

I jumped up, Tolek covering my back and scanning the ceiling-less cavern as I raced toward my pegasus, tossing an orb of Angel-light in the air to see by. In its golden glow, Zanox, Dynaxtar, and the sphinx landed with echoing booms.

One of Sapphire's wings draped across the ground, her beautiful feathers stained a deadly red, and an onyx arrow pierced the tip.

Looking into her eye I whispered, "I'm going to fix it, Sapphire. I promise. I'm going to make it feel better. But it might hurt for a moment first."

She blinked, not even making a sound, like she understood what I meant.

"Need help?" Rina asked, appearing at my side, her wrist wrapped and cradled against her chest. The rest of the group surrounded us, weapons drawn and waiting for the attackers to expose themselves.

"Keep her calm," I said. My heart pounded against my bones, hands threatening to shake, but with precise, quick movements, I tugged the arrow free and sent a burst of healing Angellight into Sapphire's wing. She jerked, but Rina held her face, whispering soothing sounds.

The gold tunneled into my pegasus even faster than it had Mora. Closing my eyes, I felt down into that source and tugged each of the seven threads, spinning a web through Sapphire's damaged wing. It stitched back together beneath my fingers, each slowed drop of blood siphoning off my panic.

"I apologize for that," a clear, commanding voice rang out. "But we could not let you go any further."

I whirled, drawing my sword, and met the shrewd, remorseless eyes of the fae queen, her form emerging from the rocky cavern wall as her glamour slowly peeled away.

"Ritalia," I growled. Stepping in front of the others, my panic solidified into iron fury. "A simple hello would have done fine."

She materialized entirely, her full gold gown out of place, the rubies of her rose diadem gleaming as red as Sapphire's blood in the shimmering Angellight. Her locks were coiled atop her head, her hands were folded primly in front of her. No amount of fae magic could convince me she fired that shot herself.

And as I watched the final trickles of her glamour fall, I thought of how Brystin had mentioned her *facade* and realized how she'd pulled this off.

"Is it truly you this time?" I spat. Tolek and Cypherion flanked me, the latter scanning the cavern and shifting in front of Vale.

"Clever warrior queen," Ritalia cooed. "You finally realized your mistake."

I scoffed. "Too late, it appears. I will be sure to include no glamours in my next bargain." With Starfire, I gestured to Mora. "It was her wasn't it? That day we made the bargain, Mora glamoured another fae of your court to look like you and strike the deal with me. And when Cypherion arrived, in all of our panic, you took her place to tell us to leave immediately."

Brystin's warning against trusting based on *what we see* echoed through my memory.

I went on, "Whoever took your place was very careful to only strike deals with the word *I*. And that's why I had to drink something to seal it, right? It was *your* magic entwined in that cup, so I was beholden to you, but only her words upheld the fae end."

"Very observant," Ritalia complemented.

It was as crafty as the fae had always been rumored. Loopholes in bargains be damned, they'd used magic against us.

I gripped Starfire's hilt tighter. "Where are the rest of your party? Will they drop their glamours, or will you fight us like cowards?"

"Who said we're here to fight?" the queen challenged. "Let us resolve this mess peacefully, Revered."

"Perhaps that was possible before you *impaled* my *horse*—"

"I believe you mean pegasus," she interrupted. "It seems you've kept many secrets, Child Kissed by Angels."

I wasn't naive enough to believe this was the first she'd heard of the woken myths, but I didn't give in to that game.

"And it seems you've told many half-truths, Bloodthirsty Queen." I assessed the air around her, but not so much as a flicker exposed how many guards she'd brought.

A cruel smile that reminded me so much of Kakias's—but with less deranged motive—broke across Ritalia's lips. And from the stone wall beside her, a second form emerged. With a wolf limping at his side.

"*Father?*" Celissia's accusatory tone sliced through the theater as Barrett blurted in a panic, "*Rebel!*"

"Fucking Angels," slipped from Malakai's lips behind me, an unconscious Mila protected behind the khrysaor.

"Hello, Celissia," Nassik said, the picture of calm. Rebel bared his teeth in a vicious growl toward the councilman. Nassik's answering flinch was satisfying.

"I knew you were a snake," Barrett insisted, voice venomous. "I knew you were slithering through my own home, plotting against *me* and my appointment, but this? And what did you do to Rebel?" At his name, the wolf looked toward his prince, adoration in those large eyes.

"He is fine," Nassik drawled. "A clumsy pup."

Behind the Engrossians, hands still tied and held in Dax's white-knuckled grip, Brystin chuckled. "I warned you."

"Did you now?" Ritalia snapped, voice the high cruelty of a ruler used to being obeyed.

Brystin shrugged, unfazed. "Only toyed with them a bit, Your Majesty."

And Ritalia smiled, long, sharp canines on display. "Excellent work." Her gaze shifted to Lancaster and Mora, to their very unbound wrists. To how Lancaster stood amid our group, and how Mora remained beside Dynaxtar.

In one swoop, Queen Ritalia catalogued every detail of the scene, and her lips twisted into a sneer, eyes flaming. "I see you two have made yourselves comfortable. What would your mother say?"

Their mother?

Both fae stood straighter, Lancaster's hands clenching at his sides. "We've done what was asked. We've kept an eye on the cursed warrior"—he jerked his head toward me—"and on the one who bears the name of the pro—"

"I understand what I asked!" Ritalia snapped. "What I don't recall is ordering you to become so...familiar with the warriors. Or the human." Her sharp stare cut to Santorina. "Though, Queen of Bounties, you seem to have done a poor job honoring your heritage."

"I claim no heritage that has any entanglement with your kind," Rina condemned.

The bloodletting queen smiled. "We do not choose our path, Queen of Bounties. It is written for us."

"A rather sorry excuse for the ruin you have brought upon the centuries."

"Much like you," Ritalia said, unbothered, "I have not had a choice in all matters of my hand. Let's hope you do not learn how that feels."

Santorina wasn't budging.

"What are you doing here?" I demanded, taking another step forward to form a barrier between my friends and the queen.

Barrett stepped beside me. Two clan rulers against a threat. "What are you doing with *him*?" He meant Nassik, but Barrett only had eyes for his wolf beside the advisor. So much larger than when I last saw the pup, Rebel sat with one gangly paw slightly elevated.

Ire twisted through me—radiated from Barrett, too—but I inhaled and tried to steady myself before the queen. To not be caught off guard again.

When Brystin showed up, Mora said that Ritalia would only adjust her plans for extreme circumstances, that the queen had learned to be patient over the centuries.

Perhaps her circumstances hadn't changed, but her opportunities had.

"You invited her to Gallantia, didn't you?" I accused Nassik. "Which one of you contacted the other?"

"Nassik wrote to me." That betrayal sank like a rock through our group. "He offered me passage through your land, and thanks to rumors from *your* ancestor, Revered—thanks to the letters he wrote to the fae asking for aid with the very curse you bare—I knew of this spot within the mountains."

Annellius had...asked the fae to help? Clearly, those rulers hadn't answered as Ritalia did. They hadn't appeased whatever plea he sent, so he re-hid the emblems instead, to become a problem for a future Alabath.

The inferno in my gut roared.

"And you claim you want to help us now?" I asked.

Ritalia nodded, but before she could answer, Celissia's voice sliced through the cavern. "How could you, Father?" Her sharp stare narrowed. "These are our people!" She pointed at Barrett. "*He* is our king!"

"He may be your friend, but that does not mean he is fit to rule."

"He's more fit than his mother ever was! And the kings before her." Nassik blanched—whether at his daughter's tone or her knowledge, it wasn't clear. "Yes, father, I know the histories. I was not sipping tea all day in the citadel for the past decade."

Nassik's eyes narrowed. "How much did you learn?"

"I learned of all the great Engrossian battles and who led them—how the dynasties crumbled. I studied the most innovative healing practices and found I had quite an affinity for them."

"Did you now?" Nassik asked, voice tight.

"I did." Celissia stood taller, strength radiating from her as she stepped in front of Barrett. "And because it is so unusual for our clan to take to healing as well as I did, my tutor helped me delve into the family line. We thought perhaps there was Bodymelder blood somewhere generations ago."

Nassik scoffed. "Must be a distant relative."

"Don't play dumb, Father." Her eyes flashed to Ritalia, then back. "You've already proven that you are; you don't need to act it on this account as well."

"Celissia!" he blubbered.

But Barrett tore his eyes from his wolf and stood beside his queen-to-be. Celissia nodded at him, and Barrett declared to the room. "Celissia's healing practice is not aided by Bodymelder blood. It is sorcia."

"*Sorcia?*" I gasped. Even Ritalia's eyes widened in surprise. Sorcia bloodlines hardly ever escaped their northern isles.

"That's why you were so advanced," Santorina echoed. "Your healing was so fluid, like another force at work, and you were able to help Vale come out of her reading in the seeing chamber when no one else could." The Starsearcher looked between Rina and Celissia, gratitude in her wide eyes. "It's not just any old, ancient bloodline in your family."

Celissia nodded, then turned a sharp stare back to her father.

"We have *sorcia* blood. And sorceress magic can be very instrumental in healing practices. And he knew all this time."

Barrett knew, as well, the two clear in their united front, as if this was something they'd discussed and planned for. A secret they meant to wield.

"Now you see, dear," Nassik said. "Now you see why, when I learned that the fae were on the outskirts of our continent, poised to challenge such a dark and devastating threat as the Mystique Revered poses, I had to answer the call."

Celissia looked down her nose at the man. "No, I do not *see*."

"What she is trying to do here"—he flung a finger at me—"it will harm everyone on Ambrisk, the gods included. It is no longer only a warrior battle, but one that challenges even our sorcia line."

"The sorcia are secluded," I argued. "They claim no part in any war we have fought."

Nassik glared at me. "This would devastate them regardless."

Celissia asked, "So you chose a line we barely know over the blood of those you have helped rule for nearly a century? Over those you work beside, live beside?" She shook her head, black waves shimmering down her back. "No, Father, I will not be like you. I will not stand for this."

Celissia whipped her head toward me. "Don't listen to them, Ophelia! No matter what poison they spew, finish what we came here for."

Ritalia scoffed. "Enough of your petty arguments! None of you warriors truly understand the threat here." And then, Ritalia's voice snapped like a whip as she said, "Hunter!"

Lancaster's body tensed, a growl slipping through his lips.

"Beautiful," she observed. "Now, enact—"

"*NO!*" And it was Santorina's voice that sliced through the queen's attempt to command a bargain from Lancaster. Santorina's throw of a blade that drowned out the queen's orders. With her injured wrist, her aim was off. The weapon soared inches away from Lancaster's heart and over his shoulder.

The male merely stared at her—at the Queen of Bounties who would have taken his life rather than allow him to call on his bargain—his dark eyes pools of intensity.

The cavern erupted, a dozen fae soldiers bursting from their glamoured positions along the walls and diving toward Rina. Warriors swept before her, meeting their blows. Engrossian axes whirled through the mix. Clashes and scrapes of metal drowned out the bargain order Ritalia tried to enact, and Zanox and Dynaxtar launched into the air above it all.

Rina spun and shoved me toward Sapphire. "Go, Ophelia! Tolek, go with her!"

Tol pulled me toward my pegasus, her blood-streaked wing now blessedly healed thanks to the Angellight.

"We can't leave you!" I yelled.

"Alabath, we have to," Tol argued, shoving me onto Sapphire. "*You* have to!"

"You're the only ones who can finish this!" Celissia added as Tol hopped up behind me.

"We can help here!" I called over a shoulder.

But I met Rina's determined stare. She gave me one tight-lipped nod, the certainty behind it saying more than words ever could.

They would do this. They would defend the mountains against the fae even if it meant their lives, while Tolek and I flew on to finish the task assigned by the Angels.

And it was Rina's and Celissia's shouts of encouragement—a human born to slay fae and an Engrossian with sorcia blood—pounding in my ears in time with Sapphire's hooves as we sped down the tunnel, their voices shouting the hopes of the warriors.

Chapter Sixty-Eight
Tolek

The raging clashes of the battle faded as Sapphire sped toward the theater buried deep in the mountains—the location the sphinx had hinted at.

One Ophelia and I had been to before.

"Do you recognize anything?" Ophelia asked as her pegasus wound through wide tunnels, following either instinct or memory.

"Not a damn thing," I admitted. The last time we were this deep in the mountains was when she'd come to rescue me and we were heading back to Damenal. I'd been riding the high of her appearance while battling off the nightmares the Mindshapers planted in my head. I'd been distracted, all the while only caring about the fact that she was inching closer toward me.

As I wrapped my arms tighter around her waist with the din of fighting melting behind us—and my prayers to the Spirits echoing for our friends' safety—it struck me that the last time we were here, I'd never thought this version of us was a possibility.

Now, those magenta eyes gazed at me over her shoulder, and I shut out the thoughts of the fae and the Angels.

I would do anything for this girl. Slaughter any Angels or gods or queens that tried to touch her and place their heads at her feet. Carve my heart from my chest if it was my blood she needed, bow to any title she claimed, and offer my hand across any realm.

I ducked to kiss Ophelia's shoulder, and for one fucking

moment, I wanted to freeze every eternity right here. Soaring through the mountains on the back of her pegasus, with those eyes on mine.

"Vincienzo?" Ophelia asked.

I blocked out all those desperate wishes and assured her, "Sapphire knows where she's headed."

As the words left my mouth, Sapphire dove. I gripped tighter to Ophelia and tightened my thighs around the pegasus' body, my stomach dropping. She swooped through an opening and landed in the center of a familiar cavern, steps carving the rounded walls on all sides but one.

Dismounting, Ophelia and I both looked up. The ceiling was a dark mass above, impossible to tell it was open as it stretched into the heart of the mountains. "Not what I expected," I commented.

"No," she agreed, shaking her head.

The theater looked exactly as I remembered, though. The seats loomed around the ring, facing the platform at the front, and arched doorways stood on either side.

And on that dais—a crumbling statue curved toward the back of the makeshift stage. A sculpture that resembled seven figures worn to time. Bowing or rising, I couldn't be sure. Few distinct features were visible.

"You're sure about this?" I asked Ophelia quietly, despite the fact that it was only us. Giving her room to confess what I saw buried in those magenta eyes.

"No," she sighed, looking to that platform, then back to me. "I don't think I have a choice, though."

Clasping a hand around the back of her neck, I hauled her to me and kissed her. *I'm with you every step*, I said without voicing it.

And for a moment, something in my gut told me not to let go. To never stop kissing her, for fear that I wouldn't get to again. For fear that everything was about to change.

But we'd learned that the gods and Angels waited for no one.

I stepped back, appreciating her flushed cheeks, and waved a hand at the statue in place of a proper stage. "Be fucking furious," I repeated what I'd said to her outside the Gates of Angeldust.

"To scorching the Angels," she said with a determined nod,

and she faced that figure. The one we studied all those months ago. The one something had called Ophelia toward on our first visit here, the stone blistering her skin upon contact.

My heart beat so ferociously against my ribs, I thought it would bruise. I stood beside Sapphire, a hand on her namesake mane, and buried all my worries, ready to watch Ophelia reclaim everything she was owed.

After everything she'd been dragged through, every fate she'd never asked for thrust upon her shoulders, I was ready to tear the Angels apart for her. To face down a trapped god with nothing but a blade and my bare hands.

As Ophelia took a step forward, I muttered, "Let's wake a god, Alabath."

CHAPTER SIXTY-NINE
OPHELIA

LET'S WAKE A GOD.

Tolek's words rang along my bones as I gripped the pouch containing the emblems at my side. As I turned back to him to pull him down to kiss me one more time, seeking his strength, and ran my fingers through Sapphire's mane.

Her ice-blue eyes bore into mine. "Let's wake a god, girl," I repeated to my pegasus.

Like I had in the other cavern, I summoned a strand of Angellight and sent it whirling above our heads, a chandelier worthy of an Angelic theater ruined by time.

Power buzzed beneath my bones—all the way down to my ravaged spirit—as I approached the front of the theater. The magic of myths brought back to life, of prophecies fulfilled and legends trapped within stone, thundered. My second pulse—the one rioting in my veins since the day I first found Malakai's spear in our clearing back in Palerman—sprang to a gallop.

It was a rhythm in the dark cave, roaring over the breathing of the man I loved and mythical creature woken beside him. Between each frantic beat, the journey that delivered us here played out in my mind.

Malakai and I, young and naive, sharing such innocent, blissful love in our clearing.

Beat, beat, beat.

Crashing to my knees in my parents' kitchen when they told me he had died during the Undertaking.

Beat, beat, beat.

The tundra wolves and the Spirits that challenged me through my own ritual.

Beat, beat, beat.

Finding Malakai...then losing him again.

Beat, beat.

Daminius and the immortality ritual, the toppling buildings and losing my father, hearing of Tolek's injuries and my heart crashing inside my chest. The time his heart stopped beating so briefly, the silence echoing in the infirmary.

Beat, beat.

Magic flooding my veins, Angellight bursting from my skin.

Beat.

Each Angel trial.

Beat.

Kakias's death. Sapphire's downy wings carrying me through the night.

Beat.

The raising of the sphinx.

Beat.

I pressed my hand to the weathered statue, and the beats went silent. And unlike all those months ago—when I'd touched the stone and it had seared my skin—this time, it flourished.

Warmth spread through my palm, seeping out along my veins, and a halo of effervescent white light radiated from the place my flesh met stone.

A welcoming *Hello, Chosen Child, it has been so long,* rang through my ears. My eyes slipped closed, and I breathed in that power, that calling.

With the inhale, the light ebbed. With my exhale, it expanded.

It was an energy unlike anything I'd felt before, the ether of the earth's core burning molten. Through it, I heard every shuffle in the massive cavern, felt every slight breath of Tolek at my back. My muscles tensed with an unusual strength.

It was warrior instinct, warrior *power*—magnified.

"Like the scrolls said," I muttered, gasping as that new sense rolled along my bones.

And if this was only a bead of it, a trigger released since I stood before the site with all emblems on my person, but the curse left unfulfilled... I shivered at the power that must lie within this stone prison. What that could do for the warriors...

My eyes snapped open, the light siphoning back into me, and I grinned over my shoulder at Tolek. "This is it."

The amber in his stare ignited at the confirmation. Could he feel the magic trapped here?

I pulled another bead of Angellight from within me and sent it twining above the statue. "It's all seven Angels," I confirmed.

"They're bowing or rising," he said.

"See this one." I pointed to a figure with its head missing, sliced clean from its neck. I remembered that identifying feature from the last time we were here, though I hadn't understood it then. "I'm certain that's Thorn."

Tolek swallowed. "He lost his head. Like a crown had ravaged his mind."

"And this here," I continued, running a hand over the deep moss covering only one Angel, "is Bant. A symbol of his deal with Kakias." The dark plant crept across the stone like those claiming, inky tendrils. "It's like the shedding of his spirit and the havoc that ensued because of it."

Tolek circled the statue, to where the Angels faced the wall in their crescent-shaped huddle. "Look at his hand."

I followed, pulling my Angellight in closer. "He actually has a hand," I observed.

"All five fingers, perfectly formed where others are worn." Tolek nodded. Sure enough, Bant held one arm out as if reaching for the wall they faced, but that hand remained bare. "Ready to host a ring."

Opening the leather pouch I kept tied to my belt, I willed my hands not to tremble. To not show a bead of fear.

I removed Bant's ring and held it up. The stone set above the axes pulsed in the glow of my Angellight, seeming to sing near its rightful home. As the emerald refracted the light, a piece of me wished Barrett was here. That he could give his permission for what I was about to do with his family heirloom.

But I was the chosen of the Angels, the descendant of a demigod, and the raiser of myths.

The power of this choice laced my blood and bones.

Stepping up to the statue, I searched Bant's form for any indication of what had driven him here. Of what—beyond an ancient, jealous feud with Damien—had dragged that moss along his skin. Weren't Angels supposed to be incapable of such feelings? Of trivial, mortal emotions?

Yet here Bant was, the features of his expression worn over time, but the foliage creeping along his facade symbol enough.

I stretched onto my toes, reaching high to match the Angel's massive form, and slipped that ring upon his finger.

And as metal slid around stone, a surge of power bolted through my veins, and the towering walls of the cave shuddered. A second tremor rolled through the land, moving like a slow, thick sludge, and sending me stumbling back into Tol. He caught me with arms around my waist, sheltering us both as small chunks of rock rained from above.

It was like those Barrett had reported during the war—the quakes in the mountains that lined up with each time I used the emblems while hunting them.

But I hadn't even bled on them this time.

The magnitude of that power settled a rock on my chest.

My eyes locked with Tol's as the shaking ceased. He nodded in encouragement.

Next, I took Gaveny's pearl from my pouch, walking along the half-moon of Angel statues.

"That one," Tolek whispered, placing a hand on my hip. I followed his gaze to a rocky figure that was broad and halfway down on one knee, what could have been a bow and arrow aimed at the ceiling.

And right at the head of that weapon, a smooth round notch waited.

Rolling the pearl between my fingers, I relished in that Angelic heat, let it fuel this choice. And I lifted the emblem.

I was about to push the second token home when a familiar cruel voice warned, "Do *not* replace any more emblems, Seraph Child!"

Immediately, my boots hit the ground, and Tolek and I had weapons in our hands. Lancaster stood with his queen, stoic. Not a blade in sight.

"*Why*, Ritalia?" I spat.

"Finishing this task will unleash a horrible plague upon the land."

"A plague for the fae, perhaps," I bit back. "Because in the millennia since the Warrior God has been locked up, he will have seen the atrocious ways *you* fought his people." Sapphire's pained whine echoed through my mind. "How you've mauled his creatures!"

The fortitude of the Engrossian emblem sliding home heated my blood, the memory of the tremors racking the earth forging my strength. "I have felt the power the god promises his warriors. It is equal to the fae—perhaps more than. And why should we be forced beneath you any longer? Why should we be at the behest of your stronger magic?"

"Because there is a reason he was sealed away!"

"Jealousy!" I roared. "The known gods were afraid of what the power he was amassing meant for *them*."

"And the things he wished to do with it," Ritalia clipped. And there was a certain desperation in her tone that stalled me. Something I'd never heard from her before. "I do not know every detail —no one does. There is a prophecy passed from fae royal to fae royal, one that threatened of a warrior who would bleed and unleash a plague, but we have never known of the warrior and have never been able to speak in depth of it. Not until your ancestor shared what he suspected, but even he could not share everything."

The queen took one step closer, continuing, "And I have been using my unique power to search for the next and uncover why this curse is twisting our magic with it. It is why I sent my hunter here. But remember what your ancestor chose. What he turned his back on, Child Kissed by Angels."

I looked over Ritalia—at the tendrils of her disheveled hair coming lose, at the thin scratch someone had struck on her cheek —and considered everything she *wasn't* saying.

The fae were our enemies; I'd been taught that since birth. Give them a sliver of an opening, and they'd raze the entirety of Gallantia. We couldn't trust Ritalia, not only with the power locked inside the emblems, but with the interest of the warriors.

But...Annellius *was* a warrior. And he had seen something in this curse so horrid, he couldn't find it in him to complete the task. He'd *asked the fae for help* after discovering what the emblems were for. *After* consuming the Godsblood and unlocking the ability to command unknown power.

Gaveny's pearl beat in my hand. I clenched my fingers around the smooth glass.

What could be so wicked that Annellius deemed it worse than death?

He was a coward.

The Angelcurse had not been resolved, it had only stopped being his problem. He'd passed the damn thing on to me, all these centuries later.

And if I didn't do this, if I didn't return these emblems to the statues and spill my own blood, that chain would continue. Jezebel's tawny eyes flashed through my mind. If I followed Annellius's footsteps, she'd bare the curse next. A girl who had already been handed untold depths of magic, who didn't deserve this pressure on her life.

And after her, it would go on to any Alabath children I bore, if I didn't die before that time. A mix of Godsblood and Angelblood —something so blessed and so cursed all in one.

I ran my thumb across the glassy edge of Gaveny's pearl. Watched Angellight reflect off the smooth surface. Behind me, Tolek awaited my decision. And across the cavern, Ritalia's stare burned into me.

I couldn't hand this task on to anyone else. If I refused—well, the world was unraveling around us. The magic was poised to burst, to take the seas and the skies.

Remember what your ancestor chose. It wasn't noble, what he had done. It was greedy.

I couldn't be as selfish as Annellius.

My gaze lifted to Ritalia again. Was she a foe...or a possible ally? A chance that could get the emblems far, far away from everyone I loved? From our continent?

But while that would be a relief of this responsibility, I couldn't take it.

Desperation clawed at my chest. *Do it*, that selfish part of my mind screamed. Assuage yourself of this damn prophecy, banish this curse.

Deep down, though, it was never an option. Not one I'd take. Because though I fought fate at every turn—though I knew I could condemn the Angels—I couldn't force the pressure of the Angel-curse off my shoulders.

The queen must have detected it, the waver in my mind. The slight, instinctual twitch of a step back toward Gaveny's statue.

Because with a sharp demand, she shouted, "Hunter!"

"*No.*" I spun, her words slicing through the cavern as I jammed the pearl of the Angel into his stony arrow and the tide of shimmering, sea-faring power washed through the cavern, abundant and roaring.

But Ritalia continued despite the rocking of the ground, like a determined boat caught on a stormy sea. As I spun back to her with the power of warriors crashing through me, the queen shouted to Lancaster, "Call in your favor."

And I was pulling Xenique's orb from my pouch as Lancaster said through gritted teeth, "Ophelia Alabath." Unwillingly, I froze. "I call in my third owed debt. I demand you stop replacing the emblems into their Angel statues." His throat bobbed on a swallow. "If you fail to comply, Tolek Vincienzo will die."

CHAPTER SEVENTY
OPHELIA

EVERY FACET OF MY BODY FROZE.

Every nerve and drop of cursed blood.

"*No,*" I gasped, barely audible, eyes meeting Tolek's. There was an answer in those chocolate depths. One I didn't want to unravel because to do so would rip my heart right from my chest.

"No!" I shouted to him.

"Ophelia—"

"Don't you dare say another word, Tolek Vincienzo," I swore, rushing toward him and fisting his leathers. "It's not worth it. *Nothing* is worth you."

"I told you I'd love you in any realm, Ophelia. That if we were somehow separated on this one, I'd find you. *Infinitely* doesn't end here."

"It doesn't end anywhere," I countered.

He gave me a sad smile. "But some things might have to."

Angels, my chest was caving in. My lungs tight and breaths short.

Did I ever have a choice in any of this? Or was every day of my life—every moment I spent learning to let myself love him—another game of the deities? That used feeling crawled along my bones like poison ivy, strangling my throat until my eyes stung.

"Ophelia," Tol coaxed, but all I could do was shake my head and blink back the tears.

I hated this. Hated that he thought this was fair—that he was willing to give up this life together because of the twisted bargains of our past. Hated more than anything the emblems weighing down our lives, dragging us to consider such dark depths.

I never had a say in any of this.

At our silence, Ritalia hummed with satisfied glee. "Now, hand over the remaining tokens, Revered."

My eyes wouldn't move from Tol's, though. Couldn't. Not with the weight of his life hanging over us. I could only watch him as he took deep breaths, telling me to mimic them.

There is a solution, I told myself with one breath.

There has to be, I encouraged on the second, timing my inhales to the rise and fall of his own chest.

I will not be their toy.

I was so lost in trying to find a way around this, I didn't see the sphinx as she swept through the open ceiling and landed upon the seats rimming the theater.

And still, I didn't look at her.

Just chocolate eyes and the saddest smirk I'd ever seen as he took a step toward me, his chest nearly brushing mine now, and he removed my hand from his leathers, cradling it between his own in some sort of quiet sympathy because Tolek Vincienzo was once again willing to give everything for me.

The warmth of his skin—he would lose that if I didn't find a way out of this. His heart wouldn't beat and his eyes wouldn't shine. Tolek would never say my name again unless I gathered myself and fought.

As my breathing steadied, my other hand—the one holding the orb—brushed the dagger at my thigh.

But one voice pierced through the blood rushing in my ears. Malakai called, "Don't give them to her, Ophelia!"

Enraged, I whipped my head toward him as he dropped off the sphinx's back with Mila in his arms. Cypherion, Vale, and Lyria were behind him.

"Don't do it!" Malakai repeated, eyes flashing from Lancaster to me and Tolek, and—he seemed so sure. His piercing green stare trying to tell me something as he set Mila down atop the seats and straightened.

The Bind pulsed beneath my elbow, but dammit, I didn't know what it *meant*.

Didn't give an Angel's breath either. I stepped protectively in front of Tolek.

"What are you *talking about*?" I shouted.

"Trust me!" And then he raced down the steps, sword singing as he and our friends dove to intercept the fae soldiers barely catching up, pouring in from the archway behind their queen, their shouts melting into the guttural, agonized roar in my mind.

The clashing of metal resounded. Zanox and Dynaxtar swooped in with our remaining party, the former dropping onto the top three rows of seats with a deep rumble.

And the presences—of the khrysaor, of my friends, of the man still staring intently at me and gripping my hand—were a different kind of armor amid this horror.

"Give the emblems over!" Ritalia ordered above the fray.

But Tolek's faint "Ophelia" was so much louder.

And now that our friends covered our backs, he was tugging me toward the statue.

With every step, his breath tightened, a bargained noose slipping around his neck. It was low—barely perceptible—but it tore at me. So much so that I was lifeless, helpless, and Tol guided my reluctant hands to lift Xenique's orb.

Cupped them ahead of the Angel's waiting palms, held before her chest.

Moon-white glass swirled with visions. And in it, my life without Tolek played out. He fell to Lancaster's bargain. I became empty, the footsteps that should shadow mine only a spirit. The halls of the Revered's Palace echoed with silence. The mountains were void of life and promise and beauty.

Reality snapped back into me, and I reared away from the statue, spinning toward Tol. "I won't do this!"

"You have to, *apeagna*. I'll be okay," he swore.

"But *I* won't be." My heart—it was cracking open in my chest.

A sharp and splitting pain. Tolek would take it with him if Lancaster's bargain struck true.

"And that hurts me more than anything else." He dragged a thumb across my cheek catching tears I didn't realize were falling. "I may not have much faith in the Angels anymore, but I have faith in us. In this. I make risky bets every day, and I never lose."

I shook my head as a promise sparked in my chest. My glassy glare shot to Lancaster and Ritalia—I swore vengeance against them for even forcing this choice upon us. And when I met the queen's stare, the gloating win pronounced in them, that desire burned like the hottest Angellight within me.

"*No*," I growled. "I've fought long enough—lost enough, Tolek! I won't have another thing taken."

And instead of whirling toward Xenique and placing the orb in her waiting hands, I drew Angelborn.

Ritalia's eyes widened as I pulled back my arm and she realized what I was about to do—where the force of my fury was going to land. With some ability I didn't understand, the bloody queen of the fae waved a hand, and my spear was ripped from my person. In shock, I pulled Starfire, but she went sailing, too.

Then, before my eyes, Ritalia snapped her fingers. And with a smile carved from an ungodly place, she melted Starfire and Angelborn down to a river of silver and gold.

And that cracking of my heart—it became a severance as she took one more thing from me.

A scream wrenched from my throat. I lunged, but strong arms caught my waist.

Starfire.

The last piece I had of my father. The gift he'd given me on my tenth birthday. The *only* sword I'd ever owned. Wiped from the world in the snap of bloodstained fingers, as his life had been taken with a blast.

I cried out for my father, my voice ragged. His loss echoed through me endlessly as my sword liquified before my eyes.

And Angelborn.

Starfire was a weapon that grew *with me*, but Angelborn was the one created *for me*. Malakai had used it, too. That spear—it had been a piece of him and a driving symbol of hope when I'd found it. A sign that he was still alive, an indication that I was right not to give up on him. To fight.

And now, as Starfire's singular gem fell to the swirling stream of molten silver and gold, it was like both weapons pierced my chest. Through bone and beating heart, all the way to their gleaming hilts.

Both parts of me I'd relied on, wiped from existence, their loss as deep as a piece of my own soul. I was a rag doll being pulled between enemies of gods and Angels, and my seams were splitting. Ripped apart as Lancaster's bargain was trying to rip Tolek from me.

The call of the debt had been the striking of a match, and now the fae queen added kindling to the fire in my roaring heart. Fury burned through me, and I heaved in breaths I hadn't even been aware of taking. My knees struck the floor and a warm chest braced my back.

Tears lashed down my cheeks. Tears for the piece of my father I'd lost, tears for Tolek, and wrathful tears for every wretched god and Angel and queen who tried to control me. Tears for the girl I'd been who'd never really had command over her life at all. Who had only been collecting these pieces—

These pieces that meant so much to her, only for higher powers to continue to tear them away. Love after love, heartbreak after heartbreak.

"I'm so sorry," Tolek muttered in my ear. His words were a gasp, a sign of Lancaster's bargain slowly taking effect.

And that spurred the tears on faster. Turned every breath guttural as fire raged within me.

Tol didn't say it was okay like he usually did when I was upset. He knew that to take a warrior's weapons was to extinguish the light in their spirit, and he knew better than anyone how this particular dousing would drown me. How they'd all been crashing down on me for months.

Luckily for us, I'd burn from those depths before I allowed them to take him. I'd burn as bright as the fucking Angels.

"Keep fighting, Ophelia," Tolek repeated. "Show her her mistake." And it was his fading voice over that last word that made me find my own.

Through my sobs, I roared, "Stay true!"

And every warrior around me called out in answer.

CHAPTER SEVENTY-ONE
CYPHERION

OPHELIA'S CRY WAS MADE OF PURE FURY, AND I answered the call. Scythe in hand, I was guarding her before I could think.

I lunged in front of Ophelia as she gathered herself on the ground, the fae guards already advancing. The Revered's teeth were bared, her eyes sharp as daggers on Ritalia. Tolek towered over her, muttering something even as he pulled his sword to defend her. He seemed steady, despite Lancaster's bargain. Winded and enraged, but alive.

As I swung my scythe behind a fae soldier's knees and drove the blade into his gut, I couldn't imagine the pain ripping through Ophelia. Not as she watched the molten silver and gold swirling before her.

I gripped my own sacred weapon tighter and continued to swing with the might of the man who had earned it.

As I took on fae after fae, defending the warriors around me, I channeled the father I didn't know—the one who earned a blade worthy of the Angels—and I picked off the enemies, my eyes on their queen.

Whatever power Ritalia had used to melt Ophelia's weapons, she didn't seem able to do it again. Our side surged toward her guard. Nassik sank into the shadows behind the remaining Engrossian soldiers.

The queen pulled a delicate dagger from her hip, surveying the fight unspooling before her.

One towering fae soldier swung an impossibly sharp, shining sword at me. I pivoted at the last moment, dodging a nasty slice to my ribs. *Fuck*, they moved like water, evading our blades as if we were simple rocks parting a current.

I brought my scythe down aiming to hook through his neck, but his long sword met the shaft. The impact jarred along my bones. He grinned down at me, canines shining.

"I've been waiting centuries to make you warriors bleed," he hissed.

"Have you?" I taunted, taking a step back to lure him in. To get his guard to falter. "Keep dreaming." At the last moment, I dropped my scythe, diving away from his blade. Coming up at his side, I swung out, fist meeting his jaw.

It was like steel against my bones, but he staggered.

And while he was recovering from the impact, I took the chance to circle him, unsheathing a small knife from the band at my chest and slicing across his throat.

"Sounds like he needs to dream bigger," Tolek said, sliding into his rightful place at my side and meeting another guard. His chest heaved with the effort, his skin a bit pale as he sucked down a breath.

Where the fuck was Lancaster with that damn bargain? I'd kill him and end it.

"Or be a bit more original, at least," Malakai added with a grunt as his own weapon caught a third fae.

I huffed a laugh. "A small-minded people, apparently."

Out of the corner of my eye, silver glinted. I spun as a fae blade was dropping toward my shoulder—

But a wall of silver-blue light exploded between us, melting the blade and freezing the fae as he collided with it.

Jezebel stood halfway up the steps, Zanox protecting her. She tossed shields of that myth-born death magic before our side of the fight where our speed wasn't a match for the fae.

I nodded in thanks, then dove back to the enemy she'd

blocked. Jezebel's magic didn't kill him. It did shock him, though. Enough for me to slide my sword into his heart.

He crashed to his knees, and I kicked him off my blade, thick crimson dripping to the cave floor.

Amid the fighting, my eyes flashed to Vale. She was braced with her short sword, a matching set of triple-bladed daggers at her hip. Her eyes glazed over for a moment. She was reading every move to know where to jump in next. A starsdamned genius, my Stargirl. I adjusted to stand in front of her while she was vulnerable.

Her magic had been so strong tonight. She told me before the Gates—after that Ascension reading and the Rites—she wanted to try to read more of the Angels, but right now, we needed her present here.

It only took her a split second to gather each reading her Fates were passing to her. Then, with a grimace, she charged at one of the fae.

And while Vale mainly used magic as her weapon, she was not inept with a blade. Far from it. She'd told us that she'd trained at the temple—that every acolyte was required to be sharp in every way that counted—but cursed fucking Angels, I hadn't expected the swiftness and accuracy to be so enhanced since the last time I'd seen her fight.

It was like with those pieces Titus had stolen, she'd taken the gaping edges around the hollows and honed them. Turned them into a hardened form of what she was before and swore to allow no one to take from her ever again.

In the blink of an eye, she launched a dagger at a fae across the cavern with his eyes set on Santorina. The three blades were a blur of silver as they spun, slicing across his neck.

"That's my fucking Stargirl!" I shouted, fighting to keep my attention on the fae advancing on me.

Barrett, Dax, and Celissia were weaving their way among the pointed-eared bastards with non-lethal blows. Enough to give the rest of us an opening, but their true target was clear: Nassik and the three Engrossian soldiers shielding him.

Over the chaos of finding my next opponent, I called to Malakai, "Mila?"

THE MYTHS OF OPHELIA

"Khrysaor" was all he grunted in response as he parried his attacker. One glance up to the theater seats showed a still-unconscious figure beneath Dynaxtar's wing.

The sphinx perched at the highest step, watching ruin unfold below, but Sapphire...

"Cursed Spirits," I murmured.

The pegasus flared her wings, no longer bleeding, and pranced impatiently in place. She may be a mythical creature, but she bore the heart of a warrior horse. And her distressed eyes were on her rider.

"Ritalia!" Ophelia shouted over the clashing of weapons. "If you want to rain blood on our soil, let it be your own." Ophelia pulled her lone remaining dagger—the one I'd gifted her for her birthday last year—from her thigh.

She'd take the queen on with nothing more than that. And as her Second, I'd hold the line.

"Tolek, Malakai," I barked, "flank me! Form a perimeter."

They fell into line, Tolek determined despite Lancaster's bargain. He'd guard Ophelia to his dying breath.

"Lyria," I instructed, "on your brother's side. Vale, Santorina, and Erista, in line."

At the edge of the skirmish, Lancaster and Mora waited, tension vibrating through their bodies. The former's eyes were trained on Tolek, watching for...I didn't know. A sign of the death he promised? A fatal string to pull?

Tolek continued to fight, panting through every strike. Nothing would get him to drop his guard in front of Ophelia—not even magic.

"Jezebel!" I spared a glance to the younger Alabath, but it wasn't necessary. She dove into the spirits of those falling around us. There were no myths here for her to slay, but Jez was manifesting shields of silver-blue light before us, blocking close calls. She threw one behind Erista as a fae charged at her back, and the male's body froze as he hit it. Like the deathly power Jezebel wielded was enough to pause his magic.

Ritalia called back to Ophelia, "You are making fatal mistakes, Revered."

A female fae nearly taller than I was charged at me. Swinging my scythe to my back, I pulled my sword and caught her blow. The metal sang as it met again, but I planted my feet and braced my arms to absorb the force.

"Why?" Ophelia spat, pacing behind us like a caged nemaxese, no doubt searching for a place to infiltrate the solid fae guard. "What is so wrong about warriors claiming our full power? About freeing a deity who is wrongfully imprisoned?"

I blocked another blow, leaning into the female. She staggered back a step, and I didn't hesitate, ripping a knife from my side and jamming it in her neck.

Around me, Tolek and Malakai each brought down another guard.

I didn't allow myself to feel guilty for the faeries falling. Their spirits would never find rest thanks to the cypher trees I was named for, but they chose that risk in attacking us. Ritalia condemned them to that fate in burning Ophelia's weapons.

"You cannot say he's wrongfully imprisoned without knowing the full story!" Ritalia shouted back, her voice strangled.

"Then, tell me!" Ophelia pleaded, tear tracks still shining on her cheeks. "Tell me the truth so I can decide if this must be done. Because from where I stand, there is *no other option*."

"I *cannot*."

Because the fae Goddess's part of the magic that forged the prison kept everyone from speaking of it.

Behind Ritalia, Dax took down two Engrossians with an ax each, leaving only one between them and Nassik.

"Why would your Goddess put such restrictions on you if not for her own advantage?" Ophelia growled, clearly frustrated, but that beseeching undertone layered her words. "Why wouldn't she want you to be able to tell us whatever it is that might convince us not to free the Warrior God? Why are we constantly left in the fucking dark, as toys and playthings for the deities?"

And that was the root of the frustration for all of us, but Ophelia especially. The answers we hadn't been given, the lies we'd been fed. Her strings had been pulled again and again, taking away any choice she had.

My blades met the advancing fae, our line inching back under their strength. The stone behind us was looming uncomfortably close. Would they demolish the statue if given the chance?

Fuck those gods for condemning us to this, I thought as I met fae swords repeatedly.

If they hadn't locked away the Warrior God and the Angels, perhaps we'd be on level footing in this fight. Perhaps the feuds wouldn't even be happening if power was equal across Ambrisk.

I'd never considered that deities could feel something as mortal as fear, but it was likely what drove their decision. And in that, the known gods sentenced the fae and warriors alike to a life of brutal warfare and prejudices.

I ducked around my opponent and jammed a knife between his ribs.

It was almost ironic, I thought, as I feinted against the next guard, that the Angels and gods were supposed to be the beings we prayed to for comfort, and yet they rained nothing but torment upon our lives.

Upon both of the rulers facing off verbally in this theater in the mountains.

And as they hurled their arguments back and forth, weapons ringing between each word, it became clear how this night would end.

With one dead queen or another.

With restless fae spirits roaming Gallantia, and perhaps, if I could get closer to Ritalia, with more than one prophecy fulfilled.

CHAPTER SEVENTY-TWO
MALAKAI

"Why are we constantly left in the fucking dark, as toys and playthings for the deities?" Ophelia had thrown at the queen.

Ritalia was trying so damn hard to tell her something without saying it. To fight through the lock the Fae Goddess put on information about the Warrior God, her mouth opening and closing in a very un-queenlike manner.

As I struck out at another fae blade, Ritalia's voice skimmed the air of the cavern, all the heaviness of her crown instilled in it. "I don't know. Trust the gods, though."

I huffed a laugh at that, ducking a swipe of my enemy's sword and parrying as my heart thudded uncomfortably. *Trust the gods?* The Angels were who we worshipped, and we couldn't even trust them. What were the gods to us?

Ophelia kept one eye on Tolek, worry and fury etched deep in the harsh lines of her face. But the way Lancaster had spoken on the sphinx while we flew over here made me trust him.

She placed rules on my sister's life that have caused her a great deal of pain, and she took more than I can name from me. I have felt the ill will of bargains that reign through the generations, and will do what is in my power to guide hands to unravel them.

And he'd healed Mila tonight. Had stood against Brystin.

The rest of these fae? They could rot with the cypher magic. But perhaps there was more to the words Lancaster had spoken—

One of Ritalia's soldiers swiped at me with a dagger. I dodged, but the fae were everywhere, and they were lightning-quick.

My heart stuttered again, and I stumbled. Something burned behind my ribs, distracting me enough for the soldier to jam the hilt of his dagger below my temple, striking the top of my cheekbone. I bit my tongue at the impact.

"Oh, fuck," I grumbled, spitting blood to the floor.

Cypherion was at the male's back, knife dragging across his throat as my vision spotted.

"He get your head?" Cyph asked over the clash of metal.

I shook out the pain, blinking to steady myself. "Barely. Fuckers have to have better aim," I said, falling back into line.

"Won't help him now," Cyph answered.

A high whinny sounded, and Sapphire swooped down, prancing sharply along fae soldier's unhelmeted heads. Careless, to come here without a hint of armor. To so gravely underestimate warrior potential.

The pegasus' wings turned the blood-streaked scene into a feathered frenzy as she fought with us. I feinted, spinning around my next opponent to get his back to Cypherion, who finished him off with a sword between his ribs.

On the seats, Zanox and Dynaxtar flared their wings as if they'd take off, too. Or open those deadly mouths and emit those white-blue flames I'd seen before. It was only once, during the final battle. The khrysaor had never done it since.

Perhaps it was a power not fully awoken or trained, one that Jezebel's hand resting on Zanox's leg said not to test in such close quarters. I didn't have time to consider it now, though.

Between opponents, I searched for Mila's hidden form.

Still there. Chest rising and falling. Fucking Spirits, whatever was in that water had really infected her to keep her down this long.

I needed to get back to her. Needed up those steps and away from this fucking battle. With a sloppy lunge, I drove my sword into the back of a soldier advancing on Santorina.

"Thanks," Rina breathed as the fae collapsed at her feet.

"Let that Bounty blood kick in," I joked.

She scowled, but we both turned back to the fight.

Or we tried to, but the body of the male I'd just killed swung up, his sword raised. I whirled, ready to strike, but his head sagged—

Jezebel. I spun toward the seats. Her stare narrow, Jez commanded the fallen's spirit with impressive speed. All the way across the cavern until he rammed straight into the lone standing Engrossian soldier, opening up the way to the councilman.

And Dax didn't wait.

The general tossed his prince an ax—wincing with the throw and clutching his scarred gut—and Rebel lunged. The wolf knocked Nassik onto his ass, and Barrett—with a vengeance I rarely saw in the prince—brought the ax down on the council-man's arm, slicing off a hand.

His wail was lost among the fight.

Immediately, I looked for Celissia, but she only glared at her father with a stare that matched Barrett's. There was no love in that look, not from the girl who had been nothing more than a pawn to the man who fathered her.

Welcome to the club.

We were denting their numbers, at least half of the fae on the floor now. Perhaps because we were on our land, so close to the source of the Angels, but luck seemed to be on our side.

I tossed my sword between my hands and jumped back into the fray.

Ophelia was still pacing in front of the statue, Tolek an all-seeing guard before her, his own breaths labored. She and Ritalia lobbied comments across the cavern, each trying to get the other to be honest or see reason.

"I don't want you as my enemy," Ophelia finally shouted. "I don't want to work against you."

"Then listen to me," she demanded, voice laced with the contempt of someone who was used to being obeyed.

"I can't trust you! Don't you understand?" Ophelia shook her head, rolling Xenique's orb in her palm. "I don't *want* you as an enemy, but we tried to work with you—we made a bargain, and you went around it."

The queen tutted. "That is your fault for not being more careful."

"Wrong fucking thing to say," I grunted beneath my breath as I lunged toward my opponent.

"A true ally would not argue whose fault it is," Ophelia yelled.

"What do you know of allies?" Ritalia spat. "Your kind has never."

Ophelia spread her arms wide. "Look around, Ritalia! Everything you see here is an alliance." She gestured to Barrett and Vale, Erista and even Lancaster and Mora. "They are our allies! But I do not think you are."

In light of everything Ophelia said, the queen still retained her cool command, announcing, "A true queen does not stoop to find allies. She collects them like prizes."

To do her bidding, no doubt.

Ritalia switched her approach. "We do not need to be allies, Revered Alabath. We do not need to stand arm in arm on a battlefield. Simply hand over the emblems. Let me remove them from this land where they are so near their locks and take them where no Chosen will ever find them again. I will not walk on your shores for all my rule if you do this."

Ophelia took a deep breath, calm washing over her. "And what about the rest of it? What about the power wrecking our world? The storms and the creatures waking?"

"What of it?"

I ducked around the fae female before me and lured her toward the steps, where Jezebel had another spirit puppet surging forward.

"The land is dying," Ophelia said sadly. "The creatures are mutinous. This is only the beginning of the effects of the godly prison unraveling. How do you propose we fight it?"

Jezzie's fae rammed a blade through the thigh of my own, and they both fell, blood mixing on the rocky floor.

"If we do away with the emblems, the known gods as you call them will bless us," Ritalia said.

Again, I scoffed. So idealistic.

Sparing a glance at Ophelia, that same doubt flashed behind her expression as she studied the emblem in one hand.

And the queen—she saw the warring gleam in Ophelia's eye. Saw that her words hadn't been enough. That not even Lancaster's bargain or melting Ophelia's weapons was going to stop her. It only fueled her, giving her less of a reason to trust Ritalia, and more of a hope to fight our way out of this.

The ancient queen of the fae had overplayed her hand—had created an enemy in Ophelia the moment she instructed her hunter to manipulate Tolek, sealed that fate in melting Starfire and Angelborn before her—and no pretty ideals of bountiful gods could stop a stubborn Alabath.

And the switch in Ritalia's understanding was like a lightning strike, a bolt of realization that drew her arm back.

"No!" Vale shouted as a reading slammed into her, and her head tipped back toward the heavens.

And Ritalia sent her dagger flying across the cavern with lethal precision and speed.

"Alabath!" Tolek warned.

Ophelia's head snapped up, eyes locking on that blade that whistled through the air, poised to strike her heart. Not quickly enough, she tried to lunge away.

But she barely flinched before someone else was there to take the dagger in her stead.

Before that sharpened sliver of silver sank into Lyria Vincienzo's heart, and a small gasp escaped her lips, her hands cupping the hilt against her chest.

Lyria, the Commander of the Mystique armies, our Master of Weapons and Warfare, fell to her knees, one of the very things that had given her her title thrust deep in her chest. Her eyes wide and lips forming a silent *o*.

And Tolek—

Tolek's scream wrenched the air unlike anything I'd ever heard.

CHAPTER SEVENTY-THREE
TOLEK

"*RIA!*"

I dove to my knees, catching my sister as she fell forward.

"Lyria," I begged. It was a broken sound. Not my voice. That wasn't my voice talking, and this wasn't my sister in my lap with a dagger in her chest.

"Lyria...Ria..." I brushed the hair that had slipped from her braid out of her face.

My hands were red.

My hands were red.

Why were they red? They shouldn't be leaving streaks on her cheeks like that. And her eyes shouldn't be so unfocused. That wasn't Lyria. Lyria was a pillar. Lyria was strong. Lyria was—

"Ria, please, please don't." I looked around frantically, and only then realized I was crying. Everything other than my sister's face was blurred. "Someone help! Santorina!" My friend's name sawed through my throat as I turned back to my sister.

A piece of me knew no one could do anything. Fate was in the flutter of Lyria's lashes, in the weak grasp she had on my arm. In the fucking fae dagger lodged in her heart.

I grappled to hold her tighter. "Lyria please," I sobbed. "We have to—we have to get our siblings still. We're going to do that together."

A warm presence wrapped an arm around me. Something I

knew was supposed to be comforting but only made me realize how quickly Lyria was losing that warmth.

Because it was all spilling out over her hand, still cupped around the hilt of the dagger.

There was so much noise around us, but I couldn't remember what any of it meant. None of it mattered, because Lyria was...my sister was...

"We didn't have time!" I yelled. "We said this was *our time*, Lyria! You can't...you can't..." My words became gasps.

Red. Everything was red.

It was all sticky and red. Except her face which paled with every struggling inhale. Each one sounded like they hurt. Each one ripped a hole wide in my chest.

If she had to go, I didn't want her last memory to be painful.

"We got the time we needed," she muttered through cracked lips. "Made amends."

"I didn't want fucking amends," I growled. "I wanted the future."

Someone knelt on her other side, but didn't touch us.

"Don't get what we want." Lyria tried to smile. "It's okay."

I shook my head, my tears falling on her. It was wrong that she was comforting me right now. I should be holding her, telling her it wasn't going to hurt anymore soon, but this was my big sister, and I suddenly felt like the smallest child, before I'd learned to look at her as competition. When all Lyria meant to me was guidance and safety and warmth.

Every memory vanished in that moment. And I was a young boy again, standing alone in a cold, empty house.

"It's not okay!" I burst.

"A warrior's death, Tol."

One at the end of a blade, protecting our cause. It was an honor to most, and maybe I should think it was for Lyria, but centuries from now. Not at twenty-four-years old. Not after surviving her second war. Not like this.

"I knew," she forced out. "The pleasure house. A Soulguider saw this happen. Hinted it was coming soon."

Lyria knew her time was coming. It was why she'd been so

shaken after the brothel. And she still walked into every battle tonight. Into the Gates of Angeldust, where she'd made sure I knew how she felt about her purpose, where she told me her goal of rescuing our siblings, so I could carry it on.

And into this battle, where she threw herself before Ophelia.

"Tell Mila—" A ragged breath. "Tell her she was the best friend I could have asked for. A sister." Another pained inhale. "The reason I kept fighting."

Mila. She was unconscious. She was going to wake to a world where her rock was taken from her.

Unfair. It was so fucking unfair. Out of all the horse shit we'd been thrown, this might be the worst piece of it all.

"I'll tell her," I whispered, voice cracked and ruined. "I promise."

The seconds were closing in now. It was in her shallow breaths. The flowing blood. So much blood.

How the fuck was anyone still moving around us when Lyria wasn't?

I had to...I had to say something. To make these final moments matter as much as all our recent ones had. But words...I couldn't... for once, I didn't have them.

"Ria, I'm sorry." My voice was hollow, but I reached down into the depths of me, dragging up every last sentiment I might regret leaving unsaid. "I'm sorry for all the years we lost. If I could go back, I'd do it all differently, but I can't, and now we're out of time. But I'm so"—my voice broke—"so fucking proud of everything you've accomplished. Of everything you've overcome. You always thought you had to be perfect and couldn't reach it, but the truth is, Ria, you *are* perfect. You're the perfect sister to me and the perfect friend to everyone here. You're the perfect you, and that's all anyone ever needed you to be."

"Tolek," she whispered, so hoarse. So...dying. "You were the purpose, Tolek." She fought for another breath. "Always were."

"Please. Please don't say goodbye, Ria. Don't go." My voice tore on that word. My sister was dying.

Dying.

Dying.

Her eyes flicked over my shoulder, to Ophelia kneeling beside me, the queen forgotten. "Take care of him. And finish this."

Ophelia's voice was barely a cracking whisper. "Forever, Lyria. Thank you."

And then, in my arms, my sister said for the last time, "I love you, baby brother."

My heart shredded, and I embedded the echo of those words into my memory, never to forget how her voice sounded saying them. "I love you."

CHAPTER SEVENTY-FOUR
MALAKAI

THE CAVERN SEEMED QUIETER WITHOUT LYRIA, BUT THE battle didn't stop. Not as Tolek sobbed over her body and they exchanged words. Not as Erista held her hand to guide her spirit to rest. Not as Ophelia ignored Ritalia's echoing barbs and only had focus for Tolek, his head cradled to her chest.

The rest of us had only been still for a moment. One singular second in which that blade sank into Lyria's heart.

And then, as if we were all fueled by the chasm Lyria would leave behind, we fought back with only her wrongful loss on our minds.

I tore through opponents with one goal—getting to Lancaster.

Tell Mila, Lyria's words played in my mind as I struck at each fae, not caring where I hit or if I killed them.

I hadn't heard the commander's message, but my heart sank like a stone in my chest. *Mila*. She was going to wake eventually, was going to find out her best friend was...

All I could see was Mila worriedly chewing her lip as she fretted over how to help Lyria. The nights she'd sat up, wondering if Lyria was sleeping okay or if the horrors of war were plaguing her, too. The joy in her eyes as her friend had returned to her these weeks and they'd walked the path to healing together.

Not everyone made it to the end of that road.

Rage poured through me at the heartbreak that awaited Mila,

but I tightened my hand around the leather grip of my sword. I'd hold her through that grief.

I used the anger to slice down the fae before me. Again and again. Let their blood bathe the chamber until I lost track of how many I'd killed.

Until my heart stuttered through my chest, and the ground trembled again. I whirled—only one thing could cause that.

Ophelia was back at the Angel statues, backing away from the Soulguider. A red-eyed Tolek urged her on from where he still held his sister. One hand clutched his chest as if struggling to draw his next breath, but he roared at her to go—an unusual steel in his voice that solidified my plan.

And as Tolek tracked Ophelia from Xenique's figure to Valyrie's, nothing but cold death lingered in his gaze—no fear at this bargain that could be his end as well, because his sister was already gone, and undiluted hatred filled the space she left behind.

No hint of dread pierced Tolek's facade as Ophelia placed the fated lovers of Valyrie's heart into position in the only statue with a face turned toward the heavens, her tall, slender body carved with long hair drifting to her waist—and a hollow in the center of her chest.

As the heart slipped into place, the earth shook again, a riotous boom like stars crashing in the sky. Shimmering, fated power burst from the statue, and Vale cried out.

It wasn't pained, though. It was a sound of true euphoria as star-laced Angellight washed over us all. And when she opened her eyes, they shone the brightest silver, amplifying the fog that had filled her stare since the Ascension reading.

I used the moment of distraction to spin back to the fight, dodging another opponent with one goal in mind.

Finally reaching the edge of the battle, I gripped Lancaster's tunic and swung him around to face me, hidden in the shadows.

"What the fuck are you doing?" I roared over clashing weapons.

"I'm not even fighting, Mystique!"

"Not the battle!" I jerked my head toward Tolek, and

Lancaster's eyes followed. "I know you're working against your queen. So, what are you doing to him?"

He'd admitted it on the flight to the mountains.

I have felt the ill will of bargains that reign through the generations, and will do what is in my power to guide hands to unravel them.

And when Santorina threw her dagger at him and the initial fight broke out, Lancaster hadn't made a move for any of us. He sank into the background.

"Guard your words, Mystique," the male muttered, brutal stare flashing to where Ritalia screamed at Ophelia.

"I know that demand is a fraud," I whispered harshly, gesturing to where Tolek held his chest.

"I assure you, it is very real. Although, there's been ways to absolve it."

"What do you mean?"

His jaw ticked. Another thing he was not allowed to share.

"I know you're powerful, Lancaster," I muttered. "I read about generational bargains—how they're hereditary when passed from your goddess. I'd bet something of the sort is laced through your blood, as fae magic tends to be passed."

I was willing to bet my life that all of these locks were tied to whatever that magic was. That whatever we'd been prying out of him and his sister went back to the gods.

Again, a muscle feathered in his jaw. I squinted at him, and he forced out, "Some things do repel—"

"Ancient magic," I whispered.

Ancient magic repelled goddess magic. We'd read about that in the books from Ritalia's library. Mora's glamoured phoenix had been nullified by Ophelia's ancient mythos magic—Lancaster's healing didn't work against the enchantment in the corpse bite on his sister's shoulder.

And they couldn't speak of their Goddess Aoiflyn, nor could they speak of the roots of their magic.

Beside us, Jezebel slammed one of the dead fae soldiers into the wall, tackling an opponent, and I shook off the budding theories. We would deal with Lancaster's secrets if we survived tonight.

The male ground his jaw, growling impatiently. He was giving me pieces, so slowly but they were there, prying them out of his locked tongue one word at a time. "Myth. Magic."

My head whipped to Ophelia, then Jezebel.

Ancient magic repels goddess magic.

"They can break it," I gasped.

"Not here," Lancaster said, my attention shifting back to him. He watched his queen, unease framing his expression. "Not in view. But they can."

Because Lancaster didn't trust Ritalia entirely, and he couldn't outright disobey her, but he could silently work against her, laying his own trap. Like insisting that Ophelia and Jezebel needed to learn how to use their magic.

"What are you doing to Tolek?"

The fae's eyes roved over Tol kneeling at his sister's side, over Ophelia at the statue, and finally his queen. "Specifications matter," he muttered.

"What was it?" I asked, eyes flicking back toward where Tolek was clearly breathing difficultly.

Lancaster's jaw ground, the words struggling to get out. "I said he would die."

My heart thudded desperately, and then I said, "Not instantly."

The slightest nod.

I nearly laughed. "So subtle, Ritalia didn't even notice." The queen would expect her loyal hunter to weave a more complicated bargain, but there was one problem she didn't foresee. Somehow, she'd turned her subject against her, and he'd used that misstep to write her own downfall.

"The breathing," I clarified, "that will get better?"

"An illusion of the deal," Lancaster said. "As a gifted crete, I created a block."

I didn't care about clarifications of the magic, waving him off and turning toward the battle. To tell Ophelia to continue with the emblems. Tolek would be perfectly fine. He'd die one day, but not right now. Not because of this.

I'd barely taken a step when Ritalia roared, "Return another emblem, Revered, and his life is next!"

"Tolek, what—" Ophelia's voice broke off abruptly, and my gaze snapped to them.

At the queen's voice, Tolek had pushed to his feet. In the flurry of Lyria's death, he'd lost his sword and dagger across the cavern, but he was rushing to Ophelia's side. Nimble fingers reached for her—

For the dagger sheathed at her thigh.

Before any of us could blink, Tolek ripped it from her and launched the blade with a silent, furious precision only grief could derive.

And that dagger—a weapon *Cypherion* had gifted Ophelia—tumbled end over end across the cavern. I swore, even over the roaring fight and clangs of weapons, the whistling of the blade pierced the air. The dagger sank between skin and bone—into the queen of the fae's heart exactly as another had Tolek's sister, sealing the debt of her death in ruby red.

The air seemed to shudder, time suspending for a moment.

Ophelia and Jezebel would not need to break the godly bargain with their mythos power. Not tonight at least. Because Ritalia's body crumbled to the ground.

Tolek stood still, breathing heavily, Ophelia blinking wide eyed at his side.

Cypherion and I locked stares, silently exchanging the weight of what had happened. Tolek had killed the queen—had ensured the demise of the royal line—thanks to a blade gifted to Ophelia by a boy named for the cyphers.

Not only was revenge sealed, but a prophecy was fulfilled.

And Tolek, without a hint of myth magic in his blood and with only pure determination and one sure, vengeance-seeking throw, severed bargains centuries in the making.

Chapter Seventy-Five
Ophelia

THE THUD OF RITALIA'S BODY HITTING THE FLOOR OF the cavern echoed. Not soft, like Lyria's slow melting to her knees, like Tolek's cracking facade as he realized what happened and caught her. Not that heartrending but natural return to the Spirit Realm of a warrior who didn't deserve to die but did so peacefully.

The queen of the fae fell with a finality that seemed to blur sound and motion.

And a heartbeat later, the remaining fae began to scream. Everything rushed back, like time catching up. They clutched their chests, their heads. Some fell to their knees and writhed. As if in their queen's death, something inside of them had severed.

The bargains, I realized. Every one she held was snapping.

"Tol!" I gasped, all care of the emblems fleeing my mind as I raced to him and pulled him around to the front of the statue where we could have some privacy in the crescent of the Angels.

He stood panting, chest heaving and eyes in the direction the queen had fallen. Gently, I cupped his cheeks, turning his face to me to catch his wild, haunted stare.

"Tolek," I murmured softly.

"Ophelia," he said back, but it wasn't right. It wasn't Tolek's warm, charismatic tone saying my name. Not the adoration layered with teasing.

It was dark and twisted, twin to the vacant stare in his dulled chocolate eyes.

"Ophelia," he repeated. And as his arms looped around my waist and his head fell to my shoulder, there was something in his tone I recognized, warped as it was: pure desperation. That feeling of being so untethered by a loss that you were grasping for something—anything—to tie yourself down.

I'd never heard it quite like this from him, with a fresh-blooming grief filling in the silence between his breaths, but he clung to me like roots gripping the soil. Like something needed to sustain life.

"I'm so sorry, Tol," I murmured, holding him tighter to remind him I was here for him. Lyria's loss was heavy—she wasn't only Tolek's sister, but my friend. An advisor, a comforting spirit among us. Someone who made rooms warmer and days brighter.

And now, she was gone. My heart split for her.

"I had to do it." He inhaled raggedly, tears staining my skin, etching paths through the dirt and sweat. "She had to die."

"I know," I assured him, my own voice cracking. "I know." I would have done the same thing if it had been Jezebel. Would kill anyone who hurt her. I'd have done it for Lyria, too.

Guilt wedged itself between my ribs. A thick reminder that it had been *me* Lyria was guarding. Another life lost to save mine. It was a pain so sharp and distinct, it carved a spot beside everything else that had been taken from us. My father, countless friends.

But I wouldn't indulge it now. That would come later, after we got out of here and could fully process the cost.

Now, though, Tolek needed me.

I bunched one hand in his leathers, the other stroking his hair, and I held him. The boy who had radiated hope our entire lives, my guiding light on all those dark nights. He'd had many of his own, but this one...this one dug its claws in the deepest.

I held him through it.

I couldn't even focus on what was happening around us. Didn't know if anyone was still fighting. All I cared about was Tol, our hearts beating in sync and breathing ragged.

Turning his face into my neck, Tolek curved his arms tighter around my back, and he whispered, "I want you to finish this."

I pulled back, cupping his cheeks and guiding his face up to look into his eyes. "What?"

"The emblems." He inhaled. "I want you to finish what we started. Lyria—she wanted you to do this."

Finish this, she had said. Right after ensuring I'd care for her brother. And dammit, I'd honor Lyria's spirit any way I could.

As soon as she'd stopped breathing, Tolek had turned to me and commanded, *Go*.

It had felt wrong to move from his side, but there was such a finality to his tone, I couldn't argue with him. Like that was the one thing that would have comforted him. And now, it was that demand that burned through his agonized stare. The heated despair that required us to finish what his sister stood for. To win a sense of freedom for the warriors she'd tirelessly protected.

And if Tolek wanted to scorch this world to ash, I'd burn beside him with the light of the Angels.

"Okay, Tol." I inhaled, and it was rough.

Pushing onto my toes, I pressed my mouth to his. *I love you*, I said with the gentle kiss, sealing my grief with his. I took the burden of all the heartache he was going to feel in the coming days and wove our souls into one because Tolek and I could survive anything the Angels threw at us so long as we were together.

Take care of him, Lyria requested. I fucking would. I'd give every drop of cursed blood in my body for Tolek Vincienzo.

Pulling back, I whispered, "For Lyria."

$\approx$

THREE MORE EMBLEMS. That was all remaining between us and fulfilling the Angelcurse.

Tolek's fingers wove through mine as we approached the statue, and I couldn't tell who was leading the other. Was it me, escorting him through his grief, or him, guiding this path with a hot vengeance?

Perhaps it was the two of us, equals.

"Thorn, Ptholenix, and Damien," I said, talking simply to fill the silence Lyria left behind.

"Damien last." Tolek's tone was too focused for what he'd endured—for how he'd been wrecked and sobbing—like he'd shoved away all emotion in light of fulfilling his sister's wish.

My gut squirmed at the cold sound and the knowledge that he'd have to feel all the grief after this, but I held tighter to him. I couldn't help him until we got out of here, so I forced myself to focus, as well.

"Malakai said Ptholenix's gilded petal came from a tattoo on his back. Between his wings."

Tolek tugged me around the statue, to the side that faced the larger cavern—

"Spirits," I gasped. A figure lay bleeding from a brutal slice to the gut at the foot of the platform.

"Good," Tol said, voice icy.

Brystin's unseeing eyes watched the chasm of a ceiling. Dead.

The only fae still alive were Lancaster and Mora, both slumped on the seats of the theater. Rina and Celissia were questioning them while Barrett and Dax dealt with Nassik, all of my friends sporting minor injuries. Jezebel scampered down the stairs toward us while Malakai passed her to get to Mila. Cypherion and Vale had joined Erista near Lyria's body, and Sapphire still hovered above us all.

I wished I could feel relieved by seeing everyone else alive, but my pulse pounded. We weren't done.

"There," Tolek said, pointing up with our locked hands and pulling my attention back to the statue.

Between Ptholenix's wings, a faint outline of a tattoo was visible, looking like nothing more than a crack in the stone. It was an orchid missing a singular petal, an indent in the stone marking it.

"How did we skim over all these details?" I asked, stretching up to return the emblem to its rightful home. Still not releasing Tol's hand, I braced for the tremor that would rack the earth as it clicked into place.

This one cracked, like the igniting of a flame. A wave of heat blistered through the chamber, licking across my scratches and bruises with a soothing kiss of fire. And like when we'd returned the others to their statues, power mounted within me. Everyone else stilled and looked our way.

No one told us to stop, though. There was an aura of retribution among us all now, a thread that tied us together after one of our own had fallen.

"We didn't know what to look for before," Tolek deadpanned as the shaking ceased.

Power thrummed through my veins, the fiery strand of Ptholenix's Angellight nearly incinerating the others at the surge. I gasped, and the light I'd sent swirling above the cavern flared orange and red, a flame being fed.

"You felt it?" Barrett called.

Warmth poured over my body as I turned to the prince. "Did you?"

But Barrett shook his head. "Not this one. But earlier, when you returned Bant's ring, I'm guessing." He exchanged a look with Dax and Celissia, the former hunched on a step and gripping his gut. "The power we felt was...it was stronger than anything we'd ever experienced."

Barrett's eyes glowed, hungry for power after being betrayed by his councilman.

"It's how we held the line for the others to get on the sphinx," Dax added, voice tight.

That surge of power from the Angel statue had saved us. How could this be the wrong choice then?

"I felt it with Valyrie's," Vale agreed. As she spoke, starlight seemed to glow from her. Her eyes swirled with silver mists, the contents of galaxies in her stare. Cyph stood attentively at her side, but fervently, Vale said, "Keep going, Ophelia."

Two more. Only two more emblems.

"Thorn," Tolek said next.

We circled back to the other side of the statue, and this time, our friends followed, filing onto the platform.

All but Malakai, who sat with an unconscious Mila and the khrysaor near the top of the seats. There was a gap in our ranks where Lyria should have leaned easily against the wall with a curious smirk, and that absence spurred me on.

I pulled both halves of Thorn's broken crown from my pouch. One I'd retrieved from the pit, the other Kakias had found and manipulated for control over the Mindshapers. It was the second half that pulsed with a power unlike my Angellight or the rest of the emblems, as if when the queen had worn it and mingled that magic with the power of Bant's spirit within her, something had snapped.

I fiddled with the two pieces, but Tolek squeezed my hand. The weight of the others' eyes bore into me. Lyria's voice wafted through my memory. *Take care of him. Finish this.*

Facing the headless statue before me, I took a step forward.

And I hung both halves of the Angel's broken crown upon the spot where his head would have been.

The earth didn't just quake this time.

A keening wail split the air, wind howling through every tunnel in the mountains. I clasped my ears against the piercing sound echoing deep within my own bones. It could have been my own voice screaming for how the shriek cleaved through me. Could have come straight from the heart of the pit in Mindshaper Territory and ripped through Gallantia.

Where the other reactions had fueled the threads of each Angel within me, Thorn's tore at it. Like he wanted to claim that power back.

It was a reckless and wily sensation, but I gritted my teeth against the pain wrenching through my body and spirit, forcing Thorn's power down into the deep hollows my Angellight flooded.

The Mindshaper's power dug through all that I was, violating and cruel, but I could do nothing against it. My back arched, a cry slipping from my throat. My friends shifted around me, but no one else crumbled beneath the Angel's clawing power.

I leaned into Tol. Was this how he suffered when captured by Aird? Was this his nightmare?

Thorn's magic dug and dug, and as the assault wrenched through me, Tolek removed his hand from mine, bracing my back and cupping my cheek with the other. He tilted my face up to his and looked at me with a little of the concerned warmth and fury at the Angels I was used to seeing in his stare.

"One more, *apeagna*," he encouraged, stroking my cheek.

"One more," I repeated, through gritted teeth.

Then, his hands slipped behind my neck. He unclasped my necklace and held the Mystique emblem out to me.

Sweat dripped along my brow as that final shard of Angelborn swung, glinting in the light. Greedily, I wanted to keep it. To find a way to extricate the power within and return that to the stone rather than give over this small piece of metal.

But the time for selfishness was past.

Swallowing that heartache and forcing the pain from the Mindshaper deep within me, I stepped toward the final of the seven figures. My heartbeat pounded through my entire body, hands shaking. In that carved stone, I searched for any hint of the Prime Warrior I'd come to know. Of Damien's lingering magic or dulcet tones. Of the wistfulness I'd seen in him once, or the scar I knew now marred the Angel's cheek.

Nothing familiar looked back at me, but it beat in my hand.

For the final time, I reached for Damien's hunched form, bowing the lowest of them all, and I clasped my necklace around his neck, the fit tight to the stone. And the shock that went through the rock, the magic surging among all of us, was as strong as a thousand lightning strikes.

It was pure, undiluted ether drenching the blood of every Mystique in that chamber. Of Tolek, Cypherion, Jezebel, and Malakai. Even Mila seemed to stir.

It burned along my muscles, through my senses, amplifying everything I knew as a warrior and all the might I'd garnered from the emblems. My pulses pounded, heart racing. The Bond at the back of my neck tugged and drowned out Thorn's painful exploration of my spirit.

And for a moment, we all silently exchanged awed glances.

"Now what?" Santorina finally asked, looking around at all of the warriors thrumming with power. There was a shift in her, too, but I wasn't sure exactly what.

"Blood," Cypherion answered.

In response, given that Tolek and I were both now weaponless, Rina pulled her dagger from her thigh. Twin to the one he had launched at the queen—the final in the set Cypherion had gifted me. Tol accepted it from her.

I held my hand between us, and for the second time in our lives, Tolek angled a blade at my flesh. This was so different than last time—when he'd been fulfilling his own worst fear.

We'd lived through another nightmare in this cavern. One that would echo for days, years. A slice to my palm to unleash a prophecy-fulfilling magic was trivial.

Only flinching slightly, Tolek dug a shallow cut. It stung, the blood welling, and one by one, I pressed the wound to each emblem in the order we'd returned them to the stone.

My heart pounded in my ears with every drop.

Paint the shards with vengeance, Damien had said to me so many months ago, following the Battle of Damenal. *Awaken the answering presence.*

He wanted me to learn the power waiting within me, had told me to master it but not allow it to be stronger than my own will. For this—to use it to absolve the curse.

With a breath and a desperate wish that we were doing the right thing for the warriors, I smeared my blood across the shard of Angelborn glinting against the worn stone.

"Blood," I said, gathering a surge of Angellight in my palm, "and magic."

Then, I blasted each emblem with a hit of golden light.

And the statues that had stood for centuries, buried in the heart of the Mystique Mountains, cracked.

Blurs of gold streaked into the air, formless masses with spots of misty lilac and stormy silver. Ocean blues and the burning of a firebird's great wings. The strands of magic wrapping through me tugged toward their sources.

Toward the essences of the Angels that had been locked away.

Toward their *spirits*, now taking shape of limbs and wings and bodies, as Bant's had in the cell of a mountain camp all those months ago.

With one final burst of almighty light that sent us all stumbling back, those spirits became solid, ethereal bodies of the Seven Angels of the Gallantian Warriors. The Primes who founded our clans, who graced us with their magic.

I could barely make out their forms through the blinding white rays, but the seven strands of Angellight within me sang like strings of a harp being plucked.

At each added note of that melody, my body burned hotter.

Hotter.

Hotter.

I cried out, the light from the Angels intensifying.

Every muscle, every damn fiber of my being, throbbed with a pain worse than anything I'd ever felt. It blazed more intensely than the fire of the Spirit Volcano, twisted my being worse than any loss I'd suffered.

Magic whirled before me and through my bones. In flashes, I was detached from this place, instead on the bridge between the realms where constellations fell from the sky and winged beings soared. Or in the dream world where I'd last seen Damien. But with another blink, I stood back in the cavern.

To ground myself, I separated the light of each Angel in this form, tracking each string they called to.

There was Ptholenix's burning fire, and Valyrie's counter of cool starlight. Gaveny, a swirl of teal tinting the gold, as wild as a roaring sea, and Xenique, whose dark depths sang with the Gods-blood she'd gifted my mother's family. Damien and Bant—those two burned brightest of all, twin whips of light lashing within me. Each a string on that delicate instrument of power.

But it was Thorn's—Thorn's swirling mass of clouded silver that I'd seen in the pit, fractured as the crown that bore his name, that didn't only play a string of my magic, but tore it.

He reached within me as he'd been trying to before and ripped the threads of my magic at the seams.

And with another echo of that keening wail, Thorn unlatched a final lock within me. He mangled, severed, and frayed some bolt that had been tampering the wild, myth-born magic and had my muscles igniting even worse than before.

It shredded skin and bone.

Unleashed something I hadn't realized was deep within me.

"Alabath," Tolek murmured.

But my only answer was an agonized scream as fire ripped down my spine, like my flesh was being flayed from my bones.

I wanted it to take me. To kill me. Because out of all the things I'd survived, this was the worst.

An aching weight settled along my shoulder blades.

"*Apeagna*," Tolek said, more urgently this time.

But I couldn't answer. All I could do was wish to succumb.

Chapter Seventy-Six
Santorina

The first instinct woke in the blink of an eye.

One moment, Ophelia was reaching toward Damien's emblem, the final of the seven, and then, everything was *brighter*. Not only did the light blazing through the chamber nearly blind us, but something within my own body shifted.

It was like stirring after a deep sleep, when your senses came back to you in misty inklings rather than a downpour, but that first one was alarmingly noticeable. A tweak in your internal stasis.

Everything within me shifted as the golden outlines of seven winged beings ascended toward the endless height of the cavern.

The theater flooded with an undeniable presence, but my attention was on everything else. On the individual specks of dust floating through the air from where the rocks crumbled. On the small scuffs of boots against stone, deciphering every grunt from each one of my friends as the force of the Angels erupting shoved us all back.

A rock caught my heel, my stomach dropping as I stumbled, but—

My hand shot out with barely a thought, steadying me against the rock wall, my reflexes sharper than ever.

I looked to Ophelia—

But my stomach jumped into my throat.

Ophelia was...

No.

The light of the Angels blared, cutting through the room and obscuring everything again.

It stirred up a wind that swirled my hair around my shoulders, and in that breeze, a sharper scent stood out among the rest, obliterating every thought in my mind.

It reeked of something centuries old and metallic. Iron and floral, like the beautiful tragedy of bloodstained roses. It called to that awakened instinct deep in my gut, stirred a sentience in my bones that I couldn't ignore.

And there was more, an ancient undertone that had my pulse racing.

Whipping my head around, my eyes instinctually landed on Lancaster and Mora, still slumped on the steps where they'd collapsed when their queen's death had shredded the bargains she held them to. When they'd felt like their bones were cracking, like their hearts were being ripped from their chests as the threads of deals unraveled.

Mora stayed seated, the Angellight Ophelia had put into place around her shoulder flaring brighter, but Lancaster...he met my gaze and slowly stood, the Angels forgotten to him, as well.

The male squared his stance, as if readying for a battle. The sharp features of his face were hauntingly exquisite as he tilted his head. Even that small movement had the air stirring around him, his brown hair swinging to his shoulders. An instinct wormed through my stomach, perking up at the faint hint of his scent stretching out to me, something warm and woodsy.

A scent *of the Gods* layering through him.

It was a reminder of bloodstained roses; of the tragedies that befell beautiful things. Of an immortal and a human committed to slaying one another.

And as all of those clues started to link together, understanding dawned, and his eyes locked to mine.

Fae, my senses said, the Bounty bloodline waking and my fingers curling toward a weapon.

Lancaster grinned at me, canines glinting razor sharp in the Angellight. It was the look of finally finding prey that was no weakling, but a huntress in and of herself. The delighted surprise of discovering a target that was an *equal*.

And the hunter said, "Hello, Queen of Bounties."

CHAPTER SEVENTY-SEVEN
VALE

THE FATES SCREAMED.

It was a glorious, glee-ridden cacophony rioting through my heart and spirit, starfire crashing through my mind at the freedom of our Angel.

And as pure, undiluted Angellight washed across the room, as it melted with the power of my nine Fate ties, the final latch on my readings snapped. And they barreled into me in one burst of starfire.

All of those moments I'd barely seen in recent weeks—all of the images I'd been trying to reach—poured out.

Annellius was on his knees, pleading before Damien. His eyes —they were a mix of brown and magenta, one fading into the next as the Godsblood took root in his spirit. But then—

"*No,*" I gasped out.

Damien lashed a branch of his power across the mountaintop, and that ether dug into Annellius. It tore up his spirit—his soul. Blood leaked from his nose and ears.

"What have you done?" Damien asked.

And as Annellius died at the hands of his Mystique Angel, he echoed, "Brother, what have *you*?"

It had been Damien. Damien who had killed Annellius after the first chosen decided not to fulfill the Angelcurse. I saw it now, in flashes as my nine Fates hurried to feed me the readings they'd been trapped with. Annellius piecing together the truth of the emblems—finding some of them, even—and the horror that sank into his gut when he learned the truth.

A man with him down in the catacombs, corpses chasing him. Killing him. And Annellius's answering rage.

How he'd written to the fae, and upon refusal, returned the emblems where he'd retrieved them from. How the earth had accepted them back—likely some spell of the God of Nature—and Annellius summoned Damien atop the mountains, knowing he would die when he told the Angel what he did.

I had to tell Ophelia. She had trusted Damien, and this was what he was capable of?

But starfire flared before me, warming me down to my toes, which, in this plane, were bare, my skin and clothes clean of the blood and gore from the cavern.

And before me, the six gods took shape in a field of burning wildflowers, ripping magic from the Angels in what I now knew was the twisted Ascension. The day the gods locked the Angels in that prison with the Warrior God in order to keep him docile.

I watched, horror sluicing through my chest, as power was siphoned from the Prime Warriors. And a part of me understood why they wanted out so badly—why they were willing to do anything to break their Angelcurse.

When the winged beings disappeared, the six gods turned to me—they could *see me*.

And I nearly fell to my knees when one of them winked. Moirenna, the Goddess of Fate and Celestial Movements. It had to be her, with the way starlight seemed to shine from her ivory skin.

"Fatecatcher," she said, and my heart leapt into a gallop, "we will see you soon."

As the session faded, I scanned the other gods. Thallia, with her cascading dark hair and willowy frame, eyed me knowingly. And there was something achingly familiar about her.

But it was Aoiflyn, the Fae Goddess, who caught my breath.

Because I'd seen her before, in a recent reading. I hadn't been able to make out her face, but I recognized the thrum of her power. Even through the starfire barrier, it echoed with the reek of blood.

It had been Aoiflyn, bleeding unto the crowds of fae in that reading.

Aoiflyn's blood, leading straight to Lancaster and Mora. Godsblood, binding their tongues and bargains. Godsblood, warring with the myth magic Ophelia bore. Godsblood, keeping that wound in Mora's shoulder from healing, because the corpse's bite was laced with ancient enchantment.

And as each god faded, taking the rolling, flaming hills of Firebird's Field with them and locking our Angels away in the past, I remembered how Valyrie had warned Ophelia not to push at the whims of the stars. Had this been what she meant? That the Angels did not want me to see the six beings now vanishing before me?

If so, I feared how close the gods had been this entire time.

And how soon we may see them again.

Chapter Seventy-Eight
Ophelia

I WAS OFF BALANCE. THAT PRESSURE SETTLED AGAINST my back, and every part of my body was tearing.

In the wash of Angellight, I'd seen a glimpse of Vale's reading. Only the first one, but Annellius had known. He had figured out all of this, what lurked in the mountains, and Damien had...

Damien had...

I gasped, trying to see through the pain still burning along my muscles—through the weight dragging me down.

"By the fucking Angels," Tol rasped.

"Are y-you," I stuttered, "okay?"

"*I'm* fine, Alabath." His voice was still stoic, though. He shifted his arms around me, and my body was racked with an agonizing shudder.

Angellight blared through the cavern, rushing like a wind so loud, I couldn't hear what anyone beyond him was saying. Could only see my friends' astounded faces as their eyes darted between me and the Angels. As Santorina and the fae stared each other down and the Engrossians huddled around Dax. As Jezebel and Erista guarded Lyria's body, still prone and bathed in the light of the Angels. As Vale was slammed with reading after reading, her eyes silvered, and Cypherion braced her.

As Malakai rose on the stairs, his eyes locked on mine, his hand clutching his hollow Bind.

My own thudded with what might have been shock.

But I couldn't try to figure it out. Because over the center of the room, the seven gold outlines solidified into bodies and wings and limbs. The Angels hovered above us.

They'd been so similar to Bant's spirit when it was released from Kakias. *And disappeared into the mountains.* The other six spirits had been encased within the stone. Bant's joined them upon the death of its shell, and when we set them free, we unlocked their bodily forms, as well.

The Angels swelled, and I was so small beneath them. So defenseless. I needed a weapon, needed—

Starfire and Angelborn were gone. The ache went through me, deep to my bones. I tried to shake it off, and another painful shudder wracked my body.

"Ophelia," Tolek said, frantic, as if he'd been repeating my name and I only just heard.

When I angled my head up to look at him, something brushed my arm and—

"*Holy fucking Angels,*" I gasped.

It wasn't a muscular ache along my back. It was a pair of glorious wings drooping along the dusty cavern floor. As white as Sapphire's downy feathers, threaded with gold and shimmering.

Wings.

I had wings.

I tried to move them—to ensure they were real and truly attached to me—but I could barely manage a flutter, and even that sent a tearing pain through my body.

Something sticky dripped down my spine. Reaching back—careful to move as little as possible—I swept my fingertips through it. When I brought them forward, my vision swimming, they gleamed crimson.

Blood. The emergence of wings had made me bleed. There was an irony in there that my mind couldn't untangle in its frazzled state.

I was a warrior. Not an Angel. I didn't want to be anything but a warrior—my entire life it had been my dream, my cause.

"Damien," I gasped. Every shred of my body hurt to turn,

trying to find a new equilibrium. Tolek held me upright, but even his arm at my waist was painful as it jostled my wings. I didn't know how to move the damn things out of the way.

But I sought out the Angel who had visited me time and again. And—

"Holy fucking Angels," I breathed again. I'd thought Damien was awash with almighty power before, but now he was an image of pure legend.

His light ebbed with visible magic, his wings dripping with shimmering gold. My pair was small in comparison, suited for my frame where as his seemed to swallow all the air around him.

Him and the six other Angels, each with their own magnificent wings. Ether poured from their forms.

Thorn roved the highest, power swirling around him like fog as his eyes crawled the cavern. On his head, a halo shone, thorned like his emblem and dripping with what resembled...*blood*.

I swallowed a bud of fear as one drop slipped from a spike, falling dozens of feet to the floor below. The other Angels watched him warily. And I could pick them all out, like the light I'd harnessed from their emblems tethered me to them.

"Hello, Ophelia," Damien said, drifting lower with a smirk that tugged at his scar. The jagged slice to his face unsettled something sinister in my gut. "Well done."

"What did you do?" I gritted out. "To Annellius."

A swarm of emotion passed across Damien's expression. Everything from sorrow to remorse to guilt. "He died, Ophelia."

"*You killed him*." Tears tore down my cheeks, both for the pain running through my muscles and for the ancestor I never knew. Damien had seen that Annellius, their Chosen, wanted to scorn the Angels, and he had killed him atop that mountain.

"We have all made mistakes," Damien said.

I shook my head and my entire body throbbed. I cried out, breathing labored.

"What's happening to her?" Tolek demanded.

"Something unprecedented" was all the Mystique Prime Warrior replied, eyes narrowed.

"I told you, Chosen Child," the sphinx said from her perch in the top corner of the theater, "on the day of your birth, two legends merged into one, thanks to the Godsblood and the Angel-curse. Together, those myths woke a breath and blood not seen in so long, they were believed lost forever. *You* awoke more myths than you know."

I opened my mouth to respond, but a clear, awed voice rang through the cavern, "Ithinix?"

From the ring of Angels watching Thorn, one emerged, feathers unspooling with a deep purple light, so dark it was almost onyx.

Xenique.

The demigoddess ancestor of my mother's line. My gaze flashed to Jezebel who was studying her from a distance. When she met my eyes, awe shone.

Xenique flapped her wings and drifted toward the sphinx. Toward *Ithinix*, the name she had not revealed until her Angel returned.

"Hello, Mistress," Ithinix cooed, her tale twitching.

Xenique laid a hand on the sphinx's cheek, something so tender in the movement. So mortal in a way legend claimed the Angels couldn't be. "I have missed you, dear friend."

"And I, you," the sphinx replied.

They were quiet for a moment, then Xenique peered around the sphinx's body. "What has happened?"

Mila.

Ithinix observed the general, prone on the stone seats behind her. "Succumbed to the heart of the Gates of Angeldust."

Xenique's brow creased, but she nodded, dismissing our unconscious friend.

Malakai stepped toward the Angel, anger clear on his face, but before he could interject, Erista said, "Prime Warrior." She crossed the cavern and kneeled at the bottom of the seats. The Soulguider opened her palms toward Xenique, gold crescent moon tattoos absorbing the Angel's light. "As a loyal warrior, I ask for your blessing in our mission to guide spirits and secrets of the dead, that you may honor my practice with the power of your Goddess, the Mother of Death and Barer of Lives Lost."

I looked to Damien, remembering the lack of reverence I showed in comparison. Though, he did have a habit of showing up at the most inconvenient times. And he apparently had *killed* the last Chosen. I leaned closer to Tolek.

With a pleasant smile on her lips, Xenique looked from Erista to Jezebel—and then to me. "Rise, child." Erista stood, tilting her chin up as the Angel floated down to her. "I have seen the good you have done in your practice. The matters you have guarded close to your heart, and the sisters you have guided back to me."

Her words sent a squirming instinct through me. Jezebel's silver-blue myth magic budded in her palms.

"With all due respect—" I gasped over the pain at my back. Before Jez could react to the Angel or her anger with Erista, I said, "My sister and I are Mystique Warriors. We may bare Soulguider blood—the blood of the gods—but we have both completed the Undertaking."

Xenique's smile was haughty, chilling my blood-and-sweat-stained skin. "I believe you have already seen how much more lies within your stories." And her gaze lingered on the wings at my back.

"Sometimes," a cool female voice added, "the Fates bear us more gifts than we realize." An Angel with hair that gleamed silver and eyes swirling in depths of navy blue fluttered her wings as she drifted beside Xenique. *Valyrie.* The Starsearcher. "But never more than we can manage."

"Holy cursed Angels," Cypherion blurted out, and we all spun toward him. His eyes were locked on Valyrie. "That voice. I've heard your voice before."

"What do you mean?" I asked.

Vale was blinking herself out of her reading, frantically scouring the cavern. She sought me out, but I gave her a grim-lipped nod. *I know*, it said. I know of Annellius.

My heart tore at the tear that slid down her cheek. At the fear blatant in her silvered eyes and how she wiped it all away. Vale cast a wary glance to Lancaster and Mora, but then, she forced herself to stand straighter and face Cypherion.

"What do you mean?" she asked.

He eyed her, clearly seeing through her front, but his expression softened and he answered, "On the night we went into the archives and you read—when Titus ambushed us—it was Valyrie's voice that spoke through you, Stargirl. When we found the book in the archives written in Endasi, she said of course she knew the language. That she was there when it was created."

"It happened tonight, too," Malakai called down from the steps, striking the Angels with accusing glares. "In the Gates."

"Valyrie?" Vale asked, her eyes still aglow but uncertain.

The Starsearcher Prime Warrior lowered herself to the ground before her warrior, her bare feet meeting rock.

And for the first time since the fated Ascension Day—since they'd gone within that prison—an Angel walked our soil. The impact of this great power returning to Gallantia rang through the stone.

"Child of many Fates," Valyrie said to Vale, and my heart stuttered at the ownership in her tone. "It is so good to see you harness your power, Fatecatcher."

"Fatecatcher," Tolek whispered to me. "That phrase was in her scrolls."

"Do you think it was talking about Vale?" I muttered, but Tol only shrugged.

Vale's frame glimmered in starlight even within this chamber. Cypherion stood a step behind her, hands within reach of his weapons, but Valyrie paid him no heed. She evaluated her warrior with the pure satisfaction only immortality could birth.

"What does that mean?" Vale asked.

Valyrie dipped her head. "In time, you shall learn." She looked around the cavern, eyes pausing on Mora and a small breath of shock leaving her lips before she stole herself. "We have much to discuss it seems. You may bear nine Fate ties and readings of higher powers, but I have not had access to my magic for a very long time. There is so much only I can impart."

"What about the Warrior God?" I asked, shifting toward Damien where he'd been whispering with Bant. Hatred and betrayal curled through me when Damien's eyes met mine.

As their muted tones slithered across the stone walls, the

Engrossian Angel watched Barrett, Dax, and Celissia with unsettling curiosity. The trio stared right back, Dax still wincing over the scar to his gut, and I swore Bant's head tilted curiously at the slight flinch.

"It seems the mortals have been playing such reckless games, brother," Bant said to Damien. The Mystique's scar twitched as his jaw ticked.

"*What. About. The. God?*" I clipped out. I was done allowing Damien to avoid me. Done being their toy.

But it was Bant, his hair and eyes as dark as the magic Kakias had manipulated from him, whose attention latched on to me, and he said, "You have cleared the way."

And at our backs, in the wall the half-moon Angel statue bowed toward, white light carved a fissure through the rock, cleaving clean through stone—

No. It *melted* it.

But stone couldn't melt. Not from any natural, easily accessible substance at least. We'd seen scorched rock before—during that first trial on the Seawatcher platforms. A result of burning Angellight, I'd thought, marking the path to the emblem.

But perhaps it hadn't been the light of Angels after all. Because even Angellight did not contain this pulsing power, melting a door where none had been before.

Flicking a lock.

Unleashing a prisoner.

This was stone touched by the hand of a god. One long-contained and ready to devour what stood in his path. The wall melted into a river of molten rock as my weapons had, and I flinched at the reminder. But I couldn't get lost to the pained memory.

Because as soon as the passage solidified, white light pouring forth and bathing every inch of the cavern, the shadow of a god filled the archway.

CHAPTER SEVENTY-NINE
OPHELIA

Somehow, the Warrior God's name came to my lips. "Echnid," I breathed, an answer long sought, the word rippling out across the cavern.

"Like in Valyrie's scrolls?" Tolek whispered in awe. Like the term Fatecatcher, this name had been there. The Starsearcher Angel had left the clues right before us, and we never realized what they meant.

I flicked a glance to her, her glowing starlight wings held high above the ground, pale blue gown drifting around her ankles, but Valyrie watched the archway. Every Angel's stare was trained on it, waiting as the Warrior God stepped from his prison realm into ours, and howls of a thousand hounds echoed in his wake.

And that ripple his name had sent through the cavern shivered across my skin, down through the rock. I had a sickening feeling it was felt all the way across Gallantia, the god of this land returning to his people after millennia locked within a realm gate through our mountains.

I thought Rebel whined, that Sapphire and the khrysaor flapped their wings, that echoes of beasts everywhere *felt* his presence beneath their skin.

Silken white hair flowed to Echnid's waist, lifting on his long-suppressed power. Skin nearly as pale glowed, white mist shooting and swirling around his being. It gathered in his palms as he lifted them, searching the ether as if he hadn't seen it this active in a very long time. Perhaps as long as he'd been caged.

When he turned his attention on us, I gasped, my wings fluttering painfully in surprise and a trembling cry catching in my throat. The Warrior God's eyes were a pure-white milky sheen, but somehow, his stare still pierced my very spirit.

A part of me wanted to bow. My bones dragged toward the earth under his scrutiny, like a moon caught in the orbit of something much stronger than itself.

Echnid scanned the theater, but those milky eyes came back to me. Evaluated every facet of my being so I felt bare and painfully vulnerable before him. The North Star Bind on my arm burned under his study, but eventually, his attention landed on those wings—my wings.

And when the Warrior God spoke, his voice had the deep timbre but effortless cadence of one who commanded obedience without needing to say anything. "The seraphs were never meant to return."

Swallowing and gripping Tolek's arm around my waist for support, I forced out, "Who are the seraphs?"

Echnid didn't answer, only smiled, and it chilled my skin.

"What does it mean, sir?" Ptholenix asked, tattoos flexing on his forearms.

"It means," Echnid drawled, "the curse of Ophelia woke your Guardian league. It will be so curious to see what else the mingling of myths can command."

The Warrior God spoke to his Angels as if none of us were present. Granted, we should probably have kneeled, but warriors had gone millennia without the knowledge of any god to guide us. We didn't know what to expect.

But we did have questions. And I forced myself to dig through the pain branching through my body, to forget the trail of blood slicking my back, and be the leader the warriors needed.

"What will happen now?" After a moment, I tacked on, "Sir? Magic has been unspooling through our land—the very magic used to lock you up. Will Gallantia replenish? The fae power regulate, the animals and storms calm?"

Would the known gods work with him to restore Ambrisk to its glory? Would he, them?

But Echnid shattered all those restorative hopes when he grinned and said, "Now, we get vengeance."

My limbs trembled. *No.* Dread encased my heart. "What?"

The Warrior God did not answer. Instead, he commanded, "We cannot stay here." My skin tingled under his attention. "Bring her to me."

"What—"

I barely got the word out before Thorn's gleeful cackle bounced off the rock. He swooped down before me, the earth shuddering at the mighty impact, and gripped my arm so bruisingly I screamed.

"What are you doing?" I stumbled forward as Thorn turned to the Warrior God, the Mindshaper's dark halo still dripping black.

"Get your fucking hands off her!" Tolek roared, holding tight to my waist.

But Thorn wrenched me from his grasp and shoved me toward Echnid. With a tearing stretch, my wings reopened the wounds on my back. Fresh blood poured, spraying Tolek as he lunged for me and painting his skin in a murderous vision.

Thorn gripped the back of Tol's hair, jerking him away from me, and that severance seemed so final—so permanent, it shoved me to teeter on the edge of my breaking point.

The Angel delivered a slap to Tolek's face with the might of an almighty deity, sending his neck snapping to the side at an odd angle.

"*TOL!*" I shrieked as Thorn discarded him.

He pushed to his feet like he'd barely felt the hit, sights only set on me—set on reaching across realms to get me. Tol charged at the Prime Warrior, but he was weaponless.

"Tolek!" Cypherion called and tossed his scythe.

Tol snatched it from the air as Thorn raised a hand, riling the power of storms. Thunder rumbled through the chamber, down to my bones, and a bolt of lightning shot toward Tolek, the scythe's glinting blade a beacon for it.

Tolek drew the weapon back, crying out as he swung forward.

The arched blade drew across the Mindshaper Angel's torso, ripping a jagged line from shoulder to hip as lightning ignited the silver steel.

"Holy fucking Angels," I breathed.

No weapon was supposed to be able to harm an Angel. Thorn still stood, but crimson blood streaked with glittering gold poured from that non-fatal wound, his surprise morphing into a sneer.

And then, everyone was screaming. The Angels were soaring down, forming a barrier between me and my friends.

Panic sank its claws into my chest.

"Tolek!" I shrieked again as he lifted Cypherion's scythe once more, and the others drew swords and axes.

Thorn fell behind his brethren, stitching his wound with a flash of Angellight. Echnid's cold hand latched around my arm.

"What are you doing?" My voice was raw and distressed as I lost sight of my friends beyond the wall of wings and ether. "*Damien!*"

He was the Mystique Angel. He was supposed to protect us, to guide us. I'd done *all of this* because he told me to. *But he killed Annellius.*

The betrayal sank into my gut. It was like being submerged into an icy river, awakening new senses that tugged my heart. It wrenched at the trust I'd handed over to our Prime Warrior, ripping up those foundations until I was a void.

I'd tried to do everything he directed. Tried to trust him.

Damien's stare met mine, gold light tumbling from his wings, and remorse darkened his purple eyes.

But I felt nothing at it. Nothing beyond the pain shredding my body, the pit of anguish I was teetering over, and the fury of a thousand Angels searing through my blood.

Echnid's milky eyes were gleeful as he tugged me closer, brushing my hair from my face. "Come, Ophelia. Let us work as a team."

His touched crawled along my skin.

"Let me go!" I staggered back a step, but his grip was solid.

"*Ophelia!*" Tolek shouted, again and again.

Rina and Cyph, too.

Jezebel was spearing her silver-blue light toward the Angels, but they threw up their own shields of Angellight to quickly swallow her myth-born magic.

My hand was gripped in the grasp of a god, my life along with it. And then, Echnid ripped a tear between here and elsewhere.

Beyond the shimmering veil, a familiar mountain view lurked. One I knew, one I loved, but when I saw the rocky peaks between stone pillars and the city spread beyond, I felt nothing. Everything worth feeling was locked on the other side of the Angels.

Echnid smiled down at me, and those milky eyes halted on my Bind.

"Wait!" he shouted, holding up a hand. I wanted to burn the tattoo from my flesh if only to keep him from seeing this piece of my soul. "Bring the boy, too."

My heart stuttered.

Bant swooped down on Malakai, lifting him right off his feet where he guarded Mila's prone body, and soaring toward the veiled tear the Warrior God had ripped in the world.

"Get your fucking hands off me!" Malakai fought, kicking wildly, but it was fruitless. His strength was nothing compared to the Angel's.

"Go!" Echnid ordered, tugging me toward the tear. He lifted me, and the movement ripped my wounds open further.

"*NO!*" My voice was gravelly through my throat. Desperation slammed into me, swallowing up the void. My strength faded with each bolt of pain through my back, but I used what was left to shout, "Tolek!"

"Ophelia!" Tolek lunged, fighting to break the barrier of Angel wings. Slicing and clawing at them where they stood as rigid as stone. "*Ophelia!*"

But the Warrior God pulled me away, shoving me over the edge and into emptiness.

And the last thing I heard as we crossed through the veil into a familiar room atop the mountains was Tolek Vincienzo's voice torn on a desperate cry of my name.

Ophelia's story concludes in the epic finale of The Curse of Ophelia series, coming 2025! Preorder now.

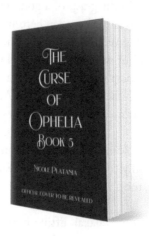

⤳

Thank you so much for reading *The Myths of Ophelia*. If you're so inclined, please consider leaving a review on Goodreads, Amazon, your favorite retailers, or social media.

And if you need some healing after that ending, take a look at what some of our favorite Engrossian Warriors were up to while they were off the page in *The Myths of Ophelia*.

Want to keep up with what's next for the Gallantian Warriors, including bonus chapters and first looks? Join Nicole's newsletter today!

ACKNOWLEDGMENTS

After that roller coaster ending, you probably don't want to hear another word from me, but I have a lot of people who deserve to be thanked, so bear with me for a page or two more.

First, I have to give the absolute biggest thank you to my family. To my mom, dad, and Chris, thank you for being endlessly supportive throughout these few hectic years. Without you, I wouldn't be able to chase this dream.

I get asked a lot if Ophelia's friends are based on anyone, and while the answer is that none of them are in particular, I always follow that up with saying that their love for each other is. I am beyond lucky to have an incredible group of ride or die friends. Thank you infinitely to my little found family who is by my side every day–you know who you are.

To all the author and reader friends who live near or far, thank you. Being a part of this community is something I never knew I needed. I am so grateful to get to share things we love so deeply and to get to cheer each other on. To every author whose path I have crossed, every artist who has brought my characters to life, and every reader who has become a friend, thank you.

Thank you to my spectacular editing team. To Kelley, Friel, and Kayla, as well as my cover designer Fran who *never* misses. I'm so sad to think we only get to do this one more time for Ophelia's story, but working with you all is a highlight of the process every time. To my agent Ezra and the EELA team as well as the audio team at Tantor, thank you for taking on my warriors and seeing the future of this series and my career.

Thank you to Maribeth at Legends Literary Management for helping smooth out all the details on the way to pub day. And thank you beyond measure to my beta readers, ARC team, and Street Team who not only helped with this stellar launch but also breathes new life into this series every day and constantly begs for more of them. It's because of you that I'm motivated to keep going on the hard days. To every Booktoker, Bookstagrammer, or reader who has picked up the series, I hope you find a home in Gallantia and know it's one you can continue to come back to.

Finally, as always, thank you to Ophelia and crew. I'd be nowhere without your story.

Infinitely yours,
Nicole

Nicole Platania was born and raised in Los Angeles and completed her B.A. in Communications at the University of California, Santa Barbara. After two years of working in social media marketing, she traded Santa Barbara beaches for the rainy magic of London, where she completed her Masters in Creative Writing at Birkbeck, University of London. Nicole harbors a love for broken and twisty characters, stories that feel like puzzles, and all things romance. She can always be found with a cup of coffee or glass of wine in hand, ready to discuss everything from celebrity gossip to your latest book theories.

Connect with her on Instagram and TikTok as @bynicoleplatania or on nicoleplatania.com.

Made in United States
Troutdale, OR
12/16/2024

26716765R10376